Harvest Moon

Harvest Moon

Zachary H. Lovelady

Table of Contents

Harvest Moon Character Sheet

CHEYENNE TRIBE

Black Bear- Cheyenne Chief
Gray Hawk- Black Bear's son
Boulder Arms – Cheyenne warrior
Fox Thoughts – Cheyenne warrior

WOODCRAFT INDIANS

Charlie- Scoutmaster
John Taylor- Oldest brother to Luther and Zack, scout, 9 years
Luther Taylor- Middle brother to John and Zack, scout, 8 years
Zack Taylor- Youngest brother to John and Luther, scout, 7 years
Kevin- Korean, scout, 5 years

KIOWA TRIBE

Lone Wolf- Kiowa Chief, Kiowa's father, Paw's brother
Grass Woman- Kiowa's mother
Kiowa- Lone Wolf and Grass Woman's son, brother of Two Moons and Weasel Tail
Two Moons- Kiowa's oldest brother
Weasel Tail- Kiowa's brother
Onendah- Kiowa tribe medicine man
Paw- Lone Wolf's brother, Kiowa's uncle
Glances Then Glares- Makes Trouble and Kida's mother
Kida- Glances Then Glares' daughter, Makes Trouble's sister
Makes Trouble- Glances Then Glares' son, Kida's brother,
Kiowa's best friend / Would-Be-Brother
Moon Beam- A Demi-God, Kiowa's pet fox

HOPI TRIBE

Kikmongwi- Hopi Chief, Anoki's father
Proud Woman- Kikmongwi's wife, Anoki's mother, kidnapped by the Navajo
Anoki- Kikmongwi's daughter, Hopi princess, Walpi and Mali's sister
Walpi- Anoki's older brother
Mali- Anoki's younger sister, kidnapped by the Navajo

CANADIANS

W.H.- Wolf Hunter, nephew to Dr. Bennet
Dr. Bennet- College Dean, uncle to W.H.
Cotton- W.H.'s horse
Bingo- W.H.'s collie dog

Harvest Moon Character Sheet

SARATOGA SPRINGS, NEBRASKA

General Lee Montgomery- Maybelle and Malice Mike's father, Kentucky militia general
Maybelle Montgomery- daughter to Gen. Lee Montgomery, twin sister to Malice Mike
Malice Mike Montgomery- aka Junior, twin bother to Maybelle
Garrick Anthony Burger- aka Rick Darling Burger

WILD WEST- CIMARRON, NEW MEXICO

Mr. Mike Mathis-Hardware store owner, married to
Frances Mathis, Jenny and Billy's father
Mrs. Frances Mather- Jenny and Billy's mother
Jenny Mathis- Daughter of Mike and Frances Mathis
Billy Mathis- Jenny's brother
Sherriff Dawson- Sherriff of Cimarron, NM

WOLVES

Kiowa- King of the Currumpaw, Heart on Fire
Anoki- Kiowa's mate, Walpi's sister
Walpi- Anoki's brother
Kida- Walpi's mate, Makes Trouble's sister
Makes Trouble- Kiowa's best friend and Would-Be-Brother, Kida's brother
Paw- Kiowa's uncle
Blue Eyes- Kiowa and Anoki's pup
Coon Eyes- Kiowa and Anoki's pup
Red Cloud- Kiowa and Anoki's pup
Cries a Lot- Kiowa and Anoki's pup

INDIAN GODS

Fire Boy
Taime
Water Boy
Hotamintanio- War God
Sun God
God of Heavens
Evil Spirit
Naukolahe

To love is to feel. To love is to grow. To love is to travel. To travel to love, has been the greatest adventure of my life! Our souls were stitched together with the needle of adversity and the thread of time. With all my heart, thank you Rebecca Lovelady.

PROLOGUE

High on a jagged mountaintop, dewdrops form on bushy pines. They collect upon the needles and drip one at a time until they fill the wild yellow daffodils to the brim. When the flowery buckets are full, they lean over and spill their nectar onto the earth. Crickets unwind their long curly tongues and lap up the ambrosia. Drunk on nature's liquor, they rub their hairy legs together and play their fiddles.

A shadow stirs in the crooked darkness. Two golden halos catch the moon's rays and glow. They hover in the infinite abyss.

A hooting owl mercifully rattles its tongue against the roof of its beak, asking, "Who? Who?" in short bursts. When no one can answer, it persists with long, drawn-out inquiries: "Whooooo? Whooooo?" The wise ol' owl warns all that danger lurks near those glowing eyes.

Restless creatures hear the warning and shy away. Those resting are fatally caught in the jaws of surprise. Predator and prey lock claws, antlers, and fangs, dancing an exhaustive tango of survival. Run, fight, or die—these are the laws of nature.

I am powerful! the wolf proudly thinks, patiently scanning the valley beneath him. He searches for his next victim. Antelope and deer think they find safety in obscure resting places, but Kiowa can see some of them.

A symphony of crickets applauds his bravado.

Corner flaps of his nostrils flare in short heaves, detecting the familiar scent of his companion among the drowning aroma of pine trees and sagebrush. The quieting crickets sober up when they feel the earth shake. They rest their fiddles and alert him that she is closer than he thinks.

He scans the valley, searching the open places where he can easily spy her. His eyes pull at the shifting shadows below the creaking trees. To mortal eyes, the report would be nothing but darkness. To the wolf's eyes, squirrels, rabbits, and skunks run as though the forest were on fire, even though clearly it is not.

Patches of white flash between breaks in the trees. Sudden flickers of motion catch his attention.

With soft excited whimpers, he lets Anoki know that he longs to see her.

Her pace increases, causing his paws to pat at the hard ground. His claws curl and scratch the earth.

All at once, she explodes through the thick shrubs. Moonlight strikes her beautiful ivory coat, eerily illuminating it. Her ghostly appearance would easily be mistaken for an apparition, were it not for her sparkling blue eyes and pink nose.

Her topaz jewels fix on Kiowa's golden glowing halos and reciprocate his anticipation.

The massive black-and-white wolf stands erect. Warm tingling sensations crackle like blue lightning in his heart and ignite a fire in those massive chambers. It is a fire that was not felt in her absence. His heart must be empty or he cannot kill. When those flames ignite, love swells and pumps across his thudding chest. He feels it spread from the tip of his black nose to the end of his white-tipped, bushy gray tail.

"Come to me!" He beckons his wife.

Anoki prances with a feminine finesse. She trots over with a giddiness in her step. She gently presses her soft cheek against his firm chest. Kiowa inhales her spirit and instantly knows from her many scents that she has hid in the musky den with the cubs, traveled by the minty spring, rolled in the wild prairie flowers, and passed through the tall evergreen forest.

She presses herself along Kiowa's side, then pauses briefly, letting her soft bushy tail delicately rest beneath his snout. She thinks of all the victims who have fallen prey to his fierce jaws. It excites her to know that only her elegance and grace are permitted to dance past those treacherous gates.

She drags the rest of her fluffy tail beneath his jaw and across his back. She turns and smiles when she feels him shudder.

"Your soul is fused to mine," he whispers.

"As yours is to mine. Why else do you think I was brought here? I felt the stitches tug," she responds, circling him. She tilts her sleek nose down and presses her forehead to his. Their ears lower. Their tails wag. They remain staring deep into each other's eyes like this until the electric emotions overwhelm him. The chambers explode, causing Kiowa to tilt his head up, exposing his pale, broad chest. With a deep heave, he unleashes a high-pitched howl, which echoes miles away. The hooting owl spreads its wings and scatters loose feathers. The coyotes tuck their tails and run. Bears snuggle up against their cubs. Raccoons shiver and climb trees. Even the cougars seek shelter inside caves to protect their young. None are safe from the King of the Currumpaw. All are meat.

Anoki tilts her head back and howls just a few octaves higher than Kiowa. The two croon the beastly song of love as the moon goes down.

Amber sun flecks dance across the towering mountain peaks, gathering in the graceful grassy valleys below. Morning birds join the howling wolves and a new day for an old love is born.

Aaaaaaarrrrrreeeeewwwww!

CHAPTER 1

"That's not scary!" a bucktoothed lad named John interrupts. His doubtful tone and squinty chestnut eyes shatter the Woodcraft Indian scoutmaster's trance over his four-man troop.

"We want to hear a scary story, not a y-u-c-k-y love story!" his brother protests, curling his fingers like claws and baring his missing front teeth. The most obvious difference between the two brothers is that Luther's hair is pitch-black and John's is light brown.

"I don't want to hear a scary story." Kevin, a five-year-old Korean boy, whimpers. He pulls his wool blanket over his bowl-cut black hair. He does this not because he's cold, but because Charlie, his scoutmaster, terrifies him.

"Me either!" Zack, John's youngest brother, shouts, almost matching Kevin's squeaky tone. He glances over his shoulder, flashing the same chestnut eyes his brothers have. The most handsome of the Taylor brothers, he moves closer to the fire and pulls his winter cap down farther, nearly covering his sandy blond hair.

"You're two years older than me," Kevin whispers to Zack. "You're supposed to be braver than I am. Who's gonna protect me in this dark, scary place?" Kevin scans the looming woods. "Run, kill, or die," he chirps. Without a doubt, he knows he would run.

Luther lifts a flaming marshmallow out of the fire and holds it to his lips. The orange flames illuminate his freckled face and scraggly black hair. "I'm not scared." He cocks his head and teases them. "You guys are titty-sucking babies!"

"Are not!" John cries out defensively, leaping off his stump.

Luther puckers his abnormally puffy lips and says, "Are sooo!" as he makes a sucking noise. He turns his attention to the scoutmaster. "Tell us the story about the one-legged man, 'Click Shaw'!"

The scoutmaster's big blue eyes and bulging gnome cheeks divide with a prominent English nose, a bushy mustache, and narrow lips. His pudgy frame fills his khaki Woodcraft Indian shirt out to the point where the buttons pucker and nearly pop off. The fifty-something man sits on a log stump near the fire and sips a steaming cup of coffee from a worn tin cup. It nearly matches the color of his silver-speckled brown hair.

"Yous fellas don't want to hear about the great Canadian wolf hunter?"

"Yeah, I wanna hear about that!" John turns to Luther with a sour face. "'Click Shaw' is a stupid story, and we've already heard it!"

Insulted by his oldest brother's protest, Luther gasps and shouts, "IS NOT!"

"IS SO!"

The two continue like this until Charlie calms them.

"It's super-duper dumb!" Zack aligns with John and makes sure he gets the last word.

"No way. It scared me so bad the last time I heard it, I slept under my mom's bed for a week." Kevin whimpers, blinking with pouting eyes. "Don't tell us scary stories in this dark forest."

"Scaredy-cat!" Kyle mocks him.

"All right, all right, settle down. It's not a scary story, Kevin. 'Chai Ma Kue' is a story of Indian love and magic."

Charlie pauses and waits for a response. When the boys' faces sag, he adds, "It has some scary parts, though!"

The boys' faces light up.

"There's a war," he emphasizes as he sets his tin cup down.

"A war?" Luther perks up, raising his brows hopefully.

"It began a long time ago. Imagine, if you can, a place where prairies stretch out like an ocean until the grasslands recede and turn into dry desert lands."

As he speaks, he reaches into his pocket and throws a handful of dry red berries into the crackling fire. They snap and pop. Thick purple smoke plumes, and the Woodcraft Indian scoutmaster masterfully stages the scene. He picks up a drum.

"Many tribes roamed these lands," he says, pounding a beat and then handing Zack the drum. The boy eagerly snatches the drum out of Charlie's hands and matches the beat.

Charlie claps his hands with arms stretched out in front and raises his hands high above his head. He sings, "These are the tribes"— he spins around and grabs a pair of rough bark sticks, smacks them together, and hands them to John—"of Indian nations."

Charlie hands Kevin his empty tin cup and flicks it with his fingernail to add a high tone to his makeshift band. The boy takes it and hums along.

"*Hi aiye, hiya.*" Charlie releases a Native American chant the boys have never heard, but they rouse and rally.

"*Hi aiye, hi aiye,*" the boys repeat in chorus.

Charlie cups his hands and pushes the purple smoke up to his face. He inhales, then blows it out in rings. Holding two fingers out, he draws them behind his ear and makes the sign of the Kiowa.

"There were many tribes that wandered these lands. The Kiowa. The Blackfoot. The Comanche. The Crow. The Sioux. The Cherokee. The Navajo, and the Hopi, to name just a few." The boys marvel at the distinct signs his hands make identifying each respective tribe.

The rotund scoutmaster claps his hands together again, making a thunderous noise that echoes off the dark trees as the purple smoke swirls above their heads and then fades against the rising pearl moon.

Charlie reaches inside his bag and removes a leather pouch. He unfolds it and reveals four brown-and-white eagle feathers. Holding one up by the stiff quill, he spins it in his fingers.

"Our story begins with the Kiowa." He hands each boy an eagle feather, then turns around, snatches up the leather pouch, and shoves his hand back in.

The boys' wondrous wide eyes zero in on whatever must be inside. Charlie slowly removes a plastic bag of hot dogs.

"Wowie zowie, hot dogs!" Zack shouts, dropping his feather and clamoring for his dinner.

Charlie takes his seat. "Scattered all across the plains are rolling rocky peaks that twist and turn into emerald mountaintops, packed limb to limb with towering pine, spruce, and Douglas fir trees as big as any you ever seen. Wild prairie flowers fill the air with sweet scents, and their purple, yellow, white, and red bodies spring up freely all around, covering the earth in a colorful quilt of beauty. Down beneath the emerald growth, beige rocky deserts span out as far as the eye can see and sometimes turn into steep winding canyons and rolling mesas. Running waters pass through at length and unite the vast land, offering life to everyone and everything. The plains are rich pastures, which are great for cattle range. This desolate beauty is known as the Currumpaw." He skewers a hot dog and lowers it into the fire. "The Kiowa were a warrior tribe," he says as the boys use red-handled Swiss Army knives to sharpen pine sticks to points and then skewer their hot dogs.

"Currumpaw was a place of prescribed beauty, but it wasn't always obvious. In the blazing summers, it was ugly as sin. Cactus and scorching sands burned the venom right out of scorpions. Spring was different. Nights were warm. Evenings were cool. It was a land of sunshine and wildflowers. The air was rich and full of songbirds' sweet music.

"The funny thing about the Currumpaw is that no matter the season, dawn and sunset transform that place into a magnificent gem. Beige mountains turn pink or tangerine orange. It is unexpected and majestic."

He pauses and stares off in the distance, as though he can actually see it.

"And terribly dangerous! Though nature poses its own challenges with bitter dry winters, there are, of course, other dangers." Charlie's voice energizes. He holds his hands up and curls his long, chubby fingers. "The claws of the grizzly bear are powerful enough to tear a man's head off with one swipe!" He swooshes his hands at Luther's face. The courageous boy flinches, which causes the other boys to duck and almost drop their weenies.

Charlie slowly scoops his hand to his mouth. "With a single bite, a bear's jaws can bite a man in half. These wild bears are known to terrorize the Indians. Oh, and there are cougars aplenty! And though they may not have the power of grizzly bears, they have speed and determination. Did any of you know a single lion was responsible for the deaths of fifty grown men bigger than me?"

The boys stare in astonishment and shake their heads in disbelief.

"Beneath almost every rock, creeping, crawling critters lurk. 'Course, the venomous fangs of rattlesnakes and the poison of scorpion tails hide from the sun and come out at night, putting the sting of their hate in whatever they can... just because they can!"

"It sounds like a terrible place!" Kevin shouts.

"Yes! It was a terrible, wonderful place. For the Kiowa, it was home."

Charlie can see that the boys are paying full attention now.

"Our story begins with an Indian raid..."

CHAPTER 2

A lone Kiowa warrior loosens rawhide straps that stitch together his shirt. The fringe on the sides accentuates each motion. He removes the garment and feels a morning chill against his muscular chest, which looks like it belongs to a chiseled statue. Enhanced by his reddish-brown skin, his rippling abdomen muscles flex.

Pink scars stand out in stark contrast to his permanently tanned skin. Some are small and indicate his skill and speed. The deepest, ugliest scars are the ones he's most proud of. "Proof of my magic," he would say when he would tell his sons war stories.

He hears the frenzied barking of dogs, which makes him suspicious. Sleepy-eyed warriors dressed in nothing but buckskin loincloths abandon the warmth of their tepees. They yawn and stretch themselves awake.

Lazy, Lone Wolf thinks to himself, wiping his grooved face.

His jaw flexed, he slowly scans the distant tree line with determination. He glances at the crackling fires and then up at the sparkling stars, which are beginning to fade in dawn's early light. His high cheekbones lift and cause his almond-shaped eyes to squint.

"Barking dogs. Predawn. This is no coincidence," Lone Wolf grumbles.

As the tribe members slip into their leggings and blouses, a brave points at the dogs and says, "They just started."

"We are about to be attacked. Awake the women and alert the warriors." Lone Wolf speaks with a calm, firm mouth and a decisive tone. His authority is not questioned. The brave leaps to action with Lone Wolf's dismissive sign.

"*Hey ya at ah hey!*" The brave runs over to a wide drum and pounds on it, whooping the war cry.

Lone Wolf wraps his long silky black hair around his fingers and twists it into a bun. He pins it in place with a thin fish bone as the war cry travels from tepee to tepee. His wife and children quickly grab his war dress and weapons.

Lone Wolf's wife, Grass Woman, appears with a noble eagle-feathered war bonnet. She proudly places it on his head and fastens the chinstrap. The tallest feathers in front represent Lone Wolf's most epic battles. The smaller feathers mean less to him, but they are still recorded victories. A long trail runs down his back and nearly touches the ground.

"I will gain many feathers today!" Lone Wolf exclaims, reaching for his weapon of choice, a bleached elk shoulder blade, which has been sharpened and spiked. Dried rust-colored bloodstains indicate the weapon's extensive use. His son holds the weapon out to him, smiling when his father receives it.

His oldest son, Two Moons, hastily paints a rectangular black square around his dark brown eyes, to keep him focused.

"My love for each of you swells with pride every time you prepare me for battle!"

"Father, it is our honor," Two Moons replies as he sharpens the corners to his war paint.

Grass Woman ties a leather pouch of magic to Lone Wolf's waistband and kisses him on the cheek. "May you kill many enemies, fill my arms with their scalps, and return without harm," she prays aloud, looking at her sons.

Lone Wolf glances at his wife. "You magnify my love for you with these sons you have given me. Ah-hoe, Grass Woman, you are my beautiful little woman."

She blushes, then scurries about grabbing this and that, anything he may need for the fight.

"Hurry. We haven't much time!" Lone Wolf orders his elite band of savage Dog Warriors.

Within moments Two Moons has his father's face, neck, chest, arms, abdomen, and back covered in red paint. Dipping his finger in black, he quickly smears a wolf's image over his father's heart.

"Darken the light areas with streaks," Two Moons orders his younger brother, Weasel Tail, as he begins covering himself in red paint. Aged sixteen and fourteen, the boys are not virgins to war, but they are not seasoned Dog Warriors, either. Two Moons looks up to his father. "I pray to the wolf that you will be swift, powerful, and deadly."

Weasel Tail rests his fingertips on his father's head. "I pray to the wise owl that you will have courage, cunning, and above all, wisdom."

Their father closes his eyes and listens to their prayers. He feels the increase in his heartbeat as it matches the beat of the drum. *Thump, thump, thump...*

He reflects on the word "wisdom" of his son's prayer and envisions his previous enemies' conquered faces. One by one he plays out the mistakes they made. He sees their leg muscles flex, their heels rising as they step too far forward or their muscles relax, heels staying on the ground as they shuffle back.

Watch the toes. Toes tell you everything! he thinks, mentally preparing himself. The drum keeps time.

Elderly women and children frantically run around and dump thick bushels of moss on crackling fires. Flames swell at first, then create a lingering smoky haze that billows and hovers.

An old woman orders a young boy, "Go fetch the medicine man, Onendah. Our smoke is not working properly. It will never mask the village like this! We need his magic."

The tribe divides itself into those who can fight and those who cannot. Some women remove their beaded buckskin tops and expose their bare breasts. With the help of their husbands and children, they paint themselves red like the warriors. The elderly, the young women, and the children hastily paint their own faces and clothes brown and green to match the colors of the forest.

"Don't forget your brother," Glances Then Glares says as she straps her son Makes Trouble to a papoose. His sister, Kida, slides her arms through the cradle's straps and secures her brother to her back. When she's finished, Glances Then Glares looks up at the enemy, then down at her daughter. She leans in and kisses her surprisingly calm daughter.

"Go now to the safe place I showed you!"

Kida retreats and dissolves into the forest with the others.

Glances Then Glares wipes a tear from her eye. She grits her teeth, grabs a bow and a stash of three-foot-long arrows with four-inch feathered fletch-and-steel tips. The arrows are painted with similar symbols of magic, which identify her tribe, her falcon god, and wavy symbols of the wind to guide her aim true. Grooves carved in the shaft allow blood to ooze out, while the tips are loosely fastened so that when the enemy pulls to extract them, they stay in place.

Chaos turns to order as the entire tribe readies for war in less than fifteen minutes. Lone Wolf raises his weapon high in the air. Painted warriors quickly circle around him.

"Put fear in their hearts before you shatter them! A heart filled with courage will not break. A heart filled with fear blows apart like withered leaves."

"*Ha hoe!*" the warriors shout in unison. Their voices echo off in the distance and send a message to their unseen enemies that the Kiowa are not afraid.

Surrounding their chief, the men show their crude weapons of war. Some hold iron-cast tomahawks, while others ready weapons of their own creation. Some have carved spikes or wrapped deer-hide tomahawks with round stone tips. Others have spears. Most warriors have shields with sacred animals painted on them.

Some greet the unseen foe with smiles, some with frowns. Everyone feels the thrill and responds accordingly.

"Father, we are ready," Two Moons shouts.

Lone Wolf stomps his foot and leads the whooping Kiowa war cry.

"*AIYE YA-AYE HI WHA YA!*"

Their voices unite in one loud roar, echoing off the distant pine trees surrounding their clearing and sending the ravens soaring. The black birds hover in the summer sky like black demons, circle appraisingly, and caw. The vile ravens perch outside of the fray, jeering at the players.

"Do you see how they would not land on those trees over there?" Lone Wolf asks his sons.

Two Moons nods.

"Why do you think that is?"

CHAPTER 3

"It is because our enemy is there." Two Moons grunts, pointing at the trees the birds avoided.

"This I know. Ravens always linger for rewards," says Raven Claw, a short but fierce warrior. His narrow face tightens and his eyes squint into slivers.

In the thick of the dense pine forest, beneath the cawing ravens, a Cheyenne chief lies flat on his belly. Covered in the hide of a black bear, he remains perfectly still and completely hidden beneath the North Pacific ferns. His stone-colored eyes shift back and forth. He exhales gruffly. Beneath his hooked nose, his abnormally large jaw clenches. He tilts his broad face to the side; the right side is painted black and the left, white.

Will they charge us? Fox Thoughts, a seasoned warrior, signs as he gives away his camouflaged position.

If they knew where we were, Black Bear signs back.

All they would have to do is look beneath the cawing ravens, Fox Thoughts signs.

An elderly Kiowa medicine man steps in front of the Kiowa tribe. His face is painted red, with stripes of black. A yellow circle is painted around his right eye to show that he has the power of future sight. A pale moon is painted around his left eye so that he does not forget the past. His long silver hair is divided into two braids. Wire copper rings widen his earlobes. Around his wrinkled neck, he wears a bear-claw necklace. Beads mesh against the claws. Each color represents a spell, and he wonders, *Which one will help the most and use the least magic?* Gold wrist couplings gleam in the morning light. He clacks them three times, summoning his power. *Fog will protect us*, he thinks. His deerskin leggings and bone breastplate are woven with the scalps of his enemies. Not all are Indian; some are white people. By the length and curl, a few are obviously women's.

Brass bells and a human scalp hang from the handle of his wand. The tip is an eagle's claw with a round clear crystal firmly fixed in place. He raises his medicine wand and chants.

"*PAHN-BAH-KHAW-BAH.*" The turquoise-encrusted handle begins to glow like blue lightning. The facets of the crystal ball illuminate his face and reflect in his pupils.

He raises his hands up and down, summoning a strong breeze that lifts loose silver strands of hair off his shoulders. The leather fringe in his worn bleached-white blouse rattles against his sides. His brown eyes gloss with a milky haze. Vapors rise from the earth. As he chants, the vapors turn into a thick fog and swirl around his firm frame. Soon the village is masked by the medicine man's magic. His wand glows like a lantern on a misty day. When his work is done, the light fades and a village that could be spotted by a sneaky enemy is now perfectly concealed in a smother as thick as a cloud.

In the pine forest, the sneaky enemy, Chief Black Bear, signs, *Do not let their medicine man fool you; they are terrified.*

Reflecting on this latest development, he's forced to reconsider his commitment to the raid. He scans the Kiowa village and admires their mind for war. The smoke screen conceals every living soul, and the barking dogs have cost him his most precious weapon, the element of surprise. Chief Black Bear pauses for a moment and wonders, *Is their magic stronger than mine?* He appraises the village, counting the tops of tepees poking out of the thick gray cloud.

Fifty tepees means fifty warriors—maybe more but probably less. The main body of their tribe is off hunting, Black Bear thinks. *What is that to my hundred?* His confidence surges, and he leans toward attack.

Gray Hawk approaches his father, Black Bear, and the two crouch together, conspiring.

"The warriors grow uneasy and want to return to camp," his son whispers. Gray Hawk, a younger and handsomer version of his father, wears a thick, bushy, dome-shaped war bonnet of gray hawk feathers. His face and muscular chest are painted black, with streaks of white.

Black Bear remains silent. He focuses intently on the stirring mist.

"Father, they sign 'bad magic' and fear for their scalps."

"Magic?" Black Bear says with a broad smile. "I have the greatest magic on earth!" He hammers his fist to his bone-plated chest armor.

The Kiowas' smoke stirs, the mist whirls, and the haze reveals a lone shadow. It is soon joined by another and another.

The numbers grow quickly, and Black Bear counts about fifty. The Kiowas' thunderous war cries make the tribe sound like hundreds, maybe even a thousand warriors. The Cheyenne chief wonders if his hundred warriors are enough for this fight.

If we leave, the warriors will lose respect for me. Surely one will challenge me. But if we fight... He steadies his heart rate, closes his eyes, and seeks vision. His eyes flutter as he searches for an answer. He knows this is the most critical piece of information any chief can ascertain before waging an attack. *How many warriors do I face?*

"Listen! Listen to your chief! Take courage! Like all of you, my heart had doubts. They blew in just now, but I have just been told by our war god, Hotamintanio, to purge our hearts of doubt and fear. Give ear to my words. In my vision Hotamintanio says the main tribe is farther north chasing buffalo. We found their tracks and followed them back here, did we not?"

A few men nod.

"Hotamintanio says no more than fifty Kiowa are in that village and if we leave, their horses and scalps will not be ours. He says to light a fire of wrath in your hearts. It is our right to raid. RAID NOW! Take from them their women, their horses, and their scalps, even their children. Make our tribe rich! Do you want to offend our god?"

The men look around, their doubting expressions mirrored all around them.

A warrior with arms as big as boulders speaks up. "I have two troubles that lean me toward leaving. Your first vision said this would be the fight to end all the Kiowa. This isn't one fight, but now two. My second trouble is with your magic. It made sense when we could stalk them, easily kill them in their sleep, and take all the spoils you promised us. How can your magic be believed now that they are awake and ready to give us a good fight? The spoils should already be in our hands. We have much to lose. Women. Children. Horses. Scalps. I say my scalp is better fixed to my head. I say it is better to kill and scalp *you* than take these risks."

Gray Hawk steps forward and speaks over his father in a hushed voice with outstretched hands. "You cannot threaten my father, Boulder Arms. Your strength will feed your family. But my father has told me something he has not yet told you. Listen to him now before your heart fails you."

The warriors' long, painted faces turn toward Chief Black Bear.

"If you leave this war party, you make peace. The Kiowa will use your peaceful kindness against you. They will make more children. We will fight again— you know this to be true. If we fight now, we take their peace from them. Do you so easily forget your hatred for what the Kiowa have done to our people? Do you forget the hell they made for us on their last raid? I say we make a hell for them. Let their women be your wives! Make their children your slaves. Imagine if our women and children never had to dress an animal or gather firewood. Our days would be made easier by the hell we make for them today."

Chief Black Bear's speech is incredibly effective. "Their horses will be yours. Boulder Arms, you can pick first of everything we take!"

This brings many agreeable nods.

Boulder Arms still isn't convinced.

As Black Bear gains steady support, his eyes flash with excitement. He raises his voice, but not loud enough to be heard by the Kiowa. "Think of the glory that will be ours. Their scalps will rest on the arms of our women, who will dance with them, singing, 'Look, here is my enemy who cursed me. What has become of him now?' Which of you would not want this honor?"

The warriors raise their weapons and celebrate with growing approval— everyone except Boulder Arms.

"I see that you do not support me, Boulder Arms, and you have challenged my magic. That is good! Who can say magic is this or that without seeing it with their own eyes?"

Boulder Arms nods with a deep, questioning frown.

"Look here!"

CHAPTER 4

Chief Black Bear leaps to his feet and answers Lone Wolf's challenge. "Behold, the Sun God has blessed me with his power!" he shouts as he unveils a supernaturally golden lance that glows like the amber flames of the sun. Brilliant light illuminates his eerie black-and-white painted face and his greedy smile. A glowing, celestial light creeps up his arms and arcs over his shoulders, then trails down his torso. His cold, hard eyes shift back and forth wildly. His long black hair blows back. Whereas Lone Wolf's war bonnet is crafted out of eagle feathers, Black Bear's war bonnet is made out of the sun.

"Warriors, hear me! Boulder Arms has asked to see my power, and here it is!"

"*Ha ya!*" the Cheyennes' whooping war cry begins.

Chief Black Bear swipes his fingers across Boulder Arms's chest to make the mark of the bear claw. Glowing light illuminates from the finger trace.

"He paints with the sun! Our chief has the power!" Boulder Arms declares.

"Let the bravest warriors touch Boulder Arms and share in my power."

One by one the strongest and bravest Cheyenne touch the magic mark and stand in awe as the amber aura passes from him to them.

Black Bear shouts, "See my power and believe my words. This is the first battle that will end the Kiowa. Tomorrow we will find the rest of their tribe and kill them all! Ready your tomahawks! Unsheathe your spears! Prepare your arrows! Spread your warrior wings and dip your feathers in the lake of their blood. Do not worry about your own scalp. Instead, let them fear the gleam of our scalping knives. Today the SUN GOD IS WITH US!"

A hundred black-and-white painted Cheyenne warriors, glowing with the light of the sun, circle around Black Bear and Gray Hawk to revel in their glory. Their hopes are high, and they are ready to attack.

Chief Black Bear steps out of the shadowy forest, parading the golden lance high above his head. Not wanting to commit his full force to the fight, he makes a strategic decision to divide his force into two groups: a main attack composed of his best warriors to wear the Kiowa down, and a reserve force he will send in later to finish them off.

Black Bear points his magic lance at the Kiowa and shouts, "TAKE COURAGE! KILL THEM ALL!"

Across the field, Lone Wolf is shocked to see a strange phenomenon emanating from within the forest, beneath the cawing raven. The sun seems to have fallen from the sky, and its rays now flicker and burst up out of the tree line.

Has the sun lost its place? Lone Wolf wonders.

The Kiowa warriors gasp at what they see. Chief Black Bear seems more like a god than a man.

Lone Wolf does something he's never done before; he takes a step back and feels a great fear tighten in his throat. His legs wobble and feel as heavy as mountains.

"Cheap tricks," Lone Wolf hears the medicine man, Onendah, protest, as he steps out of the mist. "If they could use that power to harm us, why wouldn't they?"

Onendah's calm voice reduces Lone Wolf's fear. As he looks heavenward, his worried eyes spy a pure white eagle soaring over the tall pointy pine trees. Its high-pitched screech scatters the ravens and sends them swarming for cover. Their cawing symphony mixes with the Kiowas' war song.

Without flapping its wings, the white eagle glides over towering evergreens that nearly touch the sky. Time seems to slow as the swaying trees lean one way, then gradually the other.

"I know not your name, White Eagle, but I must understand: Have you come to take me to the happy hunting grounds?" Lone Wolf questions.

Lone Wolf watches the elegant creature tilt its wings. His eyes grow heavy and drop to the earth; he watches the eagle's shadow slowly circle around him. He looks up and feels an avalanche of emotions crash inside him. For the first time in his life, he feels the frost of death nipping at his heels. As quickly as the fear came, it melts. Lone Wolf feels an immediate sense of calm that erases the pettiness of this world. For a tranquil moment, it is evident that his circle is complete.

"They sound close. Should we not step out of the mist and greet them?" Two Moons asks, breaking Lone Wolf's tranquility.

Lone Wolf takes a deep breath and looks beyond this life. He rests his weapon against his thigh. His massive shoulders rise and flex. The veins in his neck contract. His biceps pulsate. His back muscles tighten. He tilts his head and cracks his neck.

"Father, can you hear me?" Two Moons asks.

"Shields up! Arrows will soon fall like raindrops," Lone Wolf answers, wiping the tears from his eyes.

"What will we do?"

Lone Wolf searches for words that will inspire his son. They form slowly in his heart and come softly from his lips. "Live your lives as though there is no tomorrow, for today is all we really have! I have spent my life fighting. I know what I must do!"

Lone Wolf ties his shield to his arm, smiles, and then charges the Cheyenne all on his own.

CHAPTER 5

Lone Wolf's hasty attack lifts the morale of his enemies. They respond by drawing the strings of their bows, eagerly awaiting the symphony notes they will add to the chorus of war cries.

"See how afraid they are, my brothers!" Black Bear shouts. "Only one warrior is brave enough to fight!"

Black Bear points his magical lance at the painted bowmen.

"Deliver death!" the Cheyenne chief orders his longbow archers.

The snap of their strings unleashes a whistling wave of arrows, which arch high in the blue morning sky.

Lone Wolf watches the distant splinters scatter like swarming locusts. They peak at a high arch, level out, and then the tips tilt and they come raining down. He sprints for a fallen tree that the men have been hollowing out for a fishing canoe.

Arrows dive into the earth. Wobbling three-foot-long shafts *thunk* as they strike the trunk. Their distinct markings identify the owners as the Cheyenne tribe. Additional markings show that they are actually several bands of the Cheyenne nation.

From Black Bear's vantage point, Lone Wolf's position is riddled with arrows. He hails his victory with a bold war cry that excites his reserves and makes them froth for the attack. The archers fire a second wave.

Flint-tipped arrows continue to strike all around Lone Wolf. He sees the arrowheads spark when they smash against the ground and snap in half.

"Thank you, Taime, for sending me an enemy that has poor craftsmanship," Lone Wolf whispers to his god. "And thank you for letting Water Boy play in the grass last night. Had he not skipped and danced all about, poorly made flint arrows could have sent your other son, Fire Boy, to destroy us."

Bodies covered in black-and-white paint sprint across a wide-open field that separates the Kiowa from the forest. Half of their bodies disappear in the tall lime-green grass.

Bushy dome-shaped war bonnets made of ravens' feathers swoosh back and forth as they go. The enormous size makes their heads seem much larger than they really are.

"*Nat hey, hey ya!*" The Cheyenne scream their war song.

Lone Wolf can tell by their aggressiveness that these relentless warriors have one ambition – to wet their weapons with Kiowa blood. The thought of his children or his brothers being harmed ignites a fire that feels like an exploding sun. Courage melts to hatred. *What can be done? They wave their weapons wildly and sing for our scalps*, he thinks.

Lone Wolf lies low against the grass and watches to see how the Cheyenne move. He intentionally placed the village a good distance from the forest for this exact reason. At the time it had seemed like a good idea, but now that he sees the quarter mile the Cheyenne must sprint across, he knows it was wonderful wisdom!

From the Cheyennes' perspective, the waist-high grass makes the village seem closer than it actually is. The bravest, most excited warriors separate from the pack.

Lone Wolf pushes his seething rage back to clear his mind. He does as his father taught him: watch, plan, act.

Most of the Cheyenne run at a similar pace, but what makes Lone Wolf happiest is seeing the increasing number of stragglers exhaust themselves and slow to a trot.

In your weakness, I will take strength! Lone Wolf thinks, biding his time.

Behind the patient, motionless warrior, the lingering hazy smoke cloud begins to clear. Seventy men and women painted blood red grip their weapons of war.

Half of the Kiowa spearmen hold long metal-tipped spears twice the length of their bodies. Archers carry fine bows and metal-tipped arrows. The Dog Warriors ready their shiny steel tomahawks and their buffalo-hide shields.

When the Kiowa can finally see the Cheyenne approaching, they release a war cry with one loud voice, which surges like a wave over the field and causes some of the Cheyenne to rethink their attack.

Chief Lone Wolf's confidence rises to elation when he sees that his enemies' arrowheads aren't the only weapons made of stone. Their tomahawks, spears, lances, and crude weapons are all crafted with some use of stone, which means they won't cut as deep, fly as far, swing as fast, or do nearly as much damage as his tribe's superior weapons.

"Bad day to be Cheyenne," Lone Wolf mumbles.

Rather than sprint toward their enemy, the Kiowa start at a steady pace that keeps their group united and focused.

Lone Wolf smiles broadly. "Now when we fight, we fight as one!"

He waits for the Cheyenne warriors to get even closer before standing up.

Gray Hawk, Chief Black Bear's son, stops in his tracks as he approaches their spent arrows. Unable to locate their kill, he looks behind him and realizes that his raiders have dispersed.

"GET UP HERE, COWARDS!" he orders the stragglers.

Though they are near, they are still too far behind.

"Wait for the others!" Gray Hawk shouts to his sprinting brothers. "We must be united!" But weapons once unleashed are hard to tame and impossible to control.

Something doesn't feel right, Gray Hawk thinks. He turns back and tries to motivate the larger separated body, but the temperature has risen to the point that they are panting.

From the safety of the forest, Black Bear revels in the soft glow of his power until he sees his youngest, and favorite son, Gray Hawk, trying to stop the assault. He watches his bloodthirsty braves within reach of the Kiowa village and wishes for his son to be with them.

Show no weakness! Glory is yours, my son! the impatient chief signs.

At the edge of the village, hidden among the tall grass, several Kiowa braves spring up from the earth and snap the strings of their bows. They quickly cycle through their stash of arrows and laugh as they watch their projectiles puncture the sinister Cheyenne bodies. One by one the raging lead element falls.

Lone Wolf watches their blood wet the grass. He patiently waits for their bold cries of war to change to the chorus of agony.

All of the Kiowa Dog Warriors, spear holders, and archers quickly reunite with the night watch and gain ground. The Dog Warriors raise their shields to make one solid protected line. Kiowa arrows rain down upon the stragglers, and soon Gray Hawk feels the effects of his divided attack.

"Here I stand," Lone Wolf shouts, goading the straggling Cheyenne.

"I see you, coward! You hide in the grass like a snake. I will separate your head from your body! That is what we do to snakes!" Gray Hawk shouts, reuniting with twenty or so warriors to press onward.

"*AH-HOE!*" Lone Wolf screams.

"*AH-HOE!*" The warriors echo his war chant.

In a blur of the chaos, Gray Hawk leads his troop in a heated attack against the full force of the Kiowa.

The Cheyenne slam against Kiowa shields. On the first impact, the Kiowa stand strong. Lone Wolf orders the Dog Warriors to kneel, and when they do, the archers fire into the horde.

Some Cheyenne fall, but the warriors do not slow in their aggressive assault. They renew with vigor. They swing their weapons wildly and hurl their spears with fatal results.

Next Lone Wolf orders the Dog Warriors to step forward and stand. As they do so, the spearmen thrust at the Cheyenne, pushing them back. For the Cheyenne, the strategy is brutal aggression. They push against the shields, probing for the weakest point. When they see a Dog Warrior fall, they focus all of their efforts on the opening. Their hand-to-hand skill is much greater than Lone Wolf had expected.

For the Kiowa, the fight is tempered calm. They work together, shield men blocking the attack, archers taking shots where they can, and spearmen puncturing warriors who get too close to the line.

Most tribes would fall back when facing this kind of skilled warfare, but not the Cheyenne. Always pushing, thrusting, attacking, they are like the red ant of the Indian nation.

With eyes fixed on Gray Hawk, Lone Wolf seeks to change the tempo of the fight. He skillfully sifts through the warring crowd, ignoring the cries of pain around him. He moves with such swiftness no Cheyenne is prepared for his aggressive attack and none can repel him. For when he seems like he's coming straight, he turns at the last minute, bends low, and strikes a leg. Then he runs past and hits an arm. His intent is not to waste his energy fighting all the warriors, just wound as many as he can to get to the leader.

As the Dog Warriors disband and follow Lone Wolf, the spear warriors spread out and form a long reverse V-shape that protects the Kiowa flanks and keeps the archers safely in the middle. It isn't long before the Cheyenne realize they are actually fighting two enemies. One body of the Kiowa uses marksmanship and control. The other uses chaos and raging hand-to-hand combat.

In truth, bloodshed sickens Lone Wolf. He detests the brutality of it. He hates the sound bones make when the tomahawk strikes. He finds no joy in the maiming of limbs or disfiguring bodies. In fact, it all disgusts him. He detests the bitter rusty taste of human blood when it splashes in his mouth. The salty aroma causes him to gag, but he knows one single truth: If the Cheyenne weren't bleeding and dying, the Kiowa would be.

It is our right to defend ourselves. No living thing when attacked rolls over and dies. That clarity forces him to hack, chop, and slash through Cheyenne warriors until he finally reaches his destination.

"Your wife and children will be my slaves, Kiowa!" Gray Hawk whoops, pointing his blood-soaked tomahawk at Lone Wolf.

Lone Wolf sees images of Grass Woman, his wife, and feels his love for her fuel his rage. He reels back his weapon and ferociously swings at Gray Hawk's blood-drenched face.

CHAPTER 6

Lone Wolf's elk blade narrowly misses Gray Hawk's throat. The young warrior dodges and feels the *swoosh* of Lone Wolf's crimson elk blade.

Gray Hawk's confidence grows. He swings his war club.

Lone Wolf defensively ducks down and swipes low at his opponent. Gray Hawk blocks. They aggressively lock weapons. Gray Hawk smiles a devilish grin, taunting Lone Wolf.

In response, the seasoned Kiowa warrior tilts his handle and smashes Gray Hawk's black-painted nose. The young man stumbles back and struggles through teary eyes to block Lone Wolf's assault. He feels a powerful gust as Lone Wolf slashes at his head but misses. Severed feathers from his headdress tickle his naked shoulders. Gray Hawk blunders his opportunity to counterattack and feels blood trickling down his lips. He regains his composure, holds his weapon up, and gets back in the fight.

Lone Wolf is thrown off-balance when his weapon fails to make contact. He feels a surge of rage. The assault he unleashes in a counterattack comes from years of experience and countless battles. Gray Hawk's inexperience shows as Lone Wolf presses the attack by swinging his elk blade, wildly striking high and low, putting the young warrior on the defense.

Gray Hawk does a sufficient job of blocking and maneuvering. The speed of the fight is a magnificent tornado of feathers and bronze muscle.

Gray Hawk strikes, and his weapon locks with Lone Wolf's. He feels the bone-rattling impact of the dense elk blade against his inferior tomahawk. His confidence wanes, yielding to exhaustion. He compensates by flexing his legs and boldly stepping forward to press the attack.

Gray Hawk sees the flash of Lone Wolf's war bonnet. This is the first sign that pain is coming. Next Gray Hawk feels the crack of Lone Wolf's weapon against his exposed shin. Gray Hawk falls to the ground. He clings to his leg, which is unnaturally bent backward. He screams in excruciating pain as he feels his splintered bone protruding from his skin. Blood spurts from the wound and stands out against the white paint on his leg. His high-pitched screams mock his earlier war cry. All traces of his courage and bravery are erased.

Like a master warrior artist, Lone Wolf paints his war with two distinct emotions: love and regret.

Safely surrounded by the cheering ravens, Chief Black Bear immediately feels his lust for power drain. He watches his hands rise in a futile attempt to stop Gray Hawk's attacker. Sheer terror manifests in the pit of Black Bear's stomach. A painful emotional hurricane swells inside the raiding chief.

"Save my son!" Black Bear shouts, releasing the Cheyenne reserve.

The reserve force follows the trampled trail left by the warriors before them.

The Kiowa cheer when they see that they've drawn out the rest of the Cheyenne warriors.

Gray Hawk cowers like a withered weed. He refuses to look up and see his doom. When the death blow he anticipates doesn't come, he can't help himself. His curiosity forces him to look up.

Oh, how death hangs in his eyes. No spark of mercy lingers in those halos, Gray Hawk thinks as Lone Wolf glares down at him. Behind the brutal Kiowa warrior, Boulder Arms emerges. He swings his tomahawk over his head and brings Dog Warriors to their knees.

Please, Boulder Arms, Gray Hawk prays. He closes his eyes and feels a surge of hope.

As Boulder Arms closes in on the unsuspecting Kiowa war chief, Dog Warriors surround him. The Dog Warriors go to work. They violently slash and smash any Cheyenne who would dare approach their great chief.

Gray Hawk slowly opens his eyes as three Kiowa warriors taunt Boulder Arms with spears. Boulder Arms fights bravely and kills one of the spearmen, but the other two are fast upon him. They stab him with their spears and draw their tomahawks. Gray Hawk's hope is dashed to pieces when he sees a tomahawk connect to Boulder Arm's pelvis.

"ARRRGGGHHH," Boulder Arms screams as his pelvic bone splits in two. He falls to his knees and drops his weapon. When he looks up, he sees those same hollow halos Gray Hawk saw. Lone Wolf's elbows lift high above his head. Boulder Arms raises his muscular arms to block the blow, but it's not enough. The elk blade severs his arm and makes a hollow crack against his skull, spilling his brains out of the side of his head. For a moment Lone Wolf can hear his thoughts; somehow he knows this man wished he had never joined the fight or even listened to the words that got him here, but it's too late for all that regret now. This is why Boulder Arms is the first victim of Lone Wolf's war brush, *regret*.

"No! Boulder Arms!" Gray Hawk shouts as he reaches for the twitching body and wails in a new kind of pain when the Cheyennes' strongest warrior joins an increasing number of lifeless casualties.

"Show me LOVE!" Lone Wolf shouts, focusing on the reserve.

"No, Father!" Gray Hawk shouts, no longer concerned for his own life.

"Father?" Lone Wolf sneers, fixated on the determined Cheyenne chief.

Gray Hawk looks around at the mangled bodies. The distant whooping cries of his cavalry bring him no peace.

"Release my spirit quickly, I beg you."

Lone Wolf grins broadly, focusing on the fast-approaching Cheyenne.

"Not quickly. Slowly." He rips Gray Hawk's war bonnet off and removes his scalping knife.

CHAPTER 7

"No! Please, mercy!" Gray Hawk begs Lone Wolf, feeling the cold blade pressed against his scalp.

"Mercy? Did you not come here for my little woman? Our children? Our scalps?"

Gray Hawk's protests turn to screams as he feels searing pain all over his crown. In one fluid motion, Lone Wolf uses his knife to cut a line from the back of Gray Hawk's right ear, then circles around his forehead and stops behind the other ear. Gray Hawk resists, but it is of no use.

"Arrrrggggghhhh!" Gray Hawk shrieks.

With a quick jerking motion, his scalp makes the same noise as cracking grass roots when the sod is separated from soil. Blood gushes down his face.

Lone Wolf holds the bloody trophy high and shouts, "Many take on few, and few win!"

He waves the son's scalp at his enraged father.

***

"Eww. He scalped him while he was alive?" Kevin gags.

Charlie adjusts his waistband and growls. "Lone Wolf's favorite weapon was the shoulder blade of an elk. With this mighty club, he fought off fifty men and prepared to fight off fifty more," the scoutmaster says, swiping his hands back and forth.

"He killed a hundred bad guys? That's not nearly as many as Alexander the Great," John blurts out.

"Yup!" Charlie responds, gulping down his coffee. "But 'bad guys' is a funny phrase. These two tribes were bitter enemies, though neither really knew why. They just knew someone scalped so-and-so and that's what started it all."

"I wanna see a scalp," Luther says with a devilish grin.

Charlie grunts and ignores him.

"How'd Lone Wolf get to be so strong?" Zack asks.

"He learned to be strong by becoming a great Indian wrestler. For sport, he would sometimes seize the ankle of his enemy, pick 'em up with one arm, swing 'em around his head, and smash 'em against a tree or a rock. You know, whichever was closer."

***

Lone Wolf does not seize an enemy by the foot but by the heart.

Black Bear sees the gleam of his son's blood-soaked skull. He watches helplessly as his son looks up and reaches for him. Chief Black Bear immediately feels his lust for power fade. His courage, conviction, and conceit evaporate. He immediately charges the Dog Warriors.

"My son! My love! My heart! Your father comes for you!" Black Bear roars.

Black Bear's ambience grows bright and temporarily blinds Lone Wolf. The brilliance of his power forces everyone to cover their eyes and shield their faces.

Lone Wolf slowly and deliberately makes eye contact with his enemy. He immediately notices that one of Black Bear's eyes is blue and the other is brown.

Dark clouds roll in. They blanket a blue sky. Cracks of lightning ignite and touch down all around Chief Black Bear. Bodies of both tribes become conductors and convulse when electricity touches them. Their torsos shake violently as their eyes glow and blue flames flicker out of their mouths before their scorched bodies fall to the ground.

The earth begins to shake and split apart. Indians struggle to keep their balance. It's useless. The grinding earth opens up and swallows warriors of both tribes. Chief Black Bear lifts the Sun God's lance to the sky. He summons a single bolt of blue lightning. The fluid crackles from far across the sky and touches the glowing lance. Sparks explode off his body and splash across Lone Wolf's shield.

In an impossible instant, the Cheyenne chief's black-and-white-painted face splits down the middle. Something terrible within fights to get out.

CHAPTER 8

Chief Black Bear's eyes flash yellow. Long black claws explode from his fingertips.

Raven Claw proves the Dog Warrior reputation. He summons all of his Kiowa courage and makes a last-ditch effort to attack. He lunges for a man, who is transitioning into a monster. Raven Claw is snatched up in a mighty bear hug. He gasps for breath and feels his ribs crack. Chief Black Bear opens his mangled mouth and roars with a beastly growl that scares Raven Claw to death.

"Kill him!" Lone Wolf commands everyone, hoping to unite both tribes in an attack against evil.

"Beware Chief Black Bear. His magic is too strong. Soon his jaws will bite. His fangs will catch and his claws will cut," Fox Thoughts bemoans.

The survivors of both tribes flee for their lives.

Defying the warning, Lone Wolf strikes the disfigured face of Chief Black Bear. He might as well be using his vital elk blade on a stone wall. All of his strength counts for nothing when he strikes the dense mass beneath flaking mortal flesh.

"I am death!" Lone Wolf screams in Black Bear's contorted face. He uses the handle of his weapon to strike Black Bear's drooping cheeks. They hang off Black Bear's face like melting wax. Lone Wolf ducks under Black Bear's swiping arm and then strikes again, ripping a portion of human flesh off the shoulder.

This cannot be. No man can take that kind of a beating and still be standing. How can one man hold all this magic? Lone Wolf thinks when he sees what's beneath. Instead of muscle and bone, it looks like moist black fur.

With a swift backswing, he slashes Chief Black Bear's throat wide open. The man should have fallen back and gurgled to his death, but instead, Chief Black Bear laughs in a deep, evil rumble. He presses his claws into the wound and starts ripping his own flesh. His muscular jugular elongates to the tone of his popping neck bones.

Lone Wolf cracks a smile, which confuses Black Bear.

"I welcome death," Lone Wolf says calmly, glaring at the beastly man. He readies his weapon and aims between Black Bear's glowing eyes.

Black Bear's moccasins split apart. Long shiny black claws protrude and curl over his foot. A tuft of black fur bursts out. The swell spreads up Black Bear's legs, which reshape into boulder-like hips.

The chief's torso solidifies in mass three times what it was before. Follicle by follicle, black fur sprouts up his back. The patches race across his stomach and thicken at his chest.

Lone Wolf readies his weapon and searches for a spot to attack just as Black Bear's arms explode into solid muscle and then disappear into fur. The mystic chief returns Lone Wolf's smile as his hands turn to paws and cover up the shiny black claws. He is no longer able to hold the golden lance, and it falls to the earth.

Lone Wolf lunges forward, then leaps back when clawed at. Black Bear's speed has also increased.

I cannot fall as easily as Raven Claw, Lone Wolf thinks, checking the placement of Black Bear's feet. *He will never let me steal the sun's power from him. No, he will kill me quickly if I even try.*

The disfigured chief tilts his head back and releases a fierce war cry that trails off into an angry bear growl. Lone Wolf sees two long white fangs poking out of a mouth that twists into a snout and distorts with bone-breaking pops. Two round bear ears spring up on top of his broad skull and wiggle back and forth, listening.

With the transformation now complete, Black Bear stands fifteen feet tall on his hindquarters and casts a shadow that touches Lone Wolf's moccasins.

Black Bear drops down on all four legs. He fixes his flaming yellow eyes on Lone Wolf and comes charging with a snarling, ferocious growl greater than the mighty grizzly bear. He closes the distance to Lone Wolf in mere seconds.

The Kiowa warrior stares blankly at the monstrosity before him. For the first time in his life, he sees a power he cannot fight, but it is a fight he cannot resist. He feels the weight of mortality lift off his shoulders, freeing him to be what he has always been: a lone warrior. When his elk blade makes contact with Black Bear, it has no effect. The strength and speed of the bear outmatch him.

A safe distance away from the fight, Lone Wolf's brother Paw shouts out. "Brother!" Paw feels deep regret for leaving his brother and his love forces him to return. He knows he stands no chance against the beast, but his love for his brother is stronger than his fear. As he throws his tomahawk, he watches the beast bite down on Lone Wolf's clavicle. The blade sinks into Black Bear's back, but nothing changes. With great force, the angry bear persists in his attack.

Paw glances at his brother and feels a great sense of pride when he watches Lone Wolf struggle his right arm free and bury a steel bowie knife in Black Bear's side. The man-beast releases his bite and cries out in morbid pain as Lone Wolf pulls the knife out. Chief Black Bear is quick to repay Lone Wolf's defense with a long, powerful swipe across his chest. His claws rip the bone breastplate off and tear the black wolf emblem painted on Lone Wolf's chest. Blood flows over his red war paint and mixes in a way that is nearly impossible to see.

Lone Wolf doesn't scream, though the excruciating pain registers in every nerve. Instead, he readies his knife and slashes Black Bear across the nose. The blade cuts deep and spews blood over Lone Wolf's face. Black Bear stumbles back and paws at his nose.

"FIGHT! FIGHT WITH ALL THE COURAGE IN YOUR HEART!" Lone Wolf commands his brother. He tries to lift his left arm, but the bite to his clavicle has rendered his arm useless.

Paw has an impossible hope that his brother stands a chance. Now he knows that the great chief's power will not protect him from harm. *I must get in this fight*, he thinks as he quickly rushes for a spear. When he turns back around, his hope is dashed. Lone Wolf slashes at Black Bear's face and misses. He exposes his back. Black Bear seizes his opportunity to attack the Kiowa chief from behind. Lone Wolf receives many brutal blows before he loses strength and falls to his knees.

"THANK YOU FOR THIS LIFE, TAIME!" Lone Wolf shouts, unable to repel the ferocious attack.

Black Bear bites down hard on Lone Wolf's open wound and

thrashes his burly head back and forth, severing Lone Wolf's shoulder. Though mere seconds have passed, Paw feels time stop. He sees the bear release his brother's mangled body, growl, circle, and attack.

A flicker of motion causes Paw to ready his spear. Two Moons has returned to help his father.

Paw looks down at his spear and up at his nephew. A single question surfaces in his mind. *Do I join my brother in the spirit world today? My love for my brother compels me to rush Black Bear. But if I do this, my nephew will follow me to my doom.*

Paw looks at his young nephew and sees his brother's eyes. Though Two Moons's features are those of a young man, he holds manly weapons and prepares to do the bidding of a man in a battle that his father has already lost.

Paw looks at his brother. He watches as Lone Wolf fights with the only weapon he has left, his bare fist.

Sorrow fills Paw's heart. He hears an eagle scream and looks up at the sky. The great white eagle has returned. It circles his brother.

Paw turns to his nephew. "Don't attack him, Two Moons. He will use the love we have for your father against us. We will become regret."

Two Moons shouts, "Father, I am so proud of you! I am here. Your son is here. I see you, Father. Tell me what to do and I will do it." Lone Wolf flails his hand to keep his son back.

With his claws and fangs, Black Bear makes a failing attempt to scalp Lone Wolf.

You put up a brave fight, brother. Soon you will know no pain. Paw holds up his fist and extends his left arm. He raises his index and middle finger, then pulls his fingers behind his left ear and makes the sign of the Kiowa. *Go in peace and walk on the wind.*

He isn't certain that his brother sees the gesture until Lone Wolf closes his fist and makes the two-finger sign. But then Lone Wolf does something else. With the last of his strength, he points. Paw looks to where he's pointing and then glances back at his brother.

When his brother's finger curls, Paw knows that the fight is close to over, though he mistakes the sign for, Leave. He watches Black Bear's massive paws press down on Lone Wolf's skull. With several repeated crushing thrusts, the Kiowa chief's life comes to an end.

"Lone Wolf saved the entire tribe," Paw tells Two Moons.

"What was he pointing at?" Two Moons asks, readying a spear to attack Black Bear.

Paw traces the path of Lone Wolf's aim and sees the golden lance lying on the ground only a short distance from him. Now he understands.

CHAPTER 9

Paw sprints for the source of Chief Black Bear's power. He greedily snatches up the lance. Surprisingly, it feels light in his hands. But something strange happens when his fingers make contact. The magic goes to work and sends a warm sensation that overpowers all fear. Courage, hope, and happiness pass through him all at once and put him in a trance.

Blinded by carnal fury, Chief Black Bear persists his ravenous attack, even though his enemy is dead.

"We are hunters, are we not?" Two Moons asks his uncle Paw, bringing him back to reality.

Paw nods.

"There is a mighty big black bear!"

"This fight is more than a war. It is something dark and evil. Something that must be dealt with now! Let us kill the man-bear and wear his scalp!" Paw grins greedily. He takes the spear in one hand and holds the lance in the other. The warriors close in and witness a terribly gruesome scene. Black Bear is in frenzy.

"As long as I live, I swear with all the blood in my veins that either you or I will separate souls from bodies!" Paw pledges a blood oath.

The two Kiowa warriors sprint toward their enemy. "VENGEANCE!" they scream.

Their screams catch the evil man-bear's attention. Unlike any other animal, this bear seems to understand humans. He presses his angry brows together and stands up. Black Bear towers over the Kiowa warriors. Saliva and blood drip out of his terrifying jaws and drool down his chest.

With a quick sprint, the grizzly charges them. Two Moons puts a short distance between him and Paw so that the bear must decide which of them to attack. When he sees the bear advance toward Paw, Two Moons circles around the massive beast and thrusts his spear into Black Bear's side. The blade punches through his thick fur and spins the heaving monster around. He extends his claws and swipes for Two Moons.

Paw seizes the moment and stabs Black Bear in the hind leg with his spear, trying to sever his tendon.

Black Bear stands up on both legs. He releases an earth-shaking roar, which echoes off the trees and reverberates through the warriors' chests.

"Your roars have no effect on hearts full of courage. And I have your magic," Paw shouts, thrusting his spear in Black Bear's belly. The point of the spear doesn't break through his thick hide. From experience, Paw knows if he can wedge the handle into the earth, the weight of the bear will send the spear through his abdomen. That thought brings a smile to his face as he thrusts and prods, constantly taunting the man-bear.

"*Het ya! Het Ya!* Your hide is your scalp and your scalp will be my trophy!" Paw shouts, tapping his spear to the ground. The bear defensively whips around and realizes the predicament he's in. He cannot attack both men at the same time, no matter how hard he tries. When he charges one, the other takes up his exposed flank and stabs him. At first, Black Bear seethes with rage. But eventually he shows signs of exhaustion. He knows it's only a matter of time before the spears strike true. To prevent a mortal wound, he breaks contact, tries to separate the Kiowa warriors, but finds himself back in the same trap over and over again.

***

Charlie acts like the bear, with his hands spread out like claws. He stands up and snarls, "RRRAAAAWWWRRR," baring his teeth.

He shifts to his normal instructive tone. "Kiowa are expert hunters. See, what they'd do is get the bear to stand up on his hind legs, and then they'd plant their spear in the ground, like this." He stomps the end of a pretend spear. "Then they'd place their foot on it, holding it at an angle. Eventually the bear would tire and come down on all fours, hopefully on the spear."

"Would that kill the bear?" John asks.

"If you catch it under the belly and have the courage to keep your foot on the spear handle as the bear falls towards you. Then it could punch right through him." Charlie thrusts his straight arm through his closed hand.

"What happens if you get real scared?" Kevin asks, shaking from the horror.

"Then Paw would have shared his brother's fate," Charlie answers macabrely.

Kevin gulps. "I would run!"

"That's 'cause you got nothin' but fear in your heart!" Luther taunts him, then whispers, "I'd run, but I'd stab you in the leg first."

"The bear would just end up eating both of you. Now listen up. I got bunches to tell."

***

Two Moons bravely places another strike in Black Bear's side, only this time he nearly gets through the ribs and to his lungs. Paw plants his spear and readies for Black Bear to fall on it. His elation turns to despair when Black Bear turns and runs into the forest. The two hunters give chase, releasing a war cry that makes the bear run faster.

CHAPTER 10

"Do not follow the devil into the night!" Paw bellows. "I am frightened that I will lose more of my precious family."

Two Moons stops at the edge of the forest and holds his position. They remain like this, hearing the heavy breathing of Black Bear for what seems an eternity.

"He hides in the shadows. He won't give up the fight."

Paw looks up at the sky and realizes why. "He's waiting for nightfall."

"Retrieve my father and I will guard you," Two Moons insists.

Paw wraps the golden lance in a buffalo hide. He ties a leather strap to it and slings it across his chest. He and Two Moons secure Lone Wolf's remains and mount two of the straggling horses, returning Lone Wolf's mangled remains to the village.

As they leave, Black Bear emerges from of the forest and stands erect on his hind legs. He lifts one paw up and down, waving good-bye.

***

"Why did they take his body?" John asks.

"Kiowa custom. They don't leave no man behind," Charlie answers.

"Did they go back for any of the other Kiowa?" Zack asks.

"Of course!" Charlie proudly proclaims.

"I wish I were Chief Black Bear." Luther snickers, thinking about the power he could have.

"I wish I were Lone Wolf," Kevin says with a heavy sigh.

"None of that matters, boys. All that matters is that Injuns is real particular about how they prepare their dead."

The boys listen intently, completely focused on their scoutmaster.

"Paw and Two Moons weren't about to let wolves or coyotes dig up Lone Wolf. That would be disrespectful and against Indian law. Now, the way Indians bury their dead is different from how we do it. First, they make a cot out of tree branches and hoist their loved one up on top of a stretched-out buffalo blanket. Next, they use tall polls to hoist the body up in the air so nothing can get to it. Then they leave behind weapons, shields, magic pouches, and even a little food for the journey ahead. Finally they kill his horse, so he will have something to ride to the happy hunting grounds."

"They killed his horse?" Zack gasps in shock.

Charlie nods and then continues. "After the attack, the Kiowa traveled far from their southern lands for many weeks, until they finally reached the northern part of where Washington is today. Except it wasn't the Olympic peninsula then. It was just called the north land, where three rivers fork and feed into the 'everywhere waters.'"

"Which rivers?" Zack wonders.

"Let's see here… I believe it was the Sol Duc, the Calawah, and Bogachiel Rivers. I could be wrong, though."

"What is 'everywhere water'?" Luther asks.

John slams his limp wrist into his chest. "That's the ocean, duh!"

Luther makes a sour face and sticks his tongue out.

"This was part of the Kiowa annual journey. During the rainy Washington winters, they would migrate down south, sometimes as far as Texas. When summer would get too hot, they'd move on back up to Washington. Year after year they would do this circuit." Charlie draws a large circle with his finger.

***

The Kiowa gather beneath a cloudy gray sky. Though the sky is dark, and the wind howls, Water Boy holds back his mighty tears. The tribe doesn't. Women release their death wails. The terrible shrieks and cries spread from one squaw to the next. They thrash their clothes and tear their hair out.

Two Moons drops a drumstick on his father's favorite drum. The dull beat and the high shrieked death rattles send the entire tribe into mournful sorrow. This ritual goes on for most of the day.

"His cunning and strength were unmatched," Paw bemoans.

"He saved our lives," Two Moons says, patting his younger brother.

"Remember the reward he has given us. His bravery brings tears to our eyes. His loss brings sorrow to our hearts," Onendah, the medicine man, crows.

Family members pass around Lone Wolf's scalping knife and cut themselves to remember him.

Paw cuts his chest deep across his heart.

Lone Wolf's body is perfectly wrapped in buffalo hides and tied to a makeshift plank. The plank is suspended high off the ground and decorated with his war bonnet, his weapons, and his magic pouch.

An elderly woman plays her flute while Two Moons lightly taps his drum. Onendah stretches his arms toward the heavens and opens his hands.

"Mount Storm Shadow and let him carry your spirit to the happy hunting grounds, where you will never starve or freeze and the sun will always shine. Follow the distant light to the place you have stored the horses you sacrificed and all the things you laid at the gods' feet. Move through these dark clouds of sorrow, till the darkness fades and the clouds turn white. This is where we will hold you, high in our hearts of happiness for the life you lived. Your life made our lives brighter, and for that we sing your name."

"Lone Wolf, our great warrior!" the tribe chants, swaying.

While they chant, Grass Woman, Lone Wolf's wife, rests her hand against a tree. She passes his scalping knife to her sister-in-law and looks away. Dancing Fawn takes the knife by the handle, then quickly slams the blade onto Grass Woman's pinkie finger and chops the digit in half.

"Arrrggghh!" the mourning widow screams. She holds her hand up and shouts, "This is how I will always remember you, Lone Wolf, my love! You were my great war chief. My greatest love. This tiny piece of me that you have taken with you is nothing compared to your death, which has taken all of my heart."

She wraps the wound, scoops up some ash from the fire, and scrubs her face black. Turning toward the sun, she howls, resuming the mourning wail.

While the tribe mourns, Onendah continues. "Father of the

heavens and the earth calls you home. He sends the great white horse, Storm Shadow, to greet you. Go to him. Go to the great creator. Find peace in your new home and wait patiently for your little woman. Your sons. And, one day, your tribe. Till we meet again." Onendah finishes the prayer and lowers his hands. "Find peace."

A rush of wind picks up and nearly blows Lone Wolf's body over. His people stabilize the pine poles. Through the clouds, a single ray of light blasts out of the darkness and rests on Lone Wolf's wrapped body. Vapors rise off his mangled chest.

Only the medicine man, Onendah, can see the vapors take form. They ascend to the heavens and gather in the light. The medicine man shakes his rattling wand and releases Lone Wolf's spirit. Off in the great distance, he sees Lone Wolf's misty image for a brief moment, riding off on the spirit horse. Clouds re-cover the sun's single ray, and Lone Wolf's bright spirit disappears in the gloomy sky.

***

Paw mourns and laments till he collapses. When he has squeezed the last ounce of sorrow out of his heart, he is determined to fulfill his promise. On his way to deliver the golden lance to Onendah, he walks through the village.

"That is a good story you paint on the side of your tepee, Grass Woman," he compliments Lone Wolf's widow.

She turns and looks at him. Her hair is a matted, tangled mess and her eyes are wild. "Arrrggggh!" she screams, leaping into her tepee like a frog leaps into a pond.

Paw continues his stroll through the tight cluster of tepees. He admires the paintings on their sides.

Children in loincloths chase half-wolf dogs through the camp. Hunters drag an elk into camp from their morning hunt. Squaw go to work stripping its hide in preparation for turning it into clothes. He strolls through the village until he reaches the center, stopping outside Onendah's white tepee. With his fingers, he traces the yellow sun, the blue mountains, and the lightning bolts painted on the side of the tepee. In just a few images, he reads the story of the medicine man's life.

"Medicine man, may I enter?" Paw calls out, alerting Onendah to his presence.

"You aren't sick!"

A quizzical expression forms in Paw's calm, wide-set eyes. He tilts his square jaw to the side and presses his high brows together.

"No, I am not."

"You are sad?"

Paw takes a deep breath and sighs. "All of us are rich with sorrow."

"Take your brother's pants to the warm springs. Wash them. Soak in the springs for two days and then wear them. His legs will become yours. You will walk from your sorrow for many days until you learn to run from it. Once you have outrun your pain, you may take his legs off and walk on your own."

For the first time since his brother's death, Paw feels tinges of hope sprout inside him. His fingers drop from the painted images to the leather bag in his hands. He wonders if he should not keep the golden lance for himself. *For it is all that is left of your brother*, he thinks.

The temptation lasts only momentarily. From the depths of his mind, his brother's face surfaces. He sees Lone Wolf in his last battle. He sees his brother fall, witnesses his sacrifice, then sees him pointing to the golden lance.

It was all for this, Paw realizes, *and I am not worthy of it.*

CHAPTER 11

"Onendah, I have a gift for you," Paw calls out.

"Leave it at the door. My eyes have seen much sorrow, and I wish to see no more of your face or anyone else's."

"I cannot leave it at the door."

"Why not?"

"Someone will take it!"

There's an excited rustling in the tent before the tepee's flap flips open. A dust cloud explodes in Paw's face.

"Gifts of worth are always welcome!" Onendah squints and deepens his sagging frown. He points down. "But your sorrow must remain at the door, with your filthy moccasins."

"But I like my moccasins. The beads were done by my wife before she died."

Onendah disappears into his tent, while Paw removes his beautifully beaded leather moccasins. Then Paw ducks down and enters the open hatch. His feet touch a soft rug comprised of rabbit, mink, and bear fur. He smacks his lips and detects the strong aroma of sage. A dull fire smolders in the center of the tepee, drying meat. It offers little light. Smoke swirls and spins out of the opening in the roof.

When his eyes adjust, Paw scans the walls of the medicine man's tepee and sees elaborate paintings of animals, people, and people-animals. Other paintings of the medicine man's greatest achievements litter the walls. The largest characters are of his deceased wife. A story forms. Paw can see how they met, where they were married under a bright moon, and the sons they had. He can tell how Onendah felt from the yellow circles in his heart in the earlier drawings, where at present there is no color in his heart. Just empty black circles where sons and a wife once had a place.

Paw turns his attention to the dream catchers hanging on the wall. He traces the woven twigs with his fingertip and admires the web-like features. Some of the dream-catchers have scalps tautly fixed in them. He wonders if the medicine man's power can actually hold the evil spirits in prison or if it draws them to the village in search of what has been taken from them.

Paw pokes at a pearl that's been dipped in silver. It symbolizes an Indian's worst nightmare, eternal internment. The jewel dangles from a string as fine as a spider web and hovers oddly in the center.

"Do you bless all of them equally?" Paw asks, wondering if the larger dream-catchers have more power than the smaller ones.

"I give them as much power as they need."

Paw sits down by the fire and crosses his legs. He sits in peace, waiting for a moment to tell Onendah what has transpired. He studies the gray-haired man's cracked face and wonders if his own hair will turn gray and if his face will crack like the mud. *Everything about this man is art. His life. His medicine. Even his curses,* Paw thinks to himself.

"I have seen things I think no man has seen before," Paw begins.

"As have I. Look upon my eyes. Do you not see the color of the sky instead of the earth?"

Paw focuses on the medicine man's hazy corn-blue eyes.

"It has not always been so. I once had the earth in my eyes as you." Onendah gently presses his thumbs to Paw's closed lids. "Many winters now, the wind has swept the earth from my eyes." He pulls his thumbs back. "Now my spirit is almost free." The old man folds his arms and leans back.

"I saw a Cheyenne chief transform into a bear."

Onendah bursts into mocking laughter. "What herb do you smoke in your pipe?"

Paw holds a straight face.

"I have seen and heard much in my lifetime, but I have never heard anything such as this. Tell me now, where can I find this herb?"

"I thought our minds would be one on this," Paw says. He slowly unwraps the golden lance. Breaks in the cloth release a soft amber glow.

Onendah gasps. "What is this?" His laughter is silenced.

An aura as powerful as the sun's light dismisses every shadow of doubt in the medicine man's mind. Onendah shields his eyes, and light emerges through the chimney hole.

Outside, the villagers circle Onendah's tepee. Braves *whoop* and women begin to chant prayers of praise for whatever spell allows Onendah to capture and hold the sun in his tepee.

"His power has grown!" Makes Trouble whispers to his sister, Kida. She nods, feeling the warmth of a beautifully woven blanket her mother wraps around her.

Kida's tender mother stands up, and stares in awe at the light blasting out of the tepee. "It must be a sign," Glances Then Glares mumbles.

"Of what?" Kida asks.

Her mother raises her hands in worship. "Only Onendah can know."

Inside the tepee, Onendah shouts at Paw, "Cover it up! The sun's power blinds me!"

Paw quickly wraps the golden lance and conceals its light. He's careful not to touch it. The warmth of the weapon is more powerful than a summer day and constantly tempts him to keep the mysterious power for himself.

"I brought it here because my brother wanted you to have it." Paw holds the wrapped weapon out with both hands, offering it to Onendah.

"What would I do with it?" Onendah places his hands beneath the wrap and accepts the gift.

"Whatever power it has, I know not. But of a few things, I am certain. The Cheyenne chief held this in his hands and repelled our arrows. It gave him power to change from a man into a bear."

Onendah pauses for a moment and thinks on the hard words Paw speaks.

"Before I answer you, I have something I need you to do," Onendah says.

"If I can do it, I will."

"I have seen in a vision that Lone Wolf's son is going to receive a demigod as a gift. I think it odd that you have shown me this power and I have had this vision."

"Very strange things are happening all at once," Paw agrees. "What is it you need?"

"I need you to go and catch a silver fox. Make sure you don't touch it. No one can touch it. Bring it back to me, and I will bless it with the lance and bind it to Lone Wolf's son. I have seen that the gods have some strange use for it."

"I have never seen a silver fox. Where would I even begin to look?" Paw questions.

"I would start in the forest or some stream. Everything must have water to live. Now, on this topic of shapeshifting. I have heard of Rugaroo, but I have never seen the shapeshifters with my own eyes." Onendah caresses the magic lance. He's mesmerized by its power. "It seems remarkably light for being crafted of gold."

"It was durable enough to fight off the man-bear," Paw informs him. He thinks for a moment. "Rugaroo are stories we tell our children to keep them frightened so they will not wander in the night. This is no fable. I speak true words."

Onendah's eyes shift from the lance to Paw. "When my medicine is not so weak from the vision I have just had, I will hold a counsel with our ancestors and see if this magic is a blessing or a curse. Thank you for bringing it to me. Is there anything else?"

"All that I ask is that you grant me its power of protection so that I may track down the man-bear and avenge my brother."

Onendah remains quiet. He studies the infinite depths of Paw's eyes. The dull fire illuminates the medicine man's leathery face. Paw holds his peace for some time, letting Onendah see what he cannot. Onendah eventually looks up to the sky, then back down at Paw. He carefully places the lance down, then lifts a stick with a hand fastened to the tip. Black feathers hang off each finger.

"Do you know what this is?" Onendah asks.

"It is a hand, attached to a stick, wrapped in deer skin. It has black feathers hanging off the fingers."

"Do you know whose hand?"

Paw shakes his head.

"It is my enemy's. The one who killed and scalped my wife and boys. He tried to reach with his magic into my soul and steal my life. But I would not let him. I used my knife to cut off his hand. Do you understand what I am saying to you?"

"I need more magic to defeat Chief Black Bear?"

Onendah sighs. "I see two paths." The medicine man swirls the wand above his head. "One is a slow, painful death. The other is a magnificent journey of life."

Paw buries his face in his hands. He sobs as he listens to the truth of Onendah's words.

"I have felt the darkness of death swirl like these black feathers. They turn into a storm as my thoughts have lingered on revenge," Paw confesses.

"What is in your heart?"

"Hatred as great as the everywhere water!"

"This is the dark path that will tease you with relief, but none will be found. Your enemies have set a trap for you and wait for you to return. The man-bear knows the death of Lone Wolf will stir such emotions. He will use your feelings to bait you. They will dangle the bait of hate in front of you. Not to kill you but to capture you, so that they may torture you for many days. They will drag your agony out until your body expires in hopes that you will confess the location of the golden lance."

"My heart *screams* for justice!"

"Justice?" Onendah says with a trailing chuckle. "Our conflict with the Cheyenne will never yield justice. Only death."

Tears well up in Paw's dark brown eyes. "The Cheyenne have taken my wife and daughter. Now they have taken my brother. What am I to do?"

"Listen."

Paw wipes the tears from his eyes.

"Like you, I have lost Indians I love. My wife's and sons' scalps fell to the Cheyenne. Replace hate with love if you can. Lone Wolf's wife is with child. That child will be walking soon. He will join the rabbit circle. I have seen in a dream that this child will walk on feet of hope and he will have all the strength of his father but none of the wisdom. You must teach him wisdom, and when this child is ready, I will grant the lance's power to him if I can understand it. For now, teach him the ways of the Kiowa. Show him how to think and not to follow the dangerous passions of his heart. Teach him our ways. Be his guardian. Bind to him as the roots bind to the earth and you will choose a path of life that is rich with love, joy, happiness, and one day, peace."

Paw laughs painfully at the thought of peace.

Onendah presses his cold hand to Paw's heart. "I know the

stones of hatred cover your ears and make it hard to hear these things. I know your wounds are fresh and deep. You must know, brother of Lone Wolf, these wounds will heal." He looks down for a moment. His hand drops to his side. He shrugs and finishes with, "The Cheyennes' won't."

Onendah's vision proves true. With death in summer comes life in spring. Grass Woman, Lone Wolf's widow, gives birth to his third and final son.

The entire tribe turns out for the baby's ceremony. The medicine man uses ash to trace the image of a sprinting wolf across his chest. The people cheer and chant, "Though Lone Wolf is gone, his spirit lives on!"

A thought cracks in the medicine man's mind. Onendah etches a thunderbolt on the calm baby's forehead. The tribe gladly welcomes Lone Wolf's gift.

"What is his name?"

CHAPTER 12

"I have no name for him," Grass Woman cries.

She struggles to hold the child up so that the tribe may see their newest member.

"Children should not be born in sorrow, and yet my heart is full of great sorrow," Grass Woman says, wiping tears from her eyes.

Onendah's face wrinkles into a sour expression, which makes the baby laugh.

"Do not name him 'Heart Full of Great Sorrow'!"

Grass Woman manages a laugh. "I would never."

Several weeks pass, and her tribal sisters begin to grow weary. They visit Grass Woman's tepee. Her voice is coarse from calling Lone Wolf's name over and over. The women complain that she's cried too much and sounds like a dove.

"I like the name Soaring Eagle."

"I don't. I like Thunderbolt," Blooming Flower, a young girl, says.

The women wrinkle their faces and shake their heads.

"That is a terrible name," Glances Then Glares says.

Yellow Sparrow shrugs. "A name is a name."

"No!" Grass Woman protests. "A name is everything!"

"If it is so important, then name him Lone Wolf!" Yellow Sparrow counters.

"Oh, I cannot do that," Grass Woman protests.

"Why not? It is a good name!" Blooming Flower encourages.

"He must earn that name. Everyone knows that!" Glances Then Glares chides her.

"Let's see. He has the love of his people. I can certainly see that," Grass Woman says. "And his father was a great warrior." She pauses for a moment, then feels the word form and slip from her lips.

"K-i-o-w-a."

The women search one another's expressions as they repeat the name.

"Kiowa."

"I think I shall call my brave little man Kiowa!"

"That's a wonderful name!" Glances Then Glares compliments Grass Woman, squeezing her shoulder in approval.

"The people will embrace him, and he will embrace his people!" Grass Woman says, pressing Kiowa's soft, warm body to her chest.

***

For two springs, Paw scours the earth in search of a silver fox. Though he unearths many foxholes, he never finds what he's looking for.

Perhaps I am approaching this wrong. Maybe I should ask my brother to guide me. He kneels down and lowers his lips to the earth. "Brother, if you can hear me, lead me to this demigod. I am tired of searching and am ready to give up."

No sooner has he finished his prayer than he feels a strong energy in his legs. It is a strength he has never felt before. His muscles want to run, so Paw cuts them loose and lets them go. He sprints through grassy meadows, across streams, and high up steep mountains. When his legs tire, he sits down, realizing he has run all day and past the night. Now the sun sends her daughters to dance fresh light across foggy mountaintops.

"Oh, how you have played a dirty trick on me, brother. Or perhaps it is some cruel Cheyenne medicine man's spell," Paw complains while he rubs his sore feet.

He looks around, finding a direction that he knows will lead him back to his village.

"At least I gave it my best effort." He stands up and bends down at the waist to tighten his moccasins.

Right next to his foot, he spots a tiny fox footprint.

I see now that my eyes cannot be trusted over my pants. Lead my feet on, brother.

He follows the trail, keeping himself concealed in case he should scare the demigod. As he goes, he sees that the tracks lead to a den.

No demigod would be trapped so easily. If I dig, I might scare it, and

I do not have the strength to chase it.

His stomach growls.

I do not have the strength to think.

He moves away from the den and makes a crude spear. After killing a rabbit, he builds a fire and roasts his breakfast in manageable chunks of meat.

When he's finished, he finds a stream and drinks until he's full. *Now I can think, but I have the same problem as before. How do I trap a demigod?*

When he returns to his fire, he spots a bushy tail with a red and black tip and a fresh set of prints.

You trap it by following its trail and feeding it.

Paw kills anything he can get his hands on. His bounty by midday includes a two squirrels and another rabbit. He sets the bodies down outside the opening of the den and hides behind a rock.

As the day wanes on, his patience pays off. A red fox pokes its head out of the hole and spots the offerings. Rather than rush out and snatch the kill, the fox decides to wait. Listen. Look. Smell. At twilight, it comes out and snatches up the squirrel, then disappears.

I know your fox thoughts. Paw squints and thinks, *You are thinking that no living thing discards meat for free. And you are right. These are gifts. So show me what my brother has led me here to see.*

The fox comes out almost upon request and snatches up another squirrel. When it comes back for the bunny, a litter of cubs slips out through the opening of the cave.

Ah, so you are a hungry mother.

Trapped between getting her cubs back inside the den and carrying home the bunny, she decides to drop dinner and take care of the babies.

"Oh, you are a good mother," Paw whispers to himself. "But why am I here? I do not see a silver fox…"

As mother gets her cubs back inside her den, one cub comes prancing out and yelps. Its silver fur nearly makes Paw's eyes leap out of his head. His mother quickly returns, catches her sacred treasure, and pulls him back into the safety of the den.

The sun sets and stars appear.

Paw withdraws to his campfire and thinks, *How am I going to catch a silver fox without touching it?*

He thinks and thinks and thinks himself to exhaustion.

I know from experience not to show myself or let the mother fox catch my scent. Ah-hoe, if she does, I will be digging for days in one hole, while she and her cubs slip out some other hole.

Paw folds his legs and thinks. *No, the fox is clever. I must be cleverer than she.*

Lost in thought, he repeatedly stabs a stick into the ground and inadvertently digs a hole.

I must dig a hole while the fox is sleeping, and I must do it tonight.

With that, Paw creeps as close as he can to the mouth of the den and carefully digs a hole. He uses rocks and sticks to carve out one handful of dirt at a time, patiently using the least amount of force as possible, for he does not want to startle the mother and make her think someone is coming for her precious silver baby.

By the next morning Paw has successfully dug a hole deep enough to hide himself. He quickly spears some fish from the stream and lays the gifts out like he did the day before. With branches and leaves, he covers himself up to match his surroundings.

Now all I need to do is stay awake.

When the mother comes out the first time, it is as before. No cubs come with her. When she comes a second time, they do what youth do – scurry away. By the third gift, the silver fox cub has appeared. His curiosity has caused him to see what brother and sister were getting that he wasn't. Cautiously, the silver fox stumbles along and then stops. The cub turns its head to the side when it sees a rise in the earth it hadn't seen before. Paw remains as still as his trembling muscles will let him. It is then that the silver fox flashes its emerald eyes at Paw.

Paw freezes. *Does he know what I am about to do?*

CHAPTER 13

Feeling more secure with the gifts, the mother fox lets the pups wander while she enjoys the meal. It would prove to be her fatal mistake. Paw watches the pups stumble this way and that. Each one scatters in a different direction. He tries to control them by throwing out little chunks of meat. They take the bait and move closer to him. He's happy to see the pups draw nearer. The demigod follows the bravest pup. Once it has come within reach, Paw carefully moves his cover out of the way. The answer to his problem, a crude basket made from twigs, slams down over the demigod.

At first Paw thinks he hurt his prize. The pup lets out such a dreadful cry that he makes Paw wonder if he's damaged the demigod in some way. He leans down and lifts the rim just enough to see that the demigod is okay. With a broad smile, he shows his teeth and terrifies the pup. It yelps even louder.

Who should respond but the brave mother. With snarling fangs and wild, worried eyes that say, *Mine*, the red mother fox explodes out of her den.

"Stay back, Mother!" the Indian tracker shouts.

She circles around him with such a dreadful look of concern he can't help but mock her.

"Ha! Ha! You, the cleverest animal of the woods, have been beaten at your own sly game. I see you putting together some plan to hurt me and take back your treasure. It won't work. He's mine!"

The mother fox scolds him with harsh chirps and reveals fangs as she steps forward and then leaps back.

"Do not worry, Mother. I am not here for them. Just this one!" Paw says while he slips twigs beneath the basket and makes a hasty lid.

Mother Fox doesn't wait to see what happens next. She snatches whatever babies she can and hides them in the cave.

Paw is so impressed with her speed and determination, he wonders if it isn't wrong to separate a child from its mother this way. Before he can finish this thought, his legs burn and rejuvenate with a newfound energy.

"There it is, Mother Fox. You keep your other little babies but I keep your greatest treasure! You also keep your hide, even though I think it would make a fine hat."

He sticks his tongue out at her and runs away.

***

Ten springs pass. Paw is now thirty-seven and Kiowa is half his height. A full-grown silver fox follows him and seems like an extension of his soul.

"You look like your father," Paw says, ruffling the boy's hair with one hand while he holds a platter of paint in the other.

"Sadly, you must go through the lessons of the rabbit before you become…"

"Become what, Uncle?" Kiowa looks up with large, round nut-brown eyes.

"Well, many moons will tell. You will have a vision, and in that vision you will see an animal. That will be your spirit and the source of your magic. Until then you are a rabbit."

"I don't like being a rabbit, Uncle. They are stupid and weak. I want to be a fox like my demigod, Moon Beam."

"Rabbits have a good life. You paint your face. You dance all day. You play games. You eat plenty. Seems like a grand old time to me."

"Yeah, I guess so. How many moons till I turn into my spirit animal?"

"Well, let's see. If it were one moon, I would say one moon from now. If it were two…"

"You would say two!"

Paw holds up all ten fingers. He flashes them repeatedly. "Many moons is this many."

"Ah-hoe, Uncle. That is a long time to be a rabbit."

Circling all around them, the silver fox inspects everything Paw does with the greatest curiosity. His emerald eyes reveal an endless silent inquiry.

Paw smiles and lifts his open hand. "Press your hand against mine."

Kiowa grins and bares his bright white teeth.

"See there, your hands are almost as big as mine. Now let me see your foot."

Kiowa hops and then sticks a foot out.

Paw swings around him and puts his foot next to his. "Ah, just as I suspected. In a few winters, your foot will be as long as mine."

"So?!" Kiowa says, sticking his tongue out and hopping away.

"So we haven't much time to teach you all that must be learned."

"Well, if I am a rabbit"—the boy hops up and down in buckskin pants and wiggles his hips—"then I hear, I smell, I shake my tail, and I hop away."

Paw laughs at his cute nephew. "All these things are true, but you must always remember that we are artists before anything else."

"Even before we are warriors?"

"Yes. Even before we are warriors," Paw says, dipping his thumbs in white paint. He presses them against the bridge of Kiowa's nose and streaks them down to the corners of his mouth.

"Why do we paint?" Kiowa asks in a soft voice.

"We paint our sacred symbols on our faces," Paw says, making paw prints on his face. "We paint our horses and our tepees so that our magic will protect us."

"Do I have magic?"

Paw nods. He waves his hands over the earth and says, "Everything has magic."

"If I have magic, can I use it against you?"

Paw rests his hands on his hips and sighs. "First I will teach you how to start fires with flint, carve arrow shafts with your knife, make arrowheads out of the white man's metals, sew moccasins, make face paint, ride horses, and wrestle. But none of these things will be as important as the art you make."

"I am eager to learn magic, Uncle!" Kiowa says with a big bright smile.

Paw smiles. "We will get there, but first"—he dips his thumb in red paint and traces it up Kiowa's right arm—"I will teach you of your father, Lone Wolf, and the great love he had for all of us..." He reaches the nook of Kiowa's arm. "The love he had for your mother…" He reaches Kiowa's armpit, then slides the red trail across his shoulder and makes a giant circle on the boy's heart. "And the love he has for you."

"I want to hear all the stories."

"One night at a time I will teach you."

One such night, Paw brings Lone Wolf's war bonnet and recounts with admiration the battles he won. He tells in great detail all of the things he saw. Kiowa laughs and sometimes cries. Paw's words swirl around Kiowa's ear canals and bring Lone Wolf's spirit to life in his mind.

"And that is how Fire Boy and Water Boy created all the stars." He looks at his nephew who seems lost. "Why do you get lost in the starry sky?" Paw asks at the end of his story.

"Me and Moon Beam wonder."

"I am more worried about you listening to these lessons I am trying to teach you, but to satisfy my curiosity, what is it you wonder?"

"I cannot say, because I do not know the words."

What Paw couldn't know, through the long campfire nights, was how close Kiowa feels to his father when he looks up at the starry sky. Though the boy isn't sure why, he howls. Paw finds the boy's high-pitched call so inviting that he joins in. As the two carry on, Moon Beam tilts his head this way and that, trying to make sense of all that his beautiful eyes see.

Over many moon-filled nights, the two got very good at the practice of howling. On more than one occasion they would trigger a roaming wolf pack, sending Moon Beam off to the tepee, where he would linger in the open doorway and tremble. This became a game for them, and it was always their intent to trick Moon Beam.

When the time has come for Kiowa to build his first bow, Paw leads him to the oak tree where he and Lone Wolf had found sturdy branches to build their first bows.

"We start with a branch that speaks to you, and then we use this." He holds out a rusty knife with a sharp blade. "With one skillful scrape after another, we will bring the spirit out and unite it with your body."

"How long will it take?"

"It does not matter how many moons. All that matters is that we find the right branch and make the right bow."

Within weeks, Paw has helped Kiowa carve his first bow. He tears a strip of deer leather from his pants and makes a sturdy grip.

"You have done well. Now we will use the sinew and tendon of the buffalo to make a string."

"When will I kill my first buffalo?"

"After you kill your first elk."

"When will I kill my first elk?"

"After you kill many bucks."

"And when will I do that, Uncle?"

"After you have killed many antelope."

Kiowa counts all the layers of the hunt and feels overwhelmed.

"But first you must kill rabbits. I bless you that when you aim with this bow, you aim with your father's hands."

Paw takes his knife and carves out finger grooves much too big for the boy's fingers.

"Now you have a hole in your pants, Uncle, and they are very worn."

"The pants I wear are your father's."

"How long will you wear my father's pants?"

"Onendah says his legs carry me. So I will wear them until I don't need his legs."

Kiowa looks from Paw's pants to his little dusty britches. "Do his legs carry me?"

Paw smiles and nods.

"But I don't have his pants. How can I be carried by his legs without his pants?"

Paw chuckles, then runs his fingers through Kiowa's long hair.

"Your legs are his legs. Now go hunt rabbits and squirrels. When you have killed enough to make a quiver for your arrows, we will make stronger arrows and hunt deer," Paw says, stringing the bow. He hands Kiowa the weapon.

"I will make you and Father proud!" Kiowa says, beaming. He wipes his nose, smearing his paint so that it now looks like he has a white mustache.

Paw licks his finger and wipes it off so that the other boys won't make a new name for him.

"Remember to aim where they are going to be, not where they are," Paw counsels.

Kiowa nods with great enthusiasm. He sprints off to the same forests his father hunted in, stalking his prey in a very patient manner. He imagines how his father may have learned to hunt and pretends to be him.

On his own, the noises of the forest intimidate him, but they also make him very curious. To calm himself, he identifies what he hears.

Raven's caw. Sparrow's chirp. Chipmunk's bark. Squirrel's squeak. I'm only in danger when everything is silent.

He sees a squirrel climb a tree so fast that by the time he takes aim, it's spun all the way around the tree three times and disappears in an explosion of pine needles. His eyebrows press together in disappointment, forcing a dissatisfied frown.

"That went differently in my mind." He *harrumphs.*

Moon Beam stares at him and seems ready to pounce at the right word.

"No, Moon Beam. You wouldn't understand. This is something I must do on my own."

With a deep breath, Kiowa breathes in the crisp pine air, and then blows all his discouragement out at once. *I am tired and that is why I am slow*, he realizes, then leaves the forest and decides to scour the open grass for rabbits.

Out in a grassy field, near the village, Kiowa spots a tall cottontail. He notches an arrow and watches its gray body move slowly at first, but then the rabbit gets excited and darts around before stopping. It seems to study him as much he studies it.

"You are cute and soft and I do not want to harm you, but I am hungry and I need to hunt deer, so you must die!"

CHAPTER 14

The bunny raises its long pointy ears and bravely stands on its hindquarters. It looks at the silver fox and cocks its head to the side. Moon Beam does the same. The rabbit rotates its head back and forth, checking Kiowa out with both eyes. Its soft pink nose rises and falls, and it reveals its long, pointy teeth. It licks both paws, then bathes its ears by bringing them down one at a time.

"You are brave," Kiowa says, drawing the bow back. He bites down on his tongue and squints one eye so tight that it puckers his face. As he's about to release the arrow, he stops and slowly relieves the tension. "It is wrong to kill you while you clean yourself. I will go and find another bunny."

He decides that if he must kill, he will strike a rabbit that is not so cute and not in the middle of its busy day. He eventually notices a fat rabbit whose belly and chest are white. He draws his arrow and aims.

Enthusiasm swells in his chest as he sees how stationary his prey remains, versus the squirrels that move as fast as lightning.

Aiming at the center of the rabbit, Kiowa releases his arrow and watches it fly toward his target. His devotion builds at the thought of striking the bunny in its furry heart. He imagines the accolades when the tribe sees his first kill.

But then the thought of hurting the bunny causes his heart to ache. Almost at the same time the arrow deviates off course, striking the ground just a few feet in front of the rabbit. It splits from the arrowhead and snaps the shaft on impact. Now mixed emotions of sympathy and anger compete for expression.

"Arrgghh!" he growls, nocking another arrow.

The rabbit continues to graze and completely ignores him.

"This time I will be quick, and you will be dead!"

As he releases an arrow, a voice interrupts his concentration.

"You are the great warrior that will embrace this people?" Kida sighs. The chubby girl looks more like an Eskimo than a Kiowa squaw. She shakes her puffy cheeks back and forth in disbelief. Her long braids flap against her fringed deerskin dress. She wraps her fingers around a carved turtle-shell necklace, made of turquoise, with two pearls pressed on either side.

Kiowa looks at the bow and arrow in her hand and laughs.

"You're just a stupid girl! Go be a stupid girl with the other stupid girls! I am learning to become a great hunter!"

"Is that so?" Kida asks haughtily.

Kiowa folds his arms and stomps his foot as he's seen the bull buffalo do. Moon Beam moves over and sits beside him.

"Let me pet your fox friend and I will teach you how to aim."

"NEVER, KIDA!"

"Why?"

"Because he is pure and you are tainted. You will ruin him!"

She squats down and smiles at Moon Beam. "But he's so cute! Come to me, Moon Beam. I will rock you in these arms and shower you with kisses."

"Leave him alone, stupid girl! You can't do anything right!"

"I can aim!" Kida stands up. She draws her arrow and releases it with accurate swiftness. She moves so fast it doesn't even appear that she takes aim. The arrow soars past Kiowa and strikes his target in the center of its chest. The rabbit falls over and kicks its hind legs violently. Blood mars its beautiful white fur. It squeals, thrashes, and does its best to get away.

Kiowa winces. Moon Beam flattens his ears. For a moment sympathy overtakes his anger. *That was my friend. See how you ruin everything, Kida?* Kiowa thinks, but he dares not say.

Kida struts past him and collects her prize. She puts her hand on his shoulder and shakes her head again. Kiowa takes note how her braids seem to emphasize her deep disappointment.

"He was eating. I was going to wait for him to finish."

"I am greatly concerned for the safety of our people," she says, then walks back toward the village.

Kiowa tosses his bow in frustration.

"Teach me how to aim, Kida!" he shouts.

"How can I? Stupid girls mustn't mingle with stupid boys. They will make stupid children, and then where will the tribe be?" She holds the rabbit by its foot. She does her best to keep the blood from dripping on her ornately beaded dress.

Frustrated with his inadequacies, Kiowa returns home and grabs his fishing spear. He sprints off to the fishing spring, where he knows he will find success—and his good friend Makes Trouble.

Certainly I will fare better in good company, he thinks, brushing Kida's bad medicine off his shoulder.

Moon Beam huffs, casting her bad magic off himself, too.

Along the banks of a fishing hole, a wild-looking, scraggly boy crouches in the shadows of a boulder. He makes every effort to conceal himself from fish that surface to swallow lazy, resting bugs.

"I thought I would find you here," Kiowa shouts.

The boy holds his finger up to his lips and whispers, "My father wanted me to gather wood and help collect berries."

Kiowa whispers back, "You had better do what he says or he will punish you again."

"I keep telling him my spirit is as *free as the wind*. Who can control the wind? I just land where my feet carry me. Besides, I am his only son. My seven sisters are perfectly capable of gathering wood and picking berries. My job is to be a great hunter."

"Have you caught anything?"

"Just ugly water bugs with big pinchers."

"Well, we can use them as bait."

Makes Trouble shrugs. "I guess so."

Kiowa spots the gray back of a rainbow trout gently swimming along the bank. He lifts his spear and aims just a little in front of its nose. "I don't think he will see it your way." Kiowa hurls his spear. It splashes through the water, striking the fish just behind the gills. Its tail flips up, the sudden commotion mixing blood and soot.

"Grab your spear before it fights off!" Makes Trouble warns.

Kiowa lunges into the water and grabs the spear with both hands. The thrill of the tugging handle forces him to push down hard, pinning the fish. Moon Beam watches from the banks. He prances up and down, chattering with excitement.

Kiowa snatches the fish by the tail, then scoops it out of the water. Moon Beam sniffs and licks its lips. It's as long as his forearm and as wide as his head.

"That's a good size. One day I hope to fish as well as you, Kiowa."

"How long have you been out here making trouble?"

"All day."

"Maybe you should take the fish. Your father will be less angry with you when you return with a catch. Your sister Kida just killed a rabbit."

"Oh, then we will have enough. You should take the fish to your mother. Besides, I won't take what I did not catch."

The boys spend the rest of the day fishing and talking about their favorite weapons. Kiowa tells Makes Trouble stories of his father. The boys act out the scenes with Kiowa playing his father and his friend playing the part of the dying, treacherous enemy.

When the sun sets, they return home.

"I wish every day could be like this."

"Me too, Makes Trouble."

"MAKES TROUBLE!"

Makes Trouble's courage evaporates when he hears the sound of his father's angry voice. His shoulders slump and his head hangs low.

"I didn't realize we were so close to my tepee."

His sisters stand in a straight line, from tallest to shortest. They each hold a switch.

"Your sisters have had to carry your weight once again. Unless that fish in Kiowa's hands is yours, you have to pay the price for your windy feet."

Kiowa offers his friend the fish, but the proud, wild boy holds up his palm and refuses to take it.

"Keep it. I have a plan."

"What is your plan?"

"The wind is my friend."

"What does this mean?"

"I'm going to run..."

CHAPTER 15

Before Makes Trouble can get away, his mother comes around the corner and catches the swift boy by the arm. She hits him with a switch several times.

"If you are the wind, then why can I catch you by your lazy arm? I am your creator. If you think you are of the wind, who do you think gave you that gift?" Glances Then Glares scolds him, hitting him between sentences.

The sisters all join in, cursing the naughty boy for abandoning them and making them double their work.

Makes Trouble winces from the force of the attack. He proudly fights back tears.

Kida swings her switch the hardest. The tip strikes bare skin and instantly leaves pink welts on her brother's chest. The boy can't help but howl in agony.

"How dare you take advantage of our kindness? You know it is in our nature to be so. You are a cruel, wretched boy to take advantage of our sweet nature and use it selfishly for idleness! Especially when you come home with nothing to show for your laziness!"

Her scolding words leave welts on his heart and bring tears of shame to his eyes.

"Forgive me, sisters!"

They ignore him and extract their ounce of justice.

You certainly are of the wind, Makes Trouble. Your cries sound like wailing willows, Kiowa thinks.

Not wanting to share in Makes Trouble's punishment, Kiowa slings his fish over his shoulder and calls for Moon Beam. For one reason or another, the silver fox does not budge. He looks down and looks up. Over and over he does this until he has Kiowa's attention.

"What is it?" Kiowa asks.

The demigod puts its foot on something as if to say, *I am playing a game. Can you guess what is beneath my paw?*

Kiowa walks over and sweeps the fox's paw out of the way and finds the most beautiful crystal.

"Is this a gift, Moon Beam?"

The fox rubs itself along his legs as a cat might.

"Is it magic?"

The fox seems to nod.

When Kiowa gets to his tepee, he can still hear Makes Trouble's cries. Kiowa is relieved that not a single switch made contact with his skin. He concludes that these events are a sign. He shows his mother and uncle the source of his protective magic, to which his mother tells him, "If it is true magic, then you must paint it with our sacred symbols and put it in a protective pouch, which Onendah will bless at the next sun dance."

Kiowa obeys her. He paints yellow zigzag lines and black circles on the stone. Then he puts it in a leather pouch he made and ties it to his belt.

"What else does my magic do for me, Moon Beam?"

The silver fox yawns, curls up in a ball, and falls fast asleep.

***

As time passes, Kiowa's skill with his bow increases. He spends many hours with Paw, learning how to inhale, hold his breath, aim at his target, then release when his muscles are relaxed. His trusty friend Moon Beam has learned to retrieve meat for him. More and more, the tribe believes in the truth of the fine animal's divinity. The fox grows to full stature but never ages one day beyond adulthood.

Before long Kiowa hits whatever he aims at: rabbits and other ground animals, birds, and reptiles. He gains confidence with each kill and even works up the nerve to hunt squirrels. After a winter, a spring, and almost an entire summer, he learns how to track their movements. Soon his uncle's words make sense. He can almost predict where his target is going to be. Even if he isn't successful, he learns something new each time. With each hunt he grows more confident. He eats more meat. And wears more skins.

Over time, Paw watches the boy turn into a young man, evidenced by the bulge in his throat, the crackle in his voice, and the traces of budding muscles. When the fall comes, it is time to take Kiowa on his first deer hunt.

"You will have to learn how to shoot while you ride," Paw informs his nephew.

The thought of riding and aiming seems impossible. Though he has seen it done dozens of times, he hasn't mastered it.

For the last year, he's gone with the warriors on their great buffalo hunts. Of course he wasn't allowed to do anything except carry arrows and ride a black mustang his uncle gave him, but it made him feel closer to being what he was destined to become.

Paw never speaks to Kiowa authoritatively and he has never struck him with his hand. He always presented options and tried to teach him to see advantages and disadvantages before forming a plan.

"Deer graze in the morning. We must either sleep in the cold grass and shiver all night or sleep in the comfort of our tepees and make our way down the pasture before dawn. Which do you prefer?" Paw asks.

Kiowa pauses thoughtfully. "Which would *you* prefer?"

Paw flicks him on the forehead. Kiowa retracts from the impact and rubs his forehead with his open palm.

"Aw, why did you do that?"

"You must think for yourself. Make your own plan and do not be influenced by others. And if you can, keep your plan to yourself before sharing it with anyone, lest they steal it from you."

Kiowa rubs the sore spot again. "Which will guarantee a kill?"

"Neither."

Growing frustrated, he draws a deep breath and grumbles, "Which path will offer the advantage?"

"Which do you think?"

"I think if we sleep out here beneath the stars, I will want to go home until the sun rises. If I stay here, I will be here when the deer graze and I will make no noise. If they show up at all, I will be prepared for them."

"And if you seek comfort?"

"Then I will make a great deal of noise when I come down in the morning, and if any deer are in this field, they will probably sprint off as the squirrels do when they hear me move in the forest."

"So, which path is best?" Paw asks, plucking the string of Kiowa's bow to test its tautness.

"I will freeze in the grass. Struggle with my desire to rest in my warm bed, and hope the deer appear in the morning."

Paw takes Kiowa's bow and carves a snake symbol in it. "And if they don't?"

Kiowa feels a frisson of frustration surge from the pit of his stomach. He clenches his fists and stomps as the feeling spreads all the way up his chest. Emotion explodes into a temper. "*Hmph.* You hate everything I say."

"I do not hate everything you say, just most of it."

"Why do you taunt me?" the frustrated boy asks, pressing his lips to a frown and squeezing his brows together until they practically touch. He tilts his head and glares at Paw so intently that his emotion cannot be mistaken.

"You think I taunt you? Look around you, son of Lone Wolf. I am the only man who is taking the time to teach you how to hunt. Did someone else show you how to carve a bow? Now, if you remain like this, I'm going to paint your sour face on your shield, and all the boys will know the bitterness that lurks inside your heart."

The thought of such embarrassment disseminates Kiowa's swelling temper almost immediately.

"Please don't do that, Uncle. They would nickname me Frowns a Lot."

Paw laughs at Kiowa's response.

"It pleases me that you can be bartered with. Can you see past your feelings yet?"

Kiowa thinks about Paw's question and knows that no answer he offers will stop him from asking another question. He also knows if he asks his uncle what he would do, he will feel another flick of his finger. The only option he has now is to put serious thought into an answer that will liberate him from his folly. Just then a simple answer surfaces in his mind.

"If the deer don't show up tomorrow, I will sleep in the grass until they make the mistake of grazing within range of my arrows."

Paw smiles at the answer he has been waiting for. He puts his hand on the young man's shoulder and says, "Boys make words. Men make actions. This is why warriors seldom speak and always listen.

Words cannot show our actions. We must be slow to use our words and quick to show our actions. When you want to move, look at this snake I carved on your bow. Remember how they sit still and wait undetected until it is too late."

Kiowa rubs his finger over the snake and listens as his uncle continues. "Actions require plans. Our plans won't always be solid like stones. The results of our actions will be. In fact, your actions will build a name for you. That name will either be a blessing or a curse. You will wear it on your shield all of the days of your life, and the tribe will never let you live beyond its shadow."

Paw leans down and lifts Lone Wolf's shield up. He displays the image on its rough hide.

"Your father's nickname was Lone Wolf because he would charge into battle on his own. You have heard my stories of him. He had no fear because he always had a plan!"

Paw hands Kiowa the shield. The boy takes it and sits down. He traces the sprinting wolf image with his fingers.

Moon Beam sits beside him and looks at the shield with a quirky smile.

"Like you, I had stones over my eyes that blinded me with fear of harm for your father. My heart would sink every time he would rush into battle, but I soon realized his plan was better than that of whomever he fought, and that is why he won!"

"So I must have a plan?"

"If you want to win and earn a name that will make your mother proud, you must not only have a plan, but you must have the *best* plan."

"How will I know if my plan is the best?"

"That is easy, Nephew. You will either be dead or alive. I must go now and leave you to your plan. This has been too many words for me. You must be honest with me and tell me which path you have taken and why."

"You aren't going to stay out here with me?"

"I won't always be with you, Kiowa. You are a young man now. You must learn to stand on your own two feet. I have killed many deer. My name is Paw because I learned to track animals by their paw prints. This is why the prints of many animals are on my shield. What image will be painted on your shield?" "Who will keep me company?"

"Moon Beam. Who else? It is getting cold. Show me who you really are."

CHAPTER 16

Kiowa shivers. "This night is the longest and coldest night of my life, Moon Beam." He pets the silver fox's head. "Something has been taken from me. There is an empty space inside me that will never be full. And it makes me so sad it hurts."

Moon Beam whimpers in short heaves.

The stars shine so brilliantly, Kiowa believes that maybe his father can see him through the portals of heaven. It gives him hope to be patient and suffer through his discomfort. He dozes off and falls asleep on the cool grass. Late into the night, his chattering teeth and uncontrollable shivering should have woken him up, but it is the rustling of the grass that disturbs him. He lies motionless, wondering what he should do.

He hears a distinct birdcall and then the familiar sound of his mother's voice. "Kiowa?"

He returns her call. "I'm over here."

Grass Woman squints and searches the darkness. "Ah, there you are."

She comes over and wraps a buffalo hide around his shaking body, then hugs him.

"I thought you might need this."

"It is late, Mother. Why are you awake?"

"Oh, I was thinking of you," she says, sitting beside him. A sprinkling of gray hair shines like Moon Beam's in the moonlight. She pats him on the back and moves her hand around in circles.

"Tell me a story," Kiowa says with a yawn that makes her yawn.

"Oh, I am not good at those," she says, pulling her son close to her side.

"Uncle tells wonderful stories."

Grass Woman begins to hum a soft song and sway back and forth. She looks up at the sky and searches for her husband's spirit. "I sometimes hear his stories. They make me happy mostly. But sometimes they make me sad."

Kiowa doses off.

When the sun rises, Kiowa feels its warm rays on his face. He opens his eyes and looks for his mother, but she is gone. Her trail leads back to the village. Beside her trail, there was another trail.

"NO!" He panics. Leaping to his feet, he shakes the warm buffalo blanket off and grabs his bow. To his complete surprise, fresh deer droppings are all around him. He missed his opportunity, and even though he doesn't want to, he quickly reports it to his uncle.

"Uncle, I remained still like the snake, but I slept like dogs and they went right past me."

"Thank you for your honesty. What have you learned?"

Kiowa is shocked that his uncle receives the news well. He makes a simple adjustment by saying, "They come and go as they please. But when the sun is up, they are nowhere to be found."

When Paw nods, he feels pleased with this experience. "But there is still a problem. I have not really done anything."

"So, what are you going to do?" Paw asks, leaning down so he's eye level with the boy.

Kiowa hesitates. He doesn't want to say, *Try again*, because last night was colder than he expected. And besides, all the other boys slept inside the comfort of their tepees, with their families, and they had all learned just as much.

"If we don't succeed, we try again," Paw whispers, patting him on the back.

"I guess..." Kiowa *humphs*.

"Are you thirsty while you stalk?"

"Yes, but I dare not get up and go drink water. It will startle my friends."

"Then put some berries in your mouth and let them roll around. Or grass. It will keep your mouth wet."

"Okay, Uncle. Thank you for your concern."

The following day the deer do not show up, but Kiowa learns why. The grass blades had all been clipped nearly in half, and though the deer could eat the grass all the way to the root, they seem to only like the grass tips.

Over the course of several weeks, Kiowa learns much about the deer. He learns that when the sun makes the earth hottest, deer generally find a place to lie down in the shade, where it is cool. He also learns how clever they are by the way they conceal themselves in undergrowth that is tall and often the same color as their fur. He learns that above all deer are quiet and patient. He watches them wrap their pink tongues around a thick blade of grass and pull it in, then thrash their heads back and forth until the herbage breaks in half. He laughs at how their lower jaws move side to side and the white fur beneath their glossy black noses looks like a mustache and beard. He becomes so close to them, he even has names for them.

"You are a mother, Black Eyes," he says to a doe whose beautiful fawn he sees nursing. He names the fawn White Eyes because of the many white spots on its side. "Feed your baby, Black Eyes. A good mother always puts milk in its baby's stomach. Oh, how you must love your baby. You let him drink milk all day long."

Kiowa learns how they move. How they speak few words, but what noises they do make sound like creaking timber, a call that brings out their young. He is shocked to see that each white-spotted fawn knows its mother's distinct call the same way he knows his own mother's call.

In his many observations and discoveries, he seems to have forgotten that he is hunting the deer. He's reached a new level of respect for his forest friends and values that bond more than his progress with the tribe. The pinnacle of his affection comes from feeding a doe by hand. He giggles when he sees his goofy reflection in her wide black eyes. He wonders why the creator put a white stripe beneath her eyes.

"I will paint this on my shield," he promises the doe, dragging the tip of his finger beneath its eye.

Kiowa learned above all that deer are incredibly gentle creatures. Doe don't have a mean bone in their bodies.

"The more affection I show you, the more affection you show me. I despise myself for wanting to harm something that can't even protect itself." His despair grows to disappointment when he thinks about a fawn losing its mother. His heart sinks at the thought of one more creature walking the earth without a parent that tenderly loved them.

"I vow here and now that I will not harm my forest friends. But only the bucks who hurt each other and sometimes scar you, Black Eyes, with their long horns." He extends this vow to all things and sees the honor in being gentle.

As with the squirrels, Kiowa learns to predict where the deer will be, not where they are. He watches them scatter in a flash when the lazy young hunters stomp down the grass and send them into flight. He even knows where the bucks will reunite with their families. Many times he creeps up on them and finds father and mother curled up in the grass and circled around their babies in the midday heat. That is when he has the most fun, because the inexperienced hunters would search and search in the fields, nearly step right on them, and the deer family would not stir. It is their greatest secret.

He laughs when the deer escape his friends' arrows. Kiowa thinks of a wonderful idea to save his furry friends. *I'll use the tops of the grass to lead them farther into the forest!*

The next day he does just that, and soon his tribe has nothing to chase. Because he spends so much time with the deer, the boys begin to mock him. His people don't value that he had learned how to observe, plan, and even speak deer. He is spared the humiliation that sent many boys out into the field and back empty-handed, but he is grouped in the same category since he had the same results. No boy is permitted to return without meat, and he knows it won't be long before his mother begins whipping him as Makes Trouble's sisters whip their brother.

Unsure of what to do, he is torn between his feelings for the deer and his uncle's instruction. Kiowa meets with his uncle to discuss the matter.

"I don't think I can kill them, Uncle."

"You have learned much, but it is now nearing winter and my patience is wearing thin. I can appreciate your bond, but your friends will abandon you when winter comes, and you and your family will be hungry."

"You are disappointed in me?"

"I am pleased in your progress, but everything must eat."

"But I have meat of plenty."

"Yes, and how did you get that meat?"

"Mother brings it to me."

"Who gives it to your mother?"

"I do not know."

Paw smiles. "Well, when you figure it out, let me know. But consider this. Boys who hide behind men's arrows can eat only so long as men are willing to share."

"What happens if they are not willing to share?"

"Then you go the way of the earth," Paw informs him, moving his hand from the earth to the sky. "I want you to hunt the buffalo. It takes as many as eight buffalo to make a tepee. I want you to feed your wife and children. Put them in a nice tepee. Make sure they are warm during the winter. If you cannot do this, I have failed you. Worse, you will fail them."

"No. I do not want that," Kiowa cries out, shaking his hands.

Which one? he asks himself. A sickening feeling rises in the pit of his stomach.

He pushes the faces of his new friends from his mind. Instead, a new image emerges. A picture on his shield of a man sprinting with a deer. He can see the shield going into battle and costing him his life because no warrior in the world would be afraid to attack a deer-painted shield, and the only magic he could get from the deer is to run fast. But even the fastest deer can't outrun a mounted Kiowa. He knows this to be true. He also knows that the wolf, the coyote, the bear, and even large eagles attack the deer. It seems that his friends have many enemies because nothing on earth is afraid of them and they are afraid of everything.

"Fear cannot be the best way," he tells Moon Beam, who is always beside him.

A plan begins to emerge in his mind. He heard a wolf howling only a short time back and thought how wonderful it would be if he could come up on a wolf and shoot it instead of his friends. In his wild imagination he thought how that would please the tribe and protect the deer. He could win both hearts in one epic battle. But then the reality of the wolf pack circling a fallen member makes him realize the impossibility of such a crazy idea. The chances of finding dozens of healthy deer were much better.

Just then Paw says something that brings his blurry thoughts into clear focus.

"Do you know where they will be tomorrow?"

Kiowa nods.

"Then we will go together, and I will be there to see for myself what delays you."

A blank stare glazes over Kiowa's eyes. He sighs. "That sounds wonderful, Uncle."

The next morning Kiowa is already in the grassy field, eager to greet his friends. He has become an expert in camouflage, and neither he nor Paw could easily be identified in the tall green grass.

Paw plucks a blade and chews on the tip. The musky flavor has a hint of mint.

"They will be here soon."

"You know what they eat?"

Paw smiles. "Doesn't everyone?"

Kiowa suddenly feels cheated, like the secret pact he has with the deer is not so secret.

An old gray-chinned deer grazes on the tops of the grass off in the distance where Kiowa has led them. It unknowingly moves toward Kiowa with slow, painful steps.

"Aim for the heart," Paw whispers.

"I will," Kiowa replies, feeling his heart sink.

He knows the old doe and takes comfort in the fact that she doesn't have any fawns to mother. As he nocks an arrow and draws the string back, the tension in his chest is as tight as the string. He pauses, feeling like he wants to cry, but he doesn't. He closes his eyes and takes several deep breaths to calm his racing heart. He slowly opens his eyes.

Kiowa fires.

CHAPTER 17

The white arrow spirals once and makes a distinct *thud* when it pierces the doe's rib cage.

The deer's muscles tighten, and it turns and sprints away.

To Kiowa's shock, he has hit his target directly in the heart.

Kiowa looks at Paw for his approval. "I hit her! My first deer!"

The pain that sank his heart and made him cry is replaced with a fire that eviscerates his sympathies. Now he is a predator and will only grow stronger with each kill. Only the thrill of the kill remains, until the deer releases a loud high-pitched squeal. Its knees buckle as blood spurts out of the wound. Its head lowers, and it struggles to rise. Its eyes blink slowly, then gloss over. Its energy slowly fades, and the light of life blows out.

Paw, invisible until he stands, pats Kiowa on the back. "Well done, Nephew!"

Kiowa tosses his bow to the ground. He sits down and wraps his arms around his knees and lets the tears flow. Moon Beam walks up beside him and rests his paw on his knee.

"Onendah was right. Your heart is stronger than your mind."

"She was my friend."

Paw glances at the deer, then back at his nephew.

"I felt as you did on my first hunt."

Kiowa looks up and wipes tears from his eyes.

"I know not why the Sun God requires us to kill, but I know that it will get easier on the next one."

"Will it ever stop hurting?"

Paw looks at Kiowa and frowns. "It is not that the pain goes away but when you kill so often, you become numb to it. That is the way of the hunter. When you are older you will seek a vision."

"What will my vision tell me?" he asks, wiping tears from his red cheeks.

"One of two things. It will show you a great medicine or it will show you the warpath. The spirits will then show you what magic symbols to paint, and that is how you will live the rest of your days."

"What symbols did they show you?"

"I could not see any animals or magic symbols. I could only see paw prints in the sand and in the sky." He motions with his hand. His long black hair catches in the wind and blows like strings of silk.

For the first time Kiowa understands the red line under his uncle's cheeks. Those were warrior marks, not medicine marks. His uncle is undoubtedly a warrior, though his knowledge of magic has convinced Kiowa that his uncle is as powerful a medicine man as Onendah.

"Do you understand?"

Kiowa nods, acknowledging that he understands, but his emotions swirl. *What if I don't want to be a great warrior?* The question shakes the foundation of everything he's been taught.

Paw interrupts his thoughts. "Your father would have wanted to be here for this. He would tell you"—he imitates Lone Wolf's voice—"'You have to be a warrior like me!' I am glad that I am here with you, so that I can tell you to be whatever your vision tells you to be."

***

Seasons pass like clouds slipping across the sky. Paw prepares Kiowa for the defining moment of his life the way a mountain lion trains its cub. He teaches Kiowa and his friend Makes Trouble how to track the buffalo herd's hoof prints.

Kiowa takes the lessons seriously.

"Every living thing that walks the earth leaves a footprint and a trail. A fresh, moist print will tell you how close you are. A dry one will tell you how many days. A deep one will most likely be a bull since they weigh more than the cows. A shallow print could be an old, weak buffalo or a starving one. Now tell me what you think." Paw instructs, then questions.

"Buffalo are similar to deer in the way mothers know their calves' calls, but not nearly as graceful. In fact, they are husky, stinky, slow-moving animals. But they are perceptive and, unlike the deer, every buffalo that can attack will. Hunting them requires incredible patience," Kiowa answers.

"And you, Makes Trouble?" Paw prods him in the ribs with his finger. "What are your troublesome thoughts?"

"I am going to keep my thoughts to myself. Kiowa has said enough," Makes Trouble replies with an empty expression.

Paw teaches the young men to stay low and stalk on their bellies. He is so accurate at reading tracks, he can predict within the hour where the buffalo will be. Among the herd's tracks, he sees an unmistakable horse print. The horse's tracks run parallel to the buffalo, and Paw gets the distinct impression that they are not alone.

Moon Beam crawls up beside them and rests as flat as he can beside Kiowa. He even flattens his ears to prove that he can lie as low. They remain like this until nightfall.

Early the next morning Kiowa whispers to Makes Trouble, "Do you know why you are here?"

"I think so. I'm here to hunt buffalo," Makes Trouble whispers back.

"That is true, but that's not why you are here."

"Why am I here?" Makes Trouble puckers up his lips and crinkles his brows together. "You must know, my would-be brother."

"My uncle asked me to pick someone to leave the rabbit circle with. I chose you."

"Does this mean we will be brothers in war for all of our days?"

Kiowa nods.

Makes Trouble smiles. "Oh, this makes me so happy. I was going to pick someone else, but when I asked, he said he already had a partner."

Kiowa frowns.

"Look there, boys. Do you see that?" Paw interrupts.

Makes Trouble and Kiowa instantly spot a white buffalo galloping across the emerald grass.

"The Sun God has sent us a sign," Paw declares.

CHAPTER 18

"He sends the white buffalo? What does it mean?" Kiowa asks.

"A long time ago, a woman appeared in the form of a white buffalo. One man was disrespectful to her and she turned him into a pile of bones. Another was respectful, and she gave him a flute and taught him special music. She also taught him special rituals that would one day bring peace," Paw teaches, handing them buffalo hides.

"Peace—that would be nice." Kiowa imagines what that might look like.

"Won't they smell us and startle?" Makes Trouble asks, doubting Paw's plan.

"They will smell us, but they will not startle. Cover yourselves up in these hides and their eyes will tell them we are one of them, while their noses will tell a different story. Some will scatter. Most will be like people—they will accept what they see."

"I don't understand," Makes Trouble says, bewildered at Paw's last remark.

"My patience grows thin. I can't wait to kill a massive bull." Kiowa grins, painting his face black and applying streaks of green paint to camouflage amongst the grass. He then wraps the buffalo hide around his back, ties a rope around his waist to hold it in place, and then immediately feels the temperature rise. The combination of the buffalo blanket and the morning sun on this spring day makes him wonder how the buffalo manage to not catch on fire.

"We will not be killing the buffalo as long as their protector is with them," Paw updates the boys.

"Then why are we here?" Kiowa asks.

"Be patient. Be still. Observe. Plan. Attack when their guardian is not with them," Paw firmly responds, applying paint to his face.

Be patient? When the Sun God's gift is before us? All I have to do is capture that trophy and my family is guaranteed meat for the rest of our days. Every Indian knows that's the reward you get when you catch a pretty white magic buffalo coat. Why do we not seize this prize? Makes Trouble wonders.

The hunters lean over on all fours and act as buffalo.

"A great lake of brown meat stretches out as far as the eyes can see," Makes Trouble whispers to Kiowa. "I am getting hungry just looking at them."

Behind them, Paw whispers, "Makes Trouble, what is your plan?"

Makes Trouble sizes up the herd from largest to smallest and decides to focus on the calves. "We should attack and scatter the young. Then it will be three against one."

Paw turns to Kiowa. "And what is your plan?"

Unsure of what to say, because his friend stole his answer, Kiowa decides to say something different. "We separate part of the herd and take some of the bigger buffalo first and some of the smaller ones when they tire from being chased."

Paw slaps the back of their heads. The boys jolt from the impact and rub their sore spots.

"Your youth is like a well of foolishness. You think the Kiowa are the only people to hunt buffalo?"

Both Kiowa and Makes Trouble shake their heads in confusion.

"If we are not here to hunt, then why are we here?"

"What does a name mean?" Paw asks.

The boys look at each other in bewilderment.

"Without it you would wander far from your parents and make nothing but great trouble," Makes Trouble responds.

"I wasn't talking to you. I was talking to my brother's son. What do you say, my would-be son?"

"Now is not the time to ask us this. We have more food and blankets roaming the field than I have ever seen. It is time to hunt," Kiowa asserts, knowing he offers the wrong answer.

"It is time to hunt when I say it is time," Paw corrects his nephew. "Now think."

"A name changes, so it is nothing." Kiowa tries again, resisting his excitement to rush the buffalo.

"Yes! This is true. Let us think on this and see if you need to know more today or if you will need to know more later. Come, follow me."

Paw crouches down and leads their stalk. They get within a hundred yards of the herd.

Kiowa hears their unusual grunts and groans and wonders what they are saying. He watches the males roll around in the dust, then approach the females and communicate in a way he can't understand. It seems to him that their disguises do not deceive the buffalo by the way the buffalo stare at them.

A bull sprints after the adorning male and smashes his massive horned head into the newcomer's horns. The clacking skulls sound like painful thunder.

"What woman is worth all that?" Makes Trouble snickers.

"Not just one woman. All of the women," Paw answers.

Makes Trouble nods in admiration. "I would smash my brains out for that reward!"

Unlike with the deer, Kiowa feels no attachment to the buffalo. To him, they are big dumb animals that should be slaughtered. They have no art, no cunning, no grace, no beauty or appeal. Even the young are ugly. To him the buffalo seem to have no other purpose than to clip grass, litter the earth with fertilizer, grow large, feed the tribe with their meat, and warm their bodies with their hides. Even their mating ritual is brutal. Bulls bellow deep roars as they charge each other and fight for breeding rights. This is the most curious thing to Kiowa. All this effort and exhaustion for the ugliest face he has ever seen.

The buffalo are the life force that sustains our people, Kiowa thinks. He readies his bow, but Paw quickly stops him. He points to an approaching Cheyenne hunting party on horseback. Their brown-and-white spotted pinto mustangs are led by a speedy horse, whose rider wears a long black bear hide. Their swift motions stir the massive herd and scatter the buffalo, exactly as Makes Trouble had anticipated.

"Ah, this is what I had hoped for," Paw tells the boys as he watches the Cheyenne pursue the white buffalo off in the distance.

"Now I see why you have led us down here in disguise," Makes Trouble whispers to Paw. "You want us to wait for them to kill the buffalo and then steal its hide."

Paw signs for them to be quiet and use only their hand signs.

The thuds of the buffalo's hooves kick up dirt clods and shake the earth so violently they rattle Kiowa's jaw. He hums and chuckles at the vibrating sound his voice makes.

A man may change his name many times in one life, but it will usually be something he does that makes his name good. Long lasting, Kiowa thinks.

Paw nods at the boys. They nod back.

Be eager to earn a name that your sons will fight for! Paw signs, nodding at the Cheyenne.

The brown buffalo act as a buffer between the Cheyenne and the white buffalo. They let the ghostly beast lead the pack.

Paw points at the leader of the Cheyenne hunting party and signs, *Him a man.*

I agree, Kiowa confidently signs back.

Him also a bear, Paw signs, pointing at the man who wears the black bear hide.

Kiowa looks confused. *How can a man be a bear?* Kiowa signs.

Not just any bear, Chief Black Bear, Paw signs back.

CHAPTER 19

"The most precious gift was taken from us. The love I had for my brother. The love he had for you. The love you had for him was ripped out of our lives. This is the man who has done it. Tonight we are going to take back a life, for the life he has taken!" Paw whispers.

Numbness washes over Kiowa and drowns his fear. A small flame ignites in his heart. He looks at Moon Beam, who seems to nod. The confirmation from his demigod fans the rising flames of rage.

"I stole this power from him." Paw pats a bundle of furs wrapped around the golden lance. "I hoped he would again be a man. The white buffalo was a sign to me that he would be here," Paw whispers. "I am glad you are here with me, Nephew. I want you to see me use this."

The rage swells and shows in Kiowa's blazing eyes. He hears his uncle's words, but his mind is elsewhere. A gust of wind whispers, "Avenge me."

Across the prairie, Black Bear encourages his hunters. "Where the white buffalo is, great magic follows. If she is not killed and sacrificed to the Sun God, she will lead the buffalo away until our people starve out. We must kill her and put to death the man of magic who has brought her here."

"*Ai hay!*" the Cheyenne hunters shout in agreement, pursuing the white buffalo with fierce whooping cries.

Kiowa's predatory gaze fixes on Chief Black Bear. The fire turns to lava, coursing through his heart and blazing through his veins. His jaw clenches and his hands tighten into fists. Now he understands why Paw has brought him to this place season after season. It wasn't to observe the buffalo but to find Chief Black Bear.

The Kiowa warriors stalk the Cheyenne as they would the buffalo, with slow, steady motions. They stay a safe distance away. They watch. They listen. They pray for justice.

"A warrior should kill at least one buffalo before he kills a man. But I have sworn an oath to kill Chief Black Bear, and I will not betray my brother now. Your father's legs carried me here, and I will follow their tracks back to camp. I will need your hands, Nephew."

"What will we do then?" Makes Trouble asks.

"Summon a war party."

"They are bound to have dogs. What will we do if we wake them?"

"Then both of you will be warriors tonight."

Paw's words fall on deaf ears.

Rage explodes inside Kiowa and forces him to his feet. With zero regard for Paw or Makes Trouble, Kiowa exposes their concealed position. He removes his buffalo hide and lets his russet chest and tawny deer-hide pants stand out in stark contrast to his green prairie surroundings. The buffalo stir at the sight of him and scamper off.

"Turn your horse around and look at my face, Chief Black Bear. My heart is full of fire! My hands turn to fury. I wear the mask of death. Come! Receive it!"

Black Bear and his hunting party are so engrossed in their hunt that they don't even notice the lone warrior. They simply pursue the herd.

Black Bear skillfully rides alongside a sprinting bull. His horsemanship is unmatched. He lifts a long spear and thrusts. His warriors fire arrows. They each take turns. The hunters know their attacks won't drop the beast. For this reason, they taunt, tease, and run the buffalo to keep its heart beating and pumping the life force out of the open wounds.

The bull staggers, drops to its knees, releases one loud bellow, and falls to its side. Black Bear thrusts his spear deep into the beast's heart. For the chief, the death blow is the greatest honor.

Kiowa releases his rage in one loud war cry. "AAAHHH-HHHOOO!"

One of the Cheyenne warriors hears the high-pitched wail. He scans the horizon and spots Kiowa. The brave halts his horse by pulling on the reins. With a swift jerk of the reins, he makes a sharp turn and points out Kiowa's distant tiny frame. He cries out to Chief Black Bear, halting the hunt's momentum.

"What, Lone Horn? Don't you realize all I have left is the hunt? After two hundred winters of life, that is all that I live for. It is the only thing that excites me," Chief Black Bear shouts. He peels off and circles around. "There is nothing but the hunt!" His disappointment shows on his frowning face. He holds his spear up and aims at Lone Horn. "My blade is thirsty for blood. I haven't even begun to whet it!"

"Chief, look over there." Lone Horn points at Kiowa. "That foolish warrior challenges you."

Black Bear strains his eyes to see the distant figure wildly waving his arms and shouting like a madman.

"He must be crazy," Sitting Elk shouts.

"He could be running from something," Spotted Fawn, the youngest of the hunters, says.

"Could be?" Sitting Elk *humphs*.

"Maybe he's running from another tribe," Spotted Fawn suggests.

Serious stone-faced men turn their painted faces toward him. All at once they burst into laughter.

"He is not alone," Black Bear grunts, knowing that Indians, like wolves, travel in packs.

"What tribe?" Lone Horn asks.

"Does it matter? My spear beckons for more blood. Can it be drawn and offer peace?" Black Bear questions. His eyes flash. Humanity disappears. It is replaced by savage, wild eyes.

"No."

"He challenges me. I accept. That is all!"

Chief Black Bear adjusts himself in his saddle and boldly peels away from the herd. He kicks hard at the side of his horse. The mustang stands up on its hind legs and cycles its front hooves. It releases a high-pitched whinny and sprints away, shaking the earth and kicking up dirt clods.

His warriors send their horses into flight and take up diagonal flanks by their chief. The Cheyenne furiously speed across the grassy plain in an arrowhead formation. Black Bear releases a war cry that lets Kiowa know he accepts his challenge.

Kiowa shouts back, "My heart is full of courage!"

"You damn fool!" Paw cries out.

"I think perhaps you have the wrong name, Kiowa," Makes Trouble says, shaking his head.

Kiowa feels the distant thuds of horses' hooves, and a great anxiety swells inside his chest as the vibrations grow.

"Do we run?" Makes Trouble asks.

Paw shakes his head. "They will scatter us like the buffalo and kill us quickly."

"What is to be done?"

"Ready your bow and die like a man!"

Makes Trouble scrambles for an arrow. His trembling hand struggles to nock it. "I haven't even had a chance to earn my name!"

"If we can kill the strongest first, the weaker ones will retreat," Paw informs his men.

"If we can't?" Makes Trouble begs, drawing the string of his bow.

"They will kill us, scalp us, and follow our tracks back to the tribe."

Once the Cheyenne are within range, Paw flips his buffalo hide off and takes a knee. Drawing an arrow, he aims high and fires.

"Ha! You see. They are never alone!" Chief Black Bear says, still unsure of the tribe he rides against. He points his spear at Kiowa. "The crazy boy's scalp is mine. The rest are yours!"

Paw's arrow strikes true, dismounting a Cheyenne warrior. The warrior tries to stand up but loses strength. Blood spurts out of his abdomen. His knees wobble as he grabs the arrow with both hands and forcefully rips it out. Parts of his intestines protrude from the incision, taking him out of the fight.

Inspired by Paw, Makes Trouble quickly fires. His arrow rises high, then falls low and strikes the earth.

"I said do as I do!" Paw rebukes him.

Paw fires again, striking a warrior's horse in the neck. The stud bucks its rider. Paw quickly aims over the man's head and misses. Within seconds, he releases a second and third arrow, eventually hitting his intended target.

Makes Trouble fires and hits an enemy in the groin. The Cheyenne brave falls off his horse, screaming so loud it scares the horses and forces them to run faster.

Paw pauses for a moment, then smiles. "Hmmm... I like your way better."

The Cheyenne are nearly upon them. Too terrified to laugh, Makes Trouble reaches for another arrow. He backs up like he's going to run, but Paw holds him in place.

"We fight as one!" he orders the young man.

Kiowa doesn't back down. Instead, he shouts, "Come to me, Chief Black Bear. I will spill your blood and make it flow like a stream on the grass. I will take your scalp and imprison your soul!"

"Kiowa…" Paw shouts, tossing him the golden lance.

Kiowa looks at his uncle and sees the powerful object glowing in midair. Instinctively, he reaches out and catches it. The second his hand touches it, the sun ignites a blinding light that slows Chief Black Bear's charge. The Cheyenne shield their eyes.

Paw wastes no time firing another arrow. He hits a horse in the leg next to Black Bear but does not reach his intended target. The horse bucks its rider and *neighs* as it sprints away.

"Ah, I know this man!" Black Bear shouts, lowering his spear. "This is the brother of Lone Wolf. We will make him sing the song of agony. Then we will scalp him alive, the way his brother scalped my son. Let us cut off his arms, his legs, and take out his eyes. He will be our living trophy!"

A soft amber glow bonds to Kiowa's tanned skin.

Black Bear lowers the point of his spear and readies his thrust. "The hunt! It really is all that's left." As he gets closer, a wild, excited grin flashes across his face. "You have not unlocked its power, or I would be facing a worse enemy than three men."

His warriors follow close behind, whooping war cries as they go.

Makes Trouble takes aim at Black Bear, but Paw pushes his arm down.

"Let Kiowa prove whose son he is."

"What if Black Bear kills him?"

Paw draws a deep breath and feels the weight of his brother's loss transfer to his nephew. "Then it is his time to reunite with his father."

Fueled by a mixture of rage and vengeance, Kiowa sprints toward his father's killer. Everything seems to slow. He sees Black Bear orient his flint-tipped gray spear toward him. The feathers tied around the shaft wave wildly. With a quick hike of his shoulder, the spear tucks firmly beneath his arm. Now Black Bear can see the weapon steady and aim directly at Kiowa's face. The horse's head rises, and its powerful hooves fall. The spotted brown-and-white mustang splashes through the marshy grass, splattering waves of cascading water with each step. Thousands of water beads form perfect spheres, then drop down as the mustang shakes the earth with each thrusting sprint.

Kiowa can hear the mustang exhale and notices how its eyes are as fiercely fixed on him as Black Bear's are.

"*Aiye-ahhh!*" Black Bear cries, lowering his shield and dropping his black-painted jaw. His eagle-feathered bonnet flattens against his head. He leans forward and prepares for the final thrust.

With every ounce of strength he has, Kiowa's arm retracts, then snaps forward. He hurls the golden lance with all his might.

Chief Black Bear glares over his raised shield.

CHAPTER 20

The golden lance leaves an ambient trail as it streaks through the sky, then disappears when it passes through Black Bear's shield.

Kiowa doesn't flinch. He doesn't run from the attack. He closes his eyes and trusts in his magic.

When nothing happens in that infinite second, he opens his eyes and sees the jagged tip of Black Bear's spear shift from his nose and dip past his chest. Kiowa's skin prickles when he feels the feathers brush past him. The spear penetrates the ground and throttles back and forth. A tingling sensation washes over him. For a moment he thinks he's passed into the next world. He rapidly blinks, expecting to see his father on a white horse, bringing another white horse for him. Instead, he sees none of that. Things are as they were, except Black Bear's body hunches over on his horse.

The hole in Black Bear's shield burns with orange embers where the lance passed clean through. As the horse continues through him, Kiowa can see the gleaming shaft poking out of his enemy's crimson back. The chief's nerves jolt as the horse walks back and forth.

"Today…" Kiowa exhales with a short breath.

Makes Trouble sees red blood spread in a perfect circle. The mighty villain's slumped body tumbles off his horse, making a terrible *thump* as it collides with the earth. "*AHHH HOOO!*" Make's Trouble cries, raising his bow above his head. He nocks an arrow and aims at the weary Cheyenne approaching, then fires. The warriors slow and turn their horses about, calling for their chief as the animals call for one another.

Kiowa walks over to greet the face responsible for all of his sorrow. When he sees the glaze of death in Black Bear's hollow eyes, which were once cold and calculating, he can't hold back his excitement. "*Ah-hoe!*" he shouts.

"*AHHH HOOO!*" Paw cries, unsheathing his scalping knife.

Kiowa kneels down and unties Black Bear's headdress. "Today you guided my hands, Father. You gave me strength I never knew I had. Thank you for today!"

Kiowa places one foot on Black Bear's chest, then forcefully rips the golden lance from his lifeless body. He looks at the Cheyenne braves, who keep a safe distance away.

"*AAAAARRRRGGGGHHHHH!!!*" Kiowa screams, lifting the bloody golden lance above his head.

The lingering Cheyenne take flight, while the blood of his enemy streams off the weapon and down Kiowa's arm. The men stop to retrieve their wounded, then speed across the plain, letting their dusty trail rest on their dead.

As the adrenaline begins to wear off, Kiowa realizes what he's just done. His knees buckle and his hands tremble. Fear and a great sense of satisfaction overpower him. The competing emotions cause tears to well in his eyes as the full impact of his kill settles like sand in his muddy mind. He looks at Black Bear's war bonnet and tries to steady his trembling hands as he wonders which feather represents his father.

Makes Trouble goes to comfort his friend, but Paw takes him by the arm. He leads Makes Trouble away and points to the fallen buffalo and the fleeing Cheyenne.

"Now you see wisdom. They hunt buffalo; we hunt them. They kill buffalo; we kill them. Now we keep the buffalo and take their scalps! Best of all, we did no harm to the white buffalo. She is free to return to the heavens. Today we are the men who treated her with respect, and she has rewarded us for it. Look here. Are we not the victors?" Paw tilts the gleaming blade of his scalping knife.

"Do you want the honor?" Paw offers Kiowa his knife.

Kiowa shakes his head. "I've never taken a scalp. I wouldn't know what to do. This lance and the headdress are all the trophies I need."

Paw moves over to Black Bear, grips the handle tightly, and kneels down. He wraps his hand around Black Bear's hair back and pulls taut. "Cut behind the ear first."

He thrusts the tip of the blade in and goes to work. "I broke my promise to you, my great enemy. I swore that it would be me who freed your spirit from your body. But today Lone Wolf's son has killed your body. I will keep my promise now. I will be the one to take your scalp. And Onendah will be the one to trap your soul!"

***

Charlie drops a log on the fire. Orange embers rise from the flames and trail off into the starry night. Luther yawns, mesmerized by the orange sparks.

"So that's it? He killed the Cheyenne chief. I thought you said it was a love story," Kevin says, wondering what he's missing.

"Yes, sir. He ran him right through with his own instrument. We ain't even close to the end of this here story, so sit tight, shut your mallow eaters, and open your ear balls," Charlie says.

"Wasn't he scared?" John asks.

"If he was he didn't show it!"

"Was it right for him to kill Chief Black Bear?" Zack asks.

"What an incredible question! In this life, I've learned two things: One, things ain't always what they seem. Two, wrong ain't always what it seems, either. Sometimes right has a way of appearing in a messy ball of wrong, but once you begin to untangle it, you see it for what it is."

"How do you know if it's right, then?" Luther asks, looking up from the flames for the first time since the story began.

"That's another great question. In this case, nothing could stop right from untangling its wrong self."

***

Grass Woman, Kiowa's mother, lays strips of elk meat out on a pine pole. Her mind drifts, and she swears she feels her husband, Lone Wolf, place his hand on her shoulder. An electric sensation fires on every nerve. It washes over her in a way that can be described only as a gust of wind. It awakens her soul with little cracks of lightning. She presses her hand to where she thinks she feels his.

"I feel you, my love," she whispers as the hairs on the back of her neck stand up. When the breeze passes, her hand slides from her shoulder to her heart. "I did not think you would want to leave the happy hunting grounds to come back and see me like this." Warmth, as powerful as the sun, rises inside her. In that moment, she knows she is not alone. Like the tide drawing back, the wave fades and her senses are again her own. But the memory of the moment remains, and though the warmth is gone, her heart is on fire.

As the day passes and the sun sets, the tribe readies for a cool night. Fog smothers the grass and fires ignite to keep the children and elderly warm.

"COME! COME!" Paw's voice interrupts the peaceful calm of the settling tribe.

Children run out of their tepees wearing sackcloth rabbit fur that conceals their gender. Their mothers chase after them with toddlers in arms. The warriors follow the women to see what all the excitement is about.

"My brother, Lone Wolf, spared us from Chief Black Bear and paid a high price for our lives. Today Chief Black Bear has been repaid equally for the hole he punched in our hearts!"

The tribe erupts in high cheers and loud praise. The warriors turn to Paw, excitedly rushing toward him. Hundreds of questions leap out of broad grinning faces.

"You *killed* Chief Black Bear?" Two Moons, Lone Wolf's oldest son, asks.

Paw immediately sets the record straight. "Kiowa killed Chief Black Bear!"

CHAPTER 21

"Kiowa killed *Chief Black Bear?*" Two Moons questions in complete disbelief.

The warriors turn their focus away from Paw, the calm muscular warrior, to the young brave, whose muscles are just beginning to bud.

.Kiowa feels the eyes of his people shift from his uncle to himself. Their silence and their gaping jaws make him feel awkward, like he's done something terribly wrong. He isn't sure what to do, so he lifts the feathered headdress and says one word. "Today!"

The tribe erupts in explosive cheers. They howl, dance, and wave their hands wildly.

Kiowa spots Kida pushing through the crowd. He smiles as she throws herself at his feet.

"You are a great warrior!" She reaches for him as though touching him might let her break a piece of his greatness off for herself.

Memories flash in her mind, from the boy who could not kill a rabbit to the man who has avenged his father and killed a great chief. She looks up at him. Her doting eyes are washed of doubt and filled with gushing admiration. She raises her hands and releases a victory cry. Soon all of the girls join in.

Kiowa blushes as his brothers Two Moons and Weasel Tail lift him on their shoulders and release victory cries so fierce, they terrify the youngest children, who scamper off after their parents like rabbits.

An explosion of praise thunders through the camp. Kiowa raises Black Bear's war bonnet high and searches for his mother. When he sees her, he tosses her the trophy. She slowly kneels down and says, "*Own, p'ayle doe,*" meaning, "Today, my love."

While the warriors carry him over to the fire and widen its warmth with logs, a few members of the tribe mount horses and speed away for the fallen buffalo.

"Listen," Paw says, hushing the tribe.

"Listen to how Lone Wolf became our greatest warrior." As Paw begins the story, the tribe circles around him. Orange firelight illuminates their proud faces. Two Moons beats on his drum. The fading sun sets the perfect stage, dimming the green pines to pointy shadows and spreading fog like a blanket over all the earth.

Kiowa listens to Paw recount the story. His uncle speaks of how he bravely stood alone and faced down his father's killer. When he assumes Kiowa's brave stance, the Dog Warriors gasp, while the ladies show their admiration through long twinkling gazes. The girls closest to him pat him on the back. All the girls tilt their heads and flutter their eyes and gush over him.

Kiowa is grateful that his uncle left out the scolding Paw gave him. He's also grateful he didn't tell the tribe about the golden lance. For though the tribe had possessions of their own, it wasn't uncommon for someone to "borrow" precious items for lengthy periods of time without returning them. It could be a lifetime before Kiowa got his turn with the lance, and since it was what his father died for, he felt especially close to it.

When Paw finishes the story, the women wipe tears from their eyes and look at their sons with high ambitions. Little girls fantasize about the sons they have yet to have and how they ought to be like Kiowa. Young men feel their arms and measure themselves against Kiowa. To look at the newest warrior, he doesn't seem to be much larger in stature than they are, which gives them hope that one day they will be as brave and as courageous as he is.

Kids lead the squaw in a dance to honor Kiowa. He'd hoped to be the hero, but he'd never suspected it would be so soon. Squaw as young as fifteen flap their arms like birds and dance around a tall pole that's covered in red paint and decorated with fresh scalps. Eagle and owl feathers form a feathery ring around the top and bottom of the pole. Beads of all kinds of colors are fastened to strings and adorn the pole from top to bottom. A short struggle ensues for the honor to carry the trophies, but Kida, being bigger, stronger, and most fierce, wins the honor. They begin to sing in a soft, sweet tone, which grows louder with the beating drum. Somehow they all keep time perfectly. As the drumbeat increases, the girls dance more wildly.

Young men shoo the girls away. They smooth out the earth while the Dog Warriors strip down to their breechcloths. They paint one another's bodies white and dress in buffalo skin. While they do this, they make buffalo noises.

Once the warriors are painted from head to toe, they dip their hands in yellow paint. Each one presses his open hand on Kiowa's body. It isn't long before Kiowa is covered in the highest honor the warriors have to offer, the compliment of the sun.

Kiowa is offered a plate of black paint. He dips his hands in and is instructed by his uncle to paint his feet. Since Kida has subdued the other females, she is permitted to tie prairie sage around Kiowa's wrists and ankles. She completes his victory outfit by placing a jackrabbit bonnet on his head.

Paw places a crow wing in one hand and blows through an eagle-bone whistle.

Kiowa sees Moon Beam watching from a distance. The silver fox seems to acknowledge Kiowa's victory through humble observation. His glittering green eyes flicker in the fire's flames. And he seems to be smiling.

Grass Woman brings his magic pouch out to him. "My son's magic is strong. I give him my blessing and the most potent magic I have, the power to blind his enemies. I have placed it in this pouch alongside his father's, and now no one can do him harm."

The tribe hoots and howls.

Kida dances and raises her hands as she shouts, "If you have eyes, let them see that this great warrior will steal your horse, take your scalp, and win your heart. He will be a ghost in the night and a spirit in the day."

"*Hey hoe!*" the Dog Warriors shout.

Kida beckons the tribe to follow her wild gyrations. Everyone dances around the fire, spinning themselves into a dizzy fray.

Warriors take turns shouting their prayers to Kiowa's idol. They say things like, "Keep our enemies asleep while we creep upon them. Let us plunder them and gain many scalps. Help us take captives to fill the empty spots of our fallen brothers and sisters. Help us steal good horses and, please, don't let us get hurt."

This praising dance lasts hours. When the children can't possibly twirl, spin, or wave their arms anymore, they sit cross-legged at the fire.

The warriors last the longest. They rattle their gourds and make use of any instrument they can contrive. Eventually the squaw and the men dance shoulder to shoulder, swaying back and forth as one tribe. A flute draws the tribe in toward the fire, and a rattle sends the circle back.

Grass Woman walks into the center of the circle. She spreads her arms out and drapes Black Bear's scalp across her back. "Whose scalp rests on my shoulders?" she asks the tribe.

The young men shout, "Our common enemy, Man-Bear."

With a spin and a turn, she displays the scalp to all of the young girls. They hiss at their enemy and spit on the moist scalp to cast off his evil spirit.

"Which of you believes yourself worthy to be my daughter? Which of you can give me grandsons?" Grass Woman challenges the young girls.

Not one squaw speaks, but the answer rests perfectly on Kida's confident face. She believes herself to be worthy of such a great honor, and though she wants to shout, "I will give Kiowa the most powerful sons," she doesn't. Instead, she slips her tongue between her teeth and bites hard enough to make herself cry.

CHAPTER 22

Two Moons takes off the bearskin and wipes his brow.

"I'm so filled with joy, I have to find a bigger drum!" He hands his bearskin to his son, then runs over to the largest drum he owns. He beats on it with such force, the bass percussion vibrates through everyone's chests.

"*Hiyah, oh, hey, ya hey!*" Two Moons sings as he pounds away. "Today we dance to Kiowa's victory. Our brother has earned his father's name!"

"*Hey hoe!*" the warriors affirm.

A heavy beat on the drum picks up the pace. Flutes blow, and Paw leaps to his feet and joins Two Moons in telling the story of Lone Wolf's death. Now he is acting himself. Uncle and nephew circle the "man-bear" and stab at him with invisible spears. The bear twists and turns. He claws at them, bites at them. Tries his best to catch them with claws that snatch and teeth that tear. The two warriors show how clever they are through dance.

"Now you see with eyes you did not have before." Onendah interrupts the dance. He materializes out of nowhere. He flips his gray hair over his shoulder and adjusts his white buckskin pants. In his hands he carries his magic wand. In the other, a large, steaming leather pouch.

Kiowa nods. "You speak what I think."

"It is my gift," Onendah says, opening the leather pouch. He thrusts his hands in and pulls out fistfuls of glistening black mud.

"We must cleanse your spirit, so that you will be pure from Black Bear's power." Onendah smears warm grit all over Kiowa's chest. He covers the boy from head to toe. Kiowa's immediate family members are the only ones permitted to touch him.

"Today a new star is born. He shines for his people and his people shine for him!" Onendah shouts.

"*Ah-hoe!*" the tribe cries out. Women spread their arms and shake their rattles. They flick their tongues on the roof of their mouths and make a high-pitched noise that endorses Kiowa with their highest honor. Kida's pitch is the highest, and her dance maneuvers are the most pronounced.

"You have earned your war bonnet, Kiowa. Now you must prove your worth, one deed at a time. Your only reward for your sacrifice will be a single feather taken from the bonnet of your fallen enemy."

Onendah holds the golden lance high above his head. Kiowa's heart sinks. *I wanted that for myself.*

The tribe sees it for the first time and they rush to touch the sun's power. Onendah holds it away and pushes them back with his other hand. Though the amber glow doesn't work for the medicine man as it did for Chief Black Bear, its luster silences their celebration.

"Do you accept your destiny?" Onendah asks Kiowa.

Kiowa slowly looks at each of his warrior brothers. One by one, they nod in affirmation. He lifts his hands and accepts the lance.

"This will be the symbol I paint on my shield: *the golden lance!*"

The tribe cheer for him.

"Your magic and your first feather," Onendah says, placing the bonnet on his head.

Now no one can take the weapon from me. It is not permitted to borrow another's magic, Kiowa thinks.

The white rabbit fur at the base of the headband is tainted with black mud as Onendah fastens it to Kiowa's head.

"Your bonnet is stained. See that your honor is not!" Onendah says, raising his hands and presenting the shadowy figure to the tribe. Only the whites of Kiowa's eyes can be seen.

"Welcome to our ranks, brother! Now you are a Dog Warrior like your father," the warriors shout. The people respond with cries of their own.

Kida grins at Kiowa. She is now a beautiful woman. A single white swan feather dangles from her silky black hair. It brushes against her beaded buckskin dress, which hugs her bulging breasts.

Now he is a warrior for his people and his people will embrace him, she thinks with a hunger in her eyes Kiowa can't ignore. Now I will fulfill my destiny and bear warriors for the tribe.

***

The Woodcraft Indians wrap their arms around their chilled legs and envision what it would be like to be at the Indian dance.

The scoutmaster clears his throat and runs his fingers along his whiskers. His eyes are focused, and he tells the story as though he were there.

"As the years pass like grains of sand in the hourglass, the Kiowa tribe grows in numbers. When the winter comes, they travel down to the southlands, where the pine forests and prairie grass recede to desert lands and red rocky mountains."

"How many miles?" John asks.

"Many."

"Did they ride horses?" he asks.

"How else do you think they got along?" Luther mocks him.

John rattles off one of many questions.

Charlie ignores him and continues. "Paw, Makes Trouble, Kiowa, Two Moons, and Weasel Tail ride their horses miles in front of their tribe, scouting for water and lurking dangers, so as to avoid ambush and such by the other tribes."

***

"Look!" Two Moons shouts, pointing to a trailing plume of smoke off in the distance.

Moon Beam sits up on the back of Night Wind. He looks at the smoke trail, then back at Kiowa. He chirps in a way that catches Kiowa's attention.

"The Hopi village," Weasel Tail says, thinking of the furs he planned to trade for beads and booze.

"Must be a war party," Paw concludes.

"Who would attack the Hopi? They seek peace, not war," Kiowa says skeptically. Kiowa has never personally traded with the Hopi—that was a right reserved for the barterers in the tribe—but he had heard stories.

For no obvious reason, Kiowa feels a swift swelling rage circle inside like a burning tornado. He isn't sure why the idea of someone hurting the innocent bothers him so much, but it reminds him of his gentle friends, the deer.

Moon Beam leaps off Night Wind and cackles. He runs away, then back. He prances in the most unusual manner.

"You have had that fox too long. He thinks himself Indian. Look how he dances." Paw points at the strangely behaving animal.

"I want to know who carries cowardice in their hearts," Kiowa growls. He looks at Moon Beam and notices that his emerald eyes seem to glow in a different way. It's as if the silver fox is saying, *Follow this way*. The demigod turns and runs off, giving no sign of coming back.

"Moon Beam, wait!" Kiowa yells.

"I think we should ride on," Makes Trouble says, kicking at his brown mustang's side.

"Moon Beam, come back!" Kiowa shouts. The silver fox takes off in a panic. He looks back to ensure he's being followed. When he sees that he's being chased, he darts toward the Hopi village.

"MOON BEAM, NO!"

"Four against how many?" Two Moons asks, wondering the size of the enemy.

Kiowa kicks at his horse's side and gives chase to Moon Beam.

Paw follows Kiowa. He turns his head and shouts over his shoulder, "Weasel Tail, warn the tribe."

CHAPTER 23

"Shear her?" whoops a Navajo warrior with a pudgy belly and crazy eyes. "Why not scalp them both?" He lifts a brown whiskey bottle. Anoki watches his pronounced Adam's apple rise and fall beneath a less-pronounced jaw. When he lowers the bottle, the devil's water erases any sign of humanity. An unquenchable rage accentuates his anger by flexing what little muscle he has.

"She is too pretty to scalp. I will be the one to shear her!" A more muscular Navajo warrior grins wickedly. He tilts his bowl-cut head and lasciviously focuses on Anoki's voluptuous chest.

"We will not get as good a price from the Mexicans if she is sheared." He looks down at his knife and grunts. His groan is followed by a drunken hiccup. "Okay, then, we're going to burn this adobe hut down and trade your whole family for more whiskey. What do you think of that, Hopi Princess?"

"WHY?!?" Anoki shrieks. She does the impossible and tries to reason with madness. Her black silk hair is braided like rope and rolled into tight wide buns on each side of her head. Her white deerskin moccasins mark her as pure. Her beaded attire glistens, making her look like a jewel. Everything about her entices her enemy. Her beauty. Her dress. Her belongings. Her rank. Her bloodline. All of it.

Tonight was supposed to be a special night. Anoki was dressed for the Hopi summer solstice dance. As princess, she was the main attraction.

An older man, her father, Kikmongwi, king chief, lies at her feet. He's been badly beaten by the drunken Navajo, who toy with their victims like cats playing with frail mice. Anoki's courage and puny tomahawk are the only things that stand between the drunken

Navajo raiders and her father's scalp.

"I told you it would be best to attack while they dance to Wuko'uyis."

"Move aside, girl!"

"I will not!" she shouts.

"We four Navajo warriors have more scalps on our belts than fingers and toes in this room. Do you really think you can stop us from adding the high king's scalp to our belt?"

"Look at her braids. She is just a single lonely girl with no husband to defend her. Ha! Ha! Ha! Ha!"

Anoki winds up her tomahawk and readies for a swing as they begin to swarm her. "GET BACK! Leave us be. Return my sister and my mother, or I will hurt you!"

The more aggressive Navajo points at himself and counts aloud. "I see one, two, three, four of us. And only two of you."

"My father is not responsible for sour meats or bad seeds."

"YOUR PEOPLE ARE RESPONSIBLE FOR EVERYTHING!" the crazy-eyed Navajo shouts, thrusting his spear into her father's leg.

Kikmongwi cries out, which causes the Navajo to cackle like a pack of coyotes.

"SAVAGES!" Anoki curses them. But they wear her insult like a badge of honor, and they feed on whiskey and misery.

Anoki puts up a good fight. But inside she is as fragile as glass, and her cracks show when her father screams. She can bear anything but the pain-filled cries of her father. Her heart sinks. She does not show her attackers. Instead, she clenches her teeth, flexes her jaw, raises her weapon, and attacks.

She leaps forward and slams the blade down on the Navajo's foot. He drops his spear and screams as he hops up and down.

"Leave us alone!" Anoki blasts, wishing she could have cracked his skull.

The Navajo laugh when the injured Indian hops up and down on one foot. He abruptly stops, turns, and slaps Anoki across the face.

She falls to the ground as though she were made of leaves instead of flesh and bone. She presses her hand to her burning cheek and reaches for her father. Instead of relenting, she grabs the tomahawk, though she feels her security slip away as the Navajo pack circle around her like wolves. She can feel her cheek swell. She can taste blood.

Now is a good time to be diplomatic, she thinks. "Please don't hurt my father. Toss him the band of mercy hanging from your wrist," she begs.

Crazy Eyes lifts the red-and-yellow band up and howls. "We have paid a high price for your trade!"

"You haven't even begun to pay, Hopi Princess!" Crazy Eyes barks, untying a knot that holds his animal-skin pants up.

Anoki gasps at the progressing horror. She feels her spirit sink to dark, unimaginable depths as she realizes the price she's about to pay for defending her father. Her head swirls. With the last bit of energy she can muster, she pushes her legs together and wraps her hands around her knees. Rocking back and forth, she prays that she has the strength to fight these vile men until life leaves her tiny little frame.

Crazy Eyes unsheathes his rust-stained scalping knife. He tears at Anoki's clothes.

"No!" she shouts, resisting his assault.

Her husky assailant responds by punching her in the face.

Her whole body convulses from the blow. She sees white flashes that nearly blind her, but she knows if she keeps up the fight, the Navajo will grow tired and stab her to death, which in her mind is better than being defiled next to her tormented father. "Oh, that this was any other day. Think of happy thoughts, Father. Do not let these be the last images you see of your precious daughter, your sweet Anoki." Darkness closes in around her.

Through hazy vision, she sees the angry Crazy Eyes raise his knife. Her stomach muscles tighten. She feels an agonizing pain and closes her eyes.

Good! she thinks. *Death is better!* She focuses on the monster's twisted face. The evil in his wide, cruel eyes maximizes her fear and makes her hope that his knife will penetrate fast and free her spirit quickly. But then his eyes suddenly seem to soften.

Among the stench of liquor, the filthy Navajo, the heat of the swelling flames, the laughing demons, her wounded father, and her imminent murder, the impossible happens. An arrow whistles past her head and punctures her attacker's beefy chest. If Anoki had gold, its value would be nothing compared to the confused expression on Crazy Eyes's face. Senseless rage turns to agony. She feels the tight tension in her face fade into a modest, righteous smile.

The Navajo drops his knife and grips the arrow. He struggles for breath, which causes blood to spurt out of the wound like a bubbling geyser.

Another arrow strikes her assailant through his arm, pinning the appendage to his chest. The knife he intended to use cannot be used to cut her now. Now it's her turn to laugh. The villain's evil face turns from agony to regret.

Anoki flashes through all the men in her tribe who could help, and she can't think of one. *What Hopi would help me when his own family is at risk? That isn't our nature. We protect ourselves first when danger is all around.*

Crazy Eyes tries to speak, but his strength fails him. Instead, he falls dead to the agonizing melody of his wicked friend's laughter. It is not a sound he likes, and his death mask indicates it.

Kiowa's bow creaks. The string twangs, and his arrow flashes through the air. His aim is deadly. Not that he would need to be accurate at such close proximity. He strikes another evil man through the flexing, laughing neck.

Choking cries surprise the other Navajo, and the last two men scramble.

Kiowa and Paw smash through the pueblo's clay wall. Anoki sees a flash of feathers attached to a bonnet. Black war paint covers their foreheads and streaks down the sides of their faces. It continues around their jawlines and ends in yellow circles at their chins.

There, see! That is what a good Indian should do. Run! Anoki thinks as she presses her hand to her head to stabilize the rocking motion.

Before the Navajo can escape, Two Moons and Makes Trouble seize their victims from behind.

CHAPTER 24

With the crook of his arm, Makes Trouble forces the man's chin high and exposes the Navajo's neck. In one swift motion he proves his name true.

Two Moons stomps the back of his opponent's knee. He feels the man's body slide into his. His steel blade slices across the man's neck. Blood spurts out of the wound and spills down the quivering man's chest. His flailing body falls to the earth, where Makes Trouble is quick to scalp him.

Anoki gags and turns away. Her head swirls even faster, and she feels like she's going to vomit. *Why? Why are these men doing this?* she thinks.

The Kiowa warriors look at each other with great satisfaction.

"Why are we here?" Two Moons asks with a broad smile.

"Because Moon Beam led us here," Kiowa answers.

"What do we do with them?" Makes Trouble demands, pointing his bloody blade at Anoki.

"What? Why?" Anoki asks Kiowa as he kneels down and reaches for her. She jerks back and resists. "I see you want to steal us from the Navajo!" She searches for her tomahawk and regrets losing it. Looking down at her stomach for the first time, she sees that she is not stabbed at all. It was just her way of anticipating the pain. *Oh, I have no appetite for this*, her face tells Kiowa as she groans.

Kiowa gently puts his hands on her arms and looks deep into her eyes. "No," is all he says.

I thought the Navajo were savage, she thinks, trying to keep her eyes open. *I see now that the Kiowa are truly savage and perfectly wild.*

Paw looks out the window. "I see plenty of Navajo moving from house to house. But I don't see Moon Beam. What is your plan now,

Nephew?"

"We will have to come back for him. No doubt the Navajo will want revenge when they see what we've done here," Two Moons warns them.

Kiowa lingers longer than he should. Where Anoki saw anarchy, Kiowa felt calm and a strange peace as he gleaned her beauty. He shakes her to keep her awake.

"Are you strong enough to walk?"

Anoki understands his foreign tongue. She doesn't answer. Instead, she focuses on his soft, gentle eyes.

Two Moons and Makes Trouble help lift Anoki's wounded father. "Come, Daughter, you must walk because I cannot run." He motions for Anoki to follow him.

She struggles to stand. Kiowa slides his arm around her small waist and helps her to her trembling feet.

The Kiowa war party is on the move. They stealthily slip in and out of the shadows as though they themselves were shadows.

Two Moons, Paw, and Makes Trouble manipulate the unsuspecting corners into death traps for the lingering drunk Navajo raiders. Their skill and oneness are things the Navajo, who feel themselves victorious, lack.

"We are swift," Makes Trouble whispers to Paw as he moves to a shadow.

"We are silent," Paw whispers back, pressing himself against the adobe wall.

"We are deadly," Two Moons says loud enough for them to hear as he unleashes an arrow that drops, but doesn't kill, a Navajo carrying an armful of Hopi skins. The wounded warrior reaches down. He wraps his fingers around Two Moons's arrow and pulls with all his might. The arrow's shaft comes out easily enough, but the arrowhead stays in. He holds it up to his face and examines the colors and markings to see if he can identify his unseen enemy.

"Kiowa? We have no quarrel with you!"

Makes Trouble sprints from the shadows and buries his tomahawk in the Navajo's skull.

Two Moons extracts his tomahawk, then swipes as he says, "Knock, knock. Is the master of the house home? If so, send him out. There is a war party here to greet him."

WHACK.

He quickly unsheathes his scalping knife and separates the man's hair from his head. He moves so fast, Paw can't help but be proud.

"See there, Makes Trouble. A little courage in your heart goes a long way, does it not?" Paw asks.

Makes Trouble smiles, forgetting it was he who wanted nothing to do with this fight.

"At the scalp dance, we will dance to your bravery instead of your fear," Two Moons says with a proud nod.

Kiowa leads Anoki and her father to his black mustang. He helps her father up and then turns to help her.

"I can get up by myself," Anoki protests. She takes several deep breaths to calm herself down.

Kiowa nods as she puts her shaking hands on the horse. He gently rests his hands on her hips and feels a pile of leaves swirl inside his stomach. *What is wrong with me?*

He lifts her up with ease. Her fear melts away like ice during the summer. A surprising giddiness replaces it. She kicks her legs several times, fluttering her moccasins up the sides of the black mustang. After she swings her leg over the horse's back, she takes a long moment to face Kiowa. She does this to calm her nerves and put on her bravest, sternest face.

Kiowa retracts his hands. *Now, that is a fine, proud, brave woman. I have never seen beauty like hers*, he thinks to himself. When he takes his hands off, she regains her senses and feels her fear return.

Caught between mixed emotions, Anoki grumbles. She's frustrated that her independence is invaded by both friend and foe. And she isn't entirely sure which one Kiowa is.

Kiowa hands her the reins and her tomahawk, a good sign, but the Navajo gave plenty of good signs, too.

Anoki grips her tomahawk with such a firmness that her fingers feel numb and begin to tingle. She isn't sure whether she should follow Kiowa or not.

She lifts the tomahawk and feels her arms tremble. *Bury this blade in his skull and then run, Anoki!* Her thoughts scream in the sanctuary of her mind. *Run like the Hopi girl you are and protect yourself, and don't forget your father.*

Kiowa looks up at her and can't help but notice how she holds the tomahawk. He smiles.

His smile keeps her in place with eyes firmly fixed on his handsome face. *You have caught me at a bad time, my would-be hero. If you are my hero? I am not very beautiful with this swollen cheek and bloody face. Certainly, you are a hero. You wouldn't help my father if you were stealing us away. Would you? No, you would kill him and rape me if you were evil,* she thinks, looking over her shoulder.

She smiles back as she sees Kiowa's band killing the Navajo with such ease that she wonders why she was ever afraid at all.

Anoki presses her hand to her throbbing cheek and looks over the blazing village. The extensive flickering flames tower and illuminate the village roads, telling a story of heartbreak. *We can rebuild. We can regrow. But what am I to do about my mother and sister?* Bodies litter the dirt roads, and the dogs waste no time in lapping up the pools of blood from masters who loved them and the enemies who would have eaten them. Both are alike to the dogs in their own deliciousness.

Anoki feels the crushing weight of the successful raid and detects the disgusting scent of her people's bodies burning in their homes. Some are still screaming. She turns away, trying to wash the images out of her mind with tears that trickle, then stream to form an ocean of deep sorrow. She trembles with fright and feels as though she's going to black out. *What can I do?*

CHAPTER 25

In that frozen moment, Kiowa steals the longest glance at Anoki. Her soft features come together in complete perfection. He overlooks her blemishes since he's used to seeing painted faces. Half of Anoki's face is as smooth as a pearl. Her eyes are a light walnut brown. Her high cheekbones give every facet of her beauty a different elegance with each turn of her slender, petite neck. His heart feels a spark, which forces his eyes to see those facets.

Am I falling, or am I flying? he wonders. He inhales, detecting the aroma of vanilla, lavender, and honeysuckle. *Do not show too much interest or she will doubt your true intentions*, he thinks, lowering his smile to a frown. *Do not show too little interest or someone else will*, he counters his thoughts. The back-and-forth lifts his frown to a flat, cornerless smile. *Think of something to say.*

"How have you trapped the wild in your skin?" he asks her, but she doesn't respond.

What is wild about my skin? Anoki thinks, then shrugs, realizing her face must be worse than she thought.

Kiowa can't help but wonder why her rustic skin has more of a red undertone than his.

Why do your lips look like two wild rose petals pressed together? He sees her small frame expand and fight for a shallow breath. *Oh, if Moon Beam were here, he would calm me. You would be the first person I would let pet him and take his sacred magic from me.*

Anoki struggles to steady her swirling head. In all the effort to keep a stern face, she held her breath too long. She blinks several times, trying to understand why the stars have lost their place and swim in her eyes. She loses strength and feels herself falling. She watches helplessly as a closing circle of darkness forms around

Kiowa's handsome face. His head turns sideways, then disappears into fading black.

Kiowa's biceps flex as he extends his arms and swiftly catches her. "You're as light as a feather and as pretty as a dove," he says softly. He wants to kiss her, but his lips recede like waves on a beach. That is against Indian law! he chastises himself.

Before this night, I did not even know a woman could be so beautiful. Fire Boy and Water Boy, are you demigods playing some trick on me? Or did you plant a heap of treasure in my hands because I killed Black Bear?

The wind catches loose strands of her fine raven hair and sweeps them across his face. They brush against his cheek. He holds her firm with one hand as he presses the tickling fibers to his skin and inhales.

"So this is how a spider catches a butterfly," he whispers, careful not to make any sudden moves. "Which of us is which? If I am the butterfly, I feel so light I could float above your string. If I am the spider, I set you free, but only to draw you back again."

He closes his eyes and inhales. He feels her spirit leap from her body into his mind and run on a never-ending coast. In his vision, she rides a white horse. Glittering stars explode like shooting comets that cross the sky with long glittering tails.

The spark catches and ignites a burning sun of passion in his heart. Warmth rises from his chest to his cheeks. "You are safe with me, little bird," he whispers between hushed whooshing. The closer he pulls her in, the warmer he feels. *What is this powerful sunlight that cascades across my sky and paints my world the colors of the sun?* For some reason, the stars do not disappear, but come closer and dazzle all around her. A moon of hope shines its powerful rays on her face. Her spirit reaches for him, and he wants nothing more than to take her hand and follow wherever she leads.

When he opens his eyes, he speaks so softly he nearly whispers, "What joyful winds do you stir inside of me?" He gently touches the palm of his hand to her cheek. "I did not know my heart could have love in it until tonight. I thought it was emptied by Chief Black Bear. Am I awake, or am I asleep? Am I hungry, or am I full? I am confused. Paw says that love is blind and it can happen at any moment. But when my eyes rest on you, I cannot help but feel your beauty pour into me and fill me up. No arrow could hit its mark if the bowman's eyes are closed. I must keep my eyes wide open. I must be hungry, but not for food. What, then?"

What time passed must have been only seconds. But in the eternities of love, time is conquered. It vanishes in a thousand moments.

You have created a starry heaven of possibility inside me, Kiowa thinks as her beauty pours into his eyes and fills him up.

He tries to hold the moment, but her short gasps bring him back to the harsh reality of this world. He is running from the Navajo. Or running to her? He can't decide. However he's doing it, he is running.

"Peace," he says. "Be not afraid. Taime blew me into your life, and I am here to protect you."

Fading in and out of reality, Anoki catches words. Glances. Impressions. All of which mix, make no sense, then evaporate. She knows only one thing for certain. She is waking in strong arms. Arms she feels supremely safe in.

Who is this man that catches this tumbleweed? she wonders. She blinks and pushes on his firm chest in a way that lets him know she can stand on her own.

Kiowa lifts her back onto his horse and asks, "Can you ride?" He hands her the reins.

Anoki takes the leather straps. A new fear emerges. It annoys her that so many fears have been revealed in one night. *What happens when he leaves?*

He swats his horse and sends wounded father and brave daughter sprinting off into the night. They disappear in the darkness.

Kiowa circles back to the village and reunites with his band. He looks at the scalped Navajos and smiles at their limp bodies.

"You are all going to pay for what you have done! One way or another, I promise that I will see it to its end!" Kiowa pledges with a blood oath.

Makes Trouble proudly holds fistfuls of bloody scalps up, along with the reins to six Navajo horses, which nearly lead him rather than him lead them. He smiles when he sees Kiowa. "They are going to be so mad when they find us."

Paw and Two Moons pull eight pinto horses by their reins. The raid is successful.

"Where's the girl?" Two Moons inquires.

"I sent them out on our horses. I think Night Wind will lead them to the last place he had good water," Kiowa answers.

"Up in the pine forest? That is good. They will be safe." Paw nods.

Makes Trouble and Kiowa mount new horses, as Paw and Two Moons ride up beside them. The group slips into the night.

"Where do we go now?" Two Moons asks his brother.

"The Hopi cannot come to our village. They are outsiders. No one will welcome them," Makes Trouble blurts out.

Kiowa's face sours. "We will decide what to do with them if we meet up with them. If we don't, they can keep our horses. We have many more than we came with. That is a good trade!"

"Look!" Paw catches a distant flicker of motion. "The Navajo are coming back. They must have felt so confident in their raid, they lit torches. They have greater numbers than us." He counts their growing lights and huffs.

"Why are they lighting torches?" Makes Trouble asks.

"They will need light to track us in the dark," Two Moons responds.

"Should we lead them back to the tribe?" Kiowa wonders.

"Yes, Kiowa, let's wake our tribe in the middle of the night with the war cry of who knows how many Navajo hot on our heels?!"

"Next time we use Cheyenne arrows. That way the Navajo will not be looking for Kiowa." Makes Trouble smirks.

Two Moons agrees. "*Aiye!* I have a quiver of Cheyenne arrows back in my tepee."

For a brief moment each man plays out several different scenarios of how their actions will bring the wrath of the Navajo. They rattle some off and come to one solid conclusion.

Paw speaks what everyone thinks. "Navajo need no reason to attack. They will just attack."

"By now they will have dispatched riders to bring the rest of the warriors, and who knows how many that will be?" Two Moons wonders.

The calmness of the warriors is remarkably out of character for the dangers they now face.

CHAPTER 26

"One set of tracks will lead them to the Hopi princess..."

"She's a princess? How do you know that?" Kiowa asks.

"Focus on escape, Kiowa!" Two Moons scolds his brother.

"If I were the Navajo, I would not chase one set of tracks. I would follow the greater number and get my ponies back," Makes Trouble says.

"Which would be our trail," Paw calmly adds as he paints his face black.

"If we go on foot, our numbers will look bigger," Makes Trouble proposes.

"True. If we dismount and send all these horses off in another direction, the Navajo may chase the men on foot or they may run after the horses," Paw contemplates.

"If I had horses, I would track down the warriors on foot." Kiowa confidently nods, seeing the pieces of his friends' plan slowly come together.

"Maybe if there are only two of us, they will feel more confident hunting us." Makes Trouble rubs his thumb on his chin and works out the final pieces to a master plan. "If we can run to the river's edge and jump in so that the currents carry us away, the Navajo will have no tracks to follow," Makes Trouble says with an "aha" expression.

Kiowa thinks it through, then nods and says, "So long as we have the night. If we don't make it by daylight, they will surely have no problem hunting us down in this vast desert and taking our scalps."

"You will need this," Two Moons says, passing his knife and flint stone to Kiowa.

"If I don't make it back, Paw, give all of these horses and treasures to my mother and sisters. Tell them I am sorry for letting the wind carry my spirit away," Makes Trouble says with a quirky smile.

Kiowa and Makes Trouble lift their bows and take only a few arrows. Two Moons and Paw sprint off with the horses and the bounty.

"I'm leaving this raid rich with many scalps and armloads of bounty. What are you leaving with, Kiowa?"

Kiowa perks up and boldly declares, "A vision that is worth a thousand raids. I have seen my future, and I am rich in love."

Makes Trouble's face puckers up with the sourest expression. "We are young and have many raids and female conquests. Why would you let one Hopi girl get in the way of all that life has to offer?"

Kiowa smiles and shakes his head. "Paw says if you chase two rabbits at the same time, you will catch neither. All you will catch is what you had to begin with, an empty hand."

Makes Trouble grumbles in contemplation.

Suddenly, Makes Trouble stomps. He looks down at his foot and says, "Kiowa! An idea has just leapt into my mind. Walk around in a small circle, like this." He motions with his finger. "Step over my tracks until we have a whole heap of tracks overlapping in a big circle."

"Makes Trouble, you have the wisdom of owls. Now the Navajo will see the horses' tracks and all these tracks and struggle over which fight will be easier to win."

Makes Trouble beams from the compliment. He stares at Kiowa with a warm smile that brightens his face in their dark hour. "You really think I am as wise as the owl?"

Kiowa nods. "I know you are! Why else would I do this?" He hoops and howls as he stomps around in a widening circle.

Shocked by his comrade's erratic behavior, Makes Trouble's smile melts away to disgust.

"If I am as wise as an owl, then you are as stupid as a squirrel. Why are you yelling? Don't you know they will find us with all that noise you are making?"

"That is my hope, my would-be brother. These deserts are vast, and they may not see our trickery."

Makes Trouble thinks on this for a moment as he watches Kiowa shout, "Beaver dung! We are here to take your scalps and all your ponies! You are falling into our trap!"

In the distance, Makes Trouble sees the Navajos' torches

consolidate into one flaming circle. He quickly counts twenty or so.

Unable to resist the invitation for trouble, Makes Trouble shouts, "Your bodies look like gopher dung and your mothers have made you like themselves."

Kiowa looks at his friend in disbelief. "Where has all this wisdom come from?"

Makes Trouble smiles and shrugs. He points to the stars. "The stars send me messages that my ears can now hear."

"Your magic is working, and I can see it in your face." Kiowa nods at the Navajo. "No Indian would stand an insult to his mother. They will most definitely find us now and probably skin us alive."

Makes Trouble rubs his arms, not wanting to part with his skin. "What do we do?"

"You are the wise one. I will follow your lead."

"Then we had better get to the river!"

The two run off as fast as their long legs will carry their muscular frames.

Within moments, the Navajo ride up on Makes Trouble and Kiowa's handiwork. They lower their torches and circle around the tracks, trying to get an idea of how many Kiowa warriors they face.

"A pack of warriors on horseback have broken off and run toward the mountains. Two men of foot run off toward the river. What would you have us do?" Jumping Bear, the father of Crazy Eyes, asks the chief.

The Navajo chief, Old Red Eagle, examines the tracks and wonders where such a large number would be. He uses his eagle-like vision for lumps in the earth, to see if the Kiowa have buried their bodies in the earth. "Be ready for anything!" When he's satisfied that no ambush awaits him, he circles around several times and wonders where such a large force would be. It doesn't take him long to realize that so many warriors could not simply disappear into thin air. *No, we would hear their whooping war cry for certain.*

"Look here. If they had all these men, they would engage in battle, and why would two sets of tracks run off?" he asks.

The Navajo search one another's blank faces.

From a distance, Old Red Eagle hears the faint shouts of Kiowa and Makes Trouble. "You are uglier than goats, and your fathers have bred with gopher mothers to make the ugliest Indians of all the Indian nations!"

"They taunt us," Jumping Bear growls at his grunting band of Navajo warriors.

"Yes, but why?" Old Red Eagle asks.

"They want a fight. There are fewer of them than those on horseback," Jumping Bear determines.

Old Red Eagle agrees. "True, and the horses are most likely leading us into an ambush. I think we catch these two fools and make them pay for the injustice they have done to our people."

"Let us pursue the men whose tongues insult our mothers," Jumping Bear shouts, swinging his large stone club.

Old Red Eagle unsheathes his knife and shouts, "By the light of the moon we will give chase. We will cut their tongues out of their mouths, slice open their bellies, and let the sun burn their entrails while they are still alive!"

"*Yet ya!*" the Navajo warriors chant.

"No, our mothers will keep them alive while ants tear their flesh down to their bones one tiny piece at a time."

"*Yet ya!*"

The Navajo mount their horses and chase their enemies.

"All Navajo are made from all the dung of every animal and bug in all the worlds!" Makes Trouble shouts, living up to his name.

"What are these other worlds you speak of?" Kiowa asks, astonished at the thought of worlds other than this one.

"I don't know. It just makes sense that the great creator made more than one. Do you have only one arrow? Do you have only one brother? Does my father only have one wife? No! Of course there are other worlds."

Kiowa stares at his transformed friend in awe. "I never knew that trouble could turn to wisdom." His awe is interrupted by the shouts of the Navajo.

"YOUR DEATH WILL BE DREADFUL, KIOWA!" Old Red Eagle hollers.

"COWARDS! STAND AND FIGHT US!" Jumping Bear *whoops.*

As the morning light begins to illuminate their activities, the wise Kiowa warriors split up.

"How are we to pursue both at the same time?" Old Red Eagle asks.

"We cannot."

"What do we do?"

"Can it be determined which is the slowest to catch? If it can, let us pursue him."

"And let the other go free? After he has killed our warriors, insulted our mothers, and led us on a wild chase?"

"Then let us break into two and run them to the ends of the earth. Be wary, though, brothers. One of these warriors might lead us back to their tribe."

The Navajo think on these words for a brief moment.

"The holy people won't stand for this. The Kiowa have disrupted our way of life. Now, because we have less, we will not be able to trade for the things we need from the Spaniards."

"And we will be out of harmony. I see. So you believe we must destroy these two warriors to bring back harmony?" Old Red Eagle asks.

Jumping Bear nods. "Two men are easier to kill than an entire tribe. One of them has killed and scalped my son. Let us ride after each of them, but if you think an ambush is possible, run for your lives. There is no honor in death. And since we are the only holy people on earth, let us live."

With that they exchange brief glances, sign to one another the directions they are going, and off they ride, chasing Kiowa and Makes Trouble, who have now had enough time to slip into the river and escape downstream.

CHAPTER 27

Thirty miles in the opposite direction, Paw and Two Moons catch up to Anoki and Kikmongwi. They lead them on a hard ride up a steep mountain. The horses heave and sweat up the rocky incline. Riders fight their horses to keep control. The morning sun raises the temperature.

Once they reach the top, they seek cover in a thick pine forest. Paw and Two Moons dismount their horses and pull them by the reins. They quickly tie them off and scan over the valley to ensure that they weren't followed.

"We will treat your wounds with our magic," Two Moons informs Kikmongwi. He grabs his pouch and opens it. "I cannot tell you what these roots are because they are sacred magic. But I assure you, your wounds will be healed."

"How do I give it to him?" Anoki asks.

"You mix it with water and let him sip it slowly."

"I'll start a fire." Anoki leans down and starts picking up pinecones. Paw and Two Moons look at each other with disapproving frowns. "If you light a fire, the Navajo are sure to find you."

"How will I warm the water so that he may drink your magic?"

Two Moons walks over to his horse. He returns with a buffalo bladder full of water. "Put this out in the sun."

"We should go back to the tribe and tell them what has transpired," Paw urges Two Moons.

"If you leave us here, all I ask is that you leave us one horse," Kikmongwi begs. He holds up one finger and points to the horse in case his broken Kiowa isn't understood. "Everything we have is in the village," he says, shaking his head.

Two Moons grunts, "What do you offer for trade?"

"What are they saying?" Kikmongwi asks his daughter.

"They want to trade something for the horses," Anoki answers.

"Tell them they can keep all of those worthless pinto ponies. Just leave that beautiful black mustang," Kikmongwi proposes.

"My father says to keep the horses. Since the black horse was given to us, we ask that you leave it with us until the owner returns to decide what should be done."

Paw squints at Anoki. His stern face does not match his thoughts. *What a good little woman, looking after her father that way. I wonder what Kiowa would want me to do. Probably keep his horse, I would imagine.*

"What do you think, Uncle?"

"Night Wind is the finest horse I have ever seen. Kiowa would be hurt to be without him."

"There it is. We keep the horse. But I think we should wait for Kiowa. He has no horse to ride," Two Moons answers, leading Kiowa's jet-black horse up the trail.

Anoki translates for her father and makes signs in Kiowa so that they will all understand.

"You sign better than you speak," Paw tells Anoki.

"Our tribe trades, and it was my duty to barter and translate deals," Anoki replies. "We will pay a high price if you help us retrieve my sister, Mali, and my mother, Proud Woman."

"Translate what I say," Two Moons tells her.

Anoki turns toward her father and signs that she's going to translate.

"Do not fear us. As I have said, we will protect you with our magic. I do not want to mislead you or to be misunderstood. Our numbers are small, and we cannot help you find your wife or your daughter. You should be grateful we were able to save you."

Anoki feels like she's going to collapse. She forces herself to be strong.

"For the harm we inflicted on their tribe, the Navajo won't stop looking for us until they catch us. It would be better for you and your daughter to stay with us until we have the force of our tribe. That is all the protection either of you will get."

Kikmongwi glances at his daughter. She remembers that her father always made better deals with the Kiowa because they were a war tribe and he wanted to stay in good favor. *Trust few Indians, but above all, trust no tribe*, he had taught her. She has immediate doubts since she overheard Makes Trouble mention that the tribe "would not accept them."

In the past, trade relations had always been good. But that was when the Hopi had things the Kiowa wanted. Anoki had never been on the side of wanting or needing anything from any tribe. She grew up privileged in the sense that she knew what independence was and she valued it. *What leverage do we have among strangers? I cannot fight. I cannot help. I have nothing to barter, and so, Mother, I will save Father. Mali, my sweet sister and cherished friend, forgive me.* Anoki presses her hand to her heart to cover up the two holes the Navajo have carved out.

"Once we return to our city, my father will show you our appreciation." Anoki doesn't like being so far from the safety of her cliff dwelling. Besides, she won't admit it, but she wants to thank Kiowa. *Oh, and see his face in the light of day.*

"You two stay here," Paw orders. "We need to go higher so we can see in all directions."

Paw and Two Moons move up a steep incline. They have to lean so far forward they could nearly kiss the earth. When they reach the cliff face, they help each other climb up the smooth beige curved sides.

Paw locks his fingers together and motions for Two Moons to step on them. He lifts his nephew up and waits for him to offer his hand in return. When Two Moons turns around, the feathers tied to his hair tickle Paw's face. He blows at them and waves them away.

"Why did we save them?" Two Moons asks his uncle. "The women of our tribe won't want a Hopi princess anywhere near them."

Paw grunts as Two Moons pulls up him the cliff. Paw pauses for a moment and reflects on what his brother, Lone Wolf, might say to his son to bring clarity to his cloudy mind. "I once killed a bobcat who caught a small yellow bird with a bright orange beak. It was such a pretty little thing, I was pleased to remove it from the jaws of death. I carefully inspected its wings and feet to ensure that if I released it, it would survive. I then held it up to my lips and whispered to it, 'Shall I let you go or use your feathers to make a bracelet?'"

Two Moons stops scanning the low lands for dust trails and looks at his uncle with a confused expression.

"I didn't know you could speak to birds."

"I can't. But I could feel its little heart pounding against my fingers and I knew that the bird wanted to live."

Paw holds his hand up and waves it over the earth, then points at Anoki and her father. "I do not know that another cat will not catch these birds. I only know that if we release them, they will fly. All creatures seem to want every moment this life has to offer, and I cannot seem to summon the dark power it takes to stop their beating hearts."

Two Moons thinks on these words. He sits down and crosses his legs. He doesn't see the Navajo below, and that gives him satisfaction that the Hopi have escaped the jaws of death. He looks behind him and sees a distant dust cloud that he believes to be his tribe. The thought of the bird being caught by a new cat disturbs him. Like his uncle, he knows that he cannot summon the dark powers to kill so beautiful a creature as Anoki. Though he wants the numbers of his tribe, he begins to wonder if that is the best path for these two birds.

***

Later that evening, as dusk is turning to night, Kiowa picks up on Anoki's trail. *Ha! I knew Night Wind would not fail me.* The excitement fades at the thought of approaching her. For some reason, an anxious feeling washes over him and makes him tremble. He stops and sits down for a moment, wondering what this strange creeping fear is that hums in his bones and numbs his chest.

I should go back to my tribe and get the numbers to take on the Navajo, he thinks, wanting to secure a sure victory. *But then again, it would be soooo nice to see Anoki.* He closes his eyes and remembers Anoki's beautiful face. He recounts every detail, from her smooth russet skin to her high cheekbones, her big round doe eyes and her rose-petal lips. He lifts his arms, reaching for her memory as if he could hold it.

"I have to get back to Pa. Back to Makes Trouble. Back to Anoki."

He stops and blinks wildly.

"Why am I always thinking of Anoki?"

His face lifts with a giddy smile. "I want to kiss those lips," he confesses with a shiver.

He lowers his hands and closes his eyes again, to see if her image remains. It does. He imagines her drawing a breath. He feels his heart pound like the war drum as he sees her press those jewels together and softly speak, "Kiowa." When he opens his eyes, he feels like the glittering stars have landed on his tongue and tickled them with frost. Then suddenly he feels the sensation leap off his tongue and transform to sun-kissed warmth burning on his lips.

What is happening to me? he wonders, wiping his lips and shaking the vapor image of Anoki out of his mind. He determines to think carefully and to plan his next move for the tribe. His people. But the problem is, no matter how hard he tries, her face returns like the reflection in a lake. For some reason, the longer he looks, the less he wants to distort his memory. He reaches for her as though she's there and finds himself in the land of confusion. When he closes his eyes, he can see his hand gently pressed against her cheek. But when he opens them, his hand is empty.

"How do you catch what cannot be caught?" He thinks on this for a moment. Excitement lifts his brows, widens his eyes, and forces a gasp. "*Ah-hoe!* I know! I must simply fill my hand with Anoki's face!" he says, grabbing on to this thought. He wraps his fingers around thin air and compresses it into his fist. He presses the idea to his heart, as though he is planting a seed.

"Father, send me Moon Beam to guide me back to your brother. I know you wanted to be my father, but this man is the only father I know. Let me learn what has become of this woman who uses her strange magic on me."

No sooner has he finished making his plea than he sees a bright star with a long glittering tail shoot across the sky in a straight line and explode like a firework over the top of the mountain where the pine forest is thickest.

"Thank you, Father!" Kiowa says, moving toward the sign.

***

Early that morning Two Moons whispers to Paw, "I hear the morning birds. The lark sings before dawn. You know, Uncle, that stupid little yellow bird that you let live. Maybe it would have been better to make a bracelet out of it after all. The Navajo will swell their numbers and certainly find us."

"If we heard nothing we would have more to fear. Perhaps they have captured your brother and he-who-is-like-a-brother."

"That would be nice. He could Make Trouble for someone else for once."

Paw frowns and looks at him. He slowly nods.

Two Moons continues. "All the more reason to leave the Hopi princess and her father here and return with our tribe. We could use them as bait, then overtake the Navajo and get more horses and scalps."

"That is a good plan," Paw confirms.

They sit motionless, weighing their options to a chorus of morning birds. Their faces are still like stone, as the dark, starry night changes from blackness and brightens ever so delicately. The stars still shine and cling to the night, refusing to surrender their place to the increasing twilight.

"Perhaps Kiowa and Makes Trouble failed. Perhaps they were captured and tortured," Paw says, choking up at the thought of his nephew who has become his son.

"If this is so, we will need the tribe to recover what remains of him. Onendah will need to free my brother's spirit."

"It would seem that all paths lead back to the tribe. Let me enjoy the morning light and music and pray to Naukolahe, that he might deliver my boy to me before we abandon the Hopi."

"I will ready the horses." Two Moons slips away without making a sound.

"Great Father of Heaven and Earth, hear my prayer. My heart is heavy with grief. It sinks to the bottom of the lake like a hard stone. I am like the stone that sinks into the lake of despair. I have worn the pants of my brother all these years in the hope that my legs would become his. They have not as of yet done much more than produce a silver fox. I do not believe they will if I cannot use them to find our son. Please light the morning sky. Reveal my son to me. Let my legs burn the way they did for Moon Beam and I will run to Kiowa. Show me a sign that I may fulfill Onendah's prophecy. This is all that I ask, and if you give me this boy back, I will never let him leave my side again! I will even take his troublesome friend under my wing. This is a mighty offering."

Paw presses his open palm to the earth and sends his message through his hand. He clenches his fist and lifts the cool sand up to his lips. With a kiss, he releases it.

Before the grains slip through his fingers, he feels Two Moons press his hand against his shoulder.

"I have said my prayer. We may go now," Paw whispers, feeling rushed.

CHAPTER 28

"But I have just returned," Kiowa says, squeezing his uncle's shoulder.

Kiowa's voice springs Paw to his feet. Excitement quivers in his heart.

"My prayer was heard. I'm am so happy!" He hugs his nephew. "Is your would-be brother with you?"

"His body is with me, but his mind is not the same. Whatever seed was planted between his ears has ripened him from a weasel to an owl. I do not even know if he makes trouble anymore."

"What happened?"

"If it were not for his quick words and cunning strategy, the Navajo would have caught us both."

Paw looks down and feels the final grains of sand slip through his fingers. "Thank you," are all the words he can muster for his god.

"Maybe it's time he gets a new name," Paw asserts.

Two Moons rejoins them.

"Maybe…" Kiowa looks away, then back at Paw before moving on to the next point of interest. "I want to bring her back to the tribe."

"They will not accept Anoki," Two Moons firmly argues.

"Surely they will accept her!" Kiowa shouts, catching Anoki's attention.

"Father, what do you think they are discussing?" Anoki asks Kikmongwi.

"Probably whether they should sell us to the Mexicans. Let me rest, Daughter. I am in much pain." He gently pats her hand as her face droops with fright.

Oh, I cannot worry about such matters. What can a little woman do against such men anyway? I am more interested in this man who saved me. She can't help but stare at him. And though she's not sure how his black war paint wiped clean from his bronze skin, she's glad that it has. His muscles have shed any trace of childhood. He is a man with a well-defined build. His abdomen ripples until it comes to a V at his waistline. His handsome face makes her feel like the intense summer heat is burning in her chest. Only when he looks at her does the heat gather in her blushing cheeks and force her to look away.

"I do not believe they will. I believe they will purge her by fire from the tribe if you take her back with you," Two Moons says with a conviction that forces Kiowa to pause and think on his words. "You will be sorry."

"I have always trusted you with all things, older brother. My heart wants to betray you, but my mind knows better. However, for my mind's curiosity, I must know why you believe this to be so." Kiowa won't back down.

"You are the greatest warrior our tribe has had since our father was slain. You alone did what the tribe could not. You challenged Black Bear in open combat and won! The tribe will expect you to marry a Kiowa woman and have Kiowa children so that we may have more great Kiowa warriors. Your job is to replace the warriors we have lost. That is the way it is. I would not be surprised if the tribe offers you every squaw of age. Wait another few years until you look on the faces of many beautiful women before you decide on this one. You will forget this woman's face soon enough." He waves Kiowa off.

Kiowa's face puckers with a sour expression. *Would I do that to her?*

"What do I do with her?" Kiowa shakes his head. *More importantly... what do I do with my vision?*

"We leave them food, a bow, and a horse. When the time is right, their men will come out of the cliff dwelling, and they can reunite with them."

Kiowa clenches his jaw and swallows the most painful truth he has heard in a long time. The roughness feels like bark scraping his throat. "What if the Navajo return?"

"They will return, and so will we. But with our tribe this time, and we will leave strong impressions on their minds that to harm the

Hopi is to harm the Kiowa. If these scalps and stolen horses aren't enough to scare them, then we will do what we do best—go to war!"

"I see the wisdom of your plan. I just don't like the heavy price I must pay." His voice trails off as he grumbles, "I've already paid a heavy price. Am I to keep paying?"

Anoki scoots closer so she can listen.

"We are warriors, Kiowa. We will always pay the heaviest price for the benefit of our tribe. What has happened here must be a secret from the tribe. You have feelings for Anoki?"

Kiowa signs, Yes.

Anoki gasps when she sees it.

"They must be your own. Share them with no one. For sure not Makes Trouble. Even if he is now an owl, he will still hoot."

"Let us go! Weasel Tail will send warriors for us soon because we have not returned. I pray that they will be bigger numbers than the Navajo," Paw says, wondering how many prayers the Sun God will answer in one day.

Kiowa walks over to Anoki, not a proud hero but with sunken shoulders and a frowning face. Her father greets them with signs and soft words.

"It has been decided that we must reunite with our tribe. I would very much like for you both to come with us."

"We would like that also!" Anoki tilts her head, smiles gently, and flutters her lashes.

Her father smiles and says, "Let this man speak. Can you not see he has much to say?"

She shakes her head and tightens her face. *Sparrows feed worms to their chicks. Fathers feed shame.*

"Tell me everything he says," Kikmongwi demands.

Anoki nods and obediently obliges. She folds her arms before she begins. With a swift motion, she signs that she is ready.

Kiowa sighs and shrugs as well. "Our tribes make us different people, and we must honor our traditions. So I must go."

Anoki translates to her father, then signs in Hopi and says in the Kiowa language, "Thank you for all that you have done for us."

Kiowa holds up two fingers. He extends them out in front of his face and then draws them behind his ear.

"I hope we will meet again."

Anoki looks away bashfully. She holds her two fingers up and makes the same sign. "Me too."

Two Moons, Makes Trouble, and Paw maneuver their glorious horse bounty into a straight line.

Kikmongwi lets a slew of Hopi slip out of his mouth. "This night has been an awful one for my daughter. She hasn't the patience to let you speak, so I will cut to the marrow of what is in my heart. You are brave warriors! I must know your names. Daughter, translate."

Anoki signs in Hopi and translates in Kiowa.

"Kiowa." Kiowa points to himself, then to his rebel band. "Paw, Makes Trouble, Two Moons."

Anoki grabs on to his name like her ears have hands and sews it to her heart.

"You are named after your people?" Kikmongwi asks.

Anoki translates. Kiowa answers with a nod.

"You have a good name. Bring me six horses, one of which must be Night Wind, and you can marry my daughter. Let her take your name, and when I die you will get more than six horses back. They will have children and so will Anoki. You would get a better deal!" Kikmongwi proudly proclaims, lifting his hands over his head.

CHAPTER 29

Anoki laughs awkwardly. Like Kiowa, she wants to follow tradition and obey her father. So she only translates, "You have a good name," to Kiowa in his language and then signs everything her father said in Hopi so that she won't get in trouble.

Makes Trouble understands all of her Hopi signs and shouts, "My name is Bluffing Owl. We are Kiowa." He speaks in a harsh tone that makes Anoki wince. "We take what we need and trade for the rest. If you were not a tribe of worthless, peaceful Hopi, you would have great warriors like us and you would not have to give your pretty daughter's flesh to anyone but the warriors in your own tribe."

"Like me?" Kiowa says, still not understanding that Kikmongwi is offering Anoki to be his bride.

"Yes, like you!" Makes Trouble answers sternly and folds his arms in front of him. His bottom lip pokes out in a proud pout.

Paw chuckles. "His name was Makes Trouble last night, and he is doing that now, so I think that will still be his name." He studies Anoki intently.

Kiowa can't take his eyes off the Hopi princess.

Anoki tilts her head, and then graciously looks up at Kiowa with the most loving brown eyes he's ever seen. "I am very grateful for your sacrifice. The Navajo would have killed us if you had not intervened. I will hold you in high esteem as a great chief." She unties her turquoise bracelet and hands it to him.

"For me?" He looks all around, then back at her. "You pick me to have this treasure?"

Anoki covers her smile with her hand and looks down.

"We will make the best deals when you return to us," Chief Kikmongwi promises.

"Kiowa would have no pretty Hopi girls to stare at and detain us if it weren't for you. Now let us ride!" Two Moons shouts.

Kiowa swats at his brother. "Shut up, you old fool!"

Anoki gathers herself and calmly says, "We are...ah..." She loses her thoughts and starts again. "We are very grateful for you, Kiowa, the great warrior."

Makes Trouble can't help but laugh.

Two Moons pats his scalps and says, "Stay in the forest, Hopi Princess. The Navajo will finish what they have started if they ever catch you."

The Kiowa rebels mount their horses and wave good-bye, taking a heap of trophy horses with them.

Kiowa points to the village. "When the smoke has cleared from the sky, Night Wind will take you home."

"He is a good and intelligent horse. He brought us here without us even knowing where we were going. How will I return him to you?" Anoki inquires, wanting to refuse the offer but knowing that would make her look like a foolish girl. Whereas right now she can see that Kiowa thinks her to be a woman.

Kiowa smiles. "When you are done with him, turn him loose. He will know where to find me."

Kiowa breaks his trance by handing Anoki his horse's reins.

"Thank you," is all Anoki can muster as her fingers brush against his.

He slowly turns away, then sprints from her and leaps onto a pinto mustang. The beast startles, stands up, and cycles its hooves as it bellows in protest to its new master.

***

"'Twas love at first sight, it was!" the scoutmaster says, resting his bearded chin on his locked fingers. He bats his eyelashes and sighs.

"You're still telling us a love story? YUCK! I think I'm going to puke!" Luther gags.

"I thought you were going to teach us how to be brave like Lone Wolf and Kiowa. Instead you're just trying to make mashed potatoes out of us!" John shouts, folding his arms and wrinkling his face.

"Mashed potato, mashed potato," Kevin sings.

"Why didn't he just fight all them Navajo? Lone Wolf would

have!" Zack asks.

"Was Anoki pretty?" Kevin asks, pushing dirt up with the tip of his boot.

"She was beautiful, and Kiowa was very handsome as well. Although it was love at first sight, you have to understand, the Kiowa tribe didn't want their leader marrying no dang Hopi. That was absolutely out of the question! They wanted him to marry Kida, the mighty huntress. Could you imagine being told who you had to marry?"

"Noooooo," the boys say in unison.

***

The inside is much different from the outside. All around his tepee are strewn bones of beaver, elk, bear, and buffalo. It is as though Kiowa wants us to think he is some wild animal, rather than a beautiful, handsome man, Kida thinks as she looks around the outside of Kiowa's tepee.

The painted symbols on his tepee tell his life's story. A young boy buries his face in his hands and cries for his father. Paw teaches the boy how to hunt. A shadow hurls a golden spear at a bear falling off a horse.

"Hello, Kiowa. I have come with gifts," Kida yells.

"Go away!"

"I have nowhere to go. Everyone has had enough to eat, and you cannot refuse a woman with a gift. That is the law."

"Ugh…" Kiowa grumbles, flipping the flap of his tepee and waving her in.

When Kida enters the tepee, she gasps. "You make darkness when it is light?"

"Darkness? It is not dark enough. If you let the light in, you are going to see much pain." Kiowa sighs. He heaves a thousandth huff to the gloomy lingering cloud of sorrow.

Kida senses it, but of course cannot touch it. But if she could, she would cut it into pieces, sweep it up, and toss it out.

"I have brought you meats, that you may gain back your strength." Kida coyly displays the food, sitting down by a fire in Kiowa's tepee.

"I am not hungry." Somberly, he lifts a brow with love-hurt eyes. He stares at the dull rolling amber flames, closes his eyes, and sees Anoki riding a white horse. Those powerful feelings shift to a sense of betrayal when he opens his eyes and sees Kida in his tepee. Alone. With just him.

"You must be sick, Kiowa. You are very quiet and you keep your thoughts to yourself," Kida purrs, obeying her mother's counsel and speaking in sweet seductive tones. She makes soft gestures instead of obeying her brutal, blunt nature.

Kiowa wants to cry an ocean of lovesick tears. Instead, he observes Kida's slow gestures and accentuated curves. She reminds him of a coiling snake. *This woman has long, pretty hair and wild, savage eyes. Her eyes are saying something, but I do not care. Her eyes are nothing like Anoki's. Sweet Anoki, who braids her hair neatly and has gentle eyes.* He smiles. *Anoki who is perfect in every way, like a white swan.* He frowns, looking directly at Kida. *Or these angry-faced Kiowa women who are like black crows to me.*

Kida feels his eyes on her. Her giddiness can hardly be contained. She pounces, seizing the moment. "I am so happy to be here with you." She beams and offers him a delightful smile.

Kiowa doesn't say anything. He plays with the bracelet Anoki gave him.

By refusing to engage or acknowledge her existence, he says a lot. The lack of attention drives Kida crazy. In complete dissatisfaction, and to Kida's utter dismay, he holds a limp bent arm out, looks away, and waves her off.

Kida takes the insult on the chin. She lifts up a log and thinks, *Surely if I cannot sweep away his gloom, I can burn it out with this fire or my flame.*

When the flames grow, Kiowa gives the tiniest comfort. "It is very good of you to come here, Kida—"

She cuts him off. "I'm glad to be here! Your tepee is the biggest in the tribe." She drags her fingers on the padded fur floor. "You have many fine furs to rest on. Magic symbols to protect you. Plenty of food. It seems all you need is..." She looks up, expecting some sort of reciprocation.

He offers a fleeting glance. "A woman?"

She bursts to life in animated excitement. "YES!" She drags the s out so long, Kiowa thinks he can see her forked tongue.

Despite his best intentions, Kida has found the grain of hope she sought. In one final burst, Kida goes too far and reveals her true intention. With a quick shift of her hips, she lies flat on her stomach and stretches herself out like a cat, showing all her enticing female curves. When he doesn't respond to her seductive advances, she seizes ground and closes the distance, now on all fours. She leans close enough to kiss him. And more than any woman ever has, she invites his kiss by tilting her head up, closing her eyes, and pushing her lips out. She doesn't know why she's supposed to close her eyes. All she knows is that her sister, who is married, told her to do this. *Oh, and don't forget to part your pretty lips! No man can refuse your lips*, was the trusted sister's council.

Kiowa shuffles around the fire. "And should I take any woman?"

Kida follows him.

Though Kiowa doesn't offer much affection, Kida clings to every word that slips through his alluring lips. She lowers her guard and answers truthfully. "No. You would betray all women if you did not pick a woman out of love. She may have children, she may cook, clean, sew, make clothes for you, but without love, she will teach her children to hate you."

"So a woman must have love from her man or his children will hate him?"

"She will die without it."

Kida feels the mood shift. She scoots closer to Kiowa and compensates by resuming her seductive game. She sits up and pulls the string to her blouse. She slides her sleeves over her shoulders and loosens her buckskin so that he can practically see her breasts.

"Touch me."

CHAPTER 30

"No!" Kiowa inches away.

"Kiss me." Kida inches closer.

"I will not!"

"Hold me?"

"I cannot!"

"Oh, you can! And you will. Tell me that you love me."

"Why? Why must I tell you I love you?"

"Will you keep your love all to yourself? Can a man hold his love inside himself?" On all fours, Kida isn't begging. She's prepping for a pounce.

"No. No man can carry love all by himself. He must give it to some woman."

"Then GIVE IT TO ME!" She closes her eyes and stalks him with her lips pressed out.

He scoots away. "I feel…" Kiowa hacks a fake cough. "I think you are right. I am sick."

"I am not asking if you are sick, and I do not care. I am begging you to love me. I want you so bad it hurts to breathe." She flips her wild hair and lets the long silky strands spill around her shoulders. She pulls her top down.

Kiowa shuffles around the fire. "I am feverish. Look, my palms are sweating."

"Let me take you in these arms"—she extends her arms—"so that you may put your love inside me." She balls her hand up into a fist and slams it against her chest. "I will take your love and I will mix it into sweet flesh and strong bone. Give me this night and I will give you a legacy."

Kiowa scoots around the fire much faster the second time. Kida is hot on his heels. When he completes the lap, he scrambles to his feet. "If I do that, it will be like a flame to the wheat grass and it will burn you to ashes." Kiowa thrusts his hands out and halts the cat's attack. "Can you not see that?"

Kida sits up. "You know this is our way, and I want to be the first woman of our tribe to have your child in this tepee." She resumes her attack, closing her eyes and parting her lips. "My body burns for you. Burn me with your flame."

"The first?" Kiowa asks in confusion.

She leans back and opens her eyes. "Don't act like you don't know. All the girls in the tribe are eager to steal away your love and make children with it. Some have even said they would trade their bones for the chance to birth your son. I have warned them that I will cut their flesh to the bone if they try. I am the best! You are the best! Today we will make the best of everything our people have to offer this Indian nation."

"I never knew."

"How could you not know?" Kida shouts, leaping to her feet. She pulls her blouse up. "If any other warrior were here right now, we would already be finished. I would have his love. I would tell my mother. And all my sisters and my mother and my grandmother would help me start making baby moccasins. It is amazing to me that the warriors let you come back at all, since none of the women will let them share their love." She points at the entrance to the village. "What do you think all us girls are doing, smiling and waving and welcoming you back by singing your name and your praises? We are like robins sitting on eggs, and nothing will ever hatch with you. Why is this? I demand to know!"

Kida isn't sure what she's supposed to do. If there were a manual written on how to catch a man, she could write a second volume on how not to.

Kiowa's sorrowful cloud returns more potent and powerful than before. It crackles with hints of hate. "Leave here, Kida. I want to spend the winter alone."

She sits up. His words sock her in the mouth. "Have I said something to offend you?"

"Everyone has said words to offend me."

"What do we say?"

"Without using your lips, you all say words that offend my very soul!"

"I don't understand you, Kiowa. You act sick, but you are in good health. You look like death with dark circles under your eyes, and yet you have no fever. But you lie around all day and night. You have no visible ailments. And you keep the entire tribe at a distance. Then, when any of us women visit you to ease your burden, you insult us and treat us with disrespect."

He buries his face and grumbles, "Please go."

"If you will only have the company of children and warriors, when spring comes, you will have neither. The warriors are going to fight, hunt, and die. That is what they do! You could die! By your own words, no man can hold his love up inside himself. Women bear children. That is what we do. Those children will grow up and fill the empty places that the warriors and hunters leave behind. Where will you be when all of this happens? Lying about in your tepee? Groaning under your buffalo blanket? Whose advice are you taking with all this time you spend by yourself? Your own? Here's some counsel from a plain and simple Indian woman: BE A MAN! GIVE ME YOUR LOVE OR GIVE ME YOUR PAIN! Either way, you must fulfill your obligation to the tribe!"

"I will be with them. I am always with them. It is my curse."

She gasps. "All of them?" For the first time in her life, Kida trembles at the thought of all the other girls being with Kiowa. "It is your blessing!" She bristles like a porcupine and does exactly what her mother warns against. "None of us are good enough for you, is that it?" she challenges him.

Insulted and humiliated, Kida leaps to her feet. She screams so loud, her mother, waiting outside the tepee, claps her hands to her face and mistakes the noise for pleasure. So do all the other girls. They scatter to their tepees, crying as they run.

"Keep the meat! I hope you choke on it!" Kida stomps out of his tepee, leaving the meat behind.

When he's certain she is gone and he won't have to look at her lustful eyes, he picks up the plate and tosses it in the fire.

"Anoki, why must you be with me when I am without you? I see your face every time I close my eyes. I smell you with every breath. Why? Why can I no longer eat?" He presses his hand to his cheek.

"What spell does your spirit cast on me that I can still feel your hair tickle my face and push me near death? Why do you hurt me so?"

He looks at the painted white figure on his tepee wall. He used porcupine quills to paint a deer's head on his demigod. This image represents the good spirit and all the good he sees. It is full of details and colors. Yellow sun rays blast kindness out of its outstretched arms. It is obvious that this good spirit is the source of everything wonderful.

"I pray to you and you do not answer me. Why? Maybe I should ask him." He points to the other side of the tepee. A black shadow figure and scary face have been sketched on his wall with charcoal. This evil spirit is colorless. Even its hollow eyes are meant to terrify anyone who looks upon it.

"When I pray to you, Evil Spirit, you tell me only to do terrible things. You are full of dirty tricks and evil ways. What do you say?"

He listens for a moment and then smiles. "That is what I thought you would say. Kill her father. Take his scalp. Kill her brother. Take his scalp. It is always the same with you. I know what you want. You want as many souls as I can bring you so you are not always lonely. You are greedy. You would call your sister, the woman in the water, to take Anoki down where it is dark and cold. If I did those things you ask, Anoki's tears would make you happy and I will not have any of that. I care only about my happiness, so I will listen to you, Good Spirit. When you are ready to speak, I will listen.

"Take me back to my vision, Fire Boy. Show me what Water Boy wants." He liked how the vision made him feel. Kiowa lies back on his side and romanticizes about Anoki. He stares at the fire. Its mesmerizing flames dull. His eyes close and he finds himself riding Night Wind on these flaming hills. Before he knows it, he is completely entranced. He yawns and dozes off to sleep.

CHAPTER 31

In Kiowa's dream, he dismounts Night Wind. When his moccasins touch the ground, it is not fire at all, but solid earth. He tries to move his legs, but they won't budge. Unsure of why or how, he finds himself firmly planted.

All around him towering trees sprout like tiny stems that continue to grow up into the sky. His horse *neighs* and runs off, leaving the warrior all on his own.

"Night Wind, come back! Do not leave me here!"

Leaves of every kind sprout out of extending branches. It frightens him that they grow so quickly.

What if one sprouts up through my feet and skewers me like a fish? He wants to run, but his feet refuse to obey him.

"Well, this is some strange end to a great warrior. Good-bye, painful world." Storming clouds billow across the blue heavens. Their ash color blackens the sky. His skin grows cold as rain pelts against his body. He struggles back and forth. Whether he wants to or not, Kiowa must stand. Try as he might, the only appendages that work are his hands and only in the slowest motion, despite his best effort.

Off in the distance, he sees lightning crackle. Rising waters swell up to his knees and cause him to shiver. Short bursts of lightning explode, and the earth shakes. With each clap of thunder, long, wiry electric strands cut loose.

"Maybe this beautiful red lightning will touch me and bring my sudden death with an exciting kiss."

Rather than succumbing to fear, he chooses to accept his fate. He rests where he has always rested, on courage. He bends down, dips his fingers in the mud, and presses them to his cheeks. Swiping down, he draws three distinct lines. One for his father. One for Paw.

One for him. When he looks at his fingers, he sees no mud at all but leaves. *Hmm… no one will fear me with leaves on my face*, he thinks, trying to wipe them off. The more he fights, the more the leaves work like a virus and spread all over his face and chest.

Off in the distance a powerful burst of light materializes and hovers in the sky. Whatever it is, it moves with the intelligence of life and is the source of all the lightning. He observes as its electric-white silhouette hovers toward him. It begins to take form. He can see that it is a woman, and he strains to make out the woman's face, feeling overwhelmed with happiness when the apparition reveals herself to be none other than Anoki.

He gasps. "Have you come for me, sweet Anoki?"

Her clothes are no longer made of buckskin and beads. Her long, flowing gown is as bright as the stars. She cups her hands and retracts the lightning. With some strange magic that Kiowa cannot begin to understand, Anoki uses her power to shape the lightning into a ball. With a gentle kiss, she blows it to him. As it approaches, branches of blue, white, yellow, and red lightning crackle off and touch the trees. They start a fire that he cannot run from or put out. He is defenseless.

The supernatural ball of energy hovers in front of his face and does not harm him. It twinkles and gyrates like a star. He licks his dry lips and can't resist the urge to touch it. He reaches up. His hands and arms are covered in withered leaves.

"What is this strange magic?"

When he extends his finger, a crackle of lightning connects. The greatest love he has ever felt overwhelms him. It feels like a tidal wave washing over his body and cleansing his soul. Warmth as powerful as the sun blankets him and makes him feel like he has finally found his place in the world.

"I am home."

A heavy wind blows hard against his face. He feels his leafy skin flutter with the breeze. When he finally summons the courage to touch the blinding light, it blasts his body apart into thousands of leaves, scattering him to the wind.

He sits up panting. He's breathing so hard he can't breathe. His chest heaves. His heart beats like a drum in his ears. He looks at his hands. Turning them back and forth he can see that they are now flesh. He smiles, clasps his hands together, and shouts, "With all my heart, I love you, Anoki!" He immediately regrets this and covers his lips with clasped hands. He carefully tiptoes over to the flap of his tepee and flings it open. It is late into the night. No one could hear him scream. Not even the night watchman pays attention to him.

"I know what that energy is," he says to himself, leaning back in his tepee. "It is the most potent happiness I have ever felt, and Anoki is the source of it. She is my home!" Kiowa closes his eyes and savors the images from his vision. *But what do the leaves mean? Was Kida right? Will Anoki blast me apart if I do not truly love her? Or will I be blasted apart if she does not truly love me?* he frets.

"If only my loving thoughts could travel faster than sunlight to sweet Anoki. Then she would know how I feel. I would ride to her"— he dips his finger in a red line and draws it up his arm—"and steal her away." He grins as he uses black paint to draw a horse on his arm. *Would she even wait for me?* He presses his hand in the yellow paint and smears a circle on his chest. *If I do have any real magic, I cast a spell on her that she will wait for me. He grins wildly at this thought. That would be true power. As my magic rests here in my pouch, it is useless to me. It only protects me in battle.* He sighs, then leans back. His body is a tapestry of emotion, manifested in color and strange images.

Several months pass, and sure as the frost melts, snowstorms turn to spring rains. Kida's words come true. The men go off to hunt. War parties raid. Most warriors return; Weasel Tail doesn't. Kiowa comes back with a harder and harder look in his eyes as he's thrust into the Indian warrior ways. War wipes his eyes clean of the pure innocence his youth preserved. The gentleness of his jaw chisels to a sharpness and makes his face insanely handsome. Each hunt and feast expand his muscles. First in his chest. Then his bulging biceps. Finally, his round shoulders look exactly like his father's. Kiowa's physique is a compliment to the man who sired him.

As time goes on, widows' death rattles rally the tribe. People mourn. People dance. People sing. The tribe is always on the move. Always going forward, never backward. Children of age take the warriors' places and help with the war parties and the hunt.

True to his word, Kiowa is there for all of it. He fights. He hunts. He kills. He carries a burden he never asked for. His only solace is the intense love he feels for Anoki growing stronger. The swirling emotions twist inside him like hurricane winds in his vision. And like hurricanes, his emotions grow stronger with each passing day. Each day of winter is more bitter without her. Snowflakes fall and freeze icicles on the trees. When he looks at the daggers, he can feel their icy pain. Not even spring eases his suffering. While all the animals are pairing off, finding love, and making children, he is alone. To the eyes of his tribe, he acts as one who is mortally wounded, since he always rests in his tepee. But those same watching, prying eyes spy no wound.

In the early part of summer, Paw cautiously enters Kiowa's tent.

"You are breaking many hearts," Paw informs Kiowa, cutting to the quick.

"They are breaking mine!"

"They want children. They want love." He looks down, then smirks. "I want children. Maybe we could go find women together and make an army of children."

Kiowa half smiles at his uncle's joke.

"I'm serious. Imagine a tiny wave of little warrior rabbits charging the enemy. They wouldn't attack because children are too cute. They are guaranteed to win."

"I have fulfilled my obligations to the tribe. You cannot ask me to marry when I do not love. Even Kida knows it is wrong."

"I know. This is why I am here. My raids have been successful. We have plenty of buffalo hides, jewelry, horses, and other things to trade with the Hopi. It is a good time for a trip. We usually trade about this time anyways, so I thought you might want to come…"

Before Paw can finish his words, Kiowa leaps to his feet and comes to life. All at once he is healed. He grabs his bow, his arrows, and a bundle of furs he uses for a bed. "Why are you sitting here, Uncle? Let us go get Anoki!"

Paw laughs. "And I thought you would need to be persuaded."

CHAPTER 32

When Kiowa comes out of his tepee, gushing squaw take notice of his improved health.

"What's that painted on your arm and chest?" Red Robin asks, batting her eyes.

Kiowa ignores her. He moves past her like she isn't even there.

"Kida said a Cheyenne medicine man used bad magic on him for killing their chief," a beautiful young squaw named Morning Dove tells the disappointed Red Robin. Morning Dove earned her name for her sweet voice and big brown eyes. She fiercely flutters her eyes at Kiowa as she pretends to chip away at a buffalo hide. *Oh, if only you were a cat and I really was a dove. I would let you catch me and my heart. You could make me your spring love, my great chief. Why not me? I have had seventeen summers. I can bear you a mighty son in a cute little body.*

"I believe it. If he met with Onendah and feels better, you know it is his special magic that healed Kiowa," Red Robin says, standing and watching Kiowa's every move. She places her hand on her cheek and sighs. *When will he notice me? I have had fewer summers than Morning Dove, but I am far prettier.*

"Onendah healed me once. He pulled a turtle out of my throat. Some enemy cast a spell on my father. When my father kissed me good night, the spell leapt from his lips on to my cheek and crawled in my mouth and down my throat. I couldn't even talk," Morning Dove says, opening her mouth and pointing to the back of her throat.

Red Robin looks in the back of the cavern, hoping to see some tracks. "How did he get the turtle out of your throat?"

"He said some prayer like, 'You can't live in here. This is not a cave. It is a little girl's mouth.' I choked and coughed until an ugly black turtle"—she holds up her hands about three inches in length—

"came out of my mouth."

Red Robin gags at the thought.

A young boy runs up to Kiowa and proudly says, "My brothers and sister, even my mother and father, have all prayed for you to be healed. Onendah did as he said. He healed you, huh? I'm glad I gave him my pet beaver!"

Kiowa looks at the boy in bewilderment and wonders what on earth Onendah would do with a pet beaver.

"Thank you, Twists My Face. I think you have earned a new name."

"What is it?" the boy eagerly asks in hopes of ridding himself of the name his mother gave him on his birth.

"Giver."

"Gives what?"

"Not Gives What? Just Giver," Kiowa answers, patting the boy on the head.

"I like it. Giver!" The boy runs off in search of something to find, so that he can give.

As Paw and Kiowa leave the village, a growing number of young, attractive, single girls cluster. They each hand Kiowa a lily and say sweet things to him like, "Trade well, and when you return, my heart is yours to do with as you please."

So many girls say the same thing that Kida decides to say something entirely different. "Find what you are looking for or do not come back here." She kisses him on the cheek and bids him farewell, but she wishes she were kissing him on the lips.

Kiowa waves farewell to his mother.

He and Paw lead a train of horses loaded with furs and buffalo hides.

Always on the move, the Kiowa tribe is now several days' journey from the Hopi village. When they finally reach the village, it is as though the Navajo raid never happened. The pink clay buildings have been restored. Plains Indians from several different tribes wander about. Traders from all over the Indian nation barter with the Hopi, seeking the best deals for beads, corn, pottery, and sugar.

"If Anoki is still here, you go find her and see what has become of her. I'll do the trading," Paw tells Kiowa.

Kiowa doesn't have to be told twice. He rides up to the tallest pueblo and locates Anoki's father.

Welcome back, Kiowa! We have many wonderful things to trade, Kikmongwi signs in the Kiowa language.

You have learned our signs well, Kiowa signs back. *I have brought you ten fine horses. Some were the Navajos'. I hope that doesn't upset you.*

Ha! Ha! No, that is more than I ask for. I will take all of them to compensate for the weaker horses. Kikmongwi waves his hand and flashes his fingers fluently.

They are all strong horses, Kiowa signs back.

That can't be true. They carried Navajo. Kikmongwi spits at the floor to curse his enemy.

Where did you learn our signs? Kiowa asks.

My daughter has taught me much over this bitter cold winter. She was very weepy and would hardly move about since last you met.

Is she sick?

Sick with no sign of sickness.

That is good, Kiowa signs. *And where is Anoki?* Kiowa mistakenly points to his heart instead of signing her name.

Kikmongwi doesn't understand.

"I, uh..." Kiowa says, losing his wits. He looks around, like he can find them skipping about on the dirt floor. "Er... uhm..." he stutters. *Why can I not sign the words I think?*

Kikmongwi smiles and rubs his hands together. He signs that his daughter is at the river.

Please sit down. I would like to show you this fine jewelry that will make a good trade for Night Wind. The Hopi chief turns and motions with an open hand to an empty seat, but when he turns back, he finds himself alone in his adobe hut.

"He is much worse than I suspected. Go get her heart. She will make you happy days and even happier nights," the Hopi chief laughs to himself.

Kiowa rides up the stream, sending his horse, Night Wind, into a full sprint. Water splashes around him as the black stallion picks up tremendous speed.

A tiny doubt twangs in the back of his mind, like a cricket plucking its fiddle.

How do I even know if she feels the same for me as I feel for her? The doubt grows.

His long raven hair whips wildly against his bare muscular back.

Looking this way and that, he searches frantically for her.

How she feels does not matter! All that matters is that I confess my love. And then... He thinks for a long time, contemplating what he should do next. *Then it won't matter, because she will confess she loves me. She must. Why wouldn't she?* His confident smile beams, straightening out to something between a flat smirk and a crooked frown.

CHAPTER 33

Up the river, Anoki washes her feet and hums a beautiful song. She carefully braids two long braids and wraps one into a bun, then looks at her brother, Walpi.

"I never hear you speak of Mali. Do you miss our sister?" Walpi asks, resting his feet in the stream.

"Of course. I think about her every day. Don't you miss her?" Anoki inquires, looking off in the distance with a somber expression. She wraps the other braid into a bun.

"No, not really."

Anoki gasps. "Why do you not miss our sister?"

Walpi shrugs. "No doubt the black robes have married her to some Mexican man by now. She has always been happy. I am sure she will be happy again."

I hadn't thought of that, Anoki thinks. "That is what they do." She gives an affirmative nod. *Probably because the black robes tell them that a woman who isn't productive will have worms grow out of her fingers. I hate the Mexicans who pay the Navajo with whiskey to steal away our fine Hopi women.*

"Soon she will have babies, and that always makes women happiest," Walpi nonchalantly replies, as he places his flute in his mouth and blows.

Anoki's eyes nearly spring out of her head. "Do you not understand a woman's mind or heart?"

Walpi looks at her with curiosity. "No. I am not a woman. How could I know a woman's thoughts?"

"Brother, I fear you have wasted too much time fishing and playing your flute. I think you are making yourself stupid. Come, listen to me." She pats the ground beside her. "A woman's heart is like a puzzle piece. When we are young like I am, women desperately want to find their place."

"How do you find your place?"

"That is not so easy. But we know it when our hearts are led to that place, because we follow the trail of love. But this is not all..."

"Love has no footprints to track. How would you ever find a woman's heart if it leaves no trail?"

"By love's bright wings."

"Love has wings? I don't think so. I think women just need to be told what to do and how to do it. They will be fine with a man who gives them babies, food, and leads them through life, with or without love."

"My worst fears are realized, Brother. You are stupid." She swats him on the head. "Without love, our sister will wish she were dead, even if her heart goes on beating and her lungs keep breathing."

"Do not tell me that. I cannot bear to think of her in pain."

"It is time for you to stop being foolish and start thinking manly thoughts. Now listen to your sister and see if you do not hear wisdom."

"Okay, I am listening."

"If the Navajo sold Mali to the Mexicans, would they not sell our mother?"

"Yes, I suppose they would."

"Do you miss our mother?"

Her words make Walpi's eyes tear up. "I miss Mother terribly. I miss bringing her presents. I miss her soothing voice. I miss her stories. No one should be without their mother. It is a hard life."

"Ah, so you know love because you love your mother. That is good. If Mother is sold, then she has a new family. Will those children make her happy?"

"I hadn't thought of that. What if she loves those children more than us? What can we do? We are a peaceful tribe." Walpi wipes tears from his eyes.

"See, love does have a trail. It is here on your cheeks. This is the concern I was looking for. Now think of how much sorrow Father must have. He loved Mother more than any man has ever loved a woman."

"How can you know?"

"You don't hear him crying all night? Where do you think the wildflowers beneath his window get their water? We live in a desert."

Walpi thinks on it for a moment, and then cries harder. "Don't tell me any more. I cannot hear your heavy words."

"But you must. Now listen. The other thing I was going to tell you about a woman is that she must not only know where her place is in the puzzle of life, but her mind will torture her until she knows what her part is in the puzzle. Here is the part we are going to play in the love for our mother. I have gathered many beads and precious yellow stones. The white men like the shiny soft gold very much. For this reason, all Indians are willing to trade with them. I will split what little we have, and I will offer every tribe we trade with a portion of the beads and yellow stone. When one of them brings us Mother, we will give them the rest. I will use the Mexicans' dirty dealings against them and offer something more valuable than whiskey. This is how we will bring our mother back to our family. This is also how we will get our sister home."

"I am even more sad for you now, Sister. How do you know they won't kill you and take what little you have?"

"Because I have learned from the gophers. I have dug holes and buried it here and there in places only I know. I will not tell anyone, not even you."

She wraps her arms around Walpi and hugs him.

"Won't Mali and Mother have children? Will they bring them here, too?"

"Yes. Everything that was ours will be ours again."

"Do you promise?" Walpi asks, sitting up and wiping his nose with his arm.

"Yes, I promise. Now let us talk about something else. I do not like to see you so sad."

"What do you want to talk about?" Walpi asks as he lifts his flute and plays a song that his mother used to ask him to play.

"Oh, I like this song," Anoki compliments him. She looks around and shakes her head like she's thinking terribly hard. "Tell me, Brother. When does a man know he loves a woman?"

"How should I know? I have never been in love."

"Never?"

"No, never!" He gives her a long, firm glance that lets her know he's not playing her game.

"Too bad," she says with a shrug. "For a woman it makes our blood boil like hot springs, and every part of our bodies comes to life with a tingling sensitivity that makes us feel like we are..."

She's succeeded in gaining his attention.

"Are...?"

"You won't know until it happens to you because you would not humor your sweet sister." She sticks her tongue out at him.

He gasps, then sticks his tongue out at her. "I knew you were teasing me. You are like the bobcat. Using crafty cunning wildcat calls that taunt and trick."

Anoki shrugs as she winds her other braid up and fastens it in place.

"It is like you are floating away." She grins and presses her hands to her mouth. "No, it is like you are flying away, even though your feet are planted on the ground."

Walpi looks at her feet. "Are you floating or flying?"

She looks down and gives it some thought. "I do not know for certain. I feel a rush of wind. I look up and I see the clouds. Then I spin around because..." She spins around, then stops.

"Because what?"

"Because... I don't know what else to do. I am just so happy! I am always moving, but then I am standing still."

Along the riverbank, Kiowa hides in the weeds. He hears what she says but cannot understand her Hopi words.

"She is the most beautiful, graceful creature I have ever seen," he whispers to Night Wind.

Where is your courage, you fool? he asks himself. *You have planned this a certain way. Why do you not rush to her and lift her up on your horse and steal her away?*

He nervously chews on his fingernails.

"Her hair is still woven in buns. She is shielded by the magic of purity." He pats his horse. "Do not laugh at me, friend. Of course I had words aplenty. We were alone in our tepee, then. In the sanctity of our home, I could say anything. Now she is there and I am here and I feel much safer behind this wall of thorny weeds."

Anoki spins around and flaps her arms like a bird.

Oh, how I wish she knew how much I love her. What am I to do?

Should I hide like a bug or charge like a mountain lion? It would be wise to first see why she is so excited.

"Father will wonder where we are if we do not return home soon," Walpi informs his sister.

"Just a few more moments," she says wistfully, looking off in the distant horizon.

"Every day you come here and bathe, more often than any woman in the town. You stop and stare off to the skies. Tell me, Sister, are you going to float or fly away?"

She shrugs, smiles, and shouts, "If I could, I would fly back into his arms." She wraps her arms around herself and pretends it is Kiowa holding her. Around and around she spins, never taking her eyes off the horizon. "Oh, Kiowa, where are you, my brave, strong chief?"

A safe distance from her, Kiowa beams with sheer delight when he hears his name. *Does she speak of me or of my tribe?* he wonders.

Walpi plays his flute faster. *This will make her fly.*

With a heart full of hope, Anoki begins singing a song she's practiced all winter.

My fingers twist around dandelion stocks. I pull them till they pop.
Then press their root to my ear. They say nothing. I frown.
The Navajo burned our crops and starved our bellies.
I smile, for my eyes don't eat unless they feast on you.
My lips thirst for yours. My ears listen for... Kiowa!
BRAVE WAR CHIEF. You charged through the walls of my heart.
If only I could go back to the night that you caught me. Catch me again!
You saved me that day. And the next day, and every day since, I have prayed for word.
Your voice is all I want, yet WINTER snowflakes fell and no words at all.
Does the howling wind blow words from you to me? Can the wind be so empty?
Or is that Night Wind rushing past me?
My love is powerful. It will float Night Wind to the sky and send word back.
Leap into heaven without regard for the moon. She is jealous!
Dance on her face. Her light makes flames upon the water.
Sprint across the sparkling stars. My eyes fix on the sky.

You have gone too far! Turn around. I am the star!
The sun's eternal flame flickers. I want to see it dance in the palm of
my hand. I reach to catch it...

Anoki doesn't finish. She reaches up for the sun and keeps her hand stretched out.

"And?" Walpi asks, breaking her spell.

"And what?" Anoki answers.

"And then what happens when you catch this flame?"

"I cannot know that. It hasn't happened yet. I can't finish my song until he finishes it for me."

"But you could just make up an ending. Then we would have another song to play at the next dance."

"Okay, then. I place my wishes on sparrows' wings." Anoki joins them by flapping her arms and pretending to fly away.

"Oh, forget it. You are wasting time with the birds. Who could know if he loves you but Kiowa himself?" Walpi interrupts.

"You cannot know what it is to be a woman and wish to be wanted."

"Of course not. I am a man. Why would I want to know such silly things?"

Anoki grunts, "What better moment can a woman have than to know her man wants her? Wants to grab her up and...?"

She captures Walpi's attention. "Yes, and...?"

"And I don't know..." She presses her hands to her lips. Her eyes burn with passion. Her heart is ablaze. *In the first spark of love, anything is possible. Fan the spark and it grows into a flame. Maybe he can even steal my heart away.* She searches the sky with hope-filled eyes. Her bright smile begins to fade. *Oh, I am tricking myself. He probably wants nothing to do with me.* She presses the back of her hand to her forehead. Her smile turns to a frown. *The Kiowa women are probably more beautiful than I am, anyway. He is from a warrior tribe. No doubt pretty women surround him. Their lips are thin. Mine are plump. Their eyes are wide like stones. Mine are oval like almonds. Their hair is wild and fine like Night Wind's. Mine is neatly braided like bread rolls stuck on both sides of my head like a ram.* She presses her hands to her buns and then thrusts her arms out. They make a *thud* when they plop against her sides.

"What?" Walpi asks.

"I'm just a plain old Hopi Indian girl." Her thoughts flicker back to the other women. She can't help but think of him with other "fine Indian women." Her frown deepens and her happiness melts to welling tears.

Here I am dreaming of that night and probably he has forgotten all about me. She shrugs and looks down to the ground, wiping tears away. *Perhaps I should just forget all about him.* She bites her bottom lip and feels it quiver between her teeth. *If that is even possible.* She looks back up to the sky.

"What are these words? You cannot even seem to find them."

She shrugs and faces her brother. "Hope has slipped from my mind. Now I am filled with doubt."

"These are dangerous times, Sister. Hope is scarce. I would choose doubt. There is an abundance of doubt. Anyone in our tribe can find doubt. It hangs on all of our faces." He frowns and pulls at the corners of his mouth with his fingers to exaggerate the doubtful expression.

"Is it so wrong for the Hopi to have hope?"

"Yes, I think so." Walpi goes back to playing his flute.

"Then we disagree. I hope Kiowa…"

Kiowa thinks, *For as many times as she's said my name, surely she's talking about me. But what is she saying?* He feels like he did in his vision. He wants to move his feet, but they won't go. *Will I blow apart like leaves?* He holds his hands up in front of his face. *Where is Moon Beam when I need him?*

Night Wind whinnies as though he is growing as bored of this as Walpi is.

Anoki gasps.

Kiowa curses his horse. "You brave fool! I will make a deal with the heavens here and now. If they send Moon Beam back, I will trade you for him in an instant." With his chest puffed out, he lets Night Wind lead the way, while he thinks of what he has rehearsed to say.

A great rustling and snapping of branches startles Anoki and Walpi.

As Night Wind picks up his pace, Kiowa orients him toward

Anoki.

Walpi panics and shouts, "RUN, SISTER!" He drops his flute and readies his hunting spear. "This time I will protect you, Anoki! I will lose no more women to the Mexicans!"

CHAPTER 34

"We have no reason to fear him." Anoki puts her hand on Walpi's spear and lowers it with a gentle press.

Kiowa's long raven hair splashes around his broad shoulders and dances off his muscular back. Each bow and rock of Night Wind impresses Anoki with the black mustang's rippling chest muscles and Kiowa's flexed arms and legs. Though it has been only one winter, Kiowa's stature has dramatically increased since last she saw him. His broad beaming smile displays winter's growth on a sharp manly jaw.

His charging stallion excites her. Anoki can feel the earth shake under her feet. She gasps and swallow a river of excitement. "See there, Brother. It is not so bad for a Hopi girl to have hope."

"This is what you want? A wild savage man running up to you?" Anoki's eyes soften. She smiles and nods.

The powerful mustang comes to an abrupt halt. A dust cloud catches up and engulfs the rider. Night Wind rears up on his bulging hindquarters and crow hops his front legs.

Neither of them says a word. Kiowa's gaze is so intense, its source cannot be mistaken. When their eyes lock, Anoki melts. She blushes and looks down bashfully. Electric emotions charge the space between them and make Walpi feel uncomfortable.

"My protector returns." Anoki looks up with gushing eyes. Her shyness demands she look away. Instead, her courage forces her to hold his gaze. She feels her rosebud lips tremble as she nervously smiles. Sage, dust, and horse offend her sense of smell. But her face doesn't show it.

Kiowa's confidence overwhelms her when he doesn't say anything. Instead, he leans down and reaches for her.

She spots a red paint line from his wrist to the center of his chest, where it meets a circle of bright yellow paint over his heart. A series of characters are smeared from his sweat. *Is this war paint?* she wonders before hesitantly taking his hand. *If it is, then am I at war?* Not wanting to be rude, she rests her palpitating hand in his. Her pulse races. *Surely he must know I'm nervous.*

It doesn't seem to matter what she is. With one swift motion, she feels his effortless strength lift her up onto his horse and draw her to him like metal to a magnet.

Swinging her leg over Night Wind's bare back, she wraps her slender arms around his waist and presses her chest against his back. Her heart beats so fast that she begs it to slow down. *Please do not leap out of my chest and run away! Why are you so nervous, Anoki? This is what I wanted! This is the man who makes me feel like I am floating. Or flying?*

"Okay, then. I guess I'm going home?" Walpi says sulkily, waving good-bye as Kiowa steals his sister away. "I could have killed him if I wanted to. Luck was with you this time, big strong Kiowa warrior man." He twirls his spear and drops it.

Kiowa and Anoki sprint across the desert floor. She releases her grip and unties her hair. Her braids quickly unfold and catch in the wind. Kiowa's long strands whip around and tickle her face. She inhales. *So that is what sunlight smells like.* She leans back and extends her arms, then looks up at the vast blue sky. Warm summer wind passes through her fingers and whooshes against her face as they blaze across the desert plains. The hot sun scorches her already blushing cheeks. Night Wind's full sprint rhythmically shakes her entire body. She beams with pure joy, then squints her eyes shut and thinks, *I was wrong, Walpi. To love is to fly.*

Kiowa kicks at Night Wind's side, making the mustang do what he does best, run as fast as the wind.

Where do we race to? Anoki thinks. *Oh, I cannot know this. I care only that it is a secret place!* This makes her joy beam even brighter. She sneaks a few kicks of her own.

After half a day's journey through flat desert lands, the distant horizon grows steep with jagged red cliffs. The cliffs shoot up through the ground and have strong streaks of brown. As they get closer to the towering walls, they find themselves enclosed in a narrowing canyon. About halfway in, the canyon widens. Leafy green foliage splashes up against the red clay cliffs. Eventually, they arrive at a murky blue-green stream. Night Wind slows to a steady trot. His heavy breathing echoes.

Upstream, thick bushy palm trees hide an oasis where a spring rests at the foot of the tallest mountain.

"Is this your secret place?" Anoki asks Kiowa.

"My uncle told me to bring you here. He said you would like it."

"He is wise. Do you know what this place is called?"

Kiowa shakes his head.

"Havasupai. These are sacred falls."

"Ah-hoe, so this is a sacred—not a secret—place?"

"Yes. It is a sacred place."

When he dismounts, he places his hands on her hips.

She rests her hands on his shoulders. *So this is what it a bird feels like to land*, she thinks as she gently slides down.

He can't help but stare at the yellow square bead patterns on her deerskin dress.

"I like these blue beads, but what are these yellow beads in a square?"

She looks down at the pattern and drags her fingers across them. "It is the sun. I have four suns in my blue sky. My father, whom you saved. My mother, whom I hope to save. My sister, whom I also hope to save. My brother, Walpi, who cannot be saved."

She looks up, tilts her head to the side, and sighs.

Kiowa lightly chuckles at her words.

Without much effort at all, she forms the most inviting expression. Her lips beg him to kiss her, right here and now, but for some reason he resists.

Am I mistaken? Anoki panics and feels sweat bead on her forehead.

Kiowa slides his hand into hers and dismisses her doubts.

She releases a breath she didn't even know she was holding. *I am not. See there, he holds my hand and I am thrilled that I can feel it.*

Kiowa leads her to a wide flowing turquoise stream. He can hear the falls rushing. *I wonder how far it is to the falls. Maybe I should kiss her now...*

Anoki looks away and points. "We are not that far away. Follow me! Follow me!" She surprises him by tugging his hand. They slip their moccasins off and leave them at the bank. When his feet hit the cool water, Kiowa is startled. *I'm confused by this conflicting temperature. The desert is an unbearable heat, whereas the river is freezing cold.*

"This is where Tawa, the creator, formed the first world out of Tokpella. Tawa formed the first humans out of clay and used his magic wind to blow breath into our nostrils. If you look just below your nose, you will still see the trail. Tawa took sun drops from the sky, turned them into corn seeds, and placed them in their hands. This is where the first Indians grew the first golden ears of corn. Most Indians have forgotten this place and their growing ways. The Hopi will always remember. That is why we are still growers and still the first Indians."

"Why do your people build cliff dwellings?"

"That is because Tawa does not like us to hurt one another. Would you like your children hurting each other? No, I don't think so. Rather than fight wars, we hide in our cliff homes."

"How long do you have to hide?"

"Until the Navajo get hungry and find someone else to raid."

"Why not just kill the Navajo, take their scalps, and teach them a lesson?"

Anoki gasps, and her face turns a pale shade. "Ah ha… we could not do that. We would not even know how to."

Sunlight cascades and exposes wild corn that grows all along the lush stream's banks. Water skippers hop on the pond's surface and glide away. Cattails stand tall out of the blue topaz water. Seeds try their hardest to hold intact to their mother stalk. No matter how hard Mother tries, her children slip off the stalk and float away. Water grass below the surface waves at Kiowa and Anoki, inviting them in.

"This is why it is our sacred place. We come back here once a year and show thanks by sacrificing the seeds from our first crop. Our sacrifices bring us back to Maawa, back to center."

"Why would you want to be center?"

"We are all looking for center, Kiowa. It is home. It is happiness. You know, it is center."

"Center is home?" Kiowa repeats.

Kiowa isn't prepared for what he finds when he gets to the falls. The stream leads to a lavish wide aquamarine pond. The turquoise pond at the center looks more like the beads in Anoki's dress than actual water.

"It is a pretty fine jewel!" Kiowa sighs.

Anoki smiles. "I am happy to be the first to bring you here."

A tall white flowing waterfall spills and roars over towering red clay cliffs. Patches of green trees line the banks. Puffy white clouds begin to sail overhead. One looks like it has lost its place in the sky where the falls meet the pond.

Kiowa stands in awe. "It is as though clouds have turned into strands of hair and blow forever. I believe you. The gods must have made this place. No doubt the first Indian man and woman were made here, too. But I believe it was Naukolahe who made it."

"Don't look at me. Spin around!" she orders him.

He obeys frantically.

She slips out of her deerskin dress. She gasps and squeals as she steps on tiny pebbles. Her svelte nude figure eases into the turquoise pool.

CHAPTER 35

Anoki releases her joy through giggles, a sound that is like a wind chime ringing in his ears. The high-pitched female tone entices his flesh and makes his heart beat like a drum. Without realizing it, her voice tempts him to turn and see more. "Are you testing my patience?"

"Maybe!"

Water wets her hair. She swims away from him and releases more joy.

No man can be expected keep his back turned on a naked woman. Surely this is a great crime! He grunts and clenches his fists as the passion in his heart sets his skin ablaze.

"Now I will turn around..." Anoki shouts, wiping water out of her cheerful eyes.

Before she can finish her sentence, he strips down to his loincloth. Her eyes widen. She gasps in a different way when she glimpses his curved buttocks and nude legs.

Kiowa extends his arms over his head, then dives into the water. His hair whips behind his head as he submerges in a splash and an explosion of air bubbles.

With a few powerful strokes he's already in the center of the pond. "This is paradise," Kiowa shouts, hearing his voice echo off the towering walls.

"Oh, you must be careful how loud you speak here," Anoki warns him.

"Why?" Kiowa wonders.

"Because the ancient woman who saw a god here and heard his name never died. She is so old her skin turned blue and her eyes went bad. She cannot catch game, so all she can eat is corn. If you call her, the last thing you will ever see is her old, evil, toothless face."

"Who is she?"

"She is the second daughter of the first Indians. She saw a god resting beneath the waterfall and singing a song about himself. When she heard his name, she called out to him. He was angry that a mortal had seen him, so he spread his eagle wings and flew away. He was so beautiful she wandered in and out of every cave searching for him. She called his name over and over again but never found him."

"What was her name?"

"I do not know her original name. But we call her Ayko. When you speak too loudly in sacred places, she repeats what she hears because she is trying to trick you into one of her caves. No one can resist repeating her words once they hear them. That's how she tricks you. She draws you nearer and nearer until she traps you and eats you alive."

Should I shout to the old evil woman that I love Anoki? Kiowa excites himself at the challenge. *Do not be foolish. Use your fox thoughts. What if Ayko shouts something back that you do not want to hear? Anoki is right. For now I must watch what I say.*

Rippling waves distort Anoki's naked frame. Kiowa catches himself staring, waiting for the ripples to stop, but they never do. Not so long as the falls pour water into the pool.

"It is always spring here," Anoki tells him. She flips her wet hair out of her face.

He laughs and takes a deep breath as he swims to the waterfall. Water slams against his head and forces him under the surface.

"Kiowa, be careful!"

"Kiowa, be careful!" Ayko calls out.

Anoki inhales sharply and covers her mouth.

He dives down, then pops back up behind the clear sheeting waterfall.

"Anoki! I think I am in love with you!" he shouts in his language as he leaps out of the white rushing falls.

Anoki gulps.

The old evil woman repeats Kiowa's words. "I love you! I love you! I love you!"

Oh no. It is true. She repeats words I cannot resist. "I LOVE YOU!"

"I love you! I love you! I love you!" Anoki's words echo.

Kiowa's body disappears beneath the water. *Ha! I have tricked the gods.*

Anoki laughs and cups her hands over her mouth. "Okay, that is enough!" She promises herself not to repeat Ayko's words. *Best not to tempt her. Ugh... the sight of her face would kill me.* She shudders at the thought.

When Kiowa surfaces, Anoki says, "Ayko heard you."

"Oh really? I forgot that you can speak my language. What did she say back?"

"I love you! I love you! I love you!" Anoki repeats in a low tone.

Her drenched black hair presses tightly against her smooth neck. She flips it back by arching her back and snapping her neck. The motion speeds up his heart and burns deep into his memory. Water droplets hang off her earlobes like diamond earrings.

He swims to her.

She pushes him away. "I will not be easily won with kind words and handsome looks. You have to prove your love to me in some worthy test."

The two laugh and play like children in the Garden of Eden until the sun sets on their sparkling oasis.

When they exit the pool, Anoki demands the same honorable decency.

"Look away!" she orders him as she wipes herself down and slips her dress back on.

Uncle warned me she would test me. This test is not so hard. Anoki is a delicate flower. Not something to thrust my love into quickly and discard. Makes Trouble cannot be right. All women do not want a quick fix of love. Well, at least Anoki is not like any woman I have ever known. She is something special. Something sacred. She is to be cherished. Protected. Respected. Honored. Anoki, your voice is sweet as honey. Your lips soft as flowers. Your hair as fine as... His thoughts cease when he catches her looking at him.

Oh, how I want to touch him, she thinks. You are the only man I know who has captured the wild in your beautiful face and hair! Your fearless dark brown eyes flash kindness towards me, so I will be sure not to make an enemy of you. My heart would break if your eyes flared fiery hatred towards me.

Kiowa wasn't sure what made Anoki smile, but he was happy to see her do it.

To hold any part of him is to pet a wolf and play with a cougar at the same time, she thinks. *I could stare at him all day with loving eyes that say, "I know you are as powerful as a grizzly bear, but with my heart, please, please be as gentle as a flower." Does he even know how fragile my heart is?*

"Are you cold?" he asks when he sees her shivering.

She nods.

"I'll gather wood and build us a fire."

"I'll pick corn."

Both do their respective tasks quickly. The fire itself is lit by twisting a stick in his bowstring and thrusting his hands back and forth until an ember ignites in a bundle of dry grass.

"I have never seen a fire built this way. You are very good at that!" Anoki compliments him as she sets the ears of corn down and twists her hair into a tight ponytail. She clenches her fists and wrings the water out.

"How do you light a fire?"

"We preserve embers as much as we can. Then, if those go out, we strike two stones together over dry grass. The sparks make a good fire. But sometimes it can take all day."

She shakes her head and lets the damp wavy strands fall all around her bare shoulders.

Kiowa stares at her in a way that makes her think, *Ha! Now you must be the one to wait.*

When the sun dips down and quickly disappears, Anoki is nearly dry. The air cools. The sky dazzles them with stars. The caw of ravens returning home and the hoot of owls welcome night's arrival.

Anoki sets the husked corn down near the fire.

"Eat this while the corn cooks." She hands Kiowa a leather pouch of pemmican she prepared for herself and Walpi. *Let us see if he appreciates Hopi meat.* She smiles when he opens the bag and sees that it is meat. When he sets it down, her face shows disappointment.

"Is something wrong?" Kiowa asks.

CHAPTER 36

"No, no. Nothing at all." Anoki forces a smile. *Why did he not like my meat?* she wonders. *Is he too good for Hopi meat?*

Before she says anything, he takes her hand and pulls her to him. She melts at his touch and immediately forgets her grievance. She tilts her head back so that her lips naturally part. He had not intended to jump right in and kiss her again, but here she is, and as Paw says, "Women need to be kissed and fish need to be caught."

Having never kissed a girl, he doesn't know if he is getting better with practice or doing worse. Anoki isn't telling him anything, but since she keeps kissing him, he keeps kissing her. His eyes remain open while she closes hers. When he feels her soft lips press against his, a surge of eagerness causes him to tremble all over. *I must be doing this right! he assures himself. If I were doing it wrong, she would not keep pushing into me with her soft lips and hot breath.* He closes his eyes, then opens his mouth and works his lips in a way that allows him to put all the burning words of love he felt from a cold lonely winter inside her mouth.

Anoki greedily receives the unspoken words from his heart. She wraps her arms around his neck and presses her lips harder to his. She feels her knees go weak and tremble like two tall trees shaking in the wind. *Why does he frighten me? Does he frighten me? Or am I afraid that he's going to hear my weak knees knocking and say something like, "What is that terrible noise coming from between your legs? Are you part cricket? Stop that, or I will stop kissing you." Oh, that would be terrible! Kiss me harder! Take my breath away! Steal my heart.*

When he doesn't say any of those things, but instead contracts his powerful muscles and pulls her closer to him, she submits. They kiss and kiss until passion grows as hot as fire, threatening to fuse them together. She fights her nature and pushes him away.

Ah, there it is. I am doing this wrong, he thinks.

"Is something wrong?" Kiowa asks.

"It's just that I hope you don't ever stop wanting me this way. Or looking at me the way you do."

"Eyes must look! My eyes cannot look away from you," Kiowa says, closing his eyes and parting his lips.

"No, I mean I want to be with you always."

He opens his eyes. "Me too." He closes his eyes and parts his lips. She pecks his lips, now with her eyes open.

"I mean I don't want to be with anyone else. Just you. Is this how you feel also?"

Kiowa sits up. *I did not expect all this talking to go on. How do I get her to be silent and keep kissing? Do I just kiss her and ignore her? No. No, she does not look like she will be ignored.*

Remembering his lessons from the deer, Kiowa decides to be gentle. He runs his fingers through her hair. "I do not understand," he says in a soft tone.

"How do the Kiowa love?" Anoki asks.

"We love like we fight, with the strongest passion! Being by you brings me more joy and passion than can be measured."

"Passion more than joy?" Anoki asks with a trickery that makes him think of Moon Beam's foxy face.

"Of course! Passion is the greatest love of all."

"That is what I was afraid of." Anoki sulks and retreats into herself.

Oh no! Kiowa thinks. *She's not going to kiss me anymore.*

She turns around and leans into him, patiently waiting for him to ask her something. Instead he runs his fingers through her hair. He eventually wraps his arms around her and thinks, *If you were buffalo, I could run you down. Tire you out. Then take from you what I want. But buffalo are ugly and you are pretty like a swan. If I chase a swan, it will fly away and I will never catch it. No, I must find what you eat and trick you into coming closer to me.*

They remain in this elated state until a blanket of bright stars twinkle above them.

Patience. Patience. Why am I always the one to be patient? Anoki thinks.

"What are you thinking?" Anoki speaks first, losing her patience.

"I am thinking about what I said when I jumped out of the falls."

"I was thinking that too."

"Then I was thinking about what you said back at the stream, when you were with your brother."

"You heard that?"

He nods. "Now I am thinking... and thinking... and thinking..." He twirls her hair around his finger. *Why are we not doing less talking and more kissing? I have been gentle.*

Anoki folds her arms and squints. "Now I will tell you what I am thinking." She sits up and faces him. "I am thinking words are easy to speak. Love is hard to find. You say you love me. Show me the tracks or the trail so that I may know it for myself."

"Tracks. Look at me. Do you see the trail of scars you have left all over my heart?" Kiowa points to his chest.

Anoki looks down. She presses her hand to his heart. "No." She sighs. *All I see is your muscle. Oh, and I want only to touch it*, she thinks. She clears her throat. "I see nothing."

"Ah, of course you don't. There are no visible wounds, but the scars are there." He puts his hand on top of hers. "Being separated from you has wounded me terribly. Moment to moment. Day by day. From one moon to the next, your absence has swollen to a bloom of pain. And now that I am with you, you peel the hurt back one petal at a time."

"You make me sound so cruel."

"Nah. You are sweet Anoki. You are all I see when I close my eyes. My heart burns with a fire that spreads through my veins and makes me fall. I cannot eat unless I know you are safe. I cannot dream unless my dreams are of your face. I miss you. I miss the sparkle in your eyes. Have you fallen in your heart the same as I have fallen in mine?"

The fire crackles.

Anoki's cheeks turn bright red. "Stop. I can see the tracks."

"I will do anything you say so long as you say stay."

"Yes, stay!"

They kiss.

AHA! Kiowa has a brilliant thought. *My words are your food, sweet Anoki. I will catch this beautiful swan yet!*

"My heart rises to my lips." She holds up her hand. "Now it sinks to my palm."

Kiowa holds up his hand, and they press their palms together. "Then I hold in my hand what cannot be caught?"

Anoki nods. Her smile reveals all. She speaks so softly her voice sounds like the twitter of morning birds. "My pledge to you is this: My love for you is as deep as the earth and as limitless as the sky. You flashed into my life like lightning, and I yearn to feel your blaze. The more of you I feel, the more of you I have."

"Till we are one?"

She nods.

"*Ah-hoe!* Sweet Anoki… I had words of plenty bursting from my heart and rushing rivers through my mind, but now that I am here with you, they have all escaped me."

Anoki, be careful. He is a man and you are woman. If you are always telling him how you feel in your heart and not pushing it deep down inside of you, he will tire of your rattling lips. Besides, Mother says, "Men who rattle their lips are like the snake who rattles its tail. Behind the lips, both have fangs and will strike." Be wise, Anoki. Be patient, Anoki. Don't rattle your lips. Lure him with your eyes, lips, and hips, never with words! Oh, it would be terrible to love him, confess it, and have my love cast aside. You must hold your tongue, Anoki. He must love me. But how can I know for certain? Anoki bites her bottom pouting lip.

"… I have a large tepee and many furs. Plenty of meat." Kiowa finishes, but Anoki hasn't heard a word of it. She tilts her head down and stares at him with an intensity that invites another kiss.

"Tell me more," Anoki begs, wanting to hear what he has to say, since she was consulting herself and not listening.

"What more can I say?"

"I must hear more now, for I have waited so long."

"What you must understand about the Kiowa is that we are artists first. Did you see the paint on my arm before I washed it off?"

When he doesn't call it "war paint," she breathes a sigh of relief. "I did." She nods and places her hand on his knee. This encourages him to go on.

Kiowa swallows, bobbing his pronounced Adam's apple. "When I paint this red line on my arm, I do it on my heart arm." He holds his left arm up and shows her where his war paint was.

She leans forward and excitedly follows his trail.

"I do this because it is the arm that leads to my heart." He makes a fist, and his eyes flash with a wildness that startles an affectionate smile out of her. *I could stare into those eyes and see something new every time I look.*

"I do this when we go to war so that the spirits know that I am ready!"

She looks confused and wants to hear nothing of war, only words of love.

"I have been fighting a war since I met you. Can you see what I have painted with red since last we met?" He turns his arm over and shows her the smeared streaks.

"Ah... Let me redraw it for you."

He picks up cooled ash from the fire and remakes the marks with the charcoal.

She watches as Kiowa draws a round smiling sun on his forearm. A horse, probably Night Wind, carries what must be a girl on its back. Farther up his arm, Anoki sees a man with outstretched arms reaching for the girl on the horse.

"I hurt when I am away from you. This sun is the light I feel when we are together. It rises in me and shines in my eyes. My lips on the sun go dry because water cannot exist on the sun, and when I am away from you, they burn hotter than the greatest fires. My eyes burn like the sun without you, but I use the sun's light to search all over the earth for you. When I think the Navajo may return and I am not there to protect you, I send Night Wind and he brings you to me." His hands tremble and his voice cracks when he points to the horse painted upon his muscled canvas.

"When I am with you, it is as though I have water and my eyes and lips do not burn. I am myself again and the wound is healed. This is the war I fight."

She gasps and is grateful for her mother's advice. Had she uttered a word, she might not have heard him confess his heart's true words.

"Did you mean that I make you feel like the sun rises inside you?" Anoki gushes to herself, *You are not a snake at all. You are something greater than I have ever known. You are the hope for a new life. You are center?*

"Yes! That is exactly what I mean." He grinds ash up and smears it on his chest. The orange fire dances around the shape of a wolf.

"This is my father, who watches my heart and tells me that I am right and it is good to confess these difficult words. I believe he is proud of me. I believe he would like you very much. I know he would want you to make his grandchildren. I cannot imagine a day without you. I cannot live another winter without you. Neither my body nor my spirit will survive it. My invisible wounds will return and I will die without you. These are my words. I write them with the smoke of my soul and whisper them with the wind of my lips. I seal them up with this kiss." He presses his lips to hers and steals her breath away.

Tears of happiness well in her eyes. "Then we must never part."

She wraps her arms around his burning neck and presses her cool lips to his. His hands no longer shake. They grow confident and travel down her slender shoulders to the small of her back. He pulls her in and breathes her winds deep into his lungs. They remain like this, as though they can never be pulled apart.

Gentle kisses. Delicate touches. Long stares. Sweet sighs. All the intricacies of love weave the fabric of their souls together in pure, innocent, adoring, coveted love.

"Tell me something, Kiowa. Why do you love me?"

Kiowa feels the fabric stretch.

CHAPTER 37

Kiowa's face goes blank. His mouth instantly dries. He goes to open his mouth, but his tongue is stuck to the roof of his mouth. *My vision is my nightmare. And my nightmare is coming true. I can't speak.*

He looks down and wiggles his finger.

There, see that? I can move my finger. But why won't my tongue work? Why do I feel frozen? He looks around, searching for the right words.

Distracted by his strange behavior, Anoki looks down and wiggles her fingers, too.

"I love you because you are so pretty!"

Impossible! He thinks... I am pretty? Me? She's utterly flabbergasted, but her face remains calm. "Is that it? You love me because of my beauty? Don't you know that at night, when husbands and wives make love, they can't see each other in the dark? To them love is blind."

His brows and lips crush together and squeeze awkwardness out of his face. His eyes blink rapidly. *She is not a spider. I am not tangled in her web. No, she is a fox. I am a blue pheasant and she has me on the run.*

Why do you make that face? You are much too handsome. Oh, see there? I love you because you are handsome, she thinks. "Did you hear my private thoughts when I was talking to my brother?" Anoki asks with a curious and cautious expression.

Not wanting this tender moment to end, but also struggling with honesty, Kiowa delicately approaches the subject. "I thought I heard you say my name."

"Is that why you came out of the bushes?"

Kiowa nods.

"Was that the first time you watched me without me knowing?"

"Yes."

That's too bad. Maybe you don't love me as much as I love you. I can hardly take my eyes off you. I want to know everything you do.

"But that was the first time I had seen you since that night."

She snuggles up against him and kisses him.

Oh, I wish you had heard my thoughts. I cannot remember any of them now. You have stolen them with my heart. Anoki yawns and shudders.

When she settles herself like a bird might shuffle its feathers, Kiowa reveals the last shadow in his heart. "Although my heart is flying, there is something that weighs it down."

Anoki's bliss instantly turns to a frown when she feels the fabric of their love tighten.

"Do not bore me with responsibilities. My whole life revolves around responsibilities. It is like I am a hawk tied to a string. Just as I am beginning to enjoy the freedom of flight, I am yanked back." Anoki huffs, then gasps for being so bold. She tilts her head to the side, clears her throat, and resumes her sweet tone. "I mean, you can tell me anything."

"My tribe values warriors above all else!"

"I thought you were artists first?"

"War is art." He puffs his chest out. "And they expect me, their 'greatest warrior' to marry a Kiowa squaw."

Anoki sits up, putting distance between them. "But you are here with me."

"Yes, but they want me there with them. Do you not understand?"

She shakes her head, "no," feeling her heart sink and her face with it.

"Okay, well, it is not just one of them. Nearly all of the girls who can have babies want to have my baby. Now do you understand?"

Anoki's loving face twists to fiery hate as she feels the fabric of their love pull tight, then tear. "You speak of flames. Of love. Are you sure you don't have fangs? I swear I feel fiery poison swelling in my veins. Why are you telling me all these things?"

"The Kiowa love is passionate. Onendah says our tribe's love is like a flame that consumes everything it touches. It appears like lightning, strikes the tree, and creates a spark. I am supposed to be the lightning, but I have seen in a vision that I am made of leaves and will blow apart."

"You can't tell me you love me, convince me of your love, and then tell me your love is like a wild fire and you want to burn me with it. I would rather hear, 'Anoki, be buried alive with your relatives. Anoki, wake up; we have left you in a cave of sleeping bears who are now waking with you. Anoki, here is a snake's den. Ha! Ha! Find your way out, but do not touch anything, BECAUSE YOU ARE SURROUNDED BY POSIONUS SERPENTS!' It is okay though, because I have thrown your heart in the cave with you. Now go find it.'" She stares at Kiowa with hurt in her eyes. "Kiowa, you saved my life. Why offer me love now when you could have just let the Navajo kill me? Oh, that would have been so much easier. Where is my strong but gentle hero?"

"I want to always speak truth to you. Love is not easy. Love is hard."

Anoki stands up, stomps her foot, and hisses, "How wrong you are. To love is to pass the test, Kiowa! Mother was right! You have words aplenty, but you are failing my test and your actions show it." She turns to run away. "He has confused love with passion. His love doesn't have the endurance of a single day. How am I supposed to build a life on this? His love crushes hope. His love cannot fuse our souls together with the eternal flame."

I am a fool. Women cannot handle truth. It cuts them to their core and makes them act like wildcats.

He catches her by the wrist.

"So you will not be true to me? I am a fool because I would be true to you. Is that it? I have shown you what is in my heart through glances, soft touches, kisses. You have shown me the same. You say you have the same feelings in your heart, and now you say you doubt love. You want to hold more than my hand. You want to kiss more than my lips. You want to capture more hearts than mine? Do you not understand that Hopi love is nothing like Kiowa love? If you want to go give your love to all the women in the world, then you will have no women. Are you a snake? Oh no, I know, it is because you think I will be the first to be burned? I have killed snakes before, and I can do it again! If I cannot trust you, I cannot have faith in you to be around and help me raise our children. Love has a price Kiowa, it is time! What woman would want such a treacherous man? To cheat my love with wicked women, I cannot endure it. Do you hear me? My heart will break." Anoki searches for a weapon. "Even robins, with the tiniest brains of birds, know this."

Kiowa sighs. *This is how I found her, searching for a weapon. I cannot be her enemy. She seems so mad. Why does she not leave? How do I control her? I could no sooner control her than I could tell the wind which way to blow. She acts on her own. Look there. She acts like she is going to leave, goes a little distance, folds her arms, stomps her pretty beaded moccasins, then turns around and nips at me. Cruel cat!* Kiowa dismisses these thoughts, knowing he will only make her angrier if he lets one word slip. He thinks a moment, chooses his words carefully, then says, "Onendah, our medicine man, says that love is the flame. Cherish it while it lasts. My uncle says I should look upon other faces. Makes Trouble says I should be with many women; that is the only way to prove to the world I am a great chief!"

"What do you want?"

"I want you!"

"To consume with fire? Ah, so your love seeks pain. Do you think I want to be burned? Oh, you cruel, cruel man. Do you not understand that love brings more love? Love cannot bring pain. Pain chases love away. Why did you even come here?"

CHAPTER 38

Before today Kiowa never knew what it was like to feel the blow of battle. Now he is more battered than any fight he has ever been in. *I could really use a shield.* He endures her assault with half a smile.

"I am here because I don't love them. I love *you.*"

His words stun her. She doesn't know what to think. "Because I am the prettiest?"

"I do not know all the reasons why. But the pain and worry disappear when I am with you. See, I can eat." He searches for the pemmican she brought. When he finds it, he snatches the pouch up, opens it, and stuffs it in his mouth. "This is all I know."

His authentic expression and the satisfied, determined look in his eyes conquer her. "You do love me!" She tries to hold up her last defense, a stern glare. *Does he even know what love is?* she thinks to herself. *He must not. I should tell him.* Anoki draws a long, deep breath. "Hopi love is as pure the pearl-white horse. Once you take my hand with love, mine will never let go. Hopi love goes on forever. It is full of color and light. We capture it and weave it in our clothes, our hair, and even our blankets. What do you think keeps us warm at night? A blanket? Ha! No. It is love. Love makes you ridiculously happy when it wraps its white wings around you and protects you. Love will take you anywhere you want to go. Love is gentleness for the one you love. Love is kindness in a limitless well. Love requires patience to raise children. When it is true, love can endure the test of time and it will outlast our cliff dwellings. Above all, it is loyal! The more you share it with other women, the less I have to give back to you. The more you share with me, the more I have to give back to you. And so you see, love is like the horizon; it goes on forever. It cannot be captured in one word. It is infinite and lacks the words to describe it because it isn't just a word. Love is also an act. It is a gesture. It is a moment. To have true love is to have the greatest treasure on earth and heaven. To have my love is to hold the most delicate and fragile part of me. Only a god could have created love. The father is the source. It is worth more than all the horses in the world. It is more desired than the best food. Love is the food of the soul. Love does not dishonor those who have it."

"I have never heard anyone use words like you do. If I am in the presence of the father's creation, am I worthy of holding this precious gift?"

"Without love, I am nothing. I am not protected. You preserved me. I could be beneath the dust of the earth and it would have been as though I had never existed if I did not have love." Her last defense is wiped clean of anger. She beams true love. "Tell me how you feel!"

"I cannot make you suffer with my envy. I am a fool to puff up and show off like the blow snake. I do not seek my happiness, but I seek yours. You speak with harsh tones, and yet I am not provoked. I cannot have one evil thought against you. My heart rejoices in this single truth. I know for certain that my love for you is a flame, and I can't share that with just anyone. You are right. We both feel the same way, and it is wrong to share it with others. Can you bear my love?"

"Yes! Now you can see. Your love brings me hope. Now I can endure anything. Love never fails, Kiowa! It is the greatest magic. Our love is perfect!" He has her full attention now. She feels tinges of guilt for thinking a bead of shame could be woven in his perfect hair.

"Your ways are right. I only want one true love to hold this hand till it withers and dies."

"We must have faith!" Anoki takes his hand.

"We must have hope!" Kiowa cups her cheek with his warm palm.

"We must have love," they say together, then kiss.

He takes her by the waist and mends the tear with his powerful arms and firm lips.

"How will I know if I am true?"

"Yes, how will you know?"

"I cannot know. I am a man. My head is full of foolish thoughts."

"Yes, I can see that. What will you do?"

"The only thing I can do. I will dance before Taime and see if I am made of leaves or if I can withstand this eternal flame you speak of. If I do not fail the ultimate test, I know he will find a way to unite us. Make us one."

"What is the ultimate test?"

"I will volunteer to dangle in front of the sun by eagle claws."

Anoki gasps. "That is the ultimate test?"

"Can you think of a harder one?"

"No. How could I?"

Kiowa holds up his hand and rests it on his heart. "My tribe's heart will always seek my strong blood to pump and course through their veins."

Anoki sighs. "My tribe will seek my blood to birth the next generation of royalty. How can I be your enemy? We are a tribe of peace. We trade with the Kiowa. Can our love not mix into Hopi and Kiowa children, without the eagle's claws? Won't they make you bleed?"

"By the blood comes more blood. You claim your duty to your tribe, so it is my duty to my tribe that binds me. That is exactly what makes you their enemy. Your power to mix blood. They will not stand for it."

Anoki tilts her head to the side and looks at him with a calm, pondering expression. "I do not understand the ways of your brutal tribe. My people will cherish this love and foster it. It scares me that your tribe will not, but I believe your words and I trust that you will find a way to keep us safe." She leans her head against his chest and realizes she must ask him one very important question as she presses her hand to his beating heart. "Kiowa, is this bud of love already nearing a winter chill? Will it wither and die like all things the Winter Woman kills with her frosty breath? Or is our love still springing in our hearts?"

"Inside my heart, I feel as though it is as hot as summer. All I know is that the tallest mountains and deepest valleys won't stop my love from bringing me to you. Surely you can believe that. I have crossed both mountains and valleys to be here with you."

She smiles and looks at him with a tender devotion that makes his soul feel whole. "Yes, I can see that."

He tucks her hair behind her ear and says, "Only the Sun God can say what our love can do." Kiowa turns away from her. What he has to say next he can't say while she stares at him. *Maybe I have said enough. Maybe I need not say more.*

She nestles back into his chest. He leans down to kiss her again. She wants him to take her breath away for the rest of her days. *Cut the string and let me fly, great war chief!*

***

"I will not be gone long, Mother," Kida says as she packs her horse. She takes extra care securing her bow.

"I do not want you to go. What if some enemy should find you and make you a captive?"

"Then at least I will be someone's wife."

"Kiowa would never allow that."

Kida smiles at the thought of him coming to save her.

"I will follow his tracks to the Hopi village. When he sees how concerned I am, he will know that I love him."

"Can you make him love you by showing him the love in your face and eyes?"

"Yes. When he sees, he will know."

"You have much to learn about men, Daughter. With bow and knife, you are undefeated. But with the arrows of the heart, you have yet to draw your string."

"Always speaking in circles, Mother. I never understand your circles."

"Kiss me good-bye and go learn for yourself. Every daughter must have her heart broken or else it cannot grow."

I do not want my heart broken. That is why I go, dear Mother, Kida thinks. She kisses her mother on the cheek.

"I will return with Kiowa."

"He will come home on his own. If you ride in with him, that does not mean you have caught him and he is yours."

"Ugh… enough of this." She mounts her horse. Kida kicks at her pinto pony and reassures herself that her presence is in fact the only way to help Kiowa come back to his senses.

When she arrives at the Hopi village, she struggles to communicate her intentions. Though she searches high and low, she can't find Kiowa or Paw. She eventually finds a Hopi girl that signs in Kiowa. The girl tells her that Paw and Kiowa split up.

She points east and signs, *the younger one went that way*. She points west, *the older one went that way*.

Kida grits her teeth as she sees a group of men lead by the Hopi Chief, riding east. *Why would Kiowa ride east, when he should be riding west? And why are those men riding east?* Kida wonders. *I should follow them.*

Though she is tired and it is already sunset, she rides late into the night and cautiously stalks up stream. She finds the group of Hopi men clustering around Kiowa's trail. She gasps and dismounts her horse.

Of course he and Paw would hide in a canyon. He is so smart. And so stupid! Why would you hide in a canyon? Now you have nowhere to run! There are too many of them. Do I get the tribe? Do I sneak attack? I'm such a fool. I left my bow on my pony, and my pony is walking away. Ugh... As she unsheathes her knife, she hears a familiar name.

"Walpi, tells me that *Kiowa* and Anoki ran off together. It is late into the night. Either I am going to have a son in-law or a grandson," the man who signed their location says.

One of the warriors chuckles and says, "Both would good."

The men laugh and follow the trail.

Kiowa, Kida thinks as she grits her teeth and clenches her knife. *They had better not harm one sacred hair on his head.* She bites her tongue hard to keep herself from screaming. *They know Kiowa. How can they know Kiowa?*

She follows the Hopi men and prepares to attack them when the time is right.

As the Hopi party moves upstream and nears the falls, they surprise the couple.

"What is this?" Kiowa shouts, leaping to his feet and searching for the weapons that are attached to his horse.

"Why did you leave your weapons fastened on that fine horse Night Wind? Don't you know he could run off or be stolen and you would never see him again?"

"It would not be hard to find him. I'm certain if he were stolen, he would end up at your house," Anoki growls at her father.

"Ha! Ha! This is a father asking what this boy's intentions are with his daughter!" Kikmongwi folds his arms and proudly stomps his foot.

Walpi doesn't say anything, but he waves at his sister, who scowls at him.

"I ugh... um..." Kiowa doesn't understand Kikmongwi's Hopi words, but judging by the look on his face, he pieces together what's upsetting him.

"If you are going to spend all night with my daughter, by Hopi law you are married. Is this what you want?" Kikmongwi pokes Kiowa in the chest.

Anoki translates. "He wants to know if you are going to make a dishonest woman out of me by keeping me out all night, or if you will make me a happy bride."

"That is the desire of my heart."

"It is the desire of my heart also!" She pecks him on the lips, then turns to her father and shouts, "We are to be married!"

"Well, then, be married!" Kikmongwi raises the whooping celebratory cry, and his warriors follow. They take one another's hands and dance in a circle around Kiowa and Anoki.

Kiowa awkwardly grins and waits for them to stop shouting before he breaks the bad news. "Tonight will not be that night. As you know, Anoki, I must pass the test."

"Will I ever see you again?" Anoki asks, feeling the string to her heart pull tight. She takes his hand and searches for evidence of his power over her.

"If I am true and if I can hold your flame the way Hopi do, then doubt me not."

"If you can't?" she asks.

"Then I will not return."

Anoki wraps her arms around his neck and sobs. "I would fill every canyon with floods from my tears if that were true. Do not make me like Ayko, wandering in and out of caves repeating your name over and over again. Please, I'm begging you, do not make me an ugly, lonely old woman."

"No, no, do not do that, sweet Anoki," Kiowa whispers.

"You are my chief. Oh, why did you have to discover us, cruel father? I only had to wait till dawn."

"Come now, Anoki. The smiling sun will shine on us tomorrow and dry your tears from this cold night." Kikmongwi pats his daughter on the shoulder.

The gentleness of this tribe is so different from Kiowa's. He's reminded of his noble deer friends. *Strange that they should have the same dignity and trusting expressions.*

Kida follows the Hopis' tracks all the way to Kiowa. She hears the whooping celebratory cry and mistakes it for the war cry. *I am coming, my love! If you must die, I want to die also!* She hurries through the shadows. She spots what she thinks to be the war party. Anticipation builds. She hears Kiowa speak calmly with no real fear in his voice. Her worries dispel. *But why are there so many Hopi warriors?*

She bites her bottom lip and maneuvers to a position where she can quickly grab one of the Hopi and slit the man's throat. As she does so, she sees that no one is threatening Kiowa at all. *I don't understand; they have the numbers.* She watches patiently and sees Kiowa embrace Anoki. A sharp pain stabs her all the way to her heart.

Is my knife sheathed in my chest? She looks down at her hand.

The agony is so swift, she hears the fractures of her breaking heart. *Oh, Mother...* she sobs. In that instant, Kida immediately understands the cause of all Kiowa's hidden pain. The happiness on his face. And the agony in her chest.

Kida seethes with rage. She bites her lip so hard, blood pools in her mouth. She points her knife at Anoki and takes a blood-spitting oath. "Your spring of love swells my river of hate. The earth is our mother, but she will soon bury you in the naval of her tomb. I will not stand for this! None of us will stand for this dishonor! You will pay with your life, foolish Hopi girl!"

CHAPTER 39

When Paw and Kiowa return to camp, the squaw line up. Their gushing eyes, pretty smiles, and waving hands welcome the men home.

"Hello, great war chief! Do you need my help putting your things away?" Dancing Fawn offers.

Now that I know what you really want, I will not even give you a sideways glance, Kiowa thinks. He proudly lifts his head and presses his lips until his jaw tightens. His eyes rest on the distant horizon as Night Wind walks straight on.

Paw collects all their presents and counts them. He laughs at the safe distance the girls keep from Kiowa. It is as though some invisible line has been drawn that they dare not cross.

"A whole heap of pretty faces will test the love in your heart by tempting your eyes. Do not feel ashamed if your eyes lead your hands. No young man could be expected to keep his hands off so much longing beauty."

"Be quiet, Uncle! If I did that, I would be an enemy to love. Always you and Makes Trouble tease me with words. My love is not drawn by my eyes or my hands, but by my deep heart."

Paw sighs. *He is dead. Stabbed through the heart by some woman's magic. He will never be the same now. If I were him, and those girls were running up to me, I would trade that one woman to hold even half of these girls, and there would be a dozen children by next spring. What a fool!*

"How are you feeling?" Willow asks, handing him a comb and her heart.

"Better!" Kiowa answers, patting his belly. "My hunger has returned to me."

"Then I will be by your tepee later and will bring you all the meat you can eat. You have been without good meat for far too long."

"Thank you, Willow. Tell your sister Kida hello for me."

Riding past his tepee, Kiowa stops at his mother's home. He dismounts Night Wind and barges into her wicker hut.

"Welcome home, Kiowa," his mother says. Grass Woman stands, dusts her buckskin skirt off, and greets her son with a huge hug and a wet kiss on the cheek. She motions toward her guest. "Kida has been telling me of her trip to trade with the Hopi."

Kiowa stiffens.

"She says she had hoped to find you and your uncle, but she only found Paw's trail."

"Yes. He was easy to find. I was able to find his trail there and followed it back," Kida says with a half-smile.

If you could follow his tracks, you could follow mine. I must find out how much this fox knows. "You have always been a good tracker, Kida."

"I can catch anything that leaves a trail!" Her half smile expands into a full smile.

"Wonderful. Mother, may I speak with you by yourself?"

Kida uncrosses her folded legs and leaps to her feet. "I was leaving. I just wanted to tell you something, Grass Woman, that I thought you must know. But I can see that Kiowa will most likely tell you himself."

Kiowa looks away.

"Kida, stay. You are like a daughter to me. Anything Kiowa has to say, he can say in front of you."

Both women turn their attention to Kiowa. Smiling mother and jealous frowning squaw make a strange mix of expressions.

"Well, since we are the family with Taime, I thought we could start the sun dance early in the spring instead of in the summer."

"What a strange request," Kida says with a scrutinizing scowl.

"Yes, indeed," Grass Woman says, looking from Kida to Kiowa. She lowers her hand and takes Kida's, thinking she's pieced together the cause of this strange request.

"I just feel like it would be better for the tribe if we had answers to questions before summer."

"Questions like?" Grass Woman grins excitedly, putting her arm around the woman she assumed was her soon-to-be daughter-in-law.

"Questions that will send me on my life's journey. If it is possible, do you think we can hold it in three—no, four—moons?"

"Why not tomorrow?" Kida smirks sourly.

Grass Woman's smile beams so wide, she shows her missing teeth. She lifts her hand to cover the blemish. "Yes! Yes, we can. I will tell Onendah. He will be cranky, but he is always that way now."

The next morning, Makes Trouble and Kiowa ride through the village.

"We begin in three days. Treat each other with honor these next few days. We do the dance of the sun. Prepare! Remember to stay away from bear, skunks, rabbits, and buffalo hearts."

Kiowa holds the magic pouch, containing the carved Taime figure, up high so everyone can see he has the power to call the dance.

Each person they greet gives a whoop of understanding and an "Ah-hoe!" vote of confidence.

After Kiowa and Makes Trouble finish informing the entire tribe, Kiowa searches for his uncle.

"Where can he be?"

"If I know your uncle, he is teaching the rabbits how to wrestle."

"Of course he is. I will come to your tepee later. Let me have words with my uncle for now."

Kiowa rides away and finds his uncle in the soft sands by a stream.

"May I speak with you?" he says, interrupting Paw's lesson.

"Wait!" Paw turns back to his student. "Grab my wrist like this," he says as he extends his arm and encourages the youth standing next to him.

The boy does as he's instructed.

"Now pull me into you and use your hip to lift me off the ground."

The boy lifts Paw's muscular body off the ground with little effort. He begins twirling Paw around. "Ha! Ha! Look at me," Snake Tongue shouts, spinning faster and faster. "I have a mighty warrior on my back."

"See, Snake Tongue, now you don't have to go spreading lies around the village. The next time Soaring Sparrow tells you lies, grab his wrist and throw him on the ground." Paw stands up and pats the boy on the head. "Size does not matter when leverage is on your side. Now, remember, we make deals like we wrestle. We always seek leverage."

"Uncle, please!" Kiowa interrupts. "I must speak with you."

His stern, frustrated expression and stomping foot make his nephew look less like a man and more like a child who needs to relieve himself.

"Of course. Go on." He motions with his hand.

"I wish to speak with you alone."

Kiowa leads his uncle away from his students. They walk in silence until they are away from unwanted ears.

"Thank you for telling me about that sacred place."

"Ah, so you found it."

"I did," Kiowa says with a relieved expression.

"So will you be having a son?"

Kiowa bits his bottom lip and shakes his head.

"What is it you want with her if you don't want that?"

"I want to be with only her…"

Paw folds his arms, an indication of a protest Kiowa had not anticipated. "You want to follow the Hopi way?"

"Hear me, Uncle, before you judge me. You have taught me since I was a rabbit, and now I am a Dog Warrior. I do not know what to do with this love I carry, so I asked my mother to sun dance. I do not know how to ask permission from the tribe. She says she will ask Onendah, but she hasn't done anything! I need to have my vision to test my manhood to know whether I am worthy of Hopi love. They have some flame that will burn me up if I am made of leaves. If not, my flame will burn her up like she is leaves. Are we both leaves, or are we both carrying the flame? Someone is bound to get burned!"

Paw says nothing for what seems like an eternity. His eyes shift from side to side as he weighs options out in his mind.

"Does any of this make sense to you, Uncle?"

"No."

"Please, Uncle! Speak your thoughts so my hope will not be crushed into shame."

Paw lifts his finger and says, "Here is what I know. But you already know what I know. Your brother said it when you wanted to bring the Hopi girl to the tribe the first time. The tribe will never allow a warrior like you to marry an outsider like her. I have seen women brought and burned at the stake before. I have seen them shot with arrows. It is always the warriors who think they can bring strange women out. It is always squaws who kill them. Maybe if you marry Kida first, have a child or two with her, then pretend to steal Anoki, she could be your second wife."

Kiowa's face twists in extreme disgust. "I could never be with Kida."

"She is the best of our women, and everyone says you will pick her."

"Who says that?"

Paw shrugs. "Everyone!"

CHAPTER 40

"Everyone is wrong! I will never be with someone I do not love. I will dance in front of Taime and find another way," Kiowa retorts.

"Even if you dance, do you think Naukolahe will show himself? Why do you think he left Taime with us?"

"I do not know. Taime is just a bundle with a painted stone in it. The Hopi have this story about the creation of Indians. Tawa is a god who grows and creates. Look around you. Can you not see all that grows? Would you rather hold a bundle in your hand or seeds that will grow?"

"Nephew, I love you dearly. Listen carefully to what I am about to say. Never! Ever! Repeat those words to me or to anyone else in the tribe. You are sure to lose favor. Ever since Taime was delivered to us by the Apache man who married into our tribe, everyone believes in its power."

"I do not know what I believe anymore."

Paw puts his hand on Kiowa's shoulder. "Believe in your power!"

"How can an Apache man marry in, but a Hopi girl cannot?"

"Does your Hopi girl have a great power she can offer the tribe?"

"No, not that I know of."

"If she did, wouldn't she have already used it to protect her father?"

"Yes, of course."

"There is your answer. She has no power. She's just a weak girl who will be tasked with cleaning animals, washing dishes, watching over children, and helping elderly."

"A slave? That is not what I would want for her."

"Kida would have to give her permission for a second marriage. As first wife, she could say no and burn Anoki at the stake."

"If Anoki has a baby before Kida, she would surely burn her at the stake." Kiowa states mournfully.

"Do you want to take that risk? Once you bring the Hopi girl to the village, her life will never be the same. And knowing Kida's wrath, she would put the fire out and start it over for days at a time. Just to teach you a lesson. That is what I see. What is your plan besides the dance?" Paw asks.

Kiowa's shoulders slump.

"Later tonight I was going to jump in the river and float down to her."

"And then?"

"I would steal a horse and we would move to the north until we reached the everywhere waters."

"I see. What would you do then?"

"I would build a canoe and sail us far away from all of this!" Kiowa says, waving his hand over the tribe. His thoughts flash back to Kida. "Has Kida told the other girls that she will cut them if they come near me?"

"How could you hear this but not hear that she loves you?"

"I didn't hear it. I just figured it out. The girls smile and wave at me. They have presents, but they keep a safe distance."

"That did not seem odd to you? You have enough furs to cover ten of them and enough meat to feed all of them. Is one wife really better than all of those wives?"

Kiowa shakes his head. "You are teasing me, Uncle."

"Maybe just a little, but the truth is this, no matter who you seek to be with, Kida will not make life easy for you. She will challenge them and scourge them with fire if she can. If she can catch you and marry you, she will."

"Then my plan is best."

"Think, Kiowa. Why is my name Paw?"

"Because anything with paws, you can find."

"Can Kida not follow two trails leading north?"

"What am I to do?"

"You need an answer to a riddle. The pieces you have now are Kida, Makes Trouble, the tribe, Anoki, her mother, her father, and me."

"I don't think I can carry all those pieces. I only want Anoki in my tepee."

Paw laughs. "When you take a woman, her parents will never let her go freely. She is not a horse that runs wherever you lead. You will take her family as well. And we are not pieces you bring into your tepee." He presses his hand to Kiowa's chest. "We are pieces inside your heart that come together for you."

"Kida is not in my heart."

Paw laughs and puts his arm around Kiowa. "Your mother does not know how to speak to Onendah. Probably she is taking her time thinking of a gift for him."

"Why would she bring him a gift to do his duty?"

"If someone asked you for a favor, would you not want something in return?"

"Of course."

"We must find a gift for Onendah or he will think us bad company. Until I can find out what he wants, you must promise not to run from us, Kiowa. You would break my heart. Your mother's heart. And, eventually, your own heart."

***

On the first day of offerings, Paw delivers ten beaver furs.

"I thought you might like to have these in the coming winter months. They will keep your feet, hands, and head warm. How is your health these days?"

Onendah glares through the slight opening in his tepee flap. He sucks his teeth and squints his eyes.

"Both are good," the medicine man grumbles, letting the tepee flap close.

I must have brought the wrong gift. Paw rubs the back of his neck and wonders what else Onendah might need. *I cannot know what an old man needs. I'm going to go watch the slaves lift the great cotton timber pole. I bet my best horse they can't do it without crushing one.*

Later that night, at the campfire, Two Moons beats a slow, steady beat on his drum.

"What did Onendah say?" Kiowa asks with great anticipation.

"He said he needs us to come back tomorrow. Old men have great needs." *What could that wise old owl need? Worse yet, how am I going to get it without my best horse?*

The second day, while the tribe gathers materials for the sweat lodge, Paw brings six otter furs.

"What do you think of otter?"

"These furs are soft and pleasing to my old bones."

Paw sees his opportunity to ask for an audience, but he is cut off just as he opens his mouth.

"What I could really use are some silky mink furs."

Because mink is a highly prized fur, Kiowa and Paw have to travel a great distance to find them.

"Of all the times to lose a bet, you chose the moment I need you most?"

"You do not have to remind me, Nephew. My bottom is sore riding this... this thing!"

"That ugly beast is what you get for being such a fool. All my life you tell me to plan for this and plan for that. What was your plan when you lost your horse?"

"I did not have one, and this is the only animal my friends would lend me. Let this be a lesson to you."

"Hee-haw! Hee-haw!" Even Paw's donkey seems to laugh at him.

"I could walk faster than that monster," Kiowa growls. *Every moon that passes by is one less moon Anoki and I will have together. How could my uncle be so foolish?*

In just a few weeks, the two catch as many mink as they can find. They trade for the rest, which takes another week.

"Uncle, there must be a better way. The sun dance is delayed and the tribe must be angry. We are nearly at the time we would have danced anyway."

"The medicine man's powers are great. My magic isn't anywhere near as strong as his. It would be like comparing an ant to a grizzly bear. He renews our power. In his vision, he was a shaman. He passed the test, and now we are all indebted to him."

"You make new fears rise in my heart."

"Why?"

"What if my vision tells me to be a shaman?"

"Why would your vision do that? You are already a warrior. In my vision you were a warrior."

"Two Moons says that no one can have a vision for you. You must have your own."

"It would be terrible for you to be a shaman. No one would let you out of their sight. You would spend your days casting spells. Searching for magic. Trapping souls. It is a hard life."

When Paw returns to Onendah's hut for the third time, the old man awaits him eagerly.

"Come in! Come in! What have you brought me now?"

Onendah leads him to an empty floor space. He points at the cold dirt.

Paw sits down.

"WHAT ARE YOU DOING?"

CHAPTER 41

Paw leaps to his feet. He looks behind him.

"THAT IS WHERE MY SPIRIT WIFE SITS!"

"I'm so sorry, Onendah. I thought you wanted me to sit there."

"If I had a bear rug here, I think my wife's spirit would be so happy to rest upon it," Onendah says with a wrinkled smile that shows his cracked yellow teeth.

"Hmmm…" Paw *humphs*. He walks over to the door, puts his moccasins on, and departs immediately.

Kiowa greets him with a broad smile. "Everything is ready for the sun dance. The pole is deep in the earth. The buffalo-calf hides have been nailed by their lips all the way up to the top. A heap of elk horns circle the base. Eagle wings are tied at the very top, but I am not certain how they got them up there. The sweat lodge is ready. What is wrong?"

"He wants a bear hide."

Kiowa's smile drops to a frown.

"And it had better not be a little bear. We are going to need to hunt the biggest bear we can find. It is a large empty space." Paw emphasizes this by opening his hands as wide as his arms can stretch.

Will the flame in your heart even burn as bright, Anoki? Or has the sun of love dimmed to a star? Maybe her father will force her to marry another, he thinks. His fear causes his heart to rage with jealousy.

In the coming week, Paw and Kiowa trap and kill a grizzly bear. As Kiowa pulls bloody meat from the bear hide, he imagines scalping some poor fool who steals his "little woman."

Though the bear hunt is much faster than the mink hunt, the tanning of the hide and the prepping of the fur take just as long.

"Now the tribe waits for Onendah. Let us drop off these gifts before the dance begins," Paw says, interrupting his thoughts and pulling him back to reality.

"If this is the only way to happiness, Uncle, then why am I so miserable?" Kiowa informs his uncle as they wrap the bear fur.

"You are on the path for certain, Nephew. This is how you get there. Did you not have to cross a dreary dry desert to get to the beautiful Havasupai falls?"

Kiowa and Paw come to Onendah with their fourth offering. When Onendah sees his gift, he welcomes Paw with open arms. Paw struggles to get the bear hide through the opening, while Onendah gleefully tugs on it. He pulls and pulls until it disappears like a mouse in a snake's mouth.

"Wait here," Paw tells Kiowa as he enters the tepee.

After adjusting the fur every way possible, Onendah finally finds a place that suits the hide and himself.

"I would ask you to stay," said the wise medicine man, "but my wife's spirit has just arrived, and we would like some privacy. Tell the tribe we will begin the dance soon."

Not wanting to be rude or to offend the great medicine man, Paw hides his frustration and leaves the tepee just as he has the previous times.

When Kiowa sees the same disappointed look on Paw's face, his rage explodes. "You tell that crazy old man that I am going to have a meeting with him! You tell him right now!" Kiowa shouts, making a scene.

Paw holds up his hands and tries to calm his nephew down, but the love-struck warrior cannot be soothed.

"Let him meet with his wife, and he will be in a better place when we come back tomorrow. Trust me, you will understand when you are married how sacred alone time is."

"I am getting my tomahawk and my scalping knife. If that old fool thinks he can make a mockery of me, he is gravely mistaken."

Kiowa keeps his word, storming off to his tepee. He promptly returns with both weapons in hand.

"Let us come back tomorrow, Nephew. Come follow me. You are tired and hungry, and this crime will only make things worse for you." Paw puts his hands up and pushes Kiowa back. "Think of Anoki," he whispers under his breath.

The sound of her name calms the young man. The fighting fires are almost immediately extinguished, but for one last spark, "We meet with him tomorrow! Or else…"

"Yes! Tomorrow."

The following morning, Kiowa stomps over to Onendah's tepee. He slaps his hand on the buffalo-hide flap and shakes the whole tepee.

"Kiowa, what a surprise. How nice it is to see you. Please come in."

Shocked by the old man's hospitality, Kiowa ducks down and nearly dives into the medicine man's tepee. One of the first things he notices is the strong scent of cedar.

"Leave your knife and tomahawk outside," Onendah orders.

"Why? In the presence of so many captive souls, do my weapons intimidate you?" Kiowa sassily responds.

"We use the knife, the arrow, and the tomahawk to raid. When you bring them into my tepee, I think you are not done raiding. However brave you think you are, you are no match for my magic."

The two stare each other down. When Kiowa sees that Onendah is as firm as stone, he turns and sets his weapons at the door.

Behind Kiowa, Paw gently taps on the door and is invited in as well.

Onendah wears a big smile on his face and invites his guests to sit down by the fire he has just lit. The early-morning light passes through an opening in the tepee and illuminates every lash of time on the medicine man's wrinkled face.

"Your uncle has been helping me improve my home. He brought me those soft furs. What do you think of them?"

Kiowa had never thought to stack so many furs on top of each other, placing the softest ones on top. "It feels really comfortable," he answers, looking about.

"Yes, your uncle brought me a bear hide as well, which we used to cover the cold earth. My wife came and visited me last night. She told me that I needed new stories to tell her. She was bored with the ones I had and went to some other fire, where they tell better stories." After a brief pause, Onendah continues. "Kiowa, you have become a great warrior. Many feathers fill your war bonnet. Tell me, will you soon marry a woman and replenish the warriors that have fallen?"

"Yes, tell us, Kiowa, who do you favor for a bride?" Paw asks with his hand stretched out and waving over the fire.

Losing all his bluster, Kiowa hesitates. He blushes and stutters. "The—the-r-e is a woman I fav-o-r."

Onendah's smile broadens. "What is her name?"

"She is the sun in my heart. I feel the warmth of her rays resting upon my face and passing into my mind. I truly desire her more than any other woman."

Onendah looks at Paw. His smile begins to fade.

"Like me, this woman will be eager to hear you utter her name. Tell me, Kiowa, few things make good stories. But love is a magic that still excites me. It will certainly excite my wife. Who is this woman you speak of?"

"Her eyes twinkle like the stars, and when she speaks, it is as larks upon my ears…"

Onendah reaches for Kiowa and pats him on the leg. "Yes, Kiowa, I understand that you favor her, but what is her name?"

"I feel afraid and at peace when I am around her. I am on fire, then cold as ice…"

Losing interest, Onendah motions toward the door and begins to speak. "Ahem…"

"Her name is Anoki. She is the Hopi princess," Paw interjects.

Onendah gasps. He sits upright and adjusts his folded legs. "The tribe will never allow you to marry a Hopi," Onendah says sternly.

Kiowa's shoulders slump, and the excitement rushes out of him.

Onendah laughs. "Oh, stop acting like a child! Is this why you have brought me all of these furs?"

Paw and Kiowa look at each other with blank expressions.

"I can see plainly that it is!" The old man pats his knee and picks up a long wooden pipe. Raven feathers hang off the end. Carvings of his wife and children tell his story. He uses a scrap of wood to light the tip. When he holds the pipe up to his mouth, he puffs on it and gets the tobacco glowing red-hot.

"If you wanted to know my thoughts on the girl, all you had to do was ask."

Kiowa shoots a death glare at his uncle. Now Paw's shoulders slump.

"Of course, I cannot refuse you now that you have helped me so much and made me and my spirit wife so happy. But there is a matter you must consider. Our people are free. We roam these plains and travel the earth and mountains acting out of necessity. When hunger causes us pain, we kill our four-legged brothers and sisters. We do this to sustain ourselves. We seek rivers because our mouths are dry and our thirst will do anything for water. We kill our enemies because they have planted hate in our hearts. But what we do for ourselves, we do out of our own desires. Neither you nor I can force another Indian to accept what nature tells him he cannot."

"Neither nature nor necessity can make me control my desire. I am telling you, Onendah, I need Anoki as the eagle needs long wings!"

Onendah draws a deep breath and exhales a plume of smoke. He hands the peace pipe to Kiowa, who takes a puff and then passes it to his uncle.

"Sudden joy has a small and dull flame, and is easy to blow out. Fire is always the victor since whatever it touches it will eat. Wouldn't you rather love hot, like fire, than cool like rain?" Onendah tempts Kiowa.

"Ah, that is what you said about lightning. I told her this and she was not happy," Kiowa confesses with regret. "Now I am not certain if I misunderstood you, but I do not want to make her sad. My heart cannot bear it."

Onendah sits up and folds his legs. "Let me say it this way. The more honey you eat, the happier you will be. Are you sure you wouldn't rather be with a few of our Kiowa women first? Looking on their pretty faces and lying in their beds might change your mind." Onendah raises a brow, testing Kiowa's devotion.

"I would rather stab my eyes out with a rock." Kiowa grimaces.

"Ha! Ha! Look there, he speaks true. I can see it in his eyes."

Paw smiles and nods in agreement, even though to him Kiowa's eyes look the same.

"Okay, Kiowa, I will consent to the sun dance. I see your wisdom now in getting it started early. Let us ask Taime what his will is concerning this forbidden love. If he favors you, then I will seek a vision. If not, there will be no vision and you will marry whoever the tribe decides."

Kiowa accepts this answer with a nod.

"Even if that is Kida?" Onendah inquires, tilting his head to the side in a way that makes Kiowa grit his teeth.

"I do not come to you because I have the answer. I come to you because I do not have any answers!" Kiowa seethes through his clenched teeth.

"Did you tell her that our love for our tribe is like a bolt of lightning? It eats everything it touches?"

Kiowa thinks back on what he said. *How can I tell these men, who think so highly of men, that I'm all made up of leaves?*

Kiowa detours the conversation back to his original concern. "My magic isn't strong enough to see what I should do next."

"You are talking about magic, and I think Onendah speaks of how we love," Paw corrects his nephew.

Kiowa's face goes numb. All of his features paralyze at once. *Where are Makes Trouble's wise thoughts when I need them? Why did Moon Beam not leave one crafty ember before he abandoned me?*

Onendah lifts his hands. "Our love consumes with a spark anything it touches. You know this. It is a beautiful violence, with passionate ends. But it is better to be the bolt than the tree. At least the lightning gets to decide which tree and how many strikes! Ha! Ha! Ha!"

Finally, a thought leaps into Kiowa's head like a prancing pony. But it appears as a question. "Is that what happened with your little woman?"

Onendah stops laughing. His face grows as serious as Kiowa's.

"He could curse you, Kiowa," Paw whispers.

CHAPTER 42

Onendah holds his hand up to silence them both.

"No, that spark did not burn my wife. Instead, it worked like a divine needle and sewed the fabric of our souls together. My greatest enemy, Time, worked his magic against me. He gave the Cheyenne many moons to brew a terrible hateful spell against me," Onendah confesses with supreme sorrow in his eyes.

If you cry, how can you have the greatest magic? Kiowa wonders, as his uncle speaks up.

"What is this spark you speak of?" Paw asks, genuinely curious.

"It is what costs you the things you love most," Onendah answers, looking for his pipe.

"So you hate the Cheyenne because they are the spark that took your wife and children from you?" Kiowa boldly asks.

"I have not had such good talk in a very long time. I am struggling for the words." Onendah looks down like he's searching for something. When he finds it, his face brightens. "Yes, the Cheyenne are my enemy, but so much time has passed that I cannot even remember their faces. Even though we found some of them and scalped them"—he waves his hand over the wall of trapped souls— "I could not even tell you which soul is in which prison."

"So who is your enemy?" Paw wonders.

"Time is the spark that took everything from me. That old devil even took my hate. Time is the enemy of everyone! With all these many moons, I have almost forgotten my wife's face. But she comes back to me sometimes, and that is nice, because it helps me remember her face and the love I have for her. That is our flame."

"A flame you can hold?" Kiowa desperately asks, reflecting on Anoki's words.

"A flame you both hold. A flame that does not burn out. Sometimes it is blue with sorrow, when one flame goes out. Sometimes it is red with passion, when both flames mix. Most of the time it blazes like the sun and it moves all about. I find it on my wife's lips. Her hands. I sometimes see it move into her eyes. She says she sees it the same way. It is always traveling from one Indian man to one Indian woman."

Kiowa and Paw listen to the old sage release the poetry of his soul.

"What is this flame?" Kiowa wonders.

"Not even I know that. No words can describe it. It is not even seen with your eyes, but *these* eyes." He points to his forehead. "It is not heard with these ears, but this one." He points to his chest. "To feel it is to truly be alive."

"Listening to this, I trust, with all my heart, that your magic is pure and true. I believe you will guide my heart, and so I put these things in your hands." Without realizing it, Kiowa signs that he has literally put his heart in Onendah's hands.

I will test your heart, Onendah signs back. *See if it is true.*

As he and Paw leave the smoke-filled tent, Kiowa can't help but notice how different the smoke and light mix in Onendah's tepee. He senses the old man's magic and trusts in his uncle's words.

"Do you think we would have gotten a different answer if we hadn't given so many gifts?"

"What do you think?" Paw challenges.

***

"I just don't know why I should care," Luther snarls, sharpening a stick with his Woodcraft Indian's knife. He holds the tip in the fire and watches it catch flame. Blowing it out, he inhales the smoke as he imagines Onendah would. It stings his young lungs. He coughs and hacks till tears well in his eyes.

"You are so stupid!" John says, turning to Charlie. "Who is 'Earth He Made It'?"

"The Kiowa call him Naukolahe. They call him, 'Earth He Made It.' He had two sons, Fire Boy and Water Boy. They came down here and killed all of the enemies so that the first humans could crawl out of the earth's naval."

John wipes his nose. He raises his hand with one arm and pokes his belly button with the other.

Charlie acknowledges him with a nod.

"Why couldn't Kiowa just marry whoever he wanted?"

"Normally, Kiowa could, but because he and his father were such great warriors, the tribe wouldn't allow him to marry a woman who didn't have Kiowa blood. To them it would be like breeding a wolf with a Labrador: Maybe you'd get a warrior, but chances are, you'd get a sweet dog that would lick an enemy's hand instead of a wolf that would bite an enemy's hand off. Since the Kiowa were a warrior tribe, they needed warriors."

Kevin swats at glowing embers that crackle from the fire. He raises his hand. "What if they just ran off and got married?"

"See, you boys are looking at this through little-boy eyes and not through Indian eyes. So let me put it into Indian perspective. Yes, it is true that Kiowa was free to do whatever he wanted. So he could have run off and married Anoki, but the tribe was equally free to do what it wanted. In this case, they would probably just hunt the couple down and kill them."

"He just told us that!" John shouts.

"Sorry! Gosh dang," Kevin shouts shrilly.

Charlie hushes his troop and continues. "For three days and three nights Onendah went without food and water. He did this to cleanse his body. Then he entered the wicker sweat lodge, so that he could cleanse his soul. All this he did so he would be purified before Naukolahe."

Zack gulps. "Did he see him?"

Charlie finishes his cup of coffee and pulls his lips up to his gums, sucking air through his teeth. "He sure did!"

***

As the final preparations are completed, Onendah strips down to his loincloth.

"*Nat aye, nah hay.*" The medicine man begins singing an ancient song and beating an old drum.

Outside of the sweat lodge, the Dog Warriors cover the woven wicker walls with buffalo hides. They weave strips of leather in and out of punched holes, stitching the skins together. One hide at a time goes up, until Onendah is sealed inside the earth's womb.

Inside the wicker hut, the temperature instantly rises.

By a camp bonfire, girls place meat down and line up in white deerskin skirts. With their faces painted white, they rest their arms on one another's shoulders and begin swaying back and forth. They offer one united prayer to Naukolahe.

"When he listens to your prayers, you will be happy. When he listens to your prayers, he listens to you. When he listens to you, you will be happy. When he listens to your prayers, you will be happy."

While they sway back and forth, the men fasten sage grass wreaths to their wrists and ankles.

Some of the Dog Warriors tie ropes to horned buffalo skulls. They march to the beat of a drum and shake their gourds. The skulls drag behind them, and buffalo teeth leave eerie grooves in the soft soil.

The elders begin beating a broad drum, while warriors quickly paint their faces and bodies.

Since Kiowa's family was keeper of the Taime, he paints his entire body with cold yellow paint that causes his skin to prickle. Everyone else paints their bodies green. He dips his fingers in green paint and draws them across his forehead and down both cheeks until he forms a triangle at his chin. The warriors do the same, but with yellow paint.

When he's ready, his mother paints a green sun and moon on his chest and back. He leans down when she finishes and allows her to slide a necklace with two eagle feathers over his head. He opens his mouth, and she places an eagle-bone flute between his lips. He blows on it and mimics the eagle's cry. After four blasts representing north, east, south, and west, she crowns him with a rabbit-skin cap and sagebrush wreath. Finally, she props a single eagle feather in his headband and whispers a prayer. "Follow your heart and release your prayer when you know exactly what to ask for."

Except for their body paint, the warriors are all decorated the same.

Concealed inside his tepee, Onendah shouts, "Naukolahe, Father of the Heavens, we thank you for creating the earth that all living things walk or crawl upon. We thank you for the creatures that fly and the winds that carry them and cool us. We thank you for the water and the creatures that swim. We know not why you created these things, but we know that we are your children and they are here to sustain us. We are grateful for your creations and their many spirits. We know you require us to kill and provide for ourselves and our families. We love our families as you love us, and we know that this time on earth is to prepare us for the greater worlds and better hunting grounds ahead, which you have also created over the vast heavens."

"*Hi ya!*" the warriors shout. Then they jump up and down, sending the girls and the entire tribe into action. The women call out, flicking their tongues and encouraging their men.

"Who has the courage to dance on the troubles of men?" Paw points to a large mushrooming boulder.

Kiowa and several Dog Warriors race up to the twelve-foot towering boulder. They fight one another for the right. With great difficulty, they claw their way to the top, until there is nowhere left to stand.

"You few have been found worthy. You many are not. Go back to the circle," Paw shouts.

"*Why ya, yi, hey ya!*" Kiowa cries out as he begins dancing on top of the mushroom rock.

"*Hey ya, hi ya,*" the warriors reciprocate in a chorus that makes the women and children smile.

And so the dance begins.

CHAPTER 43

The men, young and old, drop their drumsticks on a large taut elk-skin drum that vibrates, sounding like thunder. Their painted bodies hop up and down and take turns spinning in place. Somehow, their timing never offsets the rhythm when they strike the drum.

"*Why ha ya. Why ha ya. Wha nay hay ya. Wha nay hay ya.*"

They bend over and thrust their arms forward, beat the drum, then lean back and spread their arms out, flexing all their muscles. They contort their fingers to look like claws and demonstrate their spirit animals.

"*Hey yo hey, hey yo, hey,*" the men shout over and over again. After three repetitions, the women sing in a loud chorus and some beat their tom-toms and shake their rattles. "*Wanna hey, wanna hey, yo, yo heeeeeyyyyy ah-hoe.*" Their pitch drops off and the men pick up.

Women dressed in beautiful elk-skin gowns bring food out for the children, then line up. One woman pretends to row. The woman behind her does the same. They form two lines. Each woman from oldest to youngest follows suit. They slowly step and emphatically flip their heads so that their long hair swirls around their shoulders. Beneath their hair, their necks are painted with war paint, which flashes colors like the underpart of a blue jay's wings.

The men sweat profusely. Their painted symbols streak and smear all over their bodies.

When the sun sets, the tribe cries out, and many overexerted warriors pass out. They are carried away, while many of the warriors let loose their prayers. "Give me strength in battle. Victory over my enemies and protection from their weapons," Kiowa hears them say.

The women are harder to understand. They always say their prayers on the first day and make sure no one can hear them. Kida's prayer is unmistakable.

"Free Kiowa from his blindness and make him see the true path," Kida shouts, releasing a fistful of her best seed as a sacrifice.

Obeying his mother, Kiowa and a small band of warriors comprised of Paw, Makes Trouble, Two Moons, and Weasel Tail dance and beat the drum all day and all night. They leap. They hop. They squat. They spread their arms and spin around in a fanciful exhausting manner that makes their legs and arm muscles spasm and their backs ache. To everyone's delight and entertainment, they pour their hearts out and shout prayers.

"Can you hear me above all these prayers, Taime?" Kiowa whispers. "I do not think it is possible to attract Naukolahe's burning eye, with so many prayers, so I will be polite and wait for my brothers and mother to finish."

On the second day, Kiowa leans back and stares at the sun. The intense light forces him to blink and close his eyes. He prays for strength, then opens his eyes and begins a ritual that only the greatest warriors pursue. He stares and stares at the sun, blinking only when he has to. He prays. He fasts. He dances. His weak arms and legs move with less enthusiasm, so he compensates with a repetitive chant. "Am I made of leaves or something else? Who am I?" He focuses on the blazing amber light in the sky, and to the best of his ability, he ignores his numb legs and shaking arms.

At the end of the day, the women line up. They spread their arms out and circle like eagles. When they touch their fingers to one another's, they smile, then spin away from one another, forming a bigger circle. The next pair of women does the same. Each woman does this, all the way down to the youngest girl. Their chorus sings a beautiful song that rises in volume with the beat of the drum. Their voices grow louder and louder, until a large circle of spinning singing women raise their arms, cross them, and finish the song in a grand finale.

"Do you hear me, Taime? Are you ready to receive my prayer?" Kiowa cries out.

When he hears nothing, he continues to dance and stare at the sun, even though his friends and family stop dancing with him. Legs go up and arms go down. Sun goes down and stars go up. All night long, Kiowa dances, until early-morning light.

Knowing how much his would-be son suffers, Paw decides to bring Kiowa's pain to an end.

"Silence!" he shouts, holding Taime figure up.

The tribe goes quiet.

"You are ready for the test?"

Kiowa nods.

"To the medicine lodge!" Paw orders.

Kiowa steps off the boulder. His legs collapse. No one dares touch him. He struggles to his feet to the steady beat of the drum. The people cry out. He trots into a large dome wicker hut. A hole cut out in the roof lets sunlight rest on a circle of sagebrush.

The tribe packs in shoulder to shoulder.

"Naukolahe, please, give him the courage of the cougar and the strength of the bear," Kida prays.

Paw and Two Moons approach Kiowa with fistfuls of sagebrush. He takes it, and they lead him into a sage circle. His body is the only body completely illuminated by the early-morning sun.

Paw holds up a tough strip of leather.

Kiowa shakes his head no.

The tribe gasps.

Two Moons holds up a bear claw. He walks around the circle and shows everyone. Finally, he stops and holds it eye level with Kiowa.

Kiowa looks away.

"*AH-HOE!*" the tribe shouts.

Paw draws a long deep breath. He lets it out slowly as he holds up a severed eagle's leg with talons still attached.

Silence fills the room.

Kiowa nods.

The women gasp. The men cheer.

Two Moons holds another eagle leg up, with the talons also attached. The tribe screams to the point of madness.

Paw and Two Moons look at each other and then at Kiowa.

Kiowa lifts up his arms and shouts, "This is the test. Let us see if I am made of leaves… or something else." He strips down to his loincloth and nods to give the go-ahead.

Paw and Two Moons thrust the eagle talons into his chest. Blood streams as Kiowa grimaces and strangles his painful cries.

"Cougar courage, bear strength," Kida repeats over and over. She presses her hands to her lips and rocks back and forth. Tears well in her eyes.

Paw and Two Moons push sharp bones through Kiowa's flesh, pinning the talons in place.

Paw lifts his hand. A rope with a loop falls from the hole in the ceiling. Two Moons does the same and another rope falls.

They slide the loops over the severed eagles' legs and cinch them down. Two Moons looks up at the men on the roof and gives a signal.

Leather scuffs on wood, tightening the slack. Kiowa steps forward. His breathing is heavy. The drum begins to beat. The slack tightens until the leather creaks. Kiowa stands on his tippy toes, supporting his weight only a little. Mostly, he hangs by the weight of his body.

"ARRRGGGHHHH!" Kiowa cries out in extreme agony.

CHAPTER 44

Paw takes the sage out of Kiowa's hand and replaces it with Kiowa's bow. Two Moons replaces the sage in Kiowa's other hand with a medicine bag.

Kiowa's chest is on fire and his flesh is tugged so tight it feels as though it is going to tear from his body. He wishes it would. Instead, it stays intact and suspends him in torment. He spreads his arms and cries out, "WHO AM I?"

As the drum picks up, Onendah shouts, "Though it is not my time to go back to you, Naukolahe, I ask special permission to meet with you face-to-face and discuss a matter of importance. When the fire is lit and burns with the white flame of love and I am found worthy, I will ask you in that special place if you will permit me to enter." While saying this prayer, Onendah pauses periodically to hear Kiowa's shouts. "What more could he offer? If he is ready, I am ready!" Onendah whispers, carefully searching his heart for any doubts.

The tribe responds by beating on the drums, shaking their rattles, pounding on their tom-toms, and blowing their flutes.

Gushing women sympathize with him. They cry out, "Kiowa!"

The rest of the tribe chants, dances, sings, and praises Kiowa's courage. Two Moons and Paw push on Kiowa's feet to spin his body around.

Children outside of the medicine man's sweat lodge spread word to their parents, who tell their neighbors, who run and tell Paw. Whispers escalate to soft voices. Imaginations begin to wonder whom he seeks and what the reward will be. When the excitement dies down, time idles. Each Indian imagines receiving a gift. Paw wishes for a wife. Makes Trouble wishes for many wives. Kida wishes for Kiowa as a husband. Women wish for more children. Children wish for more food. Everyone wishes for more and more. Nothing less.

Having fasted for many days before the sweat lodge, Onendah's body is completely empty of food and waste. As Kiowa hangs in the medicine lodge and the sun sets, Onendah feels it is the right time to light the sacred fire.

"It gives me comfort to know that the warrior who has asked me to suffer suffers with me."

A smile lifts his wrinkled cheeks.

"Help me. Help me, Mink Woman. Send your spirit wife. You are the harvester of love, and I need your spirit and strength to find the answers that this young couple seek."

As he leans in to light the fire, the pile of moist wood explodes into flames that burn orange at first. He chants, "Way ah hey, ah, hey."

The tribe circles his wicker hut and watches smoke plume out from underneath. They lock hands and sway, repeating his words.

All day long, Kiowa hangs and stares into the sun. Once the sun sets, Two Moons gives the order to drop Kiowa.

The ropes release. Kiowa's limp body falls. Instead of hitting earth, his spirit passes through his body and splashes into water.

Kida rushes to him and hoists up his head. She pours water down his open mouth and wets his face with her tears.

"Now you see! You see that it is me who will catch you!"

Outside, a red cloud of smoke plumes out the top of Onendah's sweat lodge. It grows thick, then changes through all the colors of the rainbow and crackles in sparks like the stars before it completely disappears.

Children run about shouting, "Onendah has vanished. We must not hurt any animals or any people till he returns."

Though the adults ignore this nonsense, one of the largest warriors, whom they call Bull, stands where Onendah's door once was. He holds a whip and lets the onlookers know that no one will trespass on these sacred grounds.

Inside the sweat lodge, the fire fades from blue to celestial sun-kissed orange. Onendah reaches out with his wand and touches the flames. Instead of burning hot, the flames freeze ice cold.

"There you are, Water Boy. Now send your brother."

Sparks fly off his wand as he thrusts it into the frozen flames. They change the flames from ice to blinding white starlight.

Inside the medicine lodge, Paw kneels down by Kida and hands her a bowl of broth. "Pour this down his throat and see that he drinks all of it." Makes Trouble kneels down by his sister. He pats Kiowa's hand and chants Kida's prayer. "Courage of the cougar, strength of the bear."

He helps her keep Kiowa's mouth open as the elder tribesmen sway their old bodies back and forth. Their leader, Two Moons, beats on a drum and keeps a steady rhythm throughout the night. He slowly blows on his eagle flute.

"Please, Naukolahe, hear my prayer," Kida prays, sensing a surreal vibe from Kiowa's body. "Bless Kiowa that he will see my love for him. Show him how true it is. Show him that I will do anything for him. I will give him the greatest gift a woman can offer. Life!"

Paw answers her with a smile and then a shrug when he sees her patting his hand. Her tears fall on Kiowa's face, mixing with his tears and trickling down his cheeks.

In his friends' and family's arms, Kiowa's body is safe, but his spirit is sinking. He exhales and sees air bubbles plume and break apart as they travel to the surface.

Down, down, down he goes, until light begins to fade. Before he ascends into infinite darkness, his spirit stops and suspends between both worlds.

Looking up at the sun, he knows he has Naukolahe's attention.

"Forgive me for doubting my magic," he begins, and sees his words written in symbols on air bubbles as they travel up toward the sky. *Ah, so that is how they reach you.* Feeling himself run out of air, he panics, but then he draws a breath underwater as easily as if he were a fish.

"I have not failed in heart or in strength. Now I humbly ask only a few things. If my love is true for a woman I am not supposed to have, let that love travel as freely as a seed in the wind. Bless it that it will find fertile soil and let this bud of love blossom into a flower."

As the bubbles travel up, Kiowa sees the sky turn amber orange, like someone lit a fire. Within seconds, the flames spread across the entire sky. He feels comforted that his spirit is under the water, but then, he feels himself rising and moving toward the flames. He turns toward the darkness but cannot force himself to sink into the depths. He tilts his head back and stretches his arms, accepting his fate. His body continues to ascend toward the fire in the sky.

Across the village, Kida has abandoned Kiowa to his uncle and her brother. She grabs her bow and arrow and disappears into the forest. No one sees her slip away, so no one can stop her. Had the law enforcer seen her, he would have whipped her. Kida's skill in clandestine escapes is equal to the men's.

"You are not a medicine man. You don't have the magic to do as Onendah does," Paw tells his unconscious nephew. "Come back to us. Do not go to the heavens, Nephew. Your place is here with your family and me. Look, there is your pretend brother, Makes Trouble. You belong with us."

Inside the sweat lodge, the medicine man's silver hair lays wet against his skin. A pool of sweat drenches the earth around him. His skin glistens. His chants become whispers. He transfixes on the coals as he shakes a rattlesnake's tail with one hand and waves an owl's wing with the other. With each breath, he seems to grow weaker. With one whooshing thrust, he tames the white flame down to a candlelight flicker. Before it can go out, he leans over it and inhales, sucking it up into his mouth. His mouth explodes with light like he's caught a star. It illuminates his face and his eyes. He uses both of his hands to push his jaw shut and keep the starlight trapped in his mouth. As the light begins to fade, he undoes the leather strings and opens the door. Instead of people, he sees stars. Instead of sky, he sees space.

As he stands up, his body is weightless. He moves slowly, because if he moves quickly, his spirit will float away. The walk in the spirit world is a walk of reverence. Onendah looks around at all the beauty the creator has made. He sees the divine's hand in everything. It humbles him.

"We truly are nothing." He sighs.

He rubs his old wrinkled eyes as thousands of stars sparkle around him. He moves forward, careful not to step on any of them. When he moves too close, they startle and fly away. Their glittering trails can be seen way off into the distant black horizon, where Onendah wonders if they reunite with their mothers.

Looking behind him, he sees Earth close enough to touch but far enough away to be seen in its glorious sphere. He looks at the moon and sees it hiding in the Earth's shadow. Beyond the moon, he sees many planets and watches all of these celestial bodies revolve around the sun. When the sun finally touches the moon, the pale light passes to him and causes his body to glow.

"Thank you, wife. I could not have done it without you. Now let us go and see what Naukolahe has in store for us."

The stars that remember him from his last visit aren't afraid of him. They draw near him and twinkle bright enough to light his way to the sun.

Onendah holds his hand up and looks away from the fireball sun.

"Great creator, I have come for wisdom. Do not be angry with me. I do not wish to stay."

Outside of the light, little children with rabbit heads and human bodies hop all around him. They stop, perk up, and use their human hands to wipe their faces clean.

"Hello, dreams. My brain is not idle tonight, so I will not play with you. I am here for a vision."

"Come play," the bunny children beg. They use their hands to bend space into playful forms like squirrels, otters, and mountain goats.

Past the rabbit people, images start to form in the Milky Way.

"Ah, there is the lake of time I have been searching for," Onendah says. He sits and folds his legs. The medicine man sees nothing but ripples.

"I will sit and wait for the waters to calm down," he decides. When the ripples of time finally settle, he sees a clear image of Kiowa marrying Anoki. He watches the tribe's response. At first they grow angry. But then their anger is amplified by a blurry-faced woman who Onendah presumes to be Kida, but this woman has no heart. Only a hole in her chest that howls with words like, "I have been wronged. I must be made right." The hole is so deep that nothing can ever fill it. The blurry-faced woman leads the tribe in persecuting Anoki.

"Come on, little woman, show me your face," he says, but the image doesn't form. He watches as the woman greets Kida with kisses and gifts. She's especially happy when Kida brings Anoki bound in ropes. The woman punishes Anoki with beatings and stabbings. When Kiowa tries to protect his love, the tribe seizes him and binds him. They force him to watch as the blurry-faced woman slowly and painfully severs Anoki's scalp while she's still alive. They chant and rejoice in her suffering. Their ferociousness offends Onendah, but it sickens him when he sees the blurry-face woman tie Anoki to a post and start a slow fire with wet bark. He shudders when the woman quickly puts out the flames and starts them again. The medicine man watches the flames scorch the Hopi princess, but what the tribe cannot see is that when they burn her, the flames burn Kiowa as well. First in his eyes, then his lips and hands, and finally his heart. His whole soul turns to ash with Anoki's body.

A cloud of darkness swirls about him. The rabbit children dance around the darkness and chant, "Avenge her! Avenge your love."

Then they hop over to Kida and hiss, "It is she! It is Mother! Mothers should not hate. Mothers should love. She has robbed herself. Robbed us all."

Kiowa seeks revenge.

When the blurry-faced woman comes into focus, it is not Kida, but Grass Woman's spirit inside Kida's body. That is where the vision stops. Onendah is not allowed to see Kiowa's revenge, only his suffering. But knowing the warrior's power, he is certain that nothing short of a massacre will come from this. With a heavy heart, the old man whispers, "Love is rough. Is this salt settled? Or can it be shaken and savored? Stirred and smoothed?"

CHAPTER 45

At first there is nothing, just the glory of space and all of the creator's majestic splendor. Onendah is about to return to his sweat lodge and awaken from his vision. But then he sees an image of the golden lance. The full moon moves over it and glows, giving the lance a peculiar power. The lake ripples and shows a new vision. Suddenly, a large gray wolf appears. Puzzled by what he sees, Onendah looks at the ghostly image and can't seem to understand it.

A flash of lighting cracks and a radiant white wolf comes from it. It is smaller than the gray wolf and sits next to the larger wolf like they are friendly with each other. The golden lance arcs over them as a full harvest moon rises behind the wolves. Briefly, Kiowa's and Anoki's human faces reflect in the glowing lake in front of the wolves.

"Now I understand," Onendah says with a weak smile.

***

Three weeks have passed since Onendah's vision. He relays everything to Kiowa in its entirety, which of course breaks the great warrior's heart.

Kiowa presses his hand to his wrapped chest to try to hold the pieces together.

"Soon you will see these scars. Was all this pain for nothing?"

"No. Let me finish." Onendah tries to comfort him, but Kiowa won't be comforted.

"I turn on my own people. How can this be? Is nothing to be done?" Kiowa asks, with frustrated tears swelling in his eyes.

"Something will be done," Onendah says, putting his hand on the great warrior's, "and I am just the man to do it."

Kiowa's sad face melts with a crooked smile.

"We will travel to the lake of life, up in the pine forest, where the wolves howl at the moon and the eagles build nests."

"But that is a day's journey. The hunters and the warriors are gathering to hunt the buffalo. Won't they notice if I am missing?"

Onendah cuts him off. "Every bird must leave its nest and fly. No one can tell it when it is ready. It must know on its own and it must summon the courage to do so. Are you ready to fly, Eagle Boy?"

Judging by Onendah's words, Kiowa realizes that he may be taking a long flight, and the thought of being without his mother saddens him.

"Let the tribe worry about its own belly; you have a destiny to seize. I suggest you use your hunger for love to flap your little wings and fly with me to the lake of flaming waters while the moon is full, or I cannot be certain my magic will work."

"I will be there," Kiowa says, looking at his mother's hut.

Later that day, Kiowa and Makes Trouble come up with a plan.

"You cannot look at your mother-in-law's face, ever!"

"Yes, I know."

"I'm serious. If you see her, you have to run away."

"I know!"

"For this reason, I will be the one to fetch Anoki."

"But her mother was taken away by the Navajo, so I can be the one to steal her away."

"You are not thinking. Think, my would-be brother. What if the black robes have returned her mother? They are not like us. They sometimes do strange things."

"You are right. I cannot take that risk. The black robes do strange things."

"Spend the evening with a mother you can look at."

When the sun sets, Makes Trouble is off and Kiowa is in his mother's hut.

"I am so happy for you," she says, handing him a plate of meat.

"You have been a wonderful mother," Kiowa says.

"You speak as though I am not going to see you all of my days, Kiowa. Give an old woman's heart peace. Never leave me to suffer the winters alone. Bring me grandbabies that I may spoil in the spring. Have you given any thought to your vision?"

"I have," Kiowa says, laying a log on the fire.

"Oh, Kida will be very happy. When will you tell her?"

Kiowa doesn't want to disappoint his mother, but he also doesn't want to lie to her.

"I think she already knows what I want."

"Oh... that is so good! I am so happy for you," Grass Woman says proudly, beaming with delight. "I am going to be the best second mother to her, Kiowa. You will see."

"You have always been a great mother to me. Do you remember when I fell asleep in the grass field hunting the deer?"

Grass Woman nods and laughs. "Oh yes. I could hear your teeth rattling like the snake's tail."

"You brought me a blanket and stayed out with me."

"Yes, I remember. We watched the sun come up."

"I want always to have sunrises with you, Mother."

"They always will shine in my heart and show me your face, brave son."

***

When Anoki receives news from Makes Trouble, she does not ask questions or waste time arguing. She simply smiles, excuses herself, and dresses in her nicest one-shouldered white cotton gown. She fastens her best bead necklace and whispers to her brother, "I will miss you."

"Where are you going?"

"To a real secret place!" Anoki smiles with a glow on her face Walpi has never seen.

"Can I come with you?"

"On one condition. You must find and ride your own horse. Night Wind is mine!"

"Oh, okay. I will go and ask Father if I can borrow one of his horses."

"You will ask Father nothing, you tattling bird. I would already be married if you had not rattled your lips like the snake rattles its tail. You will not interfere this time, dear brother. Either you will come with me now or Makes Trouble will add your scalp to his belt."

Anoki signs the last part, hoping that Makes Trouble doesn't see her signs.

Walpi swallows deeply and takes shallow breaths. "I will go with you, Sister."

"You are wise beyond your years."

With the small hours waning on, Kiowa bids good-bye to his aging mother. He watches her eyelids flicker before she falls asleep. When she begins to snore, he covers her with a buffalo blanket and kisses her on the cheek. "I will miss you terribly, Mother. Maybe in a few winters I will bring you children and you will accept them. For now I cannot let you rob me of my happiness. I will never be far from you, Mother. I am flesh of your flesh, heart of your heart. If you knew what was inside my heart, I know you would want this for me. It is true happiness, and I cannot help but be drawn to it."

He leans in and kisses his mother on the cheek.

"I will have Onendah watch out for you, and you will have Two Moons and Weasel Tail to protect you until *I return*."

A chilling thought crosses his mind. If I return.

With that, he rises to his feet, takes a sweeping glance, then wipes tears from his eyes.

Why all these tears? Tears for Mother. Tears for Anoki. Women drink our tears and force us to choose between them. Then they shed tears. What cruel creatures. Kiowa sprints to his tepee and fetches his bleached buckskin pants, some war paint, and a wolf-cap headdress. He plops his war bonnet on and exits the tepee.

Paw and Onendah are already mounted on their horses.

"Look at this pretty white stallion. Onendah found him just for you."

"You will need all of the sacred magic you can gather, and this white horse has more potency than any mustang on the prairie," Onendah whispers.

The three mounted riders make for a late-night band. They draw Kida's attention. Not because it looks like the three are going to do a raid—no, that would be normal—but because she watches Kiowa's tepee like a hawk. She has even found herself circling it, not really knowing why, but having a constant curiosity of all things he does. An impulse she can never ignore and can satisfy only by seeing him or being close enough to smell him.

CHAPTER 46

Never in my life have I seen the great medicine man Onendah ride off on a night raid. Why does he do this now? Kida wonders. She feels the impulse to follow them surge to its pinnacle and tip over to action. This sets curiosity off inside her mind, which reflects in her squinting eyes.

I am going to follow them and learn what they are doing, she thinks, racing for her horse.

Kiowa, Onendah, and Paw ride late into the night. They are the first to arrive at the sparkling lake, way up in the pine forest. As their horses come to a sudden halt, the Indians watch the sun rise. They relax and sing songs and wait for Anoki and Makes Trouble well into the afternoon and finally into the lingering sunset. Orange colors splash across the sky, turning clouds pink and blessing the pine trees with a powerful golden haze. Birds sing farewell to the day while crickets begin their nightly symphony. Firebugs ignite here and there. A wolf howls. An owl hoots. Racoons steal acorns from the squirrels.

"Are you nervous?" Paw asks with a teasing grin.

Kiowa nods. His emotions hurdle from one elated extreme to the other. The boy in him seeks his mother, but the man wants the woman who is replacing his mother. His stomach feels like it is flying and leaving the rest of him behind, which causes him to smile. But then his face stiffens, turning serious, and his eyes seem to be looking through the earth. Then the smile returns.

"It was the same when I took a little woman," Paw says with a comforting smile. "Between your father's death, her death, and the child she took with her, I am surprised my heart has any room left in it."

"You have a big heart and I have made a place in it."

"You have taken all the space in it, and now you have not told me your plan. Will you be leaving me as well? Can I come with you?"

"Onendah hasn't said, Uncle."

Paw searches Kiowa's face for the prospect of hope. He doesn't find what he's looking for. All he sees is his nephew looking for some sign of Anoki.

Off in the distance, where Kiowa can't see, Kida halts her horse. She ties him to a tree and paints her face and arms black. She crouches low and runs her fingers along the sharp edge of her rusty scalping knife. "If you are here and casting spells on Kiowa, Hopi girl, I will break your spell, steal your magic, and cast a spell of my own." She grabs her magic pouch and knife.

"I will gather wood and light a fire," Paw says, stepping off into the forest.

"I should have sent you to fetch her, Uncle. Makes Trouble is probably off creating some mischief."

"Change into your wedding clothes, Kiowa. We won't want any distractions when the ceremony begins," Onendah orders him.

Kiowa nods and removes the roll on the back of his brown-and-white pinto pony. He fastens a wampum around his neck and paints his horse.

Kida can hear their voices but cannot make out their words. Onendah has a habit of signing his words while he speaks, so she thinks she understands him to motion "ceremony," but she can't be certain.

Thoughts swirl in Kida's mind. *Surely Kiowa wouldn't be stupid enough to marry the Hopi girl and bring her back to the tribe?* She surveys the men and realizes that is their intent. She laughs and thinks, *Perhaps I should just go home and tell his mother what treachery her son plans. They will not be able to stop a herd of angry women.* She presses the cold blade against her cheek and shifts her calculating eyes. She slides it down to her chin and taps the tip of her bottom lip. She feels her heart burn with rage and decides to stay. *I will be swift! I will be silent! I will be deadly!*

Many hours pass, and the howls of the coyotes, the hoots of the owls, and the chirps of the crickets wear on Kida. She grows very sleepy and can't help but nod off.

Soon, the large pale moon takes on an orange hue. A blanket of stars glitters all around it and shine unnaturally bright. Aside from the sounds of nature, the only signs of humans are the crackling fire and the flute Paw plays. With a huff of his chest, he pushes out his cheeks and keeps a constant pressure on a small opening in the pine flute. As he wiggles his fingers in a slow, smooth pattern, the notes of a love song the Kiowa have played ever since there were Kiowa dance off his pipe and beckon the bride.

"I have done many things I should have been afraid to do but for some reason was not. Tonight, I am not certain why, but I have great fear," Kiowa confesses with a broad, nervous smile.

"It was the same for me when my little woman and I made promises to each other," Onendah says, nodding and blowing rings of smoke, one through the other.

On the opposite side of the lake, Kida is awakened by the distant *thud* of horses' hooves.

She sits up and sees a sight that turns her hateful flames into spewing lava.

"I don't know how you know where to go, Night Wind, but carry my precious heart to him! *Ya! Ya!*" Anoki wraps her fingers in Night Wind's mane. She leans forward and kicks his side harder. He goes from a trot to a sprint.

Makes Trouble, covered in black-and-white war paint and wearing his bonnet, rides a pinto pony, leading the most beautiful woman Kida has ever seen. What's worse is that she expertly handles Kiowa's horse, Night Wind.

It is as though he was made for her to ride him. I could never ride bareback that fast. I would fall off and die, Kida thinks enviously.

Kida tallies Anoki's beauty the way all women do: face, figure, and clothes. *I hate that your face is prettier than mine! I hate that your waist is smaller than mine. I hate that your breasts are larger than mine. I hate that you are more beautiful than I ever will be. I hate the gold arm bracelet on your slender arm. I hate your plain-woven dress. I could have made one just like it. It is a simple white dress with pretty beaded patterns. So what? Any woman could do that. After tonight, it will be blood red.* Kida seethes, placing her knife in her mouth. She smears black paint on her dress and feels the flames of jealousy burn until the veins in her eyes crackle red. She quietly crouches down until her belly rests on the cool earth, then slithers along. *Let us see if he loves you when I cut out your heart. No man can love a cold, dead woman, no matter how much his heart tells him to. Before morning light, your scalp will be woven into my dress,* Kida thinks as she quietly stalks Anoki.

Drawn to Kiowa like iron to magnetic love, Anoki works the mane and furiously attacks Night Wind's side with her heels. She lets him loose. His front legs fully extend. His back legs spring with a powerful thrust that cuts the earth and kicks soft soil up behind him. She makes the stallion live up to his wild name and sends him into a full sprint. The enthusiastic rider sails past Makes Trouble's inferior horse. He cackles and whips his horse for speed, but no animal is comparable to Night Wind.

Anoki's smile broadens and beams as bright as the moon. Her eyes sparkle like the stars above her head and brim with absolute joy. Her cheeks burn with bright hope. Her rich raven hair whips wildly behind her. She can feel the wind push hard against her face. Her lips part and she shouts her joy. "Kiowa, my great chief! Anoki is here!"

"Anoki!" Kiowa shouts. He lifts his arms to the sky. His face explodes with righteous conviction.

He holds his muscular arms out toward her. "Come to me!" Kiowa passionately proclaims. He watches her reflection in the lake. In the sparkling crystal reflection, he sees her majestic spirit. She doesn't seem like a mere mortal woman at all, but more like an angel riding a shooting star.

"Is it possible to catch a star?" Kiowa asks his uncle.

"With magic, anything is possible," Paw answers.

Paw watches as the warrior's features soften and turn to angst. At this moment he looks so much like his father, Paw can hardly tell the two apart.

"She is here, Uncle! Makes Trouble, my almost brother, has brought me the greatest treasure. He did it! She is here. Now I have everything!"

"He did," Paw says, patting Kiowa on the back. "Is that her brother way behind Makes Trouble?"

CHAPTER 47

Paw puts his arm around his nephew and feels reunited with Lone Wolf, his brother. He pulls Kiowa in tight and doesn't say anything, but part of him feels like he's losing a son.

When Kiowa breaks free from Paw's grip, the emptiness brings an immediate sorrow. As the warmth from his nephew leaves, Paw cherishes the honor he had in raising his "would-be son." For though he did not know the meaning of all the lessons and all the sacrifices, it is now that his purpose as provider, protector, and surrogate parent has come together. *My circle is complete. I was preparing this boy to be a man. The man is moving toward a beautiful woman. What could I offer greater than this?*

"Go from love to love," are all the words that dance off his lips. He draws a deep breath, raises his flute, and blows every emotion he's ever had for the boy into the most beautiful notes Kiowa has ever heard.

A bright yellow-orange harvest moon hovers over the dark pine forest. Anoki dismounts Night Wind once she brings him to a skidding stop. His coat is wet with sweat. He heaves and *neighs* as she dismounts. When her feet hit the ground, fireflies share her joy in exploding bursts of excitement. Her slender left shoulder is completely exposed and glistens in the moonlight. Her face is calm and determined. Her soul vibrates like a plucked string. Her hands rest by her sides. Her face wears a delicate expression. The way she looks at Kiowa is how every man wants his woman to look at him, not just on his wedding night, but every night. Her female power is wrapped in desire and absolute want. Where her gaze rests is the unmistaken object of her affection.

Kiowa's nervous smile melts away when he receives her power.

It is as though she is challenging him in a new way, and he does not shrink from the invitation, but embraces it. He points to his healed scars and wins a smile from her.

The way he looks at Anoki is the way every woman wants a man to look at her. A tender look that says, *You alone can quench this terrible thirst.* A confident look that ensures he will not shrink from love or manly duties, but will raise her up to multiply their love. A bold look that shows he will protect her and stomp her fear out with steadiness. A look of such love, he answers the eternal question her heart yearns to hear. The answer is, she knows now, she will never be alone again. Kiowa will always be there for her.

With her hair down and strewn all around her, she signals to the world that she is no longer single. Her beauty is magnified a thousand times by those silky black strands.

Kiowa is so taken aback by her loveliness, he doesn't rush up and sweep her off her feet like she expects. Instead, he admires her with an expression that she doesn't know how to interpret.

A gust of wind blows her hair around her face. She tilts her head and looks at him with inviting eyes and alluring lips. No man on earth could resist her.

He takes a step forward, then back.

Anoki blushes and flips her hair the way she imagines it will entice him. By the rise of his brows and the lift of his lips, she knows she has hit her mark.

His feet feel like needles on a compass, pulling him to his true north. Remembering his lessons with the deer, Kiowa approaches reverently.

"Kiowa!" Onendah shouts. He shakes his head and motions with his hand.

The two stand only feet from each other, and though they both want to embrace, the ceremony forbids man and wife from touching until they have made sacred promises to each other. Between the space that separates them, everyone present can feel their electric love crackling off the couple's tingling bodies.

Onendah steps between them. He carries the wrapped lance.

With an eagle wing in one hand he motions for Kiowa to stand closer to his right and then Anoki on his left. The two obey.

A million jitters explode in trembles of excitement off the bride and groom.

"The love you two share for each other is most pleasing to my eyes. Kiowa, I have never seen your face shine like the sun. It does your spirit much good." He turns to her and tickles her face with eagle feathers. "Her beauty glows like no moon I have ever seen." Onendah smiles and circles the eagle wing over his head. "I have seen in vision that your love is forbidden. Because you are Hopi, the Kiowa will do you harm. For this purpose, we have met in secrecy, to summon Naukolahe's magic. Do you both agree of your own free will that this is the reason we are here?"

The two look at each other and nod.

"Naukolahe will not allow love to die. It is his most precious magic. When a man and a woman find it, he shines his light so that you may grow it. It is his desire that you both be protected and preserved. He has shown me what must be done and I am prepared to do it. But before I do, I would like for you both to express your feelings for each other."

Paw places paint bowls at their feet.

Kiowa lunges forward and flexes his muscles as he throws his arms up over his head. He lowers them so that his hands are pointed at Anoki. He claps his hands together and locks his fingers.

"I have caught something that could not be caught."

His power overwhelms her and causes her to spin around in an excited twirl. Her hair lifts and twirls with her dress. She holds up her right hand. "And I have received your love."

She dips her finger in white paint and paints the shape of a heart on her palm.

"And I draw it on my hand and offer it back to you"—she extends her arm—"as my most precious gift."

She walks over to him and tenderly presses her hand to his heart, where there are three distinct scars. "Oh, how deep my love is for you. I put it here in your heart because this is where I know you will keep it safe. The bear marks the tree and so I mark my man."

Kiowa looks down at her hand, then back up at her. "In my vision, you were the fire and I was the sky. I have caught your flame."

He dips his hand in yellow paint.

"And?" Anoki asks with a hint of fear on her trembling lips.

"I am not made of leaves at all. I know now that I can hold your flame firm in my sky. It is not just a flame. It is a great fire, but it will not consume me. I will use my sky magic to fuse the fabric of our souls together and protect our flame from blowing out," he says as he draws from his heart, down his arm, and up her arm. "Staring at the sun, I went blind. My spirit eyes could see that our love for each other is as bright as the blinding sun. What power could be greater than that? With my magic and the power of the sun, I connect myself to you. You are my center. You are my home." He puts his palm on her heart, leaving his yellow handprint on her chest.

A broad smile lifts his high cheekbones and enhances his sharp jaw and strong neck. With his eyes he asks if she feels the same as he does. With his trembling hands and his words, he shines his light on every inch of her.

"These words do please me," she says, beaming with confidence. "The more love you give to me, the more I will have to give back to you. I will take the thread of time and stitch our souls together with the needle of adversity. We will be like the lake that reflects the stars. No one can tell where one begins and the other ends, and so it will be the same for our love. Our fire sky will burn forever!"

He takes her hand. They stare into each other's eyes, making a deep connection that only two lovers can understand and reciprocate.

Onendah looks at the painted couple. "Oh, Great Spirit, hear my words. We small, weak children need your wisdom. Let these my children walk in your strength. Let their paints mix like the reds and purples in your sunsets. Make their hands kind to each other. Their ears open to their needs. Their voices soft, with kind words always. Let them learn the secrets you have hidden under rocks. Show them how to conquer their enemies. Teach them how to keep their spirits clean so that when they return to you, they will not wear the blanket of shame. With this prayer, I now use my power to seal them as one." He raises a bundle that he's wrapped the lance in. His old hooked fingers untie the leather strands. When he unveils the weapon, the moonlight creates an arch, and it activates with a sun-kissed celestial glow.

Anoki and Kiowa gasp. Their emotions for each other are amplified in the weapon's presence.

"*Na he, no, na we nah ha*," Onendah chants. "Give me the power to bless their lives. I have done as you've asked, Naukolahe. I have brought these two before you and humbly request that you use your power on them now."

As he finishes his prayer, the lance grows so bright it forces them to shield their eyes. An arch of light rises over Onendah and cascades with beams of moonlight that illuminate the entire forest and turn night into day. A strange vibration echoes off the lance like pulsating crystal. The trebles are so powerful they shake the earth. Mist vapors rise off the forest floor and enhance the clean pine scent.

Onendah's irises glow.

"I pray for this gift," Kiowa says.

"I also pray for this gift," Anoki says.

Paw and Makes Trouble chant, "NAT HAY NAY HOE!"

"Anoki, don't do it!" Walpi shouts.

Anoki takes Kiowa's hand, terrified that he might fly away. She sees with her eyes, but she can't believe what her eyes tell her.

The lance's light touches the magic symbols Kiowa painted on her, and they begin to glow like sunlight. Her handprint transforms on Kiowa's chest and glows as well.

"Look," she says, pointing to the marks. "Our love is true. We are connected!"

Paw, Makes Trouble, and Walpi look away from the blinding light. Despite the difficulty, Anoki and Kiowa keep their eyes on each other, gasping as they are overwhelmed by the sun's radiant blessing.

"As Indians, you will be tracked and killed, but as animals, your tribe will never find you," Onendah shouts. "Kiowa, you have chosen this woman to be one with. She has accepted your decision. Now you must both choose to be something else. Tonight and every night after, you shall not be alone. You must touch what you desire to become and skinwalk into the animal you desire to be."

"What is skinwalk?" Walpi asks.

"Naukolahe, protect my children!" Onendah shouts. He lowers the radiant lance so that it divides Kiowa from Anoki.

With his other hand, he plucks an eagle feather from his bonnet and demonstrates what it means to skinwalk. Onendah closes his eyes. His irises glow behind his eyelids. He tilts his head to the heavens like he's concentrating. When he opens his eyes, the white turns yellow.

CHAPTER 48

In an instant his arms grow feathers and pop out of their joints at obtuse angles. They bend in the shape of an eagle wing and sprout feathers all over. His face elongates and his nose and mouth combine, protruding into a yellow beak. His eyes roll back. As he blinks, his human eyelids transform into leathery, yellow eagle's eyelids. His mortal speech is replaced with an eagle's piercing screech. He releases a long, drawn-out eagle's cry. He drops the lance when his hands turn entirely into wings, but he catches it with a newly formed eagle's claw.

"I cannot believe my eyes," Paw says, falling to his knees. "You have unlocked the lance's magic. My brother must have known you could. Why else would it have meant so much to him?"

Onendah latches on to the lance with his other foot and flaps his mighty wings. He circles around the couple, trailing a sacred aura of sunlight.

He releases an eagle cry that frightens Anoki and excites Kiowa.

As he hovers above them, Kiowa looks down at his father's symbol and knows instantly what he wants to be. He points to the glowing wolf and feels a rush of anticipation when Anoki nods. He passionately kisses her for the last time as a man.

"What I sacrifice now, I sacrifice for you!"

He reaches up with an open hand. With his other hand, he touches his wolf cap, tilts his head back, and howls. Onendah drops the lance in his hand.

The second his fingers make contact with the lance, the power overwhelms him and surges up his arm. A deep burning sensation washes over him. He is paralyzed by a tingling wave of indescribable feelings over his body .

"He holds the sun!" Anoki cries out.

At first he feels fire, but then everything goes cool as ice. He feels a wind as strong as a hurricane blow his skin apart, but it doesn't hurt, not even when his bones pop. Instead, every nerve opens up and fires the greatest feelings he's ever felt all at once. Now he is connected to everything wild and disconnected from everything human.

This is what it feels like to hold the sun and lightning at the same time.

He smiles at Anoki as two wolf ears protrude atop his head, nestled among his black hair. A thick mane bursts from his chest. His hearing increases. The acuteness is so clear, he can hear the crickets stepping on the ground. He can hear Paw's racing heart. Anoki screams. He covers his ears because it feels like his head is going to explode.

His eyelids close over brown eyes, then retract over yellow irises. Colors fade. Now the world is black-and-white. He can see deeper into the forest. He can see more stars than his human eyes could ever see. The only color that remains in his vision is in the things that move. His eyes shift to Anoki. He can feel, see, and hear her pulsating jugular veins rushing blood into deep pink veins that spread throughout her face like vines.

Though Anoki sees Kiowa's eyes turn yellow and fangs explode out of his elongating snout, she doesn't turn away. Every physical sense she has tells her to run—every sense except her heart. The love and courage contained within those chambers welds her firmly toward her decision to be with Kiowa.

"I will pay any price!"

His sense of smell changes again. The potency of the pine forest, the flowers and animals, can be easily detected. He can smell Anoki like she has somehow crawled up his nose and danced all around. He can smell Paw, Makes Trouble, Anoki's brother, and distantly, Kida. Fur bristles up his contorting snout and covers his face, chest, and stomach.

He reaches for his mouth and tries to speak to Anoki, but he can't. His teeth seem to break apart and extend. His tongue grows long and retracts in and out on its own, bringing new scents. Scents he can't discern. It overwhelms him. Panicked by the transformation, he extends his hands. His fingernails grow and transform into long claws that immediately curl under his popping fingers and change into the shape of a paw. He hunches over and feels his legs snap as they arch and then straighten into hindquarters. Oddly, his bottom half seems to grow indefinitely, until finally stopping. It jostles back and forth as though it has a mind of its own. He looks back at his tail and feels a deep rumble in his diaphragm that reverberates off his lungs. He tilts his head back, drops his ears, and releases a long, deep howl.

"I am scared." Anoki weeps.

Kiowa stops howling and looks at her with words in his eyes, but he can no longer communicate with her.

"Does it hurt?" she asks.

Kiowa shakes his head.

With that last hurdle removed, she touches his side and tilts her head back, releasing a soft and delicate howl as she gently presses her fingers to the lance.

She feels the same energy overwhelm her. Every sensation comes more alive. She feels her lips part and a pressure in her nose, like she has to sneeze, but instead of sneezing, her snout grows and grows until it doesn't. All at once, white fangs push through the roof of her mouth and her front teeth file down to pointed peaks. Two pointed ears lift off her hair. She looks away from Kiowa, not wanting him to see her hideous features. As she blinks, her beautiful brown eyes transform like snowflakes. A drop of blue expands from her pupil and continues through her brown iris until her eyes are as blue as topaz. She blinks rapidly, seeing things she has never seen before. She sees a family of owls, a bat chasing insects, thousands of stars she didn't even know existed. She can even see craters on the moon. She can hear Kiowa's voice, but she can't understand his words.

"Stop resisting the magic," he tells her.

She doesn't even realize that she's fighting the transformation, but now that she realizes it's taking her longer than Kiowa, she submits. An eerie feeling comes over her as white fur follicles sprout up her face and down her arms. She feels her torso shrink and her breasts flatten out. Her lower body collapses inside her dress. Soon she feels something shaking between her legs.

"Anoki, are you hurt?" Kiowa asks.

She shakes back and forth, feeling more alive than she's ever felt before. Her sense of smell and taste are so vastly different from her human senses. She struggles to decipher all of the intensities.

"Tell me that you are well."

Anoki slowly turns and faces her husband.

Her piercing blue eyes lock with his yellow eyes, and though they say nothing to each other with words, their minds are connected in a way that they can practically read each other's thoughts.

"My love for you is stronger than an animal," she says as she stands on all fours and slips out of her white deerskin dress.

Kiowa tilts his head back and howls loud and hard. Anoki joins in with him, and all who came to witness the wedding now tilt their heads and howl with the couple.

When Onendah sees the transformation is complete, he looks to the wolves and speaks in a way that fascinates Anoki. Though his beak hardly breaks open, his voice is clearly heard.

"Speak with humility. Feel with infinity. You will find in this world a new happiness. With this joy will come new struggles: Some will be good; some will be bad. Like a seed, your love will grow."

"My prayer has been answered. Thank you, Naukolahe!"

"We will live as wolves the rest of our days?" Anoki asks, feeling pangs of regret.

"Only if you do not change back to human form by the harvest moon. Then will you be as wolves for all time. I encourage you to change back, but the choice is yours. Always remember where you came from. That is the only way to know where you are going. Time will heal the tribes' wounds, and it would be a great tragedy to lose my human children."

***

Charlie stands and flaps his wings like the great white eagle Onendah. He pretends to speak from high above the campfire circle.

"Suddenly Paw, Makes Trouble, and Walpi sprint out of the forest and transform into... guess what?"

"What?" Kevin asks, biting down on his fingernails.

"They all turned into wolves. Paw turned into a black one. Dark as night he was. Makes Trouble transformed into an auburn wolf. He looked just like autumn. Walpi turned into a golden wolf with black stripes down his back." Charlie describes the pack.

The boys gasp.

"They're werewolves?" Zack whimpers, looking side to side, as though the wolves could be anywhere.

"No... no... they turned into real wolves!"

"So wait. When they turn into wolves they can only turn human on a harvest moon?" John asks, with a perplexed look on his face.

"Legend has it that they have to turn into humans on the harvest moon," Charlie answers, pointing up to the harvest moon. "Then they have to decide by morning if they are going to be wolf or human until the next harvest moon. Don't forget, though, this story is about a wolf hunter."

"Eh?" Kevin squints his face so tight, he looks like he's licked a lemon.

"Yeah, when I started I asked you boys if you wanted to hear a story about a wolf hunter."

"But that was before we knew the wolves were skinwalkers," John protests.

"JUST LET HIM TELL THE STORY!" Luther shouts, slapping his hands together.

"Boys... shush up. Now, listen here. Do any of you know how a mountain is formed?" Charlie asks, sitting back down on the log, the flames reflecting in his lenses. The boys are immediately silenced, eager to know how the saga will continue.

"No!?" Zack answers, rubbing his chin with his fingers.

"It has to start out as a small pebble, doncha know. With a little time and patience, the stone gets a little bigger and a little bigger until one day—"

"It's a mountain," Kevin interrupts, leaping off his log and throwing his hands high.

"That's right. And so it was with the great wolf hunter, W.H."

CHAPTER 49

Roughly fourteen hundred miles north of Cimarron, New Mexico, a town in Canada called Winnipeg experienced a sudden boom. Only their development occurred in 1811. It was propelled forward by a man named Thomas Douglas, a proud Scotsman and the fifth Earl of Selkirk. He had received a land grant of a hundred and sixteen thousand square miles just off the Red River basin. His intent was to refine a decades-old trading post, where two rushing rivers met. Douglas thought it to be "the perfect location for an agricultural settlement for retired Hudson's Bay Company employees."

Now in that fair town sits a young man at a bar in a very old pub. King's Pub, to be exact. Then and now, it is the oldest pub in town. He holds his beer mug up to his lips and mumbles something like, "Leave her alone. That's all I ask."

Though he sits at an empty bar, with no women in sight, he mumbles the phrase repeatedly, allowing the beer foam to tickle his mustache before he presses the cold brew to his lips and lets the sour ale swell in his cheeks before pushing it down. The glass empties, and so too do his scruffy cheeks. His pointy Scottish nose and rosy cheekbones echo the genetic mix of French and Scottish ancestry.

He adjusts his round glasses and squints his sapphire eyes. With one last swallow, he uses his black cotton sleeve to wipe beer foam off his mustache, and then holds up one finger.

"Hit me, Alfred," he says to a bald bartender polishing a stack of gleaming shot glasses. The fiftysomething man smiles, lifting the dark corners of a short, trim black mustache that matches the rim of his gleaming head. His white shirt, apron, and black tie identify his profession.

"Last one, W.H. I don't let my customers wobble out of here.

It's bad for business," the bartender sternly warns, pulling a silver tap forward until the yellow liquid fills the glass to the rim. Foam spills over and empties onto the floor.

The glass liquor bottles behind the bartender vary in color, size, and shape, but they all seem to sparkle in the candlelight, enticing consumers with a hint of pixie power.

The only other patron at the bar is a large man in a red and black checkered flannel shirt. He turns so that he's facing W.H. "He's been callin' you 'W.H.' all night. What gives?" When the man looks back at his mug, scruff from his jawline catches on his shirt and leaves fibers in the bristle.

"That's his name," Alfred answers, picking up another glass and polishing it, even though it's clean.

The lumberjack adjusts his brown suspenders, which pull tightly on his khaki cotton trousers. He glances back at the scrawny fellow dubbed W.H. and shakes his head, obviously becoming more agitated at the sight of the scrawny man. A man who is on the cusp of being a handsome "pretty boy."

"What doncha get aboot it?" W.H. asks with a smile as his head wobbles back and forth.

"He's Alfred. I'm Little John. Doesn't seem fittin' to be usin' letters fer a *name*."

W.H. turns and stares at the man. For a long, uncomfortable moment, neither says anything to the other.

"He's known around these parts as 'Wolf Hunter,'" Alfred answers, mediating the tension between both men. He glances back and forth, keeping one eye on each, and lowers his hand for a short club.

"SWEET BISCUITS AND GRAVY, HA! HA! HA!" Little John, who is not at all little, laughs boisterously, slapping his bear-like paw to his bulging knee. Clouds of dust plume between each breath and mocking laugh.

"You… you're a wolf hunter? I'll be… What next, Injuns?"

W.H. gets up, exposing his Colt 1851 Navy six-shooter. It's a revolving, black powder pistol.

"Injuns run on up the river to trade. Everyone knows they slip right by Winnipeg," the bartender says, moving from the billy club to a double-barreled sawed-off shotgun.

The lumberjack sits upright, then manages a few more laughs at W.H.'s expense. He lifts his mighty mug and prepares to throw the contents in W.H.'s face if he reaches for his gun.

"I ain't afraid of a man with a gun. I've always been a fair fight kinda fella," Little John says, keeping his eyes on W.H. through the bartender's mirror.

W.H. looks down. "Ain't no fair fightin' with wolves, fella. There's only dead and alive."

W.H. reaches in his pockets and pulls out some crumbled bills.

"I'll be at the east end of the maple forest, where the rivers meet, tomorrow morning. Why don't you come see for yourself?" W.H. says as he turns and stumbles for the door.

"I might just do that. We'll be cuttin' some hard blond in that area. Usually start pretty early in the mornin'. Ain't heard no wolves, though. Shouldn't be hard to see you catch a snipe."

"He ain't goin' on a wild-goose chase. If W.H. is there, you better believe wolves are in the area," Alfred says, with a respected brow raised.

"Sure, sure, ol' man. Wolves as big as polar bears! Can't wait to see 'em!"

CHAPTER 50

The following morning, a group of lumberjacks wearing thick winter coats of many colors finish their breakfast and prepare for work as the sun rises.

Dark spruce trees mingle with tall maples. The spruce are distinct from the maple in that their branches hang low, making them almost frown. Autumn had stripped the trees of their leaves. Wind had brought both frost and a heavy snow and made the trees bend, so that they looked like they were kissing each other. Where sunlight couldn't penetrate the density of the forest, ominous shadows warned onlookers to beware.

"Can lungs freeze?" Chris, a gnome-looking fellow whose nickname is derived from his appearance, asks. He rubs his bright red nose and exhales thick clouds of steam through his full beard. Moisture catches on the fibers and forms into ice crystals.

"Can't be. You're blowing dragon's breath," an old man replies. He's managed to keep his given name a mystery, which brings him boatloads of delight. His peers have dubbed him Father Time because of the long white beard that goes to his waist and the cracks in his face.

The five men fasten their snowshoes and gather their axes, saws, and hammers. The tight geometric webs of twine in their snowshoes serve their purpose and keep the lumberjacks from falling through the nine-foot powder base.

Little John sticks out like a sore thumb. His height and girth make him look more like a giant than a man. On the rusted head of his steel ax, a gleaming blade indicates a fresh grind.

"Tools sharp, boys," he says, licking his finger and running it along the blade. "Me and Biscuit are ready to make some gravy. You ever hear of any wolves out here, Gnome?" he asks Chris.

"Can't say that I have. I imagine if you went out farther in the woods you wouldn't have any trouble finding 'em. I'd rather not, though!" Gnome puckers his lips and nods his head, picking his teeth.

"Why do you ask?" Father Time asks, wrapping his arms around his ax blade. He spins back and forth and rotates his hips.

"Oh, this kook at King's was spinnin' my marbles yesterday. Said he was hunting wolves in our neck of the woods."

"If there was wolves here, we woulda heard them by now," Father Time says, combing his fingers through his beard.

Bob, the quiet man they call Silent Slim, leans back and howls. One by one the other men join in. They pause and keep quiet in the white winter's day to see if their wild call is answered.

When there is no response, they have a good laugh.

"I think we got a fella who's cryin' wolf!" Little John roars, slapping his dusty knee.

"Where'd you boys wanna start today?" Father Time asks, changing the subject.

"I'll scout for fallen timber north of the forest," Little John answers, winding up his ax and taking some practice blows.

"We might'in want to stay in pairs," Father Time suggests as he slides his hand into a cotton mitten. "Ya never wanna be alone in these woods. Getting lost out in this rugged wilderness and freezin' to death would a far worse end than comin' upon a pack of wolves."

"Nah. I don't need a partner to scout. With just the five of us, we'll have two saw teams. I'll head on up that ridge to sample and mark the trees."

"You got enough paint to mark 'em?" Gnome asks.

Little John removes a half-charred cigar and tosses it in his mouth. He nods as he strikes a match with his thumbnail.

"We should be able to get about ten out today, doncha think?" Silent Slim asks, hoisting a large two-handled saw blade on his shoulder.

"That would be a good day, eh, Foreman?" Gnome asks Little John, as they shoulder their six-foot blades.

"Yep, that sure would make the owners happy, wouldn't it?"

The men greedily nod, counting Canadian pounds that haven't been earned and already scheming ways to spend them.

As the men part ways, Little John tramples a path up the ravine. He pulls the branches back on the snow-packed maple trees and inspects the bases for ice. With the back of his hammer, he taps on a long spike to see if he can drive it into the tree. If he can, he measures the tree with his arm span, because any tree that is wider than his arms belongs to the King of England, Edward VII.

He finds almost an inch of ice on the first few inspections, which discourages him, forcing him farther down the high ridge and into a deep ravine. There he hopes the frost hasn't had as strong an effect.

After a few attempts, he finally finds one worth chopping. He winds his hefty ax up over his head and slams it against the tree trunk. With several chops, he chips off the bark in an X shape, then uses orange chalk to "paint" the tree.

"Got one here, boys!" he hollers at a saw team that meanders over an adjacent ridge and drops down into a draw.

"Ain't no wolves out here, just ice, snow, trees, and an empty heaven, with no God," Little John says, moving away from his team over to another tree.

A one-time Christian, Little John lost his faith when he lost his wife and six-month-old baby boy to the croup.

As the day wanes on, he gets farther from his team. Around noon, he's located eight trees after surveying thirty or so.

Feeling the sweat press against his black wool cap, he pulls it off and wipes his forehead with his frosty sleeve. Icicles have begun to form on his mustache. He breaks them off and removes his mitten. With his glove off, he flexes his fingers and reaches inside his warm pants pocket. Fumbling around, he removes a silver flask and unscrews the lid.

It ain't encouraging drinking on the job if the boys can't see. He chuckles to himself and takes a long swallow of whiskey. The liquid travels down his throat, lava hitting his stomach and coursing through his veins. Like antifreeze, the spirits regulate the temperature in his core, and with another shoulder-wrenching swallow, he feels completely cozy.

As he screws the cap back on and goes to put his hand back in his mitten, he sees something he has never seen before.

Beneath a tall evergreen, the skirt moves and the snow collapses on its own. He looks around to see if maybe a gust of wind caused the disturbance, but all of the treetops are perfectly still, and all of the branches retain their snow.

CHAPTER 51

He feels a creeping fear but waves it off, mostly because liquid courage runs his common sense off-course and amplifies his bravado.

"So you're not wind. That much I've figured out. If you be living, then let's put steel to flesh and find what lurks beneath."

As he approaches the skirt, his snowshoes sink deeper than he expected. He takes another step forward and sinks up to his waist.

"Aw, fiddlesticks," he bemoans, thrusting his ax forward. It disappears in the snow, making a perfect indentation in the white surface.

"Grrr…"

He hears a loud, deep grumble from beneath the tree.

"Come on, fellas, this is getting old!"

Suddenly, his courage plummets and the shiny rim of his blade is less powerful than he thought, especially now that it's buried and out of reach.

"Come on, W.H. You've had your fun. I got no understanding why you'd carry on like this, but I'll buy ya a beer and you can tell me how ya got the drop on me."

Before the lumberjack can finish his sentence, two large golden eyes are illuminated in the shadows of the tree's base. The snarling grows stronger and the snow breaks off the skirt as a massive timber wolf's gray snout protrudes.

The next things Little John spies are the wolf's large curved, clenched fangs.

With a heavy growl from its abdomen, the wolf snarls in a way that puts the fear of God in a man who thought heaven was empty. Yet a prayer slips from his heart and flies off his lips. It isn't a complicated prayer. Little John just asks that God allow him to retrieve his "gravy maker" and save his biscuits.

The two-hundred-pound wolf leans down and prepares to lunge.

Up on the other side of the ridge, the saw team works diligently. The team closer to camp fells a tree.

"TIMBER!" Gnome shouts, warning the team up the ridge so that they can make clear.

Bark breaks and the creaking tree falls to the ground. Seeing that they're clear of any harm, the diligent team up the ridge gets back to work.

"Wanna break for lunch?" Father Time asks Chris.

"Nah. I gotta get my pounds or my old lady's gonna tear my hide."

"All right, then. Let's get on over that ridge and find Little John."

On the other side of the ridge, Little John feels like he's outfoxed the wolf. He manages to use the depth of the snow to his advantage. Neither the wolf nor the man can put their entire weight on the frosty powder without sinking through. Because the wolf hasn't found a way to get to him, the lumberjack has just enough time to swipe snow away with flailing arms until his hands touch the solid handle.

His efforts to retrieve his weapon only entice the wolf as Little John appears to be more like a wounded animal than a man.

With weapon in hand, Little John readies his ax and summons enough courage to swipe at the wolf. He misses but finds that the wolf isn't as brave as he thought.

The beast stops snarling and backs up. He circles around Little John's flank and begins the horrible process again. Mane standing up, teeth bared, yellow eyes fixed – the predator becomes fiercely determined.

Little John swings again. A deadly dance ensues. For though the hefty man's stamina is strong, the wolf is no fool. He playfully pounces close, sinks in the snow, then lowers his head to make it seem like he can be reached. Then he snarls and lunges forward, snapping at Little John when he winds up. The inexperienced man falls for the bait every time. Little by little, the wolf establishes himself as the taunting superior. It does an excellent job of tiring out the man and simultaneously packing the snow.

When the towering lumberjack pauses to take a breath, the wolf steps up its attack, probing for the advantage with snarling fangs and snipping jaws that keep the man always on the defense.

As Gnome and Father Time breach the ridgeline, they look down and see Little John fighting for his life and obviously losing.

"Please! HELP ME!" Little John pleads.

"We have to do something!" the old man cries.

The men point at something that makes Little John look from them to the top of the ridge. Two more gray wolves slither down the decline and move in for the kill.

"STAY CALM!" Gnome shouts as though temperament were enough for him to survive.

When Gnome shouts, he catches the attention of one of the charging wolves. For a brief moment, the wolves pause and stare at Gnome. Gnome stares back.

"Get outta here!" Gnome screams, waving his arms.

By flailing his arms, Gnome taps into the primal mind of the wolf and sets in motion gears that decipher all actions as healthy or wounded. In an instant, the wolf charges through the snow and up the steep incline. Gnome turns and runs, confirming the predator's instincts.

This energetic wolf moves through the snow much quicker than the larger wolf that's attacking Little John does.

Unlike Little John, Gnome is the exact opposite of calm. He is terribly frightened.

"There's a rifle in the lodge," Gnome yells to Father Time.

"Race ya for it!" Father Time shouts, taking off for the lodge.

"No. Don't do that!"

"Last one to the lodge is a rotten egg," the old man croaks as he shuffles his snowshoes like he's a train.

When the wolf makes it to the top of the ridge, he's forced to decide between the two. He looks left, at Gnome, then right, at the healthy lumberjack who isn't showing a hint of weakness. Glancing back at Gnome, it lunges forward and puts its padded paws to use.

Though the stalking wolf doesn't have snowshoes, its thick fur divides its weight across its four paws more evenly than the duck-footed men putting distance between each other.

When Silent Slim and Jim see a gray streak in hot pursuit of their friends, neither wastes time asking questions. Both men abandon their saws and head for the lodge, thinking the same thing as Father Time. *Get to a gun.*

The wolf closes in on Gnome and bites down on his ankle. The lumberjack screams and tumbles in an explosion of snow. His severed Achilles sprays blood on the winter sand and pools crimson. He slowly backs away from the wolf, keeping his blade between him and the snapping bite.

CHAPTER 52

"I ain't afraid to die!" Little John shouts, heaving heavily as he swings his ax with less and less force.

He finally sees that the wolf is getting careless and putting himself within striking distance. He lifts his ax over his head and prepares to lower it into the charging monster's skull, but when he tries to release his wrath, the ax seems frozen in place. He turns around with a "what gives?" expression on his face.

A fresh-to-the-fight, clever wolf is behind Little John. It stands with a proud-seeming smile, like, "Gotcha!"

With a fierce shake of his head, the wolf snaps the wooden ax handle in half, stealing Little John's defense away, and along with it, his hope.

Now, with two wolves circling him and readying for the kill, Little John has finally lived up to his name.

He feels a crushing pain on his right calf and looks down to discover that the third wolf has returned. Its bloodstained muzzle has taken him by surprise. He releases a carnal scream that excites the pack.

"Please, God, spare me!"

He falls to his side and covers his face with his arms, as he has no fight left to give to the master butchers.

Between the break in his arms, he sees the leader leaping for him and acknowledges with the Lord's Prayer that the end has arrived. The wolf that discovered the lumberjack happens to be the alpha wolf. When he sees a weakness and latches on to Little John's coat, the other wolves latch on to his side, stretching his skin so tight he thinks it will rip in two. He's totally cognitive of the carnage but wishes he isn't. He knows now that he underestimated their strength and sheer ferocity. It will take only seconds for them to sever his arms and legs. He wonders how much of this barbarism he'll be forced to suffer before the lights go out and peaceful death sets his reborn Christian soul free.

BOOM!

He feels the full, powerful impact of the alpha wolf as it slams against his chest, and he refuses to see if his intestines are sprawled out before him. "Thank you, God!" he mumbles to himself, managing a smile as the thought of his men returning with a rifle brings a rushing wave of hope.

A wrenching, ripping noise makes him scream and think, *Is my flesh being torn apart?* He lets loose a long scream. "Ahhhh! Ahhh! Ahhh!"

A second shot echoes off in the distance, hitting the wolf who had snapped the ax in half. Blood and brains spray all over the white snow. The wolf lifts its paws twice, then falls dead with its mouth agape and tongue extended toward Little John's exposed abdomen.

The third wolf gets wise and releases the lumberjack's leg. It darts back underneath the pine skirt, disappearing out the other end. With a quick howl, it calls for the pack, then vanishes in the snowy forest.

From the top of the ridgeline, W.H. chambers a third round by cocking his lever-action, Henry Big Boy .44-caliber, 1860 rifle. Cordite plumes out the barrel. He leans in and inhales. Vapors slip into his nostrils. He steadies his racing heart, holds the rifle up to his lips, and kisses it. He slides the weapon into his shoulder socket and lines his eye up with the long tin scope. His pupils narrow. The six-power lens brings him so close, it makes him feel like he's down there with Little John.

"Help! Help. He's got me!"

W.H. scans the scene. A limp alpha wolf, a second wolf in pieces, and a thrashing Herculean man. He flips the weapon on safe but keeps the hammer cocked as he rises from his prone position with a crooked smile.

"I'm dyin'! I'm dyin'!" Little John shouts between hacking gasps and teary-eyed sobs. "He got me. He's tearing my guts out!"

Although it takes W.H. a few minutes to work his way down the ridge, he can't help but laugh, thinking back to the burly man who spewed courage like a volcano.

"Where's all that courage now?" W.H. says and slaps the brawny lumberjack across the face to restore him to his senses.

When Little John sees two bright blue eyes grinning behind round gold-framed lenses, he stops spewing fear.

"How can you laugh at a dying man?" he asks, holding his blood-soaked hands up. "Ain't any part of you Christian?"

W.H. presses his fist against his short auburn mustache, hiding a smile.

As Little John pieces together what has happened, he begins to calm down.

"Ain't nothin' more enticing to a wolf than live bait," W.H. says.

Little John shakes his head in confusion. "Whad'ya mean?"

W.H. extends his hand. "Whad'ya mean, 'whad'ya mean'?'"

"Who's the bait?"

With a heavy tug, W.H. pulls his companion to his feet.

The pawn slowly pats himself down and finds blood everywhere. He examines his clothes and realizes the ripping he heard was not in fact his flesh but only his thick wool coat. He looks to the ground and spies W.H.'s brutal work. A small hole on one side of the wolf indicates the entry, whereas a devastating wound the size of his fist shows the exit.

The third wolf howls long and hard in the forest, desiring an update on its pack members.

"Follow your friends' tracks outta here. I got a job to finish," W.H. says, cocking his rifle.

"You're going after him?" he asks incredulously.

W.H. faces him and smiles with wild eyes. "Got me two hundred cartridges and fifty pounds of bounty on them two wolves. Might be as much as five hundred pounds of reward money out here, all said and done." He cocks his head and smiles wryly.

"You're crazy! You're really nuts!" Little John shouts. He quickly fastens his snowshoes and scuffles up the ridgeline in time to greet most of his friends. Father Time holds a rifle.

"We heard shots!" Silent Slim says.

"Are you okay?" Father Time asks.

"I'd be dead if it wasn't for…" He looks past Father Time and sees Gnome's bloody, mangled body in a disfigured pile. The tracks and divots in the snow tell the heavy-hearted story.

That coulda been me, Little John thinks but dares not say aloud.

Alone in the forest, W.H. follows the wolves' tracks back up the ridgeline from whence they came.

"Don't wanna be low; gotta get high. Can't see 'em creeping up on you when you're low." He huffs and puffs as he goes.

When he hears the cackling cries of the pack, he sighs and drops down into the prone position to take careful aim. He glances back at the lumberjacks and waves good-bye as they disappear.

"Don't need you fellas anymore, anyway," he hollers.

SNAP.

CHAPTER 53

A wolf trap clamps down on W.H.'s foot.

"AAAGGGHHH! Dadgum trap. I'm caught in my own contraption." He thrashes from the catch, but doesn't feel any pain because the heel of his boot absorbs the impact. He tries to set himself free with one hand and hold the rifle with the other. The balancing act results in him tumbling over.

SNAP.

Another trap clamps down on his arm. He immediately regrets being a zealot. Shadows approach. The rumbling growls grow louder and louder.

W.H. tries to aim his rifle, but can't align it to his eye with his arm trapped.

A wolf howls again, much closer this time. He can see flashes in the forest, and he knows it's circling. Circling and closing in with each pass.

***

"Wolves have distinct howls. One howl that is unmistakable is the rally call. The wolf's howl is answered by the pack, because the strength of the wolf is the pack and the strength of the pack is the wolf."

The boys repeat the catchy expression with inattentive mumbles.

"Soon they begin to surround W.H.," Charlie says, rising to his feet, "and they are everywhere."

The boys watch and wonder what happens next as Charlie stretches out his hands.

***

Winding and winding around, the growls get louder as they close in.

"For though I walk through the valley of the shadow of death, I shall fear no evil."

W.H. lifts his rifle with his free limb and fires a shot into a small and starved wolf's chest.

"Because all wolves are evil!"

He rests the barrel in the snow while he slides the bolt back with one hand and manages to lock another round. Just as he raises the barrel, a wolf explodes from underneath the evergreen canopy. It successfully flanks him but mistakes the barrel for W.H.'s arm. It clamps down on the warm metal barrel and runs off with it. A second wolf runs up to partake in the "kill." It gnaws at the trigger housing, and its bottom teeth find the free space between the trigger and the guard. It bites hard and applies enough pressure to decompress the trigger.

"AND I AM DEATH!"

BOOM!

W.H. feels a rush of joy when the weapon explodes in a cloud of red mist and blows the top of the starved wolf's head off.

On the other side of the ridge, a horse's *neigh* catches the attention of the pack. The magnificent white Appalachian thrashes back and forth and makes such a commotion, it forces the wolves to decide between revenge and dinner. Caving to their carnal instincts, the majority of the pack divides and runs off toward the saddled pony. Two stay behind.

Baring fangs, snarling, and drooling, the wolves move in for the kill just as they had with Little John.

W.H. reaches for his bowie knife and quickly unsheathes it.

"One of you is goin' with me!" he shouts, readying the blade.

As one wolf goes for the wolf hunter's exposed side, he stabs the knife into its throat and feels it sink deep. The wolf bites at the blade and puts up a brutal defense until it loses its strength and goes limp.

The other wolf uses its cold claws to tear through the hunter's thick coat and connect with his bare flesh. W.H. screams, which only encourages the wolf.

Unable to distinguish between wool and flesh, the wolf bites down hard on the coat collar and viciously thrashes it with such force that W.H. can't help but feel like his jolted neck is broken. Leaning at the waist, he slips his arm out of the sleeve and pushes the coat down his trapped arm. The sleeve slides down to where the trap clamps on to W.H.'s wrist and catches there. W.H. gasps for air and cracks a slanted smile as he realizes he's fooled the wolf into thinking it's torn his flesh off him. The beast rips the sleeve and separates the garment from its master.

Suddenly a collie leaps on the wolf, snarling and tearing at its thickly furred throat. The clack of fangs chip both animals' teeth, and the snarls cause W.H. to try to protect his buddy Bingo.

"Bingo, no! Skin outta here, boy!" W.H. shouts at his only true friend, a black-and-white-patched dog with a single brown ring around his right eye.

W.H. uses his free hand to reach for his six-shooter. His traps work against him and restrict his movements. He twists himself around until his spine nearly snaps, but he manages to get a finger and thumb on the handle. All the while Bingo and the timber wolf viciously trash each other's hides with fierce bites and pouncing claws. Mustering the most pressure he can in this awkward position, the wolf hunter manages to unholster his pistol. He cocks the weapon and fires so fast that he isn't sure if he's hit his precious collie or the wolf.

Pressing down on the hammer, he watches the chamber rotate. He uses the front sight to aim at the wolf and fires a second shot, which severs the wolf's spinal cord. The wolf can't move anything but its snapping jaws, and those seek justice. Its pink tongue slips between its broken teeth, and before W.H. can fire a third shot, the wolf dies.

A brief, silent pause makes W.H. feel like part of his soul has been lost in the battle of savagery versus civilization.

But then a spotted tail stirs. Fear turns to elation when two shaggy black ears point up. Bingo shuffles out from under the wolf. His black nose is now frosted white with snow. He limps over to W.H., whimpers, and presents a wounded paw for his master to see.

Hurt here, his eyes seem to say.

"Did he tear you up, buddy?" W.H. asks the panting dog.

CHAPTER 54

"I got us into one heck of a mess, Bingo. Yer my best friend and a dang fool. I gotta get us outta here or we're gonna end up as supper."

Bingo licks W.H.'s face the entire time he pushes on the traps and struggles to set himself free. Once he releases the tension, he's able to slide his arm out.

"I'm hurtin' all over, boy, but it ain't my face. You don't need to go on like that." W.H. pushes Bingo away.

The pair quickly scramble to their feet. W.H. picks up his rifle and reloads it with fourteen shiny brass shells. He cocks it and peers through the scope to ensure that it wasn't damaged.

"Fangs and claws ain't no match for the Reaper," he says, patting the butt stock like it's a baby.

Bingo looks up and notices that the sun will be down in a couple hours, giving the wolves the advantage. He whimpers as W.H. searches for his bowie knife. He finds it in a pool of bloodstained snow next to the maimed wolf. He wipes the blade off on the wolf's hide and holsters it.

"I know. I want to get the bounty, too. But we'll just have to come back for their hides at early light."

He follows the lumberjacks' tracks out of the killing fields and looks for his horse. "I sure hope Cotton made it out all right." He whistles for her.

Rattled from the fight and freezing cold, Bingo shivers.

As the dog and man work their way down the ridge, W.H. sings, "B-I-N-G-O. and Bingo was his name-o…"

The dog prances to his master's tune, proudly displaying himself with puffed-up chest.

"Bingo, you're my hero! With all the money we'll fetch for the bounty, I'm gonna buy you a big steak dinner!"

The thought of a warm steak makes him lick his lips.

***

Kiowa's wolf eyes present the world in a way a man could never understand. Everything has a trail and is marked clearly by a heat signature in tracks that fade or hold strong.

He detects faint traces of golden light in fresh deer tracks. Every living creature has a distinct scent all its own. Between how he sees and smells the world, the wolf could find anything he wanted.

He follows them and sees the tracks of everything that's ever stepped on the earth's cool surface. Tiny squirrel imprints run along the forest floor and scamper up the trees. They disappear in tiny hollows, but he can see their gleaming eyes and hear their beating hearts. He logs their location in the back of his mind, and for some reason, he wants more than ever to punish them.

Rabbit tracks frantically dash across the pine needles, going this way and that with no discernible direction. Bobcat tracks follow close behind. A dried pool of crimson blood shows where that story ends.

Elk tracks are distinct and deep. They move steadily and become frantic, like the rabbit's. He identifies why. A cougar made a wide stalking circle and discovered its prey. He assumes that the cougar tracks end the elk's story, the same as the bobcat ended the rabbit's. To his surprise, he discovers bear tracks. The deep grooved foot traffic indicates that a fight occurred. But where the elk's end, the bear's resume. The bear must have won, because the bloody elk body was dragged away.

Now he can see history and the present at the same time. As he searches around, he sees tracks glow brightest where a deer recently stepped. He inhales and detects its gamey scent, approximating where a deer is hiding. The aroma of pine and musky water are so pronounced in his nose and mouth, he can't help but see where the animal has been all day. Its sex is given away by a faint hint of sweetness. Judging by the tracks' width and length, she's not much older than the doe he grew fond of when he was a boy. *Do not worry. We can still be friends… I hope.*

A new truth is revealed to this animal world he's been birthed into. Everything searches for food. Some seek grass, berries, and nuts. Everything else must eat *meat!*

His ears instinctively shift back and forth and bring the acoustic sounds into focus with each turn. When his ears turn out, he can hear the wind blow. The trees creak as they sway. When they turn in slightly, he can hear an owl's hoot and the deer's heavy breathing. When they turn so that they point straight up, he can hear her heart beating to the symphony of crickets that are loud all around her and quiet near her.

"I think I know exactly where she is," he whispers to Anoki, who trots up behind him.

Having never hunted, Anoki's senses are overwhelming.

"I am confused and pleased at the same time."

She sees many of the same things as Kiowa, but she could never think as a hunter thinks. To her, all is beauty. All is life.

"What do you hear?"

"I hear everything. I can even hear your heart. It beats like a drum."

"I hear crickets. I hear owls. I can even hear the bat's wings. For me it is the same, but more of it and much, much louder!"

The two wolves look at each other, laugh, then sprint off playfully through the forest.

The speed with which four legs carry a body is much greater than two ever could. Anoki runs as fast as she can, but in her wildest dreams, she could never keep up with Kiowa. He sprints far ahead of her and disappears into the woods. She can hear him leaping over fallen trees and maneuvering through the forest as though he has always been a wolf. She blinks and suddenly he is beside her. He pounces all around her.

"I circled back. I didn't want to leave you, but I had to see how fast I could go! We are as fast as the wind!" Kiowa shouts, circling around Anoki so many times it makes her anxious to follow him.

I could never be as fast as you. She lowers her ears and drops her tail.

"I could never move this fast on my horse!"

"Always promise me that you will wait for me, Kiowa!"

"Anoki, you are my soul. Wherever you go, there will I be also," he says with yellow eyes that both spook and excite her.

"You are my heart. Where you go, my body must follow."

Kiowa has so much energy that he leaps from thought to thought. "We are free from duty! Free from tribes! Free from everyone and everything!"

"We are free to be with each other," she says, lowering her nose and testing his meaning.

Kiowa feels an explosion of excitement swell in him. He draws a deep breath, tilts his head back, lowers his ears, and howls so loudly it silences the crickets, sends the owls inside their shelter, and alerts all living things that a new master owns the night. Masters that are man, woman, and wolf.

The deer sprints out of its hiding place and flees for its life. All animals smaller and within range clear out of his kingdom. For miles and miles they move, seeking shelter elsewhere.

Unable to resist, Anoki joins in.

"Thanks be to Onendah for his great magic!" Kiowa howls in a new voice, which echoes through the forest.

When he's finished singing praises, he presses his head to Anoki's and stares deep into her blue eyes, sinking into her ocean. He presses his paw to her heart. She does the same to him. They stare at each other like this as lovers often do when they build love with glances and gentle touches. The energy passes from one to the other, heightening new senses that excite, tickle, and charge.

"I know it isn't possible, but are we flying?"

"Anoki, can you not see? With our magic, anything is possible!"

CHAPTER 55

The couple is trapped in their bliss, a dance ensues. The wolves circle each other and nuzzle noses.

Kiowa presses his lips to her face and tries to kiss her, but his lips don't work the same.

"I wish with all my heart that I could kiss you."

"I wish you could hold me. Your arms are strong and made me feel safe."

The wolves go from howling gratitude to whimpering loss.

"It seems in our desperate escape, we have sacrificed our first night as man and wife."

"What shall we do?" Anoki asks with her hungry eyes fixed on his.

Her seductive stance makes his hind legs go weak, forcing his bottom to the ground. His tail flops all around, picking up pine needles as it pats the earth. His ears flatten.

"A warrior so brave and so fierce must have other passions," she says, stepping toward him, the huntress, now hunting the hunter.

Kiowa tries to think of ways to show his love to his new wife, but the reality of the situation is that the exchange they made has robbed him of his most human element, mortal affection. Thoughts of him dragging his fingers through her hair are displaced as he examines his paws and realizes that his claws will most likely hurt her. His tongue goes in and out of his mouth as the sweet words he wishes to say to her won't form on this large, cumbersome animal tongue. He puckers his lips to kiss hers, but instead bumps his snouts with hers. Wrecking everything, he presses his head to her neck and wonders what it would have been like to touch her breasts. The agony of the loss makes him draw a long deep breath and release slowly. He whimpers.

Careful, you fool. This is your wedding night, and if you keep this up, she's going to name you Whimpers a Lot. The thought of having such a weak name reminds him of his youthful days when he was going to paint a deer on his shield.

"Wolf or woman, I am your wife, am I not?"

"I am thinking of a way to treat you as my wife."

"Have you not grown up near animals?"

"Yes," he says, clenching his teeth and closing his eyes. He releases one last remorseful whimper.

"Are they so different than we?"

Yes! he thinks to himself, reflecting on his loss.

He knows better than to list the human features he already misses.

The two stand close to each other and eventually maneuver into positions that allow them to consummate their marriage.

***

Back in the pine forest, the Indians stare at the glowing magic.

"We shouldn't," Paw says, looking at the wolf paw and the golden lance.

"Onendah isn't here to stop us." Makes Trouble smirks.

Before he can finish his words, Walpi lunges for the lance and touches the wolf paw and lance.

"I will not let you eat my sister," Walpi shouts. He immediately collapses and disappears beneath the glowing mist.

"Hopi? Hopi!" Makes Trouble shouts in a jealous rage. He watches Walpi's hand rise up above the mist like he's reaching for the sky. Wolf claws protrude out of his fingertips and his hand sprouts light brown fur, but the transformation doesn't appear as swift. A shadow stirs inside the mist. Two wolf eyes glow. A growl is heard. The vapors swirl. A man's frame with a wolf's head startles Makes Trouble.

"Well, if Hopi can change, then why not us?" Makes Trouble asks Paw. He does as Onendah showed them. The transformation does not go as smoothly. His hands grow long black claws and sprout golden fur, but the popping sound doesn't occur. His head twists and configures into a wolf's, but his heart lacks courage during the transformation and his body begins resisting the change.

Makes Trouble swipes at a tree and leaves a huge gash in the trunk.

Splinters spray against Paw's calm face. "Don't fight the magic, Makes Trouble."

Makes Trouble's fearful heart keeps his chest, arms, and legs human. He looks at Paw with a wolf's head and gurgles as his snout protrudes and his teeth elongate.

"AAAARRRRGGGHHRRRROOOO." Makes Trouble unleashes a terrifying evil howl. His back broadens and triples in size. His chest doubles in bulging mass. In an instant, he grows muscles so thick he doesn't resemble a man or a wolf, but something in between. He spreads his massive arms out and sees coiling golden wolf hair spread all over his body in patches instead of one smooth coat. He holds his hands up and examines his mutilated fingers, then presses them to his cheeks and shakes his head. His eyes flutter, then glow bright green. He looks down at his feet and sees black claws protruding out of his splitting moccasins. In a rage, he sprints into the forest, slashing tree trunks as he goes.

Paw grumbles and shakes his head. "He makes trouble, even with magic." Paw thinks it odd that Makes Trouble resists. Now he is stuck with the head and hands of a wolf but the body of a man. "How awful and dreadful. Not even a woman's love could look upon that monster's face."

With no one left to stop Paw, and since he has no one left to live for, he sighs and reaches down to pick up the lance. As soon as his fingertips make contact, he feels the sun's power. A sun-kissed glow transfers from the lance to his body.

"Ah-hoe, this feels amazing!" he says with a bright smile. His teeth glow white. "All that is left for me now is magic."

Not far away, Makes Trouble's growls and screams mix between beast and man.

"I'm not so sure I want to be a wolf." Paw reflects on Makes Trouble's transformation. He thinks of every animal he could be.

"Life as a happy river otter would be short. But I might find love again and hold hands with a lady otter. That would be nice."

"Grrrraaaawwwrrrr…" Makes Trouble screams into the night.

"Or maybe a powerful cougar? I've always wondered what it might be like to be a soaring eagle."

"Help me!" Makes Trouble speaks.

"Leave me to make up my own mind, Makes Trouble. You had your turn. Now it's mine. Let's see. I could be a bear." Paw taps his finger to his temple. *Oh no. Anything but a bear.* He reflects on Black Bear. "I could dangle from the web as a spider or I could crawl on my belly as a snake. Perhaps I could be a large fish and swim in the everywhere waters to find out things no one will ever know." Feelings of excitement surge, but with each thought, images of the predator who eats that animal follows.

"No, I suppose I cannot be any of those things. I could never be eaten. That is the worst of things." He turns the lance over and over and thinks, *If only I had my cougar furs.*

Not really sure why, he decides against being a mountain lion. Leaning down with true ambivalence, he touches the wolf hide. He immediately transforms into a husky black wolf with gray eyes. His brother's pant legs split off him and fall to the damp forest ground.

He hears Makes Trouble's heavy breathing.

"Paw, help me! This is bad magic. Something is wrong," Makes Trouble shouts as he returns.

Paw stumbles out of the mist. The two stare at each other, blinking in disbelief.

"Can you understand me?" Makes Trouble snarls.

Paw tilts his head but doesn't answer.

Makes Trouble signs. *Your black fur and gray eyes make me wonder how many wolves have watched me without my ever knowing.*

"Your green eyes frighten me," Paw responds.

My eyes? What about yours? Makes Trouble signs his response.

"I think I would like to be an eagle like Onendah; do you think it is too late to reverse this spell?" Paw asks.

Makes Trouble stares at him blankly, his distorted jaws gaping.

"Do not eat me, monster. I did not cast the spell. You did it of your own free will."

Where's the lance? I have to change back. I would rather be a cricket than this... this... Makes Trouble thinks, scrambling for the golden lance, but its glow has faded. *Oh no. It's too late. What have I done?* His jaw pops and elongates his distorted mouth.

Walpi, now a hefty golden wolf with a black raccoon mask that connects to long black streaks down his back, appears out of nowhere. He snarls and leaps on Makes Trouble. In one swift motion, he manages to knock the hideous creature down. The brownish wolf bites hard on the monster's ear. "Run, Father of Kiowa. I will protect you against this ravenous man-wolf."

Makes Trouble screams from the dreadful pain.

"The love I have for my nephew has taken me to strange places..." Paw glances down at the ground, ignoring the scuffle. He sees his golden heat signal fade from the torn deerskin breeches that have acted as his brothers' legs carrying him all the way to here.

"This is the place where I stand on new legs?" He chuckles as he wobbles forward unsteadily on four feet. He leans down and detects the faint scent of his brother beneath the overwhelming sour scent of years of wear.

"Run, Black Wolf, before this monster eats you!" Walpi shouts. He clamps down on Makes Trouble's crooked ear.

"Please, please let go of my ear. You are hurting me terribly." Makes Trouble snarls, then swipes. The last change to his jaw has made it so that his words only come out in drooling growls and snarls. When Walpi doesn't let go, he signs, *Help.*

Looking up, Paw laughs when he sees Makes Trouble's sign. "That is not a monster, Hopi. That is Makes Trouble."

Walpi releases his bite. "I doubt that. Are you certain?"

Paw looks down at his long sleek black legs. "Onendah said new legs would carry me. I wonder if he knew they would be wolf legs," he says in a tone so low, only animal ears could hear.

Of course he knew! He has great power, Makes Trouble signs.

Paw sits down and lowers his ears. He sees his brother's image in his mind as clearly as if he were standing in front of him. He feels his eyes water and then laughs at the thought of a crying wolf.

"Do you hear that?" Walpi asks, leaping off Makes Trouble's chest.

I do! Makes Trouble signs, feeling a strange sensation electrify him as his mane stands up on the back of his mortal neck.

"What is it?" Walpi asks Paw, but the black wolf is lost in his thoughts.

"It sounds like crying or..."

"Whimpering!"

"Give me peace, boys. I mourn and feel happy for my lost brother, all at the same time."

They both look at him and tilt their furry heads to the side.

"They are happy tears! That is all."

"Warriors cry?" Walpi asks.

Yet I still hear it, Makes Trouble signs, walking over to the fading mist. He looks down and sees Kiowa's fading prints, Anoki's, and a separate set of wolf prints, which glow much brighter than both of the others. The tracks move in the same direction.

Makes Trouble tilts his head up and sniffs the air.

Paw, I do not think we are the only wolves in the forest, he signs, sniffing the tracks and jogging down the trail. He shakes the earth with his massive frame.

Paw, do you hear me? Makes Trouble signs.

Paw remains lost in memories of his brother. "I did not, but I can see that you will not allow me a single moment of reverence."

"These tracks follow Kiowa's and Anoki's trail," Walpi says.

"Kill," they hear a voice say.

CHAPTER 56

Paw stands up, turns around, and clumsily falls over. He can't seem to coordinate his legs. "Don't just stand there; follow them!" he orders the monstrous man-wolf.

Makes Trouble runs off and scans the brush. His hearing is superior to the other wolves and catches the voice saying, "Kill you! I hate you!" But he can't understand who would be this far from the tribe and why they would want to do harm. He grows angry and lashes out in a roar that sends a colony of bats soaring.

"Do you hear that high-pitched noise?" Walpi asks, sprinting toward Makes Trouble. "I can hear the bats chirping like they are in my ears." He runs with his sidekick.

I hear a different song and I recognize it. Makes Trouble motions with terrifying claws and human-like hands.

"What song is that?"

Makes Trouble holds out two long gnarled fingers and draws them behind his towering pointed wolf ears. *Kiowa.* He holds his other gruesome hand up and pats his mouth, signing, *War song.*

The two stop and look at each other. With a nod, they tear off down the trail, catching glimpses of two yellow eyes and a white fanged grin vanishing among the shadows.

"Whoever you are, you cannot run and hide. We track you as you track them," Walpi shouts.

The uncanny duo follows the trail out into an open prairie.

"Look there!" Walpi says, spotting a red wolf in full sprint.

Makes Trouble growls and races after the beast.

Walpi easily forgets his peaceful upbringing and caves to his new carnal instinct. He leads the chase since Makes Trouble can run only on two immense, lumbering legs. Their thudding paws shake the moist grass.

Walpi closes the distance quickly.

"You have nowhere to run or hide!" Makes Trouble shouts to himself, only a hundred feet away.

As the red wolf scales a hill, Walpi presses the charge. He uses his newfound muscles and seemingly inexhaustible energy to close on this intruder. Instead of sending her tumbling as he had Makes Trouble, he stops short, awkwardly finding himself in the middle of his sister's honeymoon. The red wolf is moving fast toward her and Kiowa, so he presses on. Yet his hesitation has cost him.

Anoki sees fiery red eyes leap for her. The impact pushes her and Kiowa over.

Completely surprised, Kiowa scrambles to his feet in time to see a red wolf thrashing its ivory fangs. He watches its reddish-gray snout snap down on her neck and devilishly try to tear at her life-supporting veins.

He locks his yellow eyes with the furious red-eyed beast.

"RELEASE HER!"

Anoki cries out. He swiftly springs into action. His attention is momentarily diverted by a flash of gold. A large golden-brown wolf is racing toward them, and it appears to him that a wolf pack is closing in.

Is our bud of love stomped out before our vows are fulfilled? he wonders.

White and red fur fills the air and float around the action. Sharp claws tear up the earth as the two fight for their lives.

Adrenaline explodes a fire in Kiowa's heart and propels him to attack. He catches the red wolf by her side and bites so hard she has no choice but to release.

With a flip of his neck and a thrust of his legs, Kiowa hurls the red wolf a good distance past the nearing gold wolf.

The red wolf rolls around in the dust, then leaps to its feet and resumes its feral attack. Again it pursues Anoki and finds the thunderous growls of the impressive gray wolf protecting his mate.

Anoki lowers her head and growls, standing behind Kiowa, whose incredible size is easily double both female wolves. His long slate mane bristles. His black lips curl back. His curved fangs are immense, and he wields them as an Indian wields a tomahawk.

He gets as low as he can and prepares to disembowel his red enemy. For a brief moment, he wonders how hard he will have to thrash in order to spill its guts.

But something halts the attack.

"Enough, Kida!" Paw shouts, just now breaching the hill.

Her red eyes turn from Kiowa to Paw. "It is enough when I say it is enough!"

"What is this?" Kiowa asks, keeping his yellow glowing eyes on the pacing red wolf. He recognizes his uncle's voice, but he doesn't recognize the pack of wolves he sees around him. His instincts take control. He lowers his head and glares at each one, readying for the next fight.

Instinctively, the closest wolves snarl back, even though they don't intend to.

Paw wobbles down the hill. "Your fight is not with us. It is not even with the red wolf."

Seeing her chance, Kida, the red wolf, lunges for Anoki.

Her attack initiates a fierce defense. Like a primed bullet, Kiowa's legs explode and shoot his two hundred pounds of imposing muscle. In seconds he is upon her. The impact of his large frame knocks Kida to the ground. He circles her and strikes. She tries to scramble to her feet but can't. She can't even catch her breath.

With his powerful gaping jaws nearing her stomach, she sees that she has no choice. She rolls over and submits. Although most wolves would cease at submission, this wolf persists. His agonizing mauling bites sap her energy. She feels her life slipping from her body and can't summon the strength to fight back. When he clenches down on her hundred-and-twenty-pound body, he thrashes her so viciously, she looks like a rag in his terrible mouth.

A gurgling growl chokes in his throat as he sees a monster that's part man, part wolf running toward him. His ears flatten.

Releasing Kida's limp body, he charges Makes Trouble and moves the hundred-and-eighty-pound man-beast with ease. A fierce fight ensues. Makes Trouble roars more like a lion than a wolf. He swipes with his powerful hands, but proves too slow. Neither sounds like a man now, only beast.

Both are precise with their agonizing bites, and both use their claws on each other's snouts and eyes, but Kiowa proves the quickest and strongest. He pushes Makes Trouble back several feet and tears up flesh with each bite. His long snout overcomes his distorted friend by landing so many bites in so many places, it is as though Makes Trouble is in a fight with a pack of wolves instead of just one. An ocean of pain overwhelms the whimpering reddish-brown monster, who lowers his ears and bows his head.

Walpi, the gold wolf, comes toward him. "It is us, Kiowa," Walpi tries to explain, but when Kiowa turns on him, his face has not even an ounce of recognition. It is as though Kiowa the man is gone and now a terrible wolf with an insane temper has been unleashed. His eyes are like glass, with a pure, evil intent. No humanity lurks in those halos, only the remains of a ruthless killer, forged in the fires of survival for thousands of years.

Kiowa tilts his bloodstained snout and snarls. Saliva and blood drip down his jaw. He charges Walpi with his beastly muscles flexed to fight. Without even so much as an ounce of fight, the gold wolf instinctively rolls over and submits. His submission only lightens Kiowa's bites but does not stop them.

"Ah! Ah! Anoki, help me!" Walpi cries out.

Anoki, the powder-white she-wolf, calmly rests on her back haunches and watches the fighting. She smiles. It pleases her tremendously that Kiowa is able to subdue so many intruders on this, her wedding night.

"ENOUGH!" Paw shouts.

"Yes, enough..." Walpi whimpers, covering his face with his burning paws.

Kiowa steps over Walpi like the hundred-and-seventy-pound wolf is sand.

"It is enough when I say it is enough!" are the first words Kiowa speaks. He charges Paw, and a brutal fight ensues that does not end quickly. They both push each other back and forth, slashing with their fangs and tearing with their claws. The battle for dominance has begun.

When a victor is not so quickly established, Kiowa nips here and there, but the black wolf bares his fangs, which are equally brutal, though Kiowa's are longer and he wields them better. Besides, youth is on his side.

Between growls and high-pitched whimpering cries, fur and

patches of flesh are torn from each wolf's hide, escalating the battle to a life-and-death fight. Paw manages to bite down so hard on Kiowa's back leg that Kiowa believes it may be soon ripped off.

With a deep rallying cry, Kiowa turns on the black wolf. He bites his uncle on top of his head, quickly readjusting his grip until he has half of the black wolf's face in his deadly jaws. With lethal crushing pressure, the two lock up in a fight it seems neither can win. Finally, Kiowa lunges forward, causing Paw's weaker back legs to fold, and he falls over.

Now in the superior position, Kiowa clamps down on his uncle's neck so tight he can feel him struggling for air. With what little effort he has left, Paw bites back, but his power is fading. The two wolves tug at each other, neither willing to give. Eventually Paw's jaw spasms to the point he can no longer hold his grip. He releases his bite. Before he passes out, he's forced onto his back.

Had Paw mastered the use of his new legs, he might have beaten Kiowa and he could have been the pack's leader. As it is, Kiowa subdued every wolf and has plenty of fight left to take on another. Oh yes, he was power. He was fear. He was death!

CHAPTER 57

"Kiowa, can you not see who that wolf is?" Anoki asks.

Somewhere in that ravaged gray beast, Kiowa was also Indian, and when his love spoke, he knew the place. It was his heart.

"That is your uncle. Release him."

Kiowa blinks several times, then opens his mouth. His whole body is on fire from where the wolves bit and clawed him.

"Anoki, it is I, your brother, Walpi," the gold wolf says, keeping a safe distance from her and Kiowa.

"I know who you are. I assume that monster is Makes Trouble. But who is this red wolf? Is this a real wolf, or a skinwalker like us?"

"What happened?" Kiowa asks, as though he has been somewhere else and has just returned.

The other wolves lower their heads and submit, except for Paw. He pants and licks his wounds. Though he won't admit it, his head aches so bad he wonders if his nephew did not fracture his skull.

"Have your senses become so much like the wolf that none of you is man?" Paw asks, wondering why his nephew has treated him so harshly.

Kiowa shakes from his snout to his big bushy tail.

"I do not know. I was here with Anoki. Now I'm here with all of you. Uncle, you are one of us!" the mighty gray wolf says, panting.

Paw tilts his head in total confusion.

"Makes Trouble? Walpi? Onendah changed you as well?"

The two playfully pounce around. Makes Trouble looks ridiculous.

You didn't think we would leave you alone in the dangerous wild, did you? he signs.

Kiowa glances at the red wolf. "Who is this?"

All eyes turn to the limp red wolf.

She is alive. I can hear her heartbeat, Makes Trouble signs.

The wolves circle Kida, growling.

As she comes to, she slowly sits up. Her cracked ribs and sore neck keep her from putting up a fight.

"Kill me quickly!" she says, lowering her head.

Anoki sits beside Kiowa. The early-morning light begins to lighten up the dramatic scene.

"A woman knows the actions of her own. You are the one who loves Kiowa?"

"KIDA!" Kiowa growls, baring his fangs.

With great effort, Kida rises to her feet, taking her most proud stance. "It is I! I am not ashamed of who I am, though now, what I am." She lifts her paw and licks it, "Abandoning our people will not save lives. Our people are excellent trackers. Come, Kiowa. Let us change back to our human forms so we can marry and be one with our people and be together"—she glares at Anoki—"and be happy."

"I am one with my people and I am more happy than I have ever been in all my life."

"The Hopi girl is not our people, and you are happy roaming the plains as a man. As nature intended you. You kill buffalo and protect our people. This is how we live. This is how we have always lived. This is just how things are!"

"Anoki is not people anymore, and neither are we. We are wolves now," Paw says, pointing out an obvious fact that Kida has overlooked.

"It doesn't have to be this way, Kiowa. But if you will not change back, I will go and tell the tribe what you have become. If you think they were angry before, wait until they see you now."

"Do the Kiowa speak wolf? Or do they kill wolves?" Anoki asks.

"Arrggghhh! They will speak to me when I change back," Kida lashes out.

Paw looks up at the rising sun. "Onendah said they would not be able to change until the next harvest moon. This means we cannot change either."

"Not allowed to shape-shift back? But I thought his power would allow us to come and go as we pleased." Kida begins to cry, which sounds like pathetic whimpers.

"Were any of you forced to change? Or have you all chosen this path?" Kiowa asks.

Each wolf reflects on their decision.

"I was the first to choose this!" Walpi proudly proclaims.

I chose the same, Makes Trouble confesses with signs.

"I wasn't sure what I wanted, and I could have been anything. No matter what I would have been, my heart is with my would-be son. Where he goes, I will follow," Paw answers.

"I only transformed into a wolf because I could not think of what kills a wolf, or I would have chosen that," Kida hisses.

"It seems one thing unites us all," Anoki concludes.

"What is that, Hopi girl?" Kida vehemently demands.

Anoki scoots toward Kiowa and rests her paw so it touches his. "Love!"

Kida snarls and skulks away, like Anoki is twisting a knife in her already-bleeding wounds.

"Think of it. I love Kiowa and he loves me. So we chose this. Makes Trouble loves Kiowa like a brother, so here he is. Paw, you could have been anything, but I can see you love your nephew. Walpi, do you love me?"

Walpi nods.

"Even Kida, twisted as her love may be, came to be a wolf through love for Kiowa."

If looks could kill, Kida's face would have killed Anoki. But as they are as harmless as words and since Kiowa already forced her into submission, all she can do is show her discontent by sticking her tongue out and making horrible angry faces.

"Your words are true, Hopi, but what do they mean?" Paw asks.

"Can't you see? We have everything a tribe would need. We have love, warriors, women, and now we have numbers."

"Uhm... Anoki, I wanted to be a lone wolf with just you," Kiowa says, hoping to resume his honeymoon.

"You are so much like your father." Paw chuckles, shaking his head and thinking of the irony in Kiowa's father's name, Lone Wolf.

"I propose this: Accept our love. We would be with a tribe if they would have allowed it. But since they will not, we can have our own tribe."

CHAPTER 58

Kida's lips curl in disgust.

"We have all lost our tribes. But it's okay, because those places can be filled." Anoki smiles and prances around as she thinks of all the children she will have under the protection of her new tribe.

"You are not as sneaky as you think. I know what you are thinking, Hopi girl," Kida declares, grimacing.

Anoki trots over to Kiowa and drags her tail under his chin.

"Yes, indeed. We must organize a pack. This will make us stronger," Paw says.

Yes, a pack. Makes Trouble signs his agreement.

"We cannot skinwalk back into our true human form as we please?" Kida asks a second time.

"No, jealous one. We are stuck this way until next fall," Walpi growls.

"Will I be stuck like this"—Makes Trouble waves his hand over his face and presents his body—"until the harvest moon?" He makes a sour face.

Paw nods.

Makes Trouble grunts out a strangled roar.

"Kiowa is the best warrior among us. He will lead us well," Anoki recommends proudly.

"The elders used to say that the strength of the wolf is the pack, and the strength of the pack is the wolf," Paw says, thinking back to the bonfire stories that once mesmerized him.

Kida slowly turns and begins to walk away.

"Where are you going, Kida?" Kiowa shouts.

She turns around and lowers her head. "I have offended you both and I don't deserve to be a part of your pack. I will make my own way until the moon turns me back to my true form. Then I will go back home."

"And then what?" Kiowa probes her.

"Tell our secret?" Paw asks.

"Of course. The tribe will want to know." She makes eye contact defiantly.

"They will kill all of us, and Onendah, if you do that," Paw tells Kida.

"Then kill me now and be done with me! I am already dead inside. Why not kill the flesh?" She turns and bristles up her mane.

No one can kill my sister, Makes Trouble signs. *You all have someone. She is all I have.*

Anoki moves in front of the men. "Kida, I forgive you."

"I do not ask for your forgiveness!" Kida roars, growling and moving closer to her.

"Nonetheless, you have it. Our numbers are few. The pack will need women to grow our numbers, and none of these fools was smart enough to bring a woman with them. So that leaves you and me."

Kida glances over at the men. "If any of them had a woman, what woman in her right mind would follow them to this life?"

"It can be no other way, Kida. Life is better than death."

Kida stops snarling.

They all look at each other for consensus.

Walpi is the first to nod his assent and, though she isn't certain, Kida thinks he winked at her.

"Fine, till the next harvest moon, then," Kida relents, seeing the wisdom in her enemies' words. Besides, her aching body won't allow her to fight any longer.

"Let this be our order, then, and let each of you show it by a vote."

One by one, the wolves circle around Kiowa.

"Put your paws together on top of mine and repeat after me."

They obey him.

Makes Trouble is the last to rest his enormous foot on top of their paws, setting it down as gently as he can.

"This is our only law. The strength of the wolf is the pack. And the strength of the pack is the wolf."

As a group, they take their oath.

"Now let us go from this place, for we must learn how to hunt with our mouths and run with four legs," Kiowa says, taking the lead.

Paw sighs. "I am going to starve, as I am clumsy with all of these legs." He hobbles away, feeling a sobering agony from his wounds. An agony all the wolves share, except Anoki.

***

John picks his nose and goes to eat it, but Charlie's disgusted expression halts him. He looks up like nothing is happening and wipes his booger on the bottom of his shoe.

Charlie gags, then takes a moment to regain his composure.

"As I've said, the Indians survived on the buffalo. So when they became wolves, they still had to rely on the buffalo for survival. But now they had to learn how to hunt as wolves."

"Wait. Wouldn't Kida still be in love with Kiowa? How can they live together?" Zack asks.

"You're thinking about this all wrong. See, the Indians saw all things as necessity. Kida did everything in her power to win Kiowa over and she failed. Now her obligation was to fill a role in the tribe."

"What happens if she doesn't?" John asks.

"You don't wanna be an Indian without an occupation. That would mean you're expendable," Charlie answers.

"So even if she did love him, she had a job to do?" Zack inquires.

"It's not a job; it's her obligation. And if she fell short on a hunt and cost the tribe food, well, then, you better believe she was going to face some punishment."

"Are you saying she didn't really love Kiowa?" Kevin asks.

"Whether she did or didn't, Kiowa chose Anoki. See, boys, it's like this: One day you will all choose a bride, and it doesn't matter if anyone else has feelings for you. All that matters is that you choose, and life goes on."

"So the Indian wolves valued occupation more than love?" John nods, answering his own question.

"That might be true for Kida. Can we get back to the story?" Charlie asks.

***

Out on a vast open prairie, the wolves crouch on a high mountain. Not a single cloud hovers in the sea-blue sky, while emerald grass stretches out like an ocean.

"Makes Trouble, I am afraid," Walpi whispers to the monster who has both taught him the Kiowa signs and become his mentor.

Makes Trouble draws a deep, growling breath. His auburn, black-flecked patches of fur add to his hideous nature. He looks at Walpi, crosses his legs, and patiently signs, *Don't be. The buffalo that lead the pack are not the buffalo that you will attack. Wolves and Indians hunt the same. Kill the old. Run the herd till it tires, then pick off the weak or young. Eat, grow stronger, live to hunt another day.*

"How can you tell the weak from the old?"

That is sometimes hard. Older buffalo have gray hairs on their chests and back. But both will separate from the herd, and that is always their biggest mistake.

"Then what?"

Then, when the herd circles around the young, the hunter among us with the greatest courage and the strongest magic will attack the largest buffalo.

"Why do we attack the largest buffalo when we can sustain ourselves off the weak and old?"

Because it is a great honor to kill the courageous ones.

"Can't we get hurt?"

Yes, but they will, too.

"I don't want to get hurt."

None of us do. That's why we use magic.

"But your magic didn't work on you. And besides, I don't have any magic."

Well, you'd better borrow some or you are going to get hurt, Hopi. I swear, all these questions end in one of two ways: Run and kill or run and die.

"One more question."

Makes Trouble growls with a dull, impatient rumble. *Yes?*

"I am afraid of more than the hunt."

What else scares you besides being mauled by buffalo hooves or stabbed by their horns?

Kida.

Makes Trouble looks at his sister and tilts his gory head to the side in confusion. *Why Kida?* he signs.

"She keeps staring at me," Walpi signs back with trembling paws.

CHAPTER 59

Makes Trouble covers his snout with his mutated hand in embarrassment.

Why do you stare at Walpi, Kida? he signs emphatically.

"I do not know." She glances away, thinking on it.

"Do you have to stare at all times?" Walpi asks.

"Yes!"

Makes Trouble laughs. He gets up and walks away, joining Paw and Kiowa.

"Do not leave me by myself, Makes Trouble. She attacked my sister. She will attack me," Walpi hisses through clenched teeth.

Makes Trouble glances at Kida. *Yes, but I do not think she is going to attack you with her teeth.*

Kida licks her lips.

Paw glances back at her and watches her crawl closer to Walpi.

"A woman's heart is like a murky creek. First she is blinded by soot, but when the dust settles, things become clear," Kida says, lowering her head and looking up at Walpi with wanton eyes. She presses her soft red fur against his side, then turns to look at him and see if it's okay.

"If you will stop staring at me, you can sit beside me," he says, scooting his hind legs away.

She looks away, then back at him.

Then away.

Then back.

Kiowa, Makes Trouble, and Paw laugh as they watch the awkwardness unfold.

"You were wise to have us hunt small game through the fall before we moved on to the herd. My legs have adjusted well and my senses are keen," Paw compliments his leader.

"I guess we are all rabbits…" Kiowa answers.

Until we are not! Makes Trouble proudly protests.

Kiowa looks at Paw and says, "The pack is only as strong as its slowest wolf."

"Slowest?" Paw questions.

What do you mean? Makes Trouble signs to Kiowa, offended.

"You are not fast enough to keep up with us, and you will only run the herd off."

But if I don't hunt, then I won't get to eat, Makes Trouble signs.

"Then you will have to eat rabbits until you figure out how to be like us."

I hate rabbits! I am so sick of eating them, and I am hungrier than I've ever been, Makes Trouble signs.

Paw turns his attention back to Kiowa. "I propose we chase the herds to the water and weaken the younglings and calves. Keep Anoki and Kida on opposite flanks to keep the herd moving, while the four of us kill the slowest. Attack any foolish enough to turn around, and leave this hideous monster here so he doesn't get hurt."

Makes Trouble bristles and storms off.

"Let us go," Kiowa says.

The wolves slither down the hill, crouching as low as they can. When they reach the thigh-high sagebrush, they completely disappear in the thick gray brush. In open spaces, they move with such stealth, the grazing buffalo fail to see their colorful coats streak across the open green places.

A very large, older male draws a crowd as he samples grass. Their tight cluster eventually spreads out.

"This grass is fresh and crisp. Move the herd closer to the spring. We can eat here and drink from the cool spring."

The herd moves closer to a shallow stream that widens in some spots and narrows in others.

"I could eat here all day, Long Horns." Blossom, his mate chews and nods.

She looks up and scans the sparkling stream and notices a cluster of cottonwood trees in a depression. As her lower jaw shifts back and forth, grinding grass, she notices that the songbirds in the trees aren't singing their usual melodies.

"Well, good morning to you, little birds," Blossom says with a snort. She shakes her long, dusty, brown-matted hide.

She looks around and notices that rabbits and gophers that usually poke their heads up curiously are scattering for their holes.

"You have nothing to fear from us. Come out, friends," Blossom encourages them.

"Do you hear that?" Long Horns asks Blossom.

"I don't hear anything."

"Not even the birds chirping?"

The two glance at each other, then at Clover, who tears up a patch of grass and shakes the clumped dirt from the roots.

"The roots are really good too. I like to chew them with the tops, because it adds an earthiness that tastes the best."

Blossom and Long Horns look out on the distant horizon but fail to see the wolf pack.

"I don't see any Indians," Long Horns says, straining his eyes to see. "'Course, you don't always. They're usually pretty sneaky."

"I hate the Indians! I can't wait for the Great White Buffalo to come from the sun and lead us all back to the safe lands," Blossom says, admiring Long Horns's lengthy beard.

"You don't believe that old ghost story, do you?" Clover asks around a mouthful of food.

"I have to, for the children. We are hunted by bears, cougars, bitten by deadly snakes, and slaughtered by Indians. The Great White Buffalo is the only hope our herd has."

"Buffalo say they have spoken to him. They say he's going to lead us all into a big cave, where he will raise and lower the sun for us."

"I heard we won't have to wander because the grass will grow right beneath our hooves as we eat it."

"Could you imagine that?"

The two move over to the taller grass, testing it first with their horns to spook the rattlesnakes.

"Lemon just doesn't understand how good the tall grass is. Let's keep it to ourselves and not tell the old cow." Clover chuckles with a wink.

With hardly a care in the world, Long Horns tears a large chunk of grass from the ground and chews it.

He leans back down, wraps his pink tongue around lime-green

stalks, and pulls them into his mouth. When he looks up, he sees something that makes him relax his grasp and snort. Two yellow eyes surrounded by a white-and-black wolf mask keep him frozen in place. Kiowa lunges for the bull, snatching down on his snout. He uses his mouth to cover Long Horn's nose to cut off his air supply.

CHAPTER 60

"Rrruuunnn!" Blossom snorts and runs off with a grunt. Clover is quick to follow.

One by one the wolves make their appearance. They leap out of the grass and bite at Long Horns's legs. Kida and Paw successfully seize both of Long Horns's hind legs and work as anchors to keep him from charging Kiowa.

Kida swiftly maneuvers around the big bull's side and latches on to a thick chunk of matted fur. Dropping down to her haunches, she brutally tugs and tugs, until Long Horns loses his balance and falls over.

Anoki leaps on top of the bison and uses her weight to help pin him. She nips at him and makes every effort to contribute. But being an inexperienced hunter, she annoys him more than hurts him. She looks up at her brother and shouts, "Do something!"

"Walpi, Anoki, charge the herd!" Kida orders the two ineffective wolves.

Walpi and Anoki look at each other with mutual baffled expressions.

"Charge them where?"

Makes Trouble shows them inadvertently by running after the beasts, two-legged. He stretches out his arms and screams, "MEAT! I NEED MEAT!" His efforts cue Walpi and Anoki. They are quick to take advantage of the gap between the monster and the herd.

Paw's and Kiowa's primal snarls terrify Long Horns. He tries to fight with powerful bucking motions, but it's pointless. His blood is already soaking the grass. Paw has begun pulling his entrails out of his abdomen.

Kiowa releases his bite and resets his powerful jaws around the groaning bull's neck. Sifting through Long Horns's thick mane for a pounding pulse, he maneuvers until he feels a beat rattle against his fangs. With one severe chomp, he punctures, twists, then pulls till he snaps the carotid artery.

The old bull releases his last breath. His tongue dangles out the side of his mouth and his big brown eyes roll up into the top of his head.

Blood stains the warriors' snouts. It mixes with their saliva and oozes down their chins.

"The honor is yours, Kiowa!" Paw commends his nephew. "You killed the biggest bull in their tribe!"

"Hurry. We must take as many as we can get," Kida shouts, already sprinting after the stampeding herd.

Kiowa leaps over the carcass and speeds past her. His paws thud as they hit the earth nearly as hard as the buffalos'. Dirt and grass kick up behind him. The powerful wolf moves with a flash. His silvery coat streaks across the green grass and is quickly ahead of his pack. Now he leads a lone attack on the frightened herd.

Blossom and Clover reunite with the herd's leader, Raging Bull.

"Raging Bull, help! Wolves attacked Long Horns."

"Impossible! Wolves wouldn't dare attack our herd in broad daylight."

"It's true! Come see for yourself."

Raging Bull follows the cows, where he comes face-to-face with Kiowa. True to his name, he lowers his head and aggressively charges the wolf leader in a heated rage. Kiowa easily darts to the side, dodging the lethal horns.

As his pack draws near, he orders them to continue the chase. The wolves obey in a flash of red, white, gold, and russet. They streak past him and continue their pursuit.

"Ha! Ha! You have not brought a large enough pack!" Raging Bull shouts, spinning his towering body abruptly.

"I'm going to stay with the herd, Clover," Blossom shouts, trotting after the buffalos' dust trail.

"What do wolves want with our herd? Shouldn't you be chasing elk and deer?"

Kiowa calmly sits down a few feet in front of his prey. "We are not wolves. We are Indians."

"You don't look like Indians. You look like wolves."

"We are skinwalkers."

"What is your name, skinwalker?"

"Kiowa, son of Lone Wolf."

"You cannot live off our herd as you once did, Kiowa. For we were once a proud many, but we are now becoming few."

"Buffalo have always been many. You are just a small herd. We will not make you much smaller."

"When have you ever seen a herd so small? I am telling you, skinwalker, we are being hunted daily by men with horses and powerful thunder sticks. I know not what we have done to offend the Sun God, but he must be angry with us to curse us this way."

Kiowa yawns, showing his pink-stained teeth.

Raging Bull glances at the sun. "I am afraid that one day there will be no more herds."

"What do your problems have to do with my tribe? As a man or a wolf, I must put meat in their mouths. It is my duty as a man. I care only that I have enough to eat. Do you plead to the grass when you eat it?"

"You are a fool. You will hunt us until we are no more, and then what will you eat?" Raging Bull shouts as he lowers his horns and presses an attack.

Kiowa leads Raging Bull, teasing him with his tail. He stays close enough to entice but far enough not to be caught. With great cunning, Kiowa leads Raging Bull to the stream bed.

When the bull tires, he hobbles down the incline into the stream and rolls around to cool off. Meanwhile the wolf remains atop of the embankment, darting to and fro energetically, to exhibit he is still fresh for a fight.

"I am not the foolish one. Without the head buffalo, the herd will run in circles and die!"

Raging Bull scampers to his hooves. He thrusts and hustles his way up the bank. Across the stream he can see his family huddled together and moving in large circles. The proud bull knows that the Indian-wolf is right. Without a leader, they will not know which direction to run, and the weak will wander to their death.

"I believe that you are Indian. You hunt as Indians, dividing us this way and that."

Kiowa turns the tables. Instead of playfully pouncing, he suddenly crouches low and bares his teeth. He releases low menacing growls, readied for a fight.

"One day the Sun God will release the Great White Buffalo. He has come before. He will come again."

Kiowa lunges and snaps at Raging Bull to get him moving. "Our magic is from the same god. He has granted us power to skinwalk. I have seen your Great White Buffalo, but he will never take our powers! Who do you think has brought me here?"

Raging Bull turns about and tries with every effort to connect his horns with Kiowa, but the wolf is too clever and too fast.

"Did you see him leading the buffalo to the great cave?" Raging Bull asks with a thrust.

"I did not see where he led the herd. But it does not matter. I will find this cave, and my pack will feast for an eternity!" Kiowa answers, snapping his savage jaws at the bull leader.

The two go back and forth, up and down the stream. Kiowa shows how he's mastered the terrain. He uses words to fan the flames of fury, then engages Raging Bull, to keep him angry and exhausted.

The pursuit takes some time, but the game comes to a regretful end for the buffalo herd.

Across the plains the herd is at the complete mercy of the wolves.

CHAPTER 61

Without their esteemed leader, Raging Bull, the herd clusters together and mills around in a disorganized circle. Dust clouds form all around their meandering traffic. It serves as cloud cover and allows the wolves to mix in and strike where they please.

"Circle back for Raging Bull," Thunderfoot shouts at the confused herd.

"Show us the way and we will follow!" a young bull answers.

Thunderfoot strains to see through the dust, but the choking air is incredibly thick, and he cannot see which way to go.

Kida disappears into the dust cloud created by the terrified buffalo.

As the young tire and separate from their mothers, the Indians are there to catch them. Kida emerges from the cloud with a wailing yearling clenched in her jaws. Makes Trouble runs up and opens his arms.

She drops the calf. "Who is faster than the wind now, ugly brother?" She grimaces and turns away. Within moments, she has another calf on its side.

Makes Trouble wants to sign an insult back, but instead, he scoops the calf up and turns to run off with it.

This is much easier than hunting with bows and arrows, Makes Trouble thinks as Paw sprints past him. He snarls at the black wolf, who returns the insult with a clacking snap.

"I will do as you tell me!" Walpi shouts to Kida, approaching the herd.

His words please her. She smiles and bares her white fangs. Her cinnamon fur glows brilliantly in the sun's setting light and makes her seem more like a fox than a wolf.

"Don't wait to be told, Hopi. Act for yourself!"

Walpi joins in the fight by biting a young buffalo on the same side as Kida.

"No, Hopi... Go for the throat. I will steady him."

Walpi hesitates. "What if I get hit by its horns?"

"He doesn't have horns. He is a child. If you want to stop being treated as Hopi, you must stop acting as Hopi! Become a wolf! Kill!"

Walpi bites down on the panicked calf's neck. He feels its pulse pound against his teeth and immediately releases.

"I'm sorry, Buffalo. I once was Hopi and grew corn. But I cannot grow corn anymore, so I must do as Kida says."

He bites down in the same place and resumes his grip.

"I prefer you as Hopi," the buffalo calf gurgles.

Walpi lacks confidence and has to reset his bite several times, causing the game a great deal of pain.

"You don't have to torture it unnecessarily, Walpi, like your beautiful fur tortures my eyes."

For the first time Walpi thinks he understands why Kida stares at him. *She wants to kill me and wear my fur as they wear scalps on their belts*, He shakes his head back and forth as he saw Kiowa do, until the buffalo eventually submits and dies. When he doesn't feel a pulse, he slowly releases. Sadness swells inside. He puts on a brave face and looks at Kida with his blood-soaked snout and paws.

"There, now I have given you reason to stare all you like!" he pants, probing to see if Kida stares at him for a different reason than the one that haunts him.

Kida smiles at him. She turns and scans the herd until she spots the white wolf going after a fatigued yearling. "Let us see what Anoki, the Hopi princess, can do."

Anoki snaps at the buffalo's hindquarters, but with no real success.

"Slow down, Buffalo!" she shouts.

"No. You're going to eat me!"

"Yes, but this is the natural way."

The calf picks up its pace and shouts, "Mama!"

Kiowa flanks the calf and charges it so quickly that both he and the buffalo collide in a bone-rattling explosion. A cloud of dust explodes around the two. Its neck bends at on oblique angle, and it falls dead.

Anoki stares at him with sparkling topaz eyes. "You are more powerful than I imagined!"

Kiowa smiles and pushes his broad chest out. "Follow me!"

Anoki capers behind him with a devilish grin.

Off in the distance, Kida sighs. She puts her head down and begins to whimper.

Paw slowly walks up beside her and lies down. He pants for a moment and then licks his blood-soaked lips.

"Kida, you must let go of your pain. Kiowa never loved you. His heart is with the white wolf. Surely your eyes can see this."

Tears well up in her eyes. "My heart aches. Will I ever love another as much as I loved him?"

Paw puts his arm around her. "In time I think you will."

***

W.H. stands on concrete steps in front of the Université de Saint-Boniface. It's Winnipeg's first Western university and was founded in 1818. The three-story rectangular building, including attic, has a gabled roof and a Colonial bell tower styled after a Roman gazebo. The decorative roof on the bell tower is of such a design and size that in comparison to the rest of the building, it makes the building seem like it's been crowned.

W.H. takes in every architectural detail first, then steps back and sees the picture in its entirety. Oak clapboard, painted white, gives the lines a symmetry that makes the building seem neat and orderly. Male students entering the front doors in their suits and ties prove that the standard of tidiness is upheld.

W.H. gazes at his reflection in the tall, lead-glass Colonial windows. He chuckles at his distorted image as he sways back and forth.

They sure did a good job matching the front turret to the bell tower, he thinks as he scans the high and low arches.

"I suppose I'm late for class," he mumbles as the bell rings. He joins the crowd of young men shuffling through the halls and into their classes. Biting his bottom lip, he shoves his hands in his brown suit pockets and tucks his belt-strapped books under his arm.

He reaches for the classroom door and opens it. With one foot out, he's about to join the last of the fluttering students, but he hesitates. He retracts his step and puts his hand on the yellow maple wainscoting, feeling the smooth surface. He isn't sure why, but his hand refuses to let go of the classroom door handle and his lead feet seem to be in communication, as they will not allow him to take one step in. The bell seems to chime, *W.H., you're late. Late to your first day of winter semester.*

He closes his eyes and imagines being on the other side of the door. He can hear it slam shut. In those stuffy classrooms, he's forced to learn algebra, geometry, finance, and Latin. The slamming door triggers an avalanche of dissatisfaction he's felt in class his entire freshman year. *If I join them, I'm never going to be anything but a man in a suit*, he cautions himself, pressing his hand to his bottom lip.

With a deep grumble, he adjusts his round, gold-framed glasses and looks up at the beautiful, artistic building.

"That's my problem. I'm too young to burden myself with all this art."

He drops his books in front of the door. With a swift grip, he swings around and marches down the wood-trimmed hallway, turning to the right toward the dean's office.

With rebellious determination in his eyes, he twists a brass door, swings it open, and boldly storms into the office. He passes a gold-etched placard with the name Dr. Bennett, PhD, Headmaster.

"How may I help you?" a middle-aged secretary with bright red hair and green eyes asks the fiery youth.

"I need to speak with the dean."

"Do you have an appointment?"

W.H. takes a step back, gets a wild look in his eyes, and says, "The art of the wild tells me I go where I want when I want! Is he in there or ain't he?"

Startled by his boisterous, unsettling behavior, the secretary takes his glasses off, showcasing a firmness he had not expected.

"Yes, but do you have an appointment?"

A red-brown mahogany door opens behind him.

"Come in." An older, gray-haired gentleman in a fine black 1800s-standard suit accepts the unsolicited appointment.

W.H. storms past the fussy secretary.

"He needs an appointment."

"This one is different, Herbert," the headmaster says, winking at her.

As W.H. enters the office, the old man rises and motions for him to sit down.

But W.H. waves him off and blurts out, "Sir, I'm here to resign my seat and scholarship."

CHAPTER 62

Dumbfounded, Dr. Bennett repeatedly blinks, then tries to bring the youth to heel by holding his hands up and shushing W.H. "Now, hold on."

W.H. clenches his fists and rocks back and forth until he stands on the tips of his toes. "I'm determined, sir!"

The wise academic takes a long, deep breath and slowly rests his body in a creaking leather desk chair.

"What reason have you to abandon such a fine institution, my good nephew?"

W.H. moves forward. His big blue eyes flash. Words practically explode off his lips. "Well, sir, I've decided that I'm a better hunter than a student."

The headmaster leans back and presses his hands together, locking his fingers. He furrows his brows disapprovingly. "So it'll be the Hudson's Bay Company for you then, eh? And how much does the fur-trap business pay?"

"Well, sir, I've decided that I'm a better hunter than most. I can make three whole dollars an antelope hide, five for buffalo, and fifteen for wolves."

"So it's the wild that calls you, is it? Dollars for hides hardly seems like a fair exchange, considering you have to extinguish lives for the furs."

An evil grin lights up W.H.'s face. "I feel almost the same way, sir. But wolves are evil, and ain't nobody gonna miss a wolf!"

"Isn't," his uncle corrects. "I, ah, see you are motivated by short-term gains versus long-term rewards..." He pauses to see if his barb will hook. When it doesn't, he works a different angle. "You esteem adventure and bounties as greater rewards than knowledge?"

W.H. holds his fingers up and rubs them together. "At present, sir, it pays better than the books."

"That is because education is like a crop. It is only of value once the seed is planted, given time to grow, and then it can be harvested. You have only begun to plant your seed and already you are saying the crop has no value? Do you realize that maybe five percent of the population is educated? Do you know what the family had to sacrifice for you to sit in that seat? Do you have any idea how many others would kill to be in your boots?"

"I'm not saying anything, sir. You know I've been hunting wolves since I was old enough to carry a rifle. I'm just a better hunter than student. Doesn't it make sense to do what you excel at?"

"So there's nothing a salty old man can say that might change your mind and convince you to exhaust your scholarship?"

"No, sir. I've already had enough success over the break that my pockets are weighed down with more pounds than I've ever had. I had to buy a new belt just to keep my britches up."

"I see. What will you do with these gains?"

"I'll invest in better equipment and start my own fur-trade company. Maybe be the next Hudson's Bay Company."

"Uh-huh, and once you've killed all the wolves?"

"That will never happen, sir."

"Perhaps, or perhaps not. These days so many men have guns, it's a wonder any critters wander the earth."

"My point exactly, sir. I gotta get while the getting is good!"

"You are a young man now. You can withdraw from the trust. But I have to warn you that seats are so competitive, you most likely will not be able to return. Plus your scholarship will go to someone else. It's not like these things remain idle." In a flurry of frustration, his uncle shows a hint of anger. "What was all this going on about you being an artist, wanting to build great coliseums? What of your writing? You know it will suffer if you abandon it." Realizing he's not getting anywhere, he transitions. Dr. Bennett leans back in his chair and locks his hands behind his head. "I'm curious. Where will your hunts take you?"

"North woods in Vancouver. They have plenty of wolves to hunt there, and the bounty is sufficient."

"Well, I wish you the best, Nephew. See to it that you write to me from time to time and inform me of this great adventure. I will do my best to see if I can secure a seat for you in the event you should change your mind."

W.H. extends his hand, "Thank you, Uncle, for your understanding. I promise I won't regret it. Or I mean, you won't."

The headmaster raises his eyebrows and reluctantly extends his hand.

***

Kevin lifts a stack of three burning marshmallows to his mouth. With several heaves, he blows them out.

"I'd quit school to shoot wolves. 'Specially if I was getting paid for it," Luther says with a greedy grin, rubbing his hands together.

"Yeah, me too. The most richest men in the world dropped out of school. I'll do the same," John affirms.

Kevin looks at the boys, then thinks over his own options. "I like school. I think I'd stay in and then hunt wolves afterward! I mean, it's not like they're going anywhere." He turns his attention to his scorched marshmallows. He stuffs the burning, ashy treats into his mouth, which simultaneously puffs out his cheeks and causes him to inhale great puffs of air to cool them down.

"W.H. probably should have stayed in boarding school. Instead, he followed his heart. Like most fools at that age, he thought he knew exactly what he wanted. Ideas are sometimes better than reality, though," Charlie says to discourage the boys from abandoning their education.

***

Several months later, W.H. sits at King's Pub.

"What will it be for you, W.H.?"

"I'll take water. I ain't got no money."

"No money? There's the door. We don't pour charity at this pub. It's whiskey and ale. Besides, it ain't even noon yet. You shouldn't even be in here."

Shocked by his buddy's response, W.H. protests. He cites all the money he's spent at the joint and all the additional customers that came to the bar just to hear his "hero" story. He made sure to comment on how he saved the lumberjack's life. It's no use. The bartender combs his fingers through his imperial mustache with one hand, while the other disappears beneath the bar.

W.H. knows that he's about to be billy clubbed or shot, and he doesn't have enough liquid courage in him to endure either. He lowers his head in shame, slouches his shoulders, and slides off the circular barstool. With a flick of his hand, he sends the wheel seat spinning all the way down to its base. Dragging his feet, he makes his way over to the glass door that reads, King's Pub.

Instead of using the bright brass handle, he presses his hand to the glass and leaves an oily palm print. For some reason, this act of resistance seems a better result to him than the arguments his lips fail to form.

When the bell rings from the breeze and the door slowly shuts behind him, he glances at his white Appalachian mountain horse. Taking a quick inventory of the pans, sleeping roll, water jugs, and rifle holster that bog down the beast, W.H. begins to regret the timing of his decision to drop out of school.

"Guess boarding in the dormitories weren't so bad after all." He pouts, wishing his home weren't strapped to his horse's back.

Bingo, his ever-faithful collie, rests at the horse's feet. He releases short whimpers to let W.H. know he's hungry. But the message gets mixed with his wagging tail.

W.H. reaches inside his pockets and turns them inside out. "Looks like we're going to have to eat out of the rubbish pail again, buddy."

Bingo barks and stands up on his hind legs. He turns around in a circle and points at the alley.

W.H. watches the alley and finds what he's looking for; the pub's overweight cook is dumping last week's chili. He waits for the worker to slip back inside his kitchen. Looking left and right to make sure no dignified persons see him, he sprints across the muddy street, trying his best to keep his feet dry. He smacks his lips as he feels his toes get wet. The drive for hunger carries a penalty of discomfort, as does rummaging through the garbage pile. Sweeping the debris away, he seizes his "kill," a mush pile of burnt chili. He scoops it up with his tin pan and tucks it under his arm as he scurries off. A breeze picks up and forces him to turn his collar up. He pushes his hands deep in his pockets to keep his hands warm.

***

The boys cup their hands to their mouths.

"Ew!"

"Gross!"

"I would have stayed in school." Zack makes a gagging noise at the thought of eating garbage.

"Me too!" John joins in.

"Yeah, I'd never eat trash!" Luther sticks his tongue out dramatically.

"Yuck!" Kevin chimes in after swallowing more marshmallows.

"Yes, sir, boys. Times were a hard for W.H. He and Bingo had to eat mice, rabbits, and squirrels for a short time, too. That is, until something happened a way down southwest. In the frontier lands, near the Mexican border."

CHAPTER 63

Kiowa and his pack perch like Lords of the Hunt on top of their mountaintop. They scan left and right and patiently wait for flashes of movement.

"This is our seventh peak in three weeks and we have seen no buffalo," Paw says, echoing Kiowa's thoughts.

"I am starving," Walpi grumbles.

"I could chew the bark off a tree," Kida says, looking at the pine trunks next to her.

Kiowa, walk with me, Makes Trouble signs, motioning for his friend.

Kiowa slowly stands up, stretching his legs. He turns and follows Makes Trouble a good distance from the pack.

A short distance away, Makes Trouble signs, *Perhaps Raging Bull was telling the truth. We have never, in all of our lives, gone so long without seeing so much as a buffalo track. Our senses are heightened and still we struggle for even a trace. Something is out of order.*

"Or perhaps Raging Bull's herd has warned all the buffalo that wolves are hunting them in lands that were once safe."

Makes Trouble nods. *Maybe.*

"Have the buffalo wings?" Kiowa asks.

Makes Trouble looks at him with a dumbfounded expression on his face.

"They cannot take to the skies, my friend. We will follow the streams until we find a trail. That is what we have always done. It is reasonable to think that animals drink water, is it not?"

This is true, and the streams are high.

"We will find something to ease our pain. Then we will find the buffalo when we have our strength back."

Though Paw can see and hear Kiowa and Makes Trouble's

conversation, there was something unsettling in that old buffalo's warning, and he feels uneasy.

I will go look for food down where the pale-face work the land, Makes Trouble decides.

"You are so ugly. Why did you resist the magic?"

Makes Trouble's shoulders droop and his long ears flatten out.

Am I to be a monster all of my days?

***

A few days later Makes Trouble hides quietly, waiting for night to fall. Earlier in the day he had detected a strong chicken scent and followed his nose to a small ranch that was recently settled and is still under construction. He nestled into the sage grass and observed them all day.

To his great delight, he sees the man of the house kiss his wife and children good-bye, mount his horse, and ride out on some business, no doubt.

What a fool. To leave all of this unprotected. His little woman. His children. His animals. I am going to talk to Kiowa about raiding these foolish, pale people. They have scalps to lose and bounty aplenty.

His lime-green glowing eyes seem to hover in the descending night. Looking through the window, he waits patiently until the candles are blown out and the lanterns dim to darkness. It is time to make trouble and move.

Fortunately for me, the moon is out and will light the way so that no snakes will surprise me and bite me. Oh, how I hate rattlesnakes.

Exercising extreme caution, he moves his massive disfigured frame across the grass with a swiftness and a stealthiness unnatural for a man.

The family bloodhound picks up the intruder's scent and charges him just as he enters the coop.

Makes Trouble releases a low growl that shakes the walls of the henhouse and starts the hens clucking.

The dog lowers his head, tucks his tail between his legs, and disappears into the night.

"Hush, hush, hush," he hisses, holding his long, gnarled fingers up to his fanged mouth. *Hush, round, tame white birds. We do not want to wake up the little woman and scare her small children, do we?* he signs.

The hens quiet down.

"What is that noise?" Anna, a hen, clucks to her neighbor, Beverly.

"Oh, I don't know. Master is so good to us. He knows a fed hen is a well-bred hen." Beverly yawns, then falls fast asleep.

"He sure does stink. More than usual. It smells like he's bathed…" Before Anna can finish her sentence, Makes Trouble scoops her up. She frantically flutters her wings and attempts to squawk. But Make Trouble's elongated fingers wrap around her beak and head. She feels a tight pressure and then…crack.

See, now, isn't that better? Makes Trouble asks as he opens his giant mouth and stuffs the limp hen in. He nearly swallows her whole.

Gathering one victim after another, Makes Trouble gorges himself. He pays no attention to the farmer's wife, who hears the hens' clucking and lights a lantern, which now illuminates the second-story window.

The intruder doesn't hear the front door slam behind her, and he doesn't hear her cock a double-barreled shotgun.

Makes Trouble is so preoccupied with filling his belly and gathering for the pack that he doesn't detect Lorraine Kelsey till it is too late.

"I'm gonna count to three, and if I don't hear an answer, I'm gonna assume you're a fox," Lorraine shouts.

"One Mississippi." She pushes the buttstock up to her shoulder.

"Two Mississippi." She closes one eye and holds the lantern out as she reaches for the door.

"Three Mississippi." She twists the handle and pulls it wide open.

CHAPTER 64

When Mrs. Kelsey opens the shed door, she is not prepared for what the devil has in store for her this wicked, enchanted night. She catches Makes Trouble with his monstrous head tilted back, jaws gaping, twitching hen going down the monster's hatch.

"ARRRRGGGGGHHHH," Lorraine shouts as she pulls both triggers, which sends her tiny frame soaring back in the air. When she lands, she hits so hard, she knocks herself out.

***

Days later, Kiowa and the pack use a stream to follow Makes Trouble's trail. He has not returned, and so they have become worried and determine it is time to go looking for him.

"It is hard for me to believe that this river is reduced to a stream in the hot days," Kida says, scanning the glittering ripples.

"In the rainy season, it rages so hard it brings down trees and cuts pathways through mountains," Walpi tells her.

"I smell something," Anoki says, tilting her wet, black nose to the sky. She takes several quick shallow breaths and detects the strong aroma of a musky animal.

"As do I," Kida says, doing the same.

Paw raises his ears. They shift back and forth, then hold steady. "I hear something," Paw says, focusing his attention.

Kiowa puts his nose to the ground and follows the strong odor. "Makes Trouble came this way."

Paw examines the tracks. He sees Makes Trouble's enormous tracks. All around them are strange, small, pointy hoof tracks that are tightly clustered together.

"I don't like this," he says.

"Don't like what?" Kida asks, detecting concern in his voice.

"It looks like all these little buffalo chased your brother."

"Chased him where?"

"I cannot say. All I can say is that he ran that way." Kiowa points with a paw and begins forming a quick plan.

"If they have harmed one hair on his ugly face, we will surprise them and kill as many as we can," Kida says.

The wolves follow the mysterious trail downstream, eager to learn what has become of their good friend and brother.

***

Farther downstream, two amiable, puffy white sheep are carefully positioned beside the gentle waters.

"You go first," a large, fluffy sheep bleats.

"No. You said you were thirsty. You go first," the second, incredibly polite sheep responds.

"No, I insist. You were here first."

As the two courteously banter back and forth, the rest of the herd begin to behave strangely. Sheep leap over one another, back to front and side to side.

Kiowa seizes a sheep and thrashes his head back forth, nearly ripping it in half. Unable to fight back, the animal goes limp and dies.

"For Makes Trouble!"

"Arrghhh, help me," the flock cry out, hopping to and fro.

The wolves circle around the sheep and herd them into a giant downy circle. Spots of black sheep make them look like a cup of salt sprinkled with pepper.

"Help us, Billy Bob," the sheep cry out.

From the center of the herd, a brown-and-white-spotted goat with wide rectangular pupils courageously leaps out to face the wolves.

"I'm ah-only gonna tell you once to put that sheep down, then I'm ah-gonna-ah ram ya!" Billy Bob shouts, stomping his hoof.

Walpi looks at the goat and cocks his head to the side.

"Fine, have it a-yer way," Billy Bob shouts. He lowers his horns and gallops in a rather odd staccato fashion.

Unsure of what the pack has encountered or what to do, Walpi freezes at the terrifying *rat-a-tat* noise the goat's hooves make. *Am I to share the same fate as Makes Trouble?*

"Ufff." The air escapes from Walpi's lungs in a rush.

"Help! Help! I have no power. I could not get magic or steal it!" Walpi yelps, struggling to catch his breath.

"Did it hurt?" Anoki asks, bounding backward in several frightened pounces.

The rest of the pack laughs at him with large toothy muzzles.

Kida quickly seizes the goat by the throat and delivers the death blow. She immediately regrets her decision.

"Yuck. It tastes worse than skunk!"

"Not the weak tiny white buffalo. They taste delicious," Anoki says, licking her bloody chops. Her white fur looks so similar to theirs. With a glance at the herd, her pupils widen and her tongue dangles out the side of her mouth, dripping saliva. "I want to kill them all!" she says, pouncing at the nearest cluster.

"Anoki, you selfish huntress. Your plan is terrible. You will scatter the herd. Let the men divide the herd. We will take the high ground, and they will drive them to us. Then they will be trapped by the high walls, and we will be able to devour them all."

The two women speak with a kindness that makes them sound more like sisters than one-time enemies.

The men go to work. Though little effort is exerted in the surging attack, the return in kills is much greater than hunting buffalo. The wolves don't seem to tire. Instead they cave to an avalanching bloodlust.

On this day only Kiowa shows restraint.

"We have enough, Anoki. Makes Trouble has been avenged."

Anoki ignores the leader and drives the sheep to the only exit, which is blocked by Kida. She welcomes the helpless bouncing flock with her white ivory fangs.

"We are doomed...*bah*...*bah*...doomed. Big bad wolves are coming for us...*bah*...*bah*..."

Together, the two females achieve their malevolent goal. As they greedily finish the last helpless animals off, they tilt their heads back and howl.

Paw and Walpi howl.

Several miles away, another wolf howls back.

CHAPTER 65

Off in the distance, Makes Trouble wakes to find himself mysteriously transformed into a copper-colored wolf. A dozen dead hens lay prostrate around him. He tries to scoop them into his dry mouth and answer the rally call at the same time, but then he decides the call is top priority.

When the pack hears a distant howl, they decide to investigate it.

"Stop! Who are you?" Kiowa demands when he discovers a handsome russet wolf, its mouth stuffed with poultry.

Makes Trouble stops and cocks his head to the side. He sits on his haunches and signs, *It is me, Makes Trouble. I have gathered all these hens for you. I am sorry that I did not return sooner. The woman fired a thunder stick, and I woke up down here...*

Before he can finish his sentence, Kida trots up to the impressive wolf and checks his scent.

"It is you, Brother!" She leaps on him and then hugs him.

"Makes Trouble? Is that you in that glorious mane of gilded fur?" Anoki asks as she goes up to greet him.

Kiowa growls, which forces all the wolves to flatten their ears and back away.

Makes Trouble drops down on all fours and rolls over.

"I did what I thought was best. I have brought meat back for the tribe."

Kiowa leans down and smells Makes Trouble. The familiar scent of his pretend brother confirms what everyone else says.

"I don't understand," Kiowa says, looking Makes Trouble over. "We aren't supposed to have enough magic to change until the next harvest moon."

"You would prefer me ugly?" Makes Trouble says and signs.

"I knew you were off making trouble, but I didn't know you were making magic, too!" Kida nudges her brother.

The tribe greets their returned, transformed friend.

***

Days later, two men examine the slaughtered flock.

Up close, a shiny silver star-shaped badge reads, "SHERIFF, CIMARRON, NEW MEXICO," in black, etched letters. Below the lettering, a rectangular name reads OFFICER DAWSON.

Beside him, a Viking-looking man in his fifties is covered in buffalo furs. He's has a stocky build and a long, blond handlebar mustache and ponytail. He cocks his head to the side and processes the crime scene with affirmative nods and squinting glances. He wears a cap made of red fox fur, and when he nods, the tail waves emphatically behind his head.

"Ain't it hot under that fur cap?" Sheriff Dawson asks.

"I ain't got no hair, so it keeps me from getting chilly."

"Yeah, but it's an extra-hot summer. Folks are saying it's an Indian summer."

"Hot is hot. Cold is cold."

"Whad'ya make of it?" Sheriff Dawson asks the trapper, a man named Dan.

The thickset man scans the scene thoroughly; the stream starts in the distance and runs down between two steep clay-colored canyon walls. The bloody massacre follows the same trail, with the worst of it inside the canyon. His jaw moves back and forth, working a bulging wad of chaw in his cheek. He spits. Nods. And says in a strangely melodic Swedish accent, "Just volves, out der, bean volves."

"What's that? Wolves. Hmm. Well, I'll be honest with you. Wolves are just a might outside my area of expertise. Poachers is fish and game. Indians have their agent, but wolves? These ranchers could sure use some experienced help."

"He didn't even eat dem. He just killed dem fer da fun ov de killin'."

"Folks down here ain't had problems with wolves. They need someone who can restore peace and give them confidence."

Trapper Dan nods and takes his fox cap off. He rubs the top of his shiny, bald head. Tightens his ponytail and squats down to get a closer glimpse at some very peculiar footprints. He measures the distance of Makes Trouble's tracks and can't believe his eyes.

"Do you have da grizzly bears down here?"

"Anything's possible. You think it's more than one predator?"

"Ya!" Trapper Dan speaks in a singsong manner, with high and low tones that make the sheriff grin. "I've heard of das volves killin' fer fun, but I h'ant never seen it. If'n the bounty is high 'nough, I might could do something to help yew."

"County will pay a two-hundred-dollar bounty for the wolf hide you bring in."

The master hunter switches his investigation back to the wolf prints and notices varying widths.

"Is that per volf hide?"

"You think there's more than one?"

"Oh, I don't know," Trapper Dan says passively. "Where der's v'one volf, der's typically more. Two hundred a pelt and yew got yerself a deal." He spits black tar out of his mouth like a grasshopper and into his extended hand.

"That's a hard bargain. Ranchers ain't gonna pay more than damages."

"Dat's my price. Take it or leave it."

From a distance, the stream flows red with sheep blood. Flies swarm the hundred or so uneaten carcasses.

***

Charlie spits in the fire and flares out his arms to show how husky Trapper Dan was.

"Trapper Dan was rumored to be a dog lover. Folks said he had so many dogs it looked like he had dogs coming out his ears. His favorite hunting hound was a pit bull and, boy oh boy, did he have a bunch of 'em."

"'Cause of their lockjaw?" John blasts, locking his fingers together and snapping them.

"Sure!" Charlie shrugs, offset by the know-it-all.

"How did he keep all those dogs together?" John asks.

"He used a bugle and he had different bursts of notes to get the dogs to do his bidding. Three blasts got them to come back. Long blasts got them to go out east, west, north, or south depending on how hard he blew."

"Are the Indians the wolves?" Luther asks, clearly not listening to the story.

"Duh! You're so stupid!" the boys shout in unison, sticking out their tongues. Luther responds in kind and contorts his face into a hateful expression.

***

"Das cavalry has arrived! Come on, Captain, find der trail," Dan shouts at his alpha dog. He presses a hollowed-out bugle horn up to his lips and releases several long bursts, which get the dogs excited.

"What do you suppose he wants us to do?" Skip, the alpha's second-in-command asks Captain, the largest pit bull Dan has ever bred.

"I'm not certain. Let's just keep sniffing around until he looks happy," Captain says. He shakes his wide jaws and gray body all the way to the tip of his white stubby tail.

As the hellhounds sniff and expose their sharp, jagged teeth, their tongues protrude out of their wide mouths.

"Hey, Captain, I think I smell something over here," a black female pit bull named Coco says.

The dogs swarm the spot and, sure enough, Trapper Dan takes notice.

"Hey, guys, he's gonna blow the bugle. Let's all run into the canyon and act like we know where were going."

"You got it, Captain," Skip says. He turns to the pack of wandering pit bulls and shouts, "Hey, Master, is going to blow the bugle, and Captain says we all need to follow him into the canyon."

"Did you find something?" asks a white pit bull named Snowflake.

"Coco thinks she—"

Just then Trapper Dan blows the bugle.

"Get 'em, boys! Get yew dat volf!"

The others quickly follow Captain, leaving a thick dust cloud behind them. Their barks echo off the steep red clay sandstone walls.

Trapper Dan mounts his horse and covers his bald head with his red fox hat. As he's about to ride off, two mini-terriers named Limpy and Beau pop their heads out of his saddlebag. They make their contribution with weak howls as the short-haired muscular pit bulls tear off through the canyon.

Trapper Dan smiles, pleased with his well-trained pack. He kicks at his horse's side and revels in the racket their thundering barks create. The brown-and-white-spotted mustang moves out and follows the pit bulls into the canyon.

"Don't vorry, Betty," Dan says to his horse. "I v'eren't telling the complete truth to Sheriff Dawson. One volf bounty is going to pay for yer new saddle." He pats the silver-studded black leather saddle. "Our profits vill be enough to replace this here Colt ring-lever carbine. Oh, von't dat be nice. I have had dis rifle since thirty-nine. Maybe cover all das gambling debts too. Prob'ly ve'll be back at das card table before da nightfall. Ve are going to ve very rich and famous. De whole town vill love us! They will stop calling me Sweed and start calling me Trapper Dan, as da good Lord intended." He grins, increasing the rosy blush in his cheeks.

Farther up the canyon, Kiowa and the wolves enjoy a midday nap. The evidence of their crime is dried all over their fur. The same scent they followed to find the herd of sheep is leading the pit bulls to them now.

CHAPTER 66

As is the custom in their tribe, one Indian remains awake while the others sleep.

Paw is on watch, and his superior wolf hearing immediately detects a sharp burst from a horn blast, followed by the savagery of hunting hounds.

"Kiowa, wicked winds blow this way," Paw growls, alerting the pack.

Kiowa lazily opens his eyes. With a quick thrust he is instantly on his feet.

"How many?" Kiowa asks, remembering the lessons of ambush.

"I cannot see them. I can only hear them."

"How far?"

"Maybe a mile?"

"What is it?" Makes Trouble asks.

"It is a dog pack," Kida says, leaning down and stretching her front legs.

"We should lead our enemy down the streambeds and use the winding canyons to divide them," Makes Trouble suggests, wanting to reduce the threat as quickly as possible.

"Are the riverbeds dry?" Paw inquires.

"It hasn't rained for many days. The canyon streambeds should be dry."

Kiowa smiles and puts a paw on his almost brother's shoulder. "Are you ready to live up to your name, Makes Trouble?"

Makes Trouble nods and bares his menacing fangs.

"Walpi!" Kiowa shouts.

Walpi stands up.

"Always last," Kida grumbles.

"Run swiftly through the riverbed. Leave a trail and meet us at the end of the north canyon. GO NOW!"

Though Walpi wants to protest that he doesn't know the way, no one dares to disobey the war chief, nor the alpha wolf.

Walpi runs down the ridgeline and begins howling as he speeds through the dry, crusted earth, which used to hold water.

Captain and his pit bull pack hear his howl and pause for a moment.

"Do you hear that?" Skip asks Captain.

"I sure do! We got something on the run, boys. Stay on me!" Captain shouts.

"We got the numbers and the law on our side!" Skip hollers, running alongside Captain.

The pit bulls give chase.

"Anoki, Kida, Paw, lower down into the north canyon and wait behind tall boulders. When we join you, they will be fewer. The strength of our pack will be great. We have magic on our side. Do not be fearful!"

"What will you do?" Anoki asks with concern welling in her eyes.

"When we whittle their numbers down, I will surprise them from behind and drive them to you."

Anoki pauses and thinks on his words for a moment.

"You are my great war chief," she says, standing proudly with her snowy chest pushed out. "I will obey, but I will be thinking of you the whole time."

As the wolves leave the cave and move up a ridgeline, Makes Trouble takes his position by Paw's side and asks, "Do you think they will be as stupid as the Navajo?"

"Let us hope!"

The pit bull posse reaches a fork in the canyon and stop.

"Which way do you want us to go, Captain?" Skip asks.

"Skip, you take half the group that way and I'll take half this way. The canyon can't go on forever. If you reach the end, turn about and rejoin the main group. If you find something, howl and we'll come to you."

"*Yipe, yipe, yow,*" Walpi wails, acting injured. His howls echo off the canyon walls and have the odd effect of seeming closer than they actually are.

"Why ain't we seen him or his trail?" Skip asks.

"We ain't got time for discussion. Master wants a dead wolf and we got him on the run! Now git!"

Skip reluctantly peels off and takes ten of the pit bulls with him.

Up on the high ground, Walpi crouches down and watches Makes Trouble's plan go into effect. *How did he know they would divide?* he wonders. Scanning the canyon maze, he can see that Skip's pack is going to face another fork. He quickly scoots away from the towering ledge and runs to gain a lead on the pit bulls. He angles his cries so that they bounce off the canyon walls, making it hard for the small pack to decipher which trail he is on. In fact, he is on none of them. But he is above them, watching them. Stalking them. Leading them.

"Whad'ya want us to do, Skip?" Coco asks when they reach another divide.

"Half of you go down that path, with Cypress. The other half, you stick with me."

"How do we even know it's a wolf, Skip?" Coco questions.

"'Cause Captain said, 'Blah, blah, get, blah, blah, wolf.' Now get the wolf!"

From Walpi's high-up perspective, the canyons create a maze for as far as the eye can see.

What would Kida do if she were me right now? he asks himself, pressing his body flat. His golden fur blends him well against the sandstone cliffs.

"She is always urging me to join the pack and fight, even though my Hopi nature tells me to do something else. I would rather plant corn, but wolves do not eat corn. She must be right. My Hopi ways must be wrong. So fight I will do!"

He turns around and starts heading back to where the pack originally divided.

Back at the canyon's entrance, Kiowa sits high on the ridgeline and patiently watches Captain's pack get divided.

BOOM!

A hundred yards into the canyon, the pit bulls stop when they hear the thunderous report of their master's rifle.

"Did you hear that?" Captain asks his pack.

"Master must have shot a wolf."

"Do you think the others will return to Master? Should we?"

"Can't be too sure 'bout them."

"*Yit-yowee*," Anoki and Kida cry out somewhere in front of the pit bull group.

"Master gives a steak to whoever captures a wolf. Who here wants steak?"

"Me!"

"I do!"

"Me too!"

Captain looks at the two weakest pit bulls in his shrunken pack of five. "Tater and Chili, get back to Master and see if he needs help. Brutus, Hector, and Achilles, you stay with me."

"Let's go earn a steak! Now, are they in front of us or behind us?"

The frothing pit bulls resume their pursuit.

Back at the canyon entrance, Trapper Dan cocks his rifle and takes aim at Kiowa. He squeezes the trigger and lets loose another shot.

CHAPTER 67

Dan looks over his front sights to see if he hit the wolf. An exploding dust cloud indicates a miss, striking earth beneath the largest gray wolf he has ever seen.

"I got yew now, yew grand fella," the crafty trapper declares, cocking his rifle.

He lines his front sight up with the wolf and aims above his right ear.

Trapper Dan takes a long deep breath, then exhales slowly. He rests his finger on the trigger and adds steady pressure.

"A little Kentucky vindage to send you to Valhalla."

"Do you see what he's shooting at?" Beau asks Limpy.

Limpy scans the ridgeline and spots Kiowa. Unable to control himself, he jerks forward and starts barking. Beau does not see Kiowa but follows suit anyway. The eruption surprises Dan, causing him to jerk the shot.

BOOM!

The bullet's impact is close enough to kick dirt and debris up in Kiowa's face, but again, the great trapper who summons thunder with a stick has missed his target. Kiowa squints and looks away but remains motionless. Instead of cutting out like a coward, Kiowa takes a brave stance and proudly displays his courage.

"Simmer down!" Trapper Dan shouts at the little terriers. The hunter swiftly pulls the lever ring and cycles the action. He realigns his square front sight. As back sights align with front, Dan squints his aiming eye and closes his other eye. He begins to squeeze the trigger and allows the wolf to come into focus.

"Yew sure is a pretty volf," he says, admiring Kiowa's stature and features.

As he prepares to feel the trigger click and the rifle kick, he sees the wolf do something he's never seen any animal do in all his years of trapping.

"Is he smiling at us?"

Dan blinks several times and opens both eyes. He shades his eyes with his hand just to be sure he's seeing what he thinks he's seeing.

"V'hy the devil are you mocking me?"

Up on the mountaintop, Kiowa sits perfectly still.

"My magic is strong. You could never shatter my courage. It is in my heart!" Kiowa hisses through clenched teeth.

"Your goose is cooked," Beau shouts back in a thick Scottish accent.

BOOM!

Again, Dan misses; it is a long shot, and the bullet's trajectory is blown off course by the canyon's side winds.

A lone ember tickles down from the weapon's top chamber and slips into the black powder cylinder.

WHA BOOM!

The rifle explodes and sends packed projectiles out the back of the gun and right through Trapper Dan's hand.

"ARRRGGGHHH!"

"On this day I have proven thunder sticks are for cowards!" Kiowa says as he turns around and maneuvers into the canyon. "Now it is my turn to use my weapons!"

Dan holsters his rifle. He claws at his shirt. He untucks it and tears a piece of fabric off, then wraps his wounded hand. He squares himself up and draws his pistol in his good hand.

"Giddyap," Dan says, kicking at Betty's sides. Seeing the wisdom in the wolf's elevated position, he shouts at his horse, "Ve gotta get closer!"

What he doesn't know is that his catastrophe was a master's move. Hunter and pack are now separated by a mile or more.

As Betty carries her master way up the steep canyon switchbacks, the terriers climb on top of her head to gain a better vantage point. "All this better be worth my new saddle," Betty complains to her best friend, Beau.

The little dogs point and then bark to greet Tater and Chili as they run up.

"Did Master kill the wolf?" Tater asks Beau.

"No," Beau responds.

"Did he see the wolf?" Chili wonders, running right behind Betty.

"We both saw him!" Limpy boasts, wagging his clipped tail. "He's bigger than any wolf we've ever seen."

"What should we do?" Tater ponders, hopping up and down excitedly.

"Get out in front of Master and let him know when you see the wolf. He will shoot him the instant you alert him, because Master is the best!"

Chili pants and looks around for water. The blazing sun makes him feel light-headed.

"I think we'll stay right here with you. Maybe Master will give us water."

"Don't vorry, boys. Ve brought das cavalry. Dis wolf ain't gonna stand no chance." Dan lifts his bugle horn to his dry lips and blows as he closes in on Kiowa's cave.

Kiowa moves down into the canyon and toward the ambush point. Across the canyon, Walpi sees the action and drops down from his side to quickly reunite with Kiowa.

Now atop of the canyon, Dan hears more than one wolf howling and yipping. He hurriedly dismounts and reaches into his leather saddle pouch to remove a brass spyglass. With great difficulty, he somehow manages to extend it one-handed.

"Oh my goodness. Oh my gracious. Der's more dan von volf." He moves the eyepiece back and forth and spots Kiowa and Walpi linking up. The hulking odd-shaped objects stand out in stark contrast to their red rock surrounding.

He holds up his fingers, counts to two, and tries to calculate his bounty using his limited education. "Let's see, two times two hundred is two hundred and tventy." His eyes widen at the thought of such riches. He eagerly runs his hand over his handlebar mustache and pats his wounded hand. The realization that more profit exists soothes the wound.

"I've got to get das boys back here now," Trapper Dan concludes. He dismounts Betty, points his pistol in the air, and hastily fires, signaling the pack to return to the master.

Unfortunately, the .44 Texas Walker Ranger Colt is much louder than his rifle and is positioned entirely too close to Betty's ear. The percussion nearly blows her eardrum out.

"OWWWIIIIEEEE," Betty shrieks, jerking several feet and wincing from the pain.

Unaware, Dan continues to fire, ensuring his brood's return.

Betty panics and instinctively jerks away. She tries to distance herself from the hand cannon but neglects to look behind her. Her hooves teeter on the flaking sandstone edge.

"Whoa, Betty!" Beau tries to calm his friend, but the horse's ears are damaged and ringing so badly she can't hear him.

Limpy leaps for Betty's reins. His little mouth snatches a mouthful of leather strap. He strains his tiny heart, tugging backward on the reins as hard as he can, but even his best efforts feel like nothing to Betty.

Betty takes one last step back. Her wobbling hoof slides on a curved and crumbling ledge. The horse tries to correct, but her metal shoes can't grip the sandy rock. Her hind legs slip out from underneath her and her bulging belly slams against the ledge. She thrusts her front hooves out, clawing at the earth as half her body dangles over the edge. With every ounce of desperate strength left, she strains to gain traction. But it's too late!

CHAPTER 68

Fortunately, Beau has enough runway to leap off Betty's snout. "Let go, Limpy," Beau shouts at his swaying brother. Limpy releases the reins and falls to the ground.

"I'm killed" are all the words the horse manages to say as her lumbering body slides over the ledge. Trapper Dan fires another shot, masking her long *neigh* before her collision with the earth.

Oblivious to Betty's dissent, Dan looks down to find Beau and Limpy pawing at his pants legs.

"I'm not saying anything," Beau says, looking sideways at Limpy.

"I won't either." Though Limpy's small brow is furrowed.

"Dat ought to bring dem home." Dan chuckles as he holsters his pistol.

When he turns around to replace the spyglass in the pouch, he finds his horse has been misplaced. He looks to his left. Then to his right. "Where da blazes did Vetty go?"

Tater and Chili whimper.

"Master, please give us water. We are terribly thirsty," Tater says, showing no interest in the devastating loss of Betty.

Dan looks down and pats his dogs on the head. "I know boys... it's hot. Why don't one of vou go find Vetty. She has das canteen..." Before he can finish his sentence, his hunter eyes spy two fresh streaks on the sandstone cliff.

"Oh no. Dis is terrible," he shouts, tossing his fox hat on the ground. "Dadgum half-breed!" he hollers as he jumps up and down, stomping the cap to death for the second time. Sweat beads down his bald head, while his pups whimper.

Deep into the winding north canyon, Kida pants and turns in circles. She whimpers and makes like she's trapped and weak.

As the posse turn a corner, they find the she-wolf all alone.

"What's this? One little wolf?" Captain mocks, shaking his head and laughing.

"Can you believe one scrawny wolf killed all them sheep, Cap?" Hector asks, looking Kida up and down.

"Please, don't hurt me," Kida whines, tilting her ruddy head down and bending her black-lined ears back. She lowers herself to the ground and makes herself as submissive as possible.

"All right, Brutus. This is going to be just like pig hunting. You get her by the ear. Achilles, you latch on to her ankle, and I'll finish the job."

"I have pups to feed. Have mercy!" Kida shouts, stretching out her paw as though to say "Stop."

The pit bulls lower their heads and snarl, ignoring her pleas. As Captain closes in on her, he moves from shadow to daylight. Kida sees his scar-littered face and instantly knows why he's giving orders. She looks his muscular frame up and down, noting possible weaknesses. *A front attack would be suicide. His broad chest and distinctive round, bulging jaws contain all of his strength. He would have no problem catching me and tearing me to pieces, she thinks. But his body is narrow. His hind legs hardly have any muscle at all. This is where I will strike!*

Kida rolls over onto her stomach and hams up the act. "Go on, finish me quickly. Fear fills my heart..." She wails.

"Oh no... no... no. We're going to take our time, just like you done with them sheep. It's going to be painful. Agonizing. Brutal!" Achilles says, maneuvering behind her.

The beastly growls grow into a ferocious thunderstorm as the pit bulls close in on her.

"Were they your sheep?" Kida asks, rolling back over onto her stomach coyly.

"They were someone's!" Captain says, waiting for his boys to do their part.

Hector and Brutus circle Kida and snap at her legs, which she masterfully keeps tucked beneath her hindquarters, so they can't gain an advantage.

"*Ya hay, nah ah hay. Yaw ah hey ah ya hey!*" The Kiowa war song echoes off canyon walls, foreshadowing a thunderous attack.

"*Ya hay, nah ah hay,*" Kida sings with him.

"Why are you doing that?" Captain asks.

Walpi appears around the bend, coming up from the rear of the canyon and chanting the war song.

Looking behind her, Kida can't help but notice how brave Walpi looks with his mane grizzled up, his fangs snapping, eyes fierce and focused. For some reason, she feels butterflies swirl in her belly.

Surprised, but eager to attack, the pit bulls continue their advance on Kida. Suddenly, Anoki appears on top of a very large boulder, positioned to the left of Kida and several feet above. Her white coat shines brilliantly.

"I killed most of the sheep myself. Will you kill me slowly?" she jabs.

The pit bulls abort their attack and huddle up. They whisper to one another.

"What's wrong? Look at them. Fear freezes their tongues to their lips. See how now they have nothing to say," Kida ridicules them.

Kiowa slowly appears from around the bend like Walpi. His towering stature is easily double that of any pit bull.

"We all killed the sheep. We hunt. We kill. We survive. Is it any different from you?" Kiowa asks.

"We are nothing like you!" Captain retorts, standing bravely in front of his crew.

Beside Brutus, the earth begins to shake. Makes Trouble rises from the dust, chanting, "*Ah hey, haya hey. Ya hey, not ta how!*"

"What kind of wolves are you?" Achilles roars.

"And what do you eat?" Paw says, rising from the sands like Makes Trouble. He is near Achilles.

The pit bulls suddenly find themselves surrounded by wolves.

"We eat what our master feeds us. It's the way we live."

"Out here we are our own masters. And we must feed ourselves."

Brutus tilts his head and howls for the pack.

"It's no use," Walpi seethes through his fangs. "I made sure your pack couldn't hear you!"

Realizing the error of his ways, Captain puffs, "You divided us and then led us into an ambush."

"*Ha, nay, yet ah hey!*" the wolf pack chants in unison.

"Join us or die!" Kiowa says, extending an olive branch.

CHAPTER 69

"What?" Kida asks in disbelief.

"Ha!" Captain shouts, puffing up his boxy chest. He paces back and forth. "I would never run with wolves! Y'all are wild and turn on your own. You got no laws, no loyalty, no master, and no *right* to wander these lands and take what ain't yours."

"*Ha, nay, yet ah hey!*" the wolves continue.

Brutus, Hector, and Achilles start barking to drown out the incessant chanting.

Kiowa does not charge as everyone had expected him to. He just stands still, frozen, waiting. His ears are pricked up. He is on alert, but waits to attack. His eyes study the curious-looking pack of animals that have just refused his offer. He has never been refused, and he has never seen such strangely put together creatures. They don't even look like dogs. Their ears are clipped and pointed, their tails come to an odd, stumpy end, and their noses are smashed into their peculiar flat faces like their masters abused them terribly. But the worst trouble is derived from their broad mouths, which pose an obvious problem in a fight.

Unwilling to accept strangers, Kida takes it upon herself to protect the integrity of the pack. Without the alpha's permission, she charges Hector. They clack teeth and claw at each other's bodies.

With the sudden action, Walpi's hair rises on his neck and spreads across his shoulders. He charges past Kiowa and catches Hector unexpectedly by the throat. His attack is ferocious; he tears through Hector's thin skin and latches on to the jugular. Blood gushes into his mouth and sends him into a blood frenzy. The thought of Kida being attacked fills his heart with rage. His growls unite with hers, and they both cave to the wild, instigating the pack's attack.

In an instant Makes Trouble answers the call. He seizes Brutus's hind leg by the meaty portion, and the pair engage and return blow for blow. Their beastly whirlwind creates a dust cloud that masks the fight.

Paw leaps forward and bites down on the back of Achilles's neck. Achilles arches wildly, shaking off the attack. He flips around and bites Paw's front leg. The crushing pain from the pit bull's jaws make him release and cry out.

To Kiowa's distress, Anoki leaps from the boulder and disappears into the fray. He wants to charge in and join the rumble, but the scars on Captain's face and body give him the distinct impression that this dog will not simply let him skirt by.

Hector puts up a decent defense, but Walpi's death blow is quick and successfully reduces the pit bulls' numbers. Now the wolves have an even greater advantage.

In all the concealed savagery, the yelping, the snarling, the snapping jaws, Kiowa can think only of Anoki, and that is his first mistake.

Captain is the only thing that stands between complete chaos and Kiowa. He waits for the alpha wolf to come to him, and when doesn't, Captain lunges forward in the battle royal. One single ambition drives him "to kill the wolf!"

He sprints toward Kiowa; his bulging cheeks lift from the momentum, exposing his teeth, and then droop once more.

Kiowa waits for the pit bull to lunge at him, then skillfully darts out of the way. He's the first to draw blood with slashing fangs that leave his mark on Captain's shoulder.

"These are not your lands. You should have stayed in Texas, Cap-i-tan," Kiowa shouts, lowering his head, exposing his fangs, and rising to the challenge.

"What do you say just you and I finish this? If I win, your boys leave the Currumpaw and only you die. If you win, the fight ends with me, and the rest of my pack agree to leave the Currumpaw forever."

"Your pack is going to die one at a time. They are lost to the badlands, miles past any water source. The Sun God has withheld his tears for much time. They have no water. No food. And if they aren't soon killing sheep, they will die too." Kiowa lunges forward. "As will you!"

Wild beast collides with tamed canine and at first the fight seems equal.

They charge one another and use their front paws to push one another down, each looking to gain an advantage. The wolf clenching down on one dog's thin, loose skin, then slashing it with ease.

Captain only laughs. "That's it? You are not gonna bite and hold on, just slash and run?"

His taunt has its intended effect. The two quickly resume the fight with a vicious vigor. Try as he might, Kiowa cannot seem to get to the soft underside of the dog's belly. Captain's narrow hindquarters are much like the buffalos' in that he pivots with an unexpected speed and changes direction faster than an animal his size should be able.

Both defend their necks by twisting their jaws back and forth with lightning speed. Kiowa slashes at Captain's face, then rips a piece out of his shoulder. All the time they are fighting, Kiowa can't help but worry about Anoki. This constant distraction saps his energy. Lost in that thought, he gives Captain an advantage that the seasoned warrior does not miss. Captain finds a vulnerable spot on Kiowa's shoulder and bites harder than the warrior had expected. Between the two, Captain bleeds far worse than Kiowa. But Captain has a tight grip, and his determination to go for the death blow blazes in his dilated brown eyes.

Captain's short tail wags enthusiastically, convincing Kiowa that he's actually having fun. The dog swings his agile hind legs here and there. He bounces back and forth, both biting and thrashing, which causes Kiowa to thrust forward and expose more of his chest. Captain successfully sifts through Kiowa's thick fur and sinks his teeth deep into Kiowa's chest. The pain is excruciating. With a mouthful of fur and flesh, Captain is forced to breathe out of his nose in trembling huffs.

Captain squats low and works his stout body like an anchor. Kiowa tries to return pain for pain, but Captain expertly darts his body back and forth so that the wolf's snapping fangs miss with each bite. Every wasted effort is followed by a paralyzing tug from the canine's locked jaws. Between his worry for Anoki and this yanking, tugging weight, Kiowa's ability to maneuver is clipped.

"Ever hear of lockjaw, wolf?" Captain grumbles through blood-soaked lips.

Kiowa can feel the pit bull's jaws reposition and strengthen their grip. They expand and contract over and over again in a chewing motion that never loses strength and never seems to tire. Captain's agonizing determination forces Kiowa to cry out, which frightens his otherwise victorious wolf pack. Never in all of the time they have known Kiowa have any of them heard their war chief yelp as he does now.

The sound tortures Anoki and forces her into action. She leaps out of the dust cloud and rushes over to join her lover's fight, only to be detained by Kida.

Tater and Chili appear off in the distance. They have finally answered Captain's call. They are late, but they have answered.

Makes Trouble and Walpi run up to higher elevation and allow the pit bulls' reinforcements to charge into the canyon.

"Captain!" Tater shouts, sprinting toward the bloody engagement. The fresh pit bulls bark and rush in like crazed matadors as Anoki and Kida sit down and stare at them.

Chili nears the fight but neither he nor Tater get very far.

Walpi and Makes Trouble strain and work together to push boulders off the cliff and start a landslide. Tumbling rocks smash against the pit bulls' bodies and pin the dogs beneath their hulking weight. Kida and Anoki are quick to end Chili. All four of the wolves turn on Tater.

Feeling the wolf's strength fade, Captain is immensely satisfied. He tenses up, hoping to finish the attack. "Ain't nothing gonna make me let go, wolf! I'm just gonna keep walking this bite up your chest and hang, like a weight, on your neck till you..."

As the dust cloud starts to settle, Kiowa finally gets eyes on Anoki and finds she is safe, to his tremendous relief. The overwhelming pain in his chest pulls him out of his savage and wild mind-set, allowing Kiowa to fall back on his human strategy. He puts his paws on the pit bull's head and uses his claws to gouge Captain's eyes.

Captain winces from the pain. He renews his determination and tries hopping and tugging at Kiowa's throat in an effort to subdue the wolf leader.

The pit bull makes the mistake of hopping in a pattern. Kiowa waits for him to set his feet on the ground and expertly executes an Indian wrestling move to trip up Captain's legs.

It works. The pit bull falls down and exposes an ear, mangled from previous fights. With all the strength he has left, Kiowa snaps down with his molars. The pit bull yipes in agonizing pain, yet refuses to let go.

Kiowa latches down repeatedly, chomping and tearing pieces of Captain's ear off. With each successful bite, Captain jerks and exposes a little of his face. He endures the pain magnificently, but when Kiowa starts tearing pieces of his cheeks off, his determination wanes.

Kiowa manages to get a lower fang in Captain's eye. Jaws that were once locked finally release.

CHAPTER 70

Feeling his carnal nature resurface, Kiowa lets the wolf take over. He works his bites down Captain's neck and repeatedly attacks until Captain's strength fades. When the pit bull stumbles onto his side, Kiowa pins him down and tears into his abdomen, disemboweling him. In seconds, Captain, the great leader of the Texas pit bull pack, gives up the ghost.

After he feels the pit bull's body go limp, Kiowa raises his blood-soaked snout and howls victoriously. The pack responds by howling with him. The echoing howls attract Coco and three other pit bulls.

High up on a mountaintop, near the wolves' cave, Trapper Dan looks through his spyglass. He catches glimpses of his dogs here and there, but can't make out what's going on.

"I can't get nvheres near dem vithout my horse," he says, looking back at the drop-off.

"I'm comin', boys!" he shouts, then blows on his horn to let them know that Master is on his way.

The pit bulls rally at the loss of Captain. They determine to avenge him but make the mistake of attacking the wolves individually or in groups of two. What Dan couldn't see is that the dogs who have managed to find the wolves wish they hadn't. Day turns to evening and the wolves' howls greet victim after victim, until the pit bulls bark no more and the dust finally settles.

"Quit dat blasted howling! Listen to das horn!" Dan shouts, blowing his horned trumpet with all of his might.

Trapper Dan works his way down the cliff, moving far slower than when Betty took him up. His feet are sore and his head aches from the day's intense sunlight and heat. "Vhy ain't dey barkin' no more? Where'd dey all go?" The terriers crouch down, putting their paws over their heads and trembling.

"Come on, Limpy, we have to stay with Master."

"I'm too tired!" Limpy complains, refusing to move.

Trapper Dan descends from the cliff and removes his canteen from his dead horse.

A full harvest moon begins to rise in the early-evening sky, quickly joined by a sea of twinkling stars.

"Oh, Betty, I'm so sorry. I should have been more careful," Dan wails, combing his handlebar mustache.

Clouds float in front of the moon and mask its ivory light. The canyon grows very, very dark.

Trapper Dan blows and blows on his horn, but hardly a hiss comes from the noisy contraption. He has exhausted himself, and no dogs heed the call. He whistles, cocks his gun, and fires, but his efforts are answered by a cold silence. Not even the wolves howl.

Now a good distance from Limpy, he hears a loud shriek. Then silence.

He claps his hands and says, "Come on, boy! Come to Dädi."

"Limpy, did you fall?" Beau asks, starting to move back up the switchback, to where he last saw his little friend.

A flash of gold fur creates the slightest gust of wind.

"Limpy? Come on, boy... come to Dädi."

Dan feels like he's dying of thirst. He pulls the cork plug on his canteen and guzzles some of his precious water. Even though it's night, he can hear the flies swarming his horse's body.

"Vat an awful mess!"

He sits down on a boulder and sobs. Cradling his wounded hand, he sets his black powder pistol against a rock. He removes his boot and turns it upside down to get the pebbles out, then leans back and tilts the canteen up for another swig.

"Come on, boys," he says, shaking the half-full canteen. "Come, drink with me."

When the terriers don't respond, he knows something isn't right. Slowly he reaches for his pistol, but it's not where he set it. He stands up and looks all around, but he can't seem to find the place he rested it.

"I'm comin' unglued." He frantically searches everywhere.

As the clouds pass, the moonlight illuminates everything. He

looks up and
 sees two glowing yellow eyes shrouded in a black-and-white wolf
mask.

CHAPTER 71

He hears a noise to his right. When he looks, Makes Trouble opens his mouth and drops Beau's body. It lands limply at Dan's feet.

"Vhat?" Dan stumbles back and frantically searches for his weapon. As he turns to run, he bumps into Paw, who carries the pistol in his mouth, like he's just retrieved a stick.

Kiowa's thunderous growls reverberate off Dan's chest. The hunter looks left to right and spots one wolf after another creeping out from behind the nearby boulders. The pack quickly seizes Dan's limbs.

"I want to be the one to kill him," Makes Trouble snarls, working his jaws like a butcher sharpens knives.

Kiowa leaps between Dan and his pretend brother. He opens his mouth and presses his full weight on Dan's wide stomach. He presses his sharp claws against Dan's burly chest and feels himself start to lose control when the man squirms under his paws. He growls so close to Trapper Dan's face that he can feel hot breath escaping his shuddering lips. He puts his paw on Dan's hairy chest, showing that his enemy has been conquered.

Dan shields his face with his hands and arms. "NO! DON'T EAT ME!"

Just as Trapper Dan thinks his goose is cooked, the cloud cover dissipates and the harvest moon's beams blast down on the wolves. Kiowa slowly shape-shifts into his natural form, starting from his feet and ending with his head.

"AAAAHHHH! AHHH! AHHH!" Trapper Dan's feels fear in its most potent form explode off his lips in terrifying wails.

The other wolves shape-shift as well, still holding Trapper Dan by his clothes with their human teeth. They continue to growl.

Kiowa slaps Trapper Dan across the face.

"We don't eat men!" he says in a language Dan can't understand.

"Verevolves... Injun verevolves!"

Kiowa steps off Dan's chest, which causes the others to release him.

Dan scrambles to his feet and clumsily sprints back toward the riverbed. He runs screaming like a madman, tripping over everything as he goes.

"Arrroooowwww." Kiowa cups his hand to his mouth and howls. The tribe laughs and howls with him.

***

W.H. sits on the steps of an icy street, shaking his tin cup. "Any spare change would be greatly appreciated."

A man walking past shields his eyes from falling snow. He looks down at the pitiful wolf hunter and says, "You're a grown man. Get a dang job!"

"Snowfall was too heavy to hunt. I'd freeze to death out there, I would, mister. Please..." W.H. sighs and lets his cup droop to the point it dangles off his trigger finger.

An older, well-dressed gentlemen walks up to W.H. and drops a penny in the cup. "Penny for your thoughts?"

"Dr. Bennett?"

"How is your expedition?"

W.H. lowers his head in shame.

"Will you come back to school, or do you still insist on trapping for a living?"

"I have seriously reconsidered my position!"

"I'd hoped you would say that, my good nephew. Nothing like a hungry stomach and a cold winter's night to bring you to your senses. Come, let us get you something warm to eat as you listen to an offer I think you will find difficult to refuse."

The pair venture into a nearby rustic, frontier-style pub. Long round logs stacked on one another make a humble building. A tin roof keeps the snow out. A river-rock fireplace stuffed with blazing logs generates a wonderful comforting heat.

A waiter with a bushy black mustache greets them. The headmaster holds up two fingers and is quickly escorted to a table. Before the waiter can hand them their menus, the headmaster orders.

"Two Dutch stews and keep the biscuits coming. I believe my nephew is close to starving."

The meaty aroma makes W.H.'s stomach grumble. He tries to maintain a calm, cool demeanor, but his eyes dart back and forth and give away his famished state.

The dean unrolls a copy of the *Squatter South*. The first paper in Atchison, Kansas.

Dr. Bennett shuffles in his seat and bops his legs. When the waiter brings two tankards of ale, he lifts his and slams it against W.H.'s. Foam spills over both and makes a frothy mess on the pine plank table.

His eyes explode with excitement. "I am adamant that you must learn the value of education."

Not wanting to hear the lecture but eager for the food, W.H. lets his eyes wander toward the kitchen. *It's really too bad that arms don't have mouths and legs. They could leap out of my sockets, run to the kitchen, and gorge themselves while my ears and hollows could oblige him.* W.H. smirks, which Dr. Bennett misinterprets as agreement.

"Ah… I knew you would be reasonable." He puts his hand on a manila envelope, postmarked NYC. "I have done some research and found several periodicals I believe may be of interest to you. Here is a letter of intent I have secured from some commissioned gentlemen of the Hudson's Bay Company. They are all masons in one way or another, you know." He leans forward and whispers, "They always want new members to keep their secrets, ugh… hum… Well, you know how they carry on, and naturally they suspected I would be a good candidate, so… where was I?"

"Research."

"Ah, yes! Research. As I was saying, you piqued my interest with your passionate pitch for the hunting endeavor. So, being the good uncle that I am, I thought I would show you the impact education can have. First, I leveraged my network on your behalf. I wrote several friends at universities and they responded in kind, might I add, with two very intriguing pieces." He slides the envelope across the table, then catches his mug and guzzles his ale. When he's downed the entire vat, he slams his tin mug down on the table and uses his brown-and-black-checkered wool coat sleeve to wipe his foamy mustache.

"I am of the firm opinion, young man, that you have redeemable qualities. Sure, you may not be the most handsome devil on the block"—he winks—"and though the ladies hardly pay you any mind, unless you tell your wolf stories and liquor them up, but where does that end? More trouble. Believe me. I have seen it a thousand times. But I digress. Here's what I believe. Your aspirations can be united with members of the lodge, commissioned gentlemen, who are the sole purpose this town was created."

W.H. combs his hands through his scruff. "You're losing me."

"Did you not know that Winnipeg was created as a place where Hudson's Bay officers could retire? Take their fortunes. Start new endeavors?"

W.H. shakes his head no and taps his foot, counting the minutes until the meal reaches his lips.

"Education, Nephew. Always measure things in principal, time, energy. Have you learned nothing? Oh never mind. Well, it would seem that you may be in just such a position to satisfy my colleagues' interest. See they always have their eye on increasing their fortune. In short, open the envelope."

W.H. opens the envelope. He unfolds a neatly handwritten letter on yellow paper in quill ink. Two newspaper articles separate from the letter and slide onto the table. He scans the letter and reads the title, LETTER OF INTENT.

"Terms?" W.H. asks bluntly.

"Your ambition is so sharp it cuts straight to the bone, eh?" The headmaster waves his curt nephew off. "Well, then, we shall skip the pleasantries and I will tell you what this first article says from the *Omaha Times*. It basically says that the United States will be giving land grants to the Union Pacific Railroad. Have you any idea what this means?"

W.H. shakes his head and searches for his food.

"What is it about youth that you are blinded to opportunity?"

CHAPTER 72

W.H. shrugs.

Lifting the letter of intent with two pinched fingers Dr. Bennett says, "These men have issued a letter of intent. They have substantial capital from their profits with the Hudson's Bay Company. They wish to send their bourgeoning prosperity into a new life. A place where the lure of even greater fortunes draws every man who can swing a pick. Carve out a farm. And build a life. Every woman can vie for a husband, some land, and a home. They're calling it the American dream. Look here."

He points to the article. W.H. lifts it up and scans it.

"I know I may have fallen on desperate times, but everyone starts hard. Why, even Moses had it rough. Besides, none of this makes sense to me. Hudson's Bay Company. American dream. It's not my dream. I hunt wolves. That's it. That's all I'm truly good at."

Dr. Bennett sighs and pushes the second article into W.H.'s view. "The retirees have organized into a board of directors and established a scholarship. This article, published by *Scientific American*, is the hunt of all hunts."

W.H. reads a headline that immediately catches his eye. NEW MEXICO'S WEREWOLF.

He reads on.

"Mrs. Lorraine Kelsey, of Cimarron, New Mexico, had her cage literally rattled when she checked on her hens in the middle of the night and found a full-grown werewolf in her chicken coop. Worried for the safety of her children and her fowl, she defended herself. In less than a second she fired two shots from her double-barreled shotgun, which lay her unconscious. *The first shot knocked me plum out.* When asked why she thought the werewolf chose not to harm her or her young 'uns, she replied, "Well, while I was flying through the air, I said a quick prayer to Jesus. Then I hit the ground. Next thing I knew, I woke up to a pail of water in my face and my young 'uns circled around me bawlin' their eyes out. All I can say is God hears prayers!" Mrs. Kelsey did not find a body, which according to locals and legend is due to lead projectiles instead of pure silver. The whereabouts of her protector and husband were earnestly established on his having honest business with the inquisition of a railroad expansion through New Mexico. "Folks will be glad to know that prices are going down on all goods. Forts will give way to Main Street. Ferry and stagecoach will be relics to our children's children." As most maids of the new lands will note, Colt Firearms is the leading craftsman of fine firearms. Repels Injuns, renegade Mexicans, mistrustful whites, runaway slaves, thieves, murderers, and now werewolves. Colt has recently announced an upcoming pure silver projectile..."

"This here is horse dung! That ain't an article. It's an advertisement designed to push sales," W.H. shouts, pushing the article back to his uncle.

"Aren't... or are not any such thing as werewolves. Scientists are men and men are flawed. Yes, they once thought the earth was flat, but we now know it to be round. Hey, do you know the difference between science and religion?"

W.H. shakes his head no.

"In science, you can be right until proven wrong. Then you can just prove yourself right again. It's fluid, see."

"And religion?"

"You can never be proven wrong!" Dr. Bennett finds this punch line so hysterical he laughs until his face turns as red as a tomato. When the headmaster calms down, he polishes his silverware with his napkin, then neatly tucks it into his shirt, properly preparing for his meal. It isn't long before the steaming stew arrives.

As soon as the slop hits his bowl, W.H. wastes no time in attacking his food.

"I don't believe in folklore or superstition," W.H. says, stuffing biscuits in his mouth as though they might grow legs, leap off the plate, and run away.

"Belief has little to do with science. Our science division is fascinated with new specimens. As you are a specimen gatherer, I have recommended your name to the board of directors for the scholarship. Combine that with the board's letter of intent and you have a substantial fortune waiting to be gathered."

W.H. swallows and says, "A wolf at my feet is worth a pack in the woods." He resumes his attack.

"Nephew, you are positively ignorant and stubborn."

"Let me see if I can get this straight: You want me to travel to Nebraska, which is no doubt packed with Indians. See if I can't find some sort of land speculation that benefits the retirees. Then travel to New Mexico to kill a werewolf, that doesn't exist in the hopes that the school may collect a specimen?"

"How's your stew?" his uncle asks him.

W.H. stops chewing, wondering if the old man's age hasn't gotten to him.

"Isn't it nice to have a warm meal and a full belly? There's a lot of warm meals that reward money can provide you. If you are the hunter you proclaim yourself to be, then prove it!"

The wolf hunter gulps down his half-chewed food and finally comes to understand the professor.

"How much?"

"One thousand dollars."

W.H. pauses for a moment, then explodes with excitement.

"Whoo-weee! That's more bounty than most outlaws is worth."

"Are worth, Nephew. Had you taken the time to read the article, you might have noticed that lots with homes are selling for twelve hundred dollars. If you appease the board, they may pay you for your efforts and you could find yourself a home right on the river for ten thousand dollars."

"What's the split?"

"Split?"

"I ain't..." He corrects himself. "I am not going fifty-fifty if I am going to do all the lifting."

"You misunderstand me. I'm in no need of money. I have a comfortable home and a rewarding career. The reward is all yours, provided you can capture, kill, and deliver the specimen or appease the board by gathering information on land grants and perhaps securing a few land deeds here and there."

"Oh, I can guarantee you that wolf is as good as dead!"

"These are my terms: Trap the 'werewolf' and the reward plus the bounty is yours. However, if you should come up empty-handed, then you must return to school for the fall semester with detailed maps, newspaper articles, and reputable contacts for the board of directors to pursue a new hedge fund. You must keep a journal and give up hunting as an occupation and commit to finishing your studies and maybe even consider taking my post when I retire."

W.H. chews his food and thinks for a moment. "Do I have to pay the scholarship back if I come up empty-handed?"

"Not if you keep a journal, take daguerreotypes, and teach one semester the following year."

"Dagoro-who?"

"It's a device they're using to take these new things called pictures. You've seen them, I'm sure."

W.H. finishes eating and packs his leftovers in a red bandana for Bingo. He clears his throat, "Well, seein' as how business is slow, I'm going to take you up on your offer. Does it matter that I don't know how to use your... what did you call it?"

"Daguerreotype. No it doesn't matter if you know how to use one. If you would like, you can stay another semester and take a class on it. Professor Higgs has room—"

W.H. holds up his hand and cuts his uncle off. "Not interested. I'll figure it out. Can't be as hard as hunting wolves. Am I expected to supply the recording materials? Quill pen? Paper? Sketch pencils? Daguerreotype?"

"No, no. The picture contraption, journal, and money are all included. Though the devices are going to require quite a bit in the way of accessories."

W.H. reluctantly agrees. "I'm a single man on a horse. I'll make room." He looks at the headmaster for a moment like he's waiting to see if this is all a joke. When he realizes that it is not, he extends his hand. His uncle takes it, and hugs his nephew.

"Thank you for this and the meal, Uncle. I love you, and I swear I won't let you down, sir."

"That's a good lad. Personally, I fancy this tall tale is nothing more than American folklore, but if dispelling some desert plains rumors gets you back in school, then so be it. And if, on the other hand, there is werewolf, our walls will be packed with spectators and students.

I'm sure a fortune can be made there."

"Whether legend or lore, if it's a wolf, I'll find it and kill it!"

***

Charlie empties rocks out of his boots.

"One thousand dollars sure is a lot of money," Luther says, thinking of the ways he would spend it.

"You'd think it was, wouldn't cha?"

"Yup!" Luther smiles greedily and nods.

"About this time, Kiowa began to understand Onendah's words, back when Onendah said he would still have troubles. Being hunted was just the beginning of his troubles. As it turns out, Raging Bull was telling the truth as well. The buffalo were being hunted to extinction."

"What's extinction?" Kevin asks.

"It means no more buffalo," Charlie answers.

"Why did the Indians hunt the buffalo to ex-tink-erton?" Zack asks, failing to pronounce the word properly.

"It wasn't just the Indians who were hunting the buffalo. It was the US Army and pale-face buffalo hunters."

"Aren't we all pale-faces?" Kevin asks.

Everyone looks at him, unsure of what to say, since his Korean features obviously set him apart. Charlie simply nods and continues with the story.

"So wait. There's Kiowa, Hopi, Navajo, Cherokee... and pale-face Indians?" John asks.

"No... no... Wait. I see why you're confused. Pale-face isn't an Indian tribe. It's an Indian term used to describe the white man." Charlie laughs. He wraps his hands around his belly and says, "We are all pale-faces to them."

Kevin nods.

"Why'd the pale-face want to kill the buffalo?"

"Oh, a lot of reasons. Probably the most important was for cattle grazing and railroads."

"No way, eh?" Kevin says in complete disbelief.

"What about the white buffalo? Was he putting all the buffalo in a cave where no one could find them?" Luther asks.

"No, stupid! Don't you understand? There is no cave. That's just hogwash the buffalo believe! It isn't true! Right?" John asks Charlie.

Charlie ignores them and continues. "I know most of yous have heard of the sun dance, but how many of you have heard of the moon dance?"

No one raises his hand.

"That's because it's a new dance and only the skinwalkers performed it."

CHAPTER 73

Back at the sacred pine forest, where the Indians first transformed into wolves, Onendah stands in front of a lean-to medicine lodge. He had crudely stretched buffalo hides over the weak beams and wetted them down. The hasty construction had gone into the night.

"Come, friends. It has been a winter, a spring, a summer, and now a fall. I have safe lodgings for you. Come." He pulls a buffalo-skin flap back. Billowing steam plumes out and obscures the brilliant harvest moon.

Paw and Makes Trouble go to work on the lodge, ensuring that it is stable.

"What am I supposed to do?" Anoki asks Kiowa.

"Be cleansed," Kiowa answers, putting his arm around his scantily clad wife.

"Why must we be cleansed?" Walpi whispers to Kida.

"Because your spirit is dirty," Kida whispers back.

Onendah beckons them and pats each one on the head as they enter the lodge. "I must hear your stories and we must all dance a new moon dance to honor the gods before dawn. I have spent a year getting ready for it. Since you have all returned unharmed, we must worship and make a sacrifice to the gods."

"But we have so little time," Walpi complains.

Everyone goes silent.

Onendah hits him with his wand. "There, you have been marked. If trouble comes, it comes to you. All the rest who want protection, we must dance and be thankful."

He leads the nearly naked, wobbling tribe into the lodge.

"Ha! You have forgotten how to walk as people. It is to be expected. I forgot how to use my people arms. But see how quickly my hands work?" He motions all around with his hands to show them what he's done.

Paintings and dream weavers litter the shelter. Walpi and Anoki wear the same dumbfounded expression, while the Kiowa walk up to the magic symbols and motion with their hands. They thank their gods and pray to them for protection. Walpi rubs the spot where Onendah hit him.

How do I shake a curse? he wonders.

A tremendous wave of heat opens every pore as Onendah spills water onto heated rocks. Inside, a large pole is painted white and decorated with bat wings strung together, taut raccoon skins, spider webs captured in time, and snakeskins frozen midslither. They all point to the sky to honor the creator.

"We must have spirits of the night with us if we are to be cleansed and receive their powers."

Onendah escorts the men to one side and the women to the other. They thank him as they dress in white Kiowa ceremonial deerskin raiment.

"What is it like to walk as wolves?"

They all look at one another and smile with an understanding that words cannot describe.

"It is—" Paw begins.

"Yes, that is wonderful." Onendah cuts him off. He waves an eagle feather fan and disperses sagebrush smoke. "It is quite amazing to be an eagle also, but I will not bore you with the greatness of flight and all the many wonderful things I have seen. Listen, dawn is fast approaching. We must move. We must dance."

"Quickly, paint your faces. Hurry, now. We mustn't waste time. The sun will be upon us, and I am sad to say that the Kiowa tribe searches for you still," the medicine man informs them as he hands them a tray of white paint.

Anoki paints a single stripe across her face. Kiowa presses his hands against both sides of his mouth and uses three fingers to leave tracks across his forehead. Each Indian paints themselves according to their visions.

Onendah motions for them to sit down once they are finished. He lights a long hollowed-out pipe and passes it around.

"*Het ya. Nay ah, hay ya.*" He begins to chant the medicine song.

He motions for them to repeat his prayer.

"Brother to the sun, we thank you, pale moon, for keeping our secrets and letting us live a life that we could not dream, but living in it feels like a dream."

Kiowa begins to sway back and forth. The men follow his lead. Kida beats her hands against a raw hide. She exaggerates the motion to show Anoki she is to do the same.

The dance takes up most of the night. Onendah brings out a leather pouch with the invaluable stone idol, Taime.

"I know we would normally dance for days, but because of our circumstances, we have only this little bit of time. I have Taime with me. Ask his blessing and be on your way."

"Let Anoki go first," Kiowa politely requests.

Anoki sits up on her knees and makes rocking motions with her cradling arms. "I would like a baby. Many winters with my loving husband. And enough game to last all of us through another winter."

Kiowa motions to his teeth and pretends to elongate them. He thanks Taime for giving him the power to defeat his enemies. He asks with hand signs that his mind will be quicker than his enemies', his heart braver, his strength increased tenfold, and his magic even more powerful.

Paw's request is quick. He thanks Taime for giving him new legs and asks that he may continue to look after one who feels like his son, Kiowa.

Makes Trouble lifts an owl wing and drags the feathers across his face. He asks that Taime will sweep doubts away from his eyes. He motions fox ears with his fingers and asks that his mind will be clever and filled with fox thoughts. He also asks for wisdom beyond the owl. He prays for the power of an entire wolf pack and asks his tribe to forgive him if he fails to transition into a gold wolf. He finishes his prayer by asking Taime that his sister stay a wolf.

All eyes turn on Kida.

She takes a moment. The stillness breeds sorrow. Tears stream down her cheeks. She points to Kiowa, then her heart, and signs like she's breaking a stick over her knee. She thanks Taime for removing the thorn from her heart and giving her a new heart. She goes to point at Walpi, then pauses for an infinite awkward second. Her cheeks blush and she quickly signs her gratitude for her mother and father and asks Taime that they will forgive her and Makes Trouble for the life they have chosen to live.

The tribe lets out soft expressions of joy.

Walpi is the last to go. He asks for only one thing, that whomever he gives his heart to will accept it.

Onendah motions for them all to rise.

"It is important to remember this. We walk in two worlds now. Never forget what it means to be people, but also, enjoy being wolves."

Anoki breaks the reverence. "How long will we be like this?"

Onendah looks to Kiowa with a harsh glance.

Kiowa raises his hand and lowers it, signing her to hold her peace.

Onendah motions for them to come closer.

Kiowa and Anoki put their arms around each other. Their flesh presses together for the first time, which excites them and causes them to blush with giddy waves of tiny tingling lightning bolts.

Onendah lifts the wolf paw and goes to transform them, but Anoki stops him. She slides her smooth hand into Kiowa's rough, firm grip. "I beg of you. Please let us use our mortal hands on mortal flesh as long as magic will permit."

Anoki wastes no time waiting for permission. Onendah's baffled expression gives her the opportunity to lead her love's beaming face off into the forest.

"Ugh..." Onendah says with a confused look on his face. "The honey of love is sticky business. The stingers of these bees' love will certainly keep all of us away."

I will stay awake and watch for the sun. Let them be husband and wife, Makes Trouble signs as he touches the lance and the wolf paw at the same time. He seamlessly transforms into an auburn wolf. Circling around the pit to find a comfortable place to rest, he lies down.

Sitting by the fire, Paw feels his eyes grow heavy. He nods once, then twice, and quickly falls asleep as Onendah rests his old bones.

The fire crackles and sways. When the sky lightens and the stars begin to fade, Paw feels a cold hand push on his arm.

"You did not think Makes Trouble would stay awake, did you?" Onendah asks the dreary-eyed man.

"You were supposed to watch for them," Onendah grumbles.

"Now an old man has lost his sleep and will never find it. Get up and quickly go get your pack together."

Paw sits up and yawns. He touches the lance and paw, stretching into a wolf as he leaves the sweat lodge. Outside, he tilts his head back and howls.

Kiowa and Anoki fumble out of the forest. The peaceful, joyous expressions on their faces reveal what their words never could.

Onendah holds the golden lance up. They each place their hand on the shaft. Then he touches each Indian with the wolf's paw. One by one they skinwalk back into wolves.

"Go, my children. Be free!" He waves them off, then returns to the lodge. "I am old and tired. Now I must..." He sits down and yawns. "Time is the enemy to us all. We think it will never run out when we are younger, but here I am, Taime, in the winter of my life. I am here with your spirit all these years later and, somehow, I lived each day as one."

He lifts the owl wing and washes smoke and steam over his head.

"Bless them, Taime. Bless my wild children that they will have great love and happiness in their lives. Do not let the Woman in the Ground take them anytime soon. Let her go find others to take to her land of cold, deep sleep. The world is full of old lazies who would rather sleep always. Lazies like me." He yawns. "So why not take me to rest, Woman in the Ground? Rest with my wife." Onendah blinks once, then falls asleep just as the sun rises.

***

Several days later, cattle move through the prairie. Fenced in a fifty-mile circuit, they circle and feed on fresh-grown grass and drink from a stream that cuts through the property.

"Yum... num... yum. The tops are so fresh and crisp. It tastes so good! Ona, try you some of this here," Ol' Bruce, the big brown bull, says, rocking his lower jaw back and forth. He grinds the grass to a pulp, then closes his eyes and swallows.

"Simply divine." The thousand-pound prize bull savors each delicious bite.

A cowbell chimes as Ona moseys on over, she's a black-and-white spotted dairy cow with short horns. She leans down and munches on the tall grass.

"Bruce, that sure is good."

Miles away from the cattle, the wolf pack hide in the shadows of a new cave they've discovered.

Paw's long black snout glances over at Kiowa. "I believe Raging Bull now. There are no more buffalo and, like a fool, I killed all the sheep."

"You didn't kill all the sheep," Anoki interjects. "I did. So did Kida."

"Perhaps he was right. So what! He's dead, and nothing can change that. Maybe the time of the buffalo is over. Thankfully, the Great Spirit has provided a new buffalo for us." Makes Trouble licks his lips and motions for the cattle.

Kida squints off in the distance and spots the cattle.

Most of the day, Makes Trouble and Kiowa prepare a plan that they run past Paw. When the three warriors come to an agreement, they run their plan past Kida and Walpi. Brief objections are met with more discussions, but eventually a plan is agreed upon. Then Anoki has her say.

"Rest now. We will need our strength when we move out."

The pack settles down. Most doze off.

Two wolves stir. Kida and Walpi. Waiting for the rest of the pack to fall sleep, Kida slips out and walks a good distance away. She climbs on top of a large cliff that overlooks the canyon and tilts her head to the glowing half-moon and diamond-like stars.

"*Arrr, arrr, eeeewwww,*" she howls softly, singing the wails of her heart. Her words are a mix of sobs and fractured sentences.

"Mother, I miss you. Father, do you miss your daughter? Makes Trouble is happy. Do you search everywhere for us and find us nowhere? We are here with Kiowa and his stupid pack!" she whimpers.

Walpi slowly makes his way up to her, then sits beside her.

"Is it good to mourn for so long?"

"You could not understand a woman's broken heart, Hopi."

CHAPTER 74

Walpi sighs and rests his fury chin on his fluffy paws. "I understand the seasons. Winter is bitter and sends frost to put out all the flames. I understand Kida's heart. Are your tears for someone other than your mother? Your father? Your tribe? Kiowa? The children you will not have? Hopi are poor warriors, but we see much and we are rich in love."

Walpi sits up and stares deep into her red eyes.

"The way Kiowa feels for Anoki…" He gulps away his fear and forces out, "Is the way I have come to feel for you."

He bristles, shuts his eyes, flattens his ears, and waits for the she-wolf to attack him.

Instead, Kida's tail wags softly between gentle whispers.

When she doesn't hurt him, he feels a surge of courage and goes on. "The desire of my heart is as the dry earth desires the Sun God's tears. I have wanted to tell you for some time, Kida, but I was too scared to say the words. My heart is not warrior, but I become warrior-hearted when I see sweet… no, *brave* Kida in danger or pain."

"That is all I ever wanted. To be loved by a great warrior."

"That is not me."

"You have just shown more courage than any man I have ever known. They all know to fear me and use their sweet words on other ladies."

"There are no other ladies."

"And that is why you are brave."

Kida scoots over to Walpi and presses herself against him. They turn their faces to each other and stare into each other's eyes. Their tails intertwine.

"I am scared."

"I am more scared."

Before dawn the pack assembles. Anoki stays behind in the cave while the pack forms in a single line. They masterfully use the terrain to their advantage by staying behind the ridgeline and scurrying along in thick patches of sagebrush. When they patrol down to the lower lands, they move along the streams until they enter the Shadow Valley.

The same way they used to hunt the buffalo, Kiowa and the pack quickly sift the yearlings away from the herd and slaughter them with such ease that every wolf has his own kill before the sun fully rises.

Horrified mothers stampede, abandoning their lifeless calves, and race toward their protector, Ol' Bruce.

A three-thousand-pound longhorn bull causes the ground to thump as he stomps his hoof to uproot grass.

"Ol' Bruce, Ona," Lucy, a new milk cow frantically cries out, "wolves slaughtered my babies!"

"I thought this was the land of milk and honey. We were told when we made the long trip from Texas that there were no wolves, bears, or cougars. Are you certain you saw wolves?" Ona wails.

"We was told a lie, Ona. Sure there's green grass and cool streams, but there's also ferocious wolves hiding in hills," Betty informs him in frantic, heaving breaths.

Bruce spits out a mouthful of grass. The veins in his eyes flush and crackle like red lightning. "Where did you see 'em?"

"Down by the stream. Oh, please hurry, before they kill all of us."

Ol' Bruce courageously trots across the grasslands. His horns cast a long shadow. Soon he sees for himself that Betty is telling no fable. Several spotted bloodstains stand out in stark contrast to the green grass. Entrails are already neatly piled next to severed heads. The calves have all been butchered, broken up into portions, and dragged off.

"We gotta get as far away from here as possible, Ona. Let's huddle up and make for the ranch. Master Geoffrey will put hot lead through these wolves."

"Circle up, y'all. We're gonna go let Rancher Geoffrey know what's happened here"

Back at the cave, the wolves return with mouths full of dripping red meat.

"That was too easy. They must be someone's pets," Paw says, dropping a severed hindquarter.

"Pale-face must raise them, as they do the little fluffy buffalo," Walpi suggests.

"You mean they raise them for food?" Anoki asks.

Walpi nods.

Anoki leans down and sniffs the meat. She turns away at the potent acrylic odor.

"I wouldn't trade all the little white fluffy buffalo in the world for the tame buffalo," she says, reluctantly taking a bite.

"Paw, if the buffalo have all been led to a cave by the Great White Buffalo, then certainly we can survive off the tame buffalo until they return," Kiowa confidently concludes with an air of logic that resonates with his pack.

"Nothing is as it once was, Nephew. These whites and Mexicans are setting up permanent homes. They chop trees and make homes that cannot be easily moved like our tepees. They kill buffalo till the Great White Buffalo is forced to lead her herd away. I do not know if they will ever return."

"No one could know that." Makes Trouble sighs.

"We have seen their iron horse blow steam along firm tracks that do not fade in snow or rain. I am greatly concerned for our tribe."

"Why?" Kiowa boldly questions.

"If we are governed by barbed fences and forced to feed off the invader's tame beasts, what are our people to do? They do not have four legs to outrun thunder sticks." Paw thinks on these changes.

"Our people will do what they have always done. Raid. Roam. Steal horses where they can find them," Kida says, offering her best thoughts.

"Yes, those are our laws. But what laws will govern us now? What will we lose?" Paw's deep questions make his heart sink. "You have sisters and nieces and nephews. Do you not think of them?"

"Of course I do. When the harvest moon comes again, we will seek Onendah's counsel. Until then, we should take only what we need and no more."

"I think we should start killing hunters!" Makes Trouble snickers.

"I see that your owl thoughts have fled from you," Kiowa rebuts.

"What do you mean?" Makes Trouble asks as though he's

offended.

"Who killed first? The Cheyenne or the Kiowa?"

"The Cheyenne, of course!" Kida belts out.

"So our fathers say. Now that we are parents, can you not see that you would say anything to protect your loved ones. Right now wolves kill to eat. If we kill a man of any color, man is certain to strike back."

"And there are more of them than us," Makes Trouble consents.

"An ocean more," Kiowa answers.

Kiowa and Anoki nod in agreement.

The wolves stick to their new code, but news of their kills meet the press on the regular. Folks organize town meetings. Wiremen tap headlines. Publishers produce books with terrifying pictures of wolves eating people. Word spreads through the territories and the old states. The decision of what to do is discussed in taverns and decided over beer.

"My herd has been whittled down by half!"

"I ain't lost half, but our loss is eroding our profit. Won't be able to raise as many cattle next year, which means I won't make enough to send my boy off to university."

"I can't afford to pay my mortgage this year, on account I lost all my sheep."

The list of complaints accumulates quickly in deafening shouts.

Although the wolves get credit for crimes they didn't commit, the blame is rightly placed for many of the things they did do.

On Sunday talk spills over into church. Some preachers preach sermons mingled with Scripture.

"And behold, it says in I Timothy, 3:5, 'For if a man knows not how to rule his own house, how shall he take care of the Church of God?' If we can't take care of our livestock, how can we take care of our homes? If we can't take care of our homes, how can we take care of our churches?"

Others preach nearly the same sermon, but with much more infatuation.

"The devil is in our midst! We must purge this Satanic Werewolf. Man beast. What have you? Sift this tare out from our wheat, by the power God has given us with these Colt forty-four, six-shootin' pistols. If the wolf seeketh to destroy our flocks, he will not stop until he devours all our animals! Our livelihoods! Our children! Our wives! Our young men! Our old! Our homes! We shall all perish with great famine, as the Egyptians did, unless we fight the righteous cause!"

"Here! Here!" were the cries of the congregation for both sermons, which put the seal needed to take strong action against Kiowa's pack.

Where preachers weren't, sermons were. Only they were mingled with more plain words and topped off with foaming beer-filled mugs in pubs and bars.

"We gotta get that wolf!"

"If I get that wolf, I'm gonna skin him and wear his pelt 'round town, see if I can't impress the ladies."

"Ain't no way a wolf coulda done this; it's a werewolf, and it's gotta die!"

"We gotta kill it!"

"Needs killin', and we're just the ones to do it."

Words, as they say, are hardly the equivalent to damages inflicted by sticks and stones. But words mixed with alcohol get folks riled up in such a way that sticks and stones actually do start to break bones. And one stick, the thunder stick as the Indians call it, was new to the prairie. In fact, Colt's brand-new invention, the rapid-fire rifle, was on its way to Cimarron. Carried by a trapper, who planned to replace printed words and whispers with thunderous echoes everywhere he saw fit.

CHAPTER 75

Cotton prances through foot-high snow like a champion stallion even though he is just a well-trained Appalachian mountain horse. The ride to Buffalo Bay was a rough and cold hundred-and-thirty-three-mile trek. What should have taken three days on horseback in good weather took nearly ten. W.H. hardly strains Cotton, but Bingo, on the other hand, does not fare as well. The cold morning is well lit. The ground is covered in a frozen blanket caused by unique snowdrifts. Skeleton trees are covered in icy crystals, which sparkle and gleam, dazzling the eyes. Fortunately, homesteaders showed Christian kindness and let the motley crew bunk in the barn to escape the cold.

W.H. turns in his saddle and looks down at his loyal dog.

"Eh, Bingo, it looks like we're saying good-bye to these snow-covered caps for a year or so."

The collie looks up at him with a dreadful expression.

W.H. laughs. "If I didn't have all this equipment, you could ride up here with me."

Bingo barks at him.

"Buddy, you can stay at the college. Dr. Bennett would take better care of you than I can."

Bingo barks his dissatisfaction in both the travel and in leaving his master's side.

"Well, then, you're caught in a pea pod of misery. Suck it up, buttercup. We just arrived."

When they approach the steamboat dock, a few ratty box buildings line the Lake of the Woods dock. Women in plaid and checked winter gowns line the dock and wooden Riverwalk which encircles the water's edge. They look like brilliant winter flowers on a white blanket. Bonnets cover their heads, and they are very particular who they make eye contact with and for how long.

Some men in handsome black, brown, and white business suits hold umbrellas and shield ladies from snow and occasional gusts of wind. Shawls hardly keep the girls warm, but to look their best and cover it up is too much to ask. Thus they endure the frigid elements and show their beautiful shivering figures.

Children dressed in their Sunday best chase one another up and down the line, hurling snowballs at one another. Girls, of course, cling to their mothers' sides and behave well. Most look like miniature versions of their mothers. Boys, on the other hand, look like something else. Their uniforms, or lack thereof, distinguish their family by class.

As W.H. rides up, he wonders what he's supposed to do with Cotton. Swinging his legs out of his saddle, he strolls up to the counter and instantly feels the cold biting at his feet.

Poor Bingo, he thinks, then dismisses his empathy with a wave.

"Hello there!"

"Howdy!" a clerk wearing a green visor, a white shirt, and a black tie hollers through a barred window.

Inside the lantern-lit office, W.H. can see a cast-iron stove and wishes he could put Bingo in there for a bit.

"I'd like to book passage."

"Final destination?"

Unable to remember where he's going, W.H. reaches inside his pocket and removes the newspaper article. He scans it for a destination.

"Cimarron, New Mexico."

"New Mexico, my goodness, sir. You are going to have quite the adventure."

"I certainly hope so! Why do you say that?"

"Well, that's the Northwest Territory! We only have steamers that go so far. You'll hop on a train that will take you to Omaha, Nebraska. From there you can catch some other carts, but don't count on it. Train robbers and Injuns is making a mess of progress."

"Is that so?" W.H. looks back at his rifle and wonders if he shouldn't bring it with him.

"You're in luck, Mister. The *Rising Star* is a livestock-friendly vessel, so you can board your horse below decks. So long as he don't get seasickness. Do you know if he gets sick or throws fits on the water?"

W.H. shakes his head. "She does not."

"Well, so long as she can be controlled, she can store below. If she can't, they might put her down and toss her overboard."

"How is a feller supposed to know?"

"I guess you will just have to wait and find out."

"That hardly seems like a fair deal."

"That's the way it is!"

The clerk tilts his green visor down and counts out six preprinted tickets, then licks his pencil and marks the destinations and transfers. "Michigan and Illinois are going to be some great stops. Have you ever been to the big city?"

"Bigger than Winnipeg?" W.H. asks.

"By a barrel and a peck."

"A barrel and a peck?"

"These are your stayovers and depots. Try not to lose these tickets. If you do, it's fine. Just remember to tell them Buffalo Bay Depot. They can wire us and I can validate your tickets. That'll be two hundred and forty-seven dollars and eighty-nine cents."

W.H. looks over the man's shoulder and catches a long view of an odd wooden-based machine with mysterious wires and brass fittings attached to its face. "Why don't you just use that contraption to let them know I'm coming? Then I won't have to worry about losing my tickets."

"Telegraph every depot? That would take entirely too much time, sir."

"Longer than it will take me to get there?"

"Ha!" The man laughs, then looks down and sees W.H.'s pistol. His face grows serious. "Would you like to see how it works?"

"Absolutely!"

The man walks around the side door, unlocks it, and greets W.H. wearing shorts instead of pants.

W.H. looks down and smiles. "You got a good deal."

"I sure do. Come on in here."

W.H. leaves the door open long enough for Bingo to slip through. The collie looks at him with so much gratitude in his eyes, W.H. can't help but grin.

"This little fellow has wires to transmit, a sender to talk, and a battery for power. A copper wire runs from the station all the way to the next depot."

"How do you transmit messages?"

"Morse code."

"What's that?"

"A series of dashes and dots that represent letters in the alphabet. See, this here is the sender. It can move up and down like this, see?" He pushes to the sender to show how a dash and a dot are represented.

W.H. stares at the clerk blankly.

"Here's how it works. This copper wire right here goes from the device all the way to the Ohio. It gets wrapped around an electromagnet and then comes back to here and completes a circuit."

W.H. tries his best to catch every detail, but he can't understand what in tarnation the man is talking about. He politely nods and does his best not to yawn, but soon he can't even control that.

"I see that I'm losing you."

"Oh no. This is all very interesting."

"Look at it from a more simple view. I can send information to whoever is on the other end of this line as fast as I can tap my finger."

"Hmm…Well, people already have access to information through the papers and books."

"Do you have any idea how long it takes a printing press to run a line of books or newspapers? By the time the information reaches its intended audience, things have changed."

"So what's your point?"

"Don't you see it?"

"'Fraid not, feller."

"All these inventions are speeding things up. Making them faster."

"But your devices aren't doing anything I can't do with my pen, paper, and trusty horse."

"You know what I'm going to do?"

W.H. shakes his head.

"I'm going to prove to you just how powerful this device is."

"How are you going to do that?"

"I'm going to send an arrest and detain order out to all these stations and see just how far you can get."

W.H. leaps to his feet, now wide-awake. "You better not!"

"Now you see how powerful information is. You youngsters can't appreciate the value of time because you think you have so much of it. Truth is, none of us really knows how long we have to live. But when your youth is threatened with bars, it stirs you. Why is that?"

"I dunno. I suppose the thought of being caged is more than my young years can bear."

"Well, anywho, pay your tab and we'll settle up and you can be on your way."

"Thank you for telling me all about that telegraph. I was mighty interested in learning about it."

W.H. reaches inside his pocket and removes a pouch containing several gold coins.

The teller's eyes light up at the clack of the coins.

W.H. pulls out a palmful of Spanish gold coins and counts out two.

"That's quite a bit of money you have there, sir. Be sure not to advertise your good fortune. Cardsharps will be sure to lift the hefty purse of a youthful man like yourself."

"Is that so?"

"Yes, sir! Also, the ships and railroads have safes, so if you will be needing a quarter-inch of steel to keep your monies and valuables secure, be sure to let the ticket master know."

"Ain't they getting robbed?"

The clerk nods. He pauses for a moment and looks down, then looks back up and sees the contradiction.

W.H. opens the door and lets in the cold. Bingo reluctantly stands up and inches his way back out into the frigid winter weather. Outside, W.H. unties his horse and takes his place in line.

Children rush Bingo and pour an ocean of sweet affections on him. W.H. is asked no less than a hundred times if he's willing to "give up his well-behaved hound." He's also asked a hundred times if "he's killed a man with his pistol." He answers no so frequently, he wonders if he shouldn't pay the wire man to type his answer into their brains. The thought makes him chuckle, then ponder if that won't be next.

With the thunderous echo of a cannon, a veiled steamer appears off on the horizon.

W.H. did not know what to expect on account he had never seen a steamer.

CHAPTER 76

A big vessel nearly a thousand feet in length and a hundred feet in width pushes through the icy, choppy waters. It has what looked to be two oversized wagon wheels attached to the middle-rear, on either side. They easily cycle through water, furiously churning the icy lake as they go. Fire spews out of two towering black tube-shaped smokestacks, which rise from the ship's middle. A cannon fires off the port side and thrills the crowd.

Children cheer and the parents light sparklers. They quickly hand them off to their excited children, who beg with all their breath for the cannon to fire once more. When it does not, the boys spin their sparklers furiously until the fire burns out.

"This is a day to be remembered!" says a middle-aged woman, gripping her Bible and saying a prayer for all to hear. "Thanks be to God, the Almighty, for he has sifted us Episcopalians out of the tears, to start a new life, in a strange new land. Full of milk and honey."

Her face shines with such bright excitement, W.H. can't help but join all the smiling folks. They join hands and dance around in circles singing a song that sounds much like Britain's anthem in rhythm, but the lyrics are clearly American.

My country 'tis of thee, sweet land of liberty, of thee I sing.
Land where my fathers died, land of the PILGRIMS' pride,
From every mountainside, LET FREEDOM RING!

At the end of the song, the men take off their hats and place them over their hearts. Soon everyone stops to salute or place their hand on their heart when they see a long flowing American flag.

Something about that blue box with bright stars lifts everyone's spirits in a way that only gospel can, W.H. thinks to himself.

"Three cheers for the free land!" a young father shouts, hoisting his son up on his shoulders.

"Hip! Hip…"

"Hooray!"

"Hip! Hip…"

"Hooray!'

"Hip! Hip…"

BOOM!

The cannon gives the boys what they've been begging for. The little boy on the man's shoulders claps his hands, his wide eyes, and shouts, "Again, again!"

As the ship nears, W.H. can't understand how that tonnage speeds itself through water. *The hull looks to be like any normal ship, but it must be strong to move through this ice.*

He is no expert in shipbuilding but was briefly educated in the art, and his beginning architect education goes to work. *Ah, yes.* His mind finds the solution. *Surely the ship is fashioned with live oak and plated with copper by the Revere press.*

The hull comes to a fine point. A fair-haired mermaid at the bow pushes her bosoms out. Her hand is raised in a permanent greeting, and her smile invites fair weather.

W.H. takes everything in, examining each detail. *Why does the boat have a sail between those smokestacks? Clearly the boilers heat up water, allow smoke to rise out of the stacks, then use the steam energy to gyrate the enormous paddle wheels with such a speed, no sail could keep up. So again, why would you sail?*

I wonder how much coal it can burn in a day. What's that pyramid of cables rising off the stern? What's more, how does that darn thing stop?

A bell rings from the deck and a uniformed man shouts, "Stand clear of the vessel. All hands, stand clear!"

W.H. expects to witness a catastrophe.

The goliath vessel casts its shadow on the crowded dock. One gear-like wheel stops moving and spills murky water all over the side of the ship, while the other gear continues churning. Slowly, the bow turns, expertly positioning the ship perpendicular to the dock. The cables run from the boom to the mast and are used to slowly lower a wide plank, which bounces on the dock, then rests firm.

"I must come to understand this!" W.H. mumbles, while the crowd wastes no time rushing to board. They nearly trample the sole ticket master.

"Tickets!" a man in a blue suit shouts at the crowd, pushing them back until he receives verification for each and every passenger.

"Be orderly. Be patient. Each of you will board in due time. We haven't set sail without a passenger, and we won't be harboring any stowaways. Tickets! Present your tickets!"

His words may have well not been spoken. No one listens. They can't help themselves. Their anticipation boils over. It's as though the motherland that bore them and reared them is the past, and their future is this new land of hope and promise.

One immigrant after another pushes, forces, kicks, pulls, tugs, and fights their way past the next. Even the woman who had said a prayer proved she knew how to use her elbows as well as her lips.

While everyone else is furiously boarding, W.H. lingers behind and studies the architecture of the vessel. He is in no rush and he finds it odd that teal water marks on the copper plating indicate that the ship has been in the water for some time.

"How could we just now be seeing this, Bingo?"

Bingo growls at the smoking cannon and barks incessantly at the man in blue. He shares none of his master's interest. And his skepticism grows as people walk to what he presumes is their bitter end.

"STOP!" Bingo barks. "'AINT SAFE! AINT RIGHT! AINT PROPER! FOR ALL YOU KNOW, YOU COULD BE FEEDING YOURSELVES TO THE FIRE!"

But not one soul listens to words that come out in barks.

"Bingo, pipe down!" W.H. hollers, forcing the collie to lower his head and flatten his ears.

W.H. gets as close as he can to the anvil-shaped cast-iron anchor and examines the artwork on it. A woman with a halo of stars around her crown hands a man a rolled-up scroll marked, liberty.

How peculiar.

Finally, all of the passengers have boarded the craft.

"Mighty fine horse you got there, feller." The ticket man compliments in a thick Boston accent.

He tips the brim of his shiny, blue octagonal hat. "He get seasick?"

"Mister, this horse pulled Titan's chariot."

"Ha! Ha! Well, okay, then, let's get 'em below decks. Tickets?"

W.H. hands him a stack of tickets. A piece is torn from one and the rest are handed back.

"I'll take good care of him." With that, the friendly fellow takes the reins and leads Cotton up the plank and down below.

Unsure of what to do, Bingo looks to his master.

"Way I see it, Bingo, you got two choices. You can stay in the cabin with me for three days on deck and let the kids pet you and pull on your ears, or keep an eye on Cotton."

I'd rather stay with my pal, Bingo barks.

He looks over the deck and realizes the scale is much larger in person, than on the dock. *So the steam combusts and...*

"Cabin tickets!" the man in the blue uniform shouts in his face.

W.H. shows him his stack.

"Follow me."

The ticket man leads W.H. down a flight of stairs to the first deck, through a narrow white hall.

"Your cabin is number one hundred and five, on the left, sir."

W.H. follows the man, a bit confused.

"You will be glad you booked first class, sir. The rest of the passengers have to sit on benches for three days and sleep wherever they can. Assuming they can get sleep. Rats run rampant at night, and if you could imagine those tiny feet crawling across your face, you'd sit right up and get no sleep."

"Sleep is good." W.H. smirks.

The steward opens the black cabin door.

"Yes, even a portal window for first class. And a bed, a wash pan, and a piss pot." The man points to each commodity.

"Well, then, that'll do."

The man sticks his hand out and tilts his head; his eyebrows hover over his bright blue eyes.

"I... ah... Can I get back to you on that?"

"Of course, sir. Tips aren't mandatory, only encouraged."

"I only have, ah..." W.H. gets hung up on words on account of the telegraph clerk's warning.

"It really isn't a problem, sir. I'll try to remember to ring you for dinner."

The man slams the door to show his discontent.

W.H. plops down on the bed and takes his glasses and boots off.

He pulls the wool blanket back and slides between two linen sheets.

***

November 22, 1859

Finally off to a grand adventure! I awoke to an evening filled with dancing, sparklers, and pistol fire. Unable to resist the festivities, I joined the celebration. I fired six shots myself. It felt great, until I realized I was surrounded by rocking darkness. I felt a queasiness in my belly. I leaned over the side of the barge and spewed my guts out. Though I hoped no one had seen me in my weakest state, I was proved wrong by children pointing and laughing. The same children that wanted me to give up Bingo. Children are awful. It's a wonder their mothers endure them.

Once I got sorted, I felt somewhat sad for the folks who won't be returning to our homeland. Most are already calling themselves American. At supper I met a supremely wonderful woman. Her name is Joanne Louise Mudry, but she goes by "Granny" and she is not a Canadian at all.

She and her brood hail from Albany, New York. She tells the wildest tales. Claims she saw her relatives fight off the British. Met George Washington when he stayed at her childhood homestead. She has buried three husbands. Buried nine of her twelve children and shed many tears as she spoke of the babies fondly. She wept particularly hard when she spoke of her mother. Her mother was her everything, as most mothers are. I could not help but tear up myself.

Granny even raised up her nephew. One day her sister-in-law kissed her baby, handed him off to Granny, and said, "I have no more milk to give. He is your child now." With that, her sister-in-law up and died, and Granny raised her thirteenth child. If anyone could make a career of mothering, it is

Granny, she has so much love in her! Of course, she repeated most of this twice to three times, but I didn't mind. I find her most amusing.

I must admit, my adventure has thrust me into the most interesting scientific inventions. The clerk did his best to explain the telegraph contraption to me. He claims it makes a series of dashes and dots, so a feller on the other side can turn that tapping confusion into words. Messages are sent across hundreds of miles no longer by pony, Uncle, but by the simple rap and tap of a very specialized operator. Can you imagine?

Currently I am on board the *Rising Star*. She is a magnificent vessel. Built out of copper and American old-growth oak, just as the texts imply. I have spent most of my day asking the crew questions that established me as a "very curious fellow." I can't help it. I simply must understand how the Americans are harnessing steam power. I was permitted to tour the engine room. What a fine mechanical marvel, Uncle. The scale of all these moving metal parts is enough to make a full-grown man feel like an ant. She's equipped with twelve boilers, one hundred furnaces, and imagine, these parts as tall as two-story office buildings. All this burns up to five hundred tons of coal per day, making her steam-power engine the fastest in the fleet. That's twenty thousand horsepower, mind you. The *Rising Star* is even said to be capable of traversing the Atlantic Ocean, though the owners are thought to be too "chicken" to risk it. Can't say that I blame them. Mechanically, the engineer explains to me that they use coal to make a fire. Run water through a "boiler," and then trap the expanding steam, which moves "push valves" up and down, forcing an axle as big as the beams in your office roof to rotate, which in turn moves the paddle wheels.

I suppose everywhere I look, scientific advancements are moving at the speed of bullets. Captain tells me we are moving equivalent to thirty miles per hour! Who knew a body could move so fast?

I was going to ask if anyone wanted his or her picture taken and then charge them for my services so as to conserve my gold allotment. But I do not know how to use the equipment just yet, so I kept my mouth shut. No need to be branded a "curious FOOL." "Curious" when said alone is still pretty much neutral.

Had corn cakes and beef for dinner. Corn-fed beef. It was quite delicious and is all the rage. The passengers on this vessel speak constantly of the opportunities in Kansas. Apparently, land is being handed out through a process Congress calls Homesteading. I seriously doubt any government is giving away land for free. These folks are poor, misled fools, and if I hadn't begun to form bonds with them, I might be led away by false pretenses and ambitious hopes. "Tools of the devil," old preacher Ahab might say. This is my first entry, and I am quite proud of myself for remembering to make it.

CHAPTER 77

Dearest Uncle,

One day on a ship goes on to the next without noticing much other than the rising and setting of the sun. Several days now we have had ham, eggs, and sweet corn cakes for breakfast. My fellow passengers are mostly Canadians. A few Americans are mixed in with us, but we stopped at Birch Beach and picked up quite a few more Yanks, as the crew calls them.

Went and fetched Bingo. He was as happy as a pup. Cotton, too, was pleased. Both hopped up and down on paws and hooves as best they could in their confined corral. By all appearances, everything seems fine except that Cotton must've got nervous and gnawed on the wood in her stable. I will be slipping her some apples to calm her down.

They are in tight quarters, as am I. In fact, I'm not sure the ferry was such a good idea. Perhaps riding my horse would have been best. No doubt it would have taken a greater amount of time to travel by horse, adding nearly six months to our journey. That would have allowed me only a couple of weeks to hunt the wolves before I would have had to turn back around and head home for school. And on second thought, poor Bingo wouldn't have no meat left on him, so I guess the barge is still the best option.

I know study is what you want for me, Uncle,

but you must know I am learning things that cannot be learned inside a classroom. I have never felt more alive. The life I am living, at this moment, couldn't be imagined, and living it feels like a dream. Which is another good reason to take the barge. Indians and vagabonds can easily single a lone man out and overtake him for his scalp, his purse, or both.

Last evening there was a dance on the top deck. Granny—remember her?—she didn't know what to make of the dancing. Says it's "of the devil for a body to gyrate about." I didn't mind, though. Everyone is in such high spirits, it would be hard to imagine that anything could dampen them.

Pounding at the cabin door forces W.H. to sit straight up.

"Yes? Who is it?" he asks as he slips his glasses on.

"Room service. Would you like your room cleaned?"

"Uh, yes, I suppose I would."

When he gets up and gets dressed, he sees that sun has barely just begun to rise.

"What the heck? Breakfast isn't for another few hours."

He hears a sheet of paper slide across the floor. He walks over to it and adjusts his suspenders so his pants won't slip down. Leaning over, he picks up the note. It reads, *Here is a tip. Rooms get cleaned when penny pinchers loosen their grip!*

"Daggone it!" W.H. grumbles, combing his hands through his handlebar mustache. He splashes water onto his face and slips his boots on. Fumbling around his room, he reaches for his brown blazer and pushes his arms through the sleeves. The pouch of gold claps against his side, giving him a sense of security the lower class will never experience.

Once dressed, he makes his way to the money exchange at the pilot cage, which is situated near the steam stacks. He slaps his palm down on a bell, which gets an immediate response.

"Hello, sir." A banker pops in brightly.

"What's the exchange rate for a gold coin?"

"Big bills or…?"

"Little ones would be fine," W.H. says, reflecting on how many times he will have to tip.

The teller slides his green visor on and counts out a hundred and fifty greenback US dollars. He licks his fingers, then says, "Don't worry, sir. Those aren't wildcat bills."

"Wildcat?"

"Oh, you aren't familiar with the term?"

W.H. shakes his head.

"That's when a bank takes in everyone's gold, then issues their own currency commensurate with the gold. The problem is, no one has tabs on the money press, you know, the printing plates. Bankers who need to expand currency print more paper money, thus causing a run on the gold."

"So why is it called 'wildcat?'"

"Because the gold will run out of the bank faster than a wild cat!"

"So why wouldn't everyone just use the greenbacks?"

"Can't get enough bills. The coach won't take the risk on account of river robbers and Indians. Rail ain't completed yet. And ferries have had a real problem with inside crew cracking the safes."

A series of whistle blasts interrupts the two and alerts the crew that they will be making a stop.

"Better get ready. We're about to dock."

W.H. passes his porter and is quick to stick out his hand. W.H. overtips him and says, "I presume this will keep call times on schedule?"

"Yes, sir. Also cleaning services, luggage services, stable services, and laundry services will all be on time. I personally guarantee!"

"Well, you do a good job and I'll match that when we get to port. Where are we now?"

"If you disembark, sir, I wouldn't be venturing far from the vessel if I was you."

"Why is that?" W.H. huffs, not wanting to be told what to do.

"INDIANS!"

"Indians? You act as though they're behind every bush and tree."

"They follow us and signal one another with smoke and mirrors. We always rotate our ports. That way they can't get our schedule or our scalps! But you better believe they're out there and they're awaiting."

"That don't hardly make sense to me." W.H. scratches his head.

"Which part, sir?"

"I can't disembark and stretch my legs, but we're picking up passengers at this port. Aren't they in danger of losing their scalps as they stand on the pier?"

"Of course, sir. But the Indians are less likely to attack them here inside Fort Mackinac, since they are guarded by a wall, fence, cannon, rifle, and fifty or so US cavalry. The red man will only attack when he has the numbers and the advantage. If he is at risk of losing his life or his scalp, he will not attack. He will run!"

"That makes more sense. So what you're saying is don't go past the gate."

"Yes, sir. And don't walk the banks. Beyond the safety of those gates is a dangerous unexplored frontier wilderness. Mongrel hordes of war-painted savages roam these plains in constant search of the buffalo, the deer, the bear, and often, one another."

They stare at each other for a serious moment.

"Thank you for your tip."

"You'll like these folks we're picking up, sir. They come from all over New England."

"Well, if the new passengers are half as fun as the folks last night, we should all be peachy."

When the steamer comes to a stop, it anchors out in deep waters. The crew goes to work loading cannon and musket, while the land crew disembark with revolving rifles and pistols. Those who want to venture ashore do so in flat-bottomed rowboats, maneuvered with long oars. Most of the passengers remain behind on account of the captain's warning, a more light-hearted version than the porter's.

W.H. looks for a better understanding of the steamboat's maneuverability. It is nothing like the flat-bottomed boats he goes to shore in. Flat-bottomed boats had only as much power as muscle could muster. The steamship on the other hand could up and go at the will of the captain's lever.

"*Bonjour!*" a lady shouts from shore, waving her handkerchief. "*Je m'appelle Helen, et vous?*"

"I wish I knew how to use that camera," W.H. whispers under his breath to Bingo. "These girls don't cover their hair with bonnets, and that makes them prettier than girls who do."

"*Bonjour!* Hello!" the ladies shout boldly.

The closer he gets, the more he can see that these New Englanders do not fancy color. Everything they wear looks well-tailored, but their dresses and shawls are entirely black. The men are dressed in fine black suits with tall black hats that have broad round brims. They are adorned with the most interesting-looking beards. Either they have bushy sideburns shaved into chops, or their beards are neatly trimmed, which in W.H.'s opinion defeats the purpose of having one. *Real Puritans?* W.H. thinks. *The porter said they was fun folks. I suppose they could be headed back from a funeral.*

His thoughts shift when he sees the younger ladies. Those who look to be sixteen and younger wear gowns that are either blue, red, or yellow satin, but those look to be the only colors allowed.

"Nellie," a woman shouts, enunciating every vowel in the most irritating New York manner, "do what your father says. Listen to him. Listen! Are you listening?"

Their pale white faces cause W.H. to wonder if these folks don't bathe in bleach instead of water.

"Look at that, Bingo. Yankee boys ain't nothing like Canadian boys. They don't run up and down the line like a bunch of wild animals. They don't pepper folks up with questions either. I would expect these finely dressed young men not to pull on your ears. Look at how they play the part of dutiful steward, tending to their families' luggage and to their younger siblings."

Bingo whimpers at the memory of tender youth tugging on his flappy black ears.

"All aboard," hollers the ticket master as the boatswain mates tie half-hitch knots onto iron anvils bolted to the pier.

Unlike the Canadians, the Americans move in a very orderly fashion and, as the ticket master said, they are well guarded by the cavalry.

Some two hundred men dressed in blue uniforms with cavalry hats perform different duties at the fort. Some stand post behind a crude, spiked wooden wall encircling the area. A few scan the prairie with goggles, while the artillery crew performs maintenance tasks on a large howitzer cannon. Others at rest, squat or lean up against the fort's whitewashed stone walls, wrapped in green wool blankets. A few officers sit outside at a table, near a fire, and play a card game, while enlisted men on the other side of the fire shoot craps.

"Remind me to make a journal entry, Bingo. I will title it, 'The life of an American soldier. To stand. To sit. To look. To lean. To gamble. To clean.'"

In this flock of New Englanders, women rule the roost. They boss the elderly and the children around with tongues as sharp as swords. Some women are even so bold as to boss men. Instead of rushing the plank, they move in a perfectly straight line.

What a pitiful sight. W.H. sighs. *Women so beautiful, with tones so ugly.*

When the boats are secure, the passengers wait patiently for W.H. and Bingo to disembark.

W.H. can't help himself. The first thing he wants to do is go outside the gate. The soldiers disapprovingly oblige him and warn him to stay within cannon range.

Outside the military's walls, wide prairie runs into a steep sand-dune bank. W.H. climbs to the top of a small bluff, huffing cloud bursts in the crisp cold. He scans the flat snow-covered landscape. The prairie is encircled all around by white winter trees.

"I don't see no Indians. Do you sense any, Bingo?"

CHAPTER 78

Later that night, W.H. is the first to arrive at supper. The interior mess hall on the first floor is decorated in the Victorian style. Mahogany wainscoting panels line the walls. Thick Turkish carpets cover the dining room hardwoods, or chow hall, as the crew call it. Oil lanterns burn a low dull flame on the gilded maple tables. The tables are spaced far enough apart for a fancied-up waiter to maneuver through them and deliver steaming meals on decorative silver platters.

Name tags are placed on a white china plate, with delicate etched gold flowers encircling the rim. He looks for his name and settles into a floral upholstered carver chair. Silverware is tin, but it is polished as though it were silver.

The rectangular windows are wide open to vent the room. Had it not been for the hurricane glass protecting its flame, the room would've been dark due to a strong breeze gusting through the space. A crew musician in a fancy dinner suit plays a fiddle; the music floats across the cool night air.

"Hello there, young man." Granny approaches W.H., and he presents her with the crook of his arm. She slowly bends at the waist, swinging one leg around, then struggling with the other. She furiously claws at her dinner dress and makes sure to tuck all the fabric under the table. "Gone are the days of my need for so much lace and exposure. I'm not a belle needing to catch a man. I've already had three. Would have been happy with the first one. Why my daughter insists that I wear all this fluff is just nonsense. Who needs these hooped gowns? I feel like a chicken in a wire coup."

"Ha! Ha! Granny. What would you wear if you weren't wearing a black gown like all these other Yankee women?"

"Pants! Same as you."

"Oh, you wouldn't like that, Granny. It isn't proper for a lady to dress like a man."

"And why not? I'm told that ranch hands in Kansas allow the ladies to wear pants."

"Pants? Unfathomable! No woman in proper civilized society would be allowed to wear pants. The laws of fashion wouldn't allow it. Neither sex would endure it, though our sex is the more patient and level-headed of the two."

A slender ghostly complexioned Yankee woman interrupts. "Oh, please excuse me. My name is Helen."

W.H. stands up and nods to the lady.

"Name's W.H. What parts of the world would you be traveling from?" He extends his hand to her husband.

"As in the letters?" Helen's tall husband asks as he draws a *W* and then an *H* with his index finger.

W.H. nods.

"Suit yourself. Name's Clarence Rockefeller the second. This is my wife," the well-to-do business man says, removing his gentleman's hat and surprising W.H. with a firm handshake.

"Yes, yes, we are kin to Mr. John D. Rockefeller. My family was the first to settle New York City. My fourth great-grandfather, Giovanni da Verrazzano, toured it when it was still inhabited by savages. No need to make a big deal of it. It's just who we are. No one can control who they were born as, and for that reason I do not feel the least bit ashamed of being born to wealth. I prefer means to meagers."

Helen pivots and turns her straight back and square shoulders to her husband. "Dearest, I am quite disappointed that we did not board the *Star of the West*. The papers all proclaim it to be 'the fastest ship in the ferry fleet. After all, I did promise the children that we would make history. It's very important to do so, don't you think?" She turns back to her company. "Anyway, we are from upstate New York. And yourselves?"

W.H. stares at the woman in disbelief. *I didn't even ask for half of that information, much less see her draw a breath.* "I'm from Winni—"

"Canada! Do they have a theater in Winnipeg?"

W.H. closes his mouth and sits back in his chair like someone has just socked him in the jaw. Before he can finish his sentence, the woman cuts him off again.

"I live for the theater. We are patrons of the Astor Opera House. Ever heard of it?"

"I can't…"

"Well, let me tell you. It is a gorgeous opera house in the Greek revival style. The theater interior is most beautifully carved and covered in twenty-four-karat gold. Oh, how I miss it. Do you fancy architecture? Italy has the best. Well, Paris has the best architecture, really. Well, I don't know. I guess it's a toss-up. We have had many a good visit to that opera house, haven't we, Clarence?"

Clarence knows better than to try to speak. He nods and reaches inside his coat pocket and withdraws two long brown cigars. Snipping off the ends, he lights one and hands it to W.H.

"Thank you."

"Did you know that in forty-nine, same year as the Gold Rush, we were involved in an opera house riot? Uhm-hmm, it's true. Tell them, Clarence." Mrs. Rockefeller's eyes are ablaze. She flips her napkin and rests it on her lap at the same time she grips a fork like it's a spear. Her teeth shine as brightly as her eyes.

W.H. has the strange sense that she is more predator than prey.

"Clarence used his pocket pistol on two rioters." She drops the fork and claps her hands together. Pointing her fingers as though they were a gun, she aims at W.H.'s belly.

"Boom!"

Then Granny's belly. "Boom!"

"Where'd he hit 'em?" Granny asks.

"Right in the gut. Wasn't anything they didn't deserve. They said, 'You are rich and snooty. We are poor and destitute.' Was my aim off, darling?" She turns to her husband.

"Colt, Baby Dragon. Forty-four caliber. Man knew what he was doing when he made that hand cannon."

"I have a Colt," W.H. begins, but no one seems to care.

"We met him. A splendid fellow!" Helen interrupts.

"You met Samuel Colt?" W.H. says admiringly.

"What brings you to the western territories?" Granny asks, breaking off a piece of bread.

"Our thriving empire. With all this westward expansion and free land, Clarence's uncle saw an opportunity. Are you familiar with industry, Mister?"

"W.H." He nods. "I saw my first telegraph machine a few days ago, and this is the finest vessel—"

"The telegraph. That old thing? Mr. Morse was at our Christmas party. Oh, you must both come to next year's Christmas party. We celebrate in the highest fashion."

She turns to look at her husband. "Clarence, please send them an invite." Then turns back to W.H. and Granny and asks, "Have you heard of phonics?"

W.H. puffs on the cigar and makes the mistake of inhaling it. He coughs and hacks while Helen continues as though nothing is out of the ordinary.

"Antonio Meucci invented a device you hold up to your ear and then, with your other hand, speak into... I believe it's called a transmitter or a speaker."

"Receiver," her husband corrects.

"Yes, that's it. Thank you, Clarence, a receiver. See, I am a woman of industry."

Clarence gets up and pats W.H. on the back until he can breathe again.

"Cubans. Uncle got two thousand of them for Christmas. Come to the party. You won't regret the gift baskets."

"I'm fine, thank you," W.H. says, reaching for a glass of water as tears trickle down his ruddy cheeks.

"Mr. Meucci believes these devices will soon be in homes. He says that we will speak and hear one another from the safety of our own homes. Can any of you fathom that? Voices in our homes instead of words on paper."

"Imagine that!" Granny blurts out. "Speaking to a person from your own home as though they were right there with you?"

"Yes, indeed, imagine. Mr. Meucci says his device works as far as three city blocks. I like you, Granny. You have a scope for imagination rare for your age. We won't need a post service anymore because no one will be writing letters. You can just pick up the handheld, press it to your ear, and speak into a receiver. It's all very modern. As are we. Very modern. Would you like to see our daguerreotype?" Helen asks. Not waiting for an answer, she spins around and claws through her bag.

"I happen to have—" W.H. begins, but Granny cuts him off.

"Yes, I would! A daguerreotype? You are modern indeed."

Helen whips around with a gold-framed black-and-white picture of her and her husband looking as still as statutes.

"Oh, how I have always wanted my daguerreotype done," Granny heaves in complete admiration.

"Is that so, Granny? I happen to have the device with me." W.H. beams proudly like he finally has something to offer.

"How proficient are you?" Clarence asks.

"Not at all."

"Then what good does it do you?" Helen waves clouds of cigar smoke out of her face.

W.H. puffs up his chest. "I'm learning."

"Clarence can show you how to use that contraption. Clarence can do anything. He met Monsieur Louis Daguerre on a business trip. Tried to offer him a fair deal for his invention. Mr. Daguerre would hear nothing of it. Can you believe he didn't want to make a penny? Said it would be better used by the masses."

"He was a proud man. Very intelligent," Clarence reflects nobly.

Helen shuffles in her seat. "Ha! Proud! Try stupid. We could have made him rich a thousand times over. He doesn't appreciate the value of wealth or time. Oh, we could have saved him so much time."

Granny turns to W.H. "If you wouldn't mind, and if you have the time, would you allow Mr. Rockefeller to take my daguerreotype?"

"Only if he shows me how the darn thing works."

"Deal. I like how you think. Whatever you charge, foot me with the bill," Clarence says, extinguishing his cigar even though he's hardly had a puff.

"I don't have much. But I would like to leave my portrait for posterity so that my descendants know where they came from. I wish I had portraits of my family. All I have of my family is framed silhouettes," Granny says, pressing her wrinkled hand to her chest.

"Granny, I wouldn't dream of charging you. It would be my pleasure and honor," W.H. proudly proclaims, winning the affection of the high-class diners. He tucks his thumb under his armpit and is more than happy to extinguish his throat-burning, eye-watering cigar.

Clarence reaches inside his jacket and removes a small notepad and a pencil. He beings scribbling and asks, "Shall we say ten o'clock tomorrow morning?"

"That would be fine with me."

"Oh, oh! How splendid," Granny exclaims, holding her shaking hand to her withered lips.

"What a fine pair of gentlemen you two are. I am honored to sit at this here table." Helen picks up her fork. "Oh, there's the food." The one-sided conversation goes on throughout supper. Even after shredded beef and mashed potatoes are delivered. Even after apple pie dessert. Helen is a walking, living, breathing encyclopedia. She has either seen or read about all the most modern devices. She is so eager to share her wealth of information, she doesn't seem to notice her entrée or dessert. And no one gets a word in. Eventually W.H. learns to follow Granny's lead. He doesn't wait for everyone to eat. He stuffs his mouth while Helen stuffs their ears.

CHAPTER 79

Dearest Uncle,

Yanks are a very boisterous bunch, especially New Yorkers! Met a couple named Rockefeller, Helen and Clarence. They claim to be of some relation to the famous oil tycoon. I was sat by them at supper and followed them around most of the evening. Yankee women speak so fast, they could lash the skin off a fast cat. The women, more than the men, fire off questions before you can answer the first. Another and another until your eyes cross and your head spins in circles. Even their luggage is quite different from everyone else's. The fabric is so fine, some say it is as fine as carpet. For this reason they are referred to as carpetbaggers.

I have no idea what a man of industry is or does, but I was asked no less than a hundred times if I was one. When I answered in the negative, I was promised a position of high rank and salary if I ever desired to become one such fella. "An opportunity to pull myself up by my bootstraps." Of course, no terms were penned to paper, so I don't reckon the offer is legitimate. However, it does raise my hopes, and I can see what got the Canadians so excited. This is truly a land of opportunity. Mr. Rockefeller didn't even want my recommendations of character or credentials. I was going to show him my letter of intent but thought better of it. Besides, he said he was "an excellent judge of character." I'm sure you would agree, Uncle.

Made one last stop, in Wheeler County, Michigan. They let us explore all around while the new passengers loaded. This time they were from as far north as Connecticut and as far south as New Jersey. The dunes were of great interest to me. It seemed that the east wind freezes and pushes the lake water, which pushes the sand up into a bank. A very steep bank that was quite difficult to climb. My feet felt as if they were stuck in mud. The sand is a fine grain and dry, despite everything else being frozen. My boots wanted to come off with every step, so I got on all fours and climbed up Mont Blanc style. My hands were freezing, but my curiosity gets the better of me every time.

When we got to the top, you could see hills and trees as far as eyes can see. With the radiant setting sun, the patches of snow were transformed in shimmering reflections, which had the appearance of water. Heck, for all I know, it was water. It was quite remarkable, but I seriously doubt that anything will come of this state. It would take too much money to develop, and no one with an ounce of common sense would endure the biting weather. This is now the longest journey I have ever made. I did not expect to be homesick so soon, but I do yearn for my pub. My forests. And my uncle.

After a delightful breakfast, W.H. and Mr. Rockefeller ignite cigars. They say very little to each other as the red eyes of their cigars glow and recede.

A waiter shows up and clears the table.

"It's mighty fine of you to make your granny's dream come true," Clarence compliments W.H.

"Oh, she's not *my* granny."

"Is that right? Well, then, that makes you a fine gentlemen in a rough outfit." Clarence laughs and blows plumes of smoke out both sides of his mouth as he pats W.H. on the back. Unsure of what to do, W.H. laughs and does the same.

Clarence breaks an awkward silence. "You gather your equipment and we'll meet here."

In a matter of moments, W.H. returns with two boxes and a bag.

"There's a certain amount of prep that goes into the slide," Clarence says, stuffing his cigar in his mouth. Billowing clouds plume out of the corners of his mouth. Removing his jacket and rolling up his sleeves, he opens up a one-foot-by-one-foot yellow pine box and examines its contents.

Clarence removes several small bottles from the box. One has white powder, and the other has red.

He walks up to the bar, his finger raised. "One whiskey."

Is it proper to tell the wealthy that hard alcohol in the morning dulls the senses for the rest of the day? W.H. wonders.

When Clarence returns, setting the bottles and whiskey in a straight line, W.H. determines it is better not to embarrass himself.

"Should be a separate bag with two buffer bars in it." Clarence looks up at W.H.

"Ah, yes, right here." W.H. presents the long velvet drawstring bag. He gulps. "Is the process all that technical?"

"Well, assuming you have everything else we need in the boxes, then yes. If not, then no. We won't have the material to take a picture. Tell me something. Can you shake shingle?"

"As good as anyone else," W.H. proudly proclaims, handing Clarence the bag.

"I was assured everything I need is in this box. I apologize for not knowing about the bumper bars."

"It's fine. And you are mostly right; everything you need is in this box." Clarence removes a shiny silver plate. He turns it over, and W.H. can see that it is made of both copper and faced with silver.

Setting his cigar down, Clarence gives an odd smile that accentuates his bushy sideburns.

"Do you know what makes America great?" Clarence asks with a raised brow.

CHAPTER 80

"I honestly hadn't thought about it," W.H. answers, blowing rings.

"See, that is precisely what I like about you. You speak your mind. The thing that makes America so incredible is inventions like the daguerreotype. Before this, my family was forced to sit for days on end while a painter did his best to portray us. Do you have any idea how many portraits my uncle has had made?"

"No, sir, I don't."

"Dozens. I can't imagine how much time he has wasted just sitting there doing nothing while a painter did his best rendition, which, on a good day, might be a close resemblance. But in practicality, the details aren't half as good as this daguerreotype. A man of such intelligence and sophistication should not be wasting his time, because his time is his money."

W.H. grips his cigar into a tight fist. *Do I say "here, here"? Or "tallyho"?* He fumbles for a word he wasn't even thinking of. "Right!"

"That's not to say that I don't have a soft spot in my heart for art. The truth is, if I wasn't forced into business and industry, I would have liked to have been a magnificent artist! Or perhaps a great architect?" His eyes shift from side to side as if the opportunity lay on one side or the other.

W.H.'s smile flattens to almost a frown. "An architect?"

"I would have liked to build something as grand as the National Mall. That would have been splendid, don't you think? I think so. Or maybe a portrait taker. Think of it like this. This pine box and these chemicals have been under Egypt's feet and they did not know how to organize it properly to take an accurate photo. Same with the Romans and any major society in existence. And we don't have to invent all this stuff. Sometimes we find it here in our own borders, but a lot of times we find it in countries as ancient as France. Then we bring it here and create an entirely new industry."

"Are you saying that because Granny offered to pay me?" W.H. asks, trying to follow Clarence's line of logic.

Without so much as a slight deviation from his thought, Clarence continues. "All walks of life are attracted to this device, and when I'm done explaining it to you, you'll see why. Making a daguerreotype is labor intensive. Mark my words, though. Someone is going to refine this here device and make it so anyone can take a picture in the future, not just the learned."

"How can that be?" W.H. asks.

"Progress, my boy. Nothing can stop it once the ripple has been made in the palms of men's hands."

He stares off into the distance, clearly seeing something that W.H. cannot.

"So!" Clarence breaks the silences. "Here's what you do first. Place the plate silver-side up on this adjustable block."

Clarence reaches inside the box and removes a smaller box. He pushes the reflective plate into a square grooved inset inside the larger box, then secures it in place by lidding the box.

"Alcohol. Rag." Clarence holds the two items up, then dips the corner of the rag in the whiskey. He sets the shot glass down, then lifts the bottle with white powder and shakes it. His bright blue eyes lighten up. "Rotten stone." He opens the bottle and spills the tiniest pile of powder onto the plate. "Don't use this on your teeth."

"Oh, I won't," W.H. assures him.

"Gotta get the surface reeeaaal clean. Be careful though. Go too fast and you will scratch the surface of the plate."

Next he lifts the red bottle and shakes it. "Rogue is applied to the buffer bar, but only buff in one direction." Clarence pulls the bar toward him, lifts it, then repeats until he seems satisfied.

W.H. pays close attention.

Clarence picks up the second buffer bar. "Use lots of elbow grease to get it off. But remember, you absolutely must go in the same direction to buff it off. Always buff with a clean pad to increase reflectivity. Now, this here plate is light reflective. Which is why we are in the dark part of the mess hall."

"Oh, yes, I see. I was wondering about that."

Clarence slowly shakes his head back and forth and draws his words out. "No you were not."

W.H.'s eyes shift back and forth. He looks down. "Okay, I wasn't."

"Pay close attention. This next part is important."

"Isn't it all important?"

"Yes! But no. Now pay attention. You will want to place the plate face down in the small box with iodized crystals. In forty-five seconds, the fumes from the iodide will react with the silver. Now we have silver iodide."

"Silver iodide, okay. I'm not a chemist. I was in school to become an architect."

"No kiddin'. Are you just saying that 'cause that's what I wanted to be?"

W.H. shakes his head no.

"I knew I liked you. Now, repeat the exact same buff process with bromine or quick stuff, as it's referred to." He removes the plate and uses a dash of brown liquid.

"Now go from the small box, or synthesizing box, to the camera box. We have to be in the shadows when we do this, because this is now bromide silver."

"Iodide silver, bromide silver. I think I understand."

"Do you?"

"No, not really."

"One is iodide, the other is bromide, but they are both silver. So don't get them confused."

"No problem there. I'm clear as mud on daguerreotypes."

Clarence laughs, picks up his cigar, takes a few puffs, and gets back to work.

W.H. watches as Clarence covers the plate with the rag, then slides the coated side down into the camera box.

"Now we remove this viewing glass. Leave that in place and you will end up pulling out an exposed plate with nothing on it. Put the plate holder where the viewing glass was—oh, and you will want to look through the viewing glass at your subject before you do all this, so you know where to set it up." Clarence finishes in one long-winded breath. He picks up his cigar, swirls it around, and takes one final look at the shot. "A bowl of fruit would add more artistic expression, but it isn't as though the plate can pick up color, so we won't be using any fancy props."

"Oh, can't it?" W.H. asks.

"Nothing is more sophisticated than the human eye, my good man." Clarence puffs on his cigar.

Unsure of what to do, W.H. imitates his mentor.

"So Granny is going to sit in that empty chair?"

"Correct. We lined everything up, so she doesn't have to be uncomfortable for all that sitting time," Clarence confirms.

"I'm glad, 'cause the chemicals kind of stink."

"That is the aroma of money, my friend. There's nothing stinky about it." Clarence inhales deeply.

W.H. does the same. "So what do I have to do to capture her image?"

"Take the camera cap off."

"That's it?"

"That's all there is to it!"

"How many of those plates did my box come with?"

"Four."

"How in tarnation am I supposed to take pictures of my journey if I'm only allowed four portraits?" W.H. huffs.

"Where are you headed?"

"Currumpaw area, New Mexico."

"Well, you are in for a shortage, that's for certain. What's your route?"

"Getting as close as I can to Kansas. Feller that booked me is sending me to Omaha."

"Omaha? Come work for me."

W.H. nervously swallows when he sees the sour expression on Clarence's face.

"Omaha is just about as far north from New Mexico as a fella can get. Why didn't you saunter straight through to Kansas? I'll get you started in Kansas and make you a fine company man. You're college educated like me. I can tell. Might as well put your education to good use."

"Thank you for that offer. I don't rightly know why I was booked through Omaha."

"Did he say why?"

"Nope, not really. All he said was Injuns and train robbers is a real threat. So I assume he sent me the safest way possible."

"That he did, my friend, if you like your scalp firmly attached to your head. 'Course, safety prevents risk. No risk, no grand reward. Listen, why don't you go fetch Granny, and then you and I will talk to the ticket master when we pull into Chicago."

"Is that in Nebraska?"

"No, Illinois. Go get the National Treasure."

Rustling up Granny and her granddaughter is more work than W.H. had anticipated. It takes Granny an additional half hour to get herself ready from the time he knocks on her door. And then an additional fifteen minutes to get to the chow hall. Knowing how much Clarence Rockefeller valued his time, W.H. grew impatient and rushed the old woman along.

"I'm a getting. I'm a getting. All you young fellers care about is pushing an old woman to her grave."

"It's not your grave, Granny. It's a daguerreotype," her granddaughter says.

"Well, why didn't you say so? I've wanted that done ever since I first saw one. Raises a body in status, you know!"

"And here is the relic of the revolution. Madam, if I may be so bold," Clarence says, taking Granny's covered hand and kissing it. His kind gesture dispels all of W.H.'s angst.

"Do I look pretty enough for my portrait?" Granny asks, patting her raven gown.

W.H. smiles and struggles for words.

"Granny, your curls are poking out of your shawl," her granddaughter says, reaching to tuck them in.

Granny swats at her hands. "Don't fuss on Granny."

"Your face is real pretty. Your clothes are very modern. I think you're as ready as you will ever be." Clarence compliments Granny, which seems to set her at ease. At least more than anyone else's pampering.

Sunlight passes through the window and rests on Granny's face.

"Okay, now, if you want to do the honors, W.H., just slide that cover off the lens, and, Granny, you be perfectly still. Like a statue."

W.H. waits for Granny to sit still and put on her best smile. He removes the lens cover.

"Now, listen to me, Granny. We want you to do this right 'cause we only have one slide. So do your best not to move or blink."

"For how long?"

"Close to an hour."

Her eyes widen. Granny hisses through her teeth, "I could be dead in an hour."

"Well, if you are, then we won't have a hard time getting this done." W.H. chuckles.

Her eyes shift, but she dares not laugh. "Is it working?" she hisses through clenched teeth and straight lips.

CHAPTER 81

"Well, would you look at that?" Granny critically reviews the daguerreotype portrait.

"With the crisp clarity of black-and-white, no less," Clarence says, handing her the finished plate.

"Thank you both so much. When we meet up for supper, I'll settle up with you. I will. You know Granny's good for it."

"Money, I have a'plenty. Smiling old ladies, well, there just aren't enough of those in my life. No need for payment, madam. It was our pleasure." Clarence leans down and bestows a kiss on her gloved hand for the second time. Granny blushes.

When supper comes, Granny shows everyone who has eyes her new portrait. Strangers "ooh" and "ahh." The old woman is right— it raises her in status, considering only the elite wealthy can afford to have one made. Of course, Helen is quick to comment on how elegant the old woman looks. W.H. sits back in his chair and has a moment he hasn't had in a long time. Supreme satisfaction.

The next morning the ship pulls into the Chicago, Illinois, port. Lake Michigan is teeming with vessels of all shapes and sizes. Additional ferries and steam engine ships crowd out sail-powered vessels of every proportion.

A tall wooden tower with cannons facing north, east, south, and west protect the harbor. Thousands of migrants offload from crowded vessels, pushing their way onto a series of winding docks. Wild turkeys greet the immigrants with an unusual call and beg for scraps. Children are all too eager to oblige.

W.H. disembarks the ferryboat and moseys on over to the train station.

When W.H. sees a ticket master, he inquires, "How many folks have been dumped at the docks by these boats?"

"Oh, I'd say twelve thousand or so."

"You don't say?" W.H. rubs his chin and takes in massive four- and five-story brick buildings that compose the industrial segment for the burgeoning city.

"More than that have come by rail. You're only seeing the ones that can afford the ferry."

"Where on earth do they all come from?"

"That is the interesting part of it. I've met folks that couldn't speak a lick of English. From Italy. Greece. France. Prussia and all over. Folks that speak English sometimes have a British, Irish, or Scottish accent. They pour like a continual stream into the bustling city of Chicago. You can always tell an immigrant by their wagon."

"What's so different about their wagons?" W.H. inquires.

"They use oxen or Clydesdales to pull these hefty carts. You can see folks of every kind, just lined up waiting for their turn to cross into the promised land. Like locusts, they swarm throughout the territories."

"How do they get by without kitchens and utensils?" W.H. asks, thinking of the women of his town.

"Dutch ovens. Or skillets. It's all you really need over a fire. 'Course, the farther west you get, the less wood there is. So you best know how to burn a buffalo chip."

"Why are they coming?"

"Land! They're giving it away out West."

"I find it inconceivable that anyone is actually going to receive a land grant. Doesn't it strike you as odd?"

"Well, they got so much of it, the government wants to collect taxes, and to do that, they need profiting landowners."

"Can all these immigrants from different backgrounds get along?"

"Most of the time they do. I've heard some mighty fine music shipped here from Louis the fifteenth. Once those violins begin, folks simmer down. Just steer clear of anyone who's drinking and wearing a gun."

"Duly noted." W.H. thinks of the many times he's been that man. *For my safety and the safety of others, I'm going to have to make some mighty big changes.*

"Will you be continuing on down the Big Muddy?"

"Hmm? What's that?"

"The 'Big Muddy.' You know, the Mississippi River?"

W.H. shrugs. "Oh no, sir. I'll be catching a train on through to Omaha."

"You'll be passing through Iowa first. I bet you'll find plenty of Easterners from the States."

"Why's that?"

"A fresh start. Land claims give everyone an equal opportunity."

"If it's half as many folks as I've seen moving about, I would be surprised if the eastern United States isn't depopulated."

"Oh, I wouldn't worry about that. Most of our gals have broods as big as dogs have puppies. Ten or more."

"I am not looking for a litter. I'm looking for an adventure. Here's my ticket."

"Well, then, I wish you best of luck. We pull out in an hour, so don't wander too far." The ticket master shakes his hand.

"What about my horse?"

"The baggage crew should have your livestock out shortly."

Dearest Uncle,

I am a Martian on another planet. I had heard of cities. I had read about them. But to see the drawings and sketches come to life in animated action before one's very eyes is beyond description. Buildings like termite hives sprawl the land as far as the eye can see. Red bricks have been organized into buildings some five stories tall! They look like boxes turned upside down, quickly erected without much thought. EVERYTHING IS MADE OF RED BRICK!!! Homes. Offices. Post offices. Stores. I imagine in these flat lands, you could build five-story redbrick buildings to the end of the earth.

Both dirt and brick make up the streets. Sleighs flow through the roads like water. The skids make the most atrocious sound when they hit the street and ignite magnificent sparks. The thermometer reached zero, so folks watered Broadway to make ice. Why they would want to risk losing horses is beyond me. The ticket master said "it's to keep the dust down." But that can't be! Unless snow is dust.

This sprawling red city is nonstop hustle and bustle. It's a wonder they don't call Chicago "the ruby city." Gentlemen in fine suits litter the streets, while laborers scurry past to build the next building. Ladies maneuver the streets without proper chaperones. Children are herded along by nuns the way mother hens skittle after their chicks.

The levee is literally crowded with whiskey pork and ready-made buildings, which are, of course, red brick. Towering boxes lean left and right and look as though they could easily fall over. Barrels, carts, and drays bow the planks of the boardwalk. It is a wonder that those boards don't give under the weight of goods and the constant flow of foot traffic from the off-loading steamers. Dozens of flat-bottomed boats swarm the steamers and offload the surplus onto a series of docks, so as to keep the traffic moving. This is a world I have never known, nor will I get to, thanks be to God.

The ticket master just announced that we should not wander from the train depot as we are likely to miss our train. I am destined for Omaha, but passing through Iowa. I will finish this crude sketch on board. Exciting news! I learned how to use the photo booth. I will no doubt come back to this place to photograph all that I have seen.

Yours truly, Nephew.

"Hello, stranger!" Clarence shouts.

W.H. spins around with a bright smile.

"You're taking the train?" Helen asks.

"In an hour or so."

"Are you sure your mind cannot be changed?" Clarence asks W.H.

"I've thought about it. If I get myself in a pickle, I can ride my horse home in the summer or fall. If I get as far down as Kansas, who knows what may happen."

Clarence extends his hand. W.H. takes it and feels hard paper scratch the palm of his hand. When he looks down, he sees an embossed linen business card.

"It was a pleasure meeting you. If you decide to go on and you need more slides, send word to the address on my business card and I will have my people in New York deliver you as many as you may need."

"Thank you for everything. It was a genuine pleasure meeting you both," W.H. says with a sincerity he hadn't expected to discover.

"Friends at last," Helen says in that terribly annoying accent.

She hugs W.H. and several other people she befriended. Clarence is fast to join her. As quickly as the Yankees blew into his life, they blow out.

"Didn't think you would like them, did you?" Granny says as her family helps her aboard a sleigh.

W.H. looks down in shame. "Was it so obvious?"

"Of course. They're New Yorkers. Nobody likes them."

"I'm sure glad I got a chance to meet you, Granny."

"Me too. Won't you let me pay you something for your fine work?"

"You've already given me so much. To think I was introduced to a woman who met General George Washington."

"Did I ever tell you, he bounced me on his lap on his victory tour to Boston. What was the year...? Seventeen eighty-six—no, nine.

Was it a six or a nine?"

Before she can finish her thought, her grandson cracks the whip. The old relic is carried away in a sleigh pulled by a trotting Clydesdale.

"It was eighty-nine!"

W.H. turns and brushes Cotton's nose as he waits for the train crew to secure his horse in a boxcar.

After a considerable wait, a train billows to a stop in deafening mechanical screeching fashion. People and animals disembark. The train is cleaned. A whistle blows long and hard.

"All aboard!" another man in a blue uniform shouts to the crowd of passengers.

CHAPTER 82

While W.H. waits for Cotton and Bingo to be secured in a livestock boxcar, he skims a fellow passenger's paper. The article reads, "Nominations announced. The National Union Party nominates Mr. Lincoln. Constitutional Union Party elects John Bell. John Breckinridge and Stephen Douglas battle it out for the Democratic nomination."

"Ugh… I hate politics." W.H. groans.

"All aboard!" the ticket master shouts.

W.H. hurries onto the passenger cart and locates his seat.

Dearest Uncle,

Forgive me for making two entries in one day. It has been only an hour or so since my last entry, but as I boarded the train, I was frozen in place by the most angelic faces I have ever seen. "Southern belles" is what I believe they are called. Ladies from the southern United States have hopped steamer, rail, steamer, and more rail, for two weeks to get to this moment. I cannot imagine they have even traveled a day they are so utterly lovely! I heard them speaking with one another and I must say, they sound nothing like the Northerners. They have a soft tone and a deep drawl. Their hair hangs freely down and flows around their naked necks and exposed shoulders. I turned bright red as I saw fabric wrap around their lifted bosoms, which gave them the very appearance of the most coveted budding flower.

"What are you looking at, Four Eyes?" a tall blond man clad in a black suit shouts.

W.H. pushes his glasses up with his index finger. He sees the man pull his blazer back and expose a shiny pistol on his belt. The stranger's diamond-blue eyes brighten when his hand rests on two nickel-plated Colt pistols, which sparkle in the sunlight. Expensive ivory handles face out and have TIFFANY & CO. stamped on the butt. The silver plating houses ornate gold vines etched and embossed in extravagant gold-leaf patterns. W.H.'s eyes follow the winding branches, which lead to the only distinguishable gold-stamped lettering on the pistols: NAVY, MODEL NUMBER 21838.

"Pardon me?" W.H. says as politely as he can.

The man's eyes soften. "What's the matter? You can't take a joke?" He wiggles his fingers in front of his pistol grips and laughs. His eyes flash again in a way that almost makes him seem unstable. "Name's Malice Mike!"

"Apologize, Junior," a refined older man in a white linen suite interjects, stealing Malice Mike's thunder. The older man is smaller in stature, yet he shares the same features and eye color as the boy.

W.H. breathes a sigh of relief. *Thank heavens he's accompanied by his father.*

The sixtysomething elder grabs his fist-shaped, silver-handled cane and thrusts it into his son's back.

Junior stiffens up from the jolt. "Pappy, he knows I was just joking."

The old man with white hair and a pointy beard raps the cane's silver knuckles against the young man's skull.

"These jokes you play are goin' to get you into a fix you can't get outta, boy!"

"I'm so terribly sorry, sir, if my behavior offended you. It's just that we don't know who we are assigned to sit next to. On account of us being plantation-owning Southerners, I wanted to be sure I wasn't sitting next to no damn Yank."

"That'll do, Junior," the elder man says in a calm Southern tone. He extends his hand and exposes the silver trim of his white suit sleeve. A silver star in the center distinguishes his rank unmistakably. "General Lee Montgomery of Kentucky's first and finest militia. Pleased to make your acquaintance."

"How do you do?" W.H. asks.

"Oh, Daddy, you needn't be putting on titles or pretenses," a voice as sweet as wind chimes sings. Over the general's shoulder, the finest woman in all the land appears.

W.H.'s heartbeat picks up. He looks down in his journal and quickly pens, *I am in love.* He looks up and slams the book shut. His cheeks flush when two sparkling emerald eyes fix on his. He struggles to swallow.

"Maybelle, quit crowdin' me!" Junior scolds his sister.

Maybelle rolls her eyes and bounces her ribbon-like blond curls. She sticks her tongue out at her brother and looks back at W.H. Her hair winds and twists around her oval face.

Helen of Troy, come to your Paris, W.H. thinks. Her perfectly pointed nose is placed properly above her petite lips. *Wait, is she Helen of Troy or an angel fallen from the sky above?* W.H. wonders.

Maybelle smiles brilliantly, and the apples of her cheeks glow, making her as pretty as a painting. W.H. struggles for breath. He steals a glance at her exposed neck and shoulders. He yearns to kiss her soft pink lips, but alas, he dare not, lest Malice Mike should put those fine pistols to work and punch holes through his body.

W.H. goes to stand, but the general puts his hand on his shoulder and shoves him back in his seat.

"These are my twins, Maybelle and Malice." The twins could not be more opposite. Maybelle, with her pixie looks and long yellow hair certainly descended from the sun. Malice Mike is incredibly handsome, but his attitude is cold and makes him seem like he was fathered by night. His pale skin even matches the moon.

"That's my nickname. Real name's Michael, as in the archangel." The young man extends his hand. "You can call me Malice Mike."

W.H. shakes hands with each man, then takes Maybelle's hand gently and kisses it.

"My two blushing pilgrims stand ready. I am so pleased to make your acquaintance, madam."

"Shakespeare? Doodle-dee-do!" Maybelle gasps, then flushes with excitement. "To be frank, sir, you are too fresh with first acquaintances." Her slow, low Southern drawl tickles his ears, which has the strange effect of raising the corners of his mouth into an awkward, trembling smile.

"May I ask what part of the South you are from?" the general asks, readying his cane.

"I'm actually from Winnipeg."

"Told ya he was a Yank. Let's go sit somewhere else." Malice Mike grumbles like a bear. He furiously scans for another seat.

"No, no, Junior. Canadians and Yanks are quite different. Did you know the only reason the greedy land-grabbing Yanks didn't expand their empire all the way up to the polar ice caps was because this fine young man's ancestors stopped them at the Canadian border? In fact, the border is literally as far as musket and hatchet could stop the Yankee state. Boy did they lick 'em good!"

The few Yanks within earshot identify themselves by rolling their eyes.

"Is that so?" Malice Mike asks, softening his demeanor to a more pleasing one. "Anyone who whoops a Yank is a friend of mine!" Malice Mike extends his hand.

W.H. shakes on his ancestors' accomplishments and makes a mental note to pen in his journal, *The men in the North are quite and polite, whereas the women are loud and boisterous. The women of the South are soft-spoken angelic creatures, whereas the men are loud and boisterous. America is an odd and perplexing mix of people.*

Maybelle flutters her eyes and says sweetly, "Our tickets put us in this row, but if y'all don't want us to burden you on account of Junior's behavior, Mister, I would certainly understand. Mister...?"

"W.H."

"What's that stand for?" Malice Mike inquires, showing his affection for nicknames.

"Wolf Hunter."

"Wolf Hunter, huh?" Malice Mike looks W.H. up and down.

"Well, that suits me, Mister. I would be much obliged to learn a thing or two about wolf hunting." Malice Mike lets slip the manly macho mask and reveals a lingering boyhood.

W.H. stands up and moves to the aisle, allowing the group to his row. He watches each member take their respective seats and hopes beyond hope that Maybelle is bold enough to sit next to him. Malice Mike cuts in front of his sister, building W.H.'s hope, and steals the window seat. Maybelle growls and pinches her brother.

"Quit that!" Malice Mike hollers as she makes him squirm.

The general is the last to take his seat, putting W.H. close to

Maybelle, but not close enough for conversation.

The train whistle blows, establishing order among all the passengers. Final calls are made. Steam billows past the rectangular widows. Every available seat on the mahogany benches is filled. The cart jerks forward and makes the yellow pine floorboards creak. A tremendous force frightens the ladies and children and rings an excited scream from the passengers. Laughter from the men follows. Soon the cart creaks forward using steam and hopes, which sync to the chug-a-chug of the train's engine. *Choo-choo. Chug-a-chug. Choo-choo.* The engine gains momentum. A boy makes the sound to his father in rhythm of the chug and choo.

A young man stands in front of the crowded cart and asks, "Would y'all like to hear a speech I've prepared?"

The crowd encourages him.

He begins with, "Down South, where the speak is easy and the minds are free, the burden of the Yanks hinder our economy with talk of ending slavery. But listen well, citizens of the free. We shall not yield our way of life nor our meager existence without a resolute fight. In these new territories, we are going to mix with the Yank and show them what it means to be gentry. Yes, the new world west is going to need leaders. For this I ask for your support when I run for Congress of the Iowa territory."

W.H. thinks nothing of the speech or of the fading ruby city, Chicago. He seizes this opportunity to rest his eyes on his darling future, Maybelle.

When the man finishes his speech, he hands around his tall black top hat, clapping his hands every time coins clank. A flock of wild geese fly up in front of the windows, stealing the stage from the would-be politician.

Oh, that I were a bird, W.H. thinks. *Then I could fly to and fro and spy every divine feature of dear Maybelle.*

CHAPTER 83

Later that night, W.H. and the upper-crust passengers are escorted to their respective cabins. He is incredibly dissatisfied to learn that he will be sharing a "private" cart with a lovely young couple from Virginia.

"What's the point of first class if I have to share a room?" he asks the ticket master.

"Well, sir, there's less room on the train. So first class gets to come and go, with bunks to sleep in, whereas the lower classes are confined to the benches."

W.H. looks down the hall and sees Maybelle resting her head on her father's shoulder. He feels bad that such a magnificent woman isn't allowed a place to rest her head. *She probably wouldn't take my spot, so there's no use in offering it.*

As he enters the room he hears the couple showering their cherubic newborn son with love. This family offers a bird's-eye view of something he's never had, a loving father and mother. *I suppose a family ain't so bad.*

W.H. steps past the couple and eyeballs the four bunks, two on the left and two on the right. Fancy down feather comforters make the mattresses look cozy. *Not too long ago I was freezing my britches off on the Winnipeg street. At least I'm warm and dry here.* He pulls in a deep breath as he takes in his surroundings, spotting a lantern, a latrine that seems more like a closet, and some candles on a dresser.

"I suppose you folks won't mind if I lie down?"

"If it's all right with you, Mister, I'd like to sleep on this here bottom bunk and my wife would like to sleep with our darling baby in that bottom bunk."

"Suits me just fine, but that leaves an empty bed." *I wonder if*

Maybelle might be interested. I ought not to ask. It wouldn't be proper.

"I overheard your name to be 'W.H.?'"

W.H. nods.

"Name's James Fallscrow, and this is my lovely jewel, Emilia."

Emilia presses their sleeping child to her chest and bows her head in recognition. She whispers, "This little sprite is the object of our affection. His name is Adam." She turns her creation and presents the child as though he were the first man ever made. W.H. smiles and feels the warmth of the parents' affection. The doting mother holds her finger up to her lips, which ends the chitchat.

W.H. climbs to the creaking top bunk and observes the couple as he might nature. He takes note how the mother dotes over the child. Every hiccup or squirm is met with her immediate attention. Father lies down on his bunk after tucking wife and child in. Then gets up to check on them through the night.

A slamming door awakens W.H. He rubs his eyes and looks about.

He finds the baby's bright blue eyes are fixed on his. Adam coos and reaches for W.H., like he is his father. Eye contact with the babe evokes complex feelings within W.H., including a sense of protection and pure love in return.

"Well, look at those pretty blue eyes!" W.H. croaks in a deep morning voice. He wiggles his fingers at the baby, which makes the child laugh.

"Would you like to eat with us, Mr. W.H?"

W.H. sits up and straps his suspenders in place. He puts his round glasses on and stretches. "What's for breakfast?"

"Ham, eggs…"

"And corn cakes?" He finishes James's sentence.

"Why, yes. Did you overhear us?"

"No, ma'am. I've gotten accustomed to your American diet. Seems like you all eat corn with every meal."

"Well, it does make for a healthy boy, doesn't it, Adam?" Emilia whispers, even though her baby is awake.

"Ticket master says we will be stopping in Saint Charles, Missouri."

Just then an ancient weathered yellow envelope slides under the door. A red wax stamp seals the envelope with the letters *G.M.*

W.H. breaks the seal and unfolds the envelope. It reads,

Dearest Friend,

We hope you settled well in your cabin. We cordially invite you to dine with us for breakfast. We pray you will forward us the opportunity to amend our first introduction and forgive us our trespasses. Again, we apologize for any offenses and we looked forward to making your acquaintance.

Sincerely yours, General Montgomery, of Kentucky's first and finest militia.

"Thank you for the offer, James, but it looks like I have a breakfast engagement." W.H. decides and presses the letter to his nose. He inhales and catches a whiff of vanilla and rose fragrance. *Ah, Maybelle, what I wouldn't give to sit next to you all night and let you rest your head on my shoulder.*

"Did you hear the gunfire last night?" James wonders.

"No. Was there a dispute?" W.H. inquires.

"It was at the card table."

"You weren't playing cards, were you, James darling?" Emilia asks, rocking her baby in a way that makes them both look at him and keeps him in check.

"No, ma'am, I wasn't. But I can say for a certainty that these rough Southerners from Texas and Tennessee mix strong drink with guns and bowie knives as freely as Northerners mix words with fists."

"The results will be early graves," Emilia professes.

"True words, wife." James pats her on the shoulder.

"Why do these men use fists, bowie knives, and guns?" W.H. reluctantly inquires.

"The men of the South carry incredibly passionate hearts. Sometimes their passions flare and they see the revolver as an honorable way to reconcile a dispute," James answers.

"Or to punish an insult," Emilia adds with a disapproving raised brow.

"Fists I get. Guns? That doesn't make much sense to me." W.H. reflects on how quick Malice Mike was to flaunt his pistols.

"Where one man may be stronger than another and subdue his peer, the use of firearms levels the playing field, even for ladies who are bold enough to learn how to shoot," James concludes.

"But that sort of logic doesn't add up if people are killed. Won't kin come searching for justice?" W.H. tries to make sense of what he's hearing.

"That, my new friend, is why we are fleeing the South. We are going to a place where we can build a peaceful life with like-minded people who forgive and forget, rather than kill and justify." James sighs and lets his eyes drift off like he's looking far away.

"Do be careful who you mix company with, sir," Emilia warns W.H., "for you never know when passions might flare."

When W.H. enters the breakfast cart, he quickly finds his new acquaintances. Maybelle wears a beautiful satin pink gown with black lace trim around the hems. Her arms are covered in white gloves, and she has a miniature umbrella hanging off her wrist. Most ladies are dressed in fine gowns and, unlike the Northerners, they flaunt their colors in every shade produced by the rainbow. They also leave their necks and shoulders bare, catching the eye of every man there.

"I am so pleased you decided to join us!" Maybelle says, flashing a smile that makes W.H. freeze in place.

He glances up and sees the snowbanks and now knows what it feels like to be frozen solid. "As am I."

Suddenly and without notice, the train grinds to a screeching, jolting halt. A chain reaction of bumps and thuds rattles the passengers and sends the women squealing.

"No need to be worried, darling." The general calms his daughter with gentle pats on her hand. "Something is most likely blocking the track."

A waiter comes by and fixes the table. He re-stands a set of salt and peppers shakers in the shapes of Mr. and Mrs. Pig and resets the silverware on top of white cotton napkins.

"No need to worry, folks. It's probably just a herd of buffalo."

"How do you know it ain't Injuns?" Malice Mike inquires. Adventure flashes in his eyes and in his wicked smile.

"Well, if it were spring, sir, then I might say draw your pistols. But on account of it being winter, most tribes is hunkering down South, where there's less snow."

"Can we take a look for ourselves?" Malice Mike begs his pa.

"Certainly. But as I warned my soldiers in the militia, never leave a rifle resting if you can hold it in your hand. Come with me. Let's fetch our guns."

"Oh, how I love adventure," Maybelle declares, batting her eyes.

"Did I mention that I am on a great adventure?" W.H. sticks out his chest and tucks his thumbs under his armpits.

"You are full of surprises." Maybelle purrs and rests her gloved hand on her cheek.

"Would you mind, waiter, preparing our breakfast in a basket? I believe we will be needing a winter picnic for our adventure."

"No, ma'am. Not at all."

"Well, I suppose I should take the general's advice and fetch my rifle."

"Do that, and we can all meet at the front of the train."

"Yes, ma'am." W.H. likes how Maybelle brings everything together with an expert plan.

At the front of the train, gunfire erupts.

CHAPTER 84

Rushing to the front of the line, Maybelle spots the action and then reports. "It is buffalo!" She hops up and down. W.H. tucks her arm under his and looks over his shoulder to ensure her father is okay with their affectionate public behavior. When he nods, W.H. is pleased to see he has permission to court!

"Well, it's a good thing it's winter," the general says to his son, handing him his rifle.

"Why's that?" Malice Mike asks.

"'Cause I do believe we are going to have a spring wedding."

"Your nuts, Pa! Maybelle's just carrying on like she does with all her other beaus."

"Maybe, but I been around longer than you, son. Do you think I might see something in my daughter that you might not?"

"Or that I may see something in my sister that you may not, Father?"

"Fair enough. What is it you see?"

"Time will tell if she has a fleeting heart!"

"Don't lose faith in your sister. And don't speak ill of it. She is the most beautiful woman in all thirty-four states. That don't even include the territories. She knows her responsibility is to bring a good wealthy man into our ranks. Sure she may have broken a few hearts here and there, but I believe Cupid's arrow will strike again. And besides, her Christian upbringing shall prevail."

"Uh-huh." Malice smirks.

"I apply the same hope for you, son."

"Don't waste any on me, Pop. Maybelle's gonna need all of it."

Outside the train at the front of the engine, a cluster of gentlemen make wagers and fire pop shots at a herd of buffalo who've taken refuge on the bare track.

"Why can't we hit 'em?" a man with a bushy mustache asks the engineer.

"Cold barrels, and they're actually on an incline. We're on a decline," the engineer shouts back.

"So what are we to do?"

"If you move closer, you'll chase them down the track. That will certainly keep us delayed. If you use your rifles instead of your pistols, you'll find more success."

"Make you a bet on who can get them buffalo." Malice Mike cocks his head to the side and puts his black hat on.

"What's the wager?" W.H. asks, ready for the challenge.

"What do you got?" Malice Mike looks W.H. up and down.

"All I got is greenbacks," W.H. answers.

"Yankee money. I should have known."

"When I exchanged my gold, the ticket master said it wasn't wildcat money. He said it was all anyone would take."

"Gold, eh? Got any more?"

W.H. doesn't answer. He pulls his bottom lip through his teeth and immediately regrets telling a man with such a bad name he had anything of worth. *Way to go, dumbo. Now you've incentivized him to shoot you.*

"What's a kiss worth?" Maybelle asks, biting her bottom lip. Her excited beaming eyes and tempting mouth entice him beyond reason.

"I dunno? Twenty dollars."

"Twenty Yank greenbacks? Are you crazy?" the man with the bushy mustache shouts.

"What's that amount to in our money, Pa?"

"Enough to buy a mule or a cow."

"Let's bet, then!" Malice Mike says, raising his rifle. "A kiss for twenty bucks."

"I accept." W.H. takes a twenty-dollar bill out of his billfold. He waves it in front of Maybelle's face. She snatches it quicker than an eagle plucking fish out of water.

Malice Mike puffs his chest up. "Although in all fairness, I must warn you that my sister and I are both great-grandchildren of Daniel Boone."

W.H. cocks his head to the side and fidgets. "Well, then, in all fairness, I must warn you that if you take your shot from down here, it won't do you any good."

"Why's that?" Malice Mike growls in youthful irritation.

"Didn't you hear the conductor? Buffalo are on an incline. You're bound to miss."

"So what do you propose?"

W.H. looks around. He spots a lofty pile of boulders leaning against one another. The stack is arranged in such a way that the tallest looks like a chimney.

"We can shoot from the top of the chimney rock."

"Superb!" Maybelle squeals. "Then we can eat breakfast on the rocks after the shooting is done."

The excitement of the challenge is enough to quiet the crowd.

"Kill 'em all and I'll give you five dollars a head. Just don't kill them on the track." The conductor adds even more incentive for the contestants.

"I'm going to get my rifle," the man with the bushy mustache declares.

"May I carry your rifles and your basket for you?" Mr. Fallscrow, W.H.'s bunkmate, asks.

"Sure!" Maybelle replies, tucking her arm under W.H.'s.

The party walks down the tracks as far as the buffalo will let them without startling. When they reach the boulders, they step off into a knee-high snowbank.

From behind them, the conductor shouts, "Dadgummit! What did I tell you about chasing them buffalo? Lookie there!" He points to the herd. The buffalo grunt and groan as they move farther up the track.

"No need to worry, sir! The situation is under control." W.H. waves at him.

"What am I to do? I can't be expected to climb around this wilderness like some savage," Maybelle cries, showing a hint of temper W.H. didn't know she had. Her cheeks flare red and her eyes glow with frustration.

"You can ride on our shoulders," Malice Mike proposes.

"Can I, Pa?"

The general looks at the growing crowd and searches their faces for acceptance. When he sees calm expressions, he gives a nod.

W.H. takes off his coat and places it on the ground.

"A true gentleman," Maybelle compliments him, stepping on his coat.

Two men come over and help her up on their shoulders. The crowd applauds the gentlemen.

"Ha! Look at me, Pa. I'm Cleopatra, the queen of the American frontier. Ushered to and fro by the strongest men in all the Western territory. Let's get three cheers for free Kansas!"

"Hip, hip!"

"Hooray!" the crowd shouts.

"Y'all can do better than that! Hip, hip!"

"Hooorrraaay!"

"One more time, y'all! HIP, HIP!"

"HOOOORRRRRAAAAYYYY!"

"Let's not get too cheeky," the general says, watching the boys escort his daughter to the boulder stack.

With each wobbling step, Maybelle warns them, "Be careful."

After carrying her to the rocks, they set her down gently, treating her like she's a prize. Malice Mike wastes no time scaling the tallest boulder, which has enough room for only one man.

"Whoo-weee! I'm the king of the frontier!" he shouts, then reaches for his rifle. James tosses him his weapon. It falls short and bangs against the rock.

"What kind of sissy toss was that?"

"Sorry about that, Mister. Let me get it."

James scurries over and digs the weapon out of the snow. The foggy breath of every passenger hangs in the air as he hands it back to its owner.

Malice Mike cocks the lever. "Better not have junked the ammo!" He seats the buttstock in his arm and takes a shot.

BOOM!

Snow kicks up in a dust pile in front of the buffalo, reporting an obvious miss. Instead of running, the beasts cluster and stare at the pack of humans.

"Your turn, W.H.," Mike says, stepping down.

W.H. scurries up the rock. He takes a knee and rests the buttstock in his shoulder. Closing his eyes, he draws a few deep breaths and opens his aiming eye. Through the scope, his crosshairs rest nearly perfectly on the buffalo's broad matted brown side. He flips the safety off and presses his finger to the trigger.

BOOM!

CHAPTER 85

When W.H.'s scope comes down from the recoil, he sees blood spurt out of the beast's side.

"My turn!" Malice Mike roars, eager to get his second shot.

"I think he hit 'im," Maybelle shouts, clapping her hands together. The buffalo stumbles off the track and falls dead in the snow.

"I got him, all right," W.H. confirms, stepping off the boulder. He takes Maybelle by the waist and pulls her in close. She squirms, but before she can protest, he plants one square on her lips. Her body quivers in his arms. Then she relents and leans back like a willow. He braces her with arms that don't seem strong but prop her tiny frame up just fine.

Malice Mike looks at his sister, then out at the herd. He sees the buffalo fall flat in the snow. He clicks his tongue. "I'll be darned. Got him on the first shot!"

When the couple stay locked longer than they ought to, the general is quick to interrupt. "That'll do. Bet obliged. Winner is paid in full. Now either get a priest or a pistol."

W.H. stands up and slowly unlocks lips with Maybelle. Her closed eyes and parted lips beg for more. She slowly opens her eyes, blinks, and plants another one him.

The crowd roars with excitement.

"Get a preacher!" the man with the bushy mustache hollers out. His wife elbows him in the side and scolds him. "Why can't you be more romantic like that?"

The man cocks up, puffs his chest out, and proclaims, "I got plenty of romance in me." He aims at the herd and opens fire. Which causes Malice and everyone with a rifle to go to work. When they're done, every fella with a willing girl plants one on his lady.

Gun smoke rises up around Maybelle and W.H. as they disobey her father and lock lips for a second time.

Having won the competition and the hearts of the Southerners, W.H. manages to raise his reputation as a man: an expert in firearms, a wallet flush with cash, and a purse weighted with gold.

Maybelle unfolds blankets on the nearly flat rock.

"Our breakfast is laid out." Maybelle bashfully pats a spot next to her, reaching for the basket. She removes a plaid napkin and unfolds two egg and ham sandwiches, set between corn cakes.

The couple stare into each other's eyes. W.H. doesn't say much of anything. His bullets and lips have said enough. Though it is a winter's day, he feels as warm as summer.

So long as I have corn cakes, ham, eggs, and this woman by my side, everything will be perfect in this righteous new world.

Dearest Uncle.

I was right! I am in love. We talked all day. Her pa let us hold hands. For the first time in my life, I kissed a girl I wasn't related to. I didn't mean to, but I made a bet I could shoot a buffalo from seventy-five yards away, and I put the slug right in his heart, while Cupid put his arrow right in mine. My reward? Maybelle Montgomery. The sweetest kiss in America was bestowed by the most beautiful woman, maybe in the entire world. Saying her name is like saying "rose." Something that is beautiful and needs protecting. To stand next to her and hold her hand is as exciting as watching stars shoot across the sky. She has made my life worth living. I had no intention of falling in love, but now that I am, I don't know what to do with myself. What's the next step after you fall in love? Marriage? Do not be surprised, Uncle, if my next entry is a wedding announcement. Things are moving mighty fast in this new world. I'm traveling thirty miles per hour deeper and deeper into the unknown. I might just be the first man married on the rail.

I believe you would like her. She is such a smart woman. She knows so much about planting crops, raising farm animals, flowers, poetry, literary arts like Shakespeare. I regret to inform you that I might be using the scholarship money on a home or a business venture. And most definitely a ring. I'm the happiest a man could possibly be. If the investors wish for a profitable venture, what could be more profitable than love?

Before W.H. leans over to turn the lantern wick down, he sees the baby staring at him.

"Oh, so that's what comes next?"

The baby gurgles, then coughs. His mother is quick to pat him on his precious back.

W.H. waves. "Good night, baby boy."

Emilia lifts Adam's hand and waves back. "Good night, W.B.H."

"W.B.H?" he asks.

"Wolf, Buffalo, Hunter."

"Ha! No. I think I will just keep it simple."

With that the lights go down. The Fallscrow family says their nightly prayers, and W.H. falls fast asleep.

BOOM!

BOOM!

Gunfire from the front of the train erupts from the engineer's cart.

A whistle blasts three times. "RAID! RAID! RAID!" a voice shouts, ringing a cowbell as it passes the door. Passengers repeat the warning.

"All men to arms! All men to arms!" another voice cries out.

W.H. rolls over and reaches for his pistol. After the buffalo shoot, he secured his rifle with his horse. *Should I go get it? What do I do?*

"James? I'm scared!" Emilia cries out. The baby detects her frantic tone and wails.

"Stay inside your cabins! Women and children, lie flat on the floor. Ladies, cover your babes with your bodies. Men, drop your windows and ready your weapons. The conductor has refused to stop the train. We are being attacked by wild Plains Indians."

"You want our scalps? Come and get 'em!" a man shouts out.

Another voice shouts, "TASTE LEAD, SAVAGES!" A volume of thunderous gunfire drowns out the crying women and children. Gun smoke fills the carts and plumes out the open windows. Children cough and grow frantic, scurrying into their mothers' arms. Absolute chaos ensues.

The savages return a larger volley of fire, which silences the passengers' guns. In the lull, the whooping native war cry can be heard.

"JAMES! DO SOMETHING!" Emilia screams.

CHAPTER 86

"Dear Lord, see us through," James prays.

The engine *chug-a-chugs* at an even faster rate. The engineer releases a long whistle blast. Each train car erupts with sporadic gunfire. Sparks fly out of hot barrels. Iron sights rise and fall. Brass levers eject smoldering shells. The exchange of gunfire bounces off the trees and echoes down the train corridors.

The Indians return fire with pistols and arrows. They press the attack with a whooping war cry that nears W.H.'s open window.

The conductor releases another loud billowing whistle blast. Its wailing horn momentarily masks the screams of the women and children.

An arrow sails through the window and lodges in W.H.'s bunk wall.

James grabs his pistols and locks eyes with W.H.

"Get your glasses on or you ain't gonna hit spit!"

W.H. turns to get his glasses.

"JAMES! THE BABY! They take children's scalps, too!"

James leans out the window and unleashes twelve rounds of his Colt's fury. Six shadowy warriors are knocked off their horses.

The baby cries from the percussion. Emilia covers his ears with her hands. The fight is on. Flashes of gunfire illuminate the cabin and strobe W.H.'s every move. Emilia looks up at W.H. Tears well in her eyes. She's gripped with fear. W.H. is inspired by Adam's father's protective actions. "You don't worry about a thing, ma'am. Nothing is going to happen to you or that baby! Not so long as I got this!"

W.H. cocks his pistol and leans out the window. A pack of Indian ponies, painted up for war, race furiously past him. He maneuvers his weapon left and then right, scanning for riders. The pack of horses sprint past his window, gaining a steady lead, as their load has been considerably lightened.

What sort of trickery is this? W.H. asks himself.

Glistening stains wet their coats and explain the lack of riders. W.H. watches a few lose momentum. They trip and fall, making a magnificent explosion of white snowy powder. The horses indicate that they were hit as well as their riders.

W.H. eases the trigger's tension, decompressing his hammer. He counts sixty or so horses and wonders how the mustangs manage to keep up in the deep snow.

"We have to cover that freezing window, or the baby is gonna catch cold!" Emilia screams.

"It's been shot out, Emilia. Can't you see all the broken glass?"

Adam unleashes his fear with a fine pair of lungs. He screams and screams, which makes his mother cry harder.

"Best reload before you do anything else, James." W.H. covers James.

James pulls every blanket off the beds he can find and cocoons his wife and child. The rushing winter wind freezes his cheeks and fingers.

BANG!

The cabin door bursts open and slams against the wall. Maybelle appears in a white linen nightgown, floating like a ghost. Two empty brass shells clank against the floor and roll around her bare feet. She snaps her double-barreled shotgun in place and cocks both hammers. The twin barrels smoke.

"I got two! And my heart screamed for you… What can I do? I am here for you!" Maybelle rhymes.

W.H. remembers with great affection their first meeting, where they exchanged Shakespeare lines. He hasn't the whit to continue the search for raiding Indians and rhyme. He lifts up his hand and invites Maybelle to slide under his arm. She gratefully obliges. They stare out the window and prepare for a second attack.

    Uncle,

       It's some dark late hour, in the early morn, and it is a mistake to attack the United States. Every citizen is armed and prepared to do their duty.

Women are armed. Children are armed. These people will fight for freedom and protect their liberty at the expense of all they hold dear. And as a result, a horde of wild Indians, an estimated eighty in strength, will release their whooping war cry no more. The Americans have silenced the attackers. Their scalps have been spared. The savages have been denied their loot. Neither tyranny nor savagery could stop the train or its progress to freedom.

Do not fret for your nephew. I am well, but a dozen passengers cannot report the same. As of yet two have passed. One was a dear and beloved mother. A prospector headed for California is dead. He has no family to speak of on the train, but that does not mean family will not mourn his loss—assuming word reaches his family, which many expect it will not. Another man is expected to die. His wife and children surround him and pray night and day for God to spare him. I don't see that's going to be the case. He has constant sweats and shakes. In addition, four adults and seven boys and girls were riddled with gunshot. One man is missing and presumed dead. In all, I am lucky to be alive. I am sorry for those poor souls who ain't. I cannot understand the savagery of the Indians, and I am grateful that Canada's tribes don't practice this particular brand of butchery. I am glad my scalp is fixed firmly to my head. Whether any of us wants it to or not, the train chugs along. It leads to new lives or, perhaps, to dreadful ends.

CHAPTER 87

Days later, at the last stop, in a little pioneer town that's too small to name, a group of people dressed in black stand in a circle.

"W.H., can I tell you how pleased we are with your decision to continue on to Saratoga, rather than stopping in Omaha." Maybelle rests her hand on his arm. She wipes a tear from beneath a black lace veil that covers her beautiful face. She looks more like a gloomy present than a woman in mourning.

"I was told it's a fine place to get a new pair of boots, and mine are plum worn out," W.H. answers.

Maybelle gasps. "Is that the only reason?"

W.H. pats her hand reassuringly and then whispers, "We'll see, darlin'. We will see."

Maybelle manages a smile beneath the veil.

Dressed in all black and surrounded by little log structures on a vast snowy prairie, the living bring their dead out to hold funeral services.

Bleak gray clouds blanket the sky. Cawing ravens welcome their newest guests and ring the alarm for wolves.

"When will the ground defrost?" James asks the landowner.

"Sometime in May," an unkempt older man grumbles. He looks at the dead baby in Emilia's arms and hangs his eyes low to the ground. The old grave keeper shuffles in his buffalo blanket like a bird might ruffle its feathers.

James looks at his broken wife and doesn't have the heart to ask Emilia if they should wait to bury their dead infant son, or just pay the man and get it over with. He makes the decision.

"Where will you keep him?" James asks, looking over the few log huts in the scant town.

"Same place as all these others. We stow them up in the barn here, so wolves and coyotes can't get at them. When the earth is soft enough, we dig and give them a proper Christian burial," the landowner turned grave keeper answers coldly.

Can't charge them too much; they've just suffered a terrible loss, the proprietor thinks. His hard, wrinkled face softens, and his eyes offer a sympathizing warmth. Then they harden and turn cold. *Can't give my land away for free neither. If they want to dig in the frozen earth and have wolves make meat out of their son, 'tis up to them. I'm providing a fair and honest service and must be compensated accordingly.* The entire time he thinks this out he notices that Emilia presses the back of her hand to the baby's cheek and whispers her findings to her husband.

"James, the baby is cold."

"I know, Emilia. I know."

"If only our window hadn't been shattered, dear one. You would have been kept warm and not caught the cough." Emilia cuts a lock of her hair and tucks it in the baby's icy fingers. "Now you are left to rest among strangers, in a strange land." Emilia traces her fingers along her baby's cheek. She rocks him and comforts him as though he were alive.

"Why aren't any of these graves marked?" James motions.

"We mark the graves with these here stakes till the families have the means to send headstones. When the headstone arrives, Mister, I promise you, I will place it myself."

Emilia kneels down at the miniature coffin resting on the snow. She wails and gently pats the lid when its shuffled into place. The grave keeper gets to work nailing it down. Each booming nail makes her jump, but it doesn't stop her from trying to comfort her child. "Rest, little one. Eternal rest. Up in heaven till Mommy comes for you."

"How did it happen so fast?" Maybelle whispers.

"The child caught cold the night of the Indian attack. Day by day it grew worse until it took to the whooping cough. After that it wasn't long before it didn't cry no more," W.H. whispers back. He struggles to hold his tears back in his welling, bloodshot eyes.

"The angel of death took their poor innocent child in just a few days? Those poor people." Maybelle wipes tears from her eyes. Her covered shoulders shiver beneath her intricate black lace gown.

General Montgomery, dressed in a fine gray coat with silver buttons, begins. "Gather 'round, folks. As the highest-ranking officer, I have been asked to say a few words. I have chosen to read Mark 4:14, 'the sower soweth the word.'"

The friends of the Fallscrow family circle around and listen to a short but sweet sermon.

"This beloved, loving couple had but moments with Adam Fallscrow. Anyone with eyes could see how much love this couple had for their child. Having buried children of my own from consumption, scarlet fever, and whooping cough, I find myself in a close hemisphere of sorrow with the bereaved. Children are the light and life of this world. A house without their laughter isn't worth much. A mother who doesn't get to see her brood increase is saddened by both the fall and decrease of her band."

"It is like it says in Mark 4:21: 'Is a candle brought to be put under a bushel or under a bed?' We put Adam in his eternal bed, but remember that Jesus Christ, the son of God, will raise him again. As it says in Matthew 5:16: 'Let your light so shine before men.' Thank you for letting your light shine, Adam, however brief a time it may have been."

With that the general waves his hand in the sign of the cross and ends the sermon. "Ashes to ashes and dust to dust."

Emilia sobs until her sobs turn to wails. She catches one of her tears on the tip of her fingers and holds it up to her husband. "See here. That is proof of all the love I have for him. It is a drop to the eye but an ocean to my heart."

Every eye in the makeshift graveyard sheds an ocean of tears for the poor deceased Adam Fallscrow. And a few others who joined him both by sickness and by murder, from the horrible Indian attack.

"Do you have anything you can give so that they don't have to suffer financial loss?" Maybelle asks W.H.

"Why, certainly!" W.H. reaches into his pocket and removes a five-dollar bill. He hands it to the caregiver and asks, "Will that be enough for expenses?" The man nods.

"Here, I don't know that it will help much, but Maybelle and I are terribly sorry for your loss." W.H. hands James a fifty-dollar bill.

"Thank you so much," James says, pocketing the money.

He walks over to his wife, scoops her up, and carries her away from her child. She screams and reaches for her son. Her curled fingers clamor for baby's cold body. She wails so loudly her voice starts to fail. Her cry is frozen in a noiseless expression.

W.H. looks away and feels the sky swirl above and the earth spin beneath. He feels his knees wobble and reaches out to brace himself against Malice Mike.

"Easy, partner," Malice says, stabilizing his pal.

W.H. leans over and tries to catch his breath. Something about Emilia's cries sickens him right to the pit of his stomach. He gags and loses control. Vomit spews out of his mouth.

Maybelle rubs his back while her twin brother steadies him.

"I'll fetch us a buggy," the general says, wandering off.

When he returns, W.H. shakes a bit, but he is mostly recovered.

"How long of a ride will it be?" the general asks the driver.

"We're a few miles from Saratoga, so we will be there in a couple of hours."

"Did you hear that, W.H.? After all this time we are less than a day's journey from the Saratoga springs. Now, as I mentioned before, I met a Mr. Dick Burger on the boat. He is a gentlemen of means and, though he is a Yank, I overheard him bragging about a business proposal."

"Just how do you know he's a man of means?" Malice Mike inquires through squinting eyes.

"He had a carpetbag, Malice!" Maybelle scowls.

In an instant her sour expression melts back into the sweetest lady W.H. ever laid eyes on. He smiles.

"Would you mind making an introduction with your letter of intent?"

W.H. can't take his eyes off Maybelle. "If you asked me to shoot the stars out of the heavens, I'd be obliged to do so. Just as long as it makes Maybelle smile. Of course, a letter is within my reach and the stars are not. As soon as they're done tying Cotton down, I'll fetch it from my saddlebag."

With the horse securely affixed to the buggy, W.H. walks over to his saddle and stares at Bingo. He pats his head and says, "I'm sorry I had to tie you up, boy. It's the only way to keep you in the saddle."

Bingo whimpers.

"I'm sorry I had to hog-tie you. If there were another way, I'd do it, buddy. But you know you can't keep up with the buggy in this winter weather."

Bingo whimpers again and rests his head against the firm leather saddle. *Another fine mess you've gotten us into, Master*, he wails. His whimpers are ignored.

W.H. opens his saddlebag and removes the letter. He helps Maybelle and the general into the buggy, then turns to see who else might be joining them. A tall, slender man with a dark complexion removes his hat to reveal a bald spot. He bows his head and says, "Mr. Garrick Anthony Burger. Most folks 'round here call me Rick Darling."

"What kind of a nickname is that?" Malice Mike chortles, mocking the stranger.

"If it were up to me I'd prefer my own name. But as you are going to learn 'round these parts, nicknames have a way of sticking."

"I'd say that's all parts." W.H. smiles and winks at Malice Mike. "What do you do for work, Rick Darling?"

"I'm a slave trader. Land holder. Jeffersonian Democrat Republican, and I am *gracious* to make your *acquiescence*."

CHAPTER 88

"You are 'courteously' 'reluctant agreement' to meet us?" W.H. scrunches up his brows in confusion and perks up his nose.

"Pleased to meet you." Maybelle greets the stranger with a polite curtsy and a sly smile.

"Yes. I am always kind to strangers I meet, but it is with reluctance I entertain strangers. So many scrupulous speculators combing over these parts, one can't be too careful." Mr. Burger pinches open a silk bag of licorice snuff. He takes a slight pinch of the sweet-smelling tobacco and holds it up to his nose. With a sniff, he inhales it, then offers it to Malice Mike.

"So, then, why are you riding in the carriage?" Malice Mike asks, rolling a toothpick from one corner of his mouth to the other with a flick of his tongue. He squints and keeps his hand close to his Tiffany pistols.

Seeing that his offer is refused, Rick Darling offers a pinch of snuff to the general. "Because your father is a respectable officer. And I presume I am in the presence of respectable people."

"How'd you get that hole in your hat?" Maybelle inquires, pointing to a perfectly round hole in the brim of the gentlemen's black silk hat.

After the general takes a pinch, Rick Darling secures the snuff. "Gunfight."

"Are you pulling my feathers?" Malice Mike's scrutiny melts into a broad, interested smile.

"I would be happy to tell you all about it. We have a ride ahead of us. Not nearly as dingy as the coal-burning city of Cincinnati, but that's a story for another time. That is, if you folks are interested in sharing a carriage." He looks over W.H.'s shoulder and nods at the last carriage on the dirt road.

"Of course we are. Junior is a might testy. Just ask W.H. Him and Junior got off to a rough start, but they're fast friends now. Wouldn't you agree, gentlemen?"

Malice Mike puts his arm around W.H. "After this feller taught me how to shoot buffalo, he might as well be my brother." Mike takes off his black cowboy hat and shoves it on W.H.'s head.

"Been meaning to give you that. Saw you eyeballing it."

And with that kind gesture, the family file into the carriage, ladies first. Strangers last.

Maybelle sits between her father and her beau. Mike sits beside Rick Darling and turns so that he faces the man.

Though his gut tells him not to let Rick Darling review the letter of intent, Maybelle's insistence is relentless. W.H. hands the letter over for careful review. He is happy to see the weight his letter carries when Rick Darling begins to ask questions.

"It says here that you have signing authority. Is that correct?"

"I have limited power of attorney."

"Can you sign deeds or loans?"

"All of that would have to be done by contract, and it would have to be reviewed by the board of directors before I could sign. Why do you ask?"

"What would they require?" Rick Darling's shifty cold brown eyes cause W.H. a hint of concern. *Why is this fella putting on airs?* W.H. asks himself. He looks out the window at the winter landscape. He counts a team of ten white canvas wagons circled about. A group of pioneers gather in its center and arrange dinner in their outdoor kitchen. There is even a blanket lying in the snow and set up like a table. As they pass a mighty lone oak, a spot of crimson reveals a cardinal grosbeak or maybe a red robin. As W.H. looks closer, the bird that catches his attention, most fitting for his present company, is the mockingbird, and it appears to be injured. In his observation, W.H. inadvertently creates a stagnant and awkward silence in the conversation.

"I would need letters of recommendation from people you do business with. My business circle extends to upstate New York." W.H. pauses, trying his best to catch a flinch or a flicker of misrepresentation. When he discovers none, he continues. "People we know. Banks and so forth. I would also have to see your portfolio.

Speak with your peers. Give your character a thorough and thoughtful review."

"The man who put this hole in my hat knows my character best. And since I'm here and he's not, that should say something." Rick Darling rests his frozen gaze on W.H.

"I'd say it does!" Malice Mike grins.

W.H. is unflinching. "So then your reputation as a gunslinger is established, but your business character has yet to be determined. Let me assure you, I will be the person to do the inspecting, and if I don't like what I see, no recommendation of mine shall be met with pen to paper."

"Well, then, Mister, have you a gander and glean what you may." Rick Darling smiles, exposing a gap between his teeth.

Maybelle takes W.H.'s hand and squeezes it so tight, she forces him to look away from Rick Darling and lock eyes with her.

"I get lost in your eyes. All my doubts melt away," Maybelle whispers, which causes Malice Mike to fake a gag.

"My character may have yet to be established, but I myself am a fine judge of character, and if I may say, madam, you have yourself a good man!" Rick Darling compliments her with a wink.

"Thank you!" Maybelle blushes. *Never had a man I wanted to keep. How do I know if he's mine?* She parts her pretty red lips, inviting a kiss. W.H. leans in to oblige her, and testing the interest of her beau, she looks away.

"Do any of you have any idea why they call Saratoga, Saratoga Springs?" Rick Darling inquires with a raised brow.

"No, sir," the general answers.

"A hot spring runs through the town."

"How do you know?" Malice Mike asks before W.H. can.

"Because I was the first iron-willed pioneer the Omaha Indians let set foot on virgin ground." Rick Darling tucks his thumbs into his belt loop and nods. "I knew how to tan. Make a harness and even my own pair of shoes. I built my own house and furniture without using one nail. My mattress is made of down feathers!"

"What is the population of the town?" The general redirects the conversation.

"A bustling fifteen thousand and growing every day! We got blacksmiths hammering iron into horseshoes and wood-burning stoves. You will have no problem finding coffee, sugar, or salt—'course, that is when the steamers bring it and the wagons pack it. Farmers here are sure to become rich. Vegetables and fruits grow big and fast. 'Course, most farmers plant flax and cotton."

"Cotton?" Maybelle beams.

"Yes, ma'am. I would even go so far as to say it is within one's destiny to become rich. But nothing comes easy in Saratoga Springs. No, gentlemen, you must do as the Bible says, till the earth. Sweat-of-your-brow sort of thing. But if your corn crops come in, the market is nearly at your front door. Oh, and you'll be needing hogs to get through the tough winters. You'll starve without a hog."

"Wouldn't it be wonderful to enjoy a hot spring during these cold winter months?" Maybelle asks W.H.

"That's what high society thinks in upstate New York, madam. Folks with fine houses, my neighbors mostly, are talking of buying a second home in Nebraska. Somewhere they can escape the towering snowbanks. A place, as one woman calls it, 'to swim through winter.'"

"In a hot spring?" Maybelle gasps.

"Uh-huh," W.H. says, exchanging simultaneous doubtful expressions with Malice Mike.

"Ice can freeze on the lakes thirty inches deep. But not in Saratoga Springs. No, sir. The water is a delightful hundred and four degrees year-round."

An orange blaze ignites and illuminates the dark carriage. The flame dulls, then touches the tip of Rick's not-so-Cuban cigar. He puffs and puffs till the tip glows like an orange eye. With each heave, the sun-kissed glow illuminates Rick's slender face. But not in the way it had Rockefeller's. No, this man was not enhanced by light, but darkness. His calculating eyes said to W.H. *I want something from you.* The wolf hunter knew to cover his trail in the wild, but Rick Darling had already caught a footprint with admission of the letter of intent.

If I know wolves, this man won't stop for one print. He will continue down the trail till he discovers that I have gold, W.H. thinks to himself. The question is, will he use force or reason to obtain what he is after? W.H. expected that inquiry about his gold and he decided then and there never to answer a direct question about money.

No sooner had he settled on this determination than the slender shadow man asked, "Have you any venture funding?"

"Yes, have you?" Maybelle leaps on the heels of Rick Darling's inquiry.

CHAPTER 89

Not wanting to answer Rick Darling but unwilling to leave Maybelle hanging, W.H. blurts out, "I have!"

Oh, what a fool I am. I have laid another print by answering the creature I adore.

Rick Darling's interest increases dramatically.

W.H. expects him to ask at any moment, "How much?" which W.H. had determined not to answer.

Instead, Rick Darling changes the conversation. "Land is why you are all here. Is it not?"

The party goes silent.

"Well, has anyone talked to you about the committees?" Rick Darling continues.

"Are you going to tell us how you got that hole in your hat?" Malice Mike interrupts.

"No, I am not. But I will tell you some of the things you all need to know before we arrive in Saratoga. The first thing you need to know is that there is no legal charter to establish official law and order. The appearance of law exists. We got a sheriff, but he ain't duly elected. He's been appointed."

"By who?" W.H. asks.

"By the senior land owners."

"That's all handy dandy, but I'd prefer to know how that bullet hole got in your tall hat," Malice Mike insists.

"Without the law that you're used to in the states, you might just be using those shiny pistols of yours sooner than you think."

Malice Mike grins. "Well that would be just fine by me!"

Rick Darling spins an interesting tale. "Have it your way. Lawlessness is how I got this hole in my hat. A hothead I was playing seven-card stud with accused me of cheating in a fair game. He was just raw 'cause I swindled most of his purse."

Maybelle leans on the edge of her seat, eyes wide and, frustrating to W.H., firmly fixed on Rick Darling.

"The man drew his gun, but I was faster."

"How fast?" Malice Mike demands.

"Fast enough I put a bullet through his chest and the only piece of me he got was this hole in my hat, as he was falling back."

"Never to rise until the dreadful day of the resurrection," Malice Mike adds in awe.

Rick Darling's cold eyes rest on Maybelle's.

W.H. looks out the window and spots thousands of geese. They mix with a flock of ducks and comb over retired corn stocks. When one stirs, hundreds take flight. They do a broad circle and land among the hoard, fighting for their daily bread.

With a shotgun, I could feed all of us for a lifetime, W.H. thinks.

For the rest of the ride, W.H. is silent. As they near town, Rick Darling plays tour guide.

"There's the finest saloon in town. I say that 'cause it's the only saloon."

"What's the game?" Malice Mike grimaces with a devilish gleam in his eye.

"Faro." Rick Darling curls a reciprocating smile.

"Is it a fair game?" the general inquires, showing where Mike acquired that evil spark.

"I've seen the house cleaned out a few times. Fairest game you'll get in town. Cheaters are shot and planted sometimes in the same night."

"Shot dead?" Maybelle asks, fanning herself. W.H. can't tell whether she's excited or curious.

"Well, yes, ma'am. That's how dealings are done here in the lawless frontier. Men brimmed with liquor seldom make compromises. Thus a brutal end."

Silence fills the air. Mike looks at his father. They share a crooked smile. The son pats his pistols while the father pats his pocket.

"That right there is the new Presbyterian Church. The panels just got painted this summer."

"They look whiter than the snow," Maybelle says with a nervous giggle.

"We got a post office. A courthouse and a jail right next to it. Steer clear from there. Especially in winter months. It ain't heated, and most men just die in that awful cage."

General Montgomery shoots a glance at his son, who smiles when he sees his father's worried expression, then looks out the window at all the passing people fluttering about to do business in half-built buildings.

"You know your town is settled when it has a piano playing. 'Course, we only have two in town, and they really only play one song well."

"What's that?" Malice Mike inquires.

"Rosalie the Prairie Flower."

"When was Saratoga settled?" General Montgomery inquires.

"It's still being settled, so no one can put a date to it as of yet. But I was one of the first to file a claim in 1854. Got here by the *Moses Greenwood* ferry. Got me a hundred and sixty acres. Only had six homes in the entire region. Some folks was under age of preemption, so I was fortunate to absorb their claims when the Pawnee ran them off."

"Why didn't they run you off?" W.H. asks, wishing they had.

"'Cause I had a steady stream of whiskey coming, which I used to gain favor and trade for furs. That's back when the Pawnee had a large and powerful tribe. But the Omaha are the town favorites now, and they killed most of the Pawnee."

"Sounds like you made out like a daisy." Maybelle compliments Rick Darling, fanning the flames of W.H.'s jealousy.

Mr. Darling points to a slew of half-finished redbrick and wooden buildings. "This here is where we held the first election. We came armed and prepared."

"Armed with what?" Malice Mike asks, showing more interest in weapons and fighting than anything else.

"Double-barreled shotguns, bowie knives, and pistols. Wasn't taking any chances with an unfair vote, and since I was the first to cast a vote for myself as town mayor, I wanted everyone to know that I supported the second amendment. I won five of the six votes. It was decided that the town would celebrate democracy in the territory by erecting Main Street around where the election occurred. I've got two of these buildings going up. Oh, look there!" He points to an

Indian woman. "That gal right there is Old Mary. She's an Omaha squaw who learned five languages trading in fur. Some preacher said she went to school, but I don't believe a wild Indian woman would ever submit herself willingly to the confines of institution." Rick Darling waves at the old woman. She stiffens, raises her hand and lowers it. Her frown never lifts.

W.H. reflects on how much he and Old Mary must have in common.

"I gave Old Mary money to make me a pair of moccasins. She just bought the beads and when I was paying her told me about a coal mine. Does that interest you at all, Mister?" Rick Darling rests his raven gaze on W.H.

"Everything interests me."

"That's wonderful. Oh, see that couple right there?" He points to a young couple. "That's Adam and Eve. 'Course that ain't their real names, but they were the first couple to be married here in town. Justice of the peace Mr. Jim Davis married them last week. Can you believe he waved his fee so they wouldn't have to start off in debt? I never would have done that, but he done it. Everyone's expecting big things from them."

As Mr. Darling continues, W.H. listens intently. He tries to pinpoint the man's accent but can't identify him as a New Yorker, even though he asks as many questions and dominates the conversation.

CHAPTER 90

"Homesteading is what folks are going to call it. Now, there's no laws on the books, because there is no law out here. So folks have formed clubs and set up rules." Rick Darling drones on.

"What kind of rules?" the general asks, leaning in.

"Well, lots of folks come out here, find out there ain't the same comforts as the States, and hightail it back," Rick Darling responds, rubbing his hands together.

"So what's the commitment to land your claim?" W.H. inquires.

"Naturally the clubs want squatters, not quitters. To curb the high-fly crowd, the clubs instituted a time commitment."

"And how long would that be?" the general asks.

Rick Darling clears his throat and keeps his eyes on W.H. "Five days."

"Five days? Folks couldn't stick it out five days without the comforts of home?" W.H. ponders.

"Between comforts and Indian attacks, yeah. Some folks weren't alive to return home."

"Five days, that's it? How much land is allotted?" Malice Mike asks.

"No limit really. I got me six hundred acres and a fine house," Rick proudly proclaims.

"Six hundred acres? Why with that much land you must have a mighty fine home," Maybelle ponders.

W.H. turns his attention back out the carriage window, showing little interest. All he can see are sparse log huts that don't seem fit for a human. "How is it, Mr. Darling, that Providence has smiled on you and spared your scalp?"

"Oh, just lucky, I guess. That and I keep a piece with me at all times. On all occasions. Especially when I'm most vulnerable, while

I sleep." Never one to linger on a sour note in a conversation, Rick Darling shifts the tone back to business. "If we can get a venture fund together big enough for a hotel, plenty of men are willing to work. Ferries are bringing in materials every day. There's a housing shortage, so the rooms would fill up right quick." Rick rubs his chin and appraises W.H.'s interest.

"Are there titles, or how is all this organized?" the general asks.

"Land is titled by 'a club.' Nebraska has a charter, even though we are not yet a state. But with that charter, we are a territory. So when Congress votes to make us a state, all titles and deeded lands will transfer. Clubs elect a sheriff. Sheriff has no power, so it's all kind of faux society, if you know what I mean. You will find most of the same privileges as in the states." Rick leans back in his chair, seemingly satisfied with the conversation.

"Oh, that's why you have a jail. How many folks have you talked to about this hot spring hotel?" the general asks.

"Two. You and me. Can't let the cat out of the bag on these sorts of things," Rick Darling responds with a wink.

The carriage comes to a stop.

"Mighty fine to meet you." Maybelle curtsies and steps out into a budding town. Square pine buildings line a muddy street that has been properly christened the "Little Muddy."

"Brrr, it's cold." Maybelle shivers, and her teeth chatter.

The noonday sun makes the snow glow so bright it nearly blinds her.

"Very nice to meet you, madam. If you folks need anything, do let me know how I may be of assistance." Rick Darling takes his hat off and politely bows. But even that is wrong to W.H. He seems to do things half right. His bow is forced. His fancy fifty-cent words have the wrong meaning. He shakes his head in disbelief, and glances sideways at Maybelle.

"Where will you be staying, W.H.?" the general inquires.

"Oh, I don't know. I thought I'd just get a tent."

"A tent?" Maybelle huffs. "How are we all supposed to fit in a tent?"

"You mean you don't have accommodations?" the general asks.

W.H. shakes his head.

Without another word, the general turns about and scurries after the slender man.

"Mister Darling. Rick!" the general hollers, waddling after him. The two exchange words.

"He's at it again. The old fool," Malice Mike grumbles.

"What is that?" W.H. asks.

"Hush up, Malice Mike! You're breaking one of the ten!" Maybelle scowls.

W.H. notices that she's shivering. He takes off his coat and wraps it around her petite frame. Her father waves for her, so W.H. goes to untie Cotton from the buggy. When he turns back around, the family waves at W.H., but not as though they are saying good-bye, so much as they are dismissing him. With horse in hand and dog on saddle, the wolf hunter awkwardly remains in this position, wondering where he is to secure accommodations.

December 31, 1859
Uncle,

I arrived near Omaha and am well pleased that I have made the journey, and I find myself in a familiar cold wind. It is not much different from Winnipeg, Uncle. They do get significantly less snow than we do. I measured three feet, and no mountains break up the constant breeze. I dined on roast turkey tonight. Of course, we had corn cakes. We always have corn cakes. Why wouldn't we have corn cakes? How could we possibly enjoy mashed potatoes and gravy when we are surrounded by corn? To make cakes out of…

Accommodations have been difficult as there is a shortage of living space and an abundance of people. Met some folks from Missouri. Call themselves the Mormons. A right friendly bunch who seem to have suffered a great many troubles. Some fine-looking dames. Hundred or more to cross the plains and join a larger party out in some desert with a large salty lake. Trials and tribulations weigh on them as they do most true believers. I reckon those are the marks of a true

Christian people.

Though space is short, food is not. Wild game runs rampant in these parts. There are literally more geese than people. On a walk with Maybelle, I spotted some river otters swimming up and down the streams. I truly enjoy watching them, though I get no joy out of watching them get trapped. Their constant high chirps and cute little faces make them the finest animals I've ever seen. You should see them swim. It is a sight to be experienced because there are not words to capture the joy. Their coats fetch a mighty fine price though, so I can see why trappers do it.

Things with Maybelle and I are hotter than ever. She and her family are living in a two-bedroom log house on Rick Darling's property. Apparently, the general had some financial troubles after his wife passed and he lost their lands. Turns out they are not pioneers on a grand adventure but fugitives from Kentucky. The debtors' prison is in hot pursuit of the general, and had it not been for his two children packing a bag and giving him advance notice, he would apparently be in prison for his debts. None of this is his fault though. He had some apple cider vinegar investment go south. I know what you may be thinking, Uncle, but as the Scriptures say, sins of the father are not passed onto the children, so I am willing to overlook these minor infractions.

Until the roads get settled, I will have to route mail through Missouri. Stagecoach is the only reliable means of travel during the winter months.

You will be happy to know that rents are rather high. For a fifteen-square-foot room, the going rate is between twenty and twenty-five dollars. Commodities are at high rates as well. Coal is six dollars per bucket. Wood is seven dollars a cord. Apples are surprisingly cheaper than in Winnipeg.

Six dollars will get you an entire barrel! Don't be too excited about the provision prices. Once this wave of immigrants gets their first crop in, prices will be driven down. No idea how that will affect rent, so as of now I can't say that an investment is worth pursuing. Also, the work force is substantially smaller. Pay rates are rather high and put all things into proportion.

Money is in surplus as well. Most people smart enough to use the gold-backed green bills do. They trade them for Winnipeg necessities that are luxuries here. Soap, for example, is a necessity at home. Here it is a luxury, and folks will go days if not weeks without a bath. Water is also a necessity I am learning to do without, as my well has been frozen and is not expected to thaw until April. I melt a great deal of snow and, unlike the others, I can afford the coal to melt enough that I will be taking a regular bath.

Tomorrow the town is throwing a grand dance at the Presbyterian Church. I am allowed to attend if I pay two dollars more than everyone else on account I am Church of England. Bought a nice brown suit that seems fitting. Got a new saddle. New ivory-handled Colt Navy .44 rotating chamber. Holds six shots, and the etch work on the chamber is of an Indian scene. I have learned that it is Colt's tribute to a Captain Jack Hays in the US Army. The six chambers have earned the pistol the nickname six-shooter. It is funny to me how nicknames stick down here. Everything has a nickname. I could write volumes on the short sayings, but I'll suffice it to say there are plenty.

I am missing you for New Year's. I find myself a bit homesick around the holidays. Tell Auntie I miss her and her fine pudding. I often remind myself that this adventure is in fact what I wanted. Some days more than others. I do not expect to see this journal reach you anytime soon since the rising rivers prevent communication from Chicago. I realize this journal is mostly empty. I have purchased a new one and thought it wise to keep you informed of my well-being. For that reason, please forgive the wasted paper. I do miss you terribly, and I wish you a blessed and happy new year.

After ending his journal entry, W.H. walks over to a mirror in the tiny room he rented from the bank and checks himself.

He pulls on his black suspender straps and looks at his pants.

"Bingo, do you think I should have bought the black pants, or do you think the brown ones look sporty enough?"

I said black. You look silly with different-color suspenders from pants, Bingo barks.

"That's what I think, too. Brown looks great with black."

Bingo drops his head between his paws and covers his eyes.

"As soon as our land deal goes through, Bingo, we'll have the house, six hundred acres, and a hotel on the hot springs. How do you like Saratoga now?"

Bingo growls.

"You been a thorn in my side ever since Maybelle and I made eyes. Listen, fella, when spring comes, I'll buy you a whole herd of sheep. A flock of chickens. A cat you can chase until your legs fall off. What else?"

Bingo rolls over on his back and exposes his belly.

BOOM!

CHAPTER 91

A cannon fires, forcing Bingo to his feet. He barks and howls.

"Simmer down, Bingo! That's just the Presbyterians telling everyone the New Year's dance is starting."

W.H. puts his black hat on and holds out his arms. "How do I look?"

He reaches into his pocket and removes a small wooden box. He takes a knee and says, "Maybelle. I spoke with your pa. He gave me permission to marry you, if you'll have me."

He smiles at Bingo, who tilts his head to the side and raises his ears.

W.H. responds, "Well, I spoke with the jeweler... What do you know about diamonds? You're a mutt."

With that W.H. slams the box shut and heads out the door. He returns, opens it, and looks in on the confused dog. "I'm sorry about that. It's just nerves is all."

Bingo whimpers.

W.H. closes the door to his room and walks through the bank, passing the closed money-counting stations, and heads out into the street. Mounting Cotton, he rides off to the church, a fine white building with an exceptional bell tower.

DING-DONG. DING-DONG.

The bell echoes.

At the church's barn, behind the main building, a violinist, a cellist, and a banjo player wait in front of two pianos, one painted blue for the North and the other red for the South, making modern music.

Southern belles in their low-shoulder, high-cleavage satin gowns twirl around and around with their fancy-dressed beaus.

Northerners lock hands. Men place a hand on the hip and ladies on the shoulder. They keep a firm distance between each other as wide as the Good Book, then dance around in spinning circles.

W.H. spots Maybelle dancing with Rick Darling. His older age and her young beauty bring a sour, puckered expression to his face.

"Oh, darlin', don't be jealous," Maybelle says, walking away from Rick in the middle of the dance. She wraps her arms around W.H.'s waist and shouts, "Spin me around and around!"

"Howdy, folks!" a man with a long gray beard yells. "I'd like to welcome y'all out to the first winter-fest dance in Saratoga Springs."

The crowd cheers and applauds.

"Thank you much. Pastor Dan and his wife of the Presbyterian Church would like to welcome y'all. On behalf of the Presbyterian Church, Pastor Dan would like to encourage y'all to make as good of an appearance at church as y'all do at the hoedowns."

The crowd erupts in laughter and applause.

"Many a fine lady in the audience tonight. Seems like a perfect opportunity to try a dance we all enjoy very much down in Savannah, Georgia, one of the original thirteen colonies."

"Shut up and play the music, old man!" a tipsy fella rudely interrupts.

"Never mind him. He ain't a fan of history."

The banjo player begins plucking away.

"Anyway, this tunes come all the way from England, where my grandpapa's grandpap taught it."

The banjo player plucks loudly, and the old man hums a loud tune.

"When the violin plays, we all dance in figure eight, two by two and four, makes it great."

The violin picks up.

"Now, it's right by right, 'round you go. And you can't go to heaven while you carry on so."

"Ha! Ha! Ha!" The young couples laugh while their parents make sour expressions.

W.H. locks arms with Maybelle. They skip around together in the square dance.

"And it's home, little gal, and do-si-do. And it may be the last time. I don't know. And oh my gosh and oh by Joe." The partners mix up. Their feet clomp and tap on the wooden floorboards. Now Maybelle is dancing with Rick Darling again. W.H. grumbles and dances with a young thirteen-year-old girl in braids who clasps her hands to his and leads him along.

The violinist steps back, lifts up a jug of whiskey with his thumb, rests it against his arm, and tips it back while the young cello player plucks deep base notes.

"Circle eight and you get up straight. And we'll all go east on a westbound freight. And knock down Sal and pick up Kate. And we'll all join hands when we circle eight."

The crowd locks hands and spins around the lantern-lit barn. Girls giggle in their calico dresses. Boys beam in their miniature suits.

The cellist stops playing, and the church lady organ player in a cornflower blue dress tickles ivory on the Northern-blue piano, which gets the Yanks hollering.

"Allemande left and allemande right. Do-si-do, we will be up all night.

"Drink your coffee, push it down, don't let your whiskey hit the ground."

As the dancers link up with their original partners, the man at the red piano brushes off his burgundy velvet jacket and pounds on the piano in an entirely different fashion.

The Southern belles jump up and down and scream, forming a straight line. They stomp twice, click their heels, spin about, and walk toward their men. When they get close, the fellas reach for their girls, but the girls turn and run away, giggling their silly heads off.

Next the men make the same move, and Malice Mike dances an Irish-like jig in the center of the room. He steals the show. His heels move so fast it looks like smoke is coming off his silver-tipped boots.

The crowd encourages him by clapping. "Show 'em how we do it back home, Malice!" Maybelle hollers. She puts her fingers between her lips and whistles so loud it pierces the piano player's music.

He obliges by kicking up his left foot and catching it with his right hand. He leaps over his caught leg. Over and over he goes to the clapping, cheering crowd.

"'Nuff of that, fancy feller," the bearded host says, inviting all the musicians to play at the same time. "Promenade left and promenade right. Lift your girls with all your might. Give 'em a twirl and hold 'em tight. Get them high, don't drop 'em low, 'cause 'round and 'round we will do-si-do."

With that he holds his hands up and ends the song.

The couples clap so loudly it shakes the barn's wood plank walls. As the night wanes on, W.H. feels a bit queasy. He chalks it up to nerves. 'Course, it doesn't help that proposals are happening all around him. Every time a fella gets on bended knee and slides a ring over a girl's finger, he feels like he did that day at sea. Maybe it's the booze. Whatever it is, it isn't good.

Maybelle presses herself tightly against W.H. and tilts her head back. She looks up beneath long eyelashes and fixes her eyes on his. "Do you maybe have something you want to ask me, hun?"

The room suddenly seems to sway back and forth. W.H. nods and cups his hands around her ears. "Mind if we step outside?"

"Not at all. I think the outdoors are terribly romantic," Maybelle says, pinching her dress and hooking her arm through his.

When they stand under a glimmering blanket of stars, W.H. kneels down in the snow. He reaches inside his pocket and struggles to find the ring.

"Darling, I just want to say that I love you."

"Oh! This is just perfect!" Maybelle interrupts. She presses her tiny hands to her mouth and strains to see the ring.

"Maybelle Montgomery, will you do me the honor of—"

BOOM!

BOOM!

BOOM!

The crowd fire their pistols to welcome in the new year. The church bell rings so loud it forces Maybelle to plug her ears. A cannon fires and briefly turns night into day. The concussion rips through their clothes and brings smiles to their faces.

"Happy New Year!" couples shout and cheer. Kids honk noise makers and bang pots and pans as noisemakers.

Six-shooters breathe fire and hot lead into the sky. A shooting star teases them and makes them believe they got a direct hit.

W.H. draws a deep breath and patiently waits for his moment. He stares into Maybelle's eyes and holds her hands.

A budding teenage girl takes the stage. She tunes her guitar and plucks the chords to "Auld Lang Syne." "Should old acquaintance be forgotten and never brought to mind," the girl sings. Her father and baby sister dance beside her while her grandfather plays the violin.

"Come on, y'all, join in."

The crowd sings along.

In the chaos of the celebration and dead of winter, W.H. remains on his knee. Sweat gathers around his forehead and trickles down his cheeks.

"HELP! HELP! HELP!" A woman swings open the tall barn door. She is covered in blood.

CHAPTER 92

Fannie lunges into the building and clings to the doorframe for support. She is clad in only her flannel nightgown, her feet shoved into oversized men's shoes. Snowflakes blow into the barn through the opening.

"Oh no, honey, someone's been hurt. I think that women is bleeding." Maybelle looks down at him with an expression on her face that sours the mood. Their special moment has passed. They rush to render aid.

"My children. All of my children are dead! And scalped..." Fannie, the frantic woman, wails. This New Year starts off with a horror too unimaginable to comprehend.

"What happened, Fannie?" Mr. Jim Davis, justice of the peace, asks.

"INDIANS IS WHAT HAPPENED!"

"Form up a posse!" General Montgomery shouts.

"I'm empty. Anyone got powder and ball?" Malice Mike yells.

"Load up your guns!" his father, the general orders. "I fought Indians, and I know what needs doin'."

"Let her finish." Pastor Dan yells so loud it brings order to the chaos. "Fannie, go on and tell us what happened."

"They were wearing dresses. Came running up to the house screaming. So's I thought they was women needin' tendin'. When my husband and I set down our rifles and opened our door, it weren't no women. It was Indians all painted up in war paint and wearing white women dresses. Ohhh, they forced their way into the cabin and... and..." She moans.

"Yes, go on."

"JUST LOOK AT WHAT'S LEFT OF MY FAMILY!" she shouts,

motioning to her bloodstained gown.

"Did they hurt Bennie?"

Fannie nods. "Scalped him, too. I don't even know if he's dead. He was screaming something awful. While the ones who snatched me was busy killing my oxen and stealing my horses, I just ran as fast as I could and came for help. My children. Oh, my poor innocent babes. They grabbed my babes by the feet..." She presses her quivering wrist to her mouth and gags out a terrifying tale so dreadfully awful, it twists the faces of all who hear it. "They took turns smashing their little bodies against the tree over and over again till their brains did come out."

Women gasp and cry, and the men growl for justice.

Anna goes on. "Poor Bennie must be tortured to death by now. I didn't know what to do. I just ran. I just ran."

"Oh, you poor thing." The preacher's wife puts her arm around Anna and pulls her in close. Empathetic and petrified ladies circle around her and usher her off into the barn.

"Bennie was a patron of this church and a member of our club!" Pastor Dan proclaims.

"If they could do it to him, they could do it to any of us," a gray-bearded singer shouts.

"They been doin' this all their lives. They are savage! Any promises they make are only as good as the danger we pose to them. Make no mistake. If the Injun is disregarding law, it is because we are allowing it. That ain't never gonna change!" a local man shouts, raising the temperature of the boiling crowd to a bubbling rage.

"What are we gonna do, sheriff?" another man asks.

"I'll tell you what we're gonna do. We're gonna get some good old-fashioned prairie justice. I want every man armed with rifles, shotguns, and pistols. Bring ropes and anything metal and sharp in case we run out of ammo."

"For what?" Rick Darling demands.

"We're gonna kill them all!" Malice Mike grins, adding his flame to the fire.

"Which ones are you gonna kill?" the pastor asks. "The Omaha are part of my flock, and I know for a fact that their men are out on a hunt. If you ride up on their village now, all you're gonna kill is women and children." He holds his arms up to calm the swelling rage.

"There is no sense in going after just any Injuns. We got three tribes out here. Some of 'em got thousands in their tribes. Plus, the Omaha are our friends."

"How do you reason with a savage people that believe we civilized whites are their enemies? They teach their children to hate us! How can you reason with hate?" a woman yells.

"Pawnee stole and killed most of the cats and dogs in town. I know for certain they're lingering about," a man shouts.

"Brothers and sisters, please be slow to anger," Pastor Dan pleads.

"Are you saying we do nothing? Turn the other cheek? Pluck the crops and move on with life?" General Montgomery challenges the preacher.

The crowd universally shake their head no.

He turns to the crowd with rifle in hand and presumptuously addresses the people as though he were their leader. "A lax response is the wrong response. Indians relish in fiendish murders. They bathe the scalping knife and tomahawk in innocent blood. They need no provocation. One day they are driven by hunger or thirst and are willing to trade. This is how they deceive us. This family has been murdered most likely by a war party that prayed to one of two deities. As you can see, the results speak for themselves. Indiscriminate killers is what they are. They will attack women, children, and unarmed men. Murder, the unrighteous cup of bitterness to us, is sweet intoxication to them. Once partaken of, they will not stop. They will get drunk on your blood, and you better believe me when I tell you, there will be more killin'. My mother had five children before me. I'm the sixth. Indians carried the torch, the tomahawk, the scalping knife to our home. They killed and scalped my older siblings and dried their scalps in front of my mother. Old Chief Pontiac gave the order to attack settlements after the bitter French and Indian War. I have seen so much blood spilled by those savages it would turn a river red. They will exploit our Christian kindness. They will use God's grace against you. Do not expect them to be anything but heathens.

"I have seen cabins set ablaze. Found countless murdered and scalped families of innocent pioneer folk. Pursued wives stolen into captivity. Retrieved daughters led away into the wilderness to suffer degradations superior to death. Discovered fathers and sons burnt to death at the pole. We have seen many a bloody attack. I've seen this all my life. I know just what needs doin', and I'm prepared to do it!"

"We don't need an Indian massacre. We have a treaty in place," Pastor Dan counters.

"Looks like they honor their treaties with the blood of your flock, Pastor!"

"Treatise with Injuns is only as good as the men and guns willing to enforce 'em."

"Their young 'uns beg for war. They paint themselves up and yearn for the notes of the war song. Nothing brings them more joy than earning feathers and scalps. They are fond of war because their fathers are fond of war. Hell, they kill each other as much as they kill us. Killin' is all they know. It's a way of life for them. If it's war they want, I say we give it to 'em!" Malice Mike shouts.

"You're right!"

"Only good Injun is a dead Injun!"

Many in the crowd nod.

"I'm not only proposing a full-scale counterattack. I'm calling upon the mayor to activate the militia! Seems we got a situation here, and the first thing we need to do is hire leadership. Now, seeing as how I'm the highest-ranking militiaman here, I will allot my services for five dollars a week," General Montgomery shouts.

Rick Darling slips away.

"I hear around their campfires they mock us by making the faces of our dead. Old men teach young men, just like Louise May was saying."

"I never said that. Y'all are plum fools." Louise May adjusts her periwinkle taffeta bonnet.

"Don't go yellow on us, wife!" Zebediah May, her husband, calls out.

"Bringing the murderers to justice is all any of us can ask. A full-scale attack on Injuns ain't right," Louise May counters.

Rick Darling resurfaces with a crucial piece of information. "Fannie says all this happened maybe a half hour ago. She reckons by their markings they're Pawnee."

"Told you, Sheriff. Same as the Indian man you killed in town a couple weeks ago."

"I had to kill him. He was dressed for war and pointing his gun at me."

"Yeah, well, he said they had a war party of hundreds. Sounds like the chickens have come home to roost," Allen Jefferson, a new arrival in town, hollers.

"For all we know, gentlemen, they could be surrounding us at this very moment," General Montgomery informs the terrified crowd. Everyone exchanges fearful glances.

"Taking our homes one at a time and burning everything to the ground."

Bullets slide into chambers. Hammers cock. Bowie knives slide into leather holsters and strap to waist belts. The men quickly arm themselves, as do the women. Even children carry guns, for none are safe from the Pawnee.

An unelected leadership converts civil hands into uncivil war.

"I figured the Omaha were too noble to do something like this." Pastor Dan defends his flock. "One of us needs to ride and alert them that a war party is going down at Otter's Creek. If they wanna join us, they can follow our tracks."

"I need a volunteer to ride a dispatch to the Indian agent and let them know what's going on here," justice of the peace Davis calls out openly to the men.

"I'll go!" Joseph, his eldest son, volunteers.

And with that, the suspected Pawnee enemy is marked for dead.

"We ain't gonna tolerate this in Saratoga. We're from Kentucky. We know how to handle Indians!" Malice Mike's words bring the boil to full flame in each man's eyes. He unholsters his gleaming Tiffany pistols and cracks a wicked grin.

"Judge Frank is the best man in the territory. We will need him to deputize us!" Clarence, the dance host, announces as he rolls his forty-four-caliber chamber along his cotton sleeve and checks his caps to make sure none have been primed or dampened.

"We ain't got time for that! Let's get over to Bennie's place and get the jump on 'em before they slip back into the woods."

CHAPTER 93

"Joseph, deliver my message to our ally, Chief Iron Eye," the pastor orders his eldest son.

The townsfolk are armed and ready for war. They huddle under the cover of surrounding tree line to assess and plan. True to Fannie's description, the painted faces and men in women's dresses were all at Bennie's cabin. Indians dance wildly around, illuminated by Fannie's burning barn. They scream victory war chants and spew liquor into the flames. They laugh and mimic Fannie's family by acting out their final death expressions. For them it is all great fun. To the posse, they look like fire-breathing demons.

"Let's lick 'em, boys!" Malice Mike cries out, firing his pistols and leading a raid.

The distinct stench of death permeates the air.

An eruption of gunfire drops several orange-illuminated bodies where they stand.

The Indians fire back.

WHOMP! BOOM!

The delayed explosion and percussion of their muskets reveals the inferiority of their weapons.

A volley of fire picks up from the posse. They gain fire superiority and send the Indians scrambling in separate directions.

W.H. hears a distinct thud and soon respects the antique weapons. He hears a man scream and glances over his shoulder. Whispering a quick prayer, he hopes it's not Mike.

Breaking away from the posse, W.H. circles around the Indians and heads into the forest, while the posse presses the attack. He believes the Indians have left their ponies tied in the forest and assumes others from the posse will follow him. But he's wrong. He's on his own.

As he rushes into the woods, Cotton's hooves sink deep into the snow. W.H. dismounts and sinks up to his knees. He unholsters both of his pistols. A shadow stirs. He fires three shots and hears a man moaning. An owl hoots. Then another. A bat squeaks. A coyote howls. A cougar roars. A bear growls. A lark sings. The forest is alive with all sorts of unnatural noises. "Damn fools. Lark's a day bird. Ain't no way it would sing at night!" He knows this, but he also knows that animals run away when gunshots ring out. They don't continue to call.

Must be Indians, W.H. thinks. He counts at least ten distinct calls. It seems like they're closing in on him. They rally, but W.H. can't see where.

An arrow trills through the air and misses him by a significant distance.

They're as blind as I am. W.H. takes comfort in this advantage. *Surely they can't maneuver through the snow any better.* He decides to mimic their owl hoot. It confuses and silences them. Two Indians panic and make the mistake of rushing toward him. He hears the snow crunch under their padded moccasins and knows if they spot him first, it will be his funeral. W.H. fires six shots directly into their torsos. With each flash of the muzzle, he sees the agony in their faces as they disappear into shallow, snowy graves.

"Who fired those shots?" Malice Mike demands to know.

"W.H.!" He calls out his name, then trails back to where he came from. He rushes a short distance and ducks behind a wide tree. Arrows strike the trees where he was standing. He can see the fletches still wobbling.

"We'll flank 'em! Stay put," General Montgomery shouts.

The posse forms a straight line. They alternate between their rifles and pistols, keeping a steady rate of fire. They gain ground fast and press the attack with superior firepower and maneuverability. As a result of their quick, decisive action, the savages push deeper into the woods.

W.H. hears their feeble attempts to get away.

"Keep at 'em, boys! For all their novelties of Injun stealth, they struggle in the snow just as much as we do!" W.H. shouts to encourage his comrades in their pursuit of justice but also to let them know that he's still in their line of fire.

He hears branches snap as the Pawnee try to pull themselves along. The noises move closer to him.

Oh, my heck, they don't know if their arrows got me or not. For all they know, I'm dead.

His hands start to shake. His throat goes dry. *I ain't never been so scared in all my life*, W.H. thinks. Adrenaline heightens every sense. He says another quick prayer, this time for himself. He summons the courage to stand and walk into danger, with pistols outstretched in the direction he believes the arrows came from.

He watches a group of shadows break up and move in separate directions. A single shadow moves toward him till it is a shadow no more. The blazing cabin fire grows, sending its dancing light across the Indian man's face. W.H. cocks his pistols, freezing the Indian in place. They stand face-to-face. Enemies glare at each other. W.H. can't help but take notice of the headdress, the leggings, and the fine, elaborate appearance, which indicate this man is important. The murderous look in his eyes and the blood spatter on his face and chest indicate this man is dangerous. The bloody tomahawk in his hand indicates W.H. has the upper hand.

"Take it easy, Chief!" W.H. says, aiming his iron sight smack-dab in the middle of the Indian's painted red and yellow face.

"How, me Corax, Chief of the Pawnee," the six-foot savage proudly proclaims, pounding his fist against his chest.

"How. Me Wolf Hunter, chief of me," W.H. says, pounding his fist against his chest.

W.H. applies the slightest pressure on his one-pound trigger. Corax feels death dancing on the pale-face's fingertip. He curls his lips and refuses to show the slightest hint of concern. "We do not fear death like you!" He draws his wet, bloodied scalping knife and prepares to attack.

A smaller figure cloaked in buffalo skin sheepishly skirts around. She holds something in her trembling hand.

"I'll shoot if you won't surrender! Stop!" W.H. yells.

She puts her hand on her husband's arm and lowers his knife. When she looks at W.H., her painted white face and black eyelids make her look more like a doll than a living, breathing human being.

The posse cheer, proving themselves victorious over the Indians.

Their victory cries cause the Indian couple to break with Indian law; they finally show fear.

"Peace," the squaw whispers. W.H. can see she holds a letter in one hand. With her other hand, she clings to an armful of loot.

"Make magic," Corax whispers, putting her letter in his hand. He motions for W.H. to do what he can't, read the letter.

W.H. steps forward with his gun pointed directly at Corax's face. He snatches the letter and struggles to read in the fire's dancing light.

> This Indian is a great foe. He took part in many war parties against white settlers and missionaries. During one such attack, he fell sick and was not able to keep up with his war party. He faced the saber or a solemn oath not to attack whites or missionaries ever again. It was in our commanding officers' interest to spare his life. Though the platoon strongly disagrees, his cruelties have been repaid with Christian kindness. He has been given food and clothing. He has been ordered to return to his tribe and lift their hearts with the mercy he has received from the United States of America.
>
> Chief Corax has made a solemn promise that he will lay down his weapons. He claims that he will not fight the white man anymore. He has sworn to depart in peace and be happy with those settlers and missionaries he encounters. If he has not done so, expect him to brandish this letter as though it were a license to kill. Should he be caught and display this letter as though it were an endorsement to attack Americans, shoot him on sight until he is dead, dead, dead.
>
> Z. T. BIBLAY, Brig.-Gen., Commanding Expedition.

W.H. looks up from the letter.

"Peace. No more war." Corax offers a man's bloodstained white cotton shirt to W.H.

"Please, peace!" The woman puts her hands together and pretends to pray.

Had it not been for a third, smaller figure, W.H. would have dropped the hammer on both of them right then and there. But a little Indian boy with a half-painted face appears from behind his father. Corax hoists him up on his hip. The savage father, caught in a murderous act, motions for W.H. to take the shirt, while he uses his son as a human shield.

"Pawnee want peace, no more war," the chief says in broken English.

W.H. blinks rapidly and tries to calm his breathing. He can't make sense of what's happening. No matter how much air he sucks in, it feels like he can't get enough. He wants to unbutton his coat, but he can't take his pistols off his prisoner.

"Mercy," the woman whimpers, falling to her knees.

BOOM!

BOOM!

BOOM!

A volley of gunfire erupts.

Just as W.H. was about to cock his pistols and take the family prisoner, he felt the world swirl around him, like at the dance, but much faster. He feels his body collapse and sink into the snow.

He tries to resist the pull of gravity, but his limbs will not oblige his will. *Dadgum Injun got the drop on me.* The cool splash against his face makes him feel like he's floating away. *So this is what it's like to die?*

CHAPTER 94

When W.H. opens his eyes, all he sees is white. His face feels wet. He reaches up to touch heaven, but he can't see his hand.

"I didn't get a chance to propose to Maybelle."

"Is that a proposal?" a voice like hers asks.

"Oh, Maybelle, they got you, too? Oh, that's terrible. I wanted to build you a house. Get some land. Farm it and make a family with you."

"That sounds like a proposal. I accept!"

W.H. thinks he hears Malice Mike's voice. "Your kids are gonna have four eyes!"

With that, W.H. succumbs to darkness.

I don't understand? Am I being tormented by the devil?

***

"Listen to this. He wrote, 'I am in love.' It was love at first sight for both of us. That was just three weeks ago."

"Good luck with that. Half the town thinks he's a coward. How's he ever gonna show his face in town?"

"Doodle-dee-do, dear brother. I doubt him not. My heart says love will prevail. These are good Christian folks. They'll see that he was just sick with the scarlet fever. Pa said his pistol was nearly empty, so I don't know how anyone could believe such a foolish thing. I think he's a hero for answering the call, even though he was in such a depressed state."

W.H. opens his eyes. He can see two blurry objects. He tries to move, but he's tucked safely in his bed.

"I'm not dead?" He moans.

"No, sugar, not even close. Just a severe case of scarlet fever.

Fever's broke, and doctor says you'll be all right."

"What was that you we're talking about? Love?"

"Don't worry, hun, I found the ring and we're engaged. See!" She holds her glittering finger out. "I'm just reading your journal to Malice. Now, go back to sleep."

"My journal?" W.H. tries to sit up. The slightest exertion knocks him out.

***

A few days later, the late afternoon brings distant rumbling thunder. Windowpanes shake, indicating the approaching storm. Droplets of rain beat down on the bank's shake-shingle roof.

"The cottage," W.H. moans in a delirious state.

"Oh yes, dearest, I realize our accommodations ain't hardly quaint, but be patient, lover. Fever's returned. Doctor says it may take a while to break," Maybelle informs him, wetting a rag down with warm water and dabbing at his head.

Blue lightning cracks and illuminates a looming figure behind Maybelle that seems more like a slender shadow than a slender man.

"No. Our children will chase gophers on the estate..." W.H. fades in and out of consciousness.

Thunder claps so close it shakes the building.

Raindrops pelt down in one large body, beating crystal sheets against the shanty structure. The clear, cold water pools and seeps in the floorboards between gaps.

"The carpet. Oh my doodledees. It's going to be ruined. Look there. Water's soaking it wet. I should have known nothing would keep in this drafty shack."

"My place was certainly better suited," the slender figure speaks.

"Because, Rick Darling"—she enunciates each syllable—"it just didn't seem proper to have my fiancé boarding with the likes of you."

"Proper? Ha! What do I care about proper?" Mr. Darling reaches inside his coat and removes an envelope. "Do you think he's well enough to sign the papers?" he asks as he watches Maybelle dote on her beau.

"Well, I don't rightly know. Can I sign for him?" Maybelle proposes politely.

"Wet papers?" W.H. grumbles. In his delirious state his words won't seem to form right, neither in his mind nor in his mouth. His face is drenched in sweat. As fast as Maybelle can wipe the droplets away, they return.

"Never you mind, darling. Just let the children chase the gophers in the grass. I gotta read this letter."

A powerful bolt touches down and splits the dead oak tree outside in half. Floating embers fade in the pouring rain. "The devil is out tonight!" Maybelle complains.

"Okay, then. We'll just sit on the porch and rock ourselves in this fine rocker. Oh, look at the steamers go by." W.H. can't make sense of the odd information, but he smiles and fades into a resplendent rest.

"Wait. Sign these papers before you drift off to fairyland." Rick Darling eagerly plops a pen in W.H.'s relaxed hand and sets them on the document.

"Oh, doodle-dee-do! I don't understand what all the fuss is over." Maybelle growls.

"Because, my darling pet, we must place an order for timber on the earliest ferry. Ferryboat captains say they aren't coming up this far anymore. They're heading down to Omaha. I have to organize a work crew. Pay them in advance. Front material costs. We have a hotel to construct, and I'd like to get the foundation in before spring. That way we can have a fully erect building by summer and we can have Easterners soaking in the Saratoga Springs by winter."

"Don't call me your pet! I'm his fiancé. Seems like I ought to be able to have some sort of say in this." She scowls.

W.H.'s hand falls limp.

The pen scratches the paper before it hits the floor.

CHAPTER 95

"Providence speaks! Lookie there, he made his mark on the deed," Rick Darling exclaims.

"You can't call that a signature," Maybelle blasts back.

"What if that's the only mark we get? He could die from the fever," Rick Darling counters.

"Die? What would that make me? A widow?"

Rick Darling rolls his eyes. "I doubt it."

"Well, then, I'd better marry him so he leaves me a decent woman."

"What will you do then?" The corners of Rick's thin lips curl up and his head tilts down. He leers at her.

"Here!" Maybelle ignores his advances. Instead she picks the pen up and puts it in W.H.'s hand. With her hand on his, she forces a mark that looks nothing like W.H.'s true signature. "He said he wanted to put me in a cottage, and this deal includes the six hundred acres on your Ponderosa Pine claim, right?"

"Yes, it does, daughter of Eve!"

"Don't call me that neither. If he wants children, they're going to need a home. Does this make us fifty-fifty partners on the hotel, and I get the estate if...?"

"If the town sees that you are married, then yes, I would imagine so. Well, you... as in *both* of you." Rick Darling motions with the pen as he inspects the tip, then pushes the cap back on.

"Well, then, here is the gold for a down payment. Now leave me to my fiancé and be on your way!"

"Does this mean you and your family will be vacating my residence permanently?"

"It means you will be vacating my premises. The cottage is

mine now, with the six hundred acres. I practically already have a husband—"

"Better get a preacher first. Town don't take too kindly to trash." Rick Darling interrupts with a wry smile.

"Why, I never! After all the things I've done for you... none of this is your concern!"

"Is this good-bye, then?"

Maybelle folds her arms and huffs. "This can be your good-bye!"

"Farewell, then, my dearest pet!" He enunciates the last word with a sneer.

"Get the hell out of here before I whoop the tarnation out of you and send you back to that hot inferno!"

Rick Darling goes to kiss Maybelle on the cheek, but she pushes him away and sticks her tongue out at him.

"Very well, then. Have it your way. I never fancied being a bug trapped in a spider's web. I'll let your well-to-do fiancé fall prey to your feminine fangs."

"Ooof. Why, I'm going to get my peacemaker and send you out in pieces if you don't git!" She leaps to her feet and scrambles the room looking for her double-barreled shotgun.

Rick Darling wastes no time letting himself out. He turns and presses his hat to his chest. "Good day, madam." He twists the dented brass knob, then opens the creaking door. With two steps he is no longer in the company of a suffering sick man but immediately in the bank. He closes the door and walks past the lines and money-counting tellers to the other side of the bank, where a sign reads, WESTERN UNION. TELEGRAPHS TEN CENTS APIECE.

"I have a wire I would like to transmit to Winnipeg."

"That'll be five cents. Here's a pencil and some paper. Just go on and write your message down, and I'll translate it for you."

Rick pulls out a crisp dollar and pays the man.

"Seeing as how I can't read or write, I'll let you keep the change if you dictate for me."

"I'd be delighted, Mr. Darling."

"Attention: Dr. Bennett. Have decided to move forward with Saratoga Springs investment. I have made a down payment with the gold you have given me. Will be sending notice for more. Very truly, your nephew, W.H."

"You can write a longer message. I won't charge you for it."

"That'll do."

With that Rick turns, puts his tall black hat on and pats the round top down. His ears poke out the sides and make him look silly. He exits the bank, whistling as he goes.

The wire man walks over to the telegraph and sits down. He begins tapping out the message in Morse code.

***

The next day folks in town are excitedly purchasing the first shipment of Ben Franklin's new lightning rods. They are busy mounting them on their roofs while Maybelle, her brother, and her father move W.H. from his "bank office quarters" to his new permanent residence, Rick Darling's two-bedroom cottage.

When W.H. finally wakes up, it's early February.

He's in the same bed but in a much bigger room. "Where am I?"

He sits up and stretches his aching body. Weak but awake, he yawns and looks around the spacious room. The half-finished bright white plaster walls glow brilliantly. He spots a beat-up old rustic mahogany dresser. A bedpan. A small end table with a lantern on it and a fine woven rug on a pinewood floor. The candle is burned down to a wax mound. He struggles to his feet and feels the cold of winter still lurking beneath the pinewood floor. He retracts his foot and wonders if he shouldn't cover it back up and lie down. The scent of bacon makes his stomach growl and his feet endure the cold floor. Coffee mixed with a hint of molasses tallies a mental bill for a fine breakfast. He looks out the bedroom window wondering where his new residence must be. There he sees Maybelle chopping wood in the snow. Bingo watches her and wags his tail as she lowers the ax.

Off in the distance Cotton trots around in a circular corral.

Scrambling to his feet, W.H. opens each drawer. Two are empty, one has his shirt and pants in it. He fastens his suspenders and opens the door. Where he expected to see bank tellers and lines of customers, he sees a blurry living room, a red velvet couch and some fine red velvet chairs to match. A kitchen area with a table. A cast-iron stove has a glowing fire burning in it.

The door flips open and Maybelle's pretty face is illuminated by the bright morning light. She carries in an armful of wood to feed the fire.

"You're finally up!" she shouts, beaming a bright smile.

She sets the wood down and gives him a big hug and a kiss.

"What's going on?" W.H. croaks and rubs his sore throat.

"You don't remember?"

He shakes his head. "Where are my glasses?"

"Right by the bedside. There was a wolf on the neighbor's ranch. I was going to tell you that to stir you and snap you out of your sleeping spell." Maybelle walks past him into the room. She opens a drawer, removes the glasses and brings them to him.

"Why would I care about a wolf?" W.H. rubs his eyes, then puts his glasses on and sees his residence in clear picture for the first time. What looks to have once been a large barn is now converted into living quarters. Gray pine planks line the ceiling and walls. Thick beams cross the ceiling and hold the roof in place. Beneath his bare feet are the same freezing pine planks that have been silvered out by time. However fine construction the roof, it is lower than most barns, which makes him question if it is a barn at all. New furniture looks crudely constructed and is haphazardly placed around the space.

"My brother was kind enough to climb up on top of your roof and patch the thatch up. A thunderstorm blew the grass patch off, and rain came pouring in. I caught the rain water with this here washtub but had to drain it more times than I care to remember," Maybelle says with a nervous smile. Her hands slide down to her waist. She spins around and asks, "Well, what do you think?"

"My roof?"

"Oh, sorry. Our roof."

W.H.'s face puckers like he's just licked a lemon.

"I thought for certain scarlet fever would be the end of you. Now, tell me what's the last thing you remember."

"Bunch of bits and pieces that don't make much sense to me. Is there any food?"

"Yes. I don't know what I should start with first. Let me make breakfast and I'll tell you over steaming ham, sizzling eggs, and fresh corn cakes."

"Oh no. Anything but corn cakes."

"What's wrong with corn cakes?"

W.H. waves her off and scratches his bearded chin.

Rather than pepper her with questions, he tries to calculate how long he's been comatose by the length of his beard.

He sits down at the table and listens as she cracks eggs, whips batter, and sizzles ham.

"It was New Year's Eve. The night the Pawnee attacked that poor family. Fannie lost everyone she loved. Injuns burned her home down. Killed all her children and her husband. She had to board a ferry and head back East to her family with nothing. No children or belongings. Poor dear. We learned later that the Pawnee had demanded ransom for 'all the wolf and deer the settlers killed.' Said if they didn't pay, they'd scalp them. 'Course, no one believed them. But there they was, all painted up in their war paint. Though I suppose an Indian doesn't have to be painted up in war paint to go to war. Half the town respects what you done." She goes quiet and sets the last prepared plate down.

Maybelle clasps her hands together and bows her head. "Dear Lord. Forgive us our trespasses and those who would trespass against our budding family. Curse those who would call this man a coward, and bless my husband..."

"HUSBAND?!?" W.H. forces his eyes open and checks his ring finger.

CHAPTER 96

"I'm just kidding, sugar—*fiancé*." She extends her hand and shows him the glittering ring. "But some in town do believe you are a coward." She bites her bottom lip.

"I don't remember proposing."

"Well, you aren't yourself right now."

"What day is it?"

"It's February. I believe today is Friday, the tenth."

"It's been nearly two months?"

Maybelle nods.

"And you've been by my side this entire time?"

She nods again. Her emerald eyes dazzle.

He smiles at her. "Thank you," W.H. says as he picks up his fork and knife. Chopping the ham into bite-size triangles, he stuffs the meat in his mouth and follows it with a clump of scrambled eggs.

"Enjoy this, 'cause we ain't got no more coffee. We have had three mails from the East." Though not married yet, the two participate in the righteous ritual of morning news as though they are a married couple.

"Deliveries arrived by ferry and skiff. I was able to acquire coffeepots, plates with beautiful blue painted flowers. Matching cups and saucers. Silver-plated knives and forks. I would prefer authentic silver, but plated will do for now. We are stocked up with fifty pounds of flour, a pound of pepper, two pounds of salt, fifteen pounds of sugar, and the Germans down the way provide plenty of eggs, milk, and butter, but I insist on getting our own cow. 'Course we ain't got the chickens they were supposed to deliver to us, but doodle-dee-do, we got everything else we need. We'll get by. How are you feeling, darling?"

"How did all this come about?" W.H. asks, waving his butter knife in a circle.

"Have some of this Turner blackberry brandy." She hands him a shot glass. "Doctor said to give it to you on the regular. I'd be so bold as to say this elixir saved your life." She pours him a glass.

"What all have I missed?"

"Here's the scoop. When you woke up, you signed a deed for the Saratoga Springs Hotel."

"I did *what?*" W.H. drops his butter knife and lifts the glass.

Maybelle's tone becomes strained. "The house came with it. I didn't know what to do, and I figured the bank room would have killed you. There was no stove to keep you warm and an awful draft. No kitchen to make meals. It made perfect sense to me."

"I can't imagine my signature was enough."

"No, it wasn't. When I was rummaging through your things looking for clothes, I found some gold."

W.H. slams the shot. His fingers curl to a fist. "That gold ain't' mine, Maybelle!" he croaks.

"Doodle-dee-day. Don't go gettin' all fl-ustrated. How was I to know? It was in your bag! The lawyer said 'possession is nine-tenths of the law.' I don't rightly know what that means and I don't know much about business." She presses the back of her hand to her head and looks as though she's going to faint.

"Lawyer?"

Maybelle nods. When she calms herself, she continues. "Mr. Darling said you needed one to finalize the filing. He found a right good one too: a Patrick O'Malley. Pa's even been down there fighting the good fight, you know. He's been yelling at them laborers, trying to get them to work, but they claim they can't work because there ain't enough materials. Got the frame up. Wind blew it down though. Then it snowed and the beams warped, so that's all I know."

"Sounds like a genuine mess. How much were they paid?" W.H. reluctantly inquires.

"Did you know the grass is pea green here? Grass is green where I'm from. Should be coming in March. What vegetables should we plant in the garden?"

"I asked you a question!"

"I TOLD YOU I AIN'T GOT A MIND FOR BUSINESS!" Maybelle

presses her hands down on the table and looks away. "There's no reason to manhandle me. Ain't it enough that I've been working around here like a slave? Look at my hands!" She holds her hands out and reveals calluses on her palms. "A lady's hands aren't meant for hard labor. They were made for caressing lovers and, perhaps, nurturing children." She bites her nails. "Certainly not for chopping wood and shoveling snow. Besides, I made a down payment. Mr. Darling took half the gold."

"HALF?"

Maybelle nods and blinks her bright, innocent eyes.

"And the workers ain't working?"

"Can't get planks to port. Pa says labor's no good. He says we need to get our slaves up here to finish the place on time. He ain't never seen men so lazy. Slaves can plank timber just fine."

"SLAVES?" W.H. growls.

"Well, it is a free territory. Ain't no laws against it, and why should we be doing the hard labor when we own a couple hundred slaves? They enjoy the work. They ain't like you and me."

"There will be no slaves under my employ, Maybelle."

Maybelle squirms in her seat.

"How much gold does my uncle have left?" W.H. asks, setting his fork down.

"Well…" She clears her throat. "By my count about a quarter of the original amount," she confesses sheepishly.

"That ain't my gold! It will all have to be paid back."

"This ain't no way to start a marriage. Pa says we ought not to quarrel over money matters."

"We ain't married yet."

"Humph! Fiddlesticks. Be that as it may, you were in need, and a body can't be expected to nurse back to health in inadequate quarters. You're welcome, by the way."

"Oh…oh…Where did it all go?"

"I'm not a businessperson. I can't rightfully say. Pa wants to talk to you about it. Eat up, hun. Your food is getting cold, and you'll need your strength."

W.H. is so angry his hands shake. He pours another shot of blackberry brandy. His eyes are bloodshot, and he stuffs his cheeks full of corn cakes.

***

The next few days move much faster. Though Maybelle tells half-truths to his more serious questions, the one thing W.H. can count on is Bingo. His dog is in good health, and though he's spent most of the winter outside on account of Maybelle moving into the guest bedroom, he's been well fed and cared for. Cotton, too. If Maybelle did anything one hundred percent right, it was to keep his little troop in good health.

When W.H. gains his strength back, he saddles Cotton and rides her into town. The cold air bothers his lungs and makes him feel a bit weak. He decides it's better to brave the elements and get things sorted before he and Maybelle tie the knot. Though she incessantly insists that they "seal the deal soon, so they can consummate as quickly as possible."

The trip to town confuses W.H. Buildings have sprouted up all over the place. Fresh coats of paint mix with partial redbrick buildings. The town is alive and bustling! A piano plays at one saloon he's familiar with and at another across the street he doesn't recognize. A steady flow of horse and carriage meander through town. *Progress comes quick on the frontier.*

He waves a fella down on the street. "Pardon me, Mister. Do you know where the new Saratoga Springs Hotel is?"

"We don't have a Saratoga Springs Hotel. I don't rightly know what you're talking about."

W.H. kicks at his horse's side and asks another man.

"Can't say that I've seen or heard anything like that," the next stranger says in a thick Southern drawl.

"Have I been bamboozled and hung out to dry?" W.H. wonders aloud.

Most of the new townsfolk are friendly, with fine families. Especially the ladies. Quite a few men he recognizes from the New Year's Eve party glare at him and make him feel uneasy. Ignoring these men, he tries to find out what's been happening in Saratoga while he was ill. He finds that most settlers seldom mix company. Within their tight circles, he discovers that mostly tradesmen have arrived in town. One man might be a blacksmith and another a tin man. The pioneer party is often led by a book-educated lawyer or a preacher. One thing he thinks odd is that the pioneers are not short on books. They often have a writer in their midst, and his trade often began with binding books or printing papers. Men lacking trades who didn't cause trouble often lacked education. If they were unrepentant troublemakers, unwilling to learn how to read or right at the local church, they were quickly branded outlaws. Everyone avoided them by scurrying across the street to steer clear from their troublesome ways.

No one seems to know anything about his hotel. What's worse is they think he's a "darn fool for losing it."

Wanting to warm up, W.H. heads to the saloon. When he slams a shot of whiskey, a fire ignites in his chest and keeps him warm in a way that a coal fire cannot.

A woman with peacock feathers in her coiffed hair plays a new modern song on the piano. She looks familiar, but he is distracted by her bare neck, pushed-up cleavage, and naked arms. *She looks just like a piece of candy!* he decides, assessing the bouncing ribbons in her springing curls and her brightly colored dress.

He finally realizes who she is. "I'm glad to see you in good spirits," he says, plopping down beside her.

Her face turns to stone and washes with guilt and shame.

"How's your husband?" W.H. persists.

She stops playing and looks at him. Her pale face and blue-gray eyes lock on his. Beneath her calm feminine mask, rage seethes.

"I ain't got no husband!" she barks. With a quick rustle, she leaps to her feet and storms off. Before she gets far, she turns back and spits on him. "You tell that no-good brother-in-law of yours this is all his doin'! And he'll burn in hell for... for what he's done..." Mrs. Fallscrow scowls, waving her hands over her head. With that, she hustles off.

W.H. returns to the bar and holds up his empty glass.

"Don't worry about her," the bartender says. "She'll settle in. They get real feisty like that when they first start out in the business."

W.H. doesn't like the way the man says business. "Ahh... what business would that be?"

"Ladies of the night, of course." The bartender winks.

"Who, her?" W.H. scoffs in disbelief. "I wouldn't be talking like that if I were you, Mister. Her husband is likely to sock you in the mouth."

The bartender chuckles and adds a second shot glass.
"Were you a friend of his?"
W.H. nods.
"Sorry for your loss."

CHAPTER 97

Dark clouds swirl in and bring the day's activities to a close. Thunder shakes the wavy windowpanes, even though the sky is blue. White clouds are tinged with gray and then quickly blacken as though they were mixed with ink and tossed on a blue canvas. A crack of lightning forks like a snake's tongue. Its powerful flash blinds everyone who sees it. An electric gleam, a crack of thunder, and an avalanche of rain begins to pour. It swells up through the floorboards in a muddy mess.

"My loss?" W.H. questions.

The bartender nods, then throws back a shot.

"Hey, what do you mean my *loss?*"

"A feller came in here with gold. Got a card game going. She begged her husband not to play, but he was so distraught over the loss of their child he got to gambling their savings away."

A flash of lightning illuminates his face in electric blue-white light.

"Who had the gold?"

"Fella calls himself Malice Mike."

Thunder rolls across the sky.

"You don't say?"

"Yep. Her husband was on the up-and-up. Played pretty good. But that feller and a few others got all liquored up. One thing led to another, and the one they call Malice let slip his gun. Poor fella died the next morning. We wanted to plant him that night, but the ground was frozen solid."

W.H. can't believe what he's hearing. Images flash in his mind of the couple doting on their baby. He thinks back to the train ride and cringes with waves of empathy when he thinks of how loving the family was.

"Where is he now?"

"Body is up in the attic. Didn't you hear me say ground is frozen solid?"

"Her husband is in the attic?"

"That's where we keep the dead till spring. I can hear her up there crying at night. Most pitiful noise you ever heard. Anywho, life goes on. He lost all her savings, so she's got to earn her living somehow."

"Where is Malice Mike?"

"Sheriff locked him up in jail."

"When did all this occur?"

"Week before last."

"I reckon I'll head on over and pay him a visit," W.H. grumbles, sliding his black hat off the counter and placing it firmly on his head. When he opens the flimsy door, lightning touches down and strikes a horse and its rider. The man convulses and the horse neighs. Their smoking bodies fall to the ground, never to rise again.

"On second thought, I don't wanna end up in an attic." W.H. returns to his warm barstool.

***

Later, at the sheriff's jail cell, W.H. finds a pitiful youth sitting behind bars on a small cot. He licks his fingers and turns pages in the Bible.

"How you holding up?" W.H. asks Malice Mike.

"You should have never lent me that money."

"What money?"

"I shouldn't have insisted. It's just that I thought I could double your investment."

"What investment?"

"The gold. I figured I would have to double your investment to cover your medical expenses. Wasn't my fault that feller got all uppity on me."

"You mean you took some of my gold?" W.H. shouts.

The sheriff interrupts. "Y'all need to keep the peace." He pats his pistol.

"Yes, sir," W.H. says, tipping his black hat.

"Who gave you my gold?" W.H. hisses through the bars.

"Maybelle. But don't be sore at her. It was me that insisted. Ain't like you didn't owe me. I saved your life that night you fell down in the snow. Injuns was gonna scalp you, but I stopped them dead to rights."

A memory stirs. W.H. sees the Indian family in his mind.

"What about the woman and the boy?"

"Ah, you might not want to ask about that," Malice Mike says with a wink. "Folks from the posse could still have sore feelings."

"All right, then. How much did you lose?"

Malice Mike gurgles. "All of it."

"Let me see if I can get this straight. You killed a man who was a friend of mine and lost a couple thousand dollars' worth of gold. Is that the gist?"

Malice nods. "My sins are forgiven me. Says so right here in the Bible."

"Is that a fact?"

"That is a righteous fact!"

"Then why are you behind them bars?"

"Well, I won't be for long. Pa is coming to fetch me. He used the remainder of the gold to hire a lawyer and set bail. Should be here any minute to spring me out."

"What?!"

Malice extends his hand between the bars. "Thanks for being your brother's keeper."

***

Rick Darling rides out to meet the foreman of the Saratoga Springs Hotel. When he arrives, he isn't pleased with what he sees.

"Why are these warped planks lying on the ground same as last week?"

"Wind keeps blowin' 'em down. No use in putting 'em up if the wind's just going to blow them back down. Ferry ain't brought materials," a red-bearded man named Patrick "Patty" O'Malley responds in a thick Irish accent. He wears a brown derby hat with a green feather in it. He grips his suspenders and bites down on his cigar like he's preparing to take a punch to the gut.

"Why ain't the ferry come?"

"Ask the wire man. He was out here day before last searching for you."

"You know I live maybe an hour's walk outside town. One would think as the foreman you would have the fortitude to contact me and keep your supervisor abreast of the goings-on here."

"Aiye. That may be." Patty's answer is an almost indistinguishable brogue. "But then who would be here making sure the workers don't strip the beams out and sell them to all these immigrants thieving for wood?"

Rick Darling wastes no time. He leaps on his horse and sprints over to the bank. He props the door open for a mother and her young. He takes off his hat and bows as they exit. When they clear the opening, they giggle when he winks at the young lady. Like hens, the women flutter off. Rick Darling doesn't take his eyes off the ladies even as he enters the bank.

"Morning, Darling," the telegraph man says when Rick raps his fingers on the counter.

"I'm advised by my foreman that you have a message for me?"

The telegraph man disappears beneath the counter. He lifts a box and sifts through it till he finds the message.

"You could save me the trouble and just tell me what it says."

"You don't want to read it for yourself?"

"I prefer you saving me the trouble. I'll make it worth your while if you keep it a secret."

The telegraph man opens the envelope and reads,

"Request denied. Improper procedure per our agreed-upon terms. (*STOP.*) Be advised, board is gravely concerned. (*STOP.*) Funds are frozen till further review. (*END OF MESSAGE.*)"

Rick bristles and snatches the note with a swipe of his hand. His eyes flash with an angry spark as he briskly turns about and marches into the street.

CHAPTER 98

Back at the cabin W.H. sits at the breakfast table with his soon-to-be father-in-law while Maybelle busily scurries about, finalizing a pot of coffee.

"But, Pa, what you're asking just don't make sense. We both want to be married, so why can't we just do it?"

"I've told you, Maybelle, your services rendered to this gentleman while he was ill must be paid in full before you can have your pappy's blessing. Is your time worth nothing? The whole time you were cooking and cleaning here, guess what I was doing."

"I'd prefer not to know! What with all the poor children the town has lost to the scarlet fever and whatnot. It's more than a female mind can handle." Maybelle presses her hand to her head and whirls like she's going to faint.

"Far be it from me to remind a daughter that her father was without while she was living in the lap of luxury. You know, dearest one, I hope when you have children, they treat you with more kindness than you've treated your old pappy."

Maybelle drops the coffeepot on the table and glares at her father. "Don't speak to me of children!" She uses a hand warmer to protect her bare hand as she snatches it and gives W.H. the distinct impression that she hasn't decided whether to pour it in the general's cup or over his head.

"Now, darling, you just calm yourself down and think of the children," the general says, pointing at her belly.

"At this rate, ain't gonna be no children, dearest *Father!*"

"Half cup for me, hold the sugar. Sugar!" The general winks at his daughter, then gulps.

"So, just for the sake of argument, what is it you calculate the bill to be?" W.H. asks, breaking a corn cake into small pieces and tossing it into his mouth.

"Glad you asked! I figure five hundred dollars oughta settle the debt."

Maybelle huffs and presses her hands to her hips. Her protruding lip hangs low enough to step on.

"Don't be upset, darling," her father says with a nudge. "I'll give you half as dowry."

She relaxes.

"Why not just call it splits, then?" W.H. asks.

"Appearances, my good man. Did you know General Washington lost more battles than he won?"

"Is that American history?" W.H. asks.

"Of course. What do they teach you boys up North?" the general prods.

"Well, we receive a general history of the crown. Arithmetic. Algebra. Latin. The sciences. Fine arts. Some—"

"That's nice." The general cuts him off. "Let me give you your first lesson, college boy. General Washington kept up the appearance that he was winning the war, when in fact he was enlisting the help of the French."

"So who are the equivalent of the French in the deal, Pa?" Maybelle snatches a strip of bacon and chews on it as she struggles with another piece of her father's puzzle.

"You give me five hundred dollars at church where everyone can see it. I kick back fifty percent for the dowry, keep fifty percent for my services, and you establish yourself as one of the richest men in town."

"Pa, that's stupid. Everyone already thinks he's the richest man in town."

"Why don't we just call it even with all those legal fees? No need for pretense," W.H. proposes.

Maybelle rolls her eyes. "He just don't understand how things work down here, Pa."

The general tilts his head to the side. "Can I be held responsible for your money-lending ways?"

"Pa's got a point, hun. People would be more likely to give us credit if they think there's more money on the way."

"What will that do?" W.H. inquires.

"I'm glad you asked. It will inch construction along and maybe even finish a few rooms. Then you can let the rooms out and use the rent to cover materials. That way, if your investors back out, you'll be protected."

"I don't think we will have anything to worry about." W.H. folds his arms and leans back confidently.

"Enough business at my table, gentlemen. Which of you is going to say grace?"

"Him!" they both say and point at each other.

"Fine. I'll say it again. Dear Lord. Thank you for this home and all the provisions in it. Thank you for looking out for us and blessing us in these dark times. Protect us as we go about our business that the savages will move along and leave us be to be peaceful plantation owners. Amen."

"We are not a plantation," W.H. corrects his fiancé.

"What did they teach you in college? Kansas-Nebraska Act nullifies the Missouri Compromise," the general corrects him.

"So?" W.H. pushes his plate away, losing his appetite.

"Hun, it means the Western territories can decide for themselves whether they'll be slave states or not. It's just labor, that's all. No real harm."

"Not here! I'll take us back to Canada."

"Doodle-dee-dee. Let's fight one battle at a time?" Maybelle says, clasping her hands together and pressing them to her lips.

W.H. retires to his room. As the day wanes on, he draws some of the things he sees. When the sun sets, he's pleased with his pictures.

Feb 23, 1860

Dearest Uncle,

I may have spoken too soon when I said I was in love. A body ought to get to know a pretty girl before jumping head over heels into a marriage. 'Course, I can't hardly remember proposing or lending money to her family. Not to say that they aren't good and reputable people. It's just that their ways are not our ways. The snow is high and the frost fairies are in full sprint. They've covered all the trees with crystals and pulled their white winter blankets high all around us.

I am again in good health and of sound mind. I didn't want to worry you, so I didn't send any word of my sickness. Had a terrible battle with scarlet fever, and though my chest is tight, my throat isn't so sore. I have had the pleasure of discussing business with the Eastern Capitalist Company. Many false representations by builders and land squatters are plaguing these parts. Good men are destroying their reputations by promising construction at prices so low it can't even be conceived. I believe the plow of deceit has plunged its greedy hook into the earth of every farmer here. Moral hazard is bound to spring up like a terrible weed strangling most of these folks' opportunities. All because of false representation.

While W.H. makes his journal entry, his peaceful evening is disturbed by a shouting voice.

"COME ON OUT, COWARD!" Rick Darling shouts. He's mounted on his horse, along with all the laborers, mounted on their horses.

"Now what?" W.H. grunts. He slides into his trousers, one leg at time, then slips his shirt on. He pokes his finger through the candleholder and heads for the bedroom door.

When he opens the door, Maybelle is dressed in her white nightgown and armed with her double-barreled shotgun.

"I'm kin of Daniel Boon. I ain't going down without a fight!" She cocks the triggers and pats her nightcap down.

"Come on out, or we'll tear the roof off!" Rick Darling holds up an iron treble hook with a long trailing chain that's attached to his saddle.

"What do they want?" W.H. asks the general, who sits up on his bed-couch, a blanket covering his legs.

"W.H., we just want to talk!" Rick Darling yells.

"Sounds like they wanna talk to you," the general answers, rubbing the sleep out of his eyes.

"Thanks!" W.H. smirks. He goes into his bedroom and sees a torch glowing back at him through the wavy glass. A pale face searches the room and spots him grabbing his pistol belt.

"He's going for his guns!" the man shouts. Stepping back, he holds his rifle up and takes aim at W.H.

CHAPTER 99

W.H. quickly blows out his candle and steps out of the room.

BANG.

BANG.

BANG.

The front door rattles from the rap of an angry fist.

W.H. runs over to the fireplace and grabs his rifle. He chambers a round, then aims at the door.

"Maybelle, you move on over behind the..."

Before he can finish his sentence, she flips the breakfast table over and ducks behind it. She pokes the gun's barrels over the top and makes herself as small a target as possible.

The general pulls the blanket back and unleashes a slew of curse words. His nightgown drops down to his ankles as he pushes his feet into his boots.

"Have it your way! Set the hooks, boys! If he ain't coming out, we're going in!"

"Don't do that!" W.H. shouts.

The general walks over to the door and opens it. "Good eve, sir. Might I have a word?" he asks as he goes to step outside.

Rick Darling and his posse point their pistols in his face and force their way into the cabin.

"Howdy, feller." Rick Darling holsters his weapon once he's in.

"Howdy," W.H. says, lowering his rifle.

Maybelle keeps her barrels pointed straight at Rick's face.

"You got a letter here says your board revokes further means." Rick Darling holds out the telegraph.

W.H. snatches it up. He strains to read the message.

"Well, what did you think was going to happen? You didn't go through the proper procedures."

"We have procedures of our own. Gonna need you to be at the church in the morning."

"For what?"

"Club meeting."

W.H. looks over Rick's shoulder. "Are they going to be there?"

"Count on it. They are part of the club."

Rick puts his gentleman's hat on and bows. "Sorry to disturb you folks, but we felt the invitation needed emphasis."

Maybelle stands up and rests her shotgun on her hip.

Rick snickers. "Woman, in your condition, you shouldn't be playing with cannons."

"You get yourself on outta here! Women in my condition has no condition except the condition to which she was born."

With that, Rick withdraws. He mounts his horse and leads the posse away.

***

The next day, Maybelle is dressed for town. The cold winter has forced her to alter her gowns. Everything must have sleeves now. She places her boot in the stirrup and reaches for W.H.'s hand.

"It ain't proper, Maybelle!" her father imbues with stronger determination than his daughter.

"Oh, doodle-dee-do, Pa! I've had enough of you!" Maybelle takes W.H.'s hand. He pulls her up, and she shifts so she's sitting sidesaddle. "There, see. It's just fine!"

As the two ride to town, W.H. feels his cough returning.

"Oh, darling, perhaps we should have sojourned another day." Maybelle wraps her arms around his waist and squeezes tightly.

He doesn't respond. In turn, Maybelle decides not to say another word to punish him the rest of the way to town. Both have plans of their own and neither are without weapons.

When they enter the church, they find that they are not the only ones to bring firearms and bowie knives.

"Howdy," Pastor Dan says, extending his hand. Even his hip is weighted with iron and lead.

W.H. shakes hands, but rather than a friendly greeting, he urges the pastor to initiate the proceedings.

The laborers, the club's director, and even the club's sheriff sit in a circle around the chair.

"Let's get on with this!" Sheriff Davis says, tapping his badge.

"What's going on?" Maybelle asks.

"Due process!" Rick Darling informs her. He closes a book he was pretending to read.

W.H. sits down, and no sooner does he sit than Rick Darling lays into him, leaving several insults and charges at once. "Listen to me, you four-eyed thieving runt! You got just one chance to save your backside."

W.H. pushes his glasses up and remains calmer than Rick expected. "What's that, eh?"

In a very low, nearly whispered tone, Rick hisses, "Get on your horse and take me back to Canada, where I can address your board of investors."

"Ha! Ha! Ha!" W.H. can't help but laugh. "It's directors, you idiot."

Rick Darling whispers, "If these men find out you claim jumped, you're going to find yourself in a pickle."

"CLAIM JUMPER?" Patrick O'Malley, the foreman, sneers. He scratches his burly chest and squints his eyes.

W.H. slaps his knee. "What in tarnation are you talking about?"

Rick Darling stands up stiff as a board and steps away from W.H. like he's confessed to carrying the plague.

"What's this about claim jumping?" Sheriff Davis asks.

"That's right," Rick Darling continues. "This man has two claims. I can prove it right here." He reaches inside his coat and removes a set of papers. "His signature is on both the Saratoga Springs claim and my Ponderosa Pine claim."

Rick hands the sheriff signed papers. The husky man flips through them to the signature.

"Is that your signature?" Sheriff Davis asks.

"Well, that's my mark, but you can't expect me to own up to it." W.H. chuckles.

"And why is that?" Rick inquires, looking at the sheriff.

"I was sick with scarlet fever when this feller harassed me for a signature."

"Is that true?" the sheriff asks. "Was he under duress?"

Rick shrinks down, and his neck disappears like a turtle pulling his head into its shell.

"Sure it's true. Listen, gentlemen, this man can't be trusted. Ask him about the Indian family I was detaining on New Year's Eve. They had a young boy with them. Where is he and his mother? Why was there no trial? See what he says about that. I bet he took their scalps for bounty."

The room goes silent. Men sit up and shuffle in their seats like flames are lapping at their legs.

"Sir! I protest! I'll tell you what happened that night. This man lost his gull. He's gutless. Turned green in the heat of battle. I saw cowardice with my own two eyes. Had the drop on the Injuns and just stood there frozen with fear. I ain't never seen—"

"Mr. Darling, with all due respect, shut the hellfire up!" Sheriff Davis orders. "Half of us was there, Mister. Anyone see a child or an Injun family?"

CHAPTER 100

"Not me," Patty mumbles.

"I was there and I found you passed out from fear," Sheriff Davis accuses W.H.

"I won't be tolerating false claims, Sheriff. I was sick with scarlet fever!" W.H. defends himself.

"Be that as it may or may not be. We found ourselves surrounded by Indians. The only reason we caught the murderers left at the barn was because the larger war party was off looting the Smiths' residence. My deputy and I conducted a thorough investigation after the attack. We tracked them all the way back to Weeping Water, where we were told by their surviving women and children that the tribe had previously returned from an unsuccessful hunt. Do you know what happens when Injuns go hungry? They raid! And guess what? They did what savages do. They see our farms as a source of sustenance when they fail in their hunts. Now I don't know why, or how, but this time they went a mite further. They murdered for pleasure, and every Pawnee savage that night did their part. So don't even hint at a massacre. We served them right good prairie justice. Get my meaning, feller?" The sheriff points his chubby finger in W.H.'s chest.

"Whoa! What's going on here, Sheriff?" Maybelle hollers, not liking the men's twisted expressions.

"This don't concern you, ma'am." The sheriff silences her as the men grow uneasy.

"Now, see here. We were attacked. Fannie came here to this church seeking refuge covered in the blood of her children. I can stand before my creator with a clear conscience for my part that night," the pastor says, checking each man's nodding face. "How about you address the charge of claim jumping and let sleeping dogs lie?"

"You buying that, Sheriff?" W.H. asks.

"I'll tell you what I am buying, feller. You don't have a real name. You come into town waving money around you say isn't yours. You signed for two claims and then report you have one. There's just one thing we do with claim jumpers like you!"

"Dissolve his claim, Sheriff, and divvy up his parcels for payment!" Patty shouts. His unpaid laborers shout in support.

"Let's not be too hasty, gentlemen," Rick Darling interrupts. "I say we get more gold to finish the Saratoga Springs Hotel before—"

"Let me tell you something. I'm the law in these parts, duly elected, might I add," the sheriff interrupts, poking his finger in Rick's chest, "and what I say goes! Got it, carpetbagger?"

"If that's so, then show me the town charter," W.H. looks at Maybelle. She shrugs and clasps her hands together.

The men grumble and exchange doubting expressions.

"You can't show a charter because there ain't no charter. Without legal documents to establish this town, you are not a real Sheriff. This is not a legal court. It's just a mish-mash of self-interested land grabbers exercising greed."

"Way I see it, you got two choices, Mr. Moneybags. Relent your claim, the timber, the rock, and all mineral rights so's we can divvy it up among these unpaid laborers, or face the wrath."

"What's the wrath?" W.H. gulps.

"You have more than enough with one of your two properties to satisfy the debt and continue construction or get run out of town. What'll it be?"

W.H. stands up. He snatches the papers out of the sheriff's hand. "I own one property. I reside on the Ponderosa Pine claim, and I have a stake in the Saratoga Springs Hotel. As far as I know, those are joined properties. That's what these papers say. That's what I was told when my fever broke. Am I to be made a fool of? Oh, why in tarnation am I explaining myself to you? You're no judge and jury. None of yins is the law."

All eyes shift to Rick Darling.

"Well, that can't be."

"What?" W.H. gasps.

"I believe I gave you the choice between one deal or the other, and it was clear that you wanted the home *and* the hotel stake. That's why I relented my claim on the house and took my partial stake in the hotel."

He turns. "Preacher, wouldn't you agree that one and a half claims is the exact same thing as owning two claims?"

"You lying snake!" Maybelle scowls.

The preacher folds his arms and shakes his head. "There you have it. By W.H.'s own admission, he lives on Ponderosa Pines and staked the hotel. He owns two properties. Nothing new under the sun! Just regular old greed."

"Not only that, but you owe all these fine men wages for labor."

"How can I owe for labor that hasn't been performed? After my fever broke, I couldn't even find the construction site."

"You promised us pay, even if materials were delayed!" Patty shouts so loud his freckled face turns red to match his hair.

Several men shift in their chairs. Their long faces and shifting eyes hint at a swelling tempest.

"How could I make a deal like that when I was bedridden with the fever?"

Rick raises his hands to calm the situation. "We are not educated men like yourself. We are honest, hardworking men."

"Ya!" the laborers shout.

"We do a job. We expect to be paid. Now, it ain't my signature on that spread. That's yours and yours alone. Work was done. Where's the pay?"

Cheers erupt so loud the windows shake.

"Pay is a separate matter. Let's get back to this claim. Now, maybe you didn't know you was in a raw deal and I'll give you that. But you know now, and the way I see it, I was elected to do a job. Law says you cannot have two claims. You have two claims. If you relent one of the two, you can walk right on out of here."

"And if I don't?"

Patty holds up a lasso.

"You can't be serious. You boys ain't gonna murder me. I ain't done nothing wrong!"

Maybelle screams and clasps her hands to her lips. Her eyes are so wide they look like they're going to spring out of her head. She shakes her head back and forth.

"I'll give every man here one percent ownership of the hotel if he continues work and forgives this man of his sins." Rick Darling does his best to lighten the blow.

"We are at church, and I have an appetite for forgiveness," the pastor says, taking his pound of flesh. He raises his hand. "You can count me in."

Most men raise their hands to get their cut. The ones that don't look to W.H. to get paid.

"I need more prompt, energetic working *men*! Those of you who want to earn a living, follow me." Rick glances at W.H. "The rest of you boys can settle your debt with this wimp. Best of luck, partner," Rick says as he puts on his top hat and marches his twiggy legs and narrow frame past Maybelle.

"Mister, are you gonna settle your debt with us or not?" Patty rallies, with laborers closing in on W.H.

"Heck no! I never made that deal, and now that I see how business has been conducted, I'm taking the deal off the table."

"Does that mean you'll relent your claim on the hotel?" Sheriff Davis asks with a focused glare.

"I put half my gold into that endeavor. I can't forsake my claim now. I need to find new laborers or get to work myself."

"Boo! Boo!" the laborers shout. They reach for him to do him harm, but the sheriff manages to push the men back.

"I already told you boys that's another matter. I gotta settle this claim. Now, go on and git."

"We'll be seeing you in town, skulker!" Patty shouts, dragging his finger across his neck.

Kneeling down so he's eye to eye with W.H., the sheriff picks up the lasso and says, "What's it going to be?"

"Please understand, sir, I have a financial obligation to the board. I have to represent their interests. I'm not rich. That ain't my gold. It belongs to officers of the Hudson's Bay Company. I can't go back to them and tell them I let their gold be stolen and used improperly."

"Then give up the house."

"I can't do that, either. I'm recovering, and I believe it was part of the original deal."

The sheriff's head droops. He looks up and clucks his tongue. "Have it your way. Fetch them buckskins. We got us a dunkin' party in the Big Muddy, boys."

Maybelle leaps to her feet. She screams so loud it attracts the attention of the preacher's wife. The righteous woman puts her arms around Maybelle, and with the help of her four daughters, scurries out of the church and into their home.

So many hands seize W.H. so quickly, his brief struggle is useless. In a matter of moments he's detained and stripped naked.

A set of decorated Indian buckskin breeches and blouse replace his fine pants and cotton shirt.

"What is this?"

The men get him to his feet and slip a rope loop around his waist. When it's in place, the sheriff pulls it tight and shouts, "If you're gonna act savage, we're gonna treat you savage! Savage!"

***

Standing in moccasins in the snowbank of a wide, muddy river, W.H. shivers as chunks of ice break apart and float past him. His mind plays over the old rhyme from elementary school, "M-i-double-s-i-double-s-i-double-p-i."

"Don't do this, boys."

"RELENT YOUR CLAIM!"

W.H. shakes his head. "You'll kill me. This is murder. I'm sick."

Without another word, Patty pushes W.H. onto the ice.

"Stop! Please, I'm begging you!"

Fractures splinter and spider web under his feet. He turns around to plead with his captors but falls through the ice.

CHAPTER 101

Freezing water seizes W.H.'s lungs. He kicks his legs and tries to find the icy ledge he fell through. His frozen hands push against the ice and finally find the edge. He tries to pull himself up, but his hands break off more ice instead. He feels a painful jerk at the waist. The men fish him back to the bank.

"RELENT YOUR CLAIM!" the sheriff orders.

"You're killing me!"

The sheriff fires his pistol, forcing W.H. off the bank and back onto the ice. A bullet shatters the ice near W.H.'s feet. He submerges and feels his body convulse. The temperature is so low, it burns rather than freezes.

The second time the posse take a little longer to fish him out.

"RELENT YOUR CLAIM, THIEF!"

W.H. slumps over and struggles for air. Before he can answer, they force him back into the water. This time he's only waist-deep. Every muscle shakes. His skin goes pale white. He looks like a corpse.

"We can slide this rope a little higher if you like," the sheriff says, pointing at W.H.'s neck.

"Gentlemen, I see my error. Please forgive me. I relent my claim."

"That'll do," the sheriff says.

When they pull W.H. to shore, the pastor wraps a blanket around him. "The truth will set you free, my son. You'll see God's hand in this."

W.H. glares at the pastor and begs the men to take him to the saloon.

"Not sure they serve your kind, but I hear there's a new lady. Her reputation is that she'll do anything for a buck. Maybe she'll take care of your sorry butt!" Sheriff Davis hollers.

The men laugh devilishly, then hoist W.H. up in a wagon. The guest of honor at the "sore parade" was one Canadian man known to the newcomers as W.H. He rode into town with confidence and pride. His status has since fallen. His new pals parade him through town, where twenty or so kids make faces and throw rocks.

Hmmm... a couple of months ago there was no young 'uns. Now Saratoga has a bolstering twenty of the worst youth I've ever seen, W.H. thinks. No passerby passes up the opportunity to shout an insult or loose a spit at the guest of honor at the humiliation parade. Fury spreads through W.H. like a wildfire till he reaches the last stop, the saloon he requested.

W.H. looks around a town that in just a few weeks has rapidly filled with gawking strangers. Town elites dressed in fine black suits point silver-handled canes and laugh at him. Their tall gentlemen's hats lean back, and their faces make the most wretched mocking expressions, which seem to hurt worse than the freezing water. A store near the Saratoga has just gone up. He watches two clerks finalize their storefront. One is Cory Collins and the other is his cousin Parley Johnson. *That should be me,* W.H. thinks to himself. *I should be opening a business and thriving. Why am I freezing and dying?*

Loose ladies are more than welcoming. They hold the door open while W.H. stumbles into the bar. They oblige him because he has a reputation of wealth. Emilia Fallscrow tends to him out of pure pity.

***

A couple of hours later, Emilia enters the small upstairs room where W.H. is resting. She sets some soup and bread down at his bedside table.

"I couldn't believe it. What happened to you?" W.H. asks.

She bristles, then turns her back to him.

"This is no place for a lady as fine as yourself."

He hears her sob before she straightens up.

"No, no, it is not."

"I'm so sorry for your loss. Tell me what happened to Mr. Fallscrow."

"Shot dead right beneath these floorboards." She goes silent. W.H. debates on whether or not he should press the matter.

"I told him not to go out. Said he needed strong drink to forget about the baby. I told him he was safe by me and that my sorrow would eventually heal. Even said we could try for another baby. He wouldn't have any of it. He yelled at me. Grabbed the money bag and came here."

W.H. stands up and puts his hands on her shoulders to console her. She jerks away.

"Please leave my pride intact. I couldn't bear it if I was expected to bare all to someone I respect."

"You misunderstand me, madam. Please go on."

"The one called Malice Mike claims he caught my husband cheating. Drew those pearly pistols and shot him dead. Next day I came searching for him. Found him up in the attic, wrapped in a bloody sheet. I didn't believe it at first, but the bartender pulled the sheet back, and his pale face didn't lie. It was him all right. Seeing as how we had debts, I didn't know how to settle them. Couldn't pay for a wire to alert my family. Debtors pressed and said they would throw me into debtors' prison if I couldn't settle. So I did what I had to. I ain't proud of it, but there it is. Plain as day for all to see."

"I'm so sorry."

She turns toward him and rests the most wounded eyes he's ever seen on him.

"I don't need pity, Mister. You'd be in your right mind to leave this place and not press them. They claim to be Christian, but as you can see from how harshly they've handled us, that just ain't so."

"And where should we go?"

"We? Ha! Don't make me laugh. I settled my debt and earned enough to buy a ticket to Kansas. Smallpox just hit the town and I can't face my family, so I'm moving to Lawrence, where sure as you are born I'll make it as a cattle ranch worker!"

She abruptly turns and walks away.

W.H. puts his hands together and thanks God that his sickness hasn't returned. The belles at the saloon nurse him back to health. He pays for a coach to take him back to the cabin and leaves a little extra something for Emilia.

How am I supposed to explain all this to Maybelle? When he opens the creaking door, he finds an empty house. The furniture is gone.

"Woof!" Bingo barks when W.H. enters his bedroom. What little belongings he has left are neatly packed and on top of his journal in the center of an empty room.

W.H. reads the first line aloud. "March 1, 1858. Dearest John."

Bingo whimpers.

"Who's John?" W.H. wonders as he reads on.

I regret to inform you that my father has called off our engagement. He says you ain't fit to be my husband on account of your hoity-toity ways. As it says in the Good Book, children must honor their father. I would return the ring, but he says it is my due since I took care of you and all. I have accepted the furniture to cover the balance of payment. Please do not come looking for me, as I have accepted another proposal and will have been wed by the time you read this. If you pass through town, you may refer to me as Mrs. Darling Burger. Forgive me. Pa explained your cowardice during the raid. How you could show your face is beyond me. I shall look to see you no more.

P.S. We had some leftovers from last night. In the stove you will find fried bread, meat, corn cakes, and Mohawk butter.

P.S.S. Your wash is hanging on the rack outside. We collected enough rain water for a bath if you so desire. I have secured your papers in the saddlebag, of which are the deed to the home and the acreage.

May God's grace be sufficient for your soul. Love always, Maybelle Montgomery.

W.H. walks over to the stove and kicks it. The cast iron doesn't move an inch because sturdy bolts hold it to the floor. "I suppose the only reason you're still here is 'cause you were bolted down." He shouts at the stove.

Bingo whimpers. *Poor, poor master.*

"Guess I got everything I asked for."

W.H. opens the stove door and removes the plate. He tosses the corn cakes to Bingo and then sits down on the empty floor to enjoy his last supper.

After dinner he opens his journal and leans against the weathered pine wall.

"Good Book says, 'Pride before the fall,' Bingo… I do not want to be the prodigal son, but we have very little gold left, and if we don't return with wolf hides, we might be laughed out of town a second time. How about we be more like King David and slay us a giant."

Bingo yawns and tilts his head to the side.

W.H. wets his pen and writes.

Dear Uncle,

By the time you read this journal, I will already be underway to my original destination. I was well cared for here, but my wife-to-be died of the consumption. Folks here believe the dead can rise up and feed off the blood of living relatives. For that reason I find it expedient to continue my adventure. I cannot write now, but I have decided to continue on to Cimarron. Saratoga is no longer a profitable prospect. Capital is limited and opportunities are secured by an irrational, armed, unreasonable mob mentality of men who have no real sense of law and order. Please send more gold so that I might be able to sustain myself.

Love always, your nephew.

With nothing left, W.H. scoops up his saddle and steps outside the cabin. He spots two large bald eagles building a nest in the tree struck by lightning. They pause and look at him as though his presence is an intrusion.

W.H. sighs and stomps toward Cotton. "And the eagles inherit the earth. Best of luck, partners. I'm going to get back to what I ought to have been doing this whole darn time! W.H. is my name and wolf hunting is my game!" he shouts at the majestic birds.

"Why, of all the stupid things I could have thought of, Bingo. A woman. Young 'uns. I hunt wolves. That's what I do. I ain't sure why the mighty eagle knows how to capture a lady friend and I don't. But I hope an Indian kills it and makes a war bonnet out of it and its young 'uns!"

He spits and straps the saddle to his horse. When he mounts Cotton, he scans the field. The sprouting grass indicates fertile soil. W.H. dismounts his horse. He stomps over to the barn and kicks in the door. There, in the dusty corner, he sees guinea sacks of corn seed. He snatches up a shovel and finds that the ground is frozen solid. He scatters the seed by hand. When he's finished, he eyeballs the shiny shovel.

"Most expensive shovel I've ever owned. I'm keeping this!" He fastens it to his bedroll and looks over the estate one last time. When he mounts Cotton, he declares, "God be my witness, I will never love again!" He whistles for Bingo. The collie comes running out of the barn, barking in eager excitement.

If ever I came close to enjoying a full life of smiling faces, this was it.

He turns and kicks at Cotton's side and gets the horse moving as he takes in one last over-the-shoulder glance. The sensation of a life he so desperately wanted causes tears to well up in his eyes. He's quick to dismiss them and not feel too sorry for himself. Heaven forbid a tear should actually spill over and stream down his untarnished cheek.

CHAPTER 102

Spring arrives. Brilliant green stems bud and blossom into beautiful prairie flowers. Colors of every kind litter the mountains freely. Wild Indian corn sprouts up through the mushy ground and lines the riverbanks.

The wolves hunt conservatively by their estimation—perhaps not by the ranchers', considering the boost in reward posters. And the doubling bounty hunter population. But the ranchers have little time. Between herding their stock and fighting legal battles over water rights, landowners overlooked the outlaws of the Currumpaw.

As the spring of 1860 begins, the reward is at a whopping three hundred dollars. Enough to buy a house, twenty acres of land, tools for farming, and plenty for savings. Though many coyotes are mistakenly killed, and bounty paid for them also, not a single wolf hide is nailed to the sheriff's furry wall.

Time passes. By end of spring, the reward triples, not because the wolves have killed more cattle, but because the animals are grazing closer to home. People of the Currumpaw do not feel safe having predators lurk around their homes. One thing the townspeople can all agree on is an overwhelming, ominous feeling of one of their own sharing the skin of mortal by day and wolf fur by night.

When cowboys and strangers pass through, they find their way to the Handy Dandy Hardware Store. Elias Mather, the hardware store owner, has quite a few words to describe the goings-on in Cimarron, one Currumpaw town.

Here's what he says: "Rifle sales have doubled. Ammunition grows wings and flies off the shelves quick as I can get it. Traps, traps, and more traps go the same way as the ammo. Best be careful with those traps, folks. Couple fellers got themselves stuck and died from exposure. Been sellin' kerosene by the gallon. Can't make candles fast enough. Got my daughter working on candles night and day. Though the profit margin is smaller, we sell more, so candles are our biggest moneymakers! Wagon shipments come and go just as quick as I get supplies on the shelf. I just can't seem to get the supplies fast enough. Soon that won't be a problem, 'cause the railroad will be connecting to Raton. Although a wagon will still have to fetch a shipment, I can get my shelves stocked within a week instead of a month. Jeremiah, the blacksmith who sells nails to the railroad, would know. He says, 'The rail will get sugar, coffee, soap of every kind ready as we need 'em.' Though most folks here is suffering, me and mine ain't. We're doin' just fine, thank you for asking!"

"Glad to hear it, Mike. Will we be seeing you and Delilah at church this Sunday?" a tall rancher with a full beard and a broad chest asks, adjusting the belt beneath his bulging belly.

"Looking forward to it, Tex."

Tex leans on the counter and says in a low tone, "You know, some folks let their superstitions get the better of them and moved on to California."

"Is that so?" Mike asks, knowing full well how many people have vacated. He doesn't say anything, but he glances at the fully stocked paint cans and wonders how long he'll have to hold them before marking them down.

Tex's big blue eyes shift back and forth. He leans close to Mike and nearly whispers, "Some folks even believe they have a desert migration. Folks is blaming their existing troubles on a more menacing belief. That the wolf is no wolf at all, but a werewolf. Read an article out of the *Evening Star* about a Mrs. Lorraine Kelsey. She claims she took chunks out of him with buckshot."

"Well, I'll be..." Mike motions with his finger for Tex to move in closer. He whispers, "I probably shouldn't say this, but ranchers and farmers say the same thing. Of course, this is all hogwash. The attacks are seasonal, and the kills are too many for just one wolf. Ain't no way it's just one wolf, but rather a large pack of wild coyotes. Fifty, maybe a hundred. I'd say that many could take down cattle. They hunt wherever they can find food. It is as simple as that."

"Just the same, I'd like to pick up a rifle and some six-shooters, as soon as you have some in stock. Say, will you be getting those new cartridge revolvers?"

Mr. Elias Mather nods. "It's all anyone wants these days. Ball and powder are antiquated." He shrugs and says, "Maybe it is a werewolf. You'll be needin' powder and ball till those rifles and pistols come in. Better buy double while you can. I got a secret stash." Elias winks and taps on his nose.

Later that night, the same conversation occurs. The same two men sit at the bar and clack glasses. They down yellow ale like it's a race. The hushed tones are now shouting matches.

Here in the Cowboy Hall, the unexplainable has a way of turning from fact to grand fiction. The result is that fewer and fewer patrons return. Week after week, folks pull out of town. Most take off in the middle of the night so they won't have to face the protests of friends or family.

The banker, Fred, is just about as well informed as Elias. In some ways his information is better, since some folks would put their keys inside an envelope instead of a mortgage payment. Fred's teller had a name for them. He called them ringers. And when he found the envelopes, he would shake them and make them jingle as he carried them into Fred's office like one carries a dead mouse. 'Course, those folks pulled out in the middle of the night, too. And it wasn't long before the teller pushed his own ringer through the mail drop.

"A creeping recession is moving in like the angel of death," Fred said one day to his wife. Soon after, Fred's wife packed her bags, snuck out the window in the middle of the night, and left for California with a handsome cowboy.

Without marital obligations, Frank decided it was time for him to mail himself a ringer instead of a mortgage payment. He moved on to a little town back East, where a cousin who worked with Samuel Morse offered him a job selling the telegraph.

These are just some of the clippings a local paper reports. Of course, talk at the bar is legitimized by the printing press. A werewolf is much more sensational than a wolf, so folks collectively begin to whisper and believe that someone among them is a man by day and a ravenous monster by night. Across the Mississippi, the United States Union has dissolved. War is imminent between the North and the South.

CHAPTER 103

Again the harvest moon hangs in the sky and again the wolves return to the pine forest. As the pale moon's rays touch their fur, Kiowa and Anoki shape-shift into man and woman.

Anoki takes Kiowa's hand and smiles. She lowers her head and nudges for him to follow her. Without saying a word to the others, he follows her lead.

Walpi brushes his tail against Kida's snout. He motions for her to follow him.

Makes Trouble and Paw skinwalk into human form. They shrug, exchanging lonely expressions and heavy sighs.

"I am jealous of Kiowa and Walpi. Will you ask Onendah to change a woman for me?"

Paw shakes his head and rubs his chin. "You express how I feel. But he does not like when I ask him things, so will you ask him for us?"

Makes Trouble gasps, "I've never asked the medicine man for anything. I have no gift. We have only until dawn to find something he will like."

"I once filled his tepee with gifts and he told me I should have just asked. Yet I still cannot find the strength to do so. I am asking you, as a friend; summon the courage to ask. I will even help you raid a village for women if we need to."

Makes Trouble leans down and picks up a rock. "Let's trick him and tell him this a magic rock."

Paw laughs and pulls the bear hide to Onendah's medicine lodge back. He motions for Makes Trouble to go in first.

Inside the dark forest, Anoki and Kiowa's faces hover above the shadows.

Beneath the tall, swaying pines, Anoki gives Kiowa an inviting glance. Both being naked, he needs no real encouragement, but the invitation from his wife certainly heats things up.

"Kiss me and don't stop!" Anoki says, tilting her head back and tossing her hair. It lifts and spills around her shoulders in a wave of silky strands. "I long for mortal lips."

The crickets sing a symphony for the lovers.

Kiowa gently touches his lips to hers. His body keeps hers warm.

"I love touching you with my hands, little woman. It is a great gift. People do not know how lucky they are."

Flesh presses against flesh. Her long tresses tickle his arms and his long hair tickles hers. Each feels the sensation morph into tingling prickles. The little bumps make them shudder.

As best they can, the two lovers use their lips to turn seconds into hours.

Anoki giggles as they kiss and move their hands all over each other. She gasps for air and then whispers, "If I were to choose between loving you as a man or a wolf, I would prefer you as a man."

"Ha! Ha!" Kiowa laughs, honoring her wish for him to kiss her and not stop.

"Do you mock my heart?" Anoki pouts.

"No! I just realized what my uncle meant when he said love is blind."

"What?"

"We cannot see each other, yet love guides our way."

"Ha! Ha! Yes, love is blind. Give me more!"

Kiowa kisses his wife passionately. Each peck and thrust causes her to moan. She curls her legs around his waist. Time escapes them. They retire to blissful eternities where true love is blind, where passionate sparking pleasure ignites a flame that builds into a bonfire. She gasps and rocks back and forth. Her moans grow louder and louder.

Across the forest, Kida covers her mouth with her paw. She and Walpi lay beside each other.

"Your sister is howling a different song tonight."

Walpi whimpers and covers his ears. "Tell me when she stops."

"I sometimes wonder if you can make me howl like that," Kida teases, knowing that he can't hear her.

Inside the tepee, Makes Trouble struggles for words.

"What is it, Makes Trouble? I can see that something upsets you," Onendah says, lighting a long pipe. He sucks his wrinkled cheeks in with heavy puffs and gets the tobacco embers glowing. With each inhale the tobacco glows bright orange and illuminates deep cracks in his face. With each exhale, smoke clouds plume out the corners of his mouth and nostrils.

"I do not know how to ask you for what I need, so I wish to speak plainly," Makes Trouble says with a tremble in his voice. He sets the "magic rock" down in front of Onendah.

"I prefer plain speak. Your friend Paw here never seems to know what he wants, but he does bring good gifts," Onendah says, waving him on. "What is this that you have brought me?"

"It is a magic rock."

Onendah's face is expressionless.

Makes Trouble continues. "Paw and I want you to turn women into wives. And wives into wolves."

Onendah tilts his head back and laughs so hard, his face turns brighter than the glowing tobacco.

Is he laughing at my gift or at my request? Makes Trouble wonders.

Paw shrugs and looks away.

Outside the tent, Kida puts her paws on Walpi's and pushes them down, "They are finished."

"For now. They'll start again."

If a wolf could smile, she would.

"Kida," Walpi says with a defeated heave. He looks at her, then looks away. Then looks back at her, then looks away again. This goes on for some time before Kida finally says, "You look like you are sick."

Walpi nods. "I like that Anoki and Kiowa hold the flame of love."

"That is not what I expected to hear. But yes, they are so devoted to each other. It sickens me sometimes. Always I see her watching him on the hunt. Everyone seems pleased with their union. Everyone watches her all the time, and it makes me so mad."

"I want that to be me and you."

CHAPTER 104

Kida sits up and blinks rapidly. Her tail shifts back and forth. "You want me to be your little woman?"

"Did I say that out loud?"

Kida eagerly nods.

"Well, then, it is too late to pretend like my thoughts did not seep out of my head. Of course I love you! For all the things I lack in courage and struggle—"

Kida interrupts him. "Do you mean strength?"

"Yes, for everything I lack in strength, the Hopi are loyal to their women. To love is to give. I want to give you the rest of my time on this Fourth World. I want to put my hand in yours till we grow old and watch the flame of life flicker out in each other's eyes."

Kida looks dumbstruck. *Never have I heard such words. And somehow, these are all the words I have ever wanted to hear.* She leans forward, accentuating her beastly curves. "Why do you say, 'to love is to give'? Why not just say I love you, here is a gift?"

Walpi glances at her. He swallows hard and widens his wolf eyes to an obvious bulge. His bushy tail gives away his excitement. "Oh, it is how we Hopi speak of love. You know, to love your wife is to give her children. To love your mother is to give her food. To love your sister is to turn into a wolf and run wild with her."

Kida tilts her head down, then lets her eyes slowly travel up to his. She stretches out on her belly, exposing the curve of her hips. "I see. For me love is to take." Kida tilts her head, flattens her ears, and narrows her gaze.

Walpi's hands tremble. "Yes, okay. I also want you to take my Hopi blood and mix it with your blood, so that you can paint our faces on our children—I mean pups. Well, whatever they are, I want them to mix with you."

She tilts her head back so far, parts her lips part and bares her fangs. "This is how wolves smile." She whimpers.

He presses his forehead to hers. "I want to kiss you so bad!" Kida growls with excitement.

"I want you to kiss me!" Walpi whimpers.

"We can't kiss. We don't have lips."

"Then this is how we kiss. Brow to brow, eye to eye, staring into each other's souls."

"Wait. We can kiss."

"How?"

"Change!"

Kida stretches out and turns human. She does just as her mother taught her. Every alluring naked curve is exposed. Walpi's eyes nearly explode out of his head.

"I want to kiss you," he says, pressing his paw to her cheek. He transforms and now cups her cheek with his warm hand.

"Stop! I do not like this."

"Wait. I am confused. Are you playing fox games with me?"

"You do not ask for a kiss, Hopi boy. You take it, like this." She grabs him by the back of the head and pulls him into her. Their lips connect. Their flesh touches. Their hearts flutter.

He shudders. His hands flail with excitement. He kisses her back and gently slides his trembling hands down to her shoulders. They disconnect. Walpi holds his hands to his lips. "That was the first time I have ever been kissed by a real woman."

"You've never kissed a girl?"

"Plenty. By that is the first time a woman has ever grabbed me and kissed me."

"Well, what do you think of it?"

"I like it!"

Kida begins to shiver uncontrollably. Her teeth rattle.

"Let me cut the stars out of the night sky and wrap you in a blanket of my love."

"You do not own a knife."

"But if I did, I would cut the—"

Kida cuts him off. "No man has ever wanted me for me. They have always wanted me for something I could not be. Or something

I could do for them. Here you are, Hopi, naked as a newborn baby and shivering, with a heart full of courage. Did you use all of it to kiss this Kiowa girl?"

"So that was your first time you grabbed a boy and kissed him?"

Kida nods. "I could not catch what could not be caught. Your sister did that."

"Then let us catch each other and never let go."

"Yes! I want this."

She presses her trembling hands to his cheeks. The two admire each other with a thousand delicate glances that need no words. Eventually, she leans forward and kisses him again. The two kiss gently at first, but the more they do it, the more they build a passionate flame. She lies back. He follows.

"I want you to be my wife. Will your medicine man unite us as he married Kiowa and my sister?"

"We should go ask. The ground is too cold for this."

They begin kissing more passionately than before.

A good distance away from them, Kiowa and Anoki lie side by side. The moon illuminates their faces. He drags his finger up and down her cheek. She tickles his chest. Where Kida feels a chill, Anoki feels nothing. Kiowa's body puts off enough heat to warm a tribe.

"Next spring you will be more than my chief and mighty hunter."

Kiowa looks at her with the most perplexed expression. "What else is there?"

"Very soon you will be chief, hunter, and *father.*"

His eyes change from doting lover to explosive excitement. "With you there was a rainbow of happiness from my heart to yours. Now there will be rays of joy between our eyes like the sun blasting through the clouds. Anoki, you have taken our love and wrapped it in flesh. You have sewn our souls together."

She nods.

"Our children will have our rainbows in their eyes and our sunlight in their hearts."

Anoki cups his face with her hand. "They will have my eyes and your nose."

"Ha! Ha! I don't think so. They will have wolf eyes and nose."

Anoki's smile turns to a frown. "I have one concern, my chief."

Kiowa takes her hand and kisses it. "Speak it so that I may kill it."

"Do I carry wolves or children?"

Kiowa draws a deep breath. His excitement is replaced with great concern.

"I do not know. Only Onendah's magic could answer that question. I must ask him."

Kiowa leaps to his feet and rushes to Onendah's tepee. Inside Onendah's tepee, the medicine man invites Kiowa to sit with his gloomy friends. He hands Kiowa his war bonnet as he blows rings of smoke from his long, fur-wrapped magic pipe.

"Why do you keep my war bonnet?"

"Because it is all that is left of you."

Kiowa puts it by his side and not on his head.

"It is made for your head, not for the earth."

"I have come to seek your counsel, great medicine man."

Onendah hands him his pipe and encourages Kiowa with a nod.

"As have your friends. Listen to this. These fools want to steal women and have me change them into wolves. Ha! Ha! Ha! Could you imagine? 'Hello. I stole you. Now you are my wife. Now you are a wolf. Now you will never see your family or tribe again, and if you do, they will kill you and skin you.' Ha! Ha! Ha! I do not think either of these two have any wisdom. I would never do this thing they ask. Especially not for the magic rock they offer me, which I know they got outside the lodge. I can just get one of my own. Their wisdom has continued to run on four legs well past them. Ha! Ha! Ha! I told them if they could convince a woman to be a wolf, I would turn her. Do you know where these two lonely men can find two women before dawn?"

Makes Trouble and Paw look down and sighs with deep carved frowns.

Kiowa ignores them and presses Onendah.

"We were blessed when you used your magic to save our lives. You said we would have troubles as wolves. Did you know that we would starve because the buffalo have been led to a big cave?"

Onendah doesn't answer. He just listens.

"These things are necessary for you to develop into a great chief, you know. No chief ever became great who wasn't forced to. It is not man's way. He will lie about idle until he is forced to become something greater by the pains of what the creator who made him wants him to become. The buffalo are not in a great cave. Their time has come to an end. This is not the right question. Ask me something else."

Kiowa thinks for a moment.

CHAPTER 105

"Anoki is with child. Does she have wolf pups or children in her belly?"

Onendah clears his throat, then slowly begins. "This is not the right question, either. Nature will sort this out for you."

Kiowa leans back and thinks for a moment. *What could be more important than food in our bellies or babies in our pack?*

His eyes shift back and forth for quite some time, as though he's searching for something. When he thinks he's found it, his face lights up. "If everything must come to an end, then what's the purpose?"

Onendah motions for his pipe, which neither Makes Trouble nor Paw have been invited to smoke.

"Good question."

The medicine man reaches down in the fire and lifts a burning stick. He holds it to the tobacco and puffs several times. When he gets it lit, he leans back and blows smoke rings.

"In my vision, I did not see hunger or pain, wolf cubs or man children. I saw only death from your tribe. I have prevented this because the Sun God permitted me to preserve your love."

"This blessing is becoming a curse. What is worse? Dying because we have nothing to eat or dying because of our love?"

"Your father was right. You have become a great chief."

Kiowa looks confused. *Has he visited with my father's spirit?*

"Here you are now, two winters a wolf, and you have more concern for your pack than for yourself. Your father is proud."

He has visited with my father's spirit. These words make me happy, Kiowa thinks.

Onendah passes Kiowa the pipe. "See now if you can blow rings."

Kiowa tries but with no real success. Onendah reaches for the pipe and blows rings with ease.

"Tell me, what do you see?"

"All I see is a hollow ring. Is there nothing more to see?"

"To answer your question, the purpose of this life is as this smoke ring. Where you see it is hollow, I see it is complete." He waves his hand around. "You must complete the circle."

"I don't understand."

"Use your wisdom, Kiowa. In time this too will profit you. For now, though, perhaps you should decide which world you belong to. I find living between two worlds is confusing. I imagine you must feel the same."

Kiowa nods. "I was afraid to say anything to Anoki, but your words are true. Must I be Indian to complete the circle, or may I remain a wolf?"

"Wearing your war bonnet doesn't make you Indian. You were born Indian."

He reaches down and lifts the war bonnet up, then places it gently on Kiowa's head.

"Like this war bonnet, there is purpose in all things. Your destiny is your decision. I see the sadness that plagues you. Enemies are circling all around. What you must ask yourself is this: How can you complete the circle, and will you be happy once your journey is at an end?"

Kiowa listens, though he still struggles to understand.

"Once you find this happiness, your next task will be to hold on to it. If your desire is to be a wolf, then you know what you must do. Do not think that the tribe is without troubles. Like the buffalo, they are now hard to find."

Kiowa gasps at Onendah's harsh words. He looks down and rests his head in his hands as tears begin to well in his eyes.

"My mother?" Kiowa grieves.

"She is Kiowa, and where they go, she follows."

"I did not want any of this. I wanted love and peace."

"I wanted a tepee full of children and grandchildren. Do you see any of them here? The Cheyenne took my happiness away from me when they killed and scalped my wife. Do I ask for things that I cannot get back?" Onendah grumbles like an old bear.

"No. You adapt to the season and survive."

Kiowa smokes the peace pipe one last time and successfully blows a ring.

"See? You are learning."

Walpi bursts into the tepee naked.

"My heart is full of love, and I want you, great medicine man, to marry me to Kida."

Onendah buries his face in his hands and shakes his head. "I am too old to see such foolishness."

"Please, marry us! I beg of you," Walpi insists.

Onendah looks at Kida and smiles. "Is this what you want, brave Kida?"

She looks at Kiowa and shrinks. "Yes."

***

Out on the open prairie, a platoon of US soldiers, mounted on cavalry horses, conceal themselves in a canyon. They wear blue dress uniforms. Their gold buttons gleam in the sun's light, making them visible for miles.

"When you get out, what endeavor will you pursue?" a private asks his platoon commander.

Major Furness is a towering man and a veteran of the war of 1812. He shrugs. "Folks is moving on over to California. I suppose I'll do the same."

"Strike it rich?" the private asks.

"Sure beats wrangling buffalo," the major answers.

"Buffalo beats tangling with Injuns."

"Amen to that, Major."

"What if the North and South ignite into war?"

"Then I suppose neither of us will be getting out."

"Whad'ya suppose they got us hunting all these buffalo fer, anyways?" the private asks.

"Gotta clear 'em out for the train. You ever seen what a thousand-pound bull does to a steam engine, son?"

The private shakes his head.

"Total devastation. Insurance companies and banks got tired of paying for the losses. They hired some lobbyists to persuade Congress that it 'is in the nation's best interests to preserve the railroads,'" Major Furness says.

"Then why not hire trappers? Why are we here instead of the Dakotas?"

"They did. Trappers aren't doing a good enough job, so they got us here to do what armies do best. Kill!"

"Just don't seem right to slaughter them for nothin'."

"Don't worry about them buffalo. They're real smart animals. Soon they'll figure out these lands are too dangerous for them and they'll move up north."

High up on a ridge, two buffalo hunters signal the soldiers with mirrors that it is time to charge.

"Here we go. Got a herd on our east flank. Let's get 'em on the run."

"Yee-haw!" the platoon sergeant shouts, unholstering his Winchester pistol and firing it in the air.

The soldiers ride out from the bluff and soon get the hairy brown beasts stampeding. At the front of the pack, Blossom leads her small herd.

CHAPTER 106

"These lands have become too dangerous for us!" Clover says.

"Run! All we can do is run!" Blossom answers.

"To where?"

"TO THE GREAT CAVE!"

Tom is one of the trappers who signaled the army. He has a long gray beard and wears a raccoon hat. Tom takes careful aim while his partner, Pierre, spots with a spy scope. The young man is dressed in a somewhat fashionable gray suit. His brand-new tall black piper hat marks him as a gentleman. Although his clothes are cheap, on the frontier he looks like a thousand bucks.

BANG!

Tom aims his black powder rifle at the lead buffalo and drops her with one shot.

"BLOSSOM!" Clover shouts. She stops and stands by her sister's side. "Dear sister, tell me what to do." Blossom's tongue hangs out, her eyes roll back, and blood trickles out her snout.

"Tom. My turn? *Oui* or no?" Pierre asks.

Tom looks confused. "Huh? I just fired. It's your turn."

"Deaf old fool, I just asked you that."

BANG! BANG!

Pierre drops Clover and another buffalo in less time than it takes Tom to fill his musket with black powder, push a ball down, and place a firing cap. Tom kisses his Henry repeating rifle. "I love you, you beautiful, .44-40-caliber bullet."

Down the butte, the soldiers continue to pursue the herd, shooting their new repeating rifles and Colt black powder six-shooter pistols as they go. A trail of smoke follows them. The animals fall down one at a time, then by twos. Soon the entire herd is wiped out.

"Pay up, *mon ami*," Pierre says, holding out his hand.

"Now, hold on just a minute, Frenchie. I'm fixin' ta get ma other musket."

"Ah, I see you're changing the rules," Pierre says, adjusting his black leather glove.

"Ain't no one changing the rules, Frenchie. The bet was on who could kill two buffalo. Stick to yer bet, fella."

"Oui, oh no, Tom." Pierre's accent is so thick he pronounces Tom's name like *Dom*. "I said two silver pieces for whoever could kill the beasts the quickest." He cocks his lever-action rifle and smiles as a smoking brass cartridge ejects and bounces off Tom's old musket.

"Now, lookie here, Pee-dang-aire, would you change the rules on a bet that's already been made? We bet who could kill the most buffalo. Soon as you let me get back to loadin' my Leman musket, I'll get my turn, and then you can take your turn."

Rather than argue with Tom, Pierre waves him off.

"Tell ya what, Pierre. Pay me the two silver pieces you owe me and next time we'll wager for speed. 'Course that wouldn't be a fair bet 'cause you got one of them fancy new lever-action rifles."

Upset more at himself for making a bet with a deaf man, Pierre reaches in his pocket and removes two silver pieces. He rubs them together and says, "*Vous etes un tricheur, Tom! FRADUER! Tu est FRADUER!*"

"EH? What's that, now? You know my French ain't so good."

Pierre turns his back on Tom.

"Don't blame me fer yer bad bettin'. If you're gonna be a poor sport about it…" Tom goes to call the bet off, but then his face lights up. "How 'bout this, ya sore loser? I'll buy yer drinks at the Cowboy Hall."

Pierre pauses. His back faces Tom.

"Wine, no whiskey?"

"Well, that's what I meant, Pee-dang-air. Quit your whining and let's go get some whiskey. Are ya deaf or something?"

Pierre shrugs. The dispute seems settled.

After a rough ride, the two find their way inside the Cowboy Hall just as the sun sets. Pierre pats himself off while Tom struts into the saloon wearing his dirty chaps and plops down at the bar in a dusty plume.

"Make my pains go away, darlin'! Give me the hardest whiskey ya got!" Tom drawls.

"Molly, can you get the piana going for these two fine gentlemen," Guy, a brunette bartender and business owner asks, reaching past a shotgun beneath the bar and grabbing a brown bottle of whiskey.

Molly stands up and pats down her pink and black silk dress. "Sure! I'll tickle some keys fer yew fellas and, for a little gold, I'll tickle more." Her thick Irish accent causes Pierre to sit up. Her green-eyed wink forces him to smile.

On the other side of the saloon, a rough mix of cowboy gamblers and townspeople check their cards and place their bets. Clacking chips and nervous gestures cue who the losers will be and excites the winners.

"Whiskey?" Guy asks Pierre.

"Wine?" Pierre orders.

"Sure. I think we got some white wine straight from Baltimore. Just came in on the train."

The bartender grabs a shot glass, pops the cork on a black bottle of chardonnay, then dumps it into the glass. He sets the bottle down and fills four beers for the gamblers.

As Pierre sips his wine, he reflects on the day's events and tallies his bounty. Just as he's about to total his profit, his concentration is broken by Trapper Dan's dramatic entrance.

"Stay indoors! Der's a pack of verevolves out der and t'isn't safe for no ones to be out on a full moon!" Trapper Dan clenches fistfuls of hair and drags his hands down his scruffy cheeks like a madman.

CHAPTER 107

Regulars at the bar turn away, as they've all heard the story a hundred times. A few table dwellers cave to their fear and give ear, on account of the night's full moon.

Seeing the men's reactions, Pierre rolls his eyes and offers his full attention to the cute redheaded Irish bar gal. He does this the French way, offering an occasional glance and a heavy sigh. She responds the Irish way, ignoring him completely.

Tom throws salt over his shoulder to ward off bad spirits and waits to hear the rest of the story.

"Killed twenty—no fifty—of my very best dogs. Ate my horse. Killed my little-bitty terriers, too." Trapper Dan covers his bald head with his red fox hat.

"If'n that's true, then how's it you're still ah standin'?" a cowboy asks. He leans over and spits in a spittoon.

"I unloaded my rifle, but it vould not stop dem, just slowed dem down a bit."

"How'd a feller of your size outrun a pack of werewolves?"

The bartender circles his finger around his temple, implying Trapper Dan is crazy. Seeing the sign but not catching the meaning, Tom goes back to drinking.

"In my country, it was once rumored that the hills were roamed by werewolves or loup-garou. But we soon found it to be untrue. It turned out to be a very large pack of evil wolves," Pierre says in a French accent that makes Molly smile.

"You want something, Trapper Dan?" Guy questions.

"Vhiskey," Dan answers, combing his fingers over his handlebar mustache.

"Uh-huh, you'll be needin' to settle your debt before you're served, Mister."

While the bartender debates with Dan, Molly makes her way over to the piano. She sits down and plays her favorite tune.

Tom puts a silver piece down on the bar and winks at the bartender.

"You buyin' drinks for this crazy fool?"

Tom mocks Dan's accent and motions at him with his thumb. "Ve ain't lazy. Ve're just enjoying da vhiskey. Get my friend a shot." Tom pats Dan on the back.

"Molly, get this man a shot."

Molly gets up from the piano and comes back to the bar. "Molly, do this. Molly, do that. Molly, get the dollars. Molly be doing all the entertaining, and Molly is just about..." She gripes until she's in earshot. "How may I be of assistance?"

Pierre nods and winks at her. She spots the silver piece and snatches it up. With a twist, a grab, and a pull, she places three beer mugs on the counter and three whiskies.

"T'anks, partner. I been ruined financially by them Injun verevolves." Trapper Dan lifts the whiskey first.

The bartender wipes down a glass and mocks Trapper Dan. "They stole your wallet as well, I suppose?"

"Not exactly. It's a long story, but as soon as I get dat bounty, I'll settle my debt and my nerves. Danke fer the drink, pardners."

Trapper Dan opens his vest and removes a puppy he named Chewy. The yellow lab sniffs around, then spots the beer foam. He leans over and laps the foam off Dan's beer.

"Well, you can rest assured you are safe here, *mon ami*," Pierre says, moving his beer and whiskey away from the dog.

"What's the reward up to, Trapper Dan?" the bartender asks, taunting his loudmouth crazy patron.

Tom's and Pierre's eyebrows rise when they hear the word

"reward." Pierre orders another whiskey for his informed new friend.

"Danke, sir. Last I heard, it vas a thousand dollars."

"One hundred dollars, eh? Hardly seems worth it," Tom says, faking interest.

He looks at Pierre and winks. Pierre smiles and wonders how much Tom hears versus pretends to hear.

"Tell me everything you know about these werewolves and leave out no detail, *mon ami*."

Trapper Dan tells them the story, minimizing his fear and maximizing his bravery.

"I vasn't terribly frightened. 'Course, it's going to take the US Army to put dem monsters down and every cannon on de continent. Dey have been all over these parts, but ranchers find most of der kills in the Currumpaw."

As the night ebbs on, Dan repeats his story so many times even Tom grows tired of it. Somewhere around one in the morning, he and Pierre creak on up the wooden staircase, ready to turn in.

"I don't think we need the US Army, Frenchie. That ol' crooked major is gonna want a hell of a lot more than we're paying him for those hides if we use his men. I say we go at it on our own."

"*Oui!* My mind is the same as yours."

Each turns the squeaky brass knobs to their respective rooms and say good night. Tom's door shuts; the boards creak every step of the way to his bed.

Pierre flips his door back open. He tiptoes through the narrow hall and down the stairs. While the card players toss hard earnings around like their meager wages mean nothing, Pierre sits down by Molly.

"*Bonjour, mon ami*."

***

Two days later and his purse lighter, Pierre rises early. He gets dressed, shaves with a pearl-handled straight razor, leaving a thin mustache on his upper lip. He scurries down the dusty main street, assessing the town not like common folks do, but more like a bourgeoisie. Seeing the town not as it is, but as it could be. Nothing catches his artistic eye like the buildings of France. The Louvre with all its fine decorations, ornate trim, soft colors, and fantastic art pieces make him wonder if he shouldn't use his earnings to open an art shop. *Would be the only one in town. I wouldn't have any competition*, he thinks. A smile lifts his thin mustache and his eyes brighten when he has a splendid thought. *Molly could be my nude model*. Walking down Dream Street, he takes in his shrinking and towering reflection through the wavy windowpanes.

One great fire is going to destroy this town, he thinks to himself as he examines the interconnected box-shaped wooden buildings that compose Main Street.

Boys run through the street and stop to toss rocks at the many empty buildings—boys who should have been in school. But since the economic bust was depriving the city of teachers, discipline lacked. It was only a matter of time before boys found rocks and rocks met windows.

Pity, Pierre thinks as he shouts at the boys in an effort to preserve the rustic relic.

As he continues his stroll downtown, Pierre stops to take in the schoolhouse.

I simply do not like it. Not enough flair, he thinks as he curls his lip and raises a pencil-thin brow.

Perhaps if it had a red coat of paint to mark it as an institution of learning rather than the semblance of a cage, it would rate merit. But now, it is simply too plain. He draws a deep breath and lets out a heavy sigh. *I might have made a superb teacher.*

Though Pierre was well educated, he detested classrooms. To this day, he grits his teeth when he thinks of the lashes he got for spelling Latin words wrong. He often confused the Latin and French translations. He looks at the rugged boys running through the streets no longer with disgust but with admiration. He checks to make sure no one is watching, then tosses a rock through the window.

The other buildings are more Pierre's style. The bank's window has just the right flash to it, its bright gold lettering spelling out Wells Fargo. Even the barbershop has its signature red, white, and blue stripes on the post.

As he progresses the short stroll down new Main Street, which is looking rather old, he finds himself again standing in front of the most prosperous business in town, the gunsmith. He pauses and looks at the business's rugged sign. He drags his fingers over the painted letters. With a sigh, he lowers his expectations. *I should have paid more attention to the sign. Father always taught me that a man who takes pride in his sign takes pride in his work.* He clenches his jaw and grinds his teeth, thinking, *I am probably going to lose my hand when I fire this craftsman's bullets.* Having nowhere else to go, Pierre gently presses his glove against a brushed and dented brass knob. As he enters, he's pleased to find that the man who took his order a few days ago remembers him.

"Mr. Pierre. Six silver bullets and a rifle repair. Let me fetch them now." The gunsmith disappears behind an oil-stained curtain. Pierre looks around the small shop. Wooden gun boxes pile from floor to ceiling. They lean precariously, looking like they could tumble at any moment. He lets out another sigh, his expectations dropping to floor and dashing to pieces.

"That'll be a nickel and a penny," the gunsmith says, setting a box of shells beside his rifle.

"Pity."

"What's that?"

"The silver shells and bullet head are pleasing to the eye. Imagine how they might look if you presented them to me in a red velvet box. It would have drawn my eye and made the metal flash."

"Whad'ya gonna do with silver bullets?" he responds, completely ignoring Pierre's flair for design.

Pierre holds his hand up in the shape of a gun. He points it at the gunsmith and pulls the trigger, then howls.

The gunsmith gets his meaning. "Oh, so you're one of those, huh? You know the Kelseys are forming a political party. They call werewolves the weeds of the west, and they're riding on a platform to weed them out. Have you seen the bounty posters?"

"*Oui.*"

"Hard to believe they're offering six hundred dollars for the wolf man."

Pierre's eyebrows rise. Clearly he hasn't seen the same posters. He removes his tan leather glove and inspects each round.

"Come on, Pee-yare!" he hears his partner, Tom, shout. Tom has tracked his partner to the gunsmith.

"Will you accept credit?"

"Sure. I didn't catch your full name, though."

"Tom Johnson, my business partner, will be covering the expense."

The gunsmith lifts his accounting book, blows dust off it and into Pierre's face, then cracks it open. With a dull pencil, he marks down *Dom*, instead of *Tom*.

Satisfied with his cleverness, Pierre takes the box of shells and his rifle and leaves. When he opens the door, the blazing light and brilliant blue sky blind him.

"Now, how many times have I told you to stick with shootin' muskets? You ain't had that rifle but two months and already you've had to send it in fer repairs."

Pierre sighs and mounts his horse, which lifts him above his dashed expectations.

As the pair trot out of town, they see a young newspaper boy posting WANTED flyers over faded reward posters.

Scanning the flyer, Pierre learns that the reward is advertised as a thousand dollars for the wolf man's body and fifteen hundred dollars if the monster is captured alive.

"Did you just hear what I said, Frenchie, or are you deaf?"

"*Oui, oui.* I should have listened *tu vieux bafoon.*"

"I got us some arsenic poison. Now we need to be gettin' some bait."

"I was just thinking the same, monsieur."

CHAPTER 108

A week later and with the help of the army scouts, the two trappers find a lone buffalo wandering the plains and calling out for its herd. Had it known it was drawing its doom instead of its salvation, the beast might have made less noise. But then again, buffalo will follow their leader off a cliff, so he might have called out just the same.

Tom carefully aims and squeezes the trigger.

FWAMP! The black powder flashes.

BANG! goes the delayed explosion.

I will never know how he does that. Beyond Pierre's reasoning, Tom manages to kill the lonely buffalo with one shot at a hundred yards' distance.

"Told ya I could find one. They love the tops of the fresh grass. If there's a buffalo within a hundred miles, you'll find 'em eatin' this here," Tom says as he reaches down and rips a handful of spring-green buffalo grass. He laughs as he opens his hand and sprinkles the grass to the wind.

"Of course, if you could hear, which you can't, you would have found him all the same," Pierre says in a low tone he knows Tom won't detect.

"Now we got bait. Let's use some o' this here special sauce." Tom shakes his bottle of poison. He walks out to his kill and pours "magic" arsenic on the hindquarters and on the head. He turns around expecting to find his partner, but he finds himself alone instead.

"Now, come on, dang Pierre, we ain't got time fer playin' games. I need yer help coverin' up the trail. Ain't no way wolves is gonna dine when they catch our scent."

Pierre doesn't respond. He's given Tom the slip. In a short amount of time, he positions himself high on the cliff tops, leaving Tom out in the open as live bait. With his spyglass, he watches Tom go back to their hasty camp and stoke the fire. Laying strips of meat on hot rocks, he warns Pierre that, "I ain't waitin' for you! I'm eating dinner!"

The aroma reaches Pierre's heights. His grumbling stomach makes him second-guess his master plan.

"Now all I have to do is wish you well, my friend. The werewolf will not be searching for me after he has eaten you."

Tom spins around, hopping up and down on one foot.

"Suit yerself. I'm eatin' a fine dinner. Gonna use the rest of this here firewood to warm maself up." Tom narrates each task like a disjointed song only he has the pleasure of hearing.

He acts as though he can hear me even though I am this far away, Pierre chuckles.

Several miles south, Kiowa and his pack scan the vast flat valley.

"I smell fire," Kida says, catching a faint scent.

"What I wouldn't trade for a buffalo!" Walpi groans, falling on his side.

Kiowa scans the valley. Off in the distance, he sees Tom's smoke trail. Always the calm, patient leader, he hears every wolf of his pack complain about hunger. He pushes his own hunger aside to find a path to food and provide for his pack.

"I see a fire. Let us see if there is anything worth taking." Kiowa heaves, standing up and shaking the dust off his thick hide.

One by one the wolves take their respective positions in the pack. As they travel, they move in an echelon similar to an arrowhead. The stronger wolves are at the front. The weaker wolves trail behind.

Of course Kiowa leads, while Makes Trouble and Paw take up the left and right flanks. They move this way so that if anything should surprise them, three wolves can immediately get in the fight while the weaker wolves can flank.

Such is life after the pit bull attack.

Anoki is the only wolf free to travel in front of the leader or trail behind. Anyone else would certainly be challenging Kiowa and maybe even face certain death. The strange nature of Indians and wolves is that every member will fight to the death to protect an expectant mother. So a mother is free to roam where she feels safest.

Across the blazing sky, the sun drops below the horizon. Stars pop out one at a time.

"Oh my darlin', oh my darlin'." Tom yawns as he sings. He plops a log down on the fire and slides his brown cowboy hat over his eyes. Lying back, he pulls his wool blanket over his burly chest.

"Oops. Nearly forgot you, Bertha." He reaches for the cold, heavy musket and tucks her in beside him. He even kisses her good night.

As the moon rises, the pale light illuminates the wolves. They keep to the shadows as best they can. Anoki's white fur looks eerily like a ghost floating over the desert. On the best of nights she could hardly be concealed. With the rising moon catching her gleaming coat, she sticks out and reveals the pack's position.

Detecting the risk, Kiowa orders the pack into a single-file line. It isn't long before they stumble upon the fallen buffalo.

"I thought they were all gone," Makes Trouble whispers, leaning down to take a whiff.

Kiowa looks at Paw. Neither knows what to make of the wasted meat.

"They killed him with their thunder sticks, but they did not skin him as they do the others," Paw surmises.

"Why?" Kiowa wonders.

The pack waits for Kiowa's opinion. He circles around the beast and smells the carcass, trying to find answers.

"What are we waiting for? Let us eat!" Walpi whimpers with ferocious appetite. He leans down to take a bite, but Kida stops him.

"How long has it been since we've seen a buffalo?" Kida asks.

"Too long," her brother, Makes Trouble, answers.

Anoki leans down and circles around the decaying meat. "Oh, I am so hungry. I am eating for two. My little ones beg me to feed them. If it were just me, then I wouldn't beg. But because it is my babes, I must feed. I MUST!"

Kiowa laughs and shakes his head.

"We are wolves, Anoki. You are probably eating for six."

She presses herself against him. "No wonder I am so hungry. I have a village inside my belly. 'Mother, Mother, feed us meat. We are hungry.' What kind of a mother am I if I do not feed my village?"

"What kind of mother are you? What kind of father am I? My children have hungry bellies, and it is a man's duty to put meat in the mother's mouth and she in the babies' bellies."

"We are two people not ready to be mother and father."

Kiowa sighs. "We are two wolves, not ready to be people."

She looks at him and thinks on his words. She had never expected to remain a wolf. The thought simply hadn't occurred to her.

"We wait for Kiowa; he is our leader. What he says, we do," Paw says, licking his lips and patiently sitting down.

Kiowa examines the buffalo closely; he notices fresh blood. He understands that the trappers kill indiscriminately, but he knows that they usually take the hide and leave the meat. *Why they do this I will never know, he thinks. And why haven't the ravens, eagles, or coyotes taken advantage? Are we the first to find the kill?*

"It's a trap," Makes Trouble says, pushing everyone back.

"How can you tell?" Walpi growls at him.

"Ants and flies eat every dead thing on the desert floor. Day and night they chew. He has been dead long enough for ants to be crawling all over him. Look here. They eat only certain parts of him. This is a trap."

"But the trappers use thunder sticks, which they have, and they leave the meat to go to waste, which they have also done," Walpi gripes, wanting to eagerly dig in.

"I can eat what the ants eat. Please, Kiowa, I too have young to feed," Kida bursts out with a yelp.

Walpi looks at her in disbelief.

"I didn't want to say anything in case we didn't have enough…" She looks away.

Walpi feels his hunger slip away and churn into guilt. He feels his growls turn to whimpers.

Kiowa leans down and smells once more.

"Kida and Anoki, eat only the center, where the ants eat. We men will hunt and find something else, even if we must take more tame buffalo."

Anoki doesn't waste time. She dives in. She and Kida grip the buffalo at separate spots and thrash until its abdomen splits open. Avoiding the entrails, they gorge themselves on its liver, then step back. In a matter of minutes, the buffalo's center is gone.

THWACK!

THWACK!

CHAPTER 109

Two silver bullets impale the buffalo carcass. A sound like distant thunder gives Pierre's position away.

Paw looks up and shouts, "No one move!"

Clouds sweep in front of the moon, drastically reducing visibility. Anoki is still easily seen.

"Anoki, lie down."

"Why? Paw said not to move."

"Because if we can see you, he can see you!" Kiowa whispers.

Anoki lies down. Her white fur is tainted by fresh blood. She has an idea. *If I roll in the blood, it will cover my coat.* It mostly works.

Pierre watches the white wolf roll around on the ground. He's certain he's killed her. He decides to wait for better visibility before firing again.

"I should lie down as well," Walpi says. "My coat is light and it will encourage him."

Eventually the clouds part. Pierre cracks the chamber with a flick of his hand. He hears the empty cartridge clank against the rocks. For a moment he shares Mona Lisa's secret. A clever smile perks on his face when he sees one wolf perfectly still. The white wolf is motionless but not so easy to see, and he isn't sure why.

As I said, they are just wolves. Not werewolves, Pierre thinks, making the sign of the cross. He slides in more rounds, just to make sure the feeding tube is full. He removes a silver medallion of Saint Dominic, father of the rosary, and kisses it.

"At least the silver will ensure their cursed souls will never rise again," he says, convinced he's hit his target. He climbs down from his elevated position to enlist Tom's help.

When he reaches the fire, Tom is nowhere to be seen.

"Tom… *pppsssttt*… Tom? *Zut alors*, Tom. I need your assistance."
Suddenly, a man's body with a beastly head emerges. It holds its long arms out and shows its curled claws.

"ROOOOAAARRRR!"

"Ahhh!" Pierre screams like an opera singer. His neck muscles flex tight and stiffen up the rest of his body. He's so overwhelmed with fear, he can't seem to move. He unloads his rifle with a quick pull of his finger and flick of his wrist.

His frantic aim scatters his silver bullets like buckshot.

"LOUP-GAROU!" Pierre frantically screams, fumbling for rounds he's buttoned in his pocket. When he realizes he's fired all but one of his silver bullets, his face turns pale and his Mona Lisa smile is wiped clean from his face. He fumbles but manages to slide the round into the feeding tube.

"AAAWWWRRRR!" the wolf man howls, seeming unscathed. He charges Pierre.

With a flick of his wrist, Pierre extends the lever. An empty shiny shell kicks out and a new one goes in. Without taking careful aim, he fires for the white of the loup-garou's eyes.

The wolf man grabs his chest like he's been shot. He spins around several times, moans dramatically, then falls down a good distance from Pierre. His legs cycle, convincing Pierre it's the last of his nerves before his damned soul leaves his body.

Sweat exudes from every pore in Pierre's face. Salty drops drip into his eyes and sting. He blinks frantically and wipes with his sleeve. With trembling hands, he cautiously approaches the monster. He furiously blinks, trying to make the stinging sweat go away, but it persists. He makes the sign of the cross.

His eyes demand to see two things. The hideousness of the loup-garou and the dramatic result of his fierce rapid fire. He unholsters his side arm and cocks his six-shooter.

"If you are loup-garou, lead won't stop you! Pierre knows this. I know this. I know this because I am Pierre. Where is Pierre? Here is Pierre. Please God of the heavens, let my silver bullets strike true." Although he says "is" he thinks "lies" and wonders if his headstone won't read the rest.

Still too nervous, he can't bring himself to check the body.

"A test!" Pierre thinks. He turns his back on the limp body and bends over to pick up a rock. When he turns back around to throw it, a surprise is waiting for him. The wolf head isn't a wolf head at all. It's a coyote's head, and it's holding Tom's musket, which is aimed directly at his face.

Click, click. The flintlock hammer locks into place.

Pierre drops the rock and his eyes bulge so big, they explode out of their sockets.

FWAMP, BOOM!

The musket fires.

Pierre's body flails back.

"Ha! HA! HA! That'll teach ya to abandon yer post, ya dirty, filthy French bastard!"

Pierre hears Tom laughing, but he doesn't understand any of this madness. He struggles with the fact that his ghost lingers inside his painful body. The thought of being terribly maimed and trapped in a paralyzed body is too much for him. He slowly opens one scorched eye at a time and presses his fingers to his powder-burned face. He pats his cheeks and forehead to ensure he still has a head. When he realizes that his face is intact, he looks at his hands and doesn't see blood but soot. He begins to sob. Tears leave white trails in his charcoaled face.

"Ah, quit yer cryin', ya big French baby. I didn't put a ball in it."

"I could have killed you, *mon ami!*"

"Naw. Ya can't shoot fer piss! Ha! Ha!"

Pierre gets up and hugs Tom. "But I can, Tom. I shot two wolves."

Hearing the news, Tom hugs him back.

Eventually they decide they've had enough excitement for one night.

"We can go look for the wolves in the morning, but if they have no bullet holes in them, I'm claiming eighty percent of the bounty."

"Fine, Tom! Fine!" As he covers his trembling frame with a blanket and lies by the fire, Pierre thinks, *My cleverness has evaded me and left me a shamble of nerves.* Pierre closes his eyes and rocks himself to a sweet repose.

When they reach the buffalo, they find no corpses. But they do see where the wolves ate around the arsenic.

Pierre removes his hat. "*Incroyable...*"

"It ain't incredible... It's unbelievable."

"That is what I said."

Tom walks away from the buffalo, scanning the terrain. He finds their tracks but can't make them out because they move in a single-file line.

"Well, one thing's for certain..."

"Loup-garou," Pierre practically whispers.

"It ain't no dang werewolf, Frenchie, but you were right. There is more than one."

Pierre looks up and over his shoulder. Tom is a good distance away from him.

"Ce qui est cette surprise? You can hear me?!?"

Tom bangs on his ear. "Well, I'll be doggone. Your bad shootin' plum fixed my hearin'."

The hunters embrace. Pierre kisses both sides of Tom's cheeks and leaves black lip impressions.

From a long distance away, a couple of cowboy, ranch hands named Hank and Juan watch the two trappers behave in the most unusual manner.

They look at each other and start laughing.

Juan chuckles. "Must be from Texas." He laughs and adjusts the straps to his wide-brimmed sombrero.

"Ha! Ha! Let's go find out," Hank says, kicking at his horse's side.

Pierre points his pistol in the air and unloads all six shots.

"Howdy," Hank hollers, putting his hand on his six-shooter.

"Did you hear that, Pierre? He said, 'Howdy.'"

"How-i-dy, cowboy," Pierre says, kicking his feet out and dancing like a circus fool.

"What's all the excitement about?"

"I was blind, and now I see," Pierre shouts.

"I was deaf, and now I hear," Tom yells, putting his hands on his broad belly and laughing.

Juan and Hank exchange perplexed looks.

"These fellers ain't all there, Juan," Hank says in a low voice.

"Werewolf... Ha! Ha! Ha!" Tom shouts, putting his coyote cap back on. He covers his face. "Roarrrr... grrrooowwwrrr..."

"I'll have some of what he's drinking," Juan says, cracking a smile at the two.

Pierre walks over to Hank, holding up an empty casing.

"Loup-garou. This will protect you."

Tom twirls in circles, acting like he's chasing his own tail.

"What is it?" Juan asks, as in, *what's the caliber?*

"Silver bullet, my friend."

Juan searches for a bullet. "But there's no bullet. It's just an empty casing," he says in a thick Spanish accent.

"Exactly!" Pierre shouts. "It is a gift for you. We are leaving this place. If anything can stop this loup-garou, it is silver. Remember that! Only silver bullets can kill a werewolf."

"Silver bullet?" Hank asks, cocking his hat to the side.

"*Oui, oui!*"

"Werewolf?" Juan curiously inquires.

Tom takes the coyote head off. "DAAANNNGGG, it's hotter than the fires of hell in there. Let's get the heck outta here, Pierre."

CHAPTER 110

Charlie cleans marshmallow goop off his stick.

"Kiowa had beaten two of the best trackers west of the Mississippi. You'd think his troubles were over, but they were just beginning. He had to make some tough decisions."

"I have big decisions to make, too. Sometimes I put my head under the sink to get my hair wet so I don't have to take a shower." Kevin snickers.

"I know I'm supposed to brush my teeth before I go to bed, but I just put a little toothpaste on my lips and make it seem like I did," John says, using his finger as a toothbrush.

"Those *are* big decisions, boys. But what I'm talking about is Kiowa deciding whether he was going to be a wolf or a man. Now that he was going to be a father, everything was changing, doncha know."

***

The wolves stand in a circle. Anoki breaks rank and transforms before Kiowa does.

"Kiowa, hurry. We have gotten here very late. The sun is almost up, and we have only a little time before you are a wolf forever."

Kiowa lies down in protest.

Anoki looks at him. Confused, she says, "I can't understand you as a wolf. You know you have to change for me to hear you as a man."

Kiowa looks at the pack.

"Each of you can choose this day who you are. As for me, I can no longer stand on two legs. The sun will never rise on my Indian face again. I am a wolf!"

"Kiowa! Kiowa! Please. I cannot hear you." Anoki makes desperate pleas.

"Kida, Makes Trouble, Paw, and I are outcasts. I believe I know what you will decide. Walpi and Anoki can return to their tribe if they must, but for me… This is my tribe now. I have fought the beast for too long and I have lost the fight."

Anoki looks at the setting moon and shivers when the sky lights up. She lifts her shirt and pats her pregnant womb. Snowflakes begin falling softly.

"I don't want to give birth to wolf babies. I want to see the faces of our babies. I have spent all spring, summer, and fall working my womanly art. Please, Kiowa, let me see our children's faces."

Kiowa turns his back on her and recedes into the forest. His soft whimpers cause tears to stream from her eyes.

"Kiowa please! I'm begging you…" Anoki wails.

For an eternal moment Kida stares at Walpi. "In spring, you will be a father. What faces do you want to see, fur or flesh?"

"I am with you and have been from the beginning. If Kiowa wants to see wolf faces on his babies, then I do, too," Walpi says, turning and following Kiowa.

Makes Trouble sighs. "I suppose it would be easier to find a female wolf than to steal some strange woman and have Onendah change her into a wolf."

Paw laughs. "Yes, I agree. Let us go find she-wolves."

Without hesitation, they join Kiowa.

The sky turns from dark to dawn.

"Kiowa, the sun is rising. Think of our children? You would choose this life for them?" Anoki shouts.

Kiowa's ears and tail drop.

"You cannot ask me to live this way forever. I won't do it. I do not mind being a wolf, but even Naukolahe made us people. Who am I to go against a god? Why go against nature and be wolves? Let us live our lives out as mother and father. I'm not saying you can't turn back to a wolf. Why can't we have the best of both worlds? I want to hold you with my hands and kiss you with my lips. Please, Kiowa, please. Let me rock my children with a mother's arms."

The pack moves into the forest, leaving Kiowa alone with Anoki. His back is turned to her. He cannot bear to look at her. Summoning all his strength, he takes a step forward and prepares to sprint after his pack.

"KIOWA!"

Anoki looks off in the distance, remembering when Kiowa brought her to this place where they were married. The sun begins to rise. Its amber light torches the sky and travels toward her at an impossible speed. Light dispels night's shadow and closes in on her. Tears stream down her cheeks.

"To love is to change," Anoki whispers as she slowly turns back into the white wolf.

"You chose me?" Kiowa says, lowering his head and whimpering. His tail swishes back and forth.

"There is no choice. I follow you because you are a thief. You have stolen my heart. I have stitched my soul to yours with all these children. We are welded together you and I."

"You changed, so you still have many moons before you make your decision final," Kiowa tells her.

"If only you hadn't made the decision for me! I will not let you abandon your children to be some wild wolf all about on your own. I will not let you. I have changed, so they can still be human, I think. I hope. My heart breaks for them. You let light rest on your snout without changing. They will never get to see your handsome Indian face again. Oh, Kiowa, why do you tug at these stitches and make your little woman so sad?"

Kiowa's yellow eyes look down. He whimpers. I had not thought of that.

"Oh, how I hate you!" She growls.

"But I love you," he huffs.

"I love you, too."

***

Charlie puts the last two logs on the fire.

"Okay. I never had to make decisions like that," Kevin says, shaking his head.

Charlie smiles.

"I would have wanted to be a wolf, too." Zack affirms Kiowa's decision.

Charlie's smile melts. "Remember what Onendah told them, though. There would always be trouble, even as wolves." He pushes his round glasses up with his finger.

CHAPTER III

Spring brings a litter of eight thriving pups. Two of Anoki's pups died of coughing sickness, one was taken by a great owl, and a cougar stole another.

"I do not want our children to suffer as Anoki's," Kida whispers to Walpi.

"Me neither. I'm glad you want to have them in the cave and not on the move. I warned Kiowa that it was dangerous to make three trips."

"I know. He would not listen. He never will. My heart breaks for would-be sister, Anoki. One of us should have stayed behind," Kida answers.

"Then one of us would have been killed by the cougar."

"I can't wait to find her and kill her cubs!"

"Me too," Walpi answers, pressing his head to hers.

"Listen," Kida whispers. "I have a little of this magic root left. I will save it for our children just in case they get sick, we will use it on them and it will heal them."

"Why did you not use it on the sick pups?"

"Because, husband, if I had, our children would have nothing."

Anoki rolls onto her side and exposes her teats, "Come Cries A Lot, eat with your brother Blue Eyes. Make room for Coon Eyes, Blue Eyes. Why are you so greedy? Red Cloud, you must eat to stay strong. If you will not eat, then you must be bathed."

"Hungry, hungry," the pups yip, searching for nature's bottle.

"First we will teach them how to hunt rabbit," Kiowa says.

Kida tucks her paws under her enlarged belly. She loves the way her restless children feel against her paws.

"Then deer," Kida proudly proclaims with a broad smile.

"A new circle." Paw parts his black lips and exposes his white teeth.

"Stop smiling at the babies. You are scaring them, Paw." Kida chastises Paw for his evil white-toothed grin, which glows against his black fur.

"Eh?" Kiowa wonders.

"This must be what Onendah was talking about when he blew circles. You have completed your circle. You have become a father."

"You're right, Uncle. I guess I have."

Kiowa steps out of the cave with his pups stumbling after. They whip their tails wildly and tip over, yipping when they fall.

"Help, Father!"

Kiowa clamps down on the backs of their necks and stands them up proud.

Paw looks at the pups. "They will hunt the tame buffalo. Surely that is the new balance."

"I am not so sure." Anoki sighs, resting her concerned blue eyes on her wobbly-legged pups.

"They will have to share the land with us. The tame buffalo roam the grasslands far and wide. We take them here and there, not too much, but enough to survive. It keeps the herd strong. Surely the mounted man with funny hats and whips can see that."

"Maybe." Anoki rests her chin on her paws.

"Come, children. Listen to Uncle tell of when we were Indians. You love hearing of my brave brother, Lone Wolf."

"I want to hear about how we were Indians," a pup with raccoon marks around his eyes chirps.

"Sshhh. Listen, Coon Eyes," Kiowa says, biting the back of his son's neck and lifting him up. The pup goes limp and curls his toes up to a perfect furry bundle. Kiowa rests his son between his paws.

"Our magic is not our own," Paw begins. "Black Bear, an evil chief, harnessed the power and left it behind when he killed your grandfather. I stole this magic and gave it to a powerful medicine man even though I was tempted to keep it for myself."

"What is 'tempted'?"

"Ssshhh. Listen, Coon Eyes," Paw says. "We were Indians then, not wolves."

Makes Trouble and Walpi stand at the front of the entrance and take turns picking the wandering pups up and carrying them back to their mothers.

***

W.H. rides into town, passing a sign as he enters that reads, WELCOME TO CIMARRON, WHERE THE ROCKIES MEET THE PLAINS." There are a few businesses on Main Street, which is surrounded by farm and cattle lands and further surrounded by red rocky mountains.

Bingo follows Cotton. W.H. halts Cotton in front of the sheriff's office. When he dismounts, he stretches, then ties the leather reins to a post. When he's secured his horse, he enters the dingy one-cell office.

"I'm here to catch the wolf pack that's terrorizing the Currumpaw," he says to Sheriff Dawson.

"Terrorizing is right. Don't think it's a pack, though. Most folks believe it's a man-wolf. Most of us call him Loup-Garou, or Louie for short. Some folks say Louie lives among us as a man and that's why he hasn't been caught yet."

W.H. shakes his head in disbelief. "I don't believe in superstitions. Ain't no such thing as werewolves. How much is a permit?"

"Where are you from?"

W.H. thinks for a moment before he answers. *If I tell him Canada, it may work against me.*

"Northern states or Southern states?" Sheriff Dawson adds before he can respond.

"I'm from Canada," W.H. relents.

"Ah, that makes sense why you think you need a permit," Sheriff Dawson says with a long Texas drawl W.H. hasn't heard yet.

"You won't be needing a permit, feller," the sheriff continues, "but keep this in mind. You ain't the first stranger to roll into town looking to collect the reward money, and you won't be the last. Most of y'all are like tumbleweeds, blowing in and out. We'll see what yer saying on the way out."

"Can you orient me to the local supply store?"

"You passed it on the way in." Sheriff points at his wall. "Find the saloon west of here and cross the street. Hardware and liquor are the only two businesses in town makin' money these days."

W.H. nods. He steps outside the municipal building and sees a boy with a handful of flyers.

It reads, WANTED, LOUIE THE WOLF. $1500 DEAD! $2500 ALIVE!

W.H. takes his black cowboy hat off and stares at the poster in disbelief. "Why would anybody want a man-wolf alive?"

The boy turns around and shouts, "Barnum's circus, Mister. Pa has a mighty good offer. Though I don't know what he will do with the devil himself."

CHAPTER 112

W.H. wastes no time checking into the saloon hotel. He's greeted by a short woman with ginger hair and a thick Irish accent.

"Make yerself at home, hun. I'm here to see that you're cared for. I'm the brand-new owner. You here to catch our werewolf?" Molly asks.

"Nope. I'm here to kill your wolf."

"If you ask me"—she leans in, exposing her cleavage, and tilts her bloodshot green eyes up—"it's Sheriff Dawson."

W.H. glances at her cleavage. "You think the sheriff is the werewolf?"

"Eyes to Jesus I do." She rises.

W.H. looks up and locks eyes with hers.

"Only a handful of us have been here since the beginning of all this mischief. Most locals have gone off to California. I know it ain't me. I know it ain't you, 'cause you just rolled into town."

"Like a tumbleweed," W.H. says with a smile. He pats the counter. Molly smirks, turns around, and tickles his nose with ostrich feathers that poke out the top of her hair. She whips around and puts two glasses on the bar. She bites down on a cork plug and yanks it out. As she tilts the brown bottle, the potent whiskey fumes make W.H. wince. He raises his glass and swallows the gold liquid fire. His throat burns so bad, his eyes water.

"That's the warmest welcome you'll get," Molly says with a smile. "First one's on the house. Tabs get paid by Friday or you won't be drinking on Monday."

"Yes, ma'am." W.H.'s hoarse vocal chords are strained from the strong drink.

"Preacher can't be possessed by the devil, 'cause he's a man of

God. 'Course, it could be Mr. Mather, the hardware store owner. That'd make a barrel of sense. He's pinchin' everyone's purse like the old crab he be."

"Wolf. It's a wolf, ma'am."

"Personally, I ain't got nothing against the werewolf. He's been great for business. If he came in here, I'd comp his drinks for life."

"Why's that?" W.H. asks, motioning for her to top him off.

"Drove the value of this property down and positioned me to be able to buy it. The O'Riley clan ain't owned land since I can't remember when. We be renters and potato farmers. Mr. Mather owns an old place out on the Currumpaw. I'd counsel you to rent first, since you know not the follies that may fall on your righteous brow. Might keep ya from going broke." She winks and slams the whiskey shot with ease.

W.H. tips his hat. "Thank you, ma'am."

As W.H. leaves, Molly cracks a smile. "My name's Molly, 'course, it don't matter much. A wimp like you ain't gonna make it a week. Least that's the bet against you."

W.H. smiles. "Did you bet against me?"

"'Course! I can't have a scrawny little runt like you driving off the classy clients, so don't come back!" she says with a cackle.

"Humph..."

Outside the hotel, he walks across the dusty street, dodging a tumbleweed as he goes. He politely tips his hat as he passes some women wearing fancy dresses.

"Howdy, ladies," he says to the only two respectable women he's seen in town. One is Mr. Mather's blooming daughter, Jenny. The other is her mother, Frances.

Jenny looks away and blushes while Mrs. Mather introduces herself and her daughter.

"Will we be seeing you at church, Mister...?"

"W.H."

"That's your name?" Jenny asks.

"Yes, ma'am. It's short for Wolf Hunter."

"Mister..." Jenny bites her bottom lip. She shakes her head. Her pretty flaxen bun sits on top of her head like frosting on a cupcake. "That's the dumbest name I have ever heard of." Jenny's sharp tongue betrays her sweet looks. "What's your real name?"

Her mother wastes no time. She puts her mother-hen arm around Jenny, which forces the young woman to straighten up. They turn their backs and swish and sway, their matching plaid hoop dresses dancing away.

"Sea-green eyes froze me; then she galloped away like a gazelle in a ball gown," W.H. mutters, thinking of tonight's journal entry.

He reaches for the hardware store's brass doorknob and turns it. The sign above reads, HouseGoods, HardWares, & Curios. A cowbell rings in his entrance.

"Howdy there, stranger," Mr. Mather, the owner, says with a welcoming hand. "What can I do you for?"

"I'm inquirin' about a place you may have available," W.H. says, half expecting the man to laugh him out of his store.

"You here for the werewolf?" Mr. Mather inquires. He reaches for a cardboard cutout of a wolf's face, which sells for one cent.

"Yes, sir. I'm here for the werewolf. Ms. O'Riley over at the saloon said you might have a place for rent near the action."

"If you're looking for credit, you've come to the wrong place. We don't give credit no more since Trapper Dan cleaned us out."

W.H. reaches into his pocket and withdraws three gold coins, which he drops on the counter.

"I'll be stayin' till the end of summer if I have to, but I hope to bag that wolf and get out in a couple of weeks, if that would be all right with you."

The merchant beams with a grin that glistens like the top of his bald head. He swipes the gold coins off the counter quicker than a Kansas twister.

"Cabin's half a day's journey north of here."

"Is it furnished?"

"Yes, sir. All the conveniences of… Where are you from?"

"Winnipeg, Canada."

"Whoo-weee, you sure came a long way, fella. How did you find out about the wolf?"

"An advertisement."

"All the way up in Canada? That makes you the farthest north a man has come here in search of Louie. How long did it take you to get here?"

"I've been on the trail since 'fore last Christmas."

"That long? Well, you'll be glad to know the rail will be finished soon and it may not take you that long to get back."

I never want to see another train again, W.H. thinks.

Mr. Mather disappears into a back room and returns with a set of keys.

"You won't be needin' to lock it. Ain't nobody out there who'd bother you, except maybe Molly herself. Between you and me, I think either she or the banker is the werewolf."

W.H. smirks and rests his elbows on the counter. He tilts his head sideways and says, "And why is that?"

"Well, only a handful of us is left in town, and it can't be Sheriff Dawson. He's the sheriff. Can't be the preacher. He's a holy man. That leaves Molly, the town whore. Plus, she beat me in a bidding war for the saloon. Makes sense that she'd want to scope out her victims, don't it? Imagine if they knew they were financing their own loss."

"And is your surplus store a charity?"

"That's exactly why I also suspect the preacher." Mr. Mather reverses himself. "What better way to gain the town's trust than to use charity? Man's in a position of trust, and I don't rightly trust him and neither should you."

"I'll keep that in mind. Here's a list of everything I'll be needing."

Mr. Mather looks it over. "Got most of these items in stock. Rest will come in on the rail. 'Course, stagecoach will have to pick them up from the rail and bring them here. It's really sped things up for us, but we still have to wagon in most of our supplies from Ol' Santa Fe."

"I'd like to get out to the cabin before dark. Wouldn't want to run into Louie."

"Ha! You don't need to worry about him hurting you—though he could if he wanted to. Apparently, he's a civilized werewolf. Never attacked a man or a woman. His hunger is confined to cattle."

W.H. turns and walks away, shaking his head. The same cowbell that welcomed him bids him farewell. He hears a scuffle behind him and tenses.

"Stick 'em up!"

W.H. reaches for his pistol.

CHAPTER 113

"I SAID STICK 'EM UP. NOW GIMME ALL YOUR MONEY!" The boy who was putting up the wanted posters spots W.H. and holds his hand up like it's a pistol.

W.H. raises his hands.

"Now gimme your loot, Four Eyes."

W.H. lowers one hand and reaches into his pocket.

"Slow, Mister."

W.H. slowly removes a copper coin. He holds it out in his hand. The little boy snatches for it, but W.H. jerks it away.

"Not so fast, slick."

He makes a fist around the coin, points his finger at it, and pretends to shoot it. When he opens his hand, the coin is gone.

"It's in your other hand."

W.H. opens his other hand, but it's also empty.

"Hey, where'd it go?"

"It's magic," W.H. says, adjusting his glasses. "What's your name?"

"Billy."

"Well, Billy, you're an ornery kid, ain't cha."

Billy nods.

"You help Mr. Mather bring me my goods and I'll give you a nickel."

"Ha! Pa told me to do it as a service, but if you're paying, Mister, I'm playing!"

He smiles and walks away, leaving the boy baffled. The boy aims at him and pretends to shoot him.

"I ain't no delivery boy! I'm a newspaperman! I got better scoops to dish than deliver…" He looks down and sees the penny on the ground. "Hey! Thanks, Mister. I'll bring your goods myself if Pa will let me."

W.H. waves as he walks away.

Later that night W.H. settles in Mr. Mather's tiny one-bedroom cabin. He lights a candle, opens his journal, licks the tip of his fountain pen, and flips the worn yellow pages to a blank page.

April 12, 1861
Dearest Uncle,

I am in love with Jenny Mather.

W.H. scratches a line through "in love" and writes: "infatuated."

My heart was set ablaze by a pair of emerald eyes that flash with excitement. I could tell she was happy to see me, but I doubt that Mrs. Mather would approve. Without so much as a howdy, she grabbed her daughter by the arm and scooted her along. My tender affection appeared wrapped in a checkered red and black dress. The lovely thing is perhaps seventeen or eighteen. She has pretty blond hair. Her lips are like two pink petals pressed to perfection. Though she is a beautiful rose in a desert wasteland, I thought better than to show affection, even though I wanted to. I have felt the prick of women and I find the Scriptures to be true. "Hell hath no fury like a woman scorned."

After spending nearly two months on the trail, I found her to be a sight for lonely eyes. Too bad mother hen was quick to guard her chick. I believe them to be Norwegian or Germanic. Their fine hair is yellow, and their eyes are of the most brilliant colors.

Jenny will be at church on Sunday. If time permits, I will be at church on Sunday as well.

"Dark o'clock," W.H. pens, too lazy to check his pocket watch. He begins his next paragraph.

Arrived in town today. My first impressions of the West are definitive. The West is an intriguing and adventurous land. I have drawn pictures of the forests I passed along the way. I sketched the ferry. The grassy plains. Towering mountains. Wildlife of every kind. Firm Fist, my first Indian friend I met in Missouri. And the train. I would have used the camera, but I only have so many slides.

I had hoped to spend more time at Fort Mackenzie with the Missouri Sioux, but that decision would have led me to break my word and land me back in the classroom. By the way, thank you for wiring me more gold. I promise to be more cautious with the rest of the grant.

I have a deep love for the frontier. If I am to be honest, Uncle, I'm not certain my heart can be trusted. It has led me into danger once already. All I know I can trust is the wild. I want nothing more than a blanket of stars over my head and the moon reflecting in my eyes. I want my face to feel the sun. Doesn't matter to me how these things come about, so long as I can see one or the other any time I please.

Before you worry yourself about my safety, remember I have a lever-action Henry rifle and a Colt six-shooter, my pal Bingo by my side for company, and a bowie knife in the event I run out of ammunition. I should be just fine. A fella's gotta make his mark in this life before it gets snuffed out by some ill-tempered drunk or a stray bullet.

It's interesting that a wolf or a pack of wolves has so decimated the town financially. I have seen them do many things, but financial ruin is not one of them. I didn't ask, but I presume the residents are Easterners migrating West. I suspect this because of their deep-rooted superstitions. If you listen to New Englanders, vampires, werewolves, and witches walk among the living. It strikes me as odd that a people so adamant about science would be equally superstitious. I either have an intriguing mystery on my hands or a ferocious wolf. Maybe a pack of wolves. One thing is for certain. If any of the townsfolk are werewolves, I would assume they'd attack one another and take that portion of property and profit. I cannot be certain which of these values Americans desire most: pistols or profits. That should be the title to a book, no doubt. Here are some odd facts.

W.H. lifts his red pen and taps it against his prickly chin.

From what Mr. Mather has said, no people have been attacked. Why is that if the wolves are within proximity? I will have to look through local newspapers to confirm that.

He circles his question about the wolves, then writes, "To be determined?"

He carries his waning candle over to a nightstand and sets it down. Hot wax trickles off and seals itself to the dusty Douglas fir desktop. After undoing his suspenders, he undresses down to his one-piece, button-up long-john undergarments. He looks around the tiny one-bedroom house and wonders why the owner has allowed such a gem to fall into disrepair. A cabinet hangs on by one hinge. Raccoons have disconnected the wood-burning stove's tall pipe. Tufts of their fur trapped in the hinge gives the burglars away.

"Keep watch, Bingo!" he shouts to his best friend, who rests on the porch.

With a long stretch and a short yawn, W.H. sits on a creaky spring mattress. He takes his glasses off and declares, "Home is where your head rests."

Bingo barks in approval before W.H. blows out the candle and goes to sleep.

The next morning shafts of the spring sun reflect off the dusty floorboards. Elias Mather and his son, Billy, knock at the door. W.H. is awake and quick to greet them. After some small talk, they deliver all the goods necessary to sustain a man.

"Go ahead and put the pigs in the pen, Billy. I'd keep the chickens in their cages until you get the coop up."

"Is there much game to be had on the prairie?" W.H. asks.

"Very little. If you need anything else, you be sure to let me know."

The first thing W.H. decides to do is build a chicken coop and free two chickens and a rooster from their cages. Next he repairs the pigpen and watches two fat hogs roll around their dusty new home. They look at him as if to say, *Where's the food? Where's the water? Where's the mud?*

"Now that we got breakfast and dinner secure, let's get to work!"

After watering and feeding the animals, W.H. wastes no time gathering his materials for his bait traps. He uses a glass jar he found in a large barn next to the small cabin. The enormous barn tempts him to move his living quarters up to the hayloft, but at present he has no time.

He carefully measures powder strychnine into the glass and then pumps water from a rusty well pump with a chipped red handle.

"Can't be too careful with wolves," he says, eagerly pouring the toxic liquid into a pan. He works the handle until the rust color in the water turns clear. His icy blue eyes fix on the cup's fill line. Once he's mixed the arsenic, he builds a fire and places the pan on it. He cuts a couple of thick strips of meat while he waits for the water to boil down his scent, then dips the meat in the poisonous brew. *If townsfolk could see me now, they might think I was a witch. Or a warlock. Or a doodledoo.*

Bingo pops his head up at the scent of meat.

"Keep back, Bingo!" W.H. shouts, pointing to the pan on the burner. "That there is poison!"

CHAPTER 114

Bingo licks his lips. He doesn't seem to care that dinner could kill. His stomach drives him to the meat.

W.H. uses metal hooks to remove the meat from the poison pan and puts long leather gloves on to keep his scent off the bait. He swaps the meats with cheese and sings, "Chicken in the fryin' pan, rooster on the grill, do-si-do." He stomps his foot and thinks of Jenny as he puts his arm out and pretends to square dance with her. "Now link your arm with that pretty little girl, ladies smile and he takes you on a twirl."

He strings the meat high up in the barn so that Bingo can't get to it.

"Change that left-hand lady by the right hand…" He sticks his tongue out and makes a sour face as he imagines himself passing her mother. Most of his day is spent prepping his gear and pretending to dance with a girl who isn't there. When the dance is over, he smirks and thinks, *She probably don't even like me.*

As the sun sets, he diligently works out every detail of his plan, then walks over to his horse and props her hooves up.

"Looks like you could use some new shoes." He leads Cotton to the barn.

Shoeing his horse, dropping a half barrel of hay, and filling her trough one bucket at a time takes the rest of his evening.

Cooking himself ham and corn mush takes longer than he expected, because he had to repair the pipe and clean the stove as well.

After a rough day of hard work, he lies back on his creaky mattress.

April 13, 1861

Thought about the weather I braved on the way down. Some of the fiercest snowfall I have ever seen. Coming from Canada, that says a lot. Sun makes me smile in ways I didn't know I could!

Prepared five poisoned baits today. Very excited to see what these baits produce. Wired Mr. Rockefeller's office for more plates, but I don't want to waste what I have until I see something worth photographing.

Gonna try real hard to keep my end of the bargain, even though I hate journalin'. Good night, Uncle.

***

Before the sun rises, the cock crows.

W.H. slowly rises and massages his aching muscles. He gets dressed and stumbles out to the chicken coop.

"Listen here, rooster. I ain't got a name for you yet, and you ain't gonna get one if you crow before dawn. I'm just gonna toss you in the skillet and go get a rooster that can crow when it's supposed to."

The rooster ruffles his feathers, cocks his head, and defiantly crows.

"Determination – that's what I like to see."

W.H. opens the cage door, grabs the rooster, carries him over to a stump, and raises a rusty hatchet.

"Cock-a-doodle…" The rooster's crow trails off into a name. "W-i-l-m-a!"

"Roger!" is the only word Wilma, the orange hen, manages before the small ax drops. She reaches for her beau with an outstretched wing.

Roger's head falls off the stump, and W.H. carries his flapping wings past his love, the only hen he truly loved.

"Wilma, I'm so sorry." Valerie, a friendly white hen with a red comb and matching wattle, comforts her. She was the only hen that truly loved Roger. What's worse is she thought Roger loved only her, but it was obvious her name was not the last to be uttered. *Never mind that*, she thinks. *Be strong for Wilma.*

W.H. returns and scatters seed for the hens. He finds two eggs under the orange hen and none under the white hen.

"You're next!" he says, pointing a bloody finger at Valerie, the heartbroken white hen.

"Don't worry, Valerie. I won't let the monster hurt you. When my nerves recover, I'll move some eggs to your nest." Wilma flutters.

"If my nerves weren't shot, I'd be able to pay the bounty. Were we brought here just to die?"

"It ain't right. They kill our men, steal our children, and keep us cooped up in prison our whole lives. We got no life living like this."

"Oh, don't say what I think you're going to say. My nerves can't take it."

"We're going to fly the coop, Valerie. I've had all I can take."

"Oh no. How will we get food? Water? Who will protect us from the coyotes? The foxes? The owls? The snakes? The werewolf?"

"What's worse, Valerie? The skillet or the jaws of the wild?"

"Oh, I just don't know!" the worried hen clucks.

CHAPTER 115

W.H. gets a fire going and makes a larger-than-usual breakfast.

He quickly saddles his horse and packs the baits.

On his first day, he sets out to place werewolf folklore into its physical locations. Upon his first investigation, ranch hands tell him about their neighbor who "lost a whole dadgum herd o' sheep."

After a brief conversation, he learns that even the ranch hands believe a werewolf is on the prowl. But unlike the townspeople who blame one another, the ranchers and laborers side with Molly. "Who else could it be but Mr. Mather? He's the one who's making all this money." A cowboy repeats her words verbatim.

I wonder if these cowboys are the high-class clientele Molly was referring to.

A couple miles away, W.H. finds the neighbor who lost his sheep to the wolf. He has a brief conversation with the man.

"I ain't never seen anything like it. They just murdered them for the fun of it," an old rancher named George says as he scratches his short gray whiskers.

"Wolves are murderers. That's all they are. That's all they'll ever be," W.H. says.

The old man nods in agreement and pats his blue coveralls. "Killing machines." He plucks a blade of grass and slips it between his lips. "Savage killers."

With the old man's permission, W.H. travels down to where the incident occurred. He lays his first bait near the stream. Then ties a white rag to a tall bush with "poison" written on it to warn anyone who might find it.

"Let's name this first stop Justice, Bingo."

Bingo barks. "Justice for all."

He moves into a canyon and sets up camp, wondering where he should place his next bait.

When morning comes, he removes what's left of the rooster from a handkerchief and finishes off Roger. Bingo cracks open the bones and practically swallows them whole. Then regrets it when he hacks them up.

The two circle five miles out from where the sheep herd was attacked. Bingo picks up the pit bulls' canyon trail and leads W.H. to their dried carcasses. At least a dozen withered pit bull bodies are found over a quarter-mile stretch. Some had their throats torn out completely. He does his best to examine each body, but the sun has baked them to a firm crisp. For the most part their story has been erased.

"We'll leave one here and call this place Vengeance," W.H. says, marking it with the same white fabric banner.

Bingo scans the ridgeline and starts barking.

"What is it, boy?" W.H. asks.

Look! Bingo says. *A den! There's a den! Right there! See it? It's right there!*

All W.H. can hear is "woof, woof, woof!" He unholsters his rifle and looks through his scope. Scanning back and forth, he finds the source of Bingo's excitement, a gaping hole in the side of the cliff.

"Good boy!" W.H. says, patting Bingo's head. "Tonight I'm giving you the bigger portion of dinner." He pats his belly, looks around, and says, "As soon as we find it."

A gust of wind picks up. Bingo catches the rotting scent of death. He gets back to tracking. He smells something so terrible, he can't help but satisfy his curiosity.

W.H. follows his energized hound, hoping to get his first shot at the wolves. He's disappointed when all Bingo leads him to is Trapper Dan's decaying horse.

"What in the world?" W.H. gags, then chokes. He covers his mouth with his handkerchief. Maggots the size of rice grains polish off the last bits of flesh, biting here and there as they scoot along. Blowflies swarm W.H.'s face and prove unbearable.

"They kill horses, too?"

W.H. is immediately concerned for Cotton. He turns around and sprints back to his horse, who he finds nibbling away at sagebrush.

"Oh, thank heavens." He places his hand over his heart.

He unties Cotton and lets her roam freely so she won't be prey. He and Bingo scale up the cliff and scout the den.

Bingo is the first to enter the dark cavern. He sniffs around, then barks to signal all clear. W.H. enters the narrow opening and flicks his weapon off safety. He aims it directly in front of him, ready to blast and work his lever action as fast as he has to.

When he sees that the den is empty, he searches around for clues and finds one that freezes him in place.

He whistles. "Dang!" Then he holds his hand to Kiowa's perfectly visible wolf track for a quick estimation. "Five and a half, maybe six inches long. Maybe four and three-fourths inches wide? This has to be the biggest wolf I've ever tracked."

He stands up and removes his cowboy hat. Scratching the top of his head, he mutters, "Wolves don't grow that big…"

Searching around, he finds other tracks and tufts of fur. *Colors don't match*, he thinks. "Could be a pack of wolves or maybe other animals lived in here. I don't know yet, Bingo, but I aim to find out," he mumbles.

W.H. drops a bait in the cave. "Let's call this place Patience."

He follows his trail back toward the ranches and talks with eager landowners, who offer up room and board and information that sounds ridiculously untrue. Each interview generates another clue. W.H. wastes no time meeting with each lead.

The next day he encounters Alejandro.

"*Bienvenido, mi amigo,*" the middle-aged, well-to-do Mexican rancher with gray hair nods to W.H. Alejandro is dressed in a fine Spanish suit with lots of flair.

The Hispanic hospitality he receives makes the pale-faced far Northerner feel like he's visiting an aunt and uncle instead of two strangers.

When they finish a large Mexican meal, Alejandro slides into a crisp, tan smoking jacket and grabs two cigars out of a cardboard box with an Indian chief on the cover.

The stern-faced Mexican strikes a match and puffs away at his cigar. When it's lit, he hands it to W.H. and then strikes another match and ignites his own. "When the ranch hands first saw Lobo, they didn't know what to call him, so they named him hombre-lobo."

"Hombre-lobo?" W.H. says, butchering the Spanish. "Is Louie the same as Lobo?"

His wife, Deserea, responds. "Sí, this is how you say 'werewolf' in Spanish. He's thinned our herd down to the point we were thinking we'd move to Texas or California," Deserea says, patting down her Spanish-style linen to knock the dust off. W.H. can't help but stare at her beautiful shiny black hair and honey-brown eyes. Time has been gracious to her.

"Haven't you tried to hunt him?"

CHAPTER 116

"Ha! Ha! Ha!" The rancher slaps his knee. "Everyone with a rifle has tried to kill Lobo! Let me ask you something, hombre. Do you...?" He turns to his wife and says, "*Como se dice, hombre-lobo?*"

"I told you, 'werewolf,'" Deserea looks out of the corner of her eye.

"This werewolf is not the monster he's been made out to be."

"None of us really are," W.H. says, feeling like he's finally found rational human beings.

Alejandro continues. "I've seen him, though. He is very wise. You can only spot him at small hours."

"Do you mean twilight?"

"Sí. I know he is a wolf. But he is not like any wolf I have ever known. His cunning and brilliance are not normal for the animal kingdom."

"But he is just a wolf?"

"Sí, 'just,'" the rancher says with a sarcastic tone and a cockeyed glance that lets W.H. know he believes the beast to be more than a wolf.

"Lobo, the wolf," W.H. says, reminding himself to make a journal entry.

They finish cigars. Alejandro gives a brief history of his family. W.H. enjoys the story.

Deserea sees to it that a warm bath is drawn for their guest. W.H. is invited to stay in their guest bedroom, which is a thousand times better than his shack. Though the floorboards creak the same way, the lady of the house had the walls decorated with watercolor paintings of lilies, roses, and dandelions. A cross-stitch on the wall with red Latin lettering reads:

S. IOANNES I:V, SI QUIS AUTEM VESTRUM INDIGENT SAPIENTIAM POSTULET A DEO. The washerwomen mixed lavender in the soap when they did laundry. They used rose petals on the pillowcases, so that when the guest pulls the covers up and rests his head, the scent from the pictures leaps into his nostrils.

No adventure can touch a man the way all these feminine qualities touch my soul. I might need a wife after all, he thinks to himself as he reflects on his stubborn position.

The next morning Alejandro has his ranch hands feed, water, comb, and saddle Cotton. Deserea has washerwomen scrub his stinky clothes, and they are dry before he wakes up. She makes fajitas and omelets and pours steaming coffee for the men, while Alejandro tells W.H. where to go next.

"Here is my card. Hand this to anyone in this town, and mis amigos will see you are treated with respect. Just remember what your Ben Franklin said about guests."

"I'm actually a Canadian."

"Sí, but that's no' what he said. He said, 'Fish and guests stink after three days.'" Alejandro lets his gaze rest on W.H. long enough to make him feel uncomfortable.

"Hey, Alejandro? *No hay una mujer entre nuestras amigas que haría de este hombre una buena esposa?*"

"*Sí, pero el debe hacerlo en tres dias o armas y rifles le acompanara al altar. No se puede esperar que un padre o una madre esperan durante mas tiempo. Ellos se quedaran dormidos el cuarto dia y el gallo encontrara su camino al gallinero!*" He tucks his arms under his armpits like wings, then chirps like a bird. "*Y luego, por la primavera, muchos chicos.*"

Deserea gasps and wrings her hands. She looks at W.H. and says, "*Hablas español?*"

He sips his coffee and says, "Sí."

Deserea gasps and throws her napkin to the floor. "*Para los santos en el cielo, ¿por qué mi esposo tiene que hablar de esta manera frente a nuestros invitados? Harás un mejor marido, ¿no?*"

Really, W.H. understands just one word of Spanish: "sí." The rest he tries to piece together through her stressed expressions.

Deserea puts her hand on his arm and squeezes tightly. "I know you will. Now let me get your supper covered in a basket so that you won't starve."

Several hours later W.H. rides out on the prairie, putting Alejandro's advice to good use. He scans the open plain at sunset and searches high and low with his collapsing telescope.

When night falls, he gets a fire going and pens a journal entry.

April 17, 1861
Dear Uncle,

   I have experienced the most exquisite food. The Mexican does not eat food the same way as any white man I have ever known. Instead of using silverware, they wrap black beans, rice, lettuce, tomato, cheese, sour cream, some spicy sauce, and whatever else they can think of in flat cornmeal they call a tortilla. These finger entrées are called burritos. They will also cook the flat dough, bend it with a metal rod, and fry it in oil. These are called tacos, and I must say are exceptionally good! Both are eaten with fingers. Tonight I ate a strange corn-husk wrap called a tamale. I cannot understand how they bite through the corn wrap. It is mushy and gross in the center and rough on the exterior. With great difficulty, I got it down. If you should ever find yourself eating Mexican food, stick with burritos or tacos.

Over the next few days he makes the rounds among the ranchers. Many Mexican and white men give him excellent advice. Most have him stay the night, and though their beautiful daughters bat their eyelashes and invite his affections, he remembers Alejandro's advice. Instead of staying for three days, he always leaves the next morning, chasing down a new lead, searching for any scrap of information that might be Lobo's undoing.

Eventually he meets Alejandro's ranch hand, Juan, the man on duty when the sheep herd was slaughtered. Juan escorts W.H. out to the site and leaves him there to search for clues. Though nothing new is discovered, W.H. drops some baits, deciding to save his last one for later. He marks them with a white rag and writes "poison" on the cotton, so no one will let their dogs or hogs accidentally eat the meat.

W.H. follows the same stream that the wolves used to lead them to the sheep. He finds himself in a tall canyon for a mile or so before he exits the mouth. He uses his spotting scope to search the wide-open valley and its surrounding red rock mountains.

To the north, a grand mesa littered with pine trees forms a thick green forest at the peak. "Whad'ya bet no one has bothered to look up there, Bingo?"

That's because it's at least ten miles away, Master. Don't make me walk all that way. The collie whimpers, longing to return to his dusty porch, but his master will have none of it. His thoroughness is exhausting.

At sunset W.H. lights a fire and chokes down the last of the stale tamales. His smoke trail stands out in the shallow valley, surrounded by tall mountains.

High on one of those mountaintops, Makes Trouble spots W.H.'s smoke plume.

"Either a man who watches over the tame buffalo is over there"— he motions with a nod—"or another enemy has come to attack us."

"Why do they come?" Kiowa asks.

"Something is bringing them here," Kida answers.

"I don't see any tame buffalo with him, but that doesn't mean he hasn't let them wander. Sometimes they will do that," Paw says in a low, serious tone.

Kiowa inhales several deep breaths and catches the man's scent. "It is a good sign for us to see him. He will lead us to his herd. Track him, Makes Trouble, and tell us what you find."

As Makes Trouble is about to leave, Paw gets up and follows him.

"You don't have to go, Uncle. Stay here with your nieces and nephews. Tell them our Kiowa stories."

"I will when I return. Two heads are better than one."

The next day, Paw and Makes Trouble track W.H. and Bingo all the way to the pine forest where they make their harvest moon change. Onendah has wisely broken down the twig huts, and winter has covered the earth.

"His dog has a good nose," Paw whispers.

"Our scent is long gone. How can he follow our trail here?" Makes Trouble asks.

"He cannot smell our trail. He can see our tracks. Even I can see them from up here. The snows did not wash them away."

W.H. drops his last bait deep in the forest, right where Bingo gives up the trail. He determines to call the bait station Certain Death, for this Lobo would certainly be dead soon. W.H. laughs at his own joke.

"What is he dropping, Paw?"

Paw shrugs. "I do not know, but no tame buffalo watchers have dropped anything before."

When W.H. is done placing his trap, he stands, turns, and comes face-to-face with Onendah.

CHAPTER 117

The medicine man is dressed in all white. He dons a beaver-pelt cap. His face is covered in black war paint, with six white dots on his right cheek signifying the wolf pack. One yellow dot on his left cheek signifies the sun's power. A brown streak in the shape of a bird spans his forehead and marks him as the eagle. He holds a long spear and watches W.H. intently.

W.H. can't help but stare at the scalps that hang off the spear's shaft. He slides his hand down but hesitates before grabbing his pistol.

Onendah lets his hand slide down and rest on a tomahawk tucked into his beaded belt.

"How," W.H. says, lifting his hand up abruptly, certain the Indian will get to his tomahawk before he can sling his pistol.

"He stinks of death!" Bingo shouts in rapid barks.

W.H. raises his right hand and repeats himself. "How."

"How what, Pale-Face?" Onendah says in nearly perfect English.

"I thought 'how' was 'hello' in Injun.'"

"For Sioux. For Kiowa it is 'ah-hoe.'" Onendah waves his arm.

"Ah-hoe," W.H. says with a broad smile, mimicking Onendah's arm gesture. "You speak good English."

"I speak nothing," Onendah says, tilting his head as he studies W.H. "My magic spell makes sense of my words to you and yours to me." Onendah shakes a rattle and pats a leather pouch around his waistband. W.H. is confused as to which one is magic.

"Magic?"

Onendah passes over the pouch and strums his fingers on top of his rust-colored tomahawk. "Why do you come to the pine forest?"

"I am looking for an evil wolf."

"What makes him evil?"

"Just bein' a wolf makes him evil."

"What does bein' Indian make me?"

"I guess a chief?"

Onendah's serious expression melts. He tilts his head back and laughs. "Ha! Ha! Ha! I don't think I will kill you, Round Eyes! You are nothing like the other hunters who have waged war on the wolf. You are funny."

W.H.'s smile is reduced to an awkward grin.

Onendah follows up with, "And funny-looking."

W.H. frowns. "Well, would you look at the time? I suppose I best be gettin' on my way. I don't wanna be out past dark."

Onendah smiles and waves good-bye. He rests his cheek on his staff and wonders what all this will mean for his dear pack of wolves.

"Bingo, he sure wasn't eagle-plumed like in the print. He was something fierce and wonderful. I don't know whether to be afraid or intrigued. I suppose it's better to be provident and prepared than intrigued and scalped."

Bingo barks. *I told you so!*

On his way back down, Bingo picks up Makes Trouble's and Paw's wolf trail. He barks ferociously and follows it all the way to town, where it ends in front of a worn-out cedar sign that reads, FAREWELL & COME AGAIN.

A safe distance away, Paw covers his snout with both paws.

"We have led him back to where he belongs. Maybe he will be wise and stay here," Makes Trouble says between snickers.

W.H. looks around in confusion. He dismounts his horse and follows the tracks.

"I don't understand. All the tracks lead to town, but they stop right here."

"Right now he is learning that you stepped back in your tracks," Paw says to Makes Trouble.

"This one is going to be fun to play with. He won't quit easy. Look how long he stands there, trying to figure out where we disappeared to."

Makes Trouble's eyes widen. He taps his head, smiles, and whispers, "Let us trace his tracks and see all the places he's been. I have the best plan I have ever had."

Bingo sniffs all around. He can smell the wolves as though they were standing right next to him. Their scent is everywhere but then nowhere.

"Unless they learned to walk backward, Bingo, I'm stumped. Let's go get some grub and a drink."

Tired and hungry, Bingo gives up the search.

Inside the Cowboy Hall, W.H. meets two cowboys passing through.

"What'll ya have?" Molly asks.

"Whiskey."

She sets the bottle on the counter. "Mather says you got gold, so you're good. I'll keep your tab open." Molly's attitude toward him has changed dramatically. She breaks a twinkling wink and a warm smile as she pops the bottle's cork.

"I got gold, Molly," Javier, a young cowboy says, showing a capped tooth.

"If you can get it outta your mouth, I'll open a tab for you, too. Otherwise y'all are gonna have to pay as you drink."

She puts her hands on her hips and stares firmly at the new guests. When she feels like she's gotten her point across, she claps her hands and shouts, "Who wants to hear a little piana?"

"Tickle them ivories, girl," a gentleman says from a table filled with rough gamblers.

Molly rocks the keys with her version of American music. She pounds away and sings, "Come on, come on, give me all them fancy things. Diamonds on my ears, gold on my fingers. Dresses galore, don't make me a whore; just give me those fancy things."

Her lyrics don't match the melody of the song at all, but the guests don't seem to mind.

After spending so long on the range, W.H. enjoys the company. After the third whiskey, Molly starts looking incredibly attractive. By the fourth whiskey, Molly is looking as good as Jenny.

The men join in the song since it's the only one Molly knows, and they've all learned it by the third time she sings it. The camaraderie between the lonely single men spreads. Some are old. Most are young. All of them sing the song of Molly, the girl who ran away from home looking for her rich love. "Her beau abandoned her and took her money. She was tossed on the street, but that didn't stop her. Ol' Molly fought her way into the room full of swine she swindled, but only after they tried to swindle her. God bless their meager souls," she sings solo.

The evening wanes on and the night turns to day.

"I haven't had this much fun in years," W.H. says, downing the last of his whiskey bottle.

"Ahh... you were but a lightweight when I first met you. Now I see you got hair on yer chest," Molly says, laughing so hard, her exposed cleavage jiggles.

The saloon doors burst open. Town and country residents pour in with some ranch cowboys. Most look familiar from all of W.H.'s investigating. They make more noise than a hurricane.

"He's done killed more cattle than all the fingers and toes in this room," Hank, a roughneck cowboy, shouts.

"You can double that number with sheep. We can't keep flocks 'cause he kills them every chance he gets," Javier follows up.

"I'd shoot him myself if I ever saw him." Jenny stands proudly, locking her double-barrel breech-loading shotgun.

"Oh no, not again," W.H. mumbles as he thinks back to the night Maybelle captured his heart with a double-barreled shotgun.

"It wouldn't do any good. He is hombre-lobo. Only silver bullets can stop the wolfman," Maria, Javier's wife, rebuts.

Jenny stomps her foot. "Who can afford silver bullets?" she demands to know.

W.H. spins around in his barstool to face her. "I just want you all to know, ain't no way Molly is a werewolf. We been here all night with her."

"Well, that's just real great, isn't it?" Jenny fumes, kicking her hip out and resting her shotgun on it. "Everyone here is real proud the mystery's solved, Mr. Capital Letters for a Name. Now let's go kill us a wolf!" she shouts, looking like a Viking goddess to the drunk hunter.

"Yew sure are purtty"—he leans forward, then hiccups—"when yer mad."

Jenny gasps. "Listen here, runt. Before you go making eyes at me, know this: If you were the last man in town, I wouldn't let you lay a finger on me."

W.H. raises the brim of his hat. "Well, fortunately for you, I'm not.

"We better organize a posse," W.H. says, scrambling for order among the chaos.

"Rest assured, gents," W.H. says, pushing his glasses up with his finger. "I am a wolf hunter, and yew can go on back to yer homes, because I"—he picks up someone's half-drunken beer and raises the mug above his head—"and I alone am going to kill that wolf!"

The bar goes silent and then erupts in laughter. Several cowboys enter the crowded saloon with Sheriff Dawson.

A card player shouts, "Ya hear that? This here boy thinks he's mightier than Mazingo the Dingo, Ol' Barb' Wire, Trapper Dan, Buffalo Tom, Frenchie Pierre, and every other tracker that's been run out of town by Lobo."

Molly laughs. "Can you even shoot a gun, Four Eyes?"

The bar explodes in mocking laughter.

CHAPTER 118

"Well, y'all can laugh, but by this time tomorrow he'll be dead and cold from—"

Mr. Mather cuts him off. "Strychnine?"

"Arsenic?" Javier says, folding his arms.

"Cyanide?" A cowboy gives a firm nod.

"Ain't none of them worked. Ever!" Mr. Mather reports.

"Well, mine's different. You'll see."

"Why do you think your bait is any different?" Sheriff Dawson folds his arms and gives a stern glare.

Not wanting to reveal his secret, W.H. blows a raspberry and spins back around in his seat.

"You deaf, runt? I asked you a question," Jenny shouts with such a harshness W.H. wonders if one of the men hasn't possessed her.

He shakes his head and raises his tone to offset hers. "It's not the bait I use; it's where I place it."

"Where'd you put it?" Jenny demands.

W.H. leaps on the counter, nearly tumbling over. After he regains his balance he hollers, "Upppppp... your arses!" He points at the onlookers.

The patrons go dead silent. Their expressionless faces show they are not impressed with his crude behavior.

"Even my arse?" Sheriff Dawson asks, with a sternness that brings order to the crowd.

Not wanting to upset local law enforcement, W.H. shrugs and says, "No, sir. Definitely not." He tries to focus his whiskey double-vision on one of the two floating Sheriff Dawsons.

"Up in the high country?" Sheriff Dawson asks.

W.H. nods and orders another bottle of whiskey.

"I think you've had enough, Mr. Wolf Hunter," Molly says. "Can anyone see him upstairs?"

"Sí," Javier says, motioning for someone to help him.

A few days later W.H. is recovered. He rides Cotton home through a seemingly empty town.

"Oh boy, Bingo, are we having the time of our lives! This is way better than school. We can drink as much as we want. Hunt wolves in our off-hours. And pretty much do whatever we want. Molly sure was kind to put us up."

It's 'cause we sing so well together, Bingo barks.

As he and Bingo trail in, he notices that the chickens have busted out of the chicken coop.

"Nothing works the way it ought to here, Bingo."

Bingo runs over and sniffs the hen house and checks to see if they did their duty. He muzzles his nose through the straw. *Not one egg.* Bingo sighs.

He follows the hen trail over to the pigpen and learns the hogs have somehow gotten free. A pile of chicken tracks surround the peg wedge. Evidence suggests the chickens pecked the peg out of the latch and freed all the prisoners.

"I guess we best skip breakfast and go check the bait stations," W.H. says, discouraged.

I'm hungry! Bingo barks.

"Well, let's get to it, boy!"

But I'm hungry now! Bingo darts back and forth, demanding food before labor.

W.H. leans over, picks up a stick and tosses it. It lands in front of his dog. Bingo growls.

"All right. All right. I'll see what I can whip up. I'm sure we got a jar of beans or something in the pantry."

A day later W.H. checks his first bait station, Justice. Broken grass blades and fresh wolf tracks indicate that an animal has been in the area.

"HA! See that, boy. They ain't as smart as everyone thinks they are." As they ride up on the flagged spot, sheer delight raises W.H.'s voice an entire octave. "Lookie there, boy. They took the bait. Do you smell anything?"

I don't smell anything dead, Bingo whines.

W.H. kicks at his horse's side and sprints to the next bait drop, Vengeance. A few hours later they arrive and find the same result.

He sees a wolf's trail. But his bait is gone and no wolf carcass can be found.

"Surely I used enough poison?" W.H. scratches his chin. He takes his hat off and fans the sweat off his face. *It's only spring and already it's hotter than the dickens. It's gonna be a roaster this year.*

Bingo barks when he finds a trail.

"Oh, we definitely have wolves. That print is unmistakable, and that is certainly Lobo!" W.H. measures with his hand to be sure. "Well, with any luck, he's eaten two baits. Maybe the sun wore him down. I bet we'll find his body just up the way."

As the sun sets, W.H. looks at Bingo. "Think that ol' rancher with the cute daughter will put us up?" Bingo tilts his head to the side and barks. "Let's get out of here. If poison can't kill the werewolf, nothing can."

Happy to abandon the search, Bingo barks rapidly.

"My thoughts exactly." W.H. mounts his horse and holsters his rifle.

***

Later that night W.H. greets the rancher Geoffrey, whom he met when previously conducting his interviews. The older man and his wife, Elizabeth, offer their accommodations most generously. They feed him, Bingo, and his horse.

Their six pretty daughters' advances go off like fireworks at the dinner table.

Yet W.H. hardly notices the oldest, Katherine's, flirtations. Even when she does as her mother instructs, bringing him dessert and lingering long enough for him steal a glance or two. Refilling his glass doesn't do much, so she gets bolder and flutters her eyelashes, to which he inquires whether she has "caught a loose eyelash."

"No, no, I'm fine," Katherine says, dismissing herself and taking her seat.

"All he seems to be interested in, Mama, is that dang wolf," Katherine whispers to her mother.

"Yes, but that's so he can get the reward money. Once he has money in his pocket, what do you reckon he'll do with it?"

"Dang if I know."

"Buy a house. Settle land. Get a wife." Elizabeth winks at her daughter.

Katherine sits up and gloats at the thought of being married before the town's toughest competition, Jenny. She makes a final attempt. "Mr. Wolf Hunter, would you like to hear us sing?"

W.H. nods.

The girls line up and sing a song Katherine wrote about a sweet little prairie bird. Their high-pitched tones and harmony get their father to fetch his fiddle. For the rest of the night, the family enjoys Katherine's pretty voice, her father's fiddle, and, occasionally, Bingo's howl.

He's sure to be mine, Katherine thinks to herself contentedly. She adjusts her bonnet's blue bow under her chin and tilts her head to the side to capture W.H.'s attention. For reasons unbeknownst to Katherine, her charms and wiles fail to hook her intended prey.

Bright and early the next day, W.H. enjoys his breakfast. He thanks the ladies and offers Katherine a poem for her next song.

"Oh, you will have to come back soon, W.H. I'll have the song ready for you, and you'll have supper with us. I'll make a fresh peach cobbler. Did I mention I can bake?"

"That sounds mighty fine. Set the date."

With a cluck of his tongue and a kick of his boot, W.H. is back on the trail.

As he rides, he can't help but think of Katherine. Then Jenny. Then Katherine again. Her pretty face haunts him, and for some reason he tastes peaches all the way to Patience, his third bait station. Katherine disappears from his mind when the white rag waves in front of his face. Again he finds wolf tracks but no body.

"This don't make no sense, Bingo!" W.H. bellows, a sinking feeling in the pit of his stomach. "That's enough poison to kill ten grown men."

Bingo whimpers. *Let's go back to the house with the pretty gals. They fed me. They let me sing with them.*

"So where's the wolf?" W.H. kicks the ground and sends an explosion of red dust flying up in the air.

Bingo walks over and puts his paw on his master's leg. *Don't worry; we will find him. You are the best wolf hunter and there is no better.*

Bingo barks, his beaming eyes communicating his thoughts.

At the fourth checkpoint, there is no bait, only the telltale wolf prints and the waving rag.

W.H. kicks at Cotton's side and forces her up the pine forest. The white horse takes the brunt of his frustration. He whips her when she slacks and drives her to the point she's gasping for air and sweating so hard she drenches his pants legs.

Expecting to find a dead wolf at any moment, he dismounts Cotton and races her to his fifth and final bait station, Certain Death. As he scans the area, his eyes rest on a scene he absolutely cannot believe.

CHAPTER 119

"Daaagggone…" W.H. lifts his glasses. He takes them off, rubs his eyes, then puts his spectacles back on just to be sure his eyes aren't playing a cruel optical trick on him.

In front of him he is astounded to find all his poisonous baits, Justice, Vengeance, Patience, Greed, and Certain Death, neatly stacked. Piles of wolf droppings on top of his baits send a clear message. Flies swarm and scatter as the wolf hunter crouches down and closely inspects exactly what the animal kingdom thinks of his hunting principles.

"Bingo, I do not believe this Lobo is an ordinary wolf," W.H. grumbles.

Makes Trouble's plan is at last revealed.

He shakes his head. "This can't be!"

"He didn't really take the bait at all. He just carried them here…" W.H. says, inspecting the pile. He winds up his leg and kicks the pile so hard it sends poisoned meat and flying feces all over the forest.

Bingo covers his snout with both paws and hides his head in shame. What W.H. can't see is all the urine Bingo notices. *Blech. Master, there's more than one wolf. Can't you see all the markings?*

"Dadgum, boy. We just got licked!"

Pacing around, W.H. looks at the trap from several different angles. He can find only one trail of tracks, because the wolves use tree branches to sweep over the rest of the pack's tracks, making it seem like only one wolf is responsible.

W.H. tosses his hat on the ground and stomps on it. Out of sheer frustration he throws his rifle.

A safe distance away, Kiowa, Paw, and Makes Trouble are well concealed in the tree line.

Makes Trouble sits up and peels his lips back. His pupils narrow and he prepares to attack the defenseless hunter.

Kiowa releases a low growl and checks him in place.

"Why? Why can we not kill Round Eyes? He cannot use his thunder stick against us. He will never be more vulnerable than he is now! Do not rob me of this honor, my would-be brother."

Kiowa growls again, making his intent clear. Makes Trouble has no choice. He must obey the alpha.

Kiowa watches W.H.'s temper tantrum with great delight. He lifts his lips, partly snarling and smiling crookedly when W.H. spends an hour or more searching for his rifle. Eventually W.H. recovers it. He mounts his tired horse and trots out of the forest with slumped shoulders.

"He is certainly our enemy and not a keeper of the tame buffalo," Kiowa whispers to his uncle. Paw nods.

"Why did we not ambush him, Kiowa?" Makes Trouble sulks. "It is not too late if you have changed your mind. Lead the raid to kill him. I will follow."

"Have all these foreign faces taught you nothing?" Kiowa asks.

Makes Trouble sighs and flattens his ears. His face puckers like he just licked a lemon.

"When we were Indians, if a wolf killed one of our tribe, would we not hunt and kill him?"

"Of course we would," Makes Trouble proudly proclaims.

"Would we be satisfied with just one wolf? Or would we hunt the entire pack?"

"I would kill the whole pack."

"Kill just one of these men, any one of them, and ten more will show up in his place."

"We could make it look like the sun took his spirit."

Paw *humphs*. "No. They have good trackers. They will find at least one print."

"My sister has pups now. As does Anoki. We cannot move as fast as we used to. I am worried, Kiowa. What is your plan to protect our tribe?" Makes Trouble demands.

"We will rob these settlers and waste their time chasing ghosts. They cannot protect their herds and grow their crops while they also pursue us."

"So?" Makes Trouble growls.

"So we will eat their crops when they tend to the tame buffalo. We will eat the tame buffalo when the crops are gone. Always we will be eating and soon they will starve."

"Ah, I see your wisdom. Eventually they will do as the village people did. They will all leave," Paw says, proud of his nephew's plan.

"I still think it would be better to kill this man savagely and let the townspeople find his body mangled. That will scare them away faster."

"Maybe you are right. Tell the pack we go on the warpath tonight. We must show the ranchers how fierce we can be." Kiowa disappears into the forest.

Paw turns and follows him while Makes Trouble remains behind and watches W.H. sidewind down the mountain.

"I would worry less if he were dead now." Makes Trouble fights the urge to attack; Kiowa's word is law.

Kiowa, Paw, and Makes Trouble return to the cave. They don't have to say a word. Anoki knows from their scent where they've been.

The warriors are greeted by yipping wolf pups.

"I saw some rabbits hopping around outside. Do you want to chase them, young ones?" Paw asks.

"*Yip, yip, yow,*" they chirp with heads down, tiny teeth bared, and tails whipping all around.

"Watch Red Cloud, Kiowa. He is already chasing rabbits," Anoki informs her chief, proud of her strongest pup.

The little pup spins circles, yaps, then falls over.

"Like this, my son. This is how you raid," Kiowa says, lowering his profile. He growls so loud it raises his mane. Every living creature feels fear at the shaking of the ground. The rabbits scamper, except one. One small bunny with a big heart does the unthinkable. He charges Kiowa.

"Arrrggghhh," Swift screams.

When the warrior bunny reaches Kiowa, it sinks its teeth into his paw. As fierce as the rabbit is, its teeth don't get past Kiowa's thick fur.

"Him brave," Paw says, lying down face-to-face with Swift, sniffing him.

Makes Trouble leans down and parts his jaws, but Kiowa stops him.

"Courage is a rare treasure, Makes Trouble. Let him be. What is your name?"

"Swift, and I'm not a-scared of any one of you!"

"You will spend all your days eating grass under the protection of this wolf named Kiowa."

Swift smiles and hops away.

"Intend to keep your word?" Anoki asks.

"Of course. But don't worry. He will bring his friends, and our hungry babies will eat them."

Kiowa lies down. The pups rush him. They bite at his nose. His tail. And his ears.

***

The next morning the townsfolk come out of their homes in shock and disbelief.

Hundreds of dead sheep line the streets. Their blood flows so thick in the dusty road, it makes crimson mud.

CHAPTER 120

The stench of death forces the townspeople to cover their faces. Windows are boarded up. More people are leaving town, their wagons filled with loved ones, furniture, and keepsakes.

Without saying a word, Sheriff Dawson walks over to the gunsmith and says, "Victor, I want a thousand rounds made out of silver and delivered by morning."

Victor nods with a determined eye for justice. "That's a big order, Sheriff. I'm going to need materials and help."

"Go on over to Mather's hardware shop. Get some sticks of dynamite. We'll blow the safe and use whatever silver is in there to make the bullets and pay the cowboys."

"What cowboys?" Victor asks.

"The ones Billy's going to go find. They work for pay and booze. Don't worry about them. Just go get your shop tooled up."

A few hours later an explosion blasts all of the windows out of the bank.

"We ought to have hung that banker for not leaving us a key to the safe before he left town."

Debris settles on an envelope marked Keys, which Fred left on his desk inside his locked office.

What few townsfolk remain stack the sheep carcasses in a pile and burn them.

"Sheriff, that BBQ you got going there will draw predators for weeks," Victor says.

"That's the plan, Victor."

Billy gets the word out, and the cowboys are quick to respond.

Summoned by duty, the remaining townsfolk show up for action. Pretty soon the gunsmith's shop is packed full of bodies. So many men show up, Victor decides to move his operation out to the street. Men line up in an assembly operation. They work in the heat and the stench. Victor runs up and down the line showing men what to do at each station. By night they have a thousand silver rounds.

Mr. Mather closes his shop, lights a torch, and cocks his rifle.

The sheriff walks over to the judge and says, "I need your permission to form a posse."

"I already deputized the men, the women, and the children old enough to carry a gun."

"Listen up, folks. Our town has been plagued long enough by this 'Louie.' Is there any doubt in anyone's mind that we're fighting a werewolf?" Sheriff Dawson scans the silent crowd, hoping to see a trace of fear in just one man's eyes. When he doesn't find a suspect, he continues. "Way I see it, we're all that's left. We got a full moon out tonight and if anyone's going to turn into Louie, you have my permission to shoot them on the spot."

"Don't you think we oughta send a search party out, Sheriff?" Alejandro asks in his thick Spanish accent.

"I most certainly do. No man is to be left alone. We move in groups. That way, if man turns to wolf, he will have to do it in plain sight of the whole town. If someone ain't with us tonight, they're the werewolf and they ain't allowed back in our town," Sheriff Dawson informs his posse.

"It's time to go to war!" a cowboy shouts.

"Hip, hip, hooray!" the people cheer.

Cowboys fire their six-shooters in the air.

"Dadgum it, boys, you're wasting ammo!" Victor scolds the mob.

***

Later that afternoon, W.H. rides into town. He notices that one of his hogs has made its way back to Mr. Mather's.

The hog roots through the dried blood on the street, searching for meat it can't find. Benches and tools from the gunsmith's shop litter the street. W.H. can't help but wonder if he's the last man in town. What few people he does see scurry indoors and slam their window shutters.

W.H. greets Elias Mather and hands him his resupply list.

"You must be a hungry fella. You already went through the

chickens? You know if you leave the chickens and rooster alone, they'll make more chicks." Elias snickers.

"Rooster crowed before dawn. Everyone's got a job to do and they ought to do it." W.H. grumbles a response, his gaze resting on gunny sacks labeled Flour, Sugar, Coffee, and Tobacco.

"Have you heard the news?" Mr. Mather asks him.

W.H. shakes his head, hoping he isn't about to hear that someone else got the wolf.

"Wolf killed a couple hundred sheep and left them in the streets."

"Are you serious?"

"See all that blood out there in the street? Why do you think I'm packin' heat?" Elias asks, patting his rifle.

"Did anybody catch him?"

"Is that all you care about? The money?"

"Mr. Mather, I ain't never seen a wolf behave this way. I am deeply concerned. The way things are escalating, it won't be long before someone gets hurt."

Mr. Mather relaxes. "To my knowledge, they haven't caught the wolf, but a posse was headed up to the pine forest, where no one's been yet. You're lucky you came into town. Sheriff has declared martial law. If your face ain't been seen in a full moon, you're the werewolf. You might want to get up there and let them know you ain't a werewolf."

"I was up there. That's where I found..." W.H. decides not to tell him about his traps, lest he seem crazy. He changes the subject. "Well, then, I suppose I won't be needing your cabin much longer."

"Don't you want to see if they catch him?"

W.H. stops. He pauses for a minute, then walks outside. "You know, I suppose I do. I found his paw print." W.H. holds up his hand. "It was as long and as wide as my hand."

"Well, you might want to tell them folks it's a wolf and not a werewolf."

"Uh-huh. I'm sure they'd believe me." W.H. gets a better idea.

"Actually, I think I'll head up to the pine forest and see if I can't link up with the posse. If they've caught the wolf, I'll take his portrait and head on out."

***

Late that night, a large group of men fans through the woods, moving in a straight line. Women hold the center of the line. Even some young boys join in. Everyone is armed. Chambers are loaded and hammers are cocked. Itchy fingers rest on hair triggers.

"Step. Step. Look right, look left," Sheriff Dawson shouts.

"Got nothing," a man at the left end of the line shouts.

"All clear," a man at the far right of the line shouts.

A loud growl like a water-powered timber saw buzzes out of the thicket.

"Louie is coming!"

CHAPTER 121

This causes everyone to fire their weapons at once. Jenny fires, and the shotgun knocks her back a few feet. She gasps, cocks her other trigger, and sends sparks out of the double barrel. The impact blows her over. Her dress looks like an upside-down bell. Her shin-high leather boots cycle in the air. She's quick to get back up, breach the chamber, and slide two shells in.

The cowboys unload their lever-action rifles and draw their pistols. In seconds the entire posse has unloaded at least a hundred rounds. As they go to reload, the grumblings grow louder.

Trees shake. Their limbs bend.

"Werewolf! We ain't hit him! Louie's in the trees," Victor the gunsmith shouts.

Some men and women panic and break from the line, while Jenny and Sheriff Dawson are determined to kill the enemy.

A few more shots are fired, and people start turning to run. Jenny isn't the first to go, but she's certainly not the last. Her mother takes her by the arm and pulls her away from the fight.

A grizzly bear slides down a tree trunk, concealed by shadows. It charges through the brush while her one-year-old cubs climb farther up the tree.

BANG! BANG! BANG!

Hank, the cowboy, unloads his six-shooter. He hits her in the shoulder. She unleashes a roar that instantly makes every mortal muscle tremble. The giant grizzly stands twelve feet tall and acts as though she hasn't been wounded. Hank falls back and breaches his chamber. He fumbles with bullets in his belt as he desperately tries to reload.

Two shadows, Kiowa and Makes Trouble, are perched safely on a cliff, watching the events unfold in the hills below. "Her attack strips the souls out of these men and sends them scampering off after their weak bodies!" Kiowa guffaws.

"Thunder sticks have no power over a heart full of courage. I would not be surprised if she kills them all." Makes Trouble smirks.

"See how they turn on her? They would do the same to us. Now you see." Kiowa nudges at the scene.

"Yes. Yes. It is better for her to kill and be killed. You are wise as the owls, Kiowa."

Down in the forest, a raspy voice yells, "Don't let it bite you. The curse can spread." Molly shakes her first.

"RUN! RUN! Get away from Louie," a cowboy shouts, waving his hands wildly.

"*Hasta luego*," Juan cries out as he draws two pistols and unloads them. When his hammers click on empty, he turns and runs. Panic and poor visibility make him miss every shot. But he sees the bear's frenzied pursuit in the townspeople's frantic muzzle flashes. With a quick swipe, the mother grizzly fells him and leaves deep lacerations across his chest.

Hank runs to Juan's aid. He points his piece at the bear's chest and cycles the chamber. He unloads all six shots. The distinct sound of hot lead slamming against muscle and fur causes the other cowboys to hone their fire. Her ribcage collapses under the wall of gunfire. Her body smokes and tufts of fur explode off her. Had it not been for the cowboys, the bear would have extinguished poor Juan's life.

She turns and roars, but her heart has been pierced and she has only enough life force to push the attack a few steps further. With a mighty roar, she falls dead.

W.H. rides up on the scene. From all the glittering casings on the ground, he's certain the town has killed themselves.

"Let's get a count!" Sheriff Dawson calls out to his deputy. One by one the townsfolk sound off.

"Well, boys, that's enough justice for one night," Sheriff Dawson says once everyone has been accounted for.

"If it's all right with you, Sheriff, I'd like to stay behind and sort out what happened here," W.H. says.

"That's fine, but no bounty will be paid for a wolf the town killed."

***

At first light W.H. scavenges the forest. Eager to see last night's outcome, he catches only a few hours of rest. Snapping sticks kept him up all night.

W.H. leans down, picks up an empty casing, and throws it. "Looks like Lobo wins again."

Without a sound, Onendah appears behind W.H. in full Indian dress. Two bear cubs run past W.H. and claw at the medicine man's legs.

W.H. flinches. "Ah-hoe, Chief. Do you always sneak up on folks?"

"They think I am their mother."

"Huh?" W.H. says, looking down. He spots the bloody mother grizzly, then looks back at the cubs.

"You were wise to avoid the war party," Onendah says. He reaches into a leather pouch and pushes bits of dried meat into a bear cub's mouth.

"Why are you here, Round Eyes?"

W.H. takes off his glasses. "I might get heat for my spectacles from everyone in town, but, Chief, I'll be put off if you make fun of me, too."

Onendah drops the rest of his meat for the bears. He walks up to W.H. and looks into the depths of his soul. "He is more than a wolf."

"I figured that after he defecated on all my baits."

Onendah laughs and shakes his head. The bear cubs follow him and beg for more food. "Maybe it would be best for you to return home."

"I will, Chief, but not until I've caught the wolf."

"Or until he catches you." He points his finger at W.H.

W.H. shrugs. "Never thought about that. I wouldn't bet on him, though. What are you going to do with them bear cubs?"

"Well, let's see. I could leave them with their dead mother, but then they might starve. I could kill them and make a fine pair of gloves out of them. Their fur is very soft to the touch. Or I could be what they want me to be."

"What's that?"

"Their mother." Onendah scoops a cub up like it's a baby.

"Chief, them's grizzly bears. One day they'll just as soon eat you as snuggle up to you."

"I guess that is where we see the world differently, Round Eyes.

The cubs say to me, 'we need a mother,' and I say back, 'I have always needed children.'"

"You're right about one thing, Chief: We don't see the world the same. I'd shoot them bears and put them out of their misery."

"Yes, but then you would be denying them the joy of life. The same life you seek to deny the wolves."

W.H. thinks about this for a moment. Without another word, the medicine man walks off with his beastly children following after him.

That evening W.H. tucks himself into bed and reports his fantastic progress.

May 21, 1861
Great news, Uncle.

Finally a break in the werewolf mystery. You can tell the board that werewolves are nothing but lore. No such creature exists. I have found positive confirmation that it is in fact a very large and very intelligent wolf. For one reason or another, his best hunting is done in the Currumpaw. That's where all the dead cattle keep turning up, anyway. 'Lobo' is so clever. I believe he uses a maze of canyons to conceal his movements during the day.

To track the mighty wolf, I've simply ridden in a wide circle, stopping and talking to ranchers, cowboys, schoolteachers, Indians (one a medicine man), pony express riders, and soldiers. My interviews have yielded success in limiting the radius of his hunting grounds. I tracked him by locating his trail in the pine forest, north of the valley. I believe he is roaming a ten-mile circuit within the lands of the Currumpaw. But he may be roaming as far west as Winslow, Arizona, and as far north as Branson, Colorado. I would have to get reports from ranchers to confirm that theory.

The funny thing is that none of the towns talk to each other. They post wanted posters in each town to spread the word. When I kill him, I'm going to make a fortune collecting on all these rewards in multiple counties across the territories.

I have found a few reputable newspapers, but the reports are either void of details or the sources don't check out. It has taken me a considerable amount of time to measure a radius, but I had extra time on my hands, considering the traps have not yet arrived.

To date I've found only one trail, which will make setting traps difficult, as I must be ever cautious with my money. Fortune is within my grasp if my resources can last.

.

CHAPTER 122

With the dawn, the rooster who should have crowed doesn't. As a result, W.H. oversleeps. When he finally wakes around noon, he is forced to skip his breakfast and head straight into town. Fortunately, he manages to make it before Mr. Mather closes shop.

"Do you have my traps?"

"Sure do. Came in late yesterday," Mr. Mather says, reading the town newspaper. On the front page is a blown-up wanted poster. There is a wolf sketch almost identical to Kiowa's likeness, and a reward now reads $3,000, Dead!

W.H. smiles and gives the shopkeeper another piece of gold. "Better order as many traps as that can get me just in case it is a werewolf." He winks.

"Glad to do so."

"I'll take a few with me now and go set them. If you could deliver the rest, I'd be much obliged."

"Anything else?" Mr. Mather asks, flipping the page.

"Could you get me another rooster?" W.H. says, making for the door.

As W.H. leaves the shop, the remaining townspeople board up their stores and hang Out of business signs on the doors and windows.

He scans the street and counts the number of buildings newly closed up. Looks like only two remain open on the west side of town. The hardware store and the Cowboy Hall saloon.

W.H. looks to the east. He spots Sheriff Dawson in front of the municipal building. He waves.

"Ain't no law that can stop a werewolf. I seen that beast hit with silver myself, and it just kept on comin'. Won't be long before he's eating people," Sheriff Dawson says, taking the silver star off his vest and handing it to the judge.

The judge holds the star in his hand and bounces it in his palm. Without a second thought, he tosses the badge over his shoulder and says, "You ain't gotta tell me twice. Fred the banker offered me a job. Came in on the wire. Says he's got more demand than he can handle. Heck, even the priest is leaving town. Says we'll all be slaughtered like the sheep for our sinnin' ways."

"So if there is a werewolf, it's either Mr. Mather, his wife, his daughter, Jenny, or Molly," W.H. hollers.

"I ain't no werewolf!" Molly shouts from the roof of the saloon. She bangs away at the wooden Cowboy Hall sign.

"What are you doing up there, Molly?" Sheriff Dawson asks.

"Name's not fittin' no more. Everyone's leaving town. Gotta change with the times. I'm very *modern*, you know!" Molly uses a hammer to knock the O loose.

"I know you boys ain't gossiping like hens out here." Jenny approaches them, creating a kaleidoscope of colors by twirling her parasol over her shoulder.

"We was just having words." W.H. straightens up and smiles.

"Most of us talk to ourselves now. Mama says that's just fine." Jenny rocks her shoulders. "Just so long as you don't answer yourself. It's not respectable." She cocks one eyebrow and smirks.

W.H. mounts his horse. "Guess I won't be seeing you at church no more."

"Papa says when the goin' gets rough, the Mathers get goin' to church."

"Ain't much of a church without a preacher, now, is it?" It's W.H.'s turn to smirk.

Jenny's spirits slump. Hope hangs on her beautiful drooping face. "Just because we don't have a preacher don't mean folks stop learning. I was thinking of teaching the youngsters, anyway. Might as well start with the Good Book."

"You need a class to be a teacher," W.H. counters.

"Well, I have Billy. Billy and a few of his friends. We'll get along just fine."

Billy nails a new reward sign up over a stack of old ones. It's the same picture in the newspaper, but under the reward it says NAME A REASONABLE PRICE.

"We'll just do Bible study. It would be mighty fine if you wanted to join us."

W.H. smiles and tips his crinkled hat. "Not if you were the last person in town, Jenny!"

Jenny's face explodes into bright red fury, a shade that nearly matches her strawberry-pink dress. She stomps her foot so hard it rattles the planks beneath her.

"You can jest—"

W.H. doesn't give her the last word. He walks off, waving her away.

"Oh… I was a darn fool for being nice to that feller." She huffs and puffs and pats her coiffed hair.

***

The summer heat pokes its blazing head through the spring showers. The fiery sunlight bakes the earth, creating cracked clay. It has the strange effect of making Main Street look like snakeskin scales. The heat is sometimes so intense it bounces off the ground and rises up through the clothes. The earth is blazing red and the sky is deep blue. Clouds dare not show their faces, lest they be eviscerated. W.H. decides to wait for a cool day before he sets his first traps.

"See, Bingo, this is my thinking. We both know that wolves move up and down rivers and streams. They use these waterways for tracking and hunting. So, if we set six or seven traps on either side of the banks, we're bound to catch something."

Even if they're dry? Bingo barks, stating the obvious.

"'Course this is a great deal of work with no known reward."

Yet to speak of, Bingo barks.

"Maybe we oughta cut and run. What do you think?"

Yes! Let's skin outta here! Bingo barks.

"That's what I like to see, fella. Determination. Have it your way. We stay."

Bingo puts his paws over his head and whimpers. *Why can't he understand me?*

"We got our work cut out for us, Bingo. Probably take a week or so to get all these traps in place, eh."

Bingo walks up and down the banks, making sure no ambushes are set to hurt his master.

"But it'll be worth it, Bingo. Man, I bet I could get paid triple the amount of the reward if I put all this in a book. Way I figure it, if the wolf is gone, the people will eventually come back. And imagine if fresh copies of the story about the greatest wolf hunter to ever live were right there on Mr. Mather's shelves just waiting to be sold."

I don't see anything suspicious! Bingo barks downstream.

"What will I do with that much loot? Probably buy a couple of these businesses and venture out on my own. Heck, we could buy the whole town, Bingo!"

Does that mean I would get to sing with Katherine every night? Bingo cocks his head to the side and lets a long whimper of excitement out.

Setting the traps takes most of the day. As W.H. and Bingo make their way back to the cabin, W.H. sings, "B-I-N-G-O, and Bingo was his name-o. Whew! We're gonna be *rich!*"

When they reach the cabin, it's late. W.H. feels compelled to make a journal entry even though he's dirty and tired.

June 1, 1860

Still haven't used the camera. Never received any slides. Been sketching pictures, though. Both Bingo and I will set traps all this week every mile or so around a ten-mile track from the pine forest, through the south canyon, all the way up to the north.

Gonna wait a week and check 'em. Won't have much time after that before I have to head on back home. You'll be proud to know, Uncle, that while I'm hoping to catch the wolf, I'm not so naive to think that I will be successful. Therefore, I am also preparing to return to school. My life as a wolf hunter just doesn't seem to be working out. At least the board was kind enough to grant me this opportunity. I detest school, but a deal's a deal. Before I make the circuit tomorrow, I'm going to drown my worries in whiskey.

He leans over and blows out the candle.

***

At twilight the next morning, rancher Geoffrey hears the cattle in a ruckus. He grabs his shotgun and heads out.

"Bulls, circle around the cows, and keep the calves in the center," Ol' Bruce, the Texas longhorn bull, bellows as he stomps his hooves.

The wolf pack has successfully killed nine yearlings in a predawn raid. Makes Trouble, Paw, Walpi, and Kiowa charge the cattle and keep them at bay, while Anoki and Kida frantically feed.

"We must take a few more of their young and bury them around the pine forest for winter," Kida shouts. Blood drips off her snout. She squints her crimson eyes.

"One more, Makes Trouble," Kiowa yells, motioning for his friend to scatter the herd.

Ol' Bruce responds by charging.

Makes Trouble skillfully turns and runs, but he keeps just enough distance between him and the bull so that the bull won't give up the chase.

Paw spots a yearling and moves in for the kill while Walpi harasses the herd.

"Hold fast, men. Circle up and hold your positions," Ol' Bruce orders. He turns around to rejoin the circle.

Makes Trouble follows him and nips at his hindquarters.

With a swift kick, Ol' Bruce's hoof connects with Makes Trouble's skull. The copper wolf drops to the ground. His lime-green eyes roll to the back of his head and his tongue droops out of the side of his mouth.

CHAPTER 123

The chaos of bellowing cattle distracts the wolf pack. They don't notice Makes Trouble, since all their energy is focused on stirring the herd.

Unlike the buffalo, the bulls circle their females in a grand defense. Their long pointy horns and hefty bodies intimidate the wolves.

"Hmmm... they have completed their circle," Kiowa says, searching for a weakness.

"Paw and Walpi, probe them and put fear in their hearts. Find a weakness!" Kiowa orders.

Each time a wolf approaches, a bull drops his horns and charges.

Walpi gets one of them to break the circle by taunting them and letting the bulls chase him, but before Paw can charge in, another bull fills the empty space. Soon Paw has a bull chasing him and the bulls have widened their circle to protect their herd.

"You want a piece of us?!" Ol' Bruce shouts, bucking his long horns and blaring, "Come see if you can get past a thousand pounds of solid steer!"

Several tall cornfields away, Geoffrey the rancher fires two shots in the air.

Realizing their ambush has been discovered, Kiowa escalates the fight.

"Ugghh..." Makes Trouble moans as he comes to. He wobbles, slowly getting to his feet. The entire world spins around him. Between rocking glimpses, he sees his fearless leader leaping on Ol' Bruce's lowered horns. He dizzily watches as Kiowa scurries up the bull's back. He drunkenly chuckles when he sees the not-so-tame buffalo conquered.

Kiowa's long claws dig deep into the bull's rippling back and send him thrusting forward. Ol' Bruce kicks his hind legs up in the air to get Kiowa off. It doesn't work. Kiowa digs in deep, lies flat, and rides the bull. When Ol' Bruce drops his lower half and rears his head straight up in the air, he cycles his hooves and brays a terrifying wail, which sounds like a mighty trumpet.

"Get 'em off!" Ol' Bruce laments, kicking his hind legs up several times. Rocking forward and backward, Ol' Bruce strains every muscle to shake the wolf.

Wolf wit conquers muscle and horn, Kiowa thinks, leaping from Ol' Bruce into the center of the herd. Kiowa exploits the chaos, snapping at the defenseless cows. His snarls send them frantically pushing to one side of the circle until their bulging bodies break their defense apart and create an opening for Paw and Walpi.

Sifting through the terrified herd, Kiowa locates the yearling Makes Trouble marked for death. "Found you!"

"Not me... her!" the young bull cries out, pointing at another calf.

The calf turns to push into the stampeding herd, which only entices the hulking wolf's instincts.

Cows call out for their babies. Bulls rage. Jaws part. White fangs snatch down on soft tender veal. A struggle ensues.

Out of rifle range, Geoffrey helplessly witnesses the slaughter of his anticipated profits. He watches the great wolf wrench its neck and slam the hefty maverick to the ground.

The cattle break apart and stampede back toward the rancher's house. The stampeding herd raises a dust cloud, masking the chaotic scene.

Ol' Bruce caves to his boiling rage. All he can see is red dust. He charges in blindly, desperately seeking a pound of Kiowa's flesh.

The King of the Currumpaw squares off with him, while the rest of his pack circles the charging steer.

Ol' Bruce takes a few swipes at Paw and Walpi before he lowers his horns and aims for Kiowa.

"I am not afraid of you, tame buffalo! You cannot break my heart," Kiowa says, charging Bruce.

"Kiowa, no!" Anoki wails.

The rancher is closing the distance.

When Ol' Bruce gets close enough, he lifts his horns and expects to crush Kiowa on impact. Sadly, that isn't what happens. Kiowa uses his weaknesses against him just as same before and ends up on his back. Instead of sliding off, he tears at the bull's back the same way he tears up the turf when he marks his territory.

"Arrrggghhh!" Bruce shrieks, bucking and thrusting forward.

Kiowa bites down hard on Ol' Bruce's neck and does his best to sever his spinal cord, but the bull's thick muscles act like armor, creating an impenetrable barrier.

Geoffrey is nearing the fray. The dust cloud chokes his nose and causes him to cough. He breaches the double-barreled shotgun, and quickly slipping two smoking shells out, he slides new two brass shells in.

"I'm gonna blow your face off, you son of a..." Geoffrey takes aim, but he can't believe his eyes. In the center of the settling dust, he witnesses the wolf riding his best bull like he's a cowboy breaking in a steer.

"Don't be fools!" Kida screams. She latches on to her kill and disappears in an ocean of sagebrush.

BANG! BANG!

Two quick shots blaze out twin barrels aimed for Kiowa. The lead balls pelt Bruce's side and cause him to jostle from the impact.

"Ol' Bruce. I'm sorry, fella," Geoffrey moans.

Kiowa rides the bull as long as he can, while his pack gathers their kills and runs off.

The rancher fumbles around in his pockets and realizes he doesn't have any more shells. "YOU DAMN DEVIL! I'LL KILL YOU!" Geoffrey rages, raising his fist at the wolf.

Kiowa lowers his ears and snarls at the old man. He leaps off Ol' Bruce and accepts the rancher's challenge.

CHAPTER 124

"No! No, you don't!" Geoffrey pleads, holding out his shaking hands. Panicked, he turns around to run home.

Kiowa caves to his carnal instincts and anticipates closing in on the frantic, flailing, feeble old man. He can visualize his teeth sinking into Geoffrey's wrinkly neck and pulling back to one quick end. The rush of blood makes him wonder if these things haven't already happened.

But Anoki's rallying howl makes Kiowa realize it was all in his mind. Bloodlust drains from the mighty wolf. The thought of tasting human blood suddenly causes him to gag.

Walpi and Paw have already ripped the last calf in half and removed its head. Each wolf carries as much as they can. Like their great raiding ancestors, they are quick to scurry off with the spoils of war.

***

Inside the C Y'all Saloon, W.H. sits at a stool and tells Molly his thoughts on who the werewolf might be.

"I think it is Mr. Mather." He winks, then thumbs over his shoulder at the hardware store.

"No!" Molly gasps. "Tell me why you be thinking that."

"I know it ain't you, 'cause I was here that night the posse formed."

"How do you know I didn't slip out the back and do Satan's bidding while you was here distracted by the demon whiskey?"

"I suppose you could have, but I would have found your tracks when you turned back and came to town. Funny thing about desert dust; it's impossible to cover a trail. There was no tracks outside of town; therefore, you are not the werewolf."

"Well done, sir! My name's finally been cleared." Molly claps her hands and victoriously lifts her arms over her head. "Praise be." She lifts her glass, clacks it to W.H.'s, then shakes her fiery mane and slams the shot.

"Whew, that'll raise the dead." She laughs as she refills the empty glasses. "Between us"—she winks—"I knew it was him the whole time."

W.H. chortles.

"Him or his pretty little girl, Jenny," Molly's suspicious kelly-green eyes squint and shift back and forth.

"Molly, weren't you listening to what I just said? Ain't no tracks all around town. Only tracks I found was wolf tracks, and they stopped at the town sign."

"Oh yeah, well, there it is, then. It's wolves. Who woulda thought?"

W.H. shrugs and shakes his head. He points his thumbs at his chest. "This guy, Molly, that's who! Ain't no werewolves. It's just plain old wolves."

"You best stay here tonight, W.H. You're too drunk to be out. What with wolves on the loose and such. Besides, I have so few paying customers now; I can't afford to lose you to the wolf man. Or wolf. Or whatever."

"I appreciate that."

W.H. stands up. He raises his glass. "To shattered dreams and empty pockets!"

"To shattered dreams, the hearts we've broken, and the love we've lost," Molly says, pounding another round.

W.H. slams the shot glass down on the bar so hard it explodes. He shrugs and turns to go to his room, when the swinging saloon doors burst open.

"Help! I need help," Geoffrey cries out as his daughter, Katherine, helps him to the bar.

"He's been mauled by the werewolf," Katherine says between frantic sobs.

"Ain't no WEREWOLF! It's a pack a wolves. I seen 'em killin' ma prized cattle."

"Ha!" W.H. says, swinging his finger through the air. "My powers of deduction have proved true by this man's eyewitness, Molly."

"W.H., shut the hell up. Let me get some water and soap. Katherine, come with me, darlin'."

Katherine glares at W.H. for his insensitivity.

W.H. reaches behind the counter and grabs a bottle of whiskey. He pops the cork and sets an empty shot glass down and quickly fills it.

"Drink up and loosen your lips, Geoffrey. I wanna hear everything you got ta say."

The rancher picks the glass up and sips it. He coughs when the liquid fire pours down his throat. W.H. pats him on the back.

"I counted six or seven of them."

CHAPTER 125

Caught off guard, W.H. sits back down and listens intently. "You don't have to talk if it's too much trouble…"

"No, no, everyone should know. One of them was so big, I thought he was a werewolf. Stands four, maybe five feet off the ground."

W.H. holds out his hand, and remembering the size of Lobo's print, he realizes this man has finally spotted the elusive killer.

"I seen him lift a four-hundred-pound maverick off the ground and snap its neck all at once. That was gonna be a blue ribbon for sure."

"That's terrible." W.H. tries to muster more empathy than interest, but his intoxication reveals his selfishness. "Tell me more about the wolves."

"Killed nine—ten of my calves total. Ain't no way I'm gonna recover from this loss. Bank's going to foreclose for sure." He tilts his head back and swallows the whole shot.

"But, Pa, the bank's been blown up." Katherine whimpers as she wipes her father's brow with a wet cloth.

"Well, soon as they put it back together, we are good as foreclosed," Geoffrey moans.

"You warm up quick," W.H. says, impressed with how fast the man overcame his initial reaction to the alcohol.

"At my age, ain't nothing quick, son." The rancher reaches for the bottle of whiskey and pours a new shot.

Molly joins Katherine. The two wipe off his dusty face and dirty hands.

"Why! There isn't a mark on you!" Molly examines the man from top to bottom. "Here I am abandoning a perfectly good drink for a man without injury. Let your daughter fret on your nerves and the whiskey can fret on mine."

"The big fella coulda got me. I didn't have time to grab extra shells before I foolishly fired off both barrels. He was riding Ol' Bruce, my prize bull..."

"The wolf rode the bull?" W.H. asks with mistrust swirling in his eyes.

The rancher nods, then continues. "I ended up peppering Ol' Bruce with buckshot. Guess I'm lucky his darn hide is so thick. That darn devil wolf was off him and glaring at me. He licked his lips, and I saw death in his yellow eyes. I probably ought not to have run away, but I knew I was a dead man, so I did the only thing I could."

"You ran from the wolf?"

The rancher nods and nurses his whiskey.

"And he didn't attack you?"

"No, sir, he did not."

"That can't be," W.H. says, squinting.

"God was watching over me. I ought not to be here, but the Almighty wants it so." Geoffrey slams the shot. "Too bad the bank won't have that kind of mercy."

W.H. shakes his head. "I don't believe it."

Molly defends him. "Geoffrey ain't a liar, Mister."

"It's just that wolves don't have control over themselves. When critters run, their instincts kick in and they give chase."

"Chase where?" Katherine asks, wiping dust off her father's frightened, weathered face.

"Not chase where, chase to kill. That's what they do. They can't help themselves. They're straight killers. That's all they are. That's all they will ever be."

"Oh, Papa." Katherine wraps her pale arms around his wrinkled, scruffy neck. Katherine realizes the reality of her father's dire situation. Tears wet her cheeks. He pats her and comforts her while he motions to Molly for a second glass.

"Well, just add that to the growing list of things that ain't normal with these wolves," Molly says, getting Katherine a glass.

W.H. drags his fingers down the side of his mouth. "Molly, I'm feeling a bit more sober. I think I'll go home."

Molly ignores him, doting on the rattled rancher and his poor daughter.

W.H. stumbles outside the saloon and tries to mount his horse. The task seems impossible as his foot slips out of the stirrup time and time again. Eventually, he mounts his horse backward and holds on to invisible reins. Cotton gets the idea. With a jerk of his head, he untangles the reins and trots home.

The next morning Bingo is incredibly excited. He runs in and out of the room. His eyes beam with joy and his tongue pants out of the side of his mouth. His tail wags so hard, it knocks against the wall.

Wake up! Wake up! Bingo barks in W.H.'s face.

When W.H. doesn't stir, Bingo runs outside.

"What did you do to him?" Bingo barks at Cotton.

"Don't blame me. It's the demon liquor."

Bingo runs back in and licks his master's face.

"This ain't natural, Jenny. We ain't properly courted." W.H. moans, puckering up for Bingo as though he were caressing the lovely blond girl's cheeks.

He slowly opens his eyes and sees Bingo's sweet face. "Eww, Bingo!" He wipes his lips with his dusty sleeve. "What in tarnation are you thinking?"

"Get up!" Bingo barks.

Scrambling to his feet, W.H. stumbles to the front door and spots his horse's condemning gaze.

"What are you looking at?"

A jackass! She neighs.

"I gotta check them traps." W.H. scrambles for his gear. When he heads into the house, his hangover hits him full force. Thunderbolts explode around his head. He presses his hands to his ears to stabilize his balance.

Shielding his eyes from the bright morning light, he stumbles into the cottage and slurs, "Soon as I get better, we will go, Bingo. I promise. Just let me sleep it off."

The following day W.H. is fresh-faced and at the top of his game. He races to their first steel traps and draws his rifle when Bingo picks up the trail.

Here! Here! He was here! Bingo barks and points at the paw prints with one foot up.

W.H. dismounts his horse and cocks his rifle so fast, the motions seem to happen at once.

"He was here, Bingo. He was here!"

Bingo tilts his head and barks. *That's what I said.*

"Well, let's go get him, boy!"

Bingo sprints off and follows the trail with his nose pressed to the ground. From his perspective, he can see paw prints that are the same color as the cool earth. *He was here.* The collie growls.

***

Bingo was right. Only days prior the wolves were at the exact same spot. They dragged their kills through the water to conceal their tracks and also because the carcasses float.

"We will use the old cave to feed our young," Kiowa informs the pack.

"I'm worried about them." Anoki whimpers, wiping red blood down her white chest.

"What if they've wandered out of the den?" Kida cries.

"Onendah is with them. You know his magic will protect them."

"Kiowa, Onendah is here," Paw says.

Kiowa looks upstream and sees the medicine man in his human form, motioning for him.

"Stay in the water. One trail is enough," Kiowa orders.

Kiowa trots over to Onendah and whimpers. "Is something wrong?"

"Don't worry, my friend. A great white owl came to me in a vision. He told me to climb on his back. His wings were as long as trees. We flew over the earth, and I did not know what he wanted. I saw many shadows circling your people until they consumed them. You were all that was left. I told the owl that I knew you.

"He asked me what I wanted. I told him to help you. I told him to fly down and pick you up. He did. Then he carried you back here. When I woke, hungry puppies wanted their mothers. I have fed them some meat."

Kiowa exhibits gratitude by pressing his paw on Onendah's leg.

"I could see that your pack was in trouble, and the owl said to me, 'Go help them.' So I have brought your little family to this home. It is all I could think to do."

CHAPTER 126

Kiowa licks Onendah's hand.

"You are welcome."

Kiowa turns around to join the pack, but Onendah stops him. "There is more. Let me get my spear." He disappears inside the cave. Whimpering puppies greet him.

"Wait here. I will be back with your mother. Oh, you puppies, how you want your mother. I know. All things want their mother. Even I want my mother. I must show your father something very important. Now is the time to be patient."

"Mama!" Cries A Lot wails.

"Mother," Coon Eyes and Blue Eyes whimper.

"Daddy," Red Cloud howls.

When Onendah comes out of the cave, he stabilizes himself by leaning on a long spear. "I am too old for all these children. They wear me out."

Kiowa sits down and listens as the medicine man goes on.

"A pale-face hunter with round glass eyes has hidden strong metal traps in the earth," Onendah says. "Walk with me down to the stream and I will show you."

With a little effort, he leads Kiowa to the spot. He lifts his spear and thrusts the handle into what appears to be nothing more than earth. The ground explodes. Dirt flies up in his face. Steel teeth snap the spear in half.

"Your paws are not as strong as this wood, and you can see the damage it does to my spear." He tugs on the broken piece of wood and shows the wolf how the trap is anchored by a long chain.

The entire device is hidden in the earth, Kiowa thinks. That is good magic.

"It can only be discovered once you step on it," Onendah explains. Kiowa leans down and smells it. The strong metallic scent registers in his mind, and he realizes he detected the scent when he exited the stream. He just didn't know what it was.

"He knows your trail, and he has placed traps all over the riverbanks and canyon." Onendah waves his hand all around. "He is a very good hunter. No one else even knew whether you were coming or going."

Kiowa sits down and lowers his ears.

Onendah kneels down and pats Kiowa's head. "My magic is weak or else I could use a speaking spell and understand your words. Even I have limits, Kiowa." The wolf rests his paw on the medicine man's leg and then his chin.

"You know the Kiowa way. We never leave our own behind. Especially our warriors." He pats the wolf's long back. "I think it is time to move north."

***

A week or so later, W.H. kneels down at a spent steel trap that's been triggered.

"Don't that beat all?" he rambles, examining the empty contraption.

Bingo sniffs it and detects a hint of rust.

"Just ain't no way. Even I get caught in these dang traps, Bingo."

Bingo nuzzles his master, trying to console him.

"We're licked, boy. They done beat us, eh. If they set off one, you know they set off all the rest." He walks around and checks just to make sure.

"Yep, right there." He points to a snapped trap. "First the poisoned meat. Now the traps? Nothing is addin' up except for expenses. I've taken an extra year longer than I was supposed to. College boy? Ha! I'm being outsmarted by a doggone wolf that can smell traps underground! How can they know about the traps? No wolf has ever escaped my traps. This... this ain't a wolf at all, Bingo. This is something else entirely."

***

"Kiowa wins?" Zack asks, literally biting his fingernails.

"Well, hold on, now..." Charlie says, raising his hands.

"Of course he wins. He's smarter than all of them. The Kiowa outfoxed the Pale-Face. I wanna be Kiowa!" Kevin shouts. Patting his hand to his mouth, he mimics the Indian war cry.

"The story ain't over yet. Don't count yer chickens 'fore they've hatched."

***

June 15, 1861

I don't know that these wolves can ever be trapped or poisoned. But I do know I'm going back to school for certain! Uncle, you will be very pleased to see how right you are. Can't say that I'm all that sad to leave either. Although I have come to love this majestic place, I miss my home. Never thought I would say that. I've managed to sketch some wonderful animals, and the science department will be happy with some of my collections. All in all, it wasn't a complete loss. I'm gonna take Bingo out to Cimarron Lake, where thousands of geese are rumored to gather before we go. After that we'll be headin' home.

Unlike so many other nights, W.H. kneels down and says a prayer.

"Thank you, Lord, for giving me the chance to come on this grand adventure. Though I will be leaving empty-handed, I ask a couple of things. First off, if you could inspire Jenny Mather to write me now and then I would be much obliged. Next I'd ask that these wolves grow tired of this area and move on. These dry lands aren't suitable for them. And I don't think I could stomach someone else cashing in on my reward. Plus they're smarter than me and I respect them for that. Last, I pray that the people who come through this place and see what I've seen will appreciate your beauty, your splendor, your handiwork in its entirety, even though it takes a while to appreciate."

He pauses for a moment, then continues. "P.S., Lord, don't let me come up empty-handed tomorrow. I truly want to see the great goose migration before I return home, that is if they ain't lost their marbles as well. Oh, and if you can, bless me that I might finally learn how to use that contraption, so I can photograph something reputable before I leave here. Amen!"

"Amen!" Bingo barks outside.

"Are you sad we're going home?" Cotton asks Bingo.

"No. I don't like this place. Will you miss it?" Bingo asks.

"Heavens, no. The heat is more than any horse should have to bear. If I have it my way, we would skip the migration and head home at first light. Heck, I'd be happy to go now."

"I've panted for so long, that's how I breathe now."

"Ha! Ha! I imagine it must be hotter than Satan's home under all that thick fur."

Bingo laughs, then lies down. His ears perk up when off in the great distance he hears the wolves singing their victorious howl. *If I didn't know any better, I'd say they was dancin'.*

"Imagine what it must be like to be a bird out here." The horse nudges him.

"We could ask them tomorrow," Bingo says, wagging his tail.

"See, Bingo, that's what you're good for. You gave me a reason to be at the lake."

The pair talk until the coyotes howl and the owls hoot.

"*Arrrooooo*," the horse howls, which is really just a whinny.

"*Arrreeewwww*." Bingo tilts his head back and joins in.

"No! No!" W.H. shouts, thrashing in his bed.

"Now you done it, Bingo," Cotton says, looking at W.H. in the throes of a nightmare. His thrashing body looks warped through the wavy windowpane.

Bingo shrugs. "I thought he couldn't hear me."

"I'll never understand why Master does that when something howls."

Inside the room, W.H. claws at his sheets. He grinds his teeth. His fists clench around the fabric and twist it into a tight knot. His feet kick at the brass footboard and shake the rack. The wolf hunter does not wake up from his nightmare.

***

In his dream, W.H. sees a beautiful chestnut-haired young woman. At first he doesn't recognize her. She struggles toward the cabin carrying a heavy armload of logs.

"And so you see, the boy who cried wolf died because he lied all the time," she says to W.H.

W.H. lifts his hands and sees that they are much smaller, like a child's.

"Why did he lie?" he asks in a full-grown man's voice.

"Because he was naughty! We must always tell the truth, eh."

W.H., as a boy, nods.

"What if he could have changed?"

"We can always change. It's never too late to do a kind deed."

"Okey dokey, Mommy, I'll try to change," he says without realizing that the woman is his mother. But once he says it, it seems to be so.

"Now, remember, you mustn't wander far from the cabin. But if you do, you must tell Mommy the truth."

"Why?"

"Because the big bad wolf is in the woods."

She tilts her head up and howls like a real wolf.

W.H. scampers for the cabin door. He pushes his way through and waves for his mother to come closer. "Come on, Mommy! Come along. I don't like this."

His mother sees something he can't. Fear fills her eyes, the same color as his own. W.H. steps outside to see what scares her. She pushes him back through the doorway and slams the door shut.

Confused, W.H. drags a chair over to the window and props himself up, just in time to see a hulking black-and-white timber wolf seize the hem of her dress.

With a powerful tug, the wolf pulls her away from the door. She claws at the ice and snow, ripping her fingernails off, as it drags her away. Her blood trails in the snow.

W.H. jumps off the chair and flings the door open. "I'm coming, Ma!" he shouts in his manly voice.

Several wolves appear within the woods.

"SHUT THE DOOR, YOU FOOL BOY!" she shouts, struggling fruitlessly to free herself. The pack circles her.

"Where's my rifle?" W.H. looks everywhere. He can't help but stare at his little hands.

His mother screams. He looks through the open door.

The wolf thrashes back and forth, ripping a chunk of her dress off.

The boy screams when wolves latch on to his mother's limbs

and begin to pull. Their snarls are so vicious, their intent cannot be mistaken.

The alpha, who grabbed her, stares with ferocious glowing golden eyes.

"*Aaaagggghhh!!!* CLOSE THE DOOR!" are his mother's final words.

W.H., the boy, slowly closes the creaking door.

CHAPTER 127

Far from the pack, Anoki and Kiowa retreat at Cimarron Lake. Tucked in a jagged canyon, a wide reflective lake ripples between towering mountain peaks. Pine trees line the banks except in spots where tall wild buffalo grass grows. Except for the ocean of mingling geese, the lake is completely isolated.

"I think twice as many have come since last year!" Anoki says, dragging her tail beneath his jaw.

"Like the sands at our feet, they cannot be numbered," Kiowa says, shuddering from the tickle.

"I want to catch enough to make a dress."

"What would you do with a dress?"

Anoki stops and thinks about it. "I used to make such fine dresses."

"Yes, but now you are always dressed in the finest fur!"

"Do you really think so?" she asks, pushing her chest out and proudly displaying her pearly coat.

Kiowa nods.

"You are the greatest wolf and, inside the wolf, the best man. I will love you forever, my grand chief."

"And I you, Anoki. Either as a wolf or a woman, the Sun God has fused us together as one."

"For how long?" she asks, sprinting ahead of him, playfully leading the way.

He runs after her. "I will love you past all the summers of my life."

Anoki smiles at his words. They circle around each other.

"I cannot believe I was worried that our love was in its spring. Look at the fiery flower it has blossomed into. Surely you will love me past winter's sorrow?"

"Sorrow?" Kiowa asks, tilting his head to the side.

She leaps to the side and pounces all around him. "Don't you know every woman's heart fills with sorrow after it floods with happiness?"

"How could I know that, Anoki?"

Anoki circles around him. The two crouch a few yards away from what looks like millions of geese.

"Then I will love you past sorrow."

Anoki nestles into him. "There's only one way to do that."

"What game are you playing?"

"Not a game. A promise," she says, leaning close enough to kiss him. "I want you to make me a promise."

"Anything," he whispers.

"Not with words but with life."

"Life?"

She nods. "I want to water these lands with the life of wolves."

"How many wolves?"

"Hundreds," she says, nipping at his nose.

"But where will they find food?"

"Do you not see all these birds?" she says, sprinting after the geese.

"WOLVES! WOLVES! WOLVES!" several geese honk as Anoki chases them with her mouth agape. She catches feathers but no meat.

The geese scatter and rise in a giant wave.

Across the wide lake, W.H. spots the geese fanning out into the air. "Guess we're in luck, Bingo." He dismounts Cotton, drops his saddle, and detaches his saddlebag.

W.H. sets up a little artist's station, where he spends his day sketching the birds. He tries his best to capture the glittering water and the setting sun. He feels sad that he's the only one to enjoy this beauty.

Careful not to startle the geese, he watches them move to the center of the lake and cover it completely. Their honking makes such a ruckus, Bingo's barks can hardly be heard.

"Did you have any idea they'd be so loud, Bingo?" W.H. asks, but the collie can't hear him.

As the day wanes on, W.H. decides that this is the place to take a picture. Reaching inside his saddlebag, he removes his camera and zooms the lens in and out, trying his best to understand how to focus.

Moving the camera back and forth, he figures out how to focus the lens. Just as he focuses the lens, he sees a flash of white.

"What in tarnation is that?"

He tries his best to locate the odd motion again, but the fluttering geese rise and block his view.

"Wonder what's got 'em spooked," he says.

"Now, stay put!" he shouts to the birds, remembering that everything has to stay perfectly still. "I'm probably just wasting a plate, Bingo."

Isn't it time we head home? Bingo asks in nudging whimpers.

"It ain't that late. Let's just get one more shot, and then we'll be on our way."

He scans the bank and sees the white flash again. This time he's able to focus in on it and track it.

"Look at that, Bingo! Someone's got a shepherd out here. Must be a female."

Bingo's head tilts to the side, and his ears stand up. He can't hear the she-wolf, and the geese mask his senses. But the thought of bumping into a lady dog causes him to lie down and wag his tale with bursts of excitement. *Tell me more.*

"Oh, she's a female, all right." W.H. goads his pal. "Look at her go! We got enough time if you want to saunter on over..." W.H. winks at Bingo.

Bingo whines.

W.H. gets up and makes all the adjustments. He puts his finger on the button and waits for Anoki to stand still.

Anoki dashes in and out of the tall sage brush, making it impossible for him to take her picture. She playfully taunts Kiowa by staying close enough to reach but too far to catch. Little does she know the game she plays keeps Kiowa out of W.H.'s focus and fools him into believing she's just a shepherd dog.

"You call yourself a mighty warrior?"

"The mightiest!"

"Show me this greatness!" She laughs and sprints away before he can chase her.

"My magic or my courage?"

"Neither. Those are nothing to a woman. My heart empties and sorrow returns."

"*Ah-hoe*, show me the cup, and I will fill it up!" Kiowa prepares to pursue her, but she makes him pause. She ducks. He ducks. She sprints. He sprints. The two play on and on.

Anoki laughs, then sprints farther down the beach.

"*What fills a woman's heart?*"

"You already know!"

Kiowa lies down and thinks about it for a moment. What fills a woman's heart?

"I'll give you a hint. When I have too much of it, it overflows… When it empties, I am filled with sorrow."

"LOVE!" Kiowa springs to his feet and sprints after her.

At that moment he makes the fatal mistake of running into W.H.'s shot just before he compresses the button.

CHAPTER 128

When W.H. sees the Terror of the Currumpaw, he realizes his mistake. "That was no shepherd dog. That right there is Lobo's mate!"

He rests his hand on Bingo's back and presses him low to the ground. "Down, boy," he whispers.

Looking behind him, he debates on whether to go for his rifle. *If I fire a shot and miss, there's a good chance I'll never see him again.*

He swallows, feeling his heart pump excitement into his veins. His pupils narrow. He can hardly contain himself. *I knew there was more than one wolf! What do I do?*

"Don't move a muscle, boy. Our fortune is running up and down the other side of this lake without a care in the world."

He watches the geese lift off as Kiowa plows into Anoki and knocks her over. Adjusting his lens, he sees the wolves lie on top of each other like they are lovers.

"What in tarnation?"

Bingo begins to whimper. *Let's just go. They aren't in range, anyway. You said it yourself, Master. Time's up and we ought to be getting on to school."*

"Shh... shh... Bingo." W.H. pats the collie's head. "There they are, boy. Look at them behavin' like they're possessed." He looks back over at his rifle and feels despair sink in as his horse turns and grazes farther out to pasture.

If I whistle, they might hear me, he thinks, biting his lip in frustration.

He turns back to the camera and searches for the wolves.

"Doggone it! Opportunity is laughing at me!"

W.H. ditches his camera and slowly retrieves his spyglass. He pops it out and watches the lovers leap to their feet and chase each other.

"You're bigger than I thought!"

Kiowa passes in front of some sagebrush and stands slightly higher than it.

"I'd say four feet easy."

Bingo covers his eyes, wishing he didn't have to hear his master narrate.

"Look at them go, boy. They're going to mate. Oh-wee… If we wait until she has pups we can get more money for them, too."

Bingo's spirits could not sink lower.

W.H. watches his prey with extreme curiosity. First he sees them move like they're going to mate, but then, rather than mount, Lobo prances around the white wolf like they're dancing. This dance, the chase, and the pursuit of the geese goes on so long, the sun sets. Before day turns into night, it seems that the wolves are going to mate, but they don't. Instead they seem to sit side by side and watch the sunset like any lovers might. The last image W.H. sees is them turning toward each other, and if it weren't for the heat signals waving, he'd swear they were trying to kiss.

When dusk turns to twilight, he strains to see the beastly couple. He wonders whether they are going to hunker down on the bank and hunt the geese or if they would leave to go somewhere else. As more geese continue descending to the lake and the shore, he presumes that wolves have left the bank.

When night comes, ghostly howls echo through the mountains and canyons until it seems they raise the moon.

W.H. carefully slides down the bank and fetches his horse.

"You best not make a peep, Bingo," he orders his pal.

They move in a wide circle, working their way through the pines and scrub brush toward the lake's opposite side.

"You ol' scoundrel. You brought your lady friend to see the birds, eh?"

W.H. measures Anoki's paw print. He fetches his spyglass. The powerful moon illuminates the desert well enough he figures he can find them by that and their cackling howls.

The collie is quick to assist his master. He sniffs along until he finds a trail. Without saying a word, he lifts his front leg and points with his nose, reporting what he's found. Quick to task, he's fast upon the wolves.

In the moonlight Anoki's white hide looks like a ghost floating over a blue desert floor. W.H. cannot spot Kiowa, but he knows wherever the she-wolf is, the alpha is not far.

"She sure is pretty for a wolf."

The two lovers disappear into tall, thick vegetation.

W.H. waits. Cattails lose their white feathery seeds and explode off the sturdy stocks. They brush past glow bugs and cause them to ignite. A trail of glittering green lights magically follows the wolves.

W.H. carefully creeps on his belly till he's out of sight, then crouches low for a hundred yards or so. When he reaches his horse, he leads her on foot for a mile before he mounts her, so as to not to shake the earth and startle the wolves.

With a cluck of his tongue and a kick of the stirrups, he races toward Geoffrey's ranch.

Rushing up to the house, he sees that all of the candles have been blown out. The family dog barks. Not wanting to waste a minute, he pounds on the door.

When Geoffrey, the old rancher, swings the door open, his wife, his daughter, and himself all have guns pointed at W.H.

"Howdy, Geoffrey," W.H. says, reaching for the sky.

"Howdy. Mighty late to be gettin' your face blown off," the old man says, cocking the trigger.

W.H. pants, "I can't waste time. I know where the wolf is and how to trap him."

The family lowers their weapons.

"Tell me what you need."

"I need you to watch after my dog. I need as many traps as you got, a dead cow and something to claw it up with."

"Traps got delivered yesterday. That ain't a problem. But them wolves got about forty-five percent of my herd. You telling me you need more of my herd to kill 'em?"

W.H. nods. "If you give me just the one, I'll give you ten percent more than market."

The rancher thinks on it, then raises his brow as a smile crosses his lips. "Bird in the hand is worth two in the bush, but you're going to have to sweeten the deal 'cause you're sweating like a hog."

"Geoffrey!" W.H. stares desperately, which he soon realizes is why the rancher is negotiating.

"I want ten percent of the reward, too." The rancher extends his hand.

"Give me everything I need and it's a deal!" W.H. spits in his hand and shakes on it.

"Everything?" Katherine his daughter asks, patting her white cotton sleeping cap.

"Not now, honey. He's about to secure your future," her mother whispers.

After Geoffrey butchers the cow, he helps W.H. hitch his hay carriage to Cotton. The two nearly break their backs getting the entire heifer in the cart.

With the moon in the middle of the starry sky, W.H. can hear his accounting professor's voice echo in his mind. *The proper way to measure risk is to understand your reward. Reward can be attained by the variables "time," "principal," and "rate." First we begin by tallying assets and comparing them to liabilities. This will allow us to determine if our assets can cover the debt.*

Back then W.H. had missed the significance of the time variable. *How could I be so stupid? Time is never so precious as when you are out of it!* At present he was running out of time.

Oh my gosh, what if the wolves aren't even there tomorrow? What if I've acted too hastily? I suppose I'll have to cover Geoffrey's costs either way. He feels tinges of regret lap at his confidence. *But if I am successful in this endeavor, I will be a free man! Experience is my teacher now, and I'm at the front of the class. The only hope I have is catching them wolves in their refuge. I must bring them to the brink of fear. How else will they make a mistake? Mistake or escape? Stakes have never been higher,* he says to himself, setting his heart on the tasks at hand.

He thinks and thinks while Geoffrey ropes down the heifer.

I'm the principal. I'm getting back there as fast as I can, so that covers my rate. I got my bullets. Borrowed some traps. I'm towing my bait. He pauses for a moment, feeling like he's missing something.

He makes a verbal note. "I gotta make it look like an animal attacked the cow or they're going to see right through me. You got anything that might take down a cow?"

"Shot a coyote yesterday," Geoffrey says.

"I'll need his feet."

Playing the scenario out, W.H. determines, *I'm giving this a fifty-*

fifty chance. Geoffrey uses a hacksaw to sever the coyote's foot.

Getting back to the wolves' trail takes much longer than W.H. had calculated. Though the moon is setting, he works furiously through the night to prep the ambush. *It's night. Wolves prowl at night. I could be in serious danger.* The chilling thought races through his mind.

He runs to his horse and unholsters his rifle. As quietly as he can, he cocks it and makes sure the weapon is on safety. *Wait a minute. Assuming they're still here, they were probably breeding all night, and since they ain't howling, that might mean they're both sleeping.*

He wonders if he shouldn't abandon this idea altogether and just go ambush them with his rifle. Mentally running the chances of success, he reasons a hasty ambush would result in an absolute failure.

He runs his fingers through his hair. *I wonder if I shouldn't set this trap closer.* Fatigue turns to crushing doubt and makes him second-guess every decision.

I already dumped the cow's body off the cart, so I guess this is the place, he reluctantly decides.

CHAPTER 129

After unfastening the snap button on his bowie knife, he unsheathes it and hacks and hacks until he severs the cow's head.

"What are they doing for food, Bingo?" W.H. whispers. He looks around for his pal, then remembers he left him with Geoffrey. With a shrug, he gets back to work and thinks, *If they've been breeding all day, they have to be hungry.* As he preps the traps, he realizes their food source. *They're not here to see the geese. They're here to eat the geese.* He stops working and has an idea bright enough to light the night. Reflecting on his business lessons, he decides, *First off, the wolves ain't the principal. Food is the principal. Second, I have competition. The geese can be captured—maybe not easily, but they can certainly be captured. How do I get the wolves to detect the heifer's scent over all these geese?*

Reeling back, he thrusts the crimson blade into the cow's abdomen and pulls the entrails out. Next he makes sure every ounce of blood flows out of the animal and onto the ground.

Now it's up to the wind.

W.H. sets seven steel traps in a staggered circle around the bloody mess. He fetches the coyote feet and claws up the hide. Next he presses the paws down in a pattern that would make it seem like a struggle ensued. As he stands up, he sees his tracks mixed with the coyote's. *I'd best sweep over my tracks, then make it look like a whole pack has been here. Certainly one coyote couldn't take down a cow.*

Focusing on his rate of speed, as his professor taught him, he carefully covers his traps with dirt. *Wait a minute. I wonder if they can detect the scent of metal.* This thought causes him to pause and reflect on the wolves' unnatural ability to escape his traps. *That's how they've been able to set them off. Maybe if I cover them with blood, meat, and coyote stink they won't be able to catch a whiff?*

A sinister thought creeps into his mind the way fog slips into night. *What if they split up?*

He cautiously walks up the hill toward the lake. He makes sure that his last trap is in the open, where he can get a clear view.

"Oh shoot. I don't think I set the anchors deep enough," W.H. mumbles to himself.

He looks around and assesses his tools. *I should set all the anchors at least two to three feet deep.*

As quietly as he can, he digs with his expensive souvenir from Iowa. Once he's about three feet down, he taps the anchor into the earth and fills the hole with rocks about a foot deep.

"That ought to do it," he tells himself as he fills the hole with earth. To keep his mind focused on final preparations, he sings "Bring your girl to the ball, put that flower on tall… Swing Jenny… 'Round and 'round she'll go, where she'll stop no one'll know… Allemande left and allemande right, do-si-do… uhmm… hmmm."

He uses the coyote paws to leave a trail and does his best to cover up his tracks. *That should make it look like the pack fought over the brains and eyes after they severed the head.* Very carefully, he leaves the coyote's imprint over the traps.

All his planning and conniving are illuminated by morning's early light.

"Time's up!" He speedily checks every detail. W.H. goes over his tasks and makes sure he hasn't accidentally dropped anything. When his scheme passes muster, he grabs his horse's reins and hauls the cart away, sweeping over the wagon tracks with sagebrush as he goes. He leads Cotton and the wagon a good half-mile before he unhitches the wagon and frees his horse. He grabs his rifle and his spotting scope, then turns back. At dawn he takes up a position where he can clearly observe the goings-on of this new day. He yawns and peers through his rifle scope, checking to make sure he has a clear shot. The rising sun chases off the cool breeze and gradually raises the temperature to a comfortable eighty degrees.

When he settles in, he covers himself with sagebrush, then rests his cheek against the buttstock of his rifle. He blinks once, then twice, and his eyelids grow heavy to the point he can't keep them open. Without realizing it, he dozes off.

When the sun's brilliant orange light turns the desert red, then peach, the geese chatter away.

Anoki hears them mention wolves so many times she puts her paws over her ears to silence them.

"I am tired of the cackling geese. Besides, their feathers turn my stomach and make me sick, and yet I think we should kill them all," she says, scanning with plotting eyes.

"So you still want the dress?"

"Yes!" She hisses.

"Well, they stay far out on the lake, which makes them hard to catch."

"Let us search for rabbit or something other than geese," she says with pouting eyes Kiowa cannot resist.

The two move far from W.H.'s ambush. Circling around the territory, they can't even find a mouse.

"The geese are chasing all the little meats away," Anoki says, panting from the rising temperature.

"I will find us something, Anoki. Go soak in the lake."

Before they separate, Kida, Makes Trouble, and Paw link up with them.

"Ranchers used their thunder stick on us yesterday and today," Paw reports.

"Where is Walpi?"

"Where he is best kept, with the children," Kida says.

"Everyone is hungry. We need a good hunt," Makes Trouble informs Kiowa.

"Well, fortune is smiling on us." Kiowa looks at Anoki and smiles. "We have more geese than we can catch, and no one will use their thunder sticks on us out here."

Anoki growls and swallows her pride.

"Have you thought about following the everywhere water up to the northlands?" Paw asks. "There are plenty of deer and elk. Maybe we could even kill a bear."

"Nah, Uncle. The grizzly is too strong for us."

"Nothing is too strong for our pack, Kiowa. Your magic protects us all." Makes Trouble beams as bright as his russet fur.

"Let us gather a little food; then we will have words with the tribe," Kiowa says, dismissing his uncle.

The pack turns back and trots over to the sparkling waters when a gentle gust of wind picks up. The faint, unmistakable salty aroma of blood mixed with a strong odor of tame buffalo makes Kida's mouth water.

"I smell meat," Kida says.

The pack circles around her and watch her follow the scent. They form up and let Kiowa take the lead when the scent is strong enough for him to follow. A very short distance from the lake, they find drops of blood.

"Kiowa, isn't this where we were yesterday?" Anoki asks. "I do not remember smelling a tame buffalo."

Kiowa doesn't answer. He strains his eyes to detect every detail.

The wolves masterfully use the terrain to mask their movements as they close in on the source. They find W.H.'s decimated cow.

"When will Round Eyes learn?" Kiowa asks, uncovering the traps.

"Look at all these coyote tracks," Paw says.

"Yes, look how they have no light in them and little drops of blood."

"And when do coyotes leave meat on a kill?" Paw asks, spotting the intact hindquarters.

"Round Eyes could be anywhere out there with his thunder stick," Makes Trouble warns. "We are at a disadvantage with all these colors that are different from our coats."

"You blend," Kida growls.

"Yes, but your red coat doesn't," her brother snarls.

Kiowa divulges his plan. "We will go back to the lake and soak in the waters until the sun is high in the sky. Then I will return and see what stirs."

"Ha! Ha! I am so proud of your wisdom, Nephew," Paw says, complimenting him. "Who would ever think to look for a wolf in a lake?"

"A fish? Yes. A goose? Certainly. A wolf? Never. I wish I had your thoughts," Makes Trouble whispers.

The pack returns to the lake. The geese immediately take off when they see the wolves slip into the water and hide under a fallen tree. They circle far overhead, honking as they wind around in a grand circle and land safely on the other side of lake.

"Wolves over there, flock over here," an old goose says, orienting the birds. "That is how we stay alive!"

The wise old bird takes the lead position in their chevron formation.
The honking geese wake up W.H.

CHAPTER 130

W.H.'s eyes lurch open.

"Oh boy am I stiff. I'm saturated plum through," he mumbles. He pats his sweat-soaked clothes. "If I didn't know any better, I'd say I just stepped out of a bath." One question haunts him. *Is moving an inch worth three thousand dollars?*

He looks through his scope, scans his trap, and struggles to keep his bloodshot eyes open.

When the sun is highest, Kiowa carefully slips out of the lake. Only a few geese startle and fly off. The rest of the flock is kept calm by huddling together in the center of the lake far away from the wolves.

"Huddle up tight, folks. Hold your position," the oldest goose orders.

"We see you there!" they shout.

"We see you and you will not surprise us!" others shout.

Careful to use the shadows, Kiowa crawls back to his vantage point. He looks, listens, and smells for any trace of Round Eyes.

My magic would warn me if danger were near. Surely I would see a sign. He continues his survey, looking for a signal from a human or a sign from the gods. When he receives neither, he decides to remain still. He lies outside the lake until the sun dries his fur. Feeling unsettled, he returns to the lake.

"I don't see anything, but there's no harm in waiting until dark."

Paw glances away, then scans the banks. "If he is down there, the geese will have raised his suspicions."

Kiowa now sees the weakness in his plan. Most of his pack is vulnerable in the water. He uses his paws to cover Anoki's white face. Paw rubs his cheeks against the muddy bank and uses his paws to cover his ears and head. They each take turns covering each other's faces and staying low in the water so that only their heads are above the surface.

"He would have spotted us by now if he were here. No skilled hunter would let the geese scatter and walk away," Makes Trouble says.

"But if he is here, the only cover we have is lying still in the water. His eyes may be weak, but the geese will eventually give us away." Paw sighs.

"That and our bobbing heads," Kida says.

"So then?" Kiowa worries about the safety of his pack.

"Don't disturb the geese," Makes Trouble says.

"Let's move closer to the brush along that bank," Paw says, moving toward the cattails.

"If he comes, everyone run in different directions. He can't kill us with his magic all at once," Kiowa orders the pack.

At a different spot, W.H. shakes uncontrollably as the sweltering heat fries him. Though he's managed to move into the shadow cast by a large boulder, he's at a great disadvantage. He can't see the lake, and he's banking on the wolves falling for his bait. He uses the geese to tell him whether the wolves have returned or not. Since they haven't flown away all day, he wonders if he shouldn't move closer to the lake and see if he's missed his opportunity. He wipes his brow and drinks the last of his water, searching all around him for scorpions, rattlesnakes, and fire ants. *Even in the shade, it's hotter than Hades out here.*

Anoki trembles from the thought of a hunter stalking them. Rather than utter her fear aloud, she whispers, "I do not mind hiding in the lake all day. It is cooler." Though she wants to leap out of the lake and sprint back to her pups, she follows her chief's lead.

The wolves do not answer her.

When the sun finally sets, the wolves move no more than an inch at a time. With very slow, calculated motions, they extract themselves at twilight.

They cautiously approach W.H.'s trap.

"I can smell his metal traps," Kiowa says.

Makes Trouble uses his mouth to pick up a rock. He tosses it. The trap snaps down. The impact triggers the trap next to it.

Kiowa draws a deep breath. He looks at Paw and says, "It will only be a matter of time before he thinks of a way to kill us."

"Or we kill him," Kida says, moving away from the cow.

"It's probably poisoned, Kiowa. Just leave it," Anoki warns them.

Makes Trouble and Kida search it over and see ants crawling all over it.

"Wait by the rocks where it's safe, Kida and Anoki. We are going to teach Round Eyes once and for all who owns these lands."

"Don't you want to hear my plan, Kiowa?" Makes Trouble asks.

"Sure. What is your plan, my would-be brother?" Kiowa answers.

"Back at the town, Paw and I saw their magic letters. We should stack the rocks in the same way."

Kiowa's eyes widen with excitement. "That is a brilliant plan."

The wolves pick up rocks with their teeth and set the traps off. Once the traps are clear, they begin to stack the rocks as best as Makes Trouble can remember. They laugh as they replicate the town sign that reads, FAREWELL AND COME AGAIN!

Kiowa stops and talks while his uncle works. "I see the wisdom in your plan, Uncle. Tomorrow we will move the pack to the northlands," Kiowa says, consenting.

Paw smiles. His white teeth shine and his yellow eyes glow in the early night.

"That fills my heart with joy!" Paw says.

Anoki walks along the path where W.H. dragged the cow's head. "The wolf has taken over the man. I say 'let's go'; he says 'you go,'" she says in a sassy tone.

Anoki unknowingly steps beside the last trap. "I say 'leave it'; he says, 'No, Anoki, you leave!'"

Her rear paw barely steps over the trap.

She turns around. "I say it's time for Anoki to put her foot down!"

She stomps her foot down directly on top of the trap.

SNAP.

CHAPTER 131

Anoki releases the long rally cry. The pack drops their rocks and sprints to her aid.

"Anoki? ANOKI..." Kiowa yelps. His voice trembles with fright.

They sprint over to her. Kiowa watches helplessly. Love is trapped. She struggles to get away. The chain pulls tight and holds her in place.

Kiowa runs to her, "Hold still, Anoki. Don't move! You'll make it worse."

"KIOWA! HELP! Please. It hurts!" She howls.

Kiowa leans down and examines her foot. On the horizon, the pack's silhouettes are highlighted by the full ivory moon.

"Oh, it hurts! I'm in terrible pain. I think my leg is broken."

"Can you stand on your leg?"

Anoki puts her trapped foot down and whimpers. "I think so."

"Is it broken?" Kida asks.

"Not if she can stand on it," Paw mewls.

"Use your magic, Kiowa!" Makes Trouble pleads.

"Onendah showed me how the traps work. I'm going to push on both sides of the jaws with my paws. When it opens, pull your paw out as quickly as you can."

Kiowa inspects the trap and sees that it is the same.

"Ready?" he asks placing his paws on the trap.

Anoki nods.

He applies pressure. The spring stretches. Jaws open. Anoki tries to slide her paw out, but Kiowa's grip slips. The trap snaps shut, clamping firm. Anoki yelps in agony.

"Stop!" Paw shouts. "The teeth will break her leg—or worse, sever it."

Kiowa looks at his paws and up at the moon. Now, more than

ever, he wishes he could shape-shift back into a human and use his hands to free Anoki. *What have I done?*

Makes Trouble bites at the chain and thrashes it with his jaws.

"What are you doing?" his sister, Kida, asks.

"Trying to bite through it."

"That will never work."

"Maybe if we all work together. Let's bite down and tug as one," Paw proposes.

The pack take their respective places and bite down on the chain. They tug together with carnal strength. The harder they pull, the more they learn that the anchor is well set.

"No, Kiowa... no more... You'll break my leg. Dig it out at the other end, and that will set me free. I can limp home."

Kiowa traces the chain back to the anchor. The wolves dig as fast they can. Their claws move the earth with swiftness. Soon they reach the rock layer. Kiowa leans down. He tries to bite the rocks and lift them, but the hole is too narrow.

"We need to dig a wider hole!" Kiowa orders the pack.

As they dig, they discover that W.H. anticipated their cleverness. He buried rocks in a wide circumference to prevent them from digging free.

"We had better watch out for him," Paw warns.

"Everyone help dig up all these rocks, so we can widen the hole and free the anchor," Kida shouts.

Kiowa is so focused on freeing Anoki, he gets tunnel vision. The pack joins in, clawing at the dirt. Clumps of sand are hurled up into a mound behind them. They find one rock after another. W.H. has set the trap well.

After several hours Kida says, "Kiowa, we need water and rest. We can all take turns to free my sister." She looks at Anoki with loving concern, an expression Anoki could not have fathomed years ago.

"No, Kida! The anchor is moving. We must continue!" Kiowa growls.

The wolves dig and dig, but their efforts slow as the night passes. Eventually Kiowa sees the wisdom in Kida's counsel. Three dig while one stays on the lookout.

When night draws its shadow back and loses the fight to morning light, the lark marks dawn with a divisive tune. W.H. catches the wolves in a trap they did not detect—time.

"I don't understand why we cannot free you. He must have a magic spell on it," Kiowa says.

"Magic?" Paw questions. "Then we need Onendah!"

"I will go," Kida volunteers, sprinting off.

Makes Trouble and Kiowa team up and jerk on the chain so hard one of Kiowa's molars cracks. He cries out, heightening Anoki's fear.

"What is it?" Anoki begs.

"Nothing. I'm just angry."

As first light peeks over the horizon, Anoki looks for the sun. Off in the distance, she sees something she has never seen before. Light catches W.H.'s scope and sparkles.

Why does this star shine in dawn's light? she wonders. Her blood turns to ice and her body begins to tremble. *Sunlight enhances it and makes it sparkle brighter. That is not normal. That is bad magic.*

Anoki looks at Kiowa and manages a nervous smile. "Go rest and drink, my love. Round Eyes has many traps to check before this one. I'm sure of it. Remember how many we found?" she says, wondering if Round Eyes is the source of the strange star.

Exhausted, Makes Trouble and Paw sprint to the lake. When they near the lake, they move slowly so as not to disturb the geese.

"I won't leave you... I can't leave you... It is Indian law. The Kiowa never leave anyone behind," Kiowa says between heavy pants.

She looks past his yellow eyes and into his soul. For a brief moment her heart turns from icy fear to the warmth of love. She searches for the right words to move him away but can't seem to find them. *I pray with all my heart to all the gods that ever were, let me hold my children with mortal hands.*

"Kiowa," she calmly says, "my foot does not hurt so bad. See, I can stand on it." She puts her foot down and suffers through the searing pain. "Your nose is dry. My nose is dry. Go soak your tail so that I may lick it and get the desert out of my mouth. You aren't leaving if you come back." She lowers her ears and tilts her head submissively. Her bright blue eyes win him over.

Kiowa hesitates to leave her side.

When Makes Trouble and Paw reach the lake, the geese spot them.

"Wolves in the open! I repeat, the wolves are in the open! Let's move out!" the old bird shouts, leading his flock in a massive exodus. Thousands of wings flutter. Loose feathers separate from wings. Gusts of wind ripple the water.

"If we starve them out, they'll leave!" their leader honks. "No one get killed!" The order honks from beak to beak.

The birds take off. Their numbers are so great, they nearly blacken the sun.

"Wolves! Wolves!" thousands of them echo, alerting every living creature for miles and miles.

"Now I can't leave you by yourself," Kiowa says, returning to the anchor.

The riotous geese wake W.H., who had passed out from exhaustion and food deprivation. He rattles his dry tongue, but it's sealed to the roof of his mouth. All he can think about is getting to the lake. He reaches for his canteen and stands up, but his numb limbs resist him.

"Oh, I shouldn't have slept on the rocks. That was stupid."

Anoki's gaze sets firmly on the strange sparkle. When she sees it move, she crouches down and caves to panicked breathing. She looks back at Kiowa, wanting to reach for him, then whimpers for her pups. *Oh, how I would want to hold my children if they ever change from pups to people. Please grant me this. Please, Maawa. Let me be their center. I want to be their home.*

W.H. decides it's "time to make the sufferin' count." He blinks several times to clear his blurred vision, then wipes the sleep out of his eyes. He looks through his scope and checks his traps from afar. His line of sight puts him directly on the dead cow. When he sees that his traps are empty, he sighs.

"Oh, dang. That's it! I'm going home. I'm done here." He stretches and rubs his spasming back. "I need breakfast. I need Bingo. Where are you, Cotton?" He yawns and blinks repeatedly.

Let's see here. I know I'm forgetting something... He struggles with a thought that dances around his memory. *Seems like I should be doing something before I go.* He scratches his chest. *Oh yeah, the cow's head. What about that?*

He pushes the thought out of his mind, not wanting to see one more empty trap. "No need to add insult to injury," he mumbles to himself, reluctant to add one more failure to the mountain. But his curiosity overcomes his pride. *'Course, it would be a crying shame to do half a job.*

W.H. musters the resolve to take one last look. He quickly holds the scope up to his eye and moves the crosshairs back and forth. "That's what I thought, empty." He grumbles, moving the scope on to the target.

Wait a minute. What's this? W.H. spies the unmistakable white fur of the she-wolf. She is crouched low on her stomach.

"No. No. No. I don't believe it!" he says, lowering the rifle and clearing his eyes in disbelief. He rests the buttstock in the hollow socket of his shoulder. Adjusting his position, he stabilizes the scope. About a hundred yards from him, he catches what once could not be caught.

"Who's afraid of the big bad wolf?" he sings as he flips his weapon off safety and takes a knee to stabilize his shot. "Dang. Had she muddied up her coat, I might not have even seen her."

An eagle screeches.

Kiowa looks up with a bright smile. "Our prayers have been answered, Onendah is here."

Onendah's eagle shadow hovers above W.H.

The wolf hunter applies the gentlest pressure on a hair trigger.

"Beware, my wolf family! I can see Round Eyes," Onendah lets out a loud high-pitched alert. He signals the wolf hunter's exact position with his circling shadow.

Anoki watches the gleaming star move back and forth. Her worst fears are confirmed when it holds still.

Tears gloss over her large cerulean eyes. In a low voice she says, "Look, Kiowa, it's Onendah. He watches from the sky. I'll be okay. Now, please, love, go get us water. I am thirsty."

Kiowa looks up at Onendah and sighs with relief. "I'll be as swift as the wind."

Anoki smiles. "You'll be faster. Go!"

As Kiowa trots away, he looks back at Anoki.

"Go, my love... Go drink," Anoki whispers. She draws a deep breath and closes her eyes.

W.H.'s scope holds still.

Anoki slowly opens her eyes and looks directly at him. "I know

now I will never be mortal again. Truly, to love is to live."
BANG.

CHAPTER 132

As Kiowa disappears over the hill, he hears a distant roll of thunder. When he looks up at the sky, he doesn't see a cloud.

As Onendah flies, he spies the cloud Kiowa searches for. It is not in the sky at all but on the earth.

Smoke explodes out of W.H.'s thunder stick.

Onendah's eyes follow the bullet's vapor trail. He bends his wings and dives with outstretched claws to catch the bullet, but the projectile is faster than his magic. He screams, seeing Anoki's body lift when the bullet pierces her chest. A puff of white fur tears from her coat. Spurting blood marks the shot. The red circle grows and stains her pure white fur. She scrambles from the shot and attempts to get back on her feet. Crushing pain overwhelms her. She tries to whimper and to howl the rally cry, but instead gurgles blood and collapses.

Anoki's eyes glaze and her muscles contract violently. Her legs stiffen. Onendah watches as her limbs go completely limp just before she dies.

Kiowa runs back over the hill. He doesn't hear the shot's impact. He hears his heart break. "AAANNNOOOKKKIII!!!"

W.H. flicks his hand and ejects the smoking brass. "For though I walk through the valley of the shadow of death, I shall fear no evil. All wolves are evil. I am death! Look at my face, Lobo, and see your doom!" W.H. pushes the lever forward. A brass shell with a copper tip locks into the chamber. He aims in on Anoki. When he sees that she's down, he scans for Kiowa.

At the top of the hill, he spots the massive gray wolf. Dropping to the prone position, W.H. slides his arm through the sling to stabilize his scope. He fires again, barely missing Kiowa because... well, he isn't certain why. The bullet strikes inches in front of the hulking wolf and kicks dirt in his face. He doesn't flinch or blink. In fact, he doesn't even move. The courage in his heart won't let him.

The love he has for Anoki drains with her blood. *But… my magic?*

Makes Trouble retreats to safety while Paw's love for the only son he's ever known forces his legs into action. He leaps in front of Kiowa and catches a second bullet, which sends him spinning to the ground. Paw yelps and tumbles, biting his back to get the burning lead out.

***

Makes Trouble hides behind the ridge and feels satisfaction at his ability to escape. But then his heart drops and sinks into an ocean of shame.

All this time Kiowa has been the brave one. Anoki's soul may be floating above my head and watching me right now. What must she think of me? Makes Trouble has made a bride out of cowardice. Guilt and shame are his children. Only his life matters? Oh no, sweet Anoki. Is it so? Am I vile? His guilt forces him to reflect on all the battles he's fought with his friend, who should have been his brother. *At my core I am terrified.* He closes his eyes. His wisdom shows him what will soon happen if he caves to the swelling rage in his heart. He ignores the fatal vision and forces the hate deep into his heart. His rage melts to courage and sears through his veins. "I am MAKES TROUBLE! I am the almost-brother of dear Kiowa, whom I love more than myself. This love has been a rough ride. But it is *my* ride! Now I must ride rough once more. Anoki, do not let your soul float off into the sky. Makes Trouble is coming for you. Your would-be brother comes for you. As bitter as my love may be, you are still my sister. Would I not fight for Kida? Then of course I will fight for you! To love is not to think, TO LOVE IS TO DO!"

When he opens his eyes, his pupils narrow and the flames of courage flicker in his lime-green irises. The blood vessels pop. Pure fiery wrath consumes them and causes them to turn red. His muscles tremble with hate. He leaps to his feet and thrusts his chest out.

"*NAH, HEY, NAT AH HEY!*" He chants the Kiowa war song and emerges a mighty warrior.

He makes his way over the ridge. "*NAH, HEY, NAT AH HEY!* I am Makes Trouble! My heart is full of courage, and what can shatter that?

Nothing!" His growl rumbles like thunder.

Off in the distance, he spots the plume from Round Eye's thunder stick.

"DO YOU HEAR ME, MY ENEMY?" the wild auburn wolf shouts, running savagely down the hill. He sprints past Anoki, past all the traps, past hope, and directly toward fate.

"I AM COMING TO MAKE A WHOLE HEAP OF TROUBLE! I SHOULD HAVE KILLED YOU LONG AGO!" He releases his passionate war cry. For a brief moment he doesn't feel his paws touch the earth. Instead his courage makes him truly feel like he's flying on the wind. He has never felt more alive than at this moment.

"THE STRENGTH OF THE WOLF IS THE PACK!" he shouts, drawing W.H.'s attention.

"Oh wow! There's four wolves. I'm getting a whole pack. Here we go! Hold steady now." W.H. fires a fourth shot.

The impact takes Makes Trouble's ear off. He refuses to succumb to the pain. His tongue waves wildly. His fangs thirst for blood. His teeth, the only weapons he has, are bare. His brave charge is poetic, his love for the pack triumphant. He is more like a war god than a wolf or a man. His eyes are filled with murder and locked on W.H.'s frame.

"This isn't what she would want, Kiowa. The wolf is nothing without the pack... Think of your children!" Paw pleads with his nephew as he limps in front of Kiowa. He offers his life to save his son's.

Kiowa's trance breaks at the thought of his children. "And the pack is nothing without the wolf."

W.H. cocks his rifle and takes careful aim. Makes Trouble tilts his head back and opens his mouth wide. He's nearly close enough to take W.H.'s head off. With one powerful thrust, he leaps for the man with all the veracity of the wild. His claws are outstretched, and his fangs anticipate tearing flesh. He is fire and fury.

BANG.

A bullet ricochets off Makes Trouble's molar and passes out the back of his neck. He falls a couple of inches in front of W.H.'s feet.

W.H. shudders. "Whew. That was close! Let's finish this, boys, whad'ya say?"

Shuck, click, the lever action victoriously sings. W.H. scans for another target.

He takes careful aim. He easily spots Paw's black coat. Behind Paw, he sees Kiowa.

"One bullet, two wolves! I'll be a legend in this town."

He squeezes the trigger and anticipates the shot, but the hammer goes *click* instead of *bang*. Before he can reload, he watches Kiowa pause, turn, and run away with the limping black wolf.

W.H. quickly slides another shell into the chamber. He fires another bullet. It hits where Kiowa was standing, but the warrior is already a phantom.

Kiowa takes a last look at Anoki. He tilts his head back and howls a long, deep, sorrowful cry.

Neither Makes Trouble nor Anoki return their leader's rally cry.

CHAPTER 133

"He killed Anoki?" Luther asks, wiping tears out of his bright red eyes.

Charlie nods and wipes tears out of his eyes. "Yep. He sure did."

There isn't a dry eye in camp.

"Remember when Onendah put the war bonnet on Kiowa and said it had a purpose?" Charlie asks while he blows his nose into a red handkerchief.

The boys nod, wiping their noses on their sleeves and blowing snot rockets.

"Well, the wolf hunter had a purpose, too."

"Poor Anoki," Kevin says as tears stream down his puffy cheeks.

***

W.H. walks up to Anoki and kicks her limp body with his dusty boot.

"A few seconds more and I would have gotten y'all, eh?"

He picks up the bloodstained corpse, carries it to Cotton, and sets it down in the empty hay cart. Then he goes to retrieve Makes Trouble's body; when he gets there he finds Makes Trouble is gone!

Kneeling down, he spots the blood trail.

"Let's see here... Would you be going back to your den or to the lake?"

W.H. scans the sky. Neither Onendah nor the geese soar in the big blue. He reloads his rifle and cocks it, putting one in the chamber. He looks down to ensure his weapon is on safety, then decides to follow the blood trail. It leads back to the traps.

"Who's afraid of the big bad wolf? The big bad wolf? The big bad wolf. Who's afraid of the big bad wolf? Certainly not me!"

W.H. inspects the wolves' handiwork. *Let's just have a look-see at what happened here.* He sees where they dropped rocks on his traps. He smiles when he finds drops of blood where he struck the black wolf. Searching around, he doesn't see a body, but he does see a lot of blood. He squints and puckers his face up in doubt when he finds the letters *F, A,* and *R* written in rocks by Makes Trouble before Anoki was snared.

That is the strangest coincidence. Someone must have... W.H. looks all around for human tracks. When he doesn't discover any, he scratches his head.

***

The wolves rally around Kiowa in the den.

"Round Eyes will come for all of us. What is your plan?" Paw shouts, licking his bleeding bullet wound.

"Where is Anoki?" Kida asks. Her desperate tone causes the pups to circle around her.

"Who's coming?" the children whimper.

"Where's is Mother?" Red Cloud whimpers. "I'm hungry."

Kiowa whimpers.

"Gather the children and hide them in the hollow log, deep in the pine forest. We have buried food all around," Walpi shouts, taking charge.

Sliding rocks at the entry to the den startle and excite the wolves. They take up attack positions, except Kiowa, who seems strangely calm.

"Help," Makes Trouble gurgles. "I am wounded badly."

"Oh brother." Kida sobs. The pups wander over and lick his wounds.

"We must enter a war pact and kill Round Eyes, Kiowa," Makes Trouble heaves.

"War is not the Hopi way. It will not bring my sister back." Walpi weeps.

"Back?" Kiowa growls.

Walpi flattens his ears. *He will only take more of us with her. We have done things the Kiowa way for long enough. Now we do what Anoki would want. We survive!*

Kiowa looks at the pack with heavy eyes. "Long Horns was right.

The Great White Buffalo is coming for us all. We are all going to the cave."

"Kiowa, tell us what to do," Kida wails.

"Round Eyes is my plague. I will deal with him alone. Makes Trouble, you are fast and fierce. You have almost been my brother. Today you are my only brother; the pack is yours now. Lead them to the mountain of Yellowstone. Stay far from thunder sticks, traps, poison, and above all, man."

Makes Trouble struggles to his feet. "Do you not have eyes? Can you not see that my spirit is slipping out of my flesh? I was wrong, Kiowa. Thunder sticks can crack a heart full of courage."

Kiowa looks at him, then looks at Paw. "What do I do, Uncle?" He whimpers, tears falling from his eyes.

"Are you a warrior or a woman? You shed tears like a woman." Paw growls.

"I-I..." Kiowa stutters from shock.

"ENOUGH OF YOUR TEARS! Do not let me see your wet eyes or I will use what strength I have to rip you into pieces. You are not wounded. All your days you proclaim your love for Anoki. You say it is deep in your heart, not in your eyes. You dance in front of the sun. You hang from the eagle's claw. You have visions. You abandon your tribe. You turn from man to wolf. You defeat all your enemies with wisdom and great strength. You dare to ask me what to do? War is confusing. It requires men to hate. Is your heart filled with something else now?"

Kiowa doesn't know how to answer.

Paw doesn't wait. "Look at your wolf pack. Can you not see that this is so? I am wounded. Makes Trouble is wounded. Anoki is wounded. Is love for the pack better than hate for Round Eyes? All Indians fight for love. We love our families, and so we go to defend them. I have never felt more love than as a wolf. I will fight for this pack to the end of my life. I cannot go back for her or I would. It is not our way to leave one of our own behind."

Paw stares Kiowa down then continues, "What will you do, son of Lone Wolf, now that Anoki needs you? Is your love true, or is it all dried up like the desert? Are you showing cracks like the clay floor? If it is so, do not ask me what to do. Wither and die. If you are my son and you truly love her, you already know what to do with your hate! I used my hate on Black Bear. I went back for your father when he fell. Go earn your father's name."

Paw's words stomp on the broken pieces of Kiowa's heart. The whimpers of the wolves bring strain the sanity of his mind.

Paw turns to the pack. "Be a good tribe and help Makes Trouble to the pine forest. If Onendah can heal him, he will. From where I stand, I see only a scratch."

All eyes fall to Makes Trouble and then return to Paw as if to say, *You have gone mad.*

Paw taunts Kiowa's band of outlaws. He lowers his black head and snarls, "But if you are going to die, Makes Trouble, Round Eyes will follow your blood trail back here and find your body. Maybe he will be satisfied with that."

"Ha! That is the worst plan I have ever heard! Take me to Onendah. If I die along the way, Round Eyes will not use my scalp to protect his body from the cold. Maybe the Winter Woman will kill Round Eyes. Ha! Ha! That would be nice."

Makes Trouble tries to stand but falls. On his third attempt, Paw brings him to his feet by nipping at his ankles.

Kida picks up the weakest pup, showing she's ready to leave. She presses her head to Kiowa's, expressing her sorrow. "You are the greatest warrior I have ever known! Your family will be safe and waiting for you." She wastes no time exiting the den. "Follow me, children. Onendah is going to help Uncle Makes Trouble." The pups' tails whip back and forth.

"Father, I want to see Mother," Coon Eyes cries.

"Go with Auntie Kida, and I will bring Mother to you soon, son."

The pup turns and howls for his mom. When she doesn't answer, he follows the line out.

"Walpi, Anoki once asked me why I love her. Do you remember?" Kiowa asks Walpi.

Walpi shakes his head.

"My love for your sister is like standing in front of the gleaming arrow tips of every Indian ever made. It is also like staring down the hollow holes of every thunder stick and instead of running like a coward, bristling up your mane and charging even though you know it is the end. I want to rise like the sun. I want to stand on all four of my feet as my heart catches on fire."

"I don't understand."

Kiowa looks out the entrance of the cave, directly into the sun. He seems to look past the blazing light to something only he can see.

"What do you see?" Paw asks.

"She is the fire and I am the sky."

"Kiowa, your magic is the strongest I have ever known. I know you will bring my sister to me. If she is alive, she will need Onendah's healing medicines. If she is dead, her spirit will need to fly from her body and rest with our Hopi people in the sky. Is this what you mean?"

"My magic is invincible!" Kiowa growls, "Anoki is not dead!"

"That is true love! I am proud of you, my son." Paw speaks from the depths of his soul. He leans down and snatches up the last cub. He puts his paw on Kiowa's shoulder and says with soul-piercing sincerity, "I wanted my last days to be with you sitting beside me, stroking my hand and calling me Father as I drew my last breath." Tears streak down his black cheeks. "But where you go, I am too wounded to follow. I will be of better use exercising the last of my life to help your children find safety. I know you will find her. I know you will return. I believe in your magic."

Paw lifts his paw and signs farewell in Kiowa by pulling his paw behind his ear.

Kiowa does the same.

"Take care of my family," are all the words Kiowa says. *If I stay, I live and Anoki will die for certain. If I go, I may die, but I may not. Moon Beam, old friend, if ever I needed your fox thoughts, it is now. After all, you are the demigod who led me to her. I must muster the strength. All this is left for me to do is collect my will, and go.*

CHAPTER 134

W.H. whistles as his horse slowly moves toward his cottage. He looks off to the horizon and watches the sun set.

"Lookie here, Bingo. We bagged one!" W.H. dismounts and heads to the barn. He slides the door with too much force, causing it to bounce ajar. He places Anoki's body inside.

As he walks away, he turns to make sure his prize is secure. When he sees the door is open, he slides it shut, locks the metal latch, and clicks a padlock on the rusted loop.

"What is this?" Bingo asks Cotton.

"I didn't have a choice. He made me stay. I'm soooo tired." The horse moans.

Kiowa's faint howl silences them all.

"Now I know for certain she was your mate, Lobo," W.H. says, waiting for the other wolves to howl. When they don't, he smiles.

"So you've come alone, have you?"

"ANNNOOOOKKKKIIII," Kiowa howls.

W.H. checks his gold pocket watch. Bingo puts his head down and covers his ears with both paws as Kiowa howls again.

"Don't worry, Bingo. It won't be long now."

W.H. slings some steel traps over his shoulder and begins to set them around the barn where he's placed Anoki's body.

"And it's one, two, slap on your shoes. Three, four, get out the front door. Five, six, pick up your sticks. Seven, eight, don't stay out late."

***

When Anoki doesn't answer by nightfall, Kiowa returns to the lake and surveys the earth where she was shot. He sniffs her blood

and rubs his cheek against a tuft of torn fur, then lies down beside it.
"Why did I listen to you? Why did you ask me to leave you?"

He wails and mourns his loss. Suddenly, a thought enters his mind.
What if Paw is right and you are not dead? he thinks, then reflects on
his magic. *Makes Trouble survived his wound and his magic is weak. So
did Paw, and his magic is strong. My magic is the strongest.* He presses
his paw on the tuft of fur. *Oh, my heart breaks to think of you in pain.*

The thought of her suffering is worse than the thought of her
death. Kiowa stands, feeling a surge of courage swell in his heart.

"I am coming, my love. Loneliness you will never know. I will fill
your heart full and chase away all your sorrows."

His pupils grow as the clouds cover the half-moon. He tilts his
huge, scruffy head back and howls.

"Anoki, I love you!" He howls long and hard. "DO YOU HEAR
ME? I LOVE YOU!"

June 17, 1861
Dearest Uncle,

You will not believe my luck! To think, a
few days ago I was going to abandon this pursuit
and return to the dreadful classroom. Early this
mornin' I trapped and shot one of the ever-elusive
Currumpaw outlaws. I bagged a pure white she-wolf.
Upon seeing her coat, the Mexicans immediately
recognized her. They call her "Blanca." That's
Spanish for "white." Apparently she has been
mistaken for a working shepherd dog, when in fact
she was a scout the entire time. I suspected she was
the mate of Lobo, as her tracks often broke rank
from the pack and even surpassed the great wolf
leader at times. Had any other wolf behaved in
such a manner, Lobo would have shredded them.

As I reflect on today's events, there were some
peculiar events that play through my mind. Like
why the great wolf was staring at his mate while
I was taking aim at him. Why didn't he run as
the other wolves did? Why did he brave my rifle
fire? Have I become enchanted by this place? Is

it possible that the tides have turned and I am no longer a stranger but fast becoming a native?

At this midnight hour, I have been awoken by Lobo's howl three times. Though I've heard the King of the Currumpaw howl on many a night, I have never heard him howl as he does now. He sounds sad, eh. I'm going to cash in on his sorrow and line my pockets with gold! I wonder how that'll make Jenny feel. Maybe she'll warm up to a rich feller.

W.H. opens his lips and howls. He takes off his glasses, leans over, and blows out the candle. Lying in his bed, he closes his eyes and falls fast asleep.

With each howl, his muscles contract. His closed eyes dart back and forth rapidly.

He's dreaming. Suddenly, he's a boy. He's back in the cabin on that dreadful day he closed the door on his own mother. Her cries make him cry. Her screams make him scream. When she stops screaming, he doesn't. His wails entice the wolves. They ram the door, trying to force their way in. W.H. manages to tie the door handle shut using a worn rope that looks like it's going to split any minute.

The wolves howl and slam their bodies against the door, which makes the walls shake. It seems like any minute his safety and security are going to fall apart.

W.H. covers his ears and screams at the top of his lungs, "MOMMY!"

The banging on the door gets louder and louder. He can't bear the noise any longer. He pushes so hard against his ears, the flaps seal shut. All he can hear is his own screams. Then he looks out the cabin window and sees the wolf that attacked his mom staring back at him. The wolf's stained muzzle is drenched in his mother's blood. It licks its lips and glares at him with glowing eyes through the wavy windowpanes.

In his bed, he swings his arms wildly.

"STOP! STOP!" he shouts, sitting straight up. Sweat beads down his forehead.

Somewhere out in the distance Kiowa howls.

"STOP! STOP IT!"

When he realizes he's in his room, he pulls his covers off and slips his boots on. He checks his watch.

"Only an hour?"

Kiowa howls.

"Well, one thing's for certain, Lobo. You ain't gonna let me get any sleep, so I might as well get to work!"

He gets up and gets dressed. With exertion, he swings the door open. Dramatically lifting his legs, he storms off to the barn, unlocks it, and flings the door open. He saddles his horse and locks the barn door to ensure his treasure, Blanca, is secure.

"Hold the fort, Bingo. I'll be back soon. I gotta set some traps for the ol' despot."

"Good luck," Bingo says to the yawning horse, Cotton.

Steel traps slung across her back rattle with each step.

"I miss sleep." She *neighs*.

W.H. slowly rides off.

Bingo runs over to the porch and lies down.

CHAPTER 135

The next morning, W.H. rides into town. He leaps off his horse with the same vigor he had on day one.

Do I tell anyone? he wonders.

A pretty girl in a yellow dress catches his attention. When she speaks, he recognizes her voice.

"Thought you were headed out of town, Mr. Capital Letters Pretending to Be a Proper Noun?" Jenny says when she spots the pep in his step.

"*W* is at the end of the alphabet, right after *V*, for victory. *H* is right about in the middle. When you put all that together, you get a proper noun. *Victorious Wolf Hunter.*" W.H. perks up.

"What's that supposed to mean?" Jenny pouts.

W.H. tips his hat and says, "Ain't you a teacher now?"

"I was for a couple weeks or so. Back when the town had children." Jenny sticks her tongue out at him, turns her nose up, and starts to saunter away. Her plaid dress swishes and sways beguilingly, like a fish with a lure.

"Hey, where you goin' anyway?"

"I'm 'bout to drown my sorrows same as you!" She scurries across the street and puts her hand on the door, then spins around before entering the saloon. "Just call me W.D., Whiskey Drinker!" She turns and disappears into the renamed C Y'all Saloon.

W.H. waves her off and goes inside the hardware store. A few ranch hands leave and walk toward Jenny. He glances out the window and feels a certain uneasiness as the eligible bachelors pursue Jenny.

"Howdy, Mr. Mather!" W.H. says.

"Howdy there, W.H. Catch any wolves yet?" Mr. Mather inquires.

"As a matter of fact, I shot and killed a white one just yesterday."

"That a fact?" Juan asks, coming up behind him with barbed wire and iron rods in his hands.

"That's a fact!" W.H. says with a big smile.

"That explains why ol' Frank heard howlin' all night. Said it was the saddest thing he ever heard," Juan says, setting his goods on the counter.

W.H. doesn't say anything. He just tips his hat and thinks, *I should have kept the werewolf rumors going. That was a hootin' good time.*

***

Bingo is curled up in his favorite corner of the porch.

In the shadows near the barn, something stirs.

Bingo rests easily.

***

W.H. waits while Mr. Mather, Jenny's dad, gets in his butcher outfit and pretends like he's the town butcher.

"Poison ain't never gonna kill that wolf," Mr. Mather says, tying off his bloody apron.

"I know, eh. I got a plan B!"

***

Bingo is having a nightmare. He's running in his sleep, searching for something unsuccessfully, he begins whimpering. His legs cycle faster and faster in his sleep.

"Woof... woof... wolf..."

He runs so fast in his sleep, he wakes himself up. With a heavy sigh, he rests his head on his paws and realizes it was all a dream.

A tumbleweed rolls through his yard and then stops.

He stares at the weed, then gets up to nudge it with his nose, intent on sending away.

As he approaches the dead sage, he freezes in his tracks.

"I knew you would come," he says, picking up a familiar foreign scent.

Dust stirs behind him.

***

W.H. whistles to Bingo's tune, "Bingo was his name-o," as he rides back to the cabin.

The town's farewell sign has changed. Now it reads DON'T COME AGAIN.

***

Bingo holds perfectly still. "I ain't afraid of you, wolf. I was just dreamin' 'bout you. Can't be afraid if you know what's gonna happen."

Suddenly Kiowa's ears poke through the dirt behind Bingo. Next his head and then his eyes with pupils dilated, as narrow as needles and completely void of emotion. His snout surfaces. His lips curl back and reveal perfect white fangs.

Without warning, he ferociously attacks.

Wolf and collie entangle. Their thrashing heads cast shadows on the pine porch. Back and forth they fight to get at each other's throats. Half Kiowa's size, Bingo struggles to hold his own.

***

Traveling the dirt road to the cabin, W.H. takes his time planting his last two traps. When he's finished, he mounts Cotton and strolls down the last stretch.

***

Realizing he's losing control of the fight, Bingo flips around and dashes toward the barn entrance. He maneuvers his footing to intentionally avoid W.H.'s traps.

SNAP.

"Gotcha, sucker! It's over now. You're stuck! Master will be home soon, and he will be so proud of me," Bingo boasts.

Kiowa's left rear paw is enclosed on the metal clamp but only for a minute. Kiowa is able to pull his foot free as the faulty trap malfunctions.

"See there, my magic protects me. Now face your doom," Kiowa shouts as he lunges for Bingo. His rage is beyond control.

Caught off guard, Bingo has nowhere to retreat.

Kiowa seizes the collie by the front paw and severs the limb with a quick bite. Completely surprised by the swift turn of events, Bingo tries to counterattack. He turns but falls when his missing foot fails to catch him. He looks at his deformed limb and then up at the savage wolf in disbelief.

Kiowa seizes the moment. Like his father, he paints regret on Bingo's face. He latches down on Bingo's tail and tears it off.

Bingo yipes so loud, Cotton stops down the road and shifts her ears back and forth, trying to focus on the source.

"What's the matter, girl?" W.H. asks. He hears Bingo's faint cries as well, but he can't make sense of them.

Kiowa moves all around the maimed collie so swiftly, it is as though he were a pack of wolves instead of just one. He bites and twists Bingo's hind leg off before the dog can bite back.

Bingo falls to his side, fighting for breath. "Where is Master? Where is my protector?"

Kiowa latches on to Bingo's side and strips rows of flesh off with patches of fur. The torn pieces look like bloody scalps.

"Help, Master!" he cries out.

The wolf thrashes the collie back and forth, finding an opening here and tearing there.

During the fight, Bingo manages a useless defense. He snips at Kiowa, but all he catches is a tuft of thick fur in his pitiful mouth. Kiowa amplifies the attack. He bites Bingo's cheek over and over again.

With what little fight he has left in him, Bingo resists Kiowa's ferocious attack by pawing at Kiowa's face with his good paw. His attempts are futile and his confidence has been wiped clean from his smiling face. His teeth are totally exposed from where Kiowa bit off part of his cheek. Sheer terror fills his eyes. Kiowa latches on to his abdomen and rips it open, disemboweling him.

Bingo gasps for air as Kiowa's bloodstained jaws slowly tighten around his neck. He is held in a death grip. Tight enough to kill, but not tight enough to kill quickly. Kiowa savors the pulsing fear that beats like a drum from Bingo's jugular against his crushing molars. He continually resets his jaws, extracting every ounce of justice he can until Bingo breathes no more. The wolf takes over the man. Kiowa's head whips back and forth with terrible force. He growls in a mad frenzy, breaking Bingo's neck.

Unleashing his carnal rage, Kiowa resumes the attack. Bingo's bones pop in Kiowa's mouth as the collie is literally ripped into pieces.

***

"He killed poor Bingo?" John asks in disbelief.

Charlie nods.

"What'd Bingo do?" Luther whines, with his hands extended straight out.

"Nothing. Bingo did nothing wrong. In fact, all he wanted was to go on home," Charlie says, snapping a stick and putting it on the fire.

"W.H. is a big fat dumbhead!" Kevin sneers.

"I can't decide if Kiowa is a good guy or a bad guy," Zack says, resting his chin on the palms of his hands.

***

A few yards away from the cabin, Cotton spots Bingo's remains. She panics and starts bucking. W.H. digs in and pulls tight on her reins, but he can't control her. He quickly dismounts and tries to rein her in, but she turns and sprints off.

"Whoa, whoa! What is it, girl?" He scans all around, expecting to see a snake. Instead he sees spots red in front of the barn.

He puts his fingers to his lips and whistles. "Come on, Bingo... C'mere, boy. Did you get a rabbit or something?"

An eerie silence fills the air.

"That ain't like Bingo."

CHAPTER 136

"You lazy dog, are you a-nappin'?"

When he gets close enough to see the horror, W.H. draws his pistol.

"Bingo! Come on, boy!" he shouts, knowing that the attack was recent by the flowing blood beating out of Bingo's body.

He runs over to Cotton and manages to get his rifle out. Blinking away tears, he draws down on the barn. He cautiously moves closer to the door. His eyes flash from the rustic gray barn to the ground, where he discovers Bingo's front paw. He follows the trail and finds Bingo's tail.

W.H. keeps his head on a swivel. He's looking in front with his rifle and aiming behind with his pistol. He tucks the pistol under his arm and checks the door. It's locked, but deep bloody claw marks in the wood give him an idea of what happened. He turns around and scours the ground looking for clues that would help him understand who murdered his best friend.

Eventually, his worst fears are realized when he stumbles on Bingo's decapitated head. Now he knows what the terrible high-pitched noise was. He looks all around, piecing the fight together, and finally spots his trap. He lifts it up to eye level and sees a tuft of Kiowa's fur trapped in the steel jaws. One set of wolf tracks causes him to remove his hat and shake his head.

"I'm sorry, Bingo. It's all my fault." He wipes his tears, seeing Bingo's brave efforts. W.H. kneels down and removes a tuft of Kiowa's fur from Bingo's mouth.

"BINGO! I'm so sorry..." He kneels down by Bingo's bloody corpse. "You were my only true friend."

When sorrow hardens into rage, he cocks his rifle and unloads it into the air as rapidly as he can. "DAMN YOU, LOBO! Damn you straight to hell! I'M COMING FOR YOU! HELL'S ON YOUR HEELS!"

He looks off on the bright blazing horizon. The sun dips below the earth and the stars begin to twinkle.

Kiowa's imminent howl gets him to move inside. He lights a candle and sits down to his open journal.

June 18, 1861

If there is a devil, Uncle, Lobo is his child! At this very moment, he taunts me with his evil howl. I am not foolish enough to go outside and face him. He has every advantage on me. I must cool my wits and wait till dawn.

I half expected Lobo to come searching for his mate, but I thought he would give up his search or maybe lose the trail along the way. I was wrong. Poor Bingo paid a high price for my complacency. Poor, dear, sweet Bingo. The best dog I've ever had. My heart has not suffered so great a loss since I was a boy. I have sworn at his graveside to destroy Lobo. With God as my witness, I shall do so. Even if that means breaking my word to you! Please understand.

Love always…

As W.H. goes to blow out the candle, he sees through the reflection two glowing wolf eyes staring back at him. He quickly scrambles for his rifle. By the time he turns around to shoot, the wolf is gone. Using the candle to light his lantern, he kicks the cabin door open and goes out with rifle cocked and finger on the trigger.

"You're no demon. You're a wolf! An evil, villainous wolf! You're empty! You're void of love, compassion, and joy. Your fate was authored at your birth, and I shall tear you piece by piece, just like you done to poor Bingo!"

He fires into the darkness, hoping to get lucky.

"I ain't scared of you! You hear me? Not one bit!"

Eventually he gives up and returns to his cabin.

Before he blows the lantern out, he checks the window to make sure Kiowa isn't looking at him. With a heave, he blows the light out and tucks his gun in his bed beside him.

Kiowa howls so close to the house, it shakes the windows. "One moment without you, Anoki, is an eternity of pain. ANSWER ME!"

W.H. pulls a pillow over his head.

Kiowa continues to howl. "Anoki, I can smell that you are here. Answer me. Tell me where you are. Are you in pain? I will come to you. I will free you. WE WILL BE ONE!"

W.H. kicks his feet and screams into his pillow.

The howling continues all night long.

The next day Onendah rides a white stallion down the dusty road to W.H.'s cabin. He's dressed in a traditional white robe. He wears a large, ornate gold necklace embedded with oval turquoise stones. Two eagle feathers dangle from his gray and white hair. The grizzly cubs are nearly full-sized. They follow behind him. All in white and yellow peace paint.

As he approaches the cabin, W.H. sits on his porch in a wooden rocking chair, dressed only in red long johns. His rifle lays across his lap. His face is scruffy and his hair is a mess. Dark circles beneath his eyes indicate his irregular sleep pattern.

Onendah dismisses his growling beast children. "Stay far from this man's thunder sticks if you value your scalps. His magic is powerful."

The grizzlies look at one another and reluctantly obey their mother.

"My eyes deceive me, Chief. I could have sworn you had two bears following you."

"I haven't seen Two Bears since he died in battle. I come in peace, Round Eyes. Do not shoot me or my children."

"You're always welcome here, Chief."

"You look like hell…"

"I got hell on ma heels!"

Onendah dismounts his horse and walks straight into W.H.'s cabin. He makes a fire in the iron stove and pours water in a pot.

"Make yourself at home, Chief." W.H. pays him no mind. He constantly scans the horizon, the barn, the horizon, hoping to catch a glimpse of Lobo.

Onendah comes out with two steaming cups of coffee. He hands

W.H. one. Neither says anything to the other as the steam slips off the rim of their cups.

Onendah eventually sits down where Bingo used to sit and sips his coffee. W.H. lets his cup go cold.

The medicine man undoes his fine necklace, takes a knee, and sets it at W.H.'s feet. "Trade with me."

W.H. looks down at the gold. "What? Trade for what?"

"This magic has been in my family as long as I have had a family. I've come for the body of the white wolf, Anoki."

CHAPTER 137

"Ha! You're even crazier than I am. That wolf and her mate are going to make me a fortune."

"Many men have come to these lands seeking riches. With these great treasures at your feet, why is the soft yellow stone not enough for you, Round Eyes?"

"It's personal now. It ain't about money no more. It's about justice."

"Ahh... forgive me, Round Eyes. My speaking spell is only so-so. What is 'justice'?"

W.H. ignores his magic implication.

"It's when you make someone pay for their crimes... Yes, sir, you give 'em the what fer. Besides, I need the white wolf to catch me the gray wolf..."

"The white wolf never wanted any of this. She wanted her man to be her great chief. In fact, she did not even want to be a wolf. She wanted to go far from here. What sense does it make that you punish the innocent for the crimes of the guilty?" Onendah stands up and takes W.H.'s cup of coffee. He holds it to his lips and sips it slowly.

"Why do you people drink these black waters? They taste terrible!"

"You have to put cream and sugar in it, Chief," W.H. says, cracking a smile for the first time.

Onendah shakes his head in confusion. "I do not know what you mean by cream and sugar. I do, however, remember that you are from cold lands."

W.H. nods.

"Ah-hoe... I see; this explains much. The coldness has seeped deep into your heart, and now you are bitter. This is why your eyes are blue."

W.H. smirks.

"This is why gold and silver have poisoned your soul against the wolves and everything that is not tame. I see now that this is the root of your hate. You cannot even see that justice will escape you when Kiowa dies. You will be left with all this rot. Surely you can see that you are no longer tame."

"Kiowa? Don't you mean Lobo?"

Onendah does not offer any confirmation for fear he has already jeopardized Kiowa's life.

"Maybe you're right, Chief."

"Pity, your blue eyes are so nice. You would do well to let love light a fire in them instead of hate."

"Desperate men do desperate things, Chief."

Off in the distance Kiowa appears on a hill and howls.

W.H. sees him and springs into action. He makes some wind speed adjustments on his scope and fires. The shot misses.

Onendah covers his ears and marvels over the thunder stick's power.

"Damn wolf's been howling all night. Didn't get a wink of sleep, and now he's going to taunt me all day."

"His magic protects him. Besides, your heart is like your aim: low."

"Just what is it you want, Chief?"

"I want the white wolf, and I want for you to enter into a peace pact with Kiowa."

W.H. laughs hysterically. "So the Indians do call him Kiowa! Is that the name for 'werewolf'?"

Onendah grits his teeth. *I am too old for this*, he thinks. He shakes his head back and forth. "I do not know what this word 'werewolf' means. But, yes, his name is Kiowa. As I have said before, he's more than a wolf."

W.H. pauses, takes a deep breath, and squints. "I could no sooner release that wolf from the jaws of justice than you could turn into an eagle and fly on outta here."

Onendah's face grows serious. He tosses the coffee out and sets the empty cup down.

"You say you have come for justice, but none of the harm Kiowa has done to the ranchers has he done to you. Yet Kiowa's love rests dead in your barn."

W.H. waves his hand, "Ahh... fiddlesticks, Chief. They don't have to be my cattle for me to do something about it."

"So you come here with poison, traps, bullets, and hate. Tell me, Round Eyes, what, if anything, have these tools profited you?"

"Ain't got no profit. Yet! I gotta kill him first, then turn them both in and collect my reward." W.H. sighs. "Lost my good ol' buddy Bingo yesterday. Buried him right there. So, as you can imagine, I'm committed."

"And still you will not let Kiowa mourn Anoki? I cannot even set her spirit free?"

"Chief, them's wolves. They ain't like you and me. They ain't got real names or real feelings."

"So little you know, Round Eyes. My time has come to an end and I must go, but before I leave, I will ask one last time. Please, give me Anoki, for your peace and mine."

"My peace... Ha!... My peace will come one scrap at a time. Ain't no peace till Kiowa's head is mounted as a *piece* on that there wall."

"Kiowa has lost his love. You have lost yours also." Onendah looks down at the dust. He sighs and lifts his sad face to the heavens. He mumbles a quick prayer and mounts his horse.

"I have prayed to Taime that the Sun God will shine his good light on your soul. When your heart is thawed and you look back at this place, you will feel nothing but pain. I pray also that you may find another path. One that suits you."

"Only path I know is the one leading to that wolf."

"Kiowa have a name for that path. It is called the War Path. On that path, two walk, but only one can finish the journey. Sometimes no one finishes."

On top of his horse, Onendah truly looks every bit the magic medicine man.

He pulls on his reins and clucks his tongue. The grizzly bears come out of their hiding place and growl so loudly it makes W.H. sit straight up.

Onendah looks over his shoulder and shouts, "Taime has told me in a dream that Round Eye's path is greater than war. Maybe when you find Kiowa the wolf, you will make peace and return with peace of mind."

Onendah rides off, taking the bears and leaving the jewelry behind. When the medicine man is out of sight, W.H. gets dressed. He goes and unlocks the barn, then saddles his horse and makes for town. On the way, he takes his shirt off and ties it around his waist. He thinks about Onendah for a brief moment, then lets his swelling rage take over. He grimaces. His eyes flash wild. He soon finds himself among the cowboys and what few townsfolk are left.

"Well, ain't you a sight?" Jenny says, folding her arms and glaring with critical doubt.

"Howdy, ma'am," W.H. says, tipping his hat and scratching his bare chest.

Inside the hardware store, Mr. Mather nervously greets him. "What can I do for ya, fella?"

W.H. drops Onendah's gold necklace on the counter.

"I want every trap ya got."

CHAPTER 138

"Still hunting the werewolf?" Mather asks.

W.H. nods his head. "Yup!"

The shopkeeper sweeps the elaborate Native American jewelry off the counter and greedily grins from ear to ear.

"Yes, sir. Do you want snap traps with teeth or without?"

"I don't wanna take his legs off. I wanna catch and hold him, so I can see into his eyes just before I start cutting him up." W.H. puts his hand on his bone-handled bowie knife.

"Alrighty, then, I suppose you're in luck. We just got two crates in on Monday. Fifty traps in each crate. I'll load 'em into the wagon and follow you back home."

"I'll be needin' the wagon, too. I'll bring it back when I'm done."

"When will that be?"

W.H. gives him a cold, hard look. "When I'm done, eh!" he growls.

"Don't do it, Pa," Jenny shouts.

Her father holds his hand up and silences her. "I need that wagon back for Monday pickups."

W.H. asserts himself. "Like I said, when I'm done!"

The trek back home takes longer. It's sunset before the wolf hunter reaches the barn. A quick inspection shows that all the traps have been sprung. The barn's door is covered in fresh claw marks and chunks of missing wood.

"He's persistent. That's good. I'm going to use that against him."

The night blankets the sky, and Kiowa's howls follow.

W.H. writes in his journal.

June 19, 1861

Met with Chief today. He tried to get me to

enter into a peace pact with Lobo. Left me a gold necklace. Crazy ol' Chief! Wonder what he'd say if the fool knew he was financing my war? Anyway, how does a man make peace with a wolf? All a wolf knows is breedin' and killin'. They're animals with a killer's instinct. They have to be destroyed when they get out of control. Lobo is way out of control. He's killed more cattle and livestock than any butcher in Currumpaw.

Haven't been able to sleep for two nights now. Ever since I killed his mate, Lobo has been a howlin' all night long. He must sleep during the day. How else could he keep at it all night long? I see now that shooting her was a foolish mistake. If I had would have trapped her and let her cry, she would have brought him to me. Then I could have got the whole pack! I had no idea they shared such a strong bond.

Tomorrow I'll set up a hundred traps near the cattle and across the prairie wherever I can find his trail. If I set eight of them, four to a line, forming an X shape, I figure I'll either trap him scavenging for food or I will trap him near water. No other way to get at him now. He's too smart to get caught near the house. He already fought his way out. I'm going to get that reward money for certain!

W.H. rests the pen on the journal. He opens a window, grabs his rifle, and climbs up a ladder to his roof. Then pulls the ladder up behind him. He straddles his roof and waits.

Kiowa howls.

W.H. screams back.

Kiowa howls louder.

W.H. howls back.

As the night wanes on, W.H. tires and nods off.

When the sun rises, W.H. yawns and looks around for Kiowa. For three days, neither has had a good night's sleep. The wolf hunter shows it in his appearance. His eyes are deep and sunken. His face is scraggy and filling in around his bushy mustache. He stinks and hasn't had bath out of fear that Kiowa might sneak up on him.

W.H. grabs the ladder and lowers it down until it touches the earth. He rests it against the weathered silver planks, then scales down.

"Get your rifle. Get your baits. Grab some arsenic. Don't be late. Gotta trap a wolf; already killed his mate. Swing those traps 'round and 'round. Bury them deep, deep in the ground. Allemande left and allemande right, do-si-do, I'm gonna fight! Fight! Fight! Two steps left and three steps right..." W.H. scratches his dirty head and thinks for a word that rhymes with "right" that isn't "fight." When he can't, he continues to hum the tune.

W.H. picks up Anoki and places her stiff corpse in the back of the wagon next to the traps. He heads out to the canyon where Kiowa fought the pit bull, thinking that is Lobo's most likely avenue of approach. He arrives in the late afternoon and gets to work. Once he's set the traps and anchors, he ties sagebrush to his feet so his tracks aren't left behind. When he's satisfied that his traps are set and tracks are covered, he slings several traps over his shoulder and enters the mouth of the canyon.

With a deep breath he bellows, "Where's that wolf? I'll work all night. Circle 'round till morning light. Sight in your scope, squeeze the trigger tight. 'Cause it's allemande left and allemande right." He laughs and shrugs. *Can't believe it took all day to think of another word that rhymed with "right." I better start reading books again or something.*

W.H. returns to the wagon and retrieves Anoki. He carefully drags her body through the booby-trapped canyon and uses her severed paws to leave fresh tracks on the trail. He removes the branches from his feet and hops on rocks back to the wagon.

At another canyon entrance he repeats the same procedure. This time he cuts squares of sod and places them around the traps. Moving to where he's previously found tracks, W.H. finalizes his ambush by booby-trapping the last entry into the canyon. He ties the traps' anchor chains around small logs or whatever he can find. Once he's finished, he returns to his wagon, being careful not to leave any tracks. Finally, he ties a rope around Anoki's tail and drags her behind his wagon all the way back home.

***

Out at the lake, Kiowa rests next to where Anoki was killed. He doesn't know why, but he keeps coming back to this place.

Kiowa heaves and expels huffs of sorrow. "You said love never fails," he whispers.

When he catches Onendah's scent, his tail begins to wag. He trots over to the medicine man's open hand and licks it.

"I spoke with him. He will not give her to me. I did not see where he is keeping her to tell you if she is alive or dead. Kiowa, you must go from this place. There is nothing but death for you here. Round Eyes will not trade."

Kiowa whimpers. He stares at Onendah, tilts his ears back, and howls loud and hard. When he's done, he looks at Onendah with eyes that are filled with immense regret.

"Round Eyes has set many traps for you. He will use your love against you."

Kiowa turns away and walks a few feet from Onendah. He looks down and claws at the earth.

"You will not be able to find them all. He will catch you and kill you. Not even my magic is strong enough to find them all. Is *your* magic strong enough?"

Kiowa looks out across the rocky horizon. The summer haze makes a mist that takes a form. Kiowa howls when he thinks he sees Anoki. He sprints across the prairie and stops, looking back at Onendah.

"Go. Complete your circle. Follow your path, Kiowa."

Kiowa tilts his head back and howls as the sun goes down. His cry is bold and proud.

CHAPTER 139

Outside his cabin, W.H. sits beneath a nearly full moon. His rifle rests over his shoulder. He writes in his journal.

> **June 19, 1861**
> Dear Uncle,
>
> It seems that the only way to catch the great monster was to use the scent of his love… I mean, mate. Oddly, now that I've read today's events in black-and-white, I can't help but feel a tinge of remorse. If one were to read yesterday's report without suffering the loss of Bingo, they may see me as the monster, rather than the wolf. Strangely, my conscience is surprisingly heavy. I can't focus on this. I have to focus on the task at hand.

W.H. closes his journal and leans up against his smokestack. He waits for Kiowa to howl, but Kiowa doesn't.

I'd be a fool to think you were in one of my traps, ol' boy. I'm just gonna sit up here and we'll see who outfoxes who. He keeps his rifle pressed up against his side.

W.H. begins to doze. He nods once, blinks twice, then falls deeply asleep. He grunts and groans. His eyes rapidly shift back and forth and his nerves fire sporadically, making his arms twitch. Then his leg. Then his other leg. Then his cheeks. Then he's back at the cabin. He's a frightened little boy again. He huddles in the corner and rocks back and forth. The door shakes again. He panics and thinks the wolf has found a way in.

"No! No! No!" he shouts as the latch lifts. Rusty hinges creek, and W.H.'s greatest fear is materializing. His whole body trembles in paralyzing quivers. The tingling effect won't allow him to run or scream. All he can do is senselessly shake and wait for the end.

When a muddy brown boot breaks the open space between outside and in, he sees it stomp down on the floor. The petrified boy screams. The shrillness forces the rest of his father into the cabin.

"I'm here!" his father says, kneeling down and reaching for his son. W.H. runs up to his father and wraps his little arms around his scruffy neck.

"How long have you been like this?" his father, a lumberjack, asks.

His boy doesn't answer. He just shakes and cries uncontrollably.

"I thought you were dead, son. I'm so sorry. I never should have left you and your mother up here in the high country by yourselves."

W.H. is soon dressed in a school uniform. He sits outside the headmaster's office. Leaning as close as he can to the door, he hears his father say, "I'll pay his tuition, but the boy deserves a better life than I can offer. Education is his best bet."

"Agreed," the headmaster says. His voice is familiar.

The headmaster escorts W.H.'s dad to the hall where W.H. is waiting.

"Things ain't the same for us no more. I need you to do as you're told and I'll send for you at Christmas."

W.H. wipes tear after tear from his eyes. He looks at his father with big blue eyes that scream, *Don't leave me here.* Instead of protesting, he nods and says, "Yes, sir."

With that, his father leaves.

W.H. sits in the chair and cries in heavy, wrenching sobs. He looks up, hoping his dad will change his mind, but the man who created him doesn't even look back.

A younger version of the headmaster consoles the distraught child. He even has his secretary bring him a box of tissues.

"Come, now, young man. If you keep rubbing your eyes like that, you'll rub them clean out of your head. Let me see if I can find you a piece of chocolate."

"Wouldn't matter. I can't hardly see out of 'em anyway."

The headmaster escorts W.H. to his office while W.H. keeps rubbing his eyes. Now he's not a boy, but a man. From W.H.'s point of view, the headmaster is blurry until he slides a pair of round gold-rimmed glasses over his eyes.

"*Bah baht p'ah hehn,*" Onendah says. He appears now dressed like the headmaster, except for his headdress.

"Huh?"

"*Bah baht p'ah hehn.*"

W.H. nods. "I understand, Chief."

***

Outside the north canyon, where the pit bulls made their last stand against Kiowa, the heartbroken wolf paces back and forth. He lowers his head and takes several deep breaths. With each huff, he immediately senses the bitter taste of metal.

He pushes the acidic taste against the roof of his mouth and detects Anoki's scent. Her aroma overwhelms him. He releases soft whimpers. *It is certainly a trap*, he thinks to himself. He paces back and forth, knowing that he's being baited, but Anoki's face appears in his mind. He howls for her, and when she doesn't respond, he feels a great loss.

"I am coming to fill your heart with my love. I will drown your sorrow with joy. You will only know the sweetest happiness, deer, kind, sweet Anoki. We will dance. We will sing. We will…"

He doesn't enter the canyon where W.H. placed the traps. Instead, he skirts a tall cliff and generates an avalanche of loose rocks by digging every few feet. At the entry to the canyon, the rocks slide and the traps snap, bursting the sandstone in half.

Once Kiowa springs the traps, he follows Anoki's scent into the narrow twists and turns of the rocky canyon.

A flash of white looks like a buffalo. He freezes in place.

"I do not hear your peace flute, Buffalo Woman." Kiowa strains his eyes to see. The flash is gone, and only darkness and the howling wind remain.

One stray vapor forms into a silver fox. Its glowing emerald eyes entice him.

"Moon Beam? Is that you? Will you lead me to Anoki?"

The smoky vapor turns and pounces down the canyon.

"Anoki… I won't leave you… I haven't slept or eaten since you…" He can't finish his sentence. "Come to me, my soul, for I am lost without you! Do you hear me, my heart? Your warrior is coming for you!"

As he turns a corner, he thinks he sees Moon Beam chase after Anoki at the end of the canyon. His tail wags with excitement. He looks down and suddenly sees her trail illuminated by soft, golden light. He puts his paw over her print and watches them begin to fade.

He gasps and feels a rush of excitement. "I knew it!"

CHAPTER 140

"K-i-o-w-a," her ghostly voice says, slipping out of sight before he can see her.

Although he can't make out Anoki's hazy white figure, it seems as though she is playfully crouching, then pouncing back and forth, teasing him. She disappears behind every canyon corner.

"I will play your game, Anoki. I will do anything you want. I will even turn back into a man. Onendah will find a way for us," he says, passing each turn, but only catching her golden prints.

Kiowa charges through the ravine. The faster he runs, the more he can see her. She runs ahead of him, leaving her scent, a vapor trail in her wake. As he's about to catch her, she ascends above the canyon cliffs. A trail of golden footprints rises up to the heavens. Her spirit hovers in front of the stars. Before she goes any farther, she stops and looks back at him. For the first time since she's passed, he sees her.

"Oh, Anoki," he says, noticing that stars shine through where her beautiful blue eyes used to be.

He breaks down and sobs uncontrollably. "Is this a vision or a dream?" he whimpers. "Is that even really you?"

She runs out of the night sky, back into the canyon.

He looks up. "Dream or not, I must find you!" He lunges forward and immediately jolts back.

SNAP.

His hind leg lands in a trap. He tries to shake it off, but the new trap holds firm.

"Wait for me, Anoki! Wait!" With a hard jerk, he pulls the trap out of the ground and feels the most excruciating pain he's ever felt as his hip bone dislocates, then pops back into its socket.

"Arrrggghhhh!" he cries out.

Anoki doesn't seem to mind. She just keeps running.

Desperate to keep up with her fading trail, he bites down hard on the trap and breaks his front fangs. A weak link in the chain gives. He tumbles, then quickly looks to the sky and seems to smile. He looks back at the trap pinching down on his spasming muscles and licks his wound. With great difficulty, he gives chase, hobbling along on three good legs.

Since my strength is being measured, I must not take great risks, he thinks to himself. He lies down on his belly and scoots himself along the dusty desert floor, sniffing for other traps as he goes.

"Why do you torture me, Wolf Hunter?" Kiowa whimpers. "Is it just for my scalp? You will find that I am my father's son and I have enough courage in my heart to pass every test you lay before me. I will go the distance for Anoki. I am the fire and she is the sky." He scoots along on his belly repeating himself. "I will crawl to the ends of the earth for you, even if I have no legs. My spirit will find you. I will do anything for you, Anoki! Anything!"

He pauses for a moment and reviews his life's most difficult challenges. Memories of his greatest achievements flash before his eyes. One feather pops up in his bonnet at a time. He sees Chief Black Bear, torn from his saddle by the golden lance. Victory in wars. Many great hunts. Saving Anoki from the Navajo. Defeating the pit bulls. Outsmarting hunters. Outplaying Round Eye's many traps. Convincing his wolf pack to hunt the cattle instead of starving to death. When he sees his children born, he not only considers it his greatest accomplishment, but his legacy.

"I have failed only at being a man. I gave up my mortal skin to be a wolf. If all you see is a wolf, even though I have forgiven you like a man, then that is all I must be to you."

He inches along.

SNAP.

An intense crushing pain sears through his stomach.

"My love is greater than my pain!" He grits his teeth and tries to bear it with pride. "I will not be stopped! I will take all of them!"

He begins to pant. "Anoki, I'm coming for you… Please… wait for me."

The path narrows.

Anoki's spirit hops up and down at the end of the canyon, enticing the husky wolf.

Kiowa howls, "I will take you to the tops of mountains. Our song will be heard throughout the lands. We will go farther north and find the buffalo. I will ask Onendah to make us Indians again. We will be with Paw. Makes Trouble awaits his would-be brother. Your brother waits, too. I will do anything you ask, sweet Anoki. I will even challenge the gods. Just don't let my faith turn to despair."

Summoning as much courage as he can, he pulls the anchor out of the ground but accidently snags another trap.

SNAP.

Then another.

SNAP.

He panics and tries to compensate by moving faster.

SNAP.

Three traps clamp down on his left side only a few inches from one another. He jerks back and bites at them, but he can't reach them. He feels gaps where his powerful teeth have broken off.

Off in the distance, beneath the full moon, he sees Anoki's bright white ghostly coat leaping back and forth, calling out his name.

"See." He sputters blood. "That wasn't so difficult..."

He heaves and begins to foam at the mouth. "I don't know if I can make it, Anoki," he says, taking an excruciating step. "My heart and soul are willing, but my feet..." He says hobbling toward her image. "My feet will not obey me." He almost reaches her when his front left paw feels the *snap* of yet another trap.

This time he has no choice but to acknowledge the pain. He cries out and tugs at the chain. It holds him in place.

With the last of his courage, he takes another step toward Anoki's spirit.

SNAP.

His right front paw is now trapped as well. Unlike the other anchors, these traps hold him in place. He's painfully stretched out and unable to move.

Inches from Anoki's ghostly image, he tilts his head down. Her spirit does the same. Slowly, their foreheads touch. He stares into her hollow eyes just before he breathes her spirit in and her spirit-slips inside of him. He passes out from the pain then comes out of it.

Frantic he whimpers and sings. "Look, my love, the light on my face, it fills your eyes, it fills this place. Your smile is mine and we are one. Let this light be our sun."

He swallows and struggles to speak.

"Tonight my name is no longer Kiowa..." He grunts. "Tonight I have earned a new name..." He summons a brave growl. "My name is HEART ON FIRE!"

The pain overwhelms him. The great wolf, blacks out.

CHAPTER 141

Still dreaming, W.H. tries to get Bingo to run up to him, but Bingo won't.

"C'mere, boy... come on."

Bingo stares at him eerily.

"You got him!" Bingo says.

W.H. tries to snap his fingers, but they're stuck together. "Got who? Why won't you come? What's going on?"

"He's trapped, but you shouldn't go. You won't like what you find."

"I must be dreaming, Bingo. You can't talk."

Bingo's face droops. In a deep and terrifying voice he growls, "DON'T KILL HIM!"

The brim of W.H.'s hat rises and falls as he snores on top of his roof. Morning light cascades across the earth and welcomes a beautiful new day. His weight shifts, and he slowly slides off the roof.

BOOM!

His rifle goes off when it hits the ground, narrowly missing his head and leaving a hole in the brim of his rumpled, black felt cowboy hat.

He scrambles to his feet and pats himself down. "No way, eh. I almost bit my own bullet!"

Around noon W.H. mounts his horse. He rides by Bingo's grave and tips his holey hat. After pausing for a moment, he draws his spy scope and scans the horizon.

"Didn't howl last night, eh? Musta been busy. Best go check my traps."

W.H. takes to the circuit. He rides around the north canyon, inspecting his traps.

"Dagnabbit!"

A sheep bleats. *Help.*

He dismounts his horse and inspects the wound. "You ain't a wolf. Why are you in my trap?"

The sheep *baas. Please, water. I'm thirsty, sir.*

W.H. inspects the sheep's leg. "Oh, I'm sorry, fella." He draws his pistol, points at the sheep's head, and pulls the trigger.

BANG!

"I ain't a sheep hunter. I'm a wolf hunter! What am I doin' out here, eh?" W.H. grumbles as he removes some paper and a pencil from his saddle.

"To whom it may concern," he scribbles. "Keep your sheep out of my traps. I have enclosed a gold piece in hopes this compensates for my mistake. Sincerest apologies, W.H."

He stomps back over to the sheep, opens its bloody mouth and stuffs the note and gold piece inside. He makes sure to leave a corner of the paper hanging outside the mouth so it will be noticed. *Sure hope your owner finds that gold piece. It's worth a whole flock of you.*

W.H. wipes his hands and searches for Kiowa's tracks.

"If you're in the canyon and I'm in the canyon and it's night, that ain't favorable. I need odds in my favor."

He gets back on his horse and looks at the setting sun.

"Last thing we need is to be trapped in the dark narrows with a pack ah angry wolves. I'll come back in the mornin'."

W.H. heads back to town as darkness falls. A few yards from the south canyon, where Heart on Fire is trapped, he suddenly halts his horse and strains to listen. He cups his hand to his ear.

"Ah... probably nuthin'..." He groans, wanting nothing more than a shot of whiskey and a glimpse of Jenny.

With a cluck of his tongue, he kicks at Cotton's side, and the pair moseys on down to the C Y'all Saloon. He arrives in the late, late hours of dark night.

A group of rough riders sit at a table, playing poker.

Molly pounds on the red piano and sings the same out-of-tune song she has always sung.

Cowboys passing through drink whiskey and tell stories at the bar.

"Down in Texas is where the prettiest gals I ever seen are!" Hank says with a wink.

"No, sir, that's where the biggest cows are. The prettiest gals I ever seen are the belles of Georgia," a Southern customer declares, raising his glass.

Molly suddenly changes her tune. She slows down and starts singing, "Home, home on the range…"

The card players play their hand and join in the tune. "Where the deer and the buffalo graze. Oh, give me a home, where the buffalo roam, and the skies are not cloudy and gray."

W.H. takes a seat at the bar.

Jenny gasps when she sees him. She tries to hide the fact that she's Molly's new bartender, but the low-cut gold satin dress and the bottle of whiskey in her hand gives her away.

"Whad'ya you think, Jenny? Prettiest girls down in Texas?" W.H. asks.

"Oh, well. I'd say the prettiest girls are right here in Cimarron, New Mexico."

"I'll drink to that," Molly shouts, raising her glass.

W.H. doesn't say anything.

"What do you think, capital letters W and H?" Jenny asks, squaring off and ready for a fight.

W.H. holds up two fingers. "Double whiskey. Say, what does your pa make of you working in a dump like this?"

Molly gasps.

"I'm my own woman," Jenny answers.

"You tell him, girl," Molly drawls with her Irish accent. She squints her eyes and pats her blazing red hair. "I happen to think this is a fine establishment, thank you, Mr. W.H."

"What's 'W.H.' stand for?" Juan asks.

"Don't ask," Jenny answers.

Juan squints at his partner. The cowboys look W.H. up and down and chuckle at his appearance.

"Sensitive subject?" Hank asks.

"Wolf Hunter, it stands for Wolf Hunter," Jenny says, putting three shot glasses down and topping them off. She picks the last one up and throws it back.

W.H. follows suit.

"Will you be staying with us, W.H.?" Molly asks.

"Yep. I'll be needin' the room upstairs."

"Jenny! Show Mr. Wolf Hunter to his room."

"I will not!" Jenny protests. "I agreed to serve drinks, but now I'm regretting that." She drops the towel on the counter, lifts the bar counter up, and storms off.

"Jenny! Jenny!" Molly shouts. "Don't go. I'll be needing your help, missy." The cowboys laugh at her. Out of embarrassment, Molly stands up and goes after Jenny. She shakes her fist. "I'll be docking your pay, missy!"

W.H. gets up and goes to his room. Once inside, he closes the door, hearing laughter. It isn't long before Molly plays a new tune she's mastered.

"Take your girl to the bar. Pony up! Pony up your dough, boys! Or stick up your hands. It won't be long till mornin' and I'm just a one-man band. Drink 'em up! Slam 'em down. Enjoy it while you can. We'll all be pushing daisies with our pistols in our hands. Get 'em up!"

The cowboys lift their glasses and shout, "Get 'em up!"

Molly continues. "Get 'em up in the sky. We'll all be drinking whiskey till the day that we die."

"Yeeeeee-haaaawwww!" the cowboys shout.

BANG.

BANG.

BANG.

They fire their pistols.

W.H. takes off his boots and hat. *Wait a minute. Where are they aiming?* He looks around the room. The floorboards are riddled with bullet holes.

With a heavy sigh, he sits at the desk and opens his saddlebag, removing his journal.

June 21, 1861
Dear Uncle,

This may be my only will and testament. If you do not hear from me, or if you receive this journal and this is my last entry, please know that I died a tired man at the C Y'all Saloon. Needed a hot bath and a nice warm bed. Wouldn't want to admit this to anyone, but I'm afraid to sleep in the cabin. I realize now that Kiowa is more than an ordinary wolf. A thin pane of glass offers me no real protection from him. Hopefully, I can find some peace with the sinners, as there is none to be had with the wolf. Poison has failed, traps have failed—even bullets are useless. Only amount of success I've ever had was luring him with his mate's body. After inspecting the traps today, it would seem that I have failed at that as well.

I'd write about this dream that convinced me it was time to go, but nobody would believe me. I'd be branded crazy and most likely institutionalized. Well, with a start like that, how can I resist? This is truly my deepest, darkest secret. I had a dream about Bingo last night. Time is running out for me. He told me to leave. Two problems with this dream. Bingo's dead. Kiowa killed him. And dogs don't talk. It's time to cut my losses. Chief was right. No victor can walk this warpath and hope to win. Just two lonely souls filled with pain, destined to face off or walk away. This wolf is too smart to be caught. I give up! Tomorrow I plan to retrieve all my traps, destroy all my baits, and cash in on whatever reward I can get for Anoki, the white wolf. I'm prepared to cut my losses and wash my hands of this. Sorry, Bingo. There can be no victor here.

***

Two days pass. The blazing sun is hot enough to bake Heart on Fire alive. He swooshes the pressing ants away with his big bushy tail and prays for the darkness. When night comes, sharp hunger pains torture him almost as much as the pain of the traps. His mouth is as dry as the desert, and he is constantly tormented by a cool stream just a short distance away.

Something stirs behind him.

CHAPTER 142

"Well, lookie here," Ol' Bruce the bull blows. He stomps his foot when he spots Heart on Fire.

"I'll be… His goose is cooked!" Louise, a dairy cow with a Southern drawl, says with a broad smirk.

Several cows gather around him.

"Is he dead?"

Ol' Bruce walks in front of the giant wolf. He cautiously sniffs Heart on Fire. "Dead as a doornail."

Suddenly, Heart on Fire seizes Ol' Bruce by the throat.

Ol' Bruce rears back, simultaneously pulling Heart on Fire's front paws loose from the traps. The pain is excruciating.

"Bruce… Bruce! What do I do?" Louise shouts.

"Oh no, Ol' Bruce… ya dun pulled him free," a distraught yellow cow shouts.

The cattle scatter and cluster a safe distance away.

Now free himself, Heart on Fire releases Ol' Bruce and hobbles toward the creek. Chains rattle with every step.

"Never has my tongue been as dry as sand," Kiowa whispers with a hoarse voice. He leans down and laps up the cool water. *How selfish of me, to think of myself. What if Anoki's mouth is dry?*

"Stay back, ladies. He's mine!" Ol' Bruce shouts.

"Ol' Bruce, if he wanted to kill ya, he had his chance. He's harmless now," Louise says.

"Harmless?" a cow doubts.

"Yeah, look at him. He can't even stand on his own four legs," another cow says.

"This is the great wolf Kiowa?" Ol' Bruce says.

Losing their fear, the cows circle him.

"He ain't nuthin', Ol' Bruce," the blond cow says.

Ol' Bruce rams Heart on Fire in the hindquarter with his horn. The wolf spins around, screaming from the impact.

"He's just a yella-belly coward." Ol' Bruce stomps his hoof and lowers his horns. "You killed our young. I still got your marks on my back. Now it's your turn to pay!"

Heart on Fire looks up at the cows with heavy eyes. "I killed, but at least I killed with honor."

His rebuttal is rewarded with laughter and insults.

He follows the stream to a pond, then slides in. The pond is shallow enough, he's able to stand at the center of the pond where the steer dare not go.

The cool water revels ever nick and cut. *Ah, yes. Pain is good. It means I am still alive. Now at least I am wet.*

"We got you now!" Ol' Bruce says, motioning for the bulls to circle up and wait the wolf out.

***

Off in the distance, two cowboys ride by.

"You ever seen bulls act like that?" Juan asks Hank.

"No, sir. Can't say that I have. Usually they circle up around cows like that to protect them. Whad'ya think's stirrin' them cattle?" Hank buzzes.

"Probably just a Texas gal," Juan says with a bright smile.

Hank laughs. "You reckon?"

"Ain't our herd."

"Ain't our problem!" Hank agrees, leading his horse away.

The two ride off.

Later that night, the two cowboys return to the C Ya'll Saloon. Hank and Juan sit at the bar and listen to Molly play "Home on the Range." Card players start a game, and Jenny has returned to serve drinks. Her number one customer is W.H., who is incredibly drunk.

"I tried to kill the wolf… I just couldn't do it," W.H. says, downing his seventh shot.

"Maybe you should change your name to Whiskey Hunter," Jenny says snidely. "You don't seem to have a problem finding whiskey."

"Don't take it so hard, W.H. You weren't the only one to fail.

653

He's not just a wolf, you know. He's part man. My ancestors from Mexico said they had heard of his kind. They call him a nagual. He is part man, part beast. Drinks the blood, eats the brains." Juan winks at W.H. while Jenny tops off his drink.

"Naga-who? Werewolves? Ain't never seen one, but that don't stop me from keepin' a silver bullet in my smoke cannon," Hank says, patting his sidearm.

"He just wouldn't die! HE WOULDN'T DIE!" W.H. says as Jenny tops him off.

"COME ON, EVERYBODY! HAPPY TRAILS... TO YOU..." Molly sings.

"You can't kill a nagual with poison, Senor W.H. Our tall, dusty friend here has the right idea. You gotta get you a silver bullet," Juan says, pointing at Hank's six-shooter.

Hank draws his pistol, which makes the bar go silent. He breaches the chamber and pulls out a silver bullet, then hands it to W.H. "That one's on me. Keep it as a souvenir."

"Drinks are on me," Juan says, holding up an empty glass.

"Perhaps you're right, eh? Maybe he is a werewolf," W.H. responds, slamming another shot.

"That he is, my boy! That he is." Jenny says sarcastically. "And maybe there's witches, ghosts, goblins, chupacabras, and vampires as well." She slaps her knee and winks at W.H. as she cocks her finger and drops the hammer with a cluck of her tongue.

W.H. waves them off. He takes the silver bullet, unloads the first round in his six-shooter, and slides the gleaming round in the chamber.

"For luck!" W.H. shouts, raising his glass.

"Until we meet again..." Molly howls.

The next day W.H. sits up in his bed with the most excruciating hangover. Most of the day passes with him in bed. When the sun sets, he feels good enough to make a journal entry.

June 22, 1861
Dear Uncle,

Whiskey is good! Music is great! I have decided not to return home. Instead I am forming a folk band dubbed Whiskey Pete. Just joshing you. Ha! Ha! Ha! Jenny is a sight for sore eyes. Sure makes this wounded soul feel better than a lonesome cabin.

Got a silver bullet and a hunting lesson from a cowboy... No wonder I couldn't kill Kiowa. He ain't a wolf... He's a...

W.H. pauses. He sets the journal down and says, "I'm too hungover for this."

Pulling the blankets over his face, he goes back to sleep.

The next day W.H. packs his belongings and, around noon, he says his good-byes.

Jenny turns her nose up at him. "You need a bath. You stink."

"I ain't got time for that, Miss Jenny."

"Too bad. Ain't nothing more foul to a woman's senses than stinky, dirty, scraggly, ol' man," Jenny jabs.

W.H. dunks his head in the horse's water trough. When he surfaces, he wipes his face and puts his hat on.

"Clean!"

As he mounts his horse, he notices that Hank is watching him.

"Maybe see you at the card table?" Hank waves and nods.

"Probably not. I'm on my way out of town," W.H. says, holding his hand up to block the sunlight.

"What 'er ya gonna do now?"

"I suppose I'm gonna hightail it outta here. You?"

"We're gonna go take a look at some cattle that were a'stirrin' yesterday. Juan and I saw some bulls acting strange. Don't feel so good about it after last night's talk with you. Know what I mean?" Hanks leans over and spits tobacco.

"Didn't have time to see what the ruckus was all about yesterday. Figure we might as well satisfy our curiosity," Juan adds, spitting tobacco.

"Where's about?" W.H. inquires, just spitting.

"The south canyon," Juan replies, reaching inside a leather pouch and pinching off some shredded tobacco. He seats it in his lip, which makes his entire lower jaw protrude strangely. W.H. looks at the bar and thinks about cashing in on his reward.

"I got me some traps out there. Suppose I could ride along with ya? Probably shouldn't just leave them about."

"Sure. The more the merrier."

The journey takes less time for the cowboys. They know of a shortcut that W.H. didn't know existed, and it saves a considerable amount of time.

As W.H. and the cowboys ride toward the canyon, they see the cattle huddled just where Hank and Juan left them.

"Yar, there's something going on out there," Hank affirms, eyeing the herd's strange behavior.

As they ride up slowly, most of the cattle peel away. Ol' Bruce the bull refuses to step aside.

"Go on. Get!" Juan cracks a whip.

A ton of solid muscle moves aside. When it does, the cowboys see the soaked wolf splash for the bank.

"Well, would ya look at that?" Hank declares.

W.H. slowly lifts the brim of his hat to watch his enemy collapse.

The wolf hunter goes into action. He kicks at Cotton's side and gallops to within a few feet of Kiowa.

"I seen what you did to Bingo. DON'T HURT ME!" Cotton *neighs*. She freezes and backs up.

W.H. dismounts and closes the distance. He pulls his six-shooter out, checks to make sure the silver bullet is in place, and carefully aims at Kiowa. "You've slaughtered hundreds of cattle! Terrorized every rancher in the Currumpaw! I've got you now!"

CHAPTER 143

W.H. closes one eye and puts his finger on the trigger. Slowly, he begins to squeeze. "And you tortured my best friend, Bingo, to death."

He's so close now he couldn't miss if he wanted to, Heart on Fire determines.

"Time to face justice for your crimes."

The closer he gets, the more he can see in Heart on Fire's eyes.

"Do it, Round Eyes; use your thunder magic and release my spirit," Heart on Fire pleads. "I am not afraid to die, and I have suffered more pain than anyone should."

W.H. opens his eyes and blinks. His hand begins to shake.

Heart on Fire stares calmly, accepting his fate. He lowers his head and moans. "Or take me to Anoki."

At that moment time slows. W.H. realizes he isn't facing a monster, a werewolf, or even an animal. Within a split second, he sees images flash through his mind of Anoki and Kiowa at the lake. They aren't playing like wolves but like lovebirds. It seems so strange to him, he can't help but release the tension on the trigger.

Also, there is something in this wolf's eyes that looks an awful lot like immense sorrow. Something that seems strangely human. He hears Onendah's words in his mind louder than the heckling cowboys beside him. *Two walk, but only one can finish the journey. Sometimes no one finishes.* Then he sees Bingo's face and hears his voice from the dream telling him not to kill the wolf. Though he can't understand why he hesitates, he does. And in that hesitation, Heart on Fire's eyes tell a story only a man's could.

"Ain't ya gonna shoot him?" Hank shouts.

"You said you were going to take him apart piece by piece, amigo.

Let's see it!" Juan taunts.

"No... no. I'm gonna shoot his picture. Ol' Lobo is worth more alive than dead," W.H. says, lowering his pistol and uncocking the hammer.

"What now?" Juan asks.

"Before we get him on my horse, let me see if I can get this dang picture taker to work."

W.H. removes the daguerreotype camera. He sets it up like Mr. Rockefeller showed him.

"This is going to take an hour or so, so you boys might want to find something else to do."

"What's it doing?" Juan asks.

"Ain't you ever seen a picture taker?" Hank responds.

Juan shrugs. "What's a picture taker?"

One hour later, W.H. inspects the plate. "I guess it took. Let's get him mounted," W.H. says.

"What is this?" Heart on Fire whimpers. "Are you cheating me of death?"

W.H. steps toward the wolf.

"Did he say he was gonna trap 'im?" Juan asks.

Hank nods.

"We should probably help him," Hank says, getting his rope.

"Easy, boy... easy," W.H. repeats, trying to calm the tormented wolf down.

"I will not go easy!" Heart on Fire protests. "I will use every advantage you give me against you!"

W.H. moves towards the wolf.

Heart on Fire stands up, as does his bristling mane. His lips curl back. He snarls ferociously at W.H., revealing his broken ivory fangs and bloody mouth.

"Even if he wanted to, he couldn't hurt us. He ain't hardly got any teeth," W.H. observes, realizing Lobo must have bitten the chains. He takes off his glove and extends his hand. The husky wolf tilts his head back and howls a mustering call. His howl reverberates off the canyon walls.

"Keep yer eyes peeled, boys. That's his rally cry," W.H. warns.

The cowboys draw their weapons and scan the cliffs.

W.H. continues to advance. Once he's within Heart on Fire's reach, he lunges at him, barely missing.

"You may not have many teeth, but I don't wanna find out which ones still hurt." The wolf hunter backs off.

"You cannot show me mercy and Anoki none." Heart on Fire whimpers. "I will allow anything but that."

"Still got the fight in ya, eh? Hank, why don't you make use of that rope?" Juan suggests.

Hank ties a lasso and swings it over his head. He lets the wide loop go and cusses when it lands in the wolf's mouth.

"Easy, boy… easy…" W.H. pulls tension on the rope.

The massive wolf thrashes his head and easily bites the rope in half.

"Kill me, Round Eyes. You cannot humiliate me to death."

"Are you sure you don't want to just shoot him?" Juan asks.

W.H. nods.

"Sure would be a mite easier," Hank observes.

Hank grabs a stick and throws it at the wolf's head. Heart on Fire clamps down on it, and before he can release it, all three men rush him. Juan uses the severed rope to tie the stick in his mouth.

It takes all three men to lift Lobo up and carry him over to Cotton. *Oh no! No! No! I'll carry anything on my back but that.* Cotton *neighs.* W.H. seizes her reins.

"He ain't gonna hurt you, Cotton. Settle down!" W.H. orders.

The three men drape Heart on Fire over Cotton's back and get on their way.

Out on the open range, from a distance, the shadows of the men stretch across the amber prairie, making them look like giants. Lobo, the outlaw wolf's shadow, can be seen right next to the Wolf Hunter's.

Heart on Fire's gaze rests on his wild home. His band of outlaws have roamed on, and his wife has vanished. He is all alone. He stares and remembers where he spent his youth as a Kiowa the Indian. Then Kiowa the wolf. Now Heart on Fire, the conquered.

He looks across the prairie and sees the pine forest. *Onendah married us there.* He smiles faintly. He remembers where they first experienced being wolves and where they danced under the moon. He remembers where they learned how to howl. He thinks of his pups and wonders if Paw will have enough life left in him to teach them everything he taught him. A thousand memories flood his mind, and although he is in great pain, his memories bring him extreme happiness. He stares until the sun sets and the light fades away. With the night, he expects W.H. to unleash some cruel revenge plot. *Probably he will come out here and skin me alive. Then tie me to a post and start a fire and put it out and start it again and again and again.*

Kiowa sighs.

At least I will finally get to see Anoki. He growls low, with a burning ember of hope.

CHAPTER 144

Late in the night, the riders arrive at the cabin. W.H. places a chain around Kiowa's neck. He plants a post in the yard and bolts the chain to it.

"Thank you fer your help, gentlemen. You're welcome to stay here for the night if ya' like."

"I think we'll git back to the Cowboy Hall," Hank says with the tip of his hat.

"It's the C Y'all Saloon now," Juan corrects.

"Since when?" W.H. asks.

"Since Molly knocked the letters off with a hammer and renamed it." Hank sighs. "I liked getting drunk at the Cowboy Hall saloon way more than I like getting drunk at the C Y'all Saloon."

"Whiskey is whiskey," Juan says with a smile so big it makes his cheeks bulge like a chipmunk. "Besides, no one is going to believe you caught the wolf alive."

"We'll check in with ya in the mornin'. Ain't nobody going to believe it weren't a werewolf." Hank waves good-bye and rides off. Juan follows.

"Thank you for your help, gentlemen!" W.H. says as they turn and ride off.

"Our pleasure!"

After the men leave, W.H. puts water in a bowl and removes the traps one at a time. Heart on Fire doesn't make a sound. He looks down at the chunk of meat W.H. places in a bowl, then back up at the pine forest.

Defeated and humiliated, the proud wolf remains motionless.

June 29, 1861

Today I am victorious! I did it, Uncle. I found the great wolf Lobo, or Kiowa, as Chief calls him, trapped in the south canyon of the Currumpaw. As I came upon him, I discovered that my plan had worked. The old fool had never stopped searching for his love, Anoki, or "Blanca," as the Mexicans call her.

Several traps tightly clenched the great wolf and held him in place. For some time he had been subject to the wrath of the elements and the justice of the cattle. What a grand old outlaw! He has led thousands of rebel raids and even killed the best friend I've ever had. He has reaped financial ruin on the town and dang near ran everyone off. Many crimes has he committed, and yet, as I closed in on him, he howled one last time. It was a muster cry, and as no wolf answered, I felt bad for him. I know it sounds absurd considering the pride I take in my name, but he and I are both alone now. He has not howled since and neither have I.

I feel as though I have aged ten years these last few days. I had him within my grasp, but I could not kill him. His eyes had an undeniable gleam of sorrow, a misery I authored. And in that moment I felt great remorse. I understand now what Chief meant when he said "make peace." If I had killed Kiowa, I may have finished the war journey, but I would have certainly lost some piece of myself that I cannot articulate, yet I know it is there. I can feel it. I now understand the general's pardon letter to the rogue Indian, Corax. It would seem as though my mother was right: It really is never too late to do a kind deed.

What to do with Kiowa now?

***

"He didn't kill him?" Kevin asks in complete shock.

"Nope," Charlie says, shaking his head.

"I would have killed him and collected the reward money. I would have killed the whole pack, too," Luther proudly boasts.

"Couldn't do it," Charlie answers, looking into the orange coals.

The boys listen intently as Charlie finishes the story.

***

The next day Hank and Juan return late in the afternoon.

W.H. spots them and greets them with a "Howdy."

"Did you catch any more of his pack?" Hank inquires.

"Nah… they ain't come yet," W.H. says, looking off in the distance.

"I'll give you two gold pieces for him right now," Juan proposes, pressing his hand against a folded reward poster in his pocket.

"I'll think on it. Let's just give him another day and see if his pack shows up," W.H. proposes back.

Heart on Fire lies still, gazing off into the distance. *Bondage is worse than death. Anoki, if you can hear my howl, let me know and I will*—he takes a deep breath, feeling the tears well in his eyes—*I will let you know that you are not alone. I will lie by your side, sweet Anoki.* He struggles to his feet, tilts his head back, and howls.

W.H. sees his glossy eyes and hears the sorrow in his voice and can't help but get emotional.

"Hey, you boys want these traps?" W.H. searches for anything that might dismiss his feelings.

"Sure!"

"Will you hitch Mr. Mather's wagon and take it back to town for me?"

"I suppose," Hank says, looking at the wolf. "Why didn't you just bring this when we went out for him?"

"I was ready to leave town. I almost did."

"What kept you?" Juan asks.

"Curiosity."

Around sunset, W.H. finishes loading the remaining traps into Mr. Mather's wagon. He slams the barn door shut and, like before, it bounces back and remains ajar.

"Good seeing you boys again."

"Come down to the saloon for a drink. The whole town is eager to see you!" Juan yells.

"Oh, I will," W.H. says, then under his breath, "Not a chance in hell."

W.H. turns and looks at his prize. "Everyone's got to eat, Ol' Lobo." W.H. walks past the wolf without the slightest hint of fear. He kicks the food bowl on his way to the cabin.

Heart on Fire watches W.H. enter the cabin. Once the wolf hunter is inside, Heart on Fire makes his move. He struggles to stand then whispers, "Anoki... Anoki, can you hear me? I can smell you everywhere. I knew you were here. Are you trapped in a cage? Does he have your mouth tied?"

He scans the perimeter, unable to see her.

"I still hear your laughter in my ears. Make a noise and I will get you out. Do not be afraid."

As he searches, the setting sun illuminates the barn. Through the barn doors, Heart on Fire can see Anoki's white body resting on the workbench.

"ANOKI!" he shouts with a trembling voice.

She doesn't answer.

"Wife... can you hear me?"

Anoki still doesn't answer.

"My love... My soul... My heart!"

Eventually, the sun's last beams fully illuminate her lifeless frame and severed paws.

At that moment, Heart on Fire feels the stitches to his soul pull so tight, they snap and stop his heart.

The next morning, W.H. rises with the *cock-a-doodle-doo* of the rooster. His conscience weighed against him all night. And though he did finally get a great night's sleep, he didn't exactly know what to do about the wolf. He knew he didn't want to kill him.

"Hey, Ol' Lobo, what is it I should do with you?" he asks, the same way he would have asked Bingo.

"It ain't like you got teeth anymore, so I guess I could give you a lift up to Yellowstone, but you are going to have one heck of a time catching game."

W.H. gets dressed and comes outside. "I bet an Indian tribe would adopt you."

When W.H. approaches he learns the wolf still hasn't eaten and his water bowl is full of dead ants.

"Come on, Lobo, you ornery old devil. You gotta at least drink some water. You're going to make yourself sick, doncha know?"

W.H. sips his coffee. "Lobo, look alive!"

Heart on Fire doesn't stir.

W.H. walks over to the wolf and pushes him with his dusty boot. His body rocks, but he doesn't respond.

The wolf hunter leans down and checks to see if the wolf is breathing. When he does, Heart on Fire's eyes roll back in his head.

Kiowa, who became Heart on Fire, is dead.

"No… no! This can't be. Lobo…? Kiowa…?"

W.H. circles around the wolf and runs his hands through his hair.

CHAPTER 145

What W.H. could not have seen, Heart on Fire shares now.

As the powerful wolf lay alone on the cool earth, he wished, more than anything, that Anoki could drag her soft tail across his chest and press herself against him.

He closes his eyes and reflects on when he first thought he loved her. The memory slips, and suddenly he has the moment of clarity Onendah spoke of. His circle completes.

He could not walk this earth without his heart. This fact strikes him like lightning. A thunderous shock follows. It rattles the electricity of his life and begins to separate spirit from flesh.

If Onendah's knowledge of the spirit world was to be believed, Heart on Fire knew it wouldn't be long before his father brought him the great white horse, Tetseya, to take him from this world to the happy hunting grounds, where he hoped to be reunited with all those he loved, but mostly, Anoki.

The massive wolf musters all of his strength to see the one single truth this life had to offer and it was this… He didn't actually love Anoki when he first saved her. How could he? He didn't even know what love was. He had no idea what she had to offer. He hardly knew her, but his heart was set ablaze by the sight of her. It was that night he felt the stars, the sun, and the moon explode into a life of hope inside him, the way life explodes at inception. Though that first glance certainly was the spark and the birth of their love, he came to love her with an intensity that was magnified through a lifetime of experiences. Experiences that connected their lives like two stars with twisting glittering tales that carry the magic of love across the sky. This is what it meant to hold the flame for her. She was the sun in his sky.

When he definitively sees her gruesome end with his own eyes, his soul shatters. Now, without a doubt, he knows the powerful force of Anoki's love. She chose to be a wolf over being a woman. She stayed by his side. She bore him children. She placed everything she had to offer on the altar of love. It was her complete sacrifice for his complete happiness.

Without her presence, her voice, her thoughts, her songs, her paints, her counsel, her gaze, her touch, and even her howl, all the glass pieces holding him together splinter and fracture apart. Most precious of all, the love she would have taken from him and mixed with her paints and put on the faces of their many children. He didn't have the strength or desire to draw another breath. As he lay on his side, spying her lifeless body in W.H.'s shed, he knew he loved her, because he could feel each moment with her turn into a vapor and slip through the cracks.

What he didn't know was that her life was the flame that fueled his life. Without her, there was no life. She was the fire and he was the sky.

Heart on Fire closes his eyes and struggles to lift a trembling paw, which feels as heavy as a mountain. The prisoner is denied a last embrace. With his dying breath, he utters, "To love is to die." And with that, he is gone. His last bit of strength was used reaching for her. His paw falls to the earth, still as a statue, never to sprint again.

He feels a hurricane of tingling wind rush inside of him. His spirit rises from his body like the morning sun. An amber glow flows over his mortal frame. The feelings of love he has for Anoki lift his spirit up, and he feels her love consume him and grow bigger than himself, bigger than this world. The separation from spirit and body is complete. He looks at his mortal hands, then at his wolf body. A bright light forces him to look up at the sky.

"Father? Is that you?"

He shields his eyes with his hand. He doesn't see his father or Tetseya, but instead, a woman glows as brightly as the sun. As she walks on the wind, he sees it is Anoki, waiting in her true form, but more beautiful than ever before. Anoki stretches out her glowing arms. White robes as soft as clouds and as bright as stars cover her and whip around her exposed arms and legs. Her silky black hair shines like the night. Her skin has a celestial sun-kissed glow. The longing look in her eyes crackles like lightning when they connect with his.

Heart on Fire reaches for her outstretched hand. And suddenly he is not dead, but more alive than he has ever been.

"*Ah-hoe.* I have kept my promise. I told you I would come for you."

She smiles and takes his hand, and as quickly as they were there, they are not.

CHAPTER 146

W.H. repeatedly runs his fingers through his hair and walks around the lifeless wolf.

"No! No! This can't be!"

The wolf hunter feels a storm of confusion brewing inside. "Why would an animal in need of food and water not eat or drink?"

He walks around the wolf one last time and stops behind Heart on Fire.

"Why's your paw stretched out like that? What in tarnation were ya reaching for?"

W.H. removes his glasses and wipes the circular lenses. He slowly puts them back on, focusing on the blurry images as they grow sharp. As he examines the distance, his eyes travel toward the shed. He sees past the gray planks and gets a clear view of Anoki's white fur, open jaws, and sprawled-out tongue.

He kneels and puts his hand on top of the wolf's paw. He stretches his fingers as one might reach for a loved one.

In a gust of wind and the flutter of wings, Onendah appears in his human form behind W.H.

"I have come for them both."

Startled, W.H. falls over, holding his hands up to shield himself from Onendah's blinding silhouette.

"Don't hurt me!" W.H. cries out.

"I am not here for you, Round Eyes. I have come for the wolves."

W.H. shakes his head back and forth in protest. "I didn't kill him. I swear I didn't kill him. I got off the warpath, Chief."

"I told you, Round Eyes: Only one can finish."

"But you said sometimes... You said sometimes two don't finish..."

"Sometimes is not this time. You are the victor and you have been paid. I will bring you more gold if you like."

W.H. feels the storm inside himself calm. It's as though he has reached the end of a journey but doesn't understand how he's arrived.

Onendah walks over to Kiowa's body. He kneels and pets the poor warrior's head.

"I sang the song of death for your father's father. I sang it for your father. Now I will sing it for you, great warrior. But before I do, I want you to know you are the greatest warrior I have ever known." Tears well in his old eyes. He leans down and whispers, "You have taught this old eagle a great lesson. I will use my magic to get you out of this dreadful place."

Onendah chants a quick spell and scoops Kiowa up with a heave. He walks over to the shed, kicks it open, and sets Kiowa by Anoki. "Now they are one again," he says in his native Kiowa language.

Onendah lifts both wolves up and walks away.

"Wait. Where are you goin'?"

The medicine man turns and gives W.H. a long hard glare before he speaks. "My magic is weak. You cannot understand me, can you?"

"Speak English, Chief!"

"That is what I thought. I will say what I have to say anyway. Their circle is complete now. You are free, Round Eyes. Go! Find a new path." Onendah flips his head, a sign W.H. cannot mistake.

The medicine man slowly turns and walks away.

"Chief, wait!"

Onendah ignores the wolf hunter and continues on until he carries the killed joys out into the golden yellow prairie.

"Oh, my poor wolves." He clasps his wrinkled hand to his heart. "Oh, my dear people. You had the greatest magic of all: true love. Anoki was patient with you. Kiowa, you were kind to her. Your love was forgiving. Your love was not puffed up like the blow snake. It was true. I saw it turn to hope. Hope grew into faith. That is why I helped you. Your faith set you free. You both have suffered greatly. Oh, my poor wolf people. My old heart breaks for you." Onendah rocks the wolves as though they were children. Tears trickle down his cracked cheeks.

"You can't...?" W.H. shouts, reaching for the wolves.

Soon Onendah is out in the vast, open prairie. He sings the Kiowa death chant as he goes. Puffy white clouds part. Powerful sun rays rest on their bodies. As the medicine man sings the ancient song, vapors rise off their fur. Soon they form a cloud.

W.H. sees their spirits rise and ascend as one. His knees buckle. He falls to the ground, crying, as Onendah disappears.

"Please... I don't understand," he shouts with his arm stretched out, reaching for something he can't catch.

***

Later that night, in his journal, W.H. wrote:

June 30, 1861

Something strange has happened to me, Uncle. I have seen things that I dare not write. Suffice it to say, Kiowa died today.

I am left wondering why.

***

The last flames of the fire roll over the glowing embers and die. The small Woodcraft Indian troop wipe tears from their eyes.

"Why'd Kiowa have to die?" Zack sobs.

Charlie looks up at the boys. He pulls his round gold glasses out of his left breast pocket and puts them on.

The fire reflects off his lenses.

"No one can say for certain. I believe once he laid eyes on Anoki's body, that was it for him."

"How do you know all this? How do you know what W.H. thought and what Kiowa did? You're Round Eyes, aren't you?" John accuses, pointing at Charlie.

Charlie takes a long deep breath and lets it out slowly. "I am."

Tears stream down Kevin's face. "MURDERER!"

"I was younger, and I didn't know my path," Charlie protests, waving his shaking hands.

Kevin buries his face in his hands.

"Did you find your path?" Zack asks, as he wipes his nose with his sleeve.

"I did. My intention was to create an outdoor school for boys. You boys are part of that school, the Woodcraft Indians. It is my intention to teach you boys how to walk a new path as they become men. A path that favors nature."

He opens a bag and removes the boys' wolf badges. They have Kiowa's image embossed on them.

"Now, raise your right hands."

The boys raise their hands.

"Repeat after me. I, state your name, promise to respect the animals of the wilderness and to always return the lands better than I found 'em, eh."

The boys speak at once. "I, John, Luther, Zack, Kevin, promise to respect the animals of the wilderness and to always return the lands better than I found 'em, eh."

"Woodcraft Indian's honor?"

"BY OUR SACRED HONOR!"

"We learn from the animals by respecting their way of life, not by destroying them. This is how I complete Onendah's circle: by honoring Kiowa's and Anoki's memory, sharing their story, and telling as many as will listen... what they have taught me. That animals love and feel love. This is my new path."

Charlie stares at the stars and focuses on his last moments in the Currumpaw.

***

An immense wave of guilt weighs the retired wolf hunter down. Charlie, the Wolf Hunter, knows his time at the Currumpaw is finished, but he can't bring himself to leave. He can't even find the strength to get off the bed. His condition becomes so depressing, he can't eat or sleep. When he closes his eyes, images of Anoki and Kiowa dancing and playing at the lake haunt him. Days turn to weeks. Weeks turn to months. Autumn turns everything brown, and the temperature becomes bearable. The place Charlie referred to as a wasteland now has an indescribable beauty he has not noticed before.

CHAPTER 147

One crisp morning, outside W.H.'s cabin, Jenny brings a gaggle of schoolchildren.

"Today, kids, we are going to meet a very brave man. His name is W.H."

"Why do we call him that?" a little girl asks.

"It's initials for wolf hunter."

"That's stupid!" the little girl says with a sour expression.

"No, it's not, Suzie. It's his name and he's earned it. Now, you mind your manners."

Jenny knocks on the faded cedar door.

"Go away!" Charlie grumbles.

Jenny clears her throat, raises her hands, and knocks louder. "It's Jenny Mather. W.H., families have returned to the Currumpaw, and their children would like to thank you."

The door swings open. "For what?"

Jenny isn't prepared for the stinky bearded monster that opens the door. A wave of body odor overpowers her.

"W.H., you smell like you haven't had a bath in months!"

"Don't call me that no more."

"Smelly? But you are!"

"W.H. My name is Charlie."

Jenny pushes her hips out and rests her hands on her sides. She tilts her head and purses her lips together. "After all this time and fussin' about capital letters for a name, you decided to be good and proper? What fer?"

"Charlie, my name's Charlie."

Charlie struggles to put his shirt on. He fastens his glasses, then looks at Jenny with a hardness in his eyes that melts her heart.

"Are you okay?" she asks, putting her hand on his shoulder.

"No!"

"Is there anything I can do to help you?"

"Miss Mather, is the smelly man going to tell us a story?" Jesse, a stout lad in a white cotton shirt, brown linen pants, and suspenders, asks, rocking back and forth.

Charlie turns his icy gaze to the children.

"So, you wanna hear the story, huh?" he growls with a hint of madness.

"Yeah! Tell us how you killed ol' Lobo," the children shout.

Charlie looks down. When he looks up, tears well in his eyes. He swallows shame down hard. It twists his mouth and ties his tongue.

"What's wrong with him?" Liza, a little brunette asks. She sways her pretty blue dress with white polka dots back and forth.

Charlie takes a deep breath. His shoulders rise, then slump. His head falls down. Defeated, he shrugs and says, "I killed him."

"But how'd you do it, Mister?" Billy, the little boy who was putting up the posters, asks.

"I don't know."

"That don't make no sense!" Billy shouts.

"Did you shoot him?" Jesse demands with an excitement in his eyes that irritates Charlie.

"No."

"Did you stab him?" Liza asks.

"No," Charlie says, looking at the ground. He lifts his foot and scuffles the tip of his boot on the porch where his pal Bingo used to sleep.

"Did you trap him or poison him?"

"He was too smart for all that," Charlie sheepishly answers.

"Then how'd you kill him, Mister?" Billy blasts, wanting to know.

He looks up at the kids. Tears leak out his eyes and disappear in a forest of facial hair. "He just died," Charlie says, shrugging as he puts his hands in his pockets.

Caught off guard by Charlie's vulnerable state, Jenny feels an immense sympathy for the man she's traded jabs with ever since they met. That part of her seems to have faded and turned to respect, which has now blossomed to sympathy.

"Well, thank you for talking with us, Charlie. Maybe I'll see you in church," Jenny says.

"Don't count on it. Only church you'll see me at is the C Y'all Saloon."

"When?"

"Tonight," Charlie says, reaching over his shoulder and scratching his back.

"It's a date, then."

"A date?" Charlie perks up, managing a smile.

"Well, I'll meet you there, I mean. Do take care of yourself." She turns, smiles to herself, and leads her class back to town.

Charlie goes back inside his cabin and looks at his bunk.

"I'm done with you!"

He packs his journal, rolls his blanket, and fetches his horse.

"I'll tell you why she wants to see me," he confides in Cotton as he straps the saddle to her. "It's 'cause she wants to ridicule me."

The horse looks at him with a calm expression that challenges him.

"Okay, maybe she ain't gonna ridicule me." He pulls tight on the saddle straps, punishing the horse with his frustration. "Maybe she wants me for something else now. Perhaps she needs some chores done or some such? Well, I ain't got nothing else. I lost Bingo. I lost all my money. I might have enough to get us home. And all I really got is you." His temper subsides like a receding tide. He gently pets her mane.

"What is it I should do, Ol' Cotton?"

The horse lowers her head and nudges him. He gets on the saddle.

"All right, then, Cotton, my destiny is in your hooves. We can go home or we can go to town. Wherever you lead, I will follow."

The horse turns and slowly walks to town.

Along the way, W.H. reflects on his time at the Currumpaw. His mind feels like a desert dust storm. He thinks of his original impressions and how with time those feelings have changed. He reflects on all the things he's learned from the animals, the Indian medicine man, the town, the ranchers, and he doesn't know what to make of it.

Memories of Bingo dance in his mind and make him sad. Before he knows it, the walk down memory lane abruptly ends at the C Y'all Saloon.

He looks down at his horse and squints. "So it's the lady, huh?"

If horses could smile, his horse would have. Instead, she lifts her head up and down, encouraging him to go inside.

"All right, then, I'm a-g'tting," he says, patting himself down and checking his reflection in the window. Behind him, the town is bustling. People ride up and down Main Street as though they own the place. Mr. Mather's store has customers swarming in and out. A work crew repairs the bank. The town is alive again.

"She won't want to see me like this. I look terrible. She tells me every time I see her that I stink. And I'm ugly."

He turns to remount Cotton. She steps away and nudges him with her head.

Before he can untie her reins, Molly shouts, "What can I do for ya, stranger?" She opens the saloon door and waves him in. The place is filling quickly. Several young women in fine dresses work the tables, and a man plays piano with the most modern of tunes.

For a moment W.H. thinks about turning around and leaving, but he feels like he owes Molly a proper good-bye.

"You don't recognize me?" Charlie inquires, holding out his arms and presenting his scraggly self.

"W.H., my word, is that you behind that lion's mane?" Molly comes around the bar and hugs the boy turned brute.

"Come sit down." She plops his shot glass down in front of him and begins filling it with whiskey. He notices that his initials have been branded in the stool he frequents.

"Did you do that for me?"

Molly shakes her head. Then she laughs and nods. "Folks wanna see where you frequent."

Charlie reaches inside his pocket to pay, but Molly stops him.

"Oh, you don't need to pay, darlin'. Drinks are on the house!"

Charlie lifts his glass and tosses the gold liquid back. These last few weeks of being sober is immediately realized by the fire stinging his cheeks. The sensation engulfs his throat and makes his whole torso radiate. He coughs, clears his throat, and slaps his hand down on the table.

"That hits the spot, Molly!"

She fills his glass, then one for herself.

"To better days," she says, clacking her glass to his.

"Amen!" Charlie toasts, wanting nothing more than to numb his aching heart.

"Town is coming back to life." Molly leans in, assessing the seats filled with paying patrons.

"Yeah, it sure is."

"Businesses are thriving again."

"Humph." Charlie grunts, slamming another shot.

"Did you ever find out who it was that was the werewolf?"

"Thought it was you!" Charlie slams another shot.

"Ah, ya be teasin' me. I see that your body is present but your mind is somewheres else, W.H." Molly winks, letting him know that she realizes she's being ignored.

"Don't mind me, Molly."

"I won't." Molly looks past Charlie and beams with delight when she sees Jenny enter the bar. "Hello, darlin'. Come sit."

Charlie turns and locks eyes with the prettiest girl in town, Jenny Mather.

CHAPTER 148

For one reason or another, Jenny and Charlie have a newfound chemistry. She feels strangely drawn to him, the way metal is drawn to a magnet.

When Jenny sees Charlie at the bar, she searches for a reason to talk to him. When she can't find one, she relies on her common sense. "I was hoping I'd find you here."

Charlie smiles. "I was hoping to find you here."

"Really?" Jenny asks.

"You seem surprised."

"Well, I…" She blushes. "I just wasn't expecting…"

"I'm sorry how I acted today. It's just that—"

"W.H.!" Sheriff Dawson shouts as he releases the double-hinged saloon doors, which swing back and forth behind him. "I thought that was you."

Jenny watches Charlie turn his back to the sheriff abruptly. His hands shake, and she isn't sure why, but when he throws back a shot, she wonders if he hasn't done something terribly wrong.

The sheriff holds up a brown guinea bag. "I got your reward money right here!"

Gamblers perk up at the announcement.

Saloon girls fresh of the stage coach push up their cleavage and fall in line behind the sheriff.

"Seven! T-h-o-u-s-a-n-d! D-o-l-l-a-r-s!"

Everyone's eyes widen. The girls gasp and heckle like excited hens. The new piano man plays a quick jingle, and the gamblers grab empty chairs and shuffle a deck of cards.

"W.H. is *the* man responsible for restoring order and peace to our town, and the ranchers have shown their appreciation by padding the bounty with a little extra something. Oh, and of course, making me an offer I couldn't refuse to return to town." He walks over and sets the bag down on the bar, then pats Charlie on the back.

Charlie extends his hand. "Name is Charlie."

"Wolf Hunter." Sheriff Dawson slams his hand into Charlie's.

"Just Charlie now. I don't want to be known as a wolf hunter no more."

Sheriff Dawson squints and cocks his head to the side. After a brief assessment, he continues. "Reporters from all across the country are wanting to talk to you! You're a hero, W.H. A real live hero!"

Hearing the title "hero" associated with his old name causes Charlie's face to droop. "Please don't call me W.H. anymore."

Jenny watches his eyes turn cold. "Told you it was a bad name," she jokes. But her prod seems to make the tempest turn and twist inside. His flickering eyes and short, jerky hand motions reveal raw nerves. His hands shake uncontrollably as he throws back another drink.

"I have never met someone so particular about their name. How about we just call you 'hero' instead of W.H.?"

"I'm not."

"Come again?" the sheriff asks.

"I'm not a hero." Charlie's shoulders slump.

"Well, sure you are. Everyone here knows it. Look at what you done for the town. By killing the werewolf, you brought the good people back."

The sheriff pats him on the back again.

The impact rattles Charlie. Rather than feel the town's pride, his face contorts in shame.

"I-I didn't save the town!"

The sheriff steps back and slowly takes a seat. "Calm down. I just came here to thank you. Heck, we all came to thank you." He turns and waves his hand at the packed saloon. Business owners and families that fled to California have returned and slipped in with baskets of pies, rolls, and roasted chicken to thank the man who deserves the honor.

Charlie looks at the bag of money as tears well in his eyes. "I don't want the money."

"Well, why not? You've earned it," the sheriff says with sincere kindness in his big blue eyes.

"I DON'T WANT THE MONEY"! Charlie roars like a lion.

Praise is replaced with a racing fear, which rips through the people's hearts and shows in their shocked, gaping faces.

"What do you want, then?"

Charlie's lips quiver, and tears uncontrollably spill over the rims of his eyes and streak down his cheeks.

"I... want... the... wolves... back." He enunciates each word.

The people gasp.

"My hearing ain't so good. Come again?" Sheriff Dawson asks, leaning in.

"Don't mind him," Molly says with a smirk. "He's on his fifth shot. Tomorrow, we will throw a big parade and Charlie here will be at the front."

"I said, I want the wolves back," Charlie says in a gruff tone, lifting his shot glass.

Jenny puts her hand on his arm. "Why would you want that?"

His eyes soften. He looks at her hand and puts his on top of it. "You don't know what I saw, Jenny."

"Tell me what you saw, Charlie. I can see that you're tormented. Let me help you." She presses her hands to his bushy cheeks, shedding sarcasm and replacing it with sincerity.

"The day I was going to leave and go back to school, I went to the lake first. That's where I found them. They were running and playing and having a grand old time. If wolves could laugh, I'd swear they did."

"That don't undo what they done," Sheriff Dawson interrupts.

"Just give us a moment, Sheriff," Jenny says, turning everyone's attention back to the wolf hunter.

"What they done?" Charlie says. He shakes his head and faces Jenny. "Jenny, I saw them for the good and the bad. Sure, they did terrible things, but I can't help asking myself, would they have done those things if our ranches weren't encroaching on their lands?"

"*Their* lands?" the sheriff asks. "These are our lands. We settled 'em. You're speaking straight hogwash."

Charlie turns to him and tilts his brow. "But if they were anywhere else, just being wolves, would any of us have minded?"

The sheriff thinks on it for a moment, then shrugs. "I suppose not, but they were here and so are we."

"See, that right there is my point. They could still be living their lives anywhere but here, and that is why I'm not a hero."

The sheriff shakes his head in confusion. "Molly's right. You've had too much to drink."

"I wanna hear more," Jenny says.

"Jenny, if you would have seen the way he looked at…" For a moment he forgets the white wolf's true name, then remembers it in an instant. "Anoki"—he snaps his fingers—"you would have known…" Charlie's eyes widen.

He has finally figured out why Kiowa died. He buries his face in his hands and starts sobbing.

Jenny puts her gentle hand on his back and rubs in soothing circles. His strong emotions overwhelm her. "I can sense that you're onto something. Just tell me what it is."

"He loved her! Pour another one, Molly. I'm gonna lose it."

"But wolves aren't people, Charlie. They can't feel like you and I feel. They can't love."

"Jenny, I saw what I saw."

Sheriff Dawson leans on the bar, he holds up a finger and orders a shot.

"But they're ravenous, Charlie," Jenny says with pout lips and searching eyes.

"That's what I thought, too. Did I ever tell you that wolves killed my mother?"

"Oh, honey, is that what all this is about?" Jenny consoles him.

"No, no…" Charlie struggles to reconcile the contradictions. "When wolves killed my mother, I thought they were just killing machines. How could I think anything different? I saw the terrible things they did to her, but I could never have imagined they were capable of real love."

Jenny gives him her full attention.

"When I first used poison"—Charlie cracks a smile—"Lobo gathered up all my baits and defecated on them. He left me a message."

The people laugh.

"Then he set off all my steel traps and left me another message."

"How did he know to set off your traps?" Sheriff Dawson asks.

"Exactly! Better yet, why?"

"I reckon he was protecting Anoki," Molly says.

"Yes! Why was he protecting Anoki?"

"Because he loved her?" Jenny says, finally dialing in on what's been tormenting him.

"The animals, they can feel love. I saw it in the rabbits. The deer. The beaver. The bear. I saw it in the birds. I seen it everywhere on the prairie, but nowhere stronger than with those two wolves. Why?"

He pauses for a moment, then throws out a random fact. "Did you know doe and bucks crouch down when they sense hunters and circle around their young. Why would they do that?"

"To survive!" Sheriff Dawson blasts.

"NO! They can feel love. Bingo could have run away this one time a wolf charged me, but he stood his ground and was willing to die protecting me. Why would he do that?"

"Who's Bingo?" Molly asks.

"His dog." Jenny sighs.

"Are you saying that by protecting their young, or in this case Lobo protecting Anoki, that was for love?" Sheriff Dawson asks.

"Bingo! That's exactly what I'm saying. But it's more than that. See, the animals experience joy within the confines of their creation. I can't describe it, but I seen them share emotions same as you and me." Charlie looks at Jenny with a newfound light in his eyes.

The moment quickly fades as he finds another truth. "That's how I caught Lobo. That's how he died. I used his love against him. I killed Anoki first and dragged her body back to Mather's place. I couldn't have caught him any other way. I knew he would follow her trail. I just knew it. But I still don't understand how he died."

"I reckon he died of a broken heart," Jenny says, wiping tears from her eyes.

That single sentence passes through Charlie like a dagger of truth to his heart. "He died of a broken heart," he repeats.

"Run. Fight. Or die. Those are nature's laws. Just the same, here's your money." Sheriff Dawson pushes the bounty toward him.

Charlie leaps to his feet, looking at the money like it's cursed.

"I ain't no Judas! Don't you see what I'm saying?" Charlie shouts.

"See what? You're rich! And drunk! And there's a purty girl hanging on your arm. Do you understand what I'm saying?"

"I might be drunk, but at least I ain't blind. I killed the wolves because of the bounty. My heart is full of regret. I cannot accept this bounty because I am certain somewhere across this beautiful wild frontier someone is killing wolves for bounty. When does it stop? Where does it end?"

"It don't. Not until there ain't no wolves," the sheriff answers.

"And the buffalo? What about them?"

"To hell with them, too!" a cowboy shouts.

"And the Indians? To hell with them?" Charlie asks.

"Hell ya!" another cowboy hollers. A minority of voices out of the crowd support him.

"Now, you know that ain't how the law stands. Indians ain't animals; they're people," Sheriff Dawson corrects him. He straightens his coat and adds, "Savage as they maybe, they are protected by the law." He leans in and says in a hushed tone, "You know, you might want to choose a different venue for your words. Folks here have been raided by the Apache. Their relatives have been scalped, skinned, burned, and tortured. I wouldn't expect someone like you to understand what it's like to face down a dozen savage Injuns."

"I'm sorry, Sheriff. My train on the way down was ambushed by Indians. We lost some good folks." A memory flashes of the covered bodies being carried off the train. He thinks of the beautiful Fallscrow child. A chain of memories go off like fireworks in W.H.'s mind. All the way to his parents' bitter end, making Charlie shudder. He doesn't know how to reconcile reality with this new found truth.

"It's the bounty, Sheriff. That's what's going to kill all this beautiful wilderness. So long as men can profit from the slaughter, the slaughter will continue. Soon there ain't gonna be a frontier!"

Charlie storms off.

"Go sober up, W.H., Charlie, or whatever your name is now. Soon you will see. This is all progress. Nothing can stand in the way of manifest destiny. The rails are gonna be laid. The wire is going to spread. No man will have the power to stop progress. Man, wicked as he might be, is going to fit into two categories: savage or civilized. Which do you think will survive?" Sheriff Dawson asks with a long stern law gaze. He looks down and sees the moneybag. "Hey, you forgot your reward money."

Charlie turns around and slowly puts his hat on. He points to

Jenny. "It's your money now, Jenny. See that rancher Geoffrey gets his ten percent. I'd like for you to open up a school and teach young 'uns a better way with the rest."

With that, Charlie leaves "W.H." branded on the barstool. He mounts Cotton and heads back to Canada.

CHAPTER 149

Dec 24, 1861
Dearest Uncle,

I regret to inform you that I will not be home for Christmas. I did not even come close to making it back. I hope you received my telegraph and you and Auntie are doing well. Merry Christmas to y'all. I am eager to start classes!

I am somewhere between Missouri and Illinois. I've made great use of this camera, and I am happy to say that I will have many pictures to incorporate into my studies, thanks be to Mr. Rockefeller, who did honor his good word and send me a crate of expensive slides.

I have used most of these pages describing my experiences in the Currumpaw. I have told the story of Lobo and Blanca—or Kiowa and Anoki, as the good Chief would call them. At church today I told my story for the first time. I wasn't expecting to take up the entire hour of church, but I did. Women and children cry as I tell the story. Even I cried. The children riddled me with questions for another hour. I think Jenny may have the right profession in mind. I think I may soon find myself on the path of teaching, but rather than sit inside a classroom, I think I will start a new school. Maybe a nature school, where I can teach children all that I have learned.

Dec 25, 1861
Dear Uncle,

Merry Christmas! This was the most wonderful Christmas of them all. The children at the church Christmas party brought me presents. They painted pictures of Lobo and Blanca. Some drew hearts in their eyes. It made me sad, but at the same time, I was happy to have shared their story. These youngsters have inspired me to write all this down and make a book out of it.

January 22, 1862
Dear Jenny,

I am officially a published author! My short story, "Harvest Moon," was run in Winnipeg's local paper. Folks here cut out copies and sent it to their relatives. One of them happened to be a publisher in New York.

I have just received a letter from that publisher asking for the draft of my novel. I wasn't going to send it, but my uncle went ahead and lay an outline from my journal entries and shipped it off before I could stop him. I surely do love that old buzzard. I truly miss your neck of the woods. I know that sounds silly since there's hardly a towering tree in your desert paradise, but the expression has meaning.

Wishing you the best,
Xoxo Charlie

April 1, 1862
Dear Uncle,

I'm resigning my Canadian citizenship and becoming an American. Ha! Ha!

April Fools' Day! On a very serious note, I'm happy to report that my book is finished selling exceptionally well. I am scheduled to do speaking tours in the provinces and parts of the United States. If there ever is a United States.

A knock at the door sends Charlie into a frenzy. He grabs his book, fixes his glasses to his face, then opens the door prepared to greet little faces who want to meet the man who killed the wild wolf and their love. Instead, he's greeted by a face he sees when he closes his eyes just about every night.

"Hello, Jenny." He sets the book down.

"I always said it was a stupid name!"

"You did, and you were right."

"Well, are you just going to stand there or invite me in?" Jenny asks.

"Idleness has never been my sin, Jenny."

"You aren't going to invite me in, are you?" Her face starts to turn red.

"I could do that. You could get cozy. We could exchange dazzled eyes. I could razzle you with tales, but we know how it's going to end."

"How's that?" Jenny huffs, making the sweetest expression.

"I'm going to kiss you."

"Is that so?" Her sternness is no longer genuine. There's a softness to her eyes that invites Charlie's next move.

"I own this piece of land in Nebraska. There are fields that need tendin'. Fresh crops to get in. They say you can soak the winter days away in the Saratoga hot springs."

She takes a step toward him. "If we had sheep, there would be wool. I could make garments."

"I didn't know you could sew." Charlie snatches her gloved hands. They're trembling.

"Oh yes. I most certainly can. I can feed animals. Milk cows. Butcher chickens. Shuck corn, make soap, cook, and clean. I can pretty much do it all."

"Can you salt apples and turnips?"

"Don't insult me."

"Can you make jam?"

She parts her lips, ready to protest.

He can't resist her. He takes her in his arms and kisses her.

Neighbors scurry by. They whisper and gossip about the young couple showing such lewd public affection.

"Let's go!" Charlie releases her, then takes her hand.

"Where?" Jenny asks, feeling fire surge into her heart.

"Justice of the peace closes his office at five. If you want to get hitched, we better get down to his office."

"If that's your idea of a proposal..."

"Jenny, I had no idea you would be here or I would have got you a fancy ring. Got down on one knee. Done the whole shebang, you know." Charlie stiffens up. "I'm famous and rich now. Do you want to get married or not?"

"Oh?" Jenny pats her hair down and wrings her hands. "Pa wouldn't appreciate a law man officiating what a man of the cloth ought'ten to. Where's the nearest church?"

April 2, 1862

Irony?!? Jenny showed up at my doorstep yesterday. Without saying a word, I swept her up and kissed her. One hour later, we went to the good old Church of England and got married by Father Lockland. We were in such a hurry to exchange vows, we had no rings to swap. She said, "Well, since I ain't got no dowry, Pa will just have to mail us a set of rings. He ain't one to pass up on a bargain."

We exchanged vows, and I never have been happier! Mr. and *Mrs.* Mors are off to honeymoon in the Saratoga Springs.

While on the ferry, the couple honeymoon in a fancy cabin, with blue toile wallpaper and ornate woodcarvings. Before she blows out the candle, Jenny reads from Charlie's journal. "I never knew you had such swelling affection and articulate writing. No wonder your book is selling like frosted cakes."

When they reach Chicago's ferry port, Jenny gasps. "It really is the ruby city. Just like you wrote. If only Pa could see me now!"

On the train she keeps looking out the window. "Can we legally move so fast? Do the laws of nature support this speed?"

Charlie smirks.

"I can hardly believe my eyes. The landscapes have transformed before us, from mountains and trees to prairies and wide rivers. What comes next, plains? Traveling by train is truly a thrilling picture of progress every American should experience!"

"What are you looking for?"

"Well, I guess I'm looking for those Indians. Says right here in your journal you had your windows blown out."

Charlie smiles. He pulls his hat over his head and tilts it just high enough so he can still peek out the window. "You'll hear 'em before you see 'em. They like to war whoop."

From the carriage, on their ride to Saratoga, the town looks alive. The population has doubled. Fancy Victorian homes nearly outnumber the log cabins. Businesses have copied Chicago's redbrick architecture sooner than Charlie had expected. The white brick bank building sticks out more than the others and rests on the ground where the Saratoga Springs Hotel should have been.

The muddy streets are crowded with horses and buggies. The raised wooden walkways are crowded with townsfolk, some old, mostly new. Fellas in fine suits go arm in arm with ladies in fancy dresses.

"Is it always so busy? I didn't realize we were moving to a major metropolis!"

Charlie shakes his head at all the people.

"Look, Charlie, Indians!" Jenny gasps at the grand ornamentation so vastly different from the Indians she's used to seeing.

"Those are the Omaha. Right noble folk in their gear, wouldn't you say?"

"Is there a circus in town?" Jenny asks, beaming.

"Certainly not. Saratoga ain't big enough for that—well, at least it wasn't. What makes you ask?" Charlie wonders.

"I thought I saw a poster, and all those folks are dressed up in their Sunday finest. I put the two together and naturally assumed folks was wearing their finest for the circus."

Charlie reads a banner out loud. "'Barnum and Bailey Circus.' You're darn straight, there is a circus in town."

"Can we go?" Jenny begs.

"Right now?" W.H. counters.

"Look! Even the Indians are headed to the circus!"

W.H. watches an Indian father hoist his son up on his shoulders.

"Who knows how long it'll be in town, Charlie. I wanna see the elephants. Oh, please, can we see the elephants? I've never seen elephants except painted on the side of boxcars. I'm going to go mad if I don't see the elephants. Oh, please, honey. Pretty please?"

"You know they have lions, too."

"LIONS?"

"Driver!" W.H. motions with his hands. "Let us out here."

Reins pull tight. The two-horse carriage comes to a skidding halt with the driver clucking his tongue and saying, "Whoa! Whoa!"

Charlie opens the carriage door and steps out. He helps Jenny down.

The second his boot touches Saratoga soil, he hears a gruff voice grumble, "I thought we ran you out of town, Four Eyes."

CHAPTER 150

Charlie ignores the angry voice. He helps Jenny by the arm, looks down, and hurries her along.

"I'm talking to you, runt!" Patty O'Malley, the Irish foreman with an accent, angrily shouts.

"Is that man hollering at you?" Jenny asks.

"Nope!" Charlie puts his arm around Jenny and scoots her farther along.

"He best not! What am I saying? Of course he's not yelling at you, darling. *No one* who knew you could speak that way to you."

"Don't you worry, fella. We'll get the boys together, come on over to your claim and have another dunking party! You hear me? I'm getting my posse and a rope."

At the circus, acrobats defy gravity. Trapeze artists steal the audience's breath with dreadful anticipation when they barely catch one another in midair. Eyes burst wide open when a handsome blond man, pretending to be Daniel, stands in the center of a caged ring, while seven lions enter and leap through rings of fire. The crowd nearly loses its mind when a strongman bends an iron rod around his neck.

Between events, Charlie delights Jenny by winning her a pink stuffed elephant at a target shooting game.

"Now you can remember the first time you saw an elephant."

She grabs it and hugs it tight. "I will never forget this day."

He wows her when he's one of the only fellas to strike a spring with a hammer and send a weight soaring up a candy-striped painted tower, ringing a bell at the top.

They eat caramel corn, candy apples, and drink enough lemonade to burst. When it's all said and done, they sit down on a bench and watch the crowd go by.

Less than a block away, two men stand out on muddy old Main Street.

"My sister is *not* the same as states' rights!" Malice Mike shouts.

"Sure she is. According to your backwoods ideology, states have a right to act in whatever way they see fit. Why should bodies be any different? It ain't like I'm the first man to hanky-panky with your sister."

"You best watch your mouth, fella!"

"Junior." General Montgomery points to his head. "Think, son. Think!"

Malice Mike puffs up his chest and tucks his thumbs under his armpits. "For a man who believes so ardently in the union, I would think you would have the decency to marry her. You said you was gonna. You proposed didn't you?"

"Sure I did, but things changed."

"Do the honorable thing and spare her good name from this dreadful guilt and shame."

"Guilt and shame don't bother you Southerners. You relish in it. Slaveholder!"

"You're the slaveholder. Stealing deeds and claims through acts of coercion and dishonest card play." Malice Mike wiggles his fingers.

Rick puffs up his chest and bolsters, "Why, sir, that offends me. I never cheated at a hand of poker. You insult my good name. You can't blame me for anything bad in your life on account I won't take credit for anything good. I insist you apologize this instant."

Back at the trumpeting elephants, Charlie hears shouting. Townsfolk run toward the attraction.

"What do you reckon all the fuss is over?" Jenny asks, tucking the pink stuffed elephant under her arm while she hand-feeds peanuts to a real elephant.

"Must be a new attraction. Wanna take in one more event, darling?"

"You had better be careful, Charlie. The elephants have my head swirling with excitement. Did you know their long trunks could be used like hands? The way that elephant picked that man up around the waist and put him in his mouth was just divine. I never seen a thing like it. Pa is going to be plumb spooked when I tell him I saw a man in an elephant's mouth."

"Spooked?"

"With all this exquisite entertainment, you are going to spoil your bride."

"Do brides sour?"

"No. We gush with delight and beam with joy," Jenny proclaims with the sweetest affection.

Charlie bends his arm. "Mrs. Mors, I would be pleased to escort you to the main attraction."

Jenny runs her arm through his. "Mr. Mors, I would be pleased to follow."

They run with the crowd. As soon as they turn down Main Street, Charlie hears a familiar voice.

Rick Darling scans the growing crowd. Two round reflecting lenses catch his attention. "You brought Four Eyes with you? What's the deal? You two think you can kill me and steal my claim, is that it? You partners? Huh? Is that it?"

"To hell with your claim. I'm interested in my sister's honor." Malice Mike turns to W.H. and shouts, "Funny you should show up, Four Eyes."

Maybelle is standing across the street, next to her father. She smiles and waves as best she can, considering she's holding twin babes, one in each arm.

Rick pulls his coat back, exposing his pistols. "Well, that's just fine by me. I got a pistol for each of you." He reaches down and draws his pistols.

"Rick, don't!" Maybelle cries out.

Charlie shoves Jenny so hard her fragile frame stumbles and falls into the muddy road. She looks over her shoulder with terrible hurt in her eyes. In a flash she sees Charlie reaching for his pistol.

Malice Mike unholsters his silver Tiffany's pistols. "VILE VILLAIN! LET LEAD FLY!"

A barrage of gunfire and pistol smoke fills the streets. Children cover their ears.

Because of their great distance from each other, Malice Mike adjusts his fire by walking the shots up to Rick. He shoots the tall gentleman's beaver-felt hat right off his head.

Rick Darling takes turns aiming and firing simultaneously at Malice

Mike and Charlie. His tongue sticks out the side of his mouth as he unloads six shots. "I AIN'T RESPONSIBLE FOR NOTHING BAD OR NOTHING GOOD IN YOUR LIVES!"

Townsfolk clear away from the shooters. Heads turn left, then right. Eager eyes fan the gunmen for the results of this violent delight.

Rick Darling hits Mike in the leg. Malice screams and falls flat on his back. Bullets kick up dust around him. The pain is overwhelming. He drops a pistol to tend to the wound. He presses on the bullet hole with one hand while he sits up and fires with his other.

Charlie draws and fires two hasty shots. He misses, but to his great fortune, Mike strikes Rick in the arm. Rick spins around. He fires at Charlie as if nothing's happened, while Mike cycles his chamber to empty.

"Pa, reload me." Mike tosses his pistol to the general.

Surprisingly, none of the townsfolks are hit. Bullet holes in the buildings make people move farther away from the shooters. To Charlie's utter amazement, no one runs. They just sort of stand there in the street and stare, waiting for someone to die.

A bullet zips past Charlie's head, causing him turn about and run in one direction until an explosion of dust sends him scampering in another. Charlie dances around Rick's bullets, making the children laugh. He doesn't have time to aim, so he just points in Rick's general direction and nervously fires off four quick shots.

Both he and Rick *click* on empty chambers.

"Nothing bad, nothing good! You hear me, Four Eyes?"

Rick drops one of his pistols. He reaches for a powder pouch in his coat pocket. Rick Darling yells, "Amnesty! I need time to reload! All bear witness, I am an unarmed, innocent man." Rick Darling braces the empty pistol under his wounded arm. Red blood pools on his white cotton shirt, proving Mike struck true. He bites down on the powder plug and spits it out as he slides lead balls into his breached chamber. Powder spills all over the chamber and his sleeve.

"I'll be ready in just a minute, now."

Charlie has no problem breaching his chamber. Colt's cartridge six-shooter is far easier to reload than Rick's black powder pistol.

Charlie has only two extra cartridges in his ammo belt. Rick Darling still nervously works through the slow steps of reloading his black powder pistol. Charlie breaches the chamber to his Colt and slides the two brass cartridges in. He spins the chamber and locks it in place.

"Nothing good and nothing bad, eh?"

"That is correct, Four Eyes. None of it! Ain't my fault! I had a rough upbringing and I'm prepared…"

Charlie lifts his gun up and closes the distance to Rick Darling, "You stole my land. Robbed me of my money. You defiled my woman."

"Four Eyes, you don't even know who you are! Who in their right mind calls himself a wolf hunter?" Rick's trembling hand slips into his burgundy velvet vest pocket. He places a cap in each chamber.

Charlie pulls the trigger.

CHAPTER 151

Click.

Charlie recocks the hammer. "I know exactly who I am."

"I saw your true name when I wired your uncle. I don't speak much Latin, but 'Mors' is Latin for 'death,' ain't it? You're an outlaw, about to commit murder. All bear witness. This man is about to do me great harm."

Charlie pulls the trigger a second time.

Click.

Rick Darling flinches.

Charlie growls. "You can try to stop me."

He pulls the trigger a third time.

Click.

Rick Darling begins to sob, "Spare me. I beg your pardon."

"You can beg for your life." Charlie's eyes are cold and hard. His face is serious and stern.

Rick's eyes narrow. His mouth goes dry and the muscles in his cheeks nervously twitch his curled black mustache back and forth. He tosses his pistol and holds his wounded hand up while he fishes for a knife tucked in his waist belt with his good hand.

"I'm unarmed!" he cries out.

"He's going for his knife, W.H.," Malice Mike shouts.

"You can never stop death." Charlie pulls the trigger a fourth time.

BANG.

Charlie hits Mr. Darling in the abdomen. The slender man tumbles to the ground, dropping his pistol. His hands press against his bleeding abdomen.

"I believe that's what you Americans call progress!" Charlie twirls his gun with his trigger finger.

"Ha! Ha!" Malice Mike laughs. "Shoot him in the face! I'm gonna call you 'M.H.' from now on. Blow his head off, Man Hunter! He deserves it. He sullied my sister while she was engaged to you!"

Charlie looks over his shoulder at Mike. When he looks back at Rick, his eyes are filled with cold murder. "You're responsible for everything awful in my life!" Charlie's thumb presses down on the hammer, cocking it. "For though I walk through the valley of the shadow of death, I shall fear no evil... because you are evil!" Charlie growls, lifting his pistol to Mr. Darling's face. He applies so much pressure on the trigger that the cuticle of his trigger finger nail flushes white.

"*You're* evil!" Rick Darling blubbers. "You shot an unarmed man in the gut. It hurts real bad. You're going to jail for assault and battery." Rick's eyes fill to the brim with fear and spill over in tears down his cheeks. "Please... I don't wanna die." He feels his last painful breath dance on the tip of Charlie's finger. "I mean it now. I just want to work my claim. Be a good man for my young 'uns. Children need a father. I don't want to die."

"Nothing ever does."

"You'll be damned if you do!" Maybelle shouts.

"For what I done down in New Mexico, I'm already damned!" Charlie shouts.

"No, you are not!" Jenny yells.

Charlie takes a deep breath. He has every intention of applying the last pound of pressure, feeling the recoil from the explosion, and ending Rick's life. His mind tells him to steady his aim. His heart tells him to strike true between the eyes. But his spirit hears an eagle cry.

He looks up and sees a white eagle circling high above him in the sky. He looks down at Rick to find the eagle's shadow eerily encircling him.

He pauses for an infinite moment and feels his hatred shake as hard as his hand.

In that space between belief and reality, he hears the rally call of a wolf's howl.

Maybelle hands her twins off to her father and runs to Charlie's side.

"He ain't the father; you are. You manhandled me when you were taken with the fever. I didn't want to fuss or anything 'cause you were out of your mind and I was hoping…"

Rick yells, "Woman, clip that lying tongue. Look at them boys. They are a spitting image of me, and they shall bear my last name."

Jenny nearly eats the gloved knuckle she's stuffed in her mouth.

"You ain't part of my circle," Charlie says, decocking his pistol hammer and cycling the chamber to an unprimed round.

Maybelle clings to Charlie's arm. Her pretty face conceals so much venom.

"I can't believe I'm saying this," Rick says with softened eyes, "but, Maybelle, I see the errors of my ways. I need my sons to have my name. Maybelle, will you marry me?"

Maybelle lets go of Charlie's hand. "Fetch a priest!" she orders the sighing crowd.

Charlie turns his back and walks away.

"Come on, Jenny. Let's get on home and settle this wild frontier."

As Charlie walks past the same men who ran him out of town the first time, they smile and lift their hats as a sign of respect.

***

The front page of the *Saratoga Press* reads:

CIRCUS TURNS INTO 3 MAN SHOOT-OUT –
FRIDAY THE 2ND OF JUNE, 1862.

Why would a three-person shoot-out occur after such a wonderful, fantastic, display of entertainment? Perhaps the rising temperature is making men ornery. Maybe it's the fact that there are now two Presidents and two separate nations. Perhaps tensions between Northern and Southern citizens are at a boil since the south succeeded. Whatever the reason, scuttlebutt from writer to reader is that a shoot-out over an engaged woman happened on the afternoon of June the 2nd.

Apparently, Maybelle Montgomery (Southern affluence) acted in a less-than-honorable fashion while engaged to Charlie Mors, aka W.H., aka Wolf Hunter (no political affiliation). All of the excitement occurred on downtown Main Street. "By God's grace, no one was killed," said former Sheriff Davis, who speaks very highly of Mr. Mors nowadays. Though two men were seriously injured from exchanged pistol fire, no one died at the scene. In the fallout, Mr. Rick Darling Burger, a pioneer and original founder of Saratoga, intended to marry Maybelle Montgomery. Said he, "I plan on a fine wedding, all the bells and whistles. Her father just needs to provide the necessary funds for our wedding." Rick declined shop owner's damages. Said Rick, "I am not to be held responsible or liable. I was an innocent unarmed victim. It is my duty to see that the Union stands strong. Of course, it will serve my claim best, so it just makes sense."

Mr. Rick Darling Burger showed interest in enlisting in the Union army, but he refused to comment on whether he had enlisted. His tarnished reputation doesn't matter since the scarlet fever claimed him while he was living all alone in the unfinished Saratoga Springs Hotel.

Mr. Darling Burger will be survived by his mistress, "Maybelle Montgomery," and twin bastards. Instead of making marital vows, Maybelle now begs for the town's forgiveness and financial support. Maybelle was recorded as saying, "Who are we to judge? All I know is these boys ain't going to have a Yankee upbringing or last name. We are headed back to Kentucky, where Pa and Mike intend to enlist in the Southern army. Pa adopted these young 'uns, and we expect to bring them up good and proper in our southern ways. Do not look to see us in present company, as we intend to retire to our plantation."

Mr. "Malice" Mike Montgomery, Rick's sworn enemy and would-be brother-in-law, is said to have enlisted with his father in the Southern army. Malice Mike already left by rail and bragged, "This war will be over in a few weeks. We could lick the Yanks with corn cobs."

The third shooter is a Canadian foreigner who gained the town's respect, after once losing it. The town mayor has asked Charlie Mors to be sheriff. Mr. Mors declined the offer on account he "wants to teach young 'uns." Tensions between Northern and Southern citizens have reached an all-time high. Pioneers have stopped migrating West on account of army enlistments. Ferryboats are expected to stop running up to Saratoga altogether. In uncertain times, we here at the *Saratoga Press* ask ourselves, "Can we not be civil toward one another in this time of civil war?"

Oct 3, 1862

Dearest Uncle,

My book is a *bestseller* in the great state of New York! Can you believe it? Jenny's expecting our first boy... I hope! With the proceeds of this book, I intend to start my own school for boys. I'm going to call it Woodcraft Indians. Jenny doesn't much like the name, but I do. Anyway, Jenny and I will teach them about nature, animals, and all that God's earth has to offer. She will teach reading, writing, and arithmetic. Somehow we will work in a message of love, but I don't think, being boys, they'll be very receptive to that. Jenny's answer, "Bring in girls." My answer, "That'll be the day!"

Room for hope has come again. And along with hope comes fear, for it is despair that fears nothing. May God guide my thoughts, may he keep my fears at bay, and may he bring my hopes to pass.

More from Zachary H. Lovelady

Harvest Moon Official Website –
for T-Shirts, Hats, & More
www.HarvestMoonOfficial.com

Prince and Princess: Into the Shadows
Buy on Amazon
www.PrinceandPrincessOfficial.com

Review Harvest Moon on Amazon

About the Author

Zachary H. Lovelady is a believer in classy brevity. He is a writer and screenwriter. An actor. A director. A sometimes poet. A scholar. An entrepreneur. A techy. A terrible scientist. A lover of math, art, and architecture. A seeker of truth. A husband. A grateful son. A traveler. And a passionate patriot.

Newsletter Sign Up

Zack's list gets sneak previews of future books, projects, and upcoming movies!

Amazon | Website | Facebook | Instagram | Email

Please feel free to follow Zack on Facebook, Instagram, or send him an email. He may answer you personally… which could be a pro or a con.